Registrar General of Marriages

Registrar General of Marriages, Births and Deaths in Ireland :

thirty-third annual report, 1896

Registrar General of Marriages

Registrar General of Marriages, Births and Deaths in Ireland : thirty-third annual report, 1896

ISBN/EAN: 9783742810458

Manufactured in Europe, USA, Canada, Australia, Japa

Cover: Foto ©Andreas Hilbeck / pixelio.de

Manufactured and distributed by brebook publishing software (www.brebook.com)

Registrar General of Marriages

Registrar General of Marriages, Births and Deaths in Ireland :

thirty-third annual report, 1896

THIRTY-THIRD
DETAILED
ANNUAL REPORT
OF THE
REGISTRAR-GENERAL (IRELAND):
CONTAINING
A GENERAL ABSTRACT OF THE NUMBERS
OF
MARRIAGES, BIRTHS, AND DEATHS
REGISTERED IN IRELAND
DURING THE YEAR
1896.

TRANSMITTED PURSUANT TO THE PROVISIONS OF THE 7 & 8 VIC., CAP. 81, S. 56; 26 VIC., CAP. 11; AND 26 & 27 VIC., CAP. 90.

GENERAL SUMMARY.

POPULATION. MARRIAGES, THEIR NUMBER AND THEIR RELATION TO POPULATION, RELIGIOUS DENOMINATIONS, AGES, AND CIVIL CONDITION. BIRTHS, THEIR NUMBER AND THEIR RELATION TO POPULATION. DEATHS, THEIR NUMBER AND THEIR RELATION TO POPULATION, AGES, AND CAUSES. EMIGRATION; WEATHER.

Presented to both Houses of Parliament by Command of Her Majesty.

DUBLIN:
PRINTED FOR HER MAJESTY'S STATIONERY OFFICE,
BY ALEXANDER THOM & CO. (LIMITED).

And to be purchased, either directly or through any Bookseller, from
HODGES, FIGGIS, and Co. (Limited), 104, Grafton-street, Dublin; or
EYRE and SPOTTISWOODE, East Harding-street, Fleet-street, E.C.; or
JOHN MENZIES and Co., 12, Hanover-street, Edinburgh, and 90, West Nile-street, Glasgow.

1897.

CONTENTS.

REPORT

TO

HIS EXCELLENCY GEORGE HENRY, EARL CADOGAN, K.G.,

&c., &c., &c.,

LORD LIEUTENANT-GENERAL AND GENERAL GOVERNOR OF IRELAND.

MAY IT PLEASE YOUR EXCELLENCY,—

I have the honour to submit, for your Excellency's consideration, the Thirty-third Annual Report on Marriages, Births, and Deaths in Ireland.

GENERAL SUMMARY.

The Marriages registered in Ireland during the year 1896 number 23,059; the Births 107,661; and the Deaths 75,700. The marriage rate although not high (5·06 per 1,000 of the estimated population) is considerably in excess of the average rate for the ten years 1886–95, and is the highest rate for any year since 1871; the birth rate (23·6 per 1,000) is somewhat above the average for the ten years 1886–95, and is the highest rate for any year since 1884; and the death rate (16·6 per 1,000) is much below the average for the ten years 1886–95, and is the lowest rate for any year since 1871.

The recorded natural increase of population, or excess of births over deaths, was 31,944; the loss by emigration amounted to 38,995; there would thus appear to have been a decrease of 7,054 in the population during the year, but against this decrease there is a set-off in immigration, of which no official record has been obtained. The estimated population in the middle of the year was 4,560,378.

TABLE I.—Showing for each of the years 1886–95, the estimated Population; the number of Marriages, Births, and Deaths registered, and the number of Emigrants enumerated, with the rates per 1,000 of the estimated Population represented thereby; and the averages for the ten years 1886–95.

Years.	*Estimated Population in the middle of each year.	Marriages (Numbers Registered)	Births (Numbers Registered)	Deaths (Numbers Registered)	Number of Emigrants as returned by the Enumerators.	Marriages (Rate per 1,000)	Births (Rate per 1,000)	Deaths (Rate per 1,000)	Emigrants (Rate per 1,000)
[illegible]	[illegible]	[illegible]	[illegible]	[illegible]	[illegible]	[illegible]	[illegible]	[illegible]	[illegible]
[illegible]	[illegible]	[illegible]	[illegible]	[illegible]	[illegible]	[illegible]	[illegible]	[illegible]	[illegible]
[illegible]	[illegible]	[illegible]	[illegible]	[illegible]	[illegible]	[illegible]	[illegible]	[illegible]	[illegible]
[illegible]	[illegible]	[illegible]	[illegible]	[illegible]	[illegible]	[illegible]	[illegible]	[illegible]	[illegible]
[illegible]	[illegible]	[illegible]	[illegible]	[illegible]	[illegible]	[illegible]	[illegible]	[illegible]	[illegible]
[illegible]	[illegible]	[illegible]	[illegible]	[illegible]	[illegible]	[illegible]	[illegible]	[illegible]	[illegible]
[illegible]	[illegible]	[illegible]	[illegible]	[illegible]	[illegible]	[illegible]	[illegible]	[illegible]	[illegible]
[illegible]	[illegible]	[illegible]	[illegible]	[illegible]	[illegible]	[illegible]	[illegible]	[illegible]	[illegible]
[illegible]	[illegible]	[illegible]	[illegible]	[illegible]	[illegible]	[illegible]	[illegible]	[illegible]	[illegible]
[illegible]	[illegible]	[illegible]	[illegible]	[illegible]	[illegible]	[illegible]	[illegible]	[illegible]	[illegible]
Ten-year Average, [illegible]	[illegible]	[illegible]	[illegible]	[illegible]	[illegible]	[illegible]	[illegible]	[illegible]	[illegible]
[illegible]	[illegible]	[illegible]	[illegible]	[illegible]	[illegible]	[illegible]	[illegible]	[illegible]	[illegible]

* See page 189.

There are 2,526 Local Registration Officers holding office directly under the Department or who have entered into bonds with the Registrar-General for the due discharge of their duties. During the year 1896, 590 cases of vacancies or appointments were dealt with.

I append a table showing the number of Searches made, and Certificates issued at the General Register Office; also the amount received as fees for same, in each year, since the commencement of the Acts for the Registration of Births and Deaths and of Roman Catholic Marriages in 1864. It will be observed that the entries under these heads in 1896 showed a considerable increase as compared with those for any preceding year.

TABLE II.—NUMBER of SEARCHES made; number of CERTIFICATES issued, and AMOUNT received as FEES for SEARCHES, &c., at the GENERAL REGISTER OFFICE, DUBLIN, during the 33 years 1864–96.

Years.	Annual Number of Searches in the Registers.	Annual Number of Certificates.	Amount received as Fees for Searches, &c., and paid into Her Majesty's Exchequer.	Years.	Annual Number of Searches in the Registers.	Annual Number of Certificates.	Amount received as Fees for Searches, &c., and paid into Her Majesty's Exchequer.
			£ s. d.				£ s. d.
[illegible]	[illegible]	[illegible]	[illegible]	[illegible]	[illegible]	[illegible]	[illegible]
[illegible]	[illegible]	[illegible]	[illegible]	[illegible]	[illegible]	[illegible]	[illegible]
[illegible]	[illegible]	[illegible]	[illegible]	[illegible]	[illegible]	[illegible]	[illegible]
[illegible]	[illegible]	[illegible]	[illegible]	[illegible]	[illegible]	[illegible]	[illegible]
[illegible]	[illegible]	[illegible]	[illegible]	[illegible]	[illegible]	[illegible]	[illegible]
[illegible]	[illegible]	[illegible]	[illegible]	[illegible]	[illegible]	[illegible]	[illegible]
[illegible]	[illegible]	[illegible]	[illegible]	[illegible]	[illegible]	[illegible]	[illegible]
[illegible]	[illegible]	[illegible]	[illegible]	[illegible]	[illegible]	[illegible]	[illegible]
[illegible]	[illegible]	[illegible]	[illegible]	[illegible]	[illegible]	[illegible]	[illegible]
[illegible]	[illegible]	[illegible]	[illegible]	[illegible]	[illegible]	[illegible]	[illegible]
[illegible]	[illegible]	[illegible]	[illegible]	[illegible]	[illegible]	[illegible]	[illegible]
[illegible]	[illegible]	[illegible]	[illegible]	[illegible]	[illegible]	[illegible]	[illegible]
[illegible]	[illegible]	[illegible]	[illegible]	[illegible]	[illegible]	[illegible]	[illegible]
[illegible]	[illegible]	[illegible]	[illegible]	[illegible]	[illegible]	[illegible]	[illegible]
[illegible]	[illegible]	[illegible]	[illegible]	[illegible]	[illegible]	[illegible]	[illegible]
[illegible]	[illegible]	[illegible]	[illegible]	[illegible]	[illegible]	[illegible]	[illegible]
[illegible]	[illegible]	[illegible]	[illegible]				

During the financial year ended 31st March last 751 cases were reported of offences against the Acts administered by this Department. On careful inquiry into the circumstances, in 217 cases prosecutions were ordered to be instituted against the offenders. In 134 of these the parties were convicted and punished; in 71 the proceedings were abandoned, the parties (in most instances) paying the costs of court and complying with the law; in 5 cases the summonses were dismissed, and there are 7 cases regarding which the result has not as yet been reported to this Office.

The cases dealt with included the following offences:—Neglect to register Births; neglect to register Deaths; neglect to furnish Certificate of Marriage; failure of Coroner to furnish Certificate of Inquest; giving false information as to age at death, as to cause of death, and as to duration of illness; giving false information as to Births, viz.—registering illegitimate children as legitimate, and misrepresenting date of birth; falsifying Medical Certificate of Cause of Death; falsifying extracts from Registers.

A general statement regarding the return of the various offences and the proceedings taken in connection therewith will be found at page 194.

TABLE III.—Showing, for each PROVINCE and COUNTY in IRELAND, the respective RATES per 1,000 of the POPULATION,* represented by the MARRIAGES, BIRTHS, and DEATHS Registered during the Year 1896.

Provinces and Counties.	Annual Rate per 1,000 of the Population, represented by			Provinces and Counties.	Annual Rate per 1,000 of the Population, represented by		
	Marriages.	Births.	Deaths.		Marriages.	Births.	Deaths.
IRELAND,	[illegible]	[illegible]	[illegible]	II. MUNSTER.			
				Clare,	[illegible]	[illegible]	[illegible]
				Cork,	[illegible]	[illegible]	[illegible]
				Kerry,	[illegible]	[illegible]	[illegible]
PROVINCES.				Limerick,	[illegible]	[illegible]	[illegible]
I. LEINSTER,	[illegible]	[illegible]	[illegible]	Tipperary,	[illegible]	[illegible]	[illegible]
II. MUNSTER,	[illegible]	[illegible]	[illegible]	Waterford,	[illegible]	[illegible]	[illegible]
III. ULSTER,	[illegible]	[illegible]	[illegible]	III. ULSTER.			
IV. CONNAUGHT,	[illegible]	[illegible]	[illegible]	Antrim,	[illegible]	[illegible]	[illegible]
				Armagh,	[illegible]	[illegible]	[illegible]
I. LEINSTER.				Cavan,	[illegible]	[illegible]	[illegible]
				Donegal,	[illegible]	[illegible]	[illegible]
Carlow,	[illegible]	[illegible]	[illegible]	Down,	[illegible]	[illegible]	[illegible]
Dublin,	[illegible]	[illegible]	[illegible]	Fermanagh,	[illegible]	[illegible]	[illegible]
Kildare,	[illegible]	[illegible]	[illegible]	Londonderry,	[illegible]	[illegible]	[illegible]
Kilkenny,	[illegible]	[illegible]	[illegible]	Monaghan,	[illegible]	[illegible]	[illegible]
King's,	[illegible]	[illegible]	[illegible]	Tyrone,	[illegible]	[illegible]	[illegible]
Longford,	[illegible]	[illegible]	[illegible]				
Louth and Co. of Town of Drogheda,	[illegible]	[illegible]	[illegible]	IV. CONNAUGHT.			
Meath,	[illegible]	[illegible]	[illegible]	Galway,	[illegible]	[illegible]	[illegible]
Queen's,	[illegible]	[illegible]	[illegible]	Leitrim,	[illegible]	[illegible]	[illegible]
Westmeath,	[illegible]	[illegible]	[illegible]	Mayo,	[illegible]	[illegible]	[illegible]
Wexford,	[illegible]	[illegible]	[illegible]	Roscommon,	[illegible]	[illegible]	[illegible]
Wicklow,	[illegible]	[illegible]	[illegible]	Sligo,	[illegible]	[illegible]	[illegible]

MARRIAGES.

The number of Marriages registered during the year is 23,055, being equal to 5·06 per 1,000, of the estimated population,* a rate which is ·01 over that for the previous year, and ·33 above the average for the ten years 1886–95.

Of the 23,055 Marriages registered during last year 15,733 were between Roman Catholics; 3,980 were celebrated according to the rites and ceremonies of the Church of Ireland; 2,486 were in Presbyterian Meeting-houses; 492 in "Registered Buildings" belonging to various religious denominations; only 368 by civil contract in the Registrars' offices; 8 were according to the usages of the Society of Friends; and 18 according to the Jewish rites.

The Roman Catholic Marriages are equal to a rate of 4·08 per 1,000 of the estimated number of Roman Catholics, being 0·47 over the corresponding average rate for the preceding ten years, and the other Marriages represent a rate of 8·33 per 1,000 of all persons other than Roman Catholics in the population, this rate being 0·60 over the corresponding average rate.

Of the 3,980 Marriages according to the rites of the Church of Ireland, 52 were by special licence, 2,271 by licence, 513 after the publication of banns, 8 on Registrar's certificate, and in 36 instances there was no information afforded as to which of these methods was adopted.

* Throughout this Report the rates for the total of Ireland are based on the estimated population in the middle of the respective years, and the rates for Provinces and Counties are based on the population according to the Census, those relating to the year 1896 being founded on the 1891 population, and those having reference to the years 1887–90 on the population by the Census of 1881.

A 2

TABLE IV.—Marriages registered in Ireland in 1896 and each of the previous ten years, according to the modes of celebration; with the rate per 1,000 of the population represented:—

Years.	Marriages registered under 7 and 8 Vic. cap. 81.							Roman Catholic Marriages.	Total Marriages Registered.	Rate per 1,000 of estimated corresponding Population represented by		
	According to the Rites of the Church of Ireland.	In Registered Presbyterian Meeting-houses.	In Registered Buildings.	In the Registrars' Offices.	Society of Friends.	Jews.	Total.			Marriages under 7 and 8 Vic. cap. 81.	Roman Catholic Marriages.	Total Marriages.
[illegible]	[illegible]	[illegible]	[illegible]	[illegible]	[illegible]	[illegible]	[illegible]	[illegible]	[illegible]	[illegible]	[illegible]	[illegible]
[illegible]	[illegible]	[illegible]	[illegible]	[illegible]	[illegible]	[illegible]	[illegible]	[illegible]	[illegible]	[illegible]	[illegible]	[illegible]
[illegible]	[illegible]	[illegible]	[illegible]	[illegible]	[illegible]	[illegible]	[illegible]	[illegible]	[illegible]	[illegible]	[illegible]	[illegible]
[illegible]	[illegible]	[illegible]	[illegible]	[illegible]	[illegible]	[illegible]	[illegible]	[illegible]	[illegible]	[illegible]	[illegible]	[illegible]
[illegible]	[illegible]	[illegible]	[illegible]	[illegible]	[illegible]	[illegible]	[illegible]	[illegible]	[illegible]	[illegible]	[illegible]	[illegible]
[illegible]	[illegible]	[illegible]	[illegible]	[illegible]	[illegible]	[illegible]	[illegible]	[illegible]	[illegible]	[illegible]	[illegible]	[illegible]
[illegible]	[illegible]	[illegible]	[illegible]	[illegible]	[illegible]	[illegible]	[illegible]	[illegible]	[illegible]	[illegible]	[illegible]	[illegible]
[illegible]	[illegible]	[illegible]	[illegible]	[illegible]	[illegible]	[illegible]	[illegible]	[illegible]	[illegible]	[illegible]	[illegible]	[illegible]
[illegible]	[illegible]	[illegible]	[illegible]	[illegible]	[illegible]	[illegible]	[illegible]	[illegible]	[illegible]	[illegible]	[illegible]	[illegible]
[illegible]	[illegible]	[illegible]	[illegible]	[illegible]	[illegible]	[illegible]	[illegible]	[illegible]	[illegible]	[illegible]	[illegible]	[illegible]
Average [illegible]	[illegible]	[illegible]	[illegible]	[illegible]	6	7	[illegible]	[illegible]	[illegible]	[illegible]	[illegible]	[illegible]
1896,	[illegible]	[illegible]	[illegible]	[illegible]	[illegible]	[illegible]	[illegible]	[illegible]	[illegible]	[illegible]	[illegible]	[illegible]

During the year 1896 there were issued by the Registrars 750 Licences for Marriages in Registered Buildings and in the Registrars' offices.

The number of Marriage Licences issued by the licensing Ministers of the several Presbyterian bodies is given in the following summary:—

Presbytery or Synod.	Number of Licensing Ministers on 31st December, 1896.	Number of Registered Meeting-houses on 31st December, 1896.	Number of Licences issued.
1. General Assembly of the Presbyterian Church in Ireland,	[illegible]	[illegible]	[illegible]
2. Remonstrant Synod of Ulster,	[illegible]	[illegible]	[illegible]
3. Presbytery of Antrim,	[illegible]	[illegible]	[illegible]
4. United Presbytery or Synod of Munster,	[illegible]	[illegible]	[illegible]
Total,	[illegible]	[illegible]	[illegible]

There being no civil restrictions as to the time or place for celebrating marriages between Roman Catholics in Ireland, a registration of the churches and chapels of the Roman Catholic Church is not necessary for the purposes of this office; but with reference to other religious bodies, a record is kept of the places of Divine worship in which marriages may lawfully be solemnized without special licence, and from this it appears that, on the 31st December, 1896, there were 1,482 churches and chapels of the Church of Ireland, 607 registered Presbyterian Meeting-houses, and 381 "Registered Buildings" belonging to various religious denominations. Compared with the previous year, these numbers show no change as regards the Church of Ireland, an increase of 2 in the number of Presbyterian Meeting-houses, and an increase of 3 in the total number of "Registered Buildings."

The following statement shows the several religious bodies having "Registered Buildings," in 1896:—

Denomination.	No. of Places of Worship.	Denomination.	No. of Places of Worship.	Denomination.	No. of Places of Worship.
Methodists,	225	Methodists, New Connexion,	7	Covenanters,	1
Reformed Presbyterians,	37	Salvation Army,	6	Welsh Presbyterians,	1
Independents,	24	Jews,	5	United Original Seceders,	1
Baptists,	23	"The Catholic Apostolic Church,"	3	"Protestant Dissenters,"	1
Christian Brethren,	14	Non-Subscribing Unitarians,	3	Non-Subscribing Christians,	1
Moravians, or United Brethren,	9	Evangelical Union,	1	Independent Protestants,	1
Quakers,	9	Unitarians,	1		
United Presbyterians,	8			Total,	381

Of the 23,055 marriages registered during the year 1896 there were recorded—in the first quarter 7,264; in the second, 5,451; in the third, 5,220; and in the last, 5,120.

The marriages of bachelors and spinsters constitute 87·4 per cent. of the total; those of widowers and spinsters 9·0 per cent.; of bachelors and widows 2·6 per cent.; and of widowers and widows 1·0 per cent. Thus, 10·0 per cent. of the men married were widowers, and 3·6 per cent. of the women were widows; and in 13 instances in every 100 marriages one or both of the contracting parties had been in the married state before.

TABLE V.—Showing by QUARTERLY PERIODS the number of MARRIAGES registered in Ireland in each of the eleven years 1886–96, and the average number for the ten years 1886–95, distinguishing the number of Roman Catholic marriages registered under the 26 & 27 Vic., cap. 90, and of Protestant and other marriages under the 7 & 8 Vic., cap. 81:—

Years.	Marriages.														
	Roman Catholic.					Others.					Total.				
	Quarter ending the last day of				Total.	Quarter ending the last day of				Total.	Quarter ending the last day of				Total.
	Mar.	June.	Sep.	Dec.		Mar.	June.	Sep.	Dec.		Mar.	June.	Sep.	Dec.	
[illegible]	[illegible]	[illegible]	[illegible]	[illegible]	[illegible]	[illegible]	[illegible]	[illegible]	[illegible]	[illegible]	[illegible]	[illegible]	[illegible]	[illegible]	[illegible]
[illegible]	[illegible]	[illegible]	[illegible]	[illegible]	[illegible]	[illegible]	[illegible]	[illegible]	[illegible]	[illegible]	[illegible]	[illegible]	[illegible]	[illegible]	[illegible]
[illegible]	[illegible]	[illegible]	[illegible]	[illegible]	[illegible]	[illegible]	[illegible]	[illegible]	[illegible]	[illegible]	[illegible]	[illegible]	[illegible]	[illegible]	[illegible]
[illegible]	[illegible]	[illegible]	[illegible]	[illegible]	[illegible]	[illegible]	[illegible]	[illegible]	[illegible]	[illegible]	[illegible]	[illegible]	[illegible]	[illegible]	[illegible]
[illegible]	[illegible]	[illegible]	[illegible]	[illegible]	[illegible]	[illegible]	[illegible]	[illegible]	[illegible]	[illegible]	[illegible]	[illegible]	[illegible]	[illegible]	[illegible]
[illegible]	[illegible]	[illegible]	[illegible]	[illegible]	[illegible]	[illegible]	[illegible]	[illegible]	[illegible]	[illegible]	[illegible]	[illegible]	[illegible]	[illegible]	[illegible]
[illegible]	[illegible]	[illegible]	[illegible]	[illegible]	[illegible]	[illegible]	[illegible]	[illegible]	[illegible]	[illegible]	[illegible]	[illegible]	[illegible]	[illegible]	[illegible]
[illegible]	[illegible]	[illegible]	[illegible]	[illegible]	[illegible]	[illegible]	[illegible]	[illegible]	[illegible]	[illegible]	[illegible]	[illegible]	[illegible]	[illegible]	[illegible]
[illegible]	[illegible]	[illegible]	[illegible]	[illegible]	[illegible]	[illegible]	[illegible]	[illegible]	[illegible]	[illegible]	[illegible]	[illegible]	[illegible]	[illegible]	[illegible]
[illegible]	[illegible]	[illegible]	[illegible]	[illegible]	[illegible]	[illegible]	[illegible]	[illegible]	[illegible]	[illegible]	[illegible]	[illegible]	[illegible]	[illegible]	[illegible]
[illegible]	[illegible]	[illegible]	[illegible]	[illegible]	[illegible]	[illegible]	[illegible]	[illegible]	[illegible]	[illegible]	[illegible]	[illegible]	[illegible]	[illegible]	[illegible]
Average for ten years, 1886–95,	[illegible]	[illegible]	[illegible]	[illegible]	[illegible]	[illegible]	[illegible]	[illegible]	[illegible]	[illegible]	[illegible]	[illegible]	[illegible]	[illegible]	[illegible]
1896,	[illegible]	[illegible]	[illegible]	[illegible]	[illegible]	[illegible]	[illegible]	[illegible]	[illegible]	[illegible]	[illegible]	[illegible]	[illegible]	[illegible]	[illegible]
Equivalent Annual Rate per 1,000 living:—															
Average, 1886–95,	[illegible]	[illegible]	[illegible]	[illegible]	[illegible]	[illegible]	[illegible]	[illegible]	[illegible]	[illegible]	[illegible]	[illegible]	[illegible]	[illegible]	[illegible]
1896,	[illegible]	[illegible]	[illegible]	[illegible]	[illegible]	[illegible]	[illegible]	[illegible]	[illegible]	[illegible]	[illegible]	[illegible]	[illegible]	[illegible]	[illegible]

A complete registry of the exact ages of the persons married would be valuable from many points of view: hence it is matter for regret that in the great majority of instances the ages are not recorded. The requirements of the law are technically complied with by the entry in the age column of "minor" or of "full age," as the case may be, and there seems to be a general and increasing inclination to take advantage of this circumstance, as in 1896 the ages of both parties were specified in 4,325 cases only, being less than one-fifth of the total number of marriages. In the year 1865, when 30,802 marriages were registered, the ages of both parties were given in 16,910 instances.

Of 23,063 men married during the year, 479, or 2·08 per cent., were minors; and of the women married, 2,004, or 8·69 per cent., were under age.

The highest proportion of husbands (2·50 per cent.) married under age in 1896, was in the province of Leinster, and in the province of Ulster there was the highest percentage of wives (9·46), not of full age.

It may be added that the per-centage of persons married in Ireland who were under age is very far below the corresponding rates in England and Scotland.

The signatures of the contracting parties in the marriage registers, or certificate, afford a rough test of the progress of elementary education. In the year 1896, 19,836, or 86·0 per cent., of the husbands, and 18,707, or 81·1 per cent., of the wives, wrote their names, and the remainder signed by marks.

These figures show a considerable improvement as compared with the corresponding results in the first of the preceding ten years, the per-centage of persons married in 1886 who wrote their names being—men 76·6, and women 74·7, and they exhibit a great advance when compared with the per-centage for the year 1864, when the general registration of marriages in Ireland was established, in which year but 61 in every 100 men, and 50 in every 100 women married wrote their names.

The per-centages for the several provinces last year range, for men, from 77 in Connaught to 86 in Leinster and Munster, and, for women, from 83 in Ulster and Connaught to 89 in Leinster and Munster.

In 1,564 cases both of the parties married signed the register by "mark," and in 3,939 the register was thus signed by either the husband or the wife, so that in 5,503 cases, or 23·9 per cent. of the total number of marriages, one or both of the parties signed by mark; and in 17,532, or 76·1 per cent., *both* parties wrote their names.

The proportion per cent. of persons married in each of the eleven years 1886–96, who wrote their names in the registers or certificates, of minors, of widowers, and of widows are given in the following Table for Ireland, and for each of the four provinces.

TABLE VI.—Showing as regards the Marriages in Ireland and in each of the Four Provinces during the years 1886–96, the proportion per cent. of Persons who signed their Names, of Persons not of Full Age, and of Re-marriages.

Province, &c.	Year	Signed their Names in Writing: Of 100 Men Married	Signed their Names in Writing: Of 100 Women Married	Persons not of Full Age: Of 100 Men Married	Persons not of Full Age: Of 100 Women Married	Re-marriages: Widowers: Of 100 Men Married	Re-marriages: Widows: Of 100 Women Married
IRELAND	1886	76·6	74·7	[illegible]	[illegible]	[illegible]	[illegible]
	1887	[illegible]	[illegible]	[illegible]	[illegible]	[illegible]	[illegible]
	1888	[illegible]	[illegible]	[illegible]	[illegible]	[illegible]	[illegible]
	1889	[illegible]	[illegible]	[illegible]	[illegible]	[illegible]	[illegible]
	1890	[illegible]	[illegible]	[illegible]	[illegible]	[illegible]	[illegible]
	1891	[illegible]	[illegible]	[illegible]	[illegible]	[illegible]	[illegible]
	1892	[illegible]	[illegible]	[illegible]	[illegible]	[illegible]	[illegible]
	1893	[illegible]	[illegible]	[illegible]	[illegible]	[illegible]	[illegible]
	1894	[illegible]	[illegible]	[illegible]	[illegible]	[illegible]	[illegible]
	1895	[illegible]	[illegible]	[illegible]	[illegible]	[illegible]	[illegible]
	1896	[illegible]	[illegible]	[illegible]	[illegible]	[illegible]	[illegible]
LEINSTER	1886	[illegible]	[illegible]	[illegible]	[illegible]	[illegible]	[illegible]
	1887	[illegible]	[illegible]	[illegible]	[illegible]	[illegible]	[illegible]
	1888	[illegible]	[illegible]	[illegible]	[illegible]	[illegible]	[illegible]
	1889	[illegible]	[illegible]	[illegible]	[illegible]	[illegible]	[illegible]
	1890	[illegible]	[illegible]	[illegible]	[illegible]	[illegible]	[illegible]
	1891	[illegible]	[illegible]	[illegible]	[illegible]	[illegible]	[illegible]
	1892	[illegible]	[illegible]	[illegible]	[illegible]	[illegible]	[illegible]
	1893	[illegible]	[illegible]	[illegible]	[illegible]	[illegible]	[illegible]
	1894	[illegible]	[illegible]	[illegible]	[illegible]	[illegible]	[illegible]
	1895	[illegible]	[illegible]	[illegible]	[illegible]	[illegible]	[illegible]
	1896	[illegible]	[illegible]	[illegible]	[illegible]	[illegible]	[illegible]
MUNSTER	1886	[illegible]	[illegible]	[illegible]	[illegible]	[illegible]	[illegible]
	1887	[illegible]	[illegible]	[illegible]	[illegible]	[illegible]	[illegible]
	1888	[illegible]	[illegible]	[illegible]	[illegible]	[illegible]	[illegible]
	1889	[illegible]	[illegible]	[illegible]	[illegible]	[illegible]	[illegible]
	1890	[illegible]	[illegible]	[illegible]	[illegible]	[illegible]	[illegible]
MUNSTER—continued	1891	[illegible]	[illegible]	[illegible]	[illegible]	[illegible]	[illegible]
	1892	[illegible]	[illegible]	[illegible]	[illegible]	[illegible]	[illegible]
	1893	[illegible]	[illegible]	[illegible]	[illegible]	[illegible]	[illegible]
	1894	[illegible]	[illegible]	[illegible]	[illegible]	[illegible]	[illegible]
	1895	[illegible]	[illegible]	[illegible]	[illegible]	[illegible]	[illegible]
	1896	[illegible]	[illegible]	[illegible]	[illegible]	[illegible]	[illegible]
ULSTER	1886	[illegible]	[illegible]	[illegible]	[illegible]	[illegible]	[illegible]
	1887	[illegible]	[illegible]	[illegible]	[illegible]	[illegible]	[illegible]
	1888	[illegible]	[illegible]	[illegible]	[illegible]	[illegible]	[illegible]
	1889	[illegible]	[illegible]	[illegible]	[illegible]	[illegible]	[illegible]
	1890	[illegible]	[illegible]	[illegible]	[illegible]	[illegible]	[illegible]
	1891	[illegible]	[illegible]	[illegible]	[illegible]	[illegible]	[illegible]
	1892	[illegible]	[illegible]	[illegible]	[illegible]	[illegible]	[illegible]
	1893	[illegible]	[illegible]	[illegible]	[illegible]	[illegible]	[illegible]
	1894	[illegible]	[illegible]	[illegible]	[illegible]	[illegible]	[illegible]
	1895	[illegible]	[illegible]	[illegible]	[illegible]	[illegible]	[illegible]
	1896	[illegible]	[illegible]	[illegible]	[illegible]	[illegible]	[illegible]
CONNAUGHT	1886	[illegible]	[illegible]	[illegible]	[illegible]	[illegible]	[illegible]
	1887	[illegible]	[illegible]	[illegible]	[illegible]	[illegible]	[illegible]
	1888	[illegible]	[illegible]	[illegible]	[illegible]	[illegible]	[illegible]
	1889	[illegible]	[illegible]	[illegible]	[illegible]	[illegible]	[illegible]
	1890	[illegible]	[illegible]	[illegible]	[illegible]	[illegible]	[illegible]
	1891	[illegible]	[illegible]	[illegible]	[illegible]	[illegible]	[illegible]
	1892	[illegible]	[illegible]	[illegible]	[illegible]	[illegible]	[illegible]
	1893	[illegible]	[illegible]	[illegible]	[illegible]	[illegible]	[illegible]
	1894	[illegible]	[illegible]	[illegible]	[illegible]	[illegible]	[illegible]
	1895	[illegible]	[illegible]	[illegible]	[illegible]	[illegible]	[illegible]
	1896	[illegible]	[illegible]	[illegible]	[illegible]	[illegible]	[illegible]

In proportion to population at all ages, the registered marriages were most numerous in the province of Ulster, in which, however, the rate was only 5·8 per 1,000 of the population, according to the Census of 1891; Leinster comes next with 5·4 per 1,000; Munster third, with 4·1 per 1,000; and Connaught last, the rate being 3·5 per 1,000.

The highest rate for any county was 8·1 per 1,000 of the population in 1891, which was the marriage rate for Antrim; and the lowest 3·3 per 1,000, for Clare and Roscommon. Between these, the most favourable were 7·3 for Dublin, and 6·1 for Down; and the least so 3·4 for Galway, and 3·5 for Waterford and Mayo.

BIRTHS.

The number of births registered during the year 1896 is 107,641—55,329 boys and 52,312 girls, or 105·8 of the former to every 100 of the latter—the rate afforded in proportion to the estimated population being 1 in 42·4, or 23·6 per thousand, which is 0·7 over the average rate per 1,000 for the ten years, 1886–95.

Of the 107,641 children whose births were registered in Ireland during the year 1896, 104,822, or 97·4 per cent. were legitimate, and 2,819, or 2·6 per cent., were illegitimate; the average per-centage of illegitimate for the preceding 10 years was 2·7. It is unnecessary to say that these results compare very favourably with the returns for most other countries.

Of the children born in wedlock during the year, 53,896 were males, and 50,926 females, being 105·8 of the former to every 100 of the latter, and of the illegitimate children 1,433 were males, and 1,386 females, or 103·4 boys to 100 girls.

Comparing the provinces, we find that the per-centage of children born in Ulster, who were illegitimate, was 3·7; in Leinster, 2·4; in Munster, 2·8; and in Connaught, 0·6.

TABLE VII.—The Per-centage of Legitimate and of Illegitimate Births registered in Ireland during the years 1892–96, by Provinces.

Provinces.	Proportion per cent. of Legitimate Births.					Proportion per cent. of Illegitimate Births.				
	[illegible year]	[illegible year]	[illegible year]	[illegible year]	[illegible year]	[illegible year]	[illegible year]	[illegible year]	[illegible year]	[illegible year]
IRELAND, . . .	[illegible]	[illegible]	[illegible]	[illegible]	[illegible]	[illegible]	[illegible]	[illegible]	[illegible]	[illegible]
Leinster, . . .	[illegible]	[illegible]	[illegible]	[illegible]	[illegible]	[illegible]	[illegible]	[illegible]	[illegible]	[illegible]
Munster, . . .	[illegible]	[illegible]	[illegible]	[illegible]	[illegible]	[illegible]	[illegible]	[illegible]	[illegible]	[illegible]
Ulster, . . .	[illegible]	[illegible]	[illegible]	[illegible]	[illegible]	[illegible]	[illegible]	[illegible]	[illegible]	[illegible]
Connaught, . . .	[illegible]	[illegible]	[illegible]	[illegible]	[illegible]	[illegible]	[illegible]	[illegible]	[illegible]	[illegible]

The respective total birth-rates for the provinces in 1896 were—Leinster 22·1 per 1,000 of the population in 1891; Munster, 21·7; Ulster, 24·6; and Connaught, 20·7.

The four counties having the highest rates are Antrim, 31·2 per 1,000 of the population in 1891; Dublin, 28·8; Down, 25·1; and Kerry, 23·1. Those with the lowest rates are—Monaghan, 15·9; Roscommon, 18·2; Fermanagh, 18·2; and Cavan, 18·5.

Of the total births, 51·4 per cent. were registered in the first six months of the year (182 days), and 48·6 per cent. in the second half of the year (184 days).

The number registered in the first quarter was 27,267; in the second, 26,108; in the third, 26,459; and in the fourth, 25,784.

DEATHS.

The number of deaths registered during the year is 75,700, being equal to 1 in 60·2 or 16·6 per 1,000 of the estimated population. The deaths of males number 37,364, and those of females 38,336, the former being equal to 16·5 in every 1,000 males living and the latter representing 16·7 per 1,000 females.

The death-rate (16·6) is 1·6 under the average rate for the preceding ten years, and 1·5 under the rate for the year 1895.

As usual, very many of the Registrars furnished at the close of each quarter valuable notes on the sanitary condition of their respective districts. These notes were embodied in the Quarterly Returns issued from this Department, and emanating as they did, from gentlemen qualified to speak decisively on the subject, it is to be hoped that they received the serious attention of the various Local Authorities intrusted with the administration of the Public Health Acts.

With respect to the death-rates for the four provinces, the rate for Connaught is only 12·3; that for Munster is 15·0; for Ulster, 17·3; and for Leinster, 17·9 per 1,000 of the population in 1891.

Of the thirty-two counties, the four having the lowest registered mortality are—Mayo, 11·6 per 1,000; Leitrim, 11·7; Kerry, 12·4; and Roscommon, 12·4.

Those in which the rate was highest are—Dublin, 23·2; Antrim, 21·3; Down, 18·6; and Waterford, 18·1.

The deaths registered in the first half of the year generally outnumber those in the second. In 1896, 53·2 per cent. of the total deaths were registered in the six months, January to June inclusive, and 46·8 per cent. in the remaining six months of the year.

The annual rates represented by the deaths registered in each quarter are as follow:—First quarter, 18·5 per 1,000 of the population; second, 16·8; third, 14·1; and fourth, 16·9. The rates for the first three quarters are below, and that for the fourth quarter is above, the corresponding average rates for the respective quarters in the ten years, 1886–95.

From the Table on pp. 174–183 it will be seen that, of the 75,700 deaths registered during the year, 2,339 took place in Infirmaries and General and Special Hospitals; 946 in Public Lunatic Asylums; 8,418 in Workhouses and Workhouse Hospitals; and 63,989 were of persons who died "At their Own Homes, &c." As in former Reports a Table (see pages 184–5) is given showing like information for those Registrars' Districts in which the principal Urban Sanitary Districts in Ireland are situated.

The deaths in "Infirmaries and General and Special Hospitals" constitute 3·1 per cent. of the total number, the per-centages for the four provinces varying from 0·4 in Connaught to 7·7 in Leinster. Over eleven per cent. of the deaths registered occurred in Workhouses or Workhouse Hospitals, the respective per-centages for the provinces being—Leinster, 13·2; Munster, 16·2; Ulster, 7·4; and Connaught, 7·9.

TABLE VIII.—Showing, by Quarterly Periods, the number of Births and Deaths registered in Ireland in each of the eleven years, 1886–96, and the average number for the ten years, 1886–95.

Year.	Births. Quarter ending the last day of March.	June.	Sept.	Dec.	Births. Total.	Deaths. Quarter ending the last day of March.	June.	Sept.	Dec.	Deaths. Total.
[illegible]	[illegible]	[illegible]	[illegible]	[illegible]	[illegible]	[illegible]	[illegible]	[illegible]	[illegible]	[illegible]
[illegible]	[illegible]	[illegible]	[illegible]	[illegible]	[illegible]	[illegible]	[illegible]	[illegible]	[illegible]	[illegible]
[illegible]	[illegible]	[illegible]	[illegible]	[illegible]	[illegible]	[illegible]	[illegible]	[illegible]	[illegible]	[illegible]
[illegible]	[illegible]	[illegible]	[illegible]	[illegible]	[illegible]	[illegible]	[illegible]	[illegible]	[illegible]	[illegible]
[illegible]	[illegible]	[illegible]	[illegible]	[illegible]	[illegible]	[illegible]	[illegible]	[illegible]	[illegible]	[illegible]
[illegible]	[illegible]	[illegible]	[illegible]	[illegible]	[illegible]	[illegible]	[illegible]	[illegible]	[illegible]	[illegible]
[illegible]	[illegible]	[illegible]	[illegible]	[illegible]	[illegible]	[illegible]	[illegible]	[illegible]	[illegible]	[illegible]
[illegible]	[illegible]	[illegible]	[illegible]	[illegible]	[illegible]	[illegible]	[illegible]	[illegible]	[illegible]	[illegible]
[illegible]	[illegible]	[illegible]	[illegible]	[illegible]	[illegible]	[illegible]	[illegible]	[illegible]	[illegible]	[illegible]
[illegible]	[illegible]	[illegible]	[illegible]	[illegible]	[illegible]	[illegible]	[illegible]	[illegible]	[illegible]	[illegible]
Average for ten years, [illegible]	[illegible]	[illegible]	[illegible]	[illegible]	[illegible]	[illegible]	[illegible]	[illegible]	[illegible]	[illegible]
[illegible]	[illegible]	[illegible]	[illegible]	[illegible]	[illegible]	[illegible]	[illegible]	[illegible]	[illegible]	[illegible]
Equivalent Annual Rate per 1,000 living:—										
Average, [illegible]	[illegible]	[illegible]	[illegible]	[illegible]	[illegible]	[illegible]	[illegible]	[illegible]	[illegible]	[illegible]
[illegible]	[illegible]	[illegible]	[illegible]	[illegible]	[illegible]	[illegible]	[illegible]	[illegible]	[illegible]	[illegible]

[TABLE IX.

B

CAUSES OF

The following TABLE (IX.) shows (1) the Number of Deaths from All Causes and from with the Average Annual Number for the ten years 1886–95, and (2) the respective

YEAR.	Total Number of Deaths.	CAUSES OF DEATH.														
		SPECIAL FEBRILE OR ZYMOTIC DISEASES.														
		[illegible]	[illegible]	[illegible]	[illegible]	[illegible]	[illegible]	[illegible]	[illegible]	[illegible]	[illegible]	[illegible]	[illegible]	[illegible]	[illegible]	[illegible]
(1.) NUMBER																
[illegible]	[illegible]	[illegible]	[illegible]	[illegible]	[illegible]	[illegible]	[illegible]	[illegible]	[illegible]	[illegible]	[illegible]	[illegible]	[illegible]	[illegible]	[illegible]	[illegible]
[illegible]	[illegible]	[illegible]	[illegible]	[illegible]	[illegible]	[illegible]	[illegible]	[illegible]	[illegible]	[illegible]	[illegible]	[illegible]	[illegible]	[illegible]	[illegible]	[illegible]
[illegible]	[illegible]	[illegible]	[illegible]	[illegible]	[illegible]	[illegible]	[illegible]	[illegible]	[illegible]	[illegible]	[illegible]	[illegible]	[illegible]	[illegible]	[illegible]	[illegible]
[illegible]	[illegible]	—	[illegible]	[illegible]	[illegible]	[illegible]	[illegible]	[illegible]	[illegible]	[illegible]	[illegible]	[illegible]	[illegible]	[illegible]	[illegible]	[illegible]
[illegible]	[illegible]	—	[illegible]	[illegible]	[illegible]	[illegible]	[illegible]	[illegible]	[illegible]	[illegible]	[illegible]	[illegible]	[illegible]	[illegible]	[illegible]	[illegible]
[illegible]	[illegible]	[illegible]	[illegible]	[illegible]	[illegible]	[illegible]	[illegible]	[illegible]	[illegible]	[illegible]	[illegible]	[illegible]	[illegible]	[illegible]	[illegible]	[illegible]
[illegible]	[illegible]	—	[illegible]	[illegible]	[illegible]	[illegible]	[illegible]	[illegible]	[illegible]	[illegible]	[illegible]	[illegible]	[illegible]	[illegible]	[illegible]	[illegible]
[illegible]	[illegible]	1	[illegible]	[illegible]	[illegible]	[illegible]	[illegible]	[illegible]	[illegible]	[illegible]	[illegible]	[illegible]	[illegible]	[illegible]	[illegible]	[illegible]
[illegible]	[illegible]	[illegible]	[illegible]	[illegible]	[illegible]	[illegible]	[illegible]	[illegible]	[illegible]	[illegible]	[illegible]	[illegible]	[illegible]	[illegible]	[illegible]	[illegible]
[illegible]	[illegible]	[illegible]	[illegible]	[illegible]	[illegible]	[illegible]	[illegible]	[illegible]	[illegible]	[illegible]	[illegible]	[illegible]	[illegible]	[illegible]	[illegible]	[illegible]
Average—ten Years [illegible]	[illegible]	[illegible]	[illegible]	[illegible]	[illegible]	[illegible]	[illegible]	[illegible]	[illegible]	[illegible]	[illegible]	[illegible]	[illegible]	[illegible]	[illegible]	[illegible]
[illegible]	[illegible]	[illegible]	[illegible]	[illegible]	[illegible]	[illegible]	[illegible]	[illegible]	[illegible]	[illegible]	[illegible]	[illegible]	[illegible]	[illegible]	[illegible]	[illegible]
(2.) RATES PER 100,000 OF																
[illegible]	[illegible]	—	[illegible]	[illegible]	[illegible]	[illegible]	[illegible]	[illegible]	[illegible]	[illegible]	[illegible]	[illegible]	[illegible]	[illegible]	[illegible]	[illegible]
[illegible]	[illegible]	[illegible]	[illegible]	[illegible]	[illegible]	[illegible]	[illegible]	[illegible]	[illegible]	[illegible]	[illegible]	[illegible]	[illegible]	[illegible]	[illegible]	[illegible]
[illegible]	[illegible]	[illegible]	[illegible]	[illegible]	[illegible]	[illegible]	[illegible]	[illegible]	[illegible]	[illegible]	[illegible]	[illegible]	[illegible]	[illegible]	[illegible]	[illegible]
[illegible]	[illegible]	—	[illegible]	[illegible]	[illegible]	[illegible]	[illegible]	[illegible]	[illegible]	[illegible]	[illegible]	[illegible]	[illegible]	[illegible]	[illegible]	[illegible]
[illegible]	[illegible]	—	[illegible]	[illegible]	[illegible]	[illegible]	[illegible]	[illegible]	[illegible]	[illegible]	[illegible]	[illegible]	[illegible]	[illegible]	[illegible]	[illegible]
[illegible]	[illegible]	[illegible]	[illegible]	[illegible]	[illegible]	[illegible]	[illegible]	[illegible]	[illegible]	[illegible]	[illegible]	[illegible]	[illegible]	[illegible]	[illegible]	[illegible]
[illegible]	[illegible]	—	[illegible]	[illegible]	[illegible]	[illegible]	[illegible]	[illegible]	[illegible]	[illegible]	[illegible]	[illegible]	[illegible]	[illegible]	[illegible]	[illegible]
[illegible]	[illegible]	—	[illegible]	[illegible]	[illegible]	[illegible]	[illegible]	[illegible]	[illegible]	[illegible]	[illegible]	[illegible]	[illegible]	[illegible]	[illegible]	[illegible]
[illegible]	[illegible]	[illegible]	[illegible]	[illegible]	[illegible]	[illegible]	[illegible]	[illegible]	[illegible]	[illegible]	[illegible]	[illegible]	[illegible]	[illegible]	[illegible]	[illegible]
[illegible]	[illegible]	[illegible]	[illegible]	[illegible]	[illegible]	[illegible]	[illegible]	[illegible]	[illegible]	[illegible]	[illegible]	[illegible]	[illegible]	[illegible]	[illegible]	[illegible]
Average—ten years [illegible]	[illegible]	[illegible]	[illegible]	[illegible]	[illegible]	[illegible]	[illegible]	[illegible]	[illegible]	[illegible]	[illegible]	16	[illegible]	[illegible]	[illegible]	[illegible]
[illegible]	[illegible]	[illegible]	[illegible]	[illegible]	[illegible]	[illegible]	[illegible]	[illegible]	[illegible]	[illegible]	[illegible]	[illegible]	[illegible]	[illegible]	[illegible]	[illegible]

I.—SPECIFIC FEBRILE OR ZYMOTIC DISEASES.

The number of deaths from Specific Febrile or Zymotic diseases registered during the year 1896 was 6,682 (3,193 males and 3,489 females), or 146 in every 100,000 of the estimated population, being 1,244 under the number for the preceding year, and 1,318 under the average for the ten years, 1886–95.

Of the 6,682 deaths from zymotic diseases 3,881, or 58·1 per cent., were amongst children under 10 years of age.

DEATH.

each of the Principal Causes registered in Ireland during each of the eleven years 1886–96, Rates per 100,000 of the estimated Population represented by these numbers.

CAUSES OF DEATH.																
[illegible]				LOCAL DISEASES.							VIOLENCE.				ALL OTHER CAUSES.	TOTAL.
				Diseases of												
[illegible]	[illegible]	[illegible]	[illegible]	[illegible]	[illegible]	[illegible]	[illegible]	[illegible]	[illegible]	[illegible]	[illegible]	[illegible]	[illegible]	[illegible]		

OF DEATHS.

[illegible]	[illegible]	[illegible]	[illegible]	[illegible]	[illegible]	[illegible]	[illegible]	[illegible]	[illegible]	[illegible]	[illegible]	[illegible]	[illegible]	[illegible]	[illegible]	[illegible]
[illegible]	[illegible]	[illegible]	[illegible]	[illegible]	[illegible]	[illegible]	[illegible]	[illegible]	[illegible]	[illegible]	[illegible]	[illegible]	[illegible]	[illegible]	[illegible]	[illegible]
[illegible]	[illegible]	[illegible]	[illegible]	[illegible]	[illegible]	[illegible]	[illegible]	[illegible]	[illegible]	[illegible]	[illegible]	[illegible]	[illegible]	[illegible]	[illegible]	[illegible]
[illegible]	[illegible]	[illegible]	[illegible]	[illegible]	[illegible]	[illegible]	[illegible]	[illegible]	[illegible]	[illegible]	[illegible]	[illegible]	[illegible]	[illegible]	[illegible]	[illegible]
[illegible]	[illegible]	[illegible]	[illegible]	[illegible]	[illegible]	[illegible]	[illegible]	[illegible]	[illegible]	[illegible]	[illegible]	[illegible]	[illegible]	[illegible]	[illegible]	[illegible]
[illegible]	[illegible]	[illegible]	[illegible]	[illegible]	[illegible]	[illegible]	[illegible]	[illegible]	[illegible]	[illegible]	[illegible]	[illegible]	[illegible]	[illegible]	[illegible]	[illegible]
[illegible]	[illegible]	[illegible]	[illegible]	[illegible]	[illegible]	[illegible]	[illegible]	[illegible]	[illegible]	[illegible]	[illegible]	[illegible]	[illegible]	[illegible]	[illegible]	[illegible]
[illegible]	[illegible]	[illegible]	[illegible]	[illegible]	[illegible]	[illegible]	[illegible]	[illegible]	[illegible]	[illegible]	[illegible]	[illegible]	[illegible]	[illegible]	[illegible]	[illegible]
[illegible]	[illegible]	[illegible]	[illegible]	[illegible]	[illegible]	[illegible]	[illegible]	[illegible]	[illegible]	[illegible]	[illegible]	[illegible]	[illegible]	[illegible]	[illegible]	[illegible]
[illegible]	[illegible]	[illegible]	[illegible]	[illegible]	[illegible]	[illegible]	[illegible]	[illegible]	[illegible]	[illegible]	[illegible]	[illegible]	[illegible]	[illegible]	[illegible]	[illegible]
[illegible]	[illegible]	[illegible]	[illegible]	[illegible]	[illegible]	[illegible]	[illegible]	[illegible]	[illegible]	[illegible]	[illegible]	[illegible]	[illegible]	[illegible]	[illegible]	[illegible]
[illegible]	[illegible]	[illegible]	[illegible]	[illegible]	[illegible]	[illegible]	[illegible]	[illegible]	[illegible]	[illegible]	[illegible]	[illegible]	[illegible]	[illegible]	[illegible]	[illegible]

THE ESTIMATED POPULATION.

[illegible]	[illegible]	[illegible]	[illegible]	[illegible]	[illegible]	[illegible]	[illegible]	[illegible]	[illegible]	[illegible]	[illegible]	[illegible]	[illegible]	[illegible]	[illegible]	[illegible]
[illegible]	[illegible]	[illegible]	[illegible]	[illegible]	[illegible]	[illegible]	[illegible]	[illegible]	[illegible]	[illegible]	[illegible]	[illegible]	[illegible]	[illegible]	[illegible]	[illegible]
[illegible]	[illegible]	[illegible]	[illegible]	[illegible]	[illegible]	[illegible]	[illegible]	[illegible]	[illegible]	[illegible]	[illegible]	[illegible]	[illegible]	[illegible]	[illegible]	[illegible]
[illegible]	[illegible]	[illegible]	[illegible]	[illegible]	[illegible]	[illegible]	[illegible]	[illegible]	[illegible]	[illegible]	[illegible]	[illegible]	[illegible]	[illegible]	[illegible]	[illegible]
[illegible]	[illegible]	[illegible]	[illegible]	[illegible]	[illegible]	[illegible]	[illegible]	[illegible]	[illegible]	[illegible]	[illegible]	[illegible]	[illegible]	[illegible]	[illegible]	[illegible]
[illegible]	[illegible]	[illegible]	[illegible]	[illegible]	[illegible]	[illegible]	[illegible]	[illegible]	[illegible]	[illegible]	[illegible]	[illegible]	[illegible]	[illegible]	[illegible]	[illegible]
[illegible]	[illegible]	[illegible]	[illegible]	[illegible]	[illegible]	[illegible]	[illegible]	[illegible]	[illegible]	[illegible]	[illegible]	[illegible]	[illegible]	[illegible]	[illegible]	[illegible]
[illegible]	[illegible]	[illegible]	[illegible]	[illegible]	[illegible]	[illegible]	[illegible]	[illegible]	[illegible]	[illegible]	[illegible]	[illegible]	[illegible]	[illegible]	[illegible]	[illegible]
[illegible]	[illegible]	[illegible]	[illegible]	[illegible]	[illegible]	[illegible]	[illegible]	[illegible]	[illegible]	[illegible]	[illegible]	[illegible]	[illegible]	[illegible]	[illegible]	[illegible]
[illegible]	[illegible]	[illegible]	[illegible]	[illegible]	[illegible]	[illegible]	[illegible]	[illegible]	[illegible]	[illegible]	[illegible]	[illegible]	[illegible]	[illegible]	[illegible]	[illegible]
[illegible]	[illegible]	[illegible]	[illegible]	[illegible]	[illegible]	[illegible]	[illegible]	[illegible]	[illegible]	[illegible]	[illegible]	[illegible]	[illegible]	[illegible]	[illegible]	[illegible]
[illegible]	[illegible]	[illegible]	[illegible]	[illegible]	[illegible]	[illegible]	[illegible]	[illegible]	[illegible]	[illegible]	[illegible]	[illegible]	[illegible]	[illegible]	[illegible]	[illegible]

The deaths from the principal zymotic diseases* registered during 1896 form 6·8 per cent. of the deaths from all causes, and are equal to 113 in every 100,000 persons living; the average annual mortality from the same diseases in the preceding 10 years represented 7·9 per cent. of the average number of deaths from all causes, and was equal to 137 deaths in every 100,000 of the population.

* Small-pox, Measles, Scarlet Fever, Typhus, Whooping-cough, Diphtheria, Simple Continued and Ill-defined Fever, Enteric Fever, Diarrhœa, Dysentery, and Cholera.

TABLE X.—Showing the Number of Deaths from the Principal Febrile or Zymotic Diseases registered in the several Provinces of Ireland during each of the ten years, 1887–96; with the Rates per 100,000 of the Population.*

Localities, Years, &c.			Small-pox.	Measles.	Scarlet Fever (Scarlatina).	Typhus.	Influenza.	Whooping-Cough.	Diphtheria.	Simple Continued and Ill-defined Fever.	Enteric Fever.	Simple Cholera.	Diarrhoea and Dysentery.
Provinces. No. of Deaths.	Leinster,	1887,	[illegible]	[illegible]	[illegible]	[illegible]	[illegible]	[illegible]	[illegible]	[illegible]	[illegible]	[illegible]	[illegible]
		1888,	[illegible]	[illegible]	[illegible]	[illegible]	[illegible]	[illegible]	[illegible]	[illegible]	[illegible]	[illegible]	[illegible]
		1889,	[illegible]	[illegible]	[illegible]	[illegible]	[illegible]	[illegible]	[illegible]	[illegible]	[illegible]	[illegible]	[illegible]
		1890,	[illegible]	[illegible]	[illegible]	[illegible]	[illegible]	[illegible]	[illegible]	[illegible]	[illegible]	[illegible]	[illegible]
		1891,	[illegible]	[illegible]	[illegible]	[illegible]	[illegible]	[illegible]	[illegible]	[illegible]	[illegible]	[illegible]	[illegible]
		1892,	[illegible]	[illegible]	[illegible]	[illegible]	[illegible]	[illegible]	[illegible]	[illegible]	[illegible]	[illegible]	[illegible]
		1893,	[illegible]	[illegible]	[illegible]	[illegible]	[illegible]	[illegible]	[illegible]	[illegible]	[illegible]	[illegible]	[illegible]
		1894,	[illegible]	[illegible]	[illegible]	[illegible]	[illegible]	[illegible]	[illegible]	[illegible]	[illegible]	[illegible]	[illegible]
		1895,	[illegible]	[illegible]	[illegible]	[illegible]	[illegible]	[illegible]	[illegible]	[illegible]	[illegible]	[illegible]	[illegible]
		1896,	[illegible]	[illegible]	[illegible]	[illegible]	[illegible]	[illegible]	[illegible]	[illegible]	[illegible]	[illegible]	[illegible]
	Munster,	1887,	[illegible]	[illegible]	[illegible]	[illegible]	[illegible]	[illegible]	[illegible]	[illegible]	[illegible]	[illegible]	[illegible]
		1888,	[illegible]	[illegible]	[illegible]	[illegible]	[illegible]	[illegible]	[illegible]	[illegible]	[illegible]	[illegible]	[illegible]
		1889,	[illegible]	[illegible]	[illegible]	[illegible]	[illegible]	[illegible]	[illegible]	[illegible]	[illegible]	[illegible]	[illegible]
		1890,	[illegible]	[illegible]	[illegible]	[illegible]	[illegible]	[illegible]	[illegible]	[illegible]	[illegible]	[illegible]	[illegible]
		1891,	[illegible]	[illegible]	[illegible]	[illegible]	[illegible]	[illegible]	[illegible]	[illegible]	[illegible]	[illegible]	[illegible]
		1892,	[illegible]	[illegible]	[illegible]	[illegible]	[illegible]	[illegible]	[illegible]	[illegible]	[illegible]	[illegible]	[illegible]
		1893,	[illegible]	[illegible]	[illegible]	[illegible]	[illegible]	[illegible]	[illegible]	[illegible]	[illegible]	[illegible]	[illegible]
		1894,	[illegible]	[illegible]	[illegible]	[illegible]	[illegible]	[illegible]	[illegible]	[illegible]	[illegible]	[illegible]	[illegible]
		1895,	[illegible]	[illegible]	[illegible]	[illegible]	[illegible]	[illegible]	[illegible]	[illegible]	[illegible]	[illegible]	[illegible]
		1896,	[illegible]	[illegible]	[illegible]	[illegible]	[illegible]	[illegible]	[illegible]	[illegible]	[illegible]	[illegible]	[illegible]
	Ulster,	1887,	[illegible]	[illegible]	[illegible]	[illegible]	[illegible]	[illegible]	[illegible]	[illegible]	[illegible]	[illegible]	[illegible]
		1888,	[illegible]	[illegible]	[illegible]	[illegible]	[illegible]	[illegible]	[illegible]	[illegible]	[illegible]	[illegible]	[illegible]
		1889,	[illegible]	[illegible]	[illegible]	[illegible]	[illegible]	[illegible]	[illegible]	[illegible]	[illegible]	[illegible]	[illegible]
		1890,	[illegible]	[illegible]	[illegible]	[illegible]	[illegible]	[illegible]	[illegible]	[illegible]	[illegible]	[illegible]	[illegible]
		1891,	[illegible]	[illegible]	[illegible]	[illegible]	[illegible]	[illegible]	[illegible]	[illegible]	[illegible]	[illegible]	[illegible]
		1892,	[illegible]	[illegible]	[illegible]	[illegible]	[illegible]	[illegible]	[illegible]	[illegible]	[illegible]	[illegible]	[illegible]
		1893,	[illegible]	[illegible]	[illegible]	[illegible]	[illegible]	[illegible]	[illegible]	[illegible]	[illegible]	[illegible]	[illegible]
		1894,	[illegible]	[illegible]	[illegible]	[illegible]	[illegible]	[illegible]	[illegible]	[illegible]	[illegible]	[illegible]	[illegible]
		1895,	[illegible]	[illegible]	[illegible]	[illegible]	[illegible]	[illegible]	[illegible]	[illegible]	[illegible]	[illegible]	[illegible]
		1896,	[illegible]	[illegible]	[illegible]	[illegible]	[illegible]	[illegible]	[illegible]	[illegible]	[illegible]	[illegible]	[illegible]
	Connaught,	1887,	[illegible]	[illegible]	[illegible]	[illegible]	[illegible]	[illegible]	[illegible]	[illegible]	[illegible]	[illegible]	[illegible]
		1888,	[illegible]	[illegible]	[illegible]	[illegible]	[illegible]	[illegible]	[illegible]	[illegible]	[illegible]	[illegible]	[illegible]
		1889,	[illegible]	[illegible]	[illegible]	[illegible]	[illegible]	[illegible]	[illegible]	[illegible]	[illegible]	[illegible]	[illegible]
		1890,	[illegible]	[illegible]	[illegible]	[illegible]	[illegible]	[illegible]	[illegible]	[illegible]	[illegible]	[illegible]	[illegible]
		1891,	[illegible]	[illegible]	[illegible]	[illegible]	[illegible]	[illegible]	[illegible]	[illegible]	[illegible]	[illegible]	[illegible]
		1892,	[illegible]	[illegible]	[illegible]	[illegible]	[illegible]	[illegible]	[illegible]	[illegible]	[illegible]	[illegible]	[illegible]
		1893,	[illegible]	[illegible]	[illegible]	[illegible]	[illegible]	[illegible]	[illegible]	[illegible]	[illegible]	[illegible]	[illegible]
		1894,	[illegible]	[illegible]	[illegible]	[illegible]	[illegible]	[illegible]	[illegible]	[illegible]	[illegible]	[illegible]	[illegible]
		1895,	[illegible]	[illegible]	[illegible]	[illegible]	[illegible]	[illegible]	[illegible]	[illegible]	[illegible]	[illegible]	[illegible]
		1896,	[illegible]	[illegible]	[illegible]	[illegible]	[illegible]	[illegible]	[illegible]	[illegible]	[illegible]	[illegible]	[illegible]
Provinces. Rate per 100,000 of Population.*	Leinster,	1887,	[illegible]	[illegible]	[illegible]	[illegible]	[illegible]	[illegible]	[illegible]	[illegible]	[illegible]	[illegible]	[illegible]
		1888,	[illegible]	[illegible]	[illegible]	[illegible]	[illegible]	[illegible]	[illegible]	[illegible]	[illegible]	[illegible]	[illegible]
		1889,	[illegible]	[illegible]	[illegible]	[illegible]	[illegible]	[illegible]	[illegible]	[illegible]	[illegible]	[illegible]	[illegible]
		1890,	[illegible]	[illegible]	[illegible]	[illegible]	[illegible]	[illegible]	[illegible]	[illegible]	[illegible]	[illegible]	[illegible]
		1891,	[illegible]	[illegible]	[illegible]	[illegible]	[illegible]	[illegible]	[illegible]	[illegible]	[illegible]	[illegible]	[illegible]
		1892,	[illegible]	[illegible]	[illegible]	[illegible]	[illegible]	[illegible]	[illegible]	[illegible]	[illegible]	[illegible]	[illegible]
		1893,	[illegible]	[illegible]	[illegible]	[illegible]	[illegible]	[illegible]	[illegible]	[illegible]	[illegible]	[illegible]	[illegible]
		1894,	[illegible]	[illegible]	[illegible]	[illegible]	[illegible]	[illegible]	[illegible]	[illegible]	[illegible]	[illegible]	[illegible]
		1895,	[illegible]	[illegible]	[illegible]	[illegible]	[illegible]	[illegible]	[illegible]	[illegible]	[illegible]	[illegible]	[illegible]
		1896,	[illegible]	[illegible]	[illegible]	[illegible]	[illegible]	[illegible]	[illegible]	[illegible]	[illegible]	[illegible]	[illegible]
	Munster,	1887,	[illegible]	[illegible]	[illegible]	[illegible]	[illegible]	[illegible]	[illegible]	[illegible]	[illegible]	[illegible]	[illegible]
		1888,	[illegible]	[illegible]	[illegible]	[illegible]	[illegible]	[illegible]	[illegible]	[illegible]	[illegible]	[illegible]	[illegible]
		1889,	[illegible]	[illegible]	[illegible]	[illegible]	[illegible]	[illegible]	[illegible]	[illegible]	[illegible]	[illegible]	[illegible]
		1890,	[illegible]	[illegible]	[illegible]	[illegible]	[illegible]	[illegible]	[illegible]	[illegible]	[illegible]	[illegible]	[illegible]
		1891,	[illegible]	[illegible]	[illegible]	[illegible]	[illegible]	[illegible]	[illegible]	[illegible]	[illegible]	[illegible]	[illegible]
		1892,	[illegible]	[illegible]	[illegible]	[illegible]	[illegible]	[illegible]	[illegible]	[illegible]	[illegible]	[illegible]	[illegible]
		1893,	[illegible]	[illegible]	[illegible]	[illegible]	[illegible]	[illegible]	[illegible]	[illegible]	[illegible]	[illegible]	[illegible]
		1894,	[illegible]	[illegible]	[illegible]	[illegible]	[illegible]	[illegible]	[illegible]	[illegible]	[illegible]	[illegible]	[illegible]
		1895,	[illegible]	[illegible]	[illegible]	[illegible]	[illegible]	[illegible]	[illegible]	[illegible]	[illegible]	[illegible]	[illegible]
		1896,	[illegible]	[illegible]	[illegible]	[illegible]	[illegible]	[illegible]	[illegible]	[illegible]	[illegible]	[illegible]	[illegible]
	Ulster,	1887,	[illegible]	[illegible]	[illegible]	[illegible]	[illegible]	[illegible]	[illegible]	[illegible]	[illegible]	[illegible]	[illegible]
		1888,	[illegible]	[illegible]	[illegible]	[illegible]	[illegible]	[illegible]	[illegible]	[illegible]	[illegible]	[illegible]	[illegible]
		1889,	[illegible]	[illegible]	[illegible]	[illegible]	[illegible]	[illegible]	[illegible]	[illegible]	[illegible]	[illegible]	[illegible]
		1890,	[illegible]	[illegible]	[illegible]	[illegible]	[illegible]	[illegible]	[illegible]	[illegible]	[illegible]	[illegible]	[illegible]
		1891,	[illegible]	[illegible]	[illegible]	[illegible]	[illegible]	[illegible]	[illegible]	[illegible]	[illegible]	[illegible]	[illegible]
		1892,	[illegible]	[illegible]	[illegible]	[illegible]	[illegible]	[illegible]	[illegible]	[illegible]	[illegible]	[illegible]	[illegible]
		1893,	[illegible]	[illegible]	[illegible]	[illegible]	[illegible]	[illegible]	[illegible]	[illegible]	[illegible]	[illegible]	[illegible]
		1894,	[illegible]	[illegible]	[illegible]	[illegible]	[illegible]	[illegible]	[illegible]	[illegible]	[illegible]	[illegible]	[illegible]
		1895,	[illegible]	[illegible]	[illegible]	[illegible]	[illegible]	[illegible]	[illegible]	[illegible]	[illegible]	[illegible]	[illegible]
		1896,	[illegible]	[illegible]	[illegible]	[illegible]	[illegible]	[illegible]	[illegible]	[illegible]	[illegible]	[illegible]	[illegible]
	Connaught,	1887,	[illegible]	[illegible]	[illegible]	[illegible]	[illegible]	[illegible]	[illegible]	[illegible]	[illegible]	[illegible]	[illegible]
		1888,	[illegible]	[illegible]	[illegible]	[illegible]	[illegible]	[illegible]	[illegible]	[illegible]	[illegible]	[illegible]	[illegible]
		1889,	[illegible]	[illegible]	[illegible]	[illegible]	[illegible]	[illegible]	[illegible]	[illegible]	[illegible]	[illegible]	[illegible]
		1890,	[illegible]	[illegible]	[illegible]	[illegible]	[illegible]	[illegible]	[illegible]	[illegible]	[illegible]	[illegible]	[illegible]
		1891,	[illegible]	[illegible]	[illegible]	[illegible]	[illegible]	[illegible]	[illegible]	[illegible]	[illegible]	[illegible]	[illegible]
		1892,	[illegible]	[illegible]	[illegible]	[illegible]	[illegible]	[illegible]	[illegible]	[illegible]	[illegible]	[illegible]	[illegible]
		1893,	[illegible]	[illegible]	[illegible]	[illegible]	[illegible]	[illegible]	[illegible]	[illegible]	[illegible]	[illegible]	[illegible]
		1894,	[illegible]	[illegible]	[illegible]	[illegible]	[illegible]	[illegible]	[illegible]	[illegible]	[illegible]	[illegible]	[illegible]
		1895,	[illegible]	[illegible]	[illegible]	[illegible]	[illegible]	[illegible]	[illegible]	[illegible]	[illegible]	[illegible]	[illegible]
		1896,	[illegible]	[illegible]	[illegible]	[illegible]	[illegible]	[illegible]	[illegible]	[illegible]	[illegible]	[illegible]	[illegible]

See Note (*) on page 8.

Small-pox.—There were but 4 deaths from Small-pox registered in Ireland during the year 1896; all occurred in the Dublin Registration District. During the preceding year the disease caused 146 deaths, and in the year 1894 there were 72 deaths from it, but the total number for the eight earlier years of the decennium, 1886–93, was 27. According to the Returns 2 of the 4 persons who died from small-pox last year were unvaccinated, and in the remaining 2 cases there was no statement as to vaccination.

Measles.—The number of deaths from Measles registered is 516, being 215 in excess of the number for the preceding year; but 360 under the average for the ten years, 1886–95. Of the 516 deaths last year, 214 or 41 per cent. were in the Union of Belfast (where 82 per cent. of the fatal cases of the disease in the year 1895 and 37 per cent. of those in 1894 occurred), 13 in [illegible] Union, 69 (equal to 1 per 1,000 of the population) in Londonderry Union, 16 in Milford Union, and 74 in other parts of Ulster, the total number for that province being 386 or 74 per cent. of the gross number for Ireland; in Munster there were 81 deaths from the disease (including 21—equal to 1 per 1,000 of the population—in Bandon Union, 17 in Clonakilty Union, 14 in Kinsale Union, and 13 in the Union of Skibbereen); in Connaught, 34, of which 16 were in Tuam Union, and in Leinster 31 only.

Scarlet Fever.—There were 758 deaths from Scarlet Fever registered, against 596 for the preceding year, and an average of 585 for the ten years 1886–95, during which period the yearly numbers ranged from 308 in the year 1891 to 973 in 1887. Nearly one-fourth of the total number for Ireland last year occurred in the Union of Belfast, where the disease caused 182 deaths, and in the two Unions of Dublin North and Dublin South there were 149 fatal cases. The only other Union in which the deaths from the disease numbered 20 or upwards, is Londonderry, in which there were 27. The total number for the province of Leinster is 242; for Munster, 63; for Ulster, 407, or 54 per cent. of the number for Ireland; and for Connaught, 46.

Typhus.—Deaths from Typhus, which, with some slight intermissions, had gradually fallen from 403 in the year 1887 to 192 in 1893, fell to 120 last year. There are only 5 Unions in which 5 or more deaths were registered, and the highest number for any of these Unions is 9, the number for Cork Union. The total number for the province of Leinster is 19; for Munster, 37; for Ulster, 38; and for Connaught, 26.

Simple continued and ill-defined Fever.—The number of deaths tabulated under this heading is 153, being 11 over the number for the preceding year, but less than that in any other of the ten years 1886–95, and 146 under the average annual number for that period. Of the 153 deaths 49 occurred in Leinster; 48 in Munster; 17 in Ulster; and 36 in Connaught.

Enteric Fever.—With the exception of that for the year 1892, which it exceeds by 2, the number of deaths (718) from enteric fever is lower than the number for any of the ten years 1886–95, and is 55 under the average for those years. The rate per 100,000 living represented by the deaths from this disease is 15·7, being 1·3 under the average rate for the ten years 1886–95. The respective rates for the four provinces for last year are, Leinster 18·9 per 100,000; Munster 10·2; Ulster 18·7; and Connaught 9·4. Of the 224 deaths from enteric fever in Leinster, 135 (equal to 0·4 per 1,000 of the population) were in the Dublin Registration District; and of the 308 deaths in Ulster, 163—equal to 0·6 per 1,000 of the population in 1891—occurred in Belfast Union. Compared with the numbers for the preceding year the deaths from enteric fever in the Dublin Registration District show an increase of 29, and those for Belfast Union a decrease of 31. In each of the ten years preceding there was a substantial decline in the Dublin number, while that for Belfast showed a slight tendency to increase. The deaths from the disease last year in the two areas combined constitute 42 per cent. of the total number from enteric fever in Ireland. More than one-half of the total number of deaths from this disease occurred in persons aged between 15 and 35 years.

TABLE XI.—Showing for the year 1896 the Deaths from the several forms of Fever at each Age-Period, with the proportion to the number of the living at each Age represented thereby.

Age Periods.	Deaths from Fever.												No. of Deaths to [illegible] of the Living at each Age.
	Typhus.			Typhoid or Enteric.			Simple [illegible]			Total.			
	M.	F.	Total.	M.	F.	Total.	M.	F.	Total.	M.	F.	Total.	
Under 5 years old,	[illegible]	–	[illegible]	[illegible]	[illegible]	[illegible]	[illegible]	[illegible]	[illegible]	[illegible]	[illegible]	[illegible]	[illegible]
[illegible]	[illegible]	[illegible]	[illegible]	[illegible]	[illegible]	[illegible]	[illegible]	[illegible]	[illegible]	[illegible]	[illegible]	[illegible]	[illegible]
[illegible]	[illegible]	[illegible]	[illegible]	[illegible]	[illegible]	[illegible]	[illegible]	[illegible]	[illegible]	[illegible]	[illegible]	[illegible]	[illegible]
[illegible]	[illegible]	[illegible]	[illegible]	[illegible]	[illegible]	[illegible]	[illegible]	[illegible]	[illegible]	[illegible]	[illegible]	[illegible]	[illegible]
[illegible]	[illegible]	[illegible]	[illegible]	[illegible]	[illegible]	[illegible]	[illegible]	[illegible]	[illegible]	[illegible]	[illegible]	[illegible]	[illegible]
[illegible]	[illegible]	[illegible]	[illegible]	[illegible]	[illegible]	[illegible]	[illegible]	[illegible]	[illegible]	[illegible]	[illegible]	[illegible]	[illegible]
[illegible]	[illegible]	[illegible]	[illegible]	[illegible]	[illegible]	[illegible]	[illegible]	[illegible]	[illegible]	[illegible]	[illegible]	[illegible]	[illegible]
[illegible]	[illegible]	[illegible]	[illegible]	[illegible]	[illegible]	[illegible]	[illegible]	[illegible]	[illegible]	[illegible]	[illegible]	[illegible]	[illegible]
[illegible]	[illegible]	[illegible]	[illegible]	[illegible]	[illegible]	[illegible]	[illegible]	[illegible]	[illegible]	[illegible]	[illegible]	[illegible]	[illegible]
[illegible]	[illegible]	[illegible]	[illegible]	[illegible]	[illegible]	[illegible]	[illegible]	[illegible]	[illegible]	[illegible]	[illegible]	[illegible]	[illegible]
75 and upwards,	[illegible]	[illegible]	[illegible]	[illegible]	[illegible]	[illegible]	[illegible]	[illegible]	[illegible]	[illegible]	[illegible]	[illegible]	[illegible]
Total,	[illegible]	[illegible]	[illegible]	[illegible]	[illegible]	[illegible]	[illegible]	[illegible]	[illegible]	[illegible]	[illegible]	[illegible]	[illegible]

Whooping-cough.—Last year as in the year preceding the mortality from whooping-cough was below the average, the number of deaths for last year being 1,040 or 288 under the average for the ten years 1886–95, during which period the annual numbers ranged from 1,047 in 1895 to 1,498 in 1890. The 1,040 deaths are equal to a rate of 22·3 per 100,000 of the population at all ages; the respective rates for the four Provinces are—Leinster, 17·8 per 100,000 of the population; Munster, 20·8; Ulster, 27·0; and Connaught, 20·1. Of the 212 deaths from whooping-cough in Leinster 108 (equal to 0·3 per 1,000 of the population) were in the Dublin Registration District. The 244 deaths in Munster comprised 33 in Waterford Union and 176 in the County of Cork, including 26 (equal to 1·2 per 1,000 of the population) in Clonakilty Union, 20 in Cork Union, 21 (equivalent to 1·4 per 1,000) in Dunmanway Union; and 29 (or 1·5 per 1,000) in the Union of Kinsale. Of the 438 in Ulster, 223 (equivalent to 0·8 per 1,000 of the population according to the Census of 1891) were in Belfast Union, 20 or 1·3 per 1,000 of the population, in Carrickmacross Union, 23 in the Union of Londonderry, and 22 in Newry Union; and the 146 deaths in Connaught comprise 15 (equal to 0·8 per 1,000 of the population) in the Union of Carrick-on-Shannon, and 18 in Sligo Union.

Diphtheria caused 329 deaths, being 18 over the number for the preceding year, but 30 below the average for the ten years 1886–95. Of the 329 deaths, 195, or 60 per cent., occurred in the province of Ulster (including 50 in Belfast Union), 52 in the province of Leinster, 49 in Munster, and 27 in Connaught.

Erysipelas.—The number of deaths from erysipelas is 179, being 37 under the number for the preceding year, and 44 under the average for the ten years 1886–95.

Puerperal Fever.—The number of deaths from this disease is 252, being 66 under the average for the preceding ten years, and 69 under the number for the year 1895.

Influenza.—For the ten years 1864–73 (during the greater portion of which period there was not any epidemic outbreak of the disease), the average annual number of deaths from influenza registered in Ireland was 166, or 0·3 per 10,000 of the population, the yearly number ranging from 311 in 1864 to 96 in 1868; for the following ten years (1874–83) the average number was 82, the highest being 134 in 1875, and the lowest 39 in 1882; and for the six years, 1884–9, the average was 34 only, the numbers varying from 21 to 44. In 1890 the deaths from the disease amounted to 1,712, or 3·6 per 10,000 of the population; in the following year they fell to 891, or 1·9 in every 10,000 living; in the year 1892 they rose to 3,742, or 8·1 in every 10,000 of the population, and equal to 4·3 per cent. of the deaths from all causes; in 1893 they fell to 1,310, or 2·8 in every 10,000 of the population; in 1894 they again rose, the number for the year being 2,032, or 4·4 in every 10,000 persons; in 1895 they fell to 1,896, or 4·1 per 10,000; and last year they declined to 720 or 1·6 per 10,000 of the estimated population. In the province of Leinster the influenza death-rate in 1896 was 2·0 per 10,000 of the population according to the Census of 1891; in Munster, 1·3; in Ulster, 1·5; and in Connaught 1·2. The county rates range from 0·2 per 10,000 in Clare County to 3·7 in Carlow.

The Table (XII.) on the opposite page shows, by Sexes and Age-Periods, the distribution of the deaths from influenza through the several counties.

TABLE XII.—Showing, by Provinces and Counties, the number of Deaths from [illegible] at each of the Age-Periods registered in Ireland during the year [illegible], with the rate per 10,000 of the population represented by the deaths at all ages.

Provinces and Counties		Population in [illegible]	Under 5 Years	5 and under 20	20 and under 40	40 and under 60	60 and upwards	Total	Deaths per 10,000 of Population
LEINSTER PROVINCE:									
Carlow County	Males, Females	[illegible]	[illegible]	[illegible]	[illegible]	[illegible]	[illegible]	[illegible]	[illegible]
Dublin	Males, Females	[illegible]	[illegible]	[illegible]	[illegible]	[illegible]	[illegible]	[illegible]	[illegible]
Kildare	Males, Females	[illegible]	[illegible]	[illegible]	[illegible]	[illegible]	[illegible]	[illegible]	[illegible]
Kilkenny	Males, Females	[illegible]	[illegible]	[illegible]	[illegible]	[illegible]	[illegible]	[illegible]	[illegible]
King's	Males, Females	[illegible]	[illegible]	[illegible]	[illegible]	[illegible]	[illegible]	[illegible]	[illegible]
Longford	Males, Females	[illegible]	[illegible]	[illegible]	[illegible]	[illegible]	[illegible]	[illegible]	[illegible]
Louth County and County of the Town of Drogheda	Males, Females	[illegible]	[illegible]	[illegible]	[illegible]	[illegible]	[illegible]	[illegible]	[illegible]
Meath County	Males, Females	[illegible]	[illegible]	[illegible]	[illegible]	[illegible]	[illegible]	[illegible]	[illegible]
Queen's	Males, Females	[illegible]	[illegible]	[illegible]	[illegible]	[illegible]	[illegible]	[illegible]	[illegible]
Westmeath	Males, Females	[illegible]	[illegible]	[illegible]	[illegible]	[illegible]	[illegible]	[illegible]	[illegible]
Wexford	Males, Females	[illegible]	[illegible]	[illegible]	[illegible]	[illegible]	[illegible]	[illegible]	[illegible]
Wicklow	Males, Females	[illegible]	[illegible]	[illegible]	[illegible]	[illegible]	[illegible]	[illegible]	[illegible]
Total	Males, Females	[illegible]	[illegible]	[illegible]	[illegible]	[illegible]	[illegible]	[illegible]	[illegible]
MUNSTER PROVINCE:									
Clare County	Males, Females	[illegible]	[illegible]	[illegible]	[illegible]	[illegible]	[illegible]	[illegible]	[illegible]
Cork	Males, Females	[illegible]	[illegible]	[illegible]	[illegible]	[illegible]	[illegible]	[illegible]	[illegible]
Kerry	Males, Females	[illegible]	[illegible]	[illegible]	[illegible]	[illegible]	[illegible]	[illegible]	[illegible]
Limerick	Males, Females	[illegible]	[illegible]	[illegible]	[illegible]	[illegible]	[illegible]	[illegible]	[illegible]
Tipperary	Males, Females	[illegible]	[illegible]	[illegible]	[illegible]	[illegible]	[illegible]	[illegible]	[illegible]
Waterford	Males, Females	[illegible]	[illegible]	[illegible]	[illegible]	[illegible]	[illegible]	[illegible]	[illegible]
Total	Males, Females	[illegible]	[illegible]	[illegible]	[illegible]	[illegible]	[illegible]	[illegible]	[illegible]
ULSTER PROVINCE:									
Antrim County	Males, Females	[illegible]	[illegible]	[illegible]	[illegible]	[illegible]	[illegible]	[illegible]	[illegible]
Armagh	Males, Females	[illegible]	[illegible]	[illegible]	[illegible]	[illegible]	[illegible]	[illegible]	[illegible]
Cavan	Males, Females	[illegible]	[illegible]	[illegible]	[illegible]	[illegible]	[illegible]	[illegible]	[illegible]
Donegal	Males, Females	[illegible]	[illegible]	[illegible]	[illegible]	[illegible]	[illegible]	[illegible]	[illegible]
Down	Males, Females	[illegible]	[illegible]	[illegible]	[illegible]	[illegible]	[illegible]	[illegible]	[illegible]
Fermanagh	Males, Females	[illegible]	[illegible]	[illegible]	[illegible]	[illegible]	[illegible]	[illegible]	[illegible]
Londonderry	Males, Females	[illegible]	[illegible]	[illegible]	[illegible]	[illegible]	[illegible]	[illegible]	[illegible]
Monaghan	Males, Females	[illegible]	[illegible]	[illegible]	[illegible]	[illegible]	[illegible]	[illegible]	[illegible]
Tyrone	Males, Females	[illegible]	[illegible]	[illegible]	[illegible]	[illegible]	[illegible]	[illegible]	[illegible]
Total	Males, Females	[illegible]	[illegible]	[illegible]	[illegible]	[illegible]	[illegible]	[illegible]	[illegible]
CONNAUGHT PROVINCE:									
Galway County	Males, Females	[illegible]	[illegible]	[illegible]	[illegible]	[illegible]	[illegible]	[illegible]	[illegible]
Leitrim	Males, Females	[illegible]	[illegible]	[illegible]	[illegible]	[illegible]	[illegible]	[illegible]	[illegible]
Mayo	Males, Females	[illegible]	[illegible]	[illegible]	[illegible]	[illegible]	[illegible]	[illegible]	[illegible]
Roscommon	Males, Females	[illegible]	[illegible]	[illegible]	[illegible]	[illegible]	[illegible]	[illegible]	[illegible]
Sligo	Males, Females	[illegible]	[illegible]	[illegible]	[illegible]	[illegible]	[illegible]	[illegible]	[illegible]
Total	Males, Females	[illegible]	[illegible]	[illegible]	[illegible]	[illegible]	[illegible]	[illegible]	[illegible]
THROUGHOUT IRELAND	Males, Females	[illegible]	[illegible]	[illegible]	[illegible]	[illegible]	[illegible]	[illegible]	[illegible]

* [illegible]

Simple Cholera.—There were 142 deaths ascribed to this disease, being 2 over the number for the preceding year, and 60 over the average for the ten years 1886–95. Those recorded in 1896 consist of 53 in Leinster, 27 in Munster, 61 in Ulster, and 1 only in Connaught.

Diarrhoea, Dysentery.—The number of deaths tabulated under this heading is 1,421, being 7 over the average for the ten years 1886–95, but 148 under the number for the year 1895. The rate per 100,000 living represented by the deaths from these causes is 31·2, being 1·2 over the average rate for the preceding ten years. The respective rates for the four provinces are—Leinster, 39·8 per 100,000; Munster, 24·8; Ulster, 25·6; and Connaught, 9·1. Seventy per cent. of the deaths under this heading in Leinster were in the Dublin Registration District, and 47 per cent. of those in Ulster occurred in the Union of Belfast.

Three males and two females died from *Hydrophobia.* One of these deaths occurred in the province of Leinster, 3 in Munster, and 1 in Ulster.

II.—Parasitic Diseases.

There were only 53 deaths from diseases of this class, but this number is 12 in excess of that for the year 1895.

III.—Dietetic Diseases.

The number of deaths from dietetic diseases is 167, including 156 from intemperance, 43 of which (40 males and 3 females) were caused by delirium tremens, and 113 (83 males and 30 females) come under the head of chronic alcoholism. The number of deaths from intemperance registered in the year 1895 was 166, and in the preceding year 146.

IV.—Constitutional Diseases.

From diseases classified as "constitutional" there resulted 15,377 deaths (7,412 males and 7,965 females), affording a rate of 1 in 4·9 of all the deaths, and equal to 337 in every 100,000 of the population.

Phthisis or Pulmonary Consumption.—Phthisis proved somewhat less fatal than usual, the number of deaths being 9,051 (4,374 males and 4,677 females), or 198·5 in every 100,000 of the estimated population, while the average for the preceding ten years was 10,081, or 212·5 per 100,000, and the lowest rate for any year in that period 204·4 per 100,000, the rate for the year 1888.

As heretofore, Leinster and Ulster yield the highest rates, and Connaught the lowest. The rates for the four provinces are as follow:—Leinster, 211 per 100,000 of the population; Ulster, 208; Munster, 184; and Connaught, 141.

Of the 3,268 deaths from phthisis in Ulster, 1,079 occurred in Belfast union, this number being equal to 373 per 100,000 of the population according to the Census of 1891; and the 2,308 fatal cases of the disease in Leinster comprise 1,073, or 307 per 100,000 of the population, registered in the unions of Dublin North and Dublin South.

Of the total number of deaths from phthisis in Ireland, 6,922, or 76 per cent., were of persons aged 15 and under 45 years of age.

Tabes Mesenterica caused 799 deaths, and *Tubercular Meningitis* 1,131, and 1,002 deaths come under the head of *Miscellaneous forms of Tuberculosis, Scrofula.*

Tuberculosis.—The deaths from phthisis and those recorded under the three headings last referred to, comprise nearly all the deaths from tuberculosis, and it may be seen that, taken together, they amount to 11,983, which number is equal to 15·6 per cent. of the deaths from all causes registered in Ireland during the year, and represents a mortality equivalent to 2·6 per 1,000 of the population.

In view of the special interest attaching to the subject at the present time, and having regard to the fact that the statistics show that this high death rate is not exceptional nor confined to the year 1896, but on the contrary, is slightly under the average rate yielded by the mortality from these causes in Ireland during a long series of years, I have had the following Table (Table XIII.), constructed. It shows the deaths from each chief form of tubercular disease during the year 1896, and each of the 25 years preceding, with the ratio of these deaths to the deaths from all causes and to the population. Decennial averages and averages for the 25 years, 1871–95, are also included. The average rate per 1,000 of the estimated population for the whole of this latter period was 2·7 per 1,000, which was also the average rate for the ten years 1881–90, and the five years 1891–5. The average for the ten years 1871–80 was slightly less, viz.:—2·6 per 1,000, but as regards this rate it may be observed that it is most probably somewhat under the actual average, as in the absence of the aid derived from the system of Burial Returns introduced in the year 1879, under the Public Health Act of 1878, the registration of deaths was not as full or satisfactory as it has become since that date. Taking the years from 1879 up to the present time, the average rate was 2·7, and it will be seen that the extreme rates were 2·9 and 2·5 per 1,000, the former being the rate for the year 1880 (in which year the general death rate was considerably above the average), and the latter that for the following year, 1881. There can be but little doubt that the distress which prevailed in the latter part of the year 1879 and the earlier months of 1880 accelerated the deaths of many delicate persons labouring under tubercular disease, and thus led to the high tuberculosis death rate in 1880, a fact which would account to a great extent for the fall in the rate in the following year. It will be observed that since the year 1881 the fluctuations in the rate have been very slight.

TABLE XIII.—Showing the Number of Deaths from the following causes, viz:—Tabes Mesenterica, Tubercular Meningitis, Phthisis, "Miscellaneous Forms of Tuberculosis, Scrofula," and from All Causes registered in Ireland in each of the twenty-six years, 1871–96, with the Rate per 1,000 of Estimated Population represented by (a) Deaths from the above-mentioned forms of Tuberculosis; (b) Deaths from all causes; and the per-centage of total Deaths caused by the tubercular diseases referred to.

Years. (1)	Number of Deaths from: Tabes Mesenterica. (2)	Tubercular Meningitis. (3)	Phthisis. (4)	"Miscellaneous Forms of Tuberculosis, Scrofula." (5)	Total Deaths from all the foregoing diseases: Number. (6)	Rate per 1,000 of Estimated Population. (7)	Total Deaths from all causes: Numbers. (8)	Rate per 1,000. (9)	Per-centage of Deaths caused by the Diseases entered in Columns 2, 3, 4, and 5. (10)
1871,	[illegible]	[illegible]	[illegible]	[illegible]	[illegible]	[illegible]	[illegible]	[illegible]	[illegible]
1872,	[illegible]	[illegible]	[illegible]	[illegible]	[illegible]	[illegible]	[illegible]	[illegible]	[illegible]
1873,	[illegible]	[illegible]	[illegible]	[illegible]	[illegible]	[illegible]	[illegible]	[illegible]	[illegible]
1874,	[illegible]	[illegible]	[illegible]	[illegible]	[illegible]	[illegible]	[illegible]	[illegible]	[illegible]
1875,	[illegible]	[illegible]	[illegible]	[illegible]	[illegible]	[illegible]	[illegible]	[illegible]	[illegible]
1876,	[illegible]	[illegible]	[illegible]	[illegible]	[illegible]	[illegible]	[illegible]	[illegible]	[illegible]
1877,	[illegible]	[illegible]	[illegible]	[illegible]	[illegible]	[illegible]	[illegible]	[illegible]	[illegible]
1878,	[illegible]	[illegible]	[illegible]	[illegible]	[illegible]	[illegible]	[illegible]	[illegible]	[illegible]
1879,	[illegible]	[illegible]	[illegible]	[illegible]	[illegible]	[illegible]	[illegible]	[illegible]	[illegible]
1880,	[illegible]	[illegible]	[illegible]	[illegible]	[illegible]	[illegible]	[illegible]	[illegible]	[illegible]
Average for 10 years (1871–80),	[illegible]	[illegible]	[illegible]	[illegible]	[illegible]	[illegible]	[illegible]	[illegible]	[illegible]
1881,	[illegible]	[illegible]	[illegible]	[illegible]	[illegible]	[illegible]	[illegible]	[illegible]	[illegible]
1882,	[illegible]	[illegible]	[illegible]	[illegible]	[illegible]	[illegible]	[illegible]	[illegible]	[illegible]
1883,	[illegible]	[illegible]	[illegible]	[illegible]	[illegible]	[illegible]	[illegible]	[illegible]	[illegible]
1884,	[illegible]	[illegible]	[illegible]	[illegible]	[illegible]	[illegible]	[illegible]	[illegible]	[illegible]
1885,	[illegible]	[illegible]	[illegible]	[illegible]	[illegible]	[illegible]	[illegible]	[illegible]	[illegible]
1886,	[illegible]	[illegible]	[illegible]	[illegible]	[illegible]	[illegible]	[illegible]	[illegible]	[illegible]
1887,	[illegible]	[illegible]	[illegible]	[illegible]	[illegible]	[illegible]	[illegible]	[illegible]	[illegible]
1888,	[illegible]	[illegible]	[illegible]	[illegible]	[illegible]	[illegible]	[illegible]	[illegible]	[illegible]
1889,	[illegible]	[illegible]	[illegible]	[illegible]	[illegible]	[illegible]	[illegible]	[illegible]	[illegible]
1890,	[illegible]	[illegible]	[illegible]	[illegible]	[illegible]	[illegible]	[illegible]	[illegible]	[illegible]
Average for 10 years (1881–90),	[illegible]	[illegible]	[illegible]	[illegible]	[illegible]	[illegible]	[illegible]	[illegible]	[illegible]
1891,	[illegible]	[illegible]	[illegible]	[illegible]	[illegible]	[illegible]	[illegible]	[illegible]	[illegible]
1892,	[illegible]	[illegible]	[illegible]	[illegible]	[illegible]	[illegible]	[illegible]	[illegible]	[illegible]
1893,	[illegible]	[illegible]	[illegible]	[illegible]	[illegible]	[illegible]	[illegible]	[illegible]	[illegible]
1894,	[illegible]	[illegible]	[illegible]	[illegible]	[illegible]	[illegible]	[illegible]	[illegible]	[illegible]
1895,	[illegible]	[illegible]	[illegible]	[illegible]	[illegible]	[illegible]	[illegible]	[illegible]	[illegible]
Average for 5 years 1891–5,	[illegible]	[illegible]	[illegible]	[illegible]	[illegible]	[illegible]	[illegible]	[illegible]	[illegible]
Average for 25 years, 1871–95,	[illegible]	[illegible]	[illegible]	[illegible]	[illegible]	[illegible]	[illegible]	[illegible]	[illegible]
1896,	[illegible]	[illegible]	[illegible]	[illegible]	[illegible]	[illegible]	[illegible]	[illegible]	[illegible]

Gout.—The number of deaths from gout is 31 (17 males and 14 females); it shows an increase of 10 as compared with the number for the preceding year.

Cancer.—Cancer caused 2,437 (1,100 males and 1,337 females), being 265 over the average for the ten years 1886–95, and 141 over the number for the last year of that period. The latter increase was chiefly in deaths of males which were 103 more numerous than in the year 1895.

The following Table shows, by Sexes and Age-periods, the deaths from Cancer registered during the year 1896, arranged according to the part of the body affected by the disease; also the number of deaths to 100,000 of the living at same age. It will be observed from the Table that the deaths entered under the first eleven headings therein, which relate to various parts of the head, neck, and throat, amount to 516, and that of these, 363, or more than two-thirds, were deaths of males. 577 of the classified cases were deaths from cancer of the stomach; 281 females died from cancer of the breast, and 169 females from cancer of the uterus. The Table shows also the total deaths from cancer in each of the ten years, 1886–95, arranged by Age-periods.

DEATHS FROM CANCER—continued.

Part Affected.		Ages at Death.												Total.
		[illegible]	[illegible]	[illegible]	[illegible]	[illegible]	[illegible]	[illegible]	[illegible]	[illegible]	[illegible]	[illegible]	[illegible]	
[illegible]														
Colon,	Males,	[illegible]	[illegible]	[illegible]	[illegible]	[illegible]	[illegible]	[illegible]	[illegible]	[illegible]	[illegible]	[illegible]	[illegible]	[illegible]
	Females,	[illegible]	[illegible]	[illegible]	[illegible]	[illegible]	[illegible]	[illegible]	[illegible]	[illegible]	[illegible]	[illegible]	[illegible]	[illegible]
	Total,	[illegible]	[illegible]	[illegible]	[illegible]	[illegible]	[illegible]	[illegible]	[illegible]	[illegible]	[illegible]	[illegible]	[illegible]	[illegible]
"Intestines,"	Males,	[illegible]	[illegible]	[illegible]	[illegible]	[illegible]	[illegible]	[illegible]	[illegible]	[illegible]	[illegible]	[illegible]	[illegible]	[illegible]
	Females,	[illegible]	[illegible]	[illegible]	[illegible]	[illegible]	[illegible]	[illegible]	[illegible]	[illegible]	[illegible]	[illegible]	[illegible]	[illegible]
	Total,	[illegible]	[illegible]	[illegible]	[illegible]	[illegible]	[illegible]	[illegible]	[illegible]	[illegible]	[illegible]	[illegible]	[illegible]	[illegible]
Peritoneum,	Males,	[illegible]	[illegible]	[illegible]	[illegible]	[illegible]	[illegible]	[illegible]	[illegible]	[illegible]	[illegible]	[illegible]	[illegible]	[illegible]
	Females,	[illegible]	[illegible]	[illegible]	[illegible]	[illegible]	[illegible]	[illegible]	[illegible]	[illegible]	[illegible]	[illegible]	[illegible]	[illegible]
	Total,	[illegible]	[illegible]	[illegible]	[illegible]	[illegible]	[illegible]	[illegible]	[illegible]	[illegible]	[illegible]	[illegible]	[illegible]	[illegible]
Rectum,	Males,	[illegible]	[illegible]	[illegible]	[illegible]	[illegible]	[illegible]	[illegible]	[illegible]	[illegible]	[illegible]	[illegible]	[illegible]	[illegible]
	Females,	[illegible]	[illegible]	[illegible]	[illegible]	[illegible]	[illegible]	[illegible]	[illegible]	[illegible]	[illegible]	[illegible]	[illegible]	[illegible]
	Total,	[illegible]	[illegible]	[illegible]	[illegible]	[illegible]	[illegible]	[illegible]	[illegible]	[illegible]	[illegible]	[illegible]	[illegible]	[illegible]
Liver,	Males,	[illegible]	[illegible]	[illegible]	[illegible]	[illegible]	[illegible]	[illegible]	[illegible]	[illegible]	[illegible]	[illegible]	[illegible]	[illegible]
	Females,	[illegible]	[illegible]	[illegible]	[illegible]	[illegible]	[illegible]	[illegible]	[illegible]	[illegible]	[illegible]	[illegible]	[illegible]	[illegible]
	Total,	[illegible]	[illegible]	[illegible]	[illegible]	[illegible]	[illegible]	[illegible]	[illegible]	[illegible]	[illegible]	[illegible]	[illegible]	[illegible]
Pancreas,	Males,	[illegible]	[illegible]	[illegible]	[illegible]	[illegible]	[illegible]	[illegible]	[illegible]	[illegible]	[illegible]	[illegible]	[illegible]	[illegible]
	Females,	[illegible]	[illegible]	[illegible]	[illegible]	[illegible]	[illegible]	[illegible]	[illegible]	[illegible]	[illegible]	[illegible]	[illegible]	[illegible]
	Total,	[illegible]	[illegible]	[illegible]	[illegible]	[illegible]	[illegible]	[illegible]	[illegible]	[illegible]	[illegible]	[illegible]	[illegible]	[illegible]
Vulva,	Males,	[illegible]	[illegible]	[illegible]	[illegible]	[illegible]	[illegible]	[illegible]	[illegible]	[illegible]	[illegible]	[illegible]	[illegible]	[illegible]
	Females,	[illegible]	[illegible]	[illegible]	[illegible]	[illegible]	[illegible]	[illegible]	[illegible]	[illegible]	[illegible]	[illegible]	[illegible]	[illegible]
	Total,	[illegible]	[illegible]	[illegible]	[illegible]	[illegible]	[illegible]	[illegible]	[illegible]	[illegible]	[illegible]	[illegible]	[illegible]	[illegible]
Uterus,	Males,	[illegible]	[illegible]	[illegible]	[illegible]	[illegible]	[illegible]	[illegible]	[illegible]	[illegible]	[illegible]	[illegible]	[illegible]	[illegible]
	Females,	[illegible]	[illegible]	[illegible]	[illegible]	[illegible]	[illegible]	[illegible]	[illegible]	[illegible]	[illegible]	[illegible]	[illegible]	[illegible]
	Total,	[illegible]	[illegible]	[illegible]	[illegible]	[illegible]	[illegible]	[illegible]	[illegible]	[illegible]	[illegible]	[illegible]	[illegible]	[illegible]
Ovary,	Males,	[illegible]	[illegible]	[illegible]	[illegible]	[illegible]	[illegible]	[illegible]	[illegible]	[illegible]	[illegible]	[illegible]	[illegible]	[illegible]
	Females,	[illegible]	[illegible]	[illegible]	[illegible]	[illegible]	[illegible]	[illegible]	[illegible]	[illegible]	[illegible]	[illegible]	[illegible]	[illegible]
	Total,	[illegible]	[illegible]	[illegible]	[illegible]	[illegible]	[illegible]	[illegible]	[illegible]	[illegible]	[illegible]	[illegible]	[illegible]	[illegible]
Penis,	Males,	[illegible]	[illegible]	[illegible]	[illegible]	[illegible]	[illegible]	[illegible]	[illegible]	[illegible]	[illegible]	[illegible]	[illegible]	[illegible]
	Females,	[illegible]	[illegible]	[illegible]	[illegible]	[illegible]	[illegible]	[illegible]	[illegible]	[illegible]	[illegible]	[illegible]	[illegible]	[illegible]
	Total,	[illegible]	[illegible]	[illegible]	[illegible]	[illegible]	[illegible]	[illegible]	[illegible]	[illegible]	[illegible]	[illegible]	[illegible]	[illegible]
Bladder,	Males,	[illegible]	[illegible]	[illegible]	[illegible]	[illegible]	[illegible]	[illegible]	[illegible]	[illegible]	[illegible]	[illegible]	[illegible]	[illegible]
	Females,	[illegible]	[illegible]	[illegible]	[illegible]	[illegible]	[illegible]	[illegible]	[illegible]	[illegible]	[illegible]	[illegible]	[illegible]	[illegible]
	Total,	[illegible]	[illegible]	[illegible]	[illegible]	[illegible]	[illegible]	[illegible]	[illegible]	[illegible]	[illegible]	[illegible]	[illegible]	[illegible]
Testicle,	Males,	[illegible]	[illegible]	[illegible]	[illegible]	[illegible]	[illegible]	[illegible]	[illegible]	[illegible]	[illegible]	[illegible]	[illegible]	[illegible]
	Females,	[illegible]	[illegible]	[illegible]	[illegible]	[illegible]	[illegible]	[illegible]	[illegible]	[illegible]	[illegible]	[illegible]	[illegible]	[illegible]
	Total,	[illegible]	[illegible]	[illegible]	[illegible]	[illegible]	[illegible]	[illegible]	[illegible]	[illegible]	[illegible]	[illegible]	[illegible]	[illegible]
[illegible]	Males,	[illegible]	[illegible]	[illegible]	[illegible]	[illegible]	[illegible]	[illegible]	[illegible]	[illegible]	[illegible]	[illegible]	[illegible]	[illegible]
	Females,	[illegible]	[illegible]	[illegible]	[illegible]	[illegible]	[illegible]	[illegible]	[illegible]	[illegible]	[illegible]	[illegible]	[illegible]	[illegible]
	Total,	[illegible]	[illegible]	[illegible]	[illegible]	[illegible]	[illegible]	[illegible]	[illegible]	[illegible]	[illegible]	[illegible]	[illegible]	[illegible]
[illegible]	Males,	[illegible]	[illegible]	[illegible]	[illegible]	[illegible]	[illegible]	[illegible]	[illegible]	[illegible]	[illegible]	[illegible]	[illegible]	[illegible]
	Females,	[illegible]	[illegible]	[illegible]	[illegible]	[illegible]	[illegible]	[illegible]	[illegible]	[illegible]	[illegible]	[illegible]	[illegible]	[illegible]
	Total,	[illegible]	[illegible]	[illegible]	[illegible]	[illegible]	[illegible]	[illegible]	[illegible]	[illegible]	[illegible]	[illegible]	[illegible]	[illegible]
[illegible]	Males,	[illegible]	[illegible]	[illegible]	[illegible]	[illegible]	[illegible]	[illegible]	[illegible]	[illegible]	[illegible]	[illegible]	[illegible]	[illegible]
	Females,	[illegible]	[illegible]	[illegible]	[illegible]	[illegible]	[illegible]	[illegible]	[illegible]	[illegible]	[illegible]	[illegible]	[illegible]	[illegible]
	Total,	[illegible]	[illegible]	[illegible]	[illegible]	[illegible]	[illegible]	[illegible]	[illegible]	[illegible]	[illegible]	[illegible]	[illegible]	[illegible]
Other specified parts,*	Males,	[illegible]	[illegible]	[illegible]	[illegible]	[illegible]	[illegible]	[illegible]	[illegible]	[illegible]	[illegible]	[illegible]	[illegible]	[illegible]
	Females,	[illegible]	[illegible]	[illegible]	[illegible]	[illegible]	[illegible]	[illegible]	[illegible]	[illegible]	[illegible]	[illegible]	[illegible]	[illegible]
	Total,	[illegible]	[illegible]	[illegible]	[illegible]	[illegible]	[illegible]	[illegible]	[illegible]	[illegible]	[illegible]	[illegible]	[illegible]	[illegible]
Part unspecified,	Males,	[illegible]	[illegible]	[illegible]	[illegible]	[illegible]	[illegible]	[illegible]	[illegible]	[illegible]	[illegible]	[illegible]	[illegible]	[illegible]
	Females,	[illegible]	[illegible]	[illegible]	[illegible]	[illegible]	[illegible]	[illegible]	[illegible]	[illegible]	[illegible]	[illegible]	[illegible]	[illegible]
	Total,	[illegible]	[illegible]	[illegible]	[illegible]	[illegible]	[illegible]	[illegible]	[illegible]	[illegible]	[illegible]	[illegible]	[illegible]	[illegible]
Total year 1896,	Males,	[illegible]	[illegible]	[illegible]	[illegible]	[illegible]	[illegible]	[illegible]	[illegible]	[illegible]	[illegible]	[illegible]	[illegible]	[illegible]
	Females,	[illegible]	[illegible]	[illegible]	[illegible]	[illegible]	[illegible]	[illegible]	[illegible]	[illegible]	[illegible]	[illegible]	[illegible]	[illegible]
	M. & F.,	[illegible]	[illegible]	[illegible]	[illegible]	[illegible]	[illegible]	[illegible]	[illegible]	[illegible]	[illegible]	[illegible]	[illegible]	[illegible]

V.—Developmental Diseases.

The number of deaths in this class is 16,460, of which 15,810 (7,1[illegible] males and 8,[illegible] females), or 20·9 per cent. of the deaths from all causes, were ascribed to "old age." Of the remaining 641 deaths, 312 are tabulated under the head of "premature birth"; 27 were caused by atelectasis, 8 by cyanosis, 32 by spina bifida; &c.

VI.—Local Diseases.

The deaths from "local diseases" amount to 30,168 (15,324 males and 14,844 females), or 39·9 per cent. of the deaths from all causes; but in the preceding year the deaths in this class amounted to 34,055, and formed 41·1 per cent. of the deaths from all causes.

Diseases of the Nervous System.—From this group of diseases there resulted 6,510 deaths—3,365 males and 3,145 females. They include 2,310 from convulsions (nearly all children), 1,185 tabulated under the head of "hemiplegia, brain paralysis"; 253 from paraplegia and diseases of the spinal cord; 1,175 from apoplexy; 410 from inflammation of the brain or its membranes; 264 from epilepsy; 634 from insanity (general paralysis of the insane); 9 (one male and 8 females) from chorea or St. Vitus's dance; 167 from softening of the brain, &c.

Diseases of the Circulatory System.—Diseases of the circulatory system caused 5,832 deaths—2,949 males and 2,883 females.

*Diseases of the Respiratory System.**—The mortality from diseases of the respiratory system* was less than in any of the ten years preceding and, allowing for decrease of population, shows a decline equivalent to 21·4 per cent. as compared with the average rate for that period. The number of deaths from the diseases in this group is 11,236—5,760 males and 5,476 females—or 246·4 in every 100,000 of the population. In the preceding year 13,918 deaths from these causes were registered, being equal to 304·9 per 100,000 living, and the average number for the ten years, 1886–95, was 14,700, or 313·5 per 100,000 living. The respective rates for the Provinces, in 1896, are—Leinster, 276 per 100,000 persons; Munster, 223; Ulster, 265; and Connaught, 195.

Of the 11,236 deaths from these causes, 6,446 (3,113 males and 3,333 females) were from bronchitis, a decline of 2,158, or 25 per cent., as compared with the number from that disease in the preceding year; 2,271 (948 males and 1,323 females) from pneumonia or inflammation of the lungs, being 342 under the number for the preceding year; 428 from croup; 187 from asthma and emphysema; 212 from pleurisy; 131 from laryngitis, &c.

Diseases of the Digestive System.—These diseases caused 3,928 deaths (2,038 males and 1,890 females), including 307 from enteritis or inflammation of the bowels; 405 from peritonitis or inflammation of the covering of the bowels; 371 from ileus or obstruction of the bowels; 130 from hernia; 5 (3 males and 2 females) from fistula; 269—169 males and 100 females—from cirrhosis of liver; &c.

Diseases of the Urinary System.—To the various affections of this order of diseases 1,431 deaths (948 males and 483 females) were ascribed. Of these deaths, 590 (232 males and 358 females) were from Bright's disease; 281 from acute nephritis or inflammation of the kidneys; 16 from suppression of urine; 14 from stone in the bladder; 30 from uraemia, &c.

The remaining deaths from Local Diseases comprise 83 from *Diseases of the Lymphatic System and of Ductless Glands*; 578 from *Diseases of the Reproductive System* (including 151 from diseases of the Organs of Generation and 427 from the Accidents of Childbirth); 276 from *Diseases of the Organs of Locomotion*; and 173 from *Diseases of the Integumentary System.*

VII.—Violent Deaths.

The number of violent deaths registered during the year is 1,976 (1,311 males and 665 females), or 43·3 in every 100,000 of the population, being somewhat higher than the average rate for the ten years 1886–95. Accidents or negligence caused 1,798 of these deaths (including 181 from burns or scalds and 330 from drowning) against an average of 1,668; the number of cases of homicide (murder and manslaughter) was 49, or 11 below the average; and the number of cases of suicide was 129 against an average of 124.

Inquests.—There were 2,690 inquests reported to the Registrars during the year 1896, being 1 inquest to every 29 deaths registered.

AGES.

Deaths of infants under 1 year old numbered 10,200, being equal to 9·5 per cent. of the number of births registered.

Amongst children under 5 years of age 16,065 deaths occurred—a mortality equal to 35·3 in every 1,000 of the estimated number of the living at that age. Of these, 8,664 were boys and 7,401 girls; the former number representing 37·5 in every 1,000 boys and the latter 33·0 in every 1,000 girls under 5 years old.

* Exclusive of Phthisis, or Pulmonary Consumption, for which see "Constitutional Diseases."

The deaths of persons aged 65 years and upwards are equivalent to 8·5 per cent. of the estimated number of the living at that age.

Among the deaths registered are 734 of persons stated to have been aged 85 years or upwards—342 males and 392 females; of these 151 (59 males and 92 females) were returned as having been 100 years or upwards. In the absence of public records for remote periods, absolute verification of the ages of very old persons is not attainable, but secondary inquiries having been made as regards persons returned during some recent years as centenarians, it was found, in almost every instance, that, so far as the Registrars could ascertain, the age was correctly stated.

EMIGRATION.

According to the Returns obtained by the Royal Irish Constabulary and the Metropolitan Police, who acted as enumerators at the several Irish seaports, the number of emigrants (natives of Ireland) who left Ireland during the year 1896 was [illegible]; of these 17,751 were males and 21,[illegible] were females. Of the whole number, [illegible] were from the Province of Leinster; 15,435 from Munster; 7,494 from Ulster; and 12,[illegible] from Connaught.

Of the total emigrants from Ireland in 1896, 5·9 per cent. were under 15 years of age; 83·7 per cent. were between 15 and 35 years old; [illegible]·4 per cent. were 35 or upwards; and in 10 instances the ages were not specified.

PRICES OF PROVISIONS, AND PAUPERISM.

The average price of the 4 lb. loaf in Dublin in the year 1896 was 5d., being [illegible] over the average price for the previous year.* Oatmeal (1st quality) averaged [illegible] per cwt. in Dublin; the average price for 1895 was 13s. 7d.; the average prices of potatoes in Dublin ranged from 1s. [illegible] to 2s. [illegible] per cwt., against 2s. 11d. to 3s. 10d. in 1895; and those of beef from 43s. 6d. to 53s. per cwt., against 46s. 6d. to 57s. 6d. in 1895.

TABLE XV.—Average Prices in Dublin of Bread, Oatmeal, Potatoes, and Beef, during the years [illegible], and the Average Number of Paupers in Ireland receiving Indoor and Out-door Relief [illegible]; also the Average Prices of Provisions and the Average Number of Paupers in Receipt of Relief during each quarter of the year 1896.

Year.	Bread, 4 lb. loaf.	Oatmeal [illegible] per cwt.	Potatoes [illegible]	Beef [illegible]	Paupers: In-door.	Paupers: Out-door.
	d.	s. d.	s. d. s. d.	s. d. s. d.		
[illegible]	[illegible]	[illegible]	[illegible]	[illegible]	[illegible]	[illegible]
[illegible]	[illegible]	[illegible]	[illegible]	[illegible]	[illegible]	[illegible]
[illegible]	[illegible]	[illegible]	[illegible]	[illegible]	[illegible]	[illegible]
[illegible]	[illegible]	[illegible]	[illegible]	[illegible]	[illegible]	[illegible]
[illegible]	[illegible]	[illegible]	[illegible]	[illegible]	[illegible]	[illegible]
[illegible]	[illegible]	[illegible]	[illegible]	[illegible]	[illegible]	[illegible]
[illegible]	[illegible]	[illegible]	[illegible]	[illegible]	[illegible]	[illegible]
[illegible]	[illegible]	[illegible]	[illegible]	[illegible]	[illegible]	[illegible]
[illegible]	[illegible]	[illegible]	[illegible]	[illegible]	[illegible]	[illegible]
[illegible]	[illegible]	[illegible]	[illegible]	[illegible]	[illegible]	[illegible]
[illegible]	[illegible]	[illegible]	[illegible]	[illegible]	[illegible]	[illegible]
1st Quarter, 1896	[illegible]	[illegible]	[illegible]	[illegible]	[illegible]	[illegible]
2nd "	[illegible]	[illegible]	[illegible]	[illegible]	[illegible]	[illegible]
3rd "	[illegible]	[illegible]	[illegible]	[illegible]	[illegible]	[illegible]
4th "	[illegible]	[illegible]	[illegible]	[illegible]	[illegible]	[illegible]

* [illegible]

† [illegible]

Surveying the period covered by several Tables in this Report, i.e., 1896, and the ten years preceding, it is found that beef was lowest in the year 1887, when the average prices ranged from 44s. to 53s. 6d. per cwt., and 1896 when they ranged from 43s. 6d. to 54s.; oatmeal (1st quality) was cheapest in 1896, in which year the average price was 12s. 7d. per cwt.; and potatoes, in 1896, when the average range of prices was from 1s. 11d. to 2s. 11d. per cwt. The highest average price of oatmeal was 16s. 7d. in 1886; the highest range for potatoes, 3s. 6d. to 4s. 3d. per cwt. in 1891, and for beef, 50s. 6d. to 62s. per cwt. in 1890.

From Returns, for which I am indebted to the Local Government Board, it appears that the average number of workhouse inmates in Ireland on Saturdays during the year 1896 was 41,920, being 271 over the average for the preceding year; and that the average number of persons receiving out-door relief was 54,296, or 8,182 under the corresponding number for 1895.

THE WEATHER.

The following particulars and those given on pages 36–40, which are inserted by the kind permission of the Editor of the Dublin Journal of Medical Science, have been derived from Returns of Meteorological Observations taken in Dublin City by J. W. Moore, Esq., M.D., F.R.C.P.I., F.R.MET. SOC.; and published in the Journal during the years 1896–97. The Tables on pages 185–188 also, are founded on Dr. Moore's observations.

The mean Atmospherical Pressure has been obtained from daily readings of the barometer at 9 A.M. and 9 P.M., corrected and reduced to 32° Fahrenheit at the mean sea level. The Mean Temperature values have been deduced from the maximal and minimal readings of the thermometer in the shade. The Rainfall is that measured daily at 9 A.M. A rainy day is one on which at least one-hundredth (·01) of an inch of rain falls within the twenty-four hours from 9 A.M. to 9 A.M.

The Mean Height of the Barometer during the year 1896 was [illegible] inches. The highest observed reading was [illegible] inches at 10 A.M. on January 6th. The lowest observed reading was [illegible] inches, at [illegible] on March 2nd. The extreme range of atmospherical pressure was [illegible] inches compared with [illegible] inches in 1895.

The Mean Temperature of the year, deduced from the arithmetical mean of the maximal and minimal readings of the thermometer in the shade was [illegible]°. The highest reading was [illegible]° on June [illegible]; the lowest reading was [illegible]° on November [illegible]. The average mean temperature for the years 1871–95, calculated in the same way, was [illegible]°. The mean temperature deduced from the daily readings of the dry bulb thermometer at 9 A.M. and 9 P.M. was [illegible]°.

Rain fell on [illegible] days, including snow or sleet on 7 days and hail on [illegible] days. The average annual number of rainy days in the years 1871–95 was [illegible]. The total rainfall amounted [illegible] inches compared with an average of [illegible] inches in the twenty years 1876–95. During the first half of 1896 (January to June, inclusive) the rainfall was [illegible] inches on [illegible] days; during the second half (July to December, inclusive) [illegible] inches fell on 110 days.

As regards the Direction of the Wind, [illegible] observations were made during the year, with the result—N., [illegible]; N.E., [illegible]; E., [illegible]; S.E., [illegible]; S., [illegible]; S.W., [illegible]; W., [illegible]; N.W., [illegible]; Calms, [illegible].

I have the honour to be

Your Excellency's faithful servant,

THOS. W. GRIMSHAW,

Registrar-General.

METEOROLOGICAL OBSERVATIONS

FOR EACH MONTH OF THE YEAR 1896.

By J. W. MOORE, ESQ., M.D., F.R.C.P.I., F.R. MET. SOC.

(Extracted from the *Dublin Journal of Medical Science*.)

JANUARY.—Proved very mild, often dull and damp, with frequent but scanty rainfall, snow on only one day, and no hail. It afforded a complete contrast in every particular to the severe January of 1895, and will be especially memorable for the record-breaking readings of the barometer on the 9th. On that day pressure exceeded 31 inches over Scotland, the North of England and the North of Ireland, and reached 31·[illegible] inches at Ardrossan, in Ayrshire. On the 20th, another area of high pressure caused the barometer to rise above 30·9 inches over the southern half of the British Isles—the extreme reading of 31·[illegible] inches being recorded at Roche's Point, Cork.

In Dublin the arithmetical mean temperature (44·3°) was much above the average (43·4°); the mean dry bulb readings at 9 a.m. and 9 p.m. were 43·[illegible]°. In the thirty-one years ending with 1896, January was coldest in 1881 (M. T. = 33·2°), and warmest in 1873 (M. T. = 46·6°). In 1868 the M. T. was 47·1°; in 1880, 43·4°; in 1880, 44·5°; in 1884, 40·1°; in 1888, 38·9°; in 1893, 40·6°; in 1894, 41·0°; and in 1895, 35·[illegible]°. As a general rule, January in Dublin is not colder, but a shade warmer, than December. This is owing to the full development in January of a winter area of low pressure over the Atlantic, to the northwestward of the British Isles, and to a resulting prevalence of S.W. winds in their vicinity. January, 1896, proved an exception to this rule, the M. T. being 2·7° above that of December, 1895 (41·6°).

The mean height of the barometer was 30·[illegible] inches, or 0·[illegible] inch above the corrected average value for January—namely, 29·874 inches. The mercury rose to 31·[illegible] inches at 10 p.m. of the 9th and fell to 29·[illegible] inches at [illegible] a.m. of the 15th. The observed range of atmospheric pressure was, therefore, 1·[illegible] inches—that is, a little more than one inch and six-tenths.

The mean temperature deduced from daily readings of the dry bulb thermometer at 9 a.m. and 9 p.m. was 43·[illegible]°, or 2·4° above the value for December, 1895. Using the formula, Mean Temp. = Min. + (max. — min. × ·[illegible]), the M. T. became 43·4°, compared with a twenty-five years' average of 41·6°. The arithmetical mean of the maximal and minimal readings was 44·3°, compared with a twenty-five years' average of 41·[illegible]°. On the 2nd the thermometer in the screen rose to 54·[illegible]°—wind, S.S.W.; on the 21st the temperature fell to 27·[illegible]°—wind, W.S.W. The minimum on the grass was 23·[illegible]°, also on the 21st.

The rainfall was only ·720 inch, distributed, however, over 14 days. The average rainfall for January in the twenty-five years, 1865-89, inclusive, was 2·200 inches, and the average number of rainy days was 17·3. The rainfall, therefore, and the rainy days were both much below the average. In 1877 the rainfall in January was very large—4·323 inches on 22 days; in 1895, also, 4·[illegible] inches fell—on, however, only 18 days. But the record rainfall for January was in 1895, namely, 5·[illegible] inches on 24 days, or nearly eight times as much as the rainfall for January of the present year. On the other hand, in 1874, only ·[illegible] inch was measured on but 9 days; and in 1880 the rainfall was only ·[illegible] inch on but 8 days.

Lunar halos were seen on the 18th and 20th. The atmosphere was foggy on the 2nd, 3rd, 4th, 5th, 7th, 10th, 20th, 21st, 22nd and 25th. High winds were noted on 9 days, reaching the force of a gale on 2 days—the 15th and 16th. Snow and sleet fell on the 10th. Temperature exceeded 50° in the screen on 12 days; while it fell to or below 32° in the screen on only 3 nights, compared with 18 nights in 1895, 7 nights in 1894, 4 nights in 1893, 18 nights in 1892, 7 nights in 1891, 1 night in 1890, and 8 nights in 1889. The minima on the grass were 32°, or less, on 9 nights, compared with 19 nights in 1895, 17 nights in 1894, 13 nights in 1893, 22 nights in 1892, 21 nights in 1891, 15 nights in 1890, and 16 nights in 1889.

Although still changeable, damp, and showery, the weather of the opening period of the month (1st–4th) showed a marked improvement when compared with that of Christmas week. It was very unusually mild, or indeed warm, for the time of year, and the rains were not heavy. The dampness of the atmosphere was attended by the formation of mist or low fog. On the 1st an area of low atmospheric pressure existed off the north of Ireland and the west of Scotland. This system threw a warm but moist south-westerly air current upon the French and British coasts. Rain fell generally and the thermometer rose to 55°, 56°, and even 57° at both English and Irish stations. In contrast to this mild weather, severe cold was felt in Russia, Austria, and Germany. At Berlin the 8 a.m. temperatures were 26°, 13°, 23°, and 33°. When the thaw set in at Berlin on Friday, the 3rd, temperature was already giving way decidedly in the British Isles, where the distribution of pressure had become anticyclonic on Thursday. Saturday was at times fair and bright, but a great deal of fog drifted in from the Irish Sea and St. George's Channel along the east coast of Ireland. In Dublin the barometer ranged from 29·[illegible] inches at 9 p.m. on Wednesday (wind S.S.W.) to 30·[illegible] inches at 9 p.m. on Saturday (wind S.E.). On Thursday the shade thermometers rose to 56·[illegible]°; on Saturday they fell to 43·[illegible]°. Rain was measured on two days, the total amount being ·[illegible] inch, of which ·[illegible] inch was registered on Thursday. The prevailing winds were S.S.W. and S.E. The mean temperature was fully 10° above the average.

The most striking features in the weather of the week ended Saturday, the 11th, were the intensity developed by an anticyclone over the British Isles on Wednesday and Thursday, and the occurrence of a bitterly cold "polar" gale in Italy and the S.E. of France about the same time. On Sunday morning an area of high atmospheric pressure, bounded by the isobar of 30·[illegible] inches, lay over the southern half of the North Sea, Holland, Belgium, and the greater part of England. By Monday morning this system had spread both westward and eastward, and the barometer had risen above 30·90 inches. On Tuesday, at 8 a.m., the isobar of 30·70 inches enclosed nearly the whole of Ireland and the central counties of England. Early on Wednesday the isobar of 31·00 inches swept in a curve south-westwards from the Hebrides to Mayo. At 8 a.m. on Thursday the isobar of 31 inches included the whole of Scotland, the Hebrides, Northumberland, Durham, Westmoreland, Cumberland, and the northern half of Ireland—the highest pressure of all being 31·09 inches at Ardrossan. In Dublin the maximum was reached at 10 a.m. and was 31·02 inches—probably the highest reading of the barometer ever recorded in the Irish capital. From this time to the close of the week pressure gave way gradually. Except on Friday morning, cold, dry weather accompanied the anticyclone, so that no severe frost occurred. At Parsonstown, however, the thermometer read only 24° in screen, on Friday. Intense cold set in at this time over Germany, the east and south-east of France, and Italy, accompanied by strong north-easterly winds and in places gales. In Dublin the mean height of the barometer was 30·753 inches, pressure ranging from 30·458 inches at 9 a.m. of Sunday (wind, N.) to 31·009 inches at 10 a.m. of Thursday (wind, E.N.E.). The corrected mean temperature was 41·4°. The mean dry bulb temperature at 9 a.m. and 9 p.m. was 41·4°. On Wednesday the screened thermometers rose to 46·1°; on Friday they fell to 33·4°. Variable, light winds prevailed. Snow and sleet fell on Friday afternoon to the amount of ·010 inch; an additional ·002 inch of rain was measured on Saturday.

Weather of the westerly type—changeable, mild, squally and showery—prevailed throughout the week ended Saturday, the 18th. At the beginning traces of the remarkable anticyclone, which had lain over the British Islands during the previous week, were still found over the South of Ireland—the barometer at 8 a.m. of Sunday reading 30·65 inches at Valentia Island and 30·64 inches at Roche's Point, Co. Cork. The barometer at this time was falling throughout Western Europe, and depressions were advancing to the North British and Norwegian coasts from the Atlantic. On Sunday the cold was intense in the South of Germany and East of France; the weather was moderately cold in England and Ireland, mild in Scotland. At 8 a.m. on Monday the barometer ranged from 28·70 inches at Bodö, in Norway, to 30·35 inches at Lyons—consequently strong westerly (S.W. to N.W.) winds swept over Western Europe, and the weather was generally unsettled, with rain in many places; especially when a secondary depression crossed England on Monday night. Temperature now became high in the south, but fell in the north, of the United Kingdom—only, however, to rise again quickly in the latter region on Wednesday morning, when the barometer was once more down to 28·93 inches at Wick. As this deep depression passed away to the eastward, the thermometer fell fast in the north. But it rose rapidly again on Friday, when a warm W. wind was blowing on the Atlantic coasts of both France and the British Isles. Saturday was springlike in the midlands, and the air was dry as well as genial. In Dublin the mean height of the barometer was 30·012 inches, pressure ranging from 30·400 inches at 9 a.m. of Sunday (wind, W.) to 29·697 inches at 9 p.m. of Wednesday (wind, W.). The corrected mean temperature was 44·9°. The mean dry bulb temperature at 9 a.m. and 9 p.m. was 45·4°. The screened thermometers fell to 30·2° on Sunday and rose to 55·1° on Saturday. The rainfall was ·268 inch on five days, ·214 inch being registered on Monday. The prevailing wind was westerly.

The changeable, cyclonic weather, so characteristic of the present winter, continued during the week ended Saturday, the 25th. Conditions were at first anticyclonic, and the weather was fine but cold and often foggy. A dense fog on Wednesday evening was followed by cyclonic conditions, and dull, damp, and mild or even warm weather. On Sunday a broad band of high atmospheric pressure (30·30 inches), stretched across Ireland, England, France, and Germany, whereas an area of low pressure (29·71 inches) lay off the North of Scotland. In Dublin the weather was at this time fine, bright, and bracing. The anticyclone steadily held its ground and developed intensity, until on Tuesday morning the barometer read 30·61 inches at Dublin. Hoar frost and fog, with fine, bright intervals during the daytime, prevailed in Dublin—a "silver thaw" following on Tuesday evening. On Wednesday a large depression passed eastwards across Scandinavia, and this caused a rise of temperature in England and Ireland, but hail, sleet and snow in Scotland, where strong N.W. winds blew on the morning of the day named. As evening the sky cleared in Dublin, and, as the air was calm, temperature fell fast, the result being the development of an exceedingly dense fog at night. Thursday was fine and mild, with a southerly wind. In the morning very sharp frost was felt in Great Britain, the shade thermometer falling to 20° at Cambridge, 21° at Loughborough, and 23° at Leith and Nairn. In a few hours a rapid rise of temperature took place, amounting to 25° at Leith, 16° at Nairn, 13° at Cambridge, and 13° at Loughborough. The week closed dull, damp, and mild. In Dublin the mean height of the barometer was 30·276 inches, pressure ranging from 30·654 inches at 9 a.m. of Monday (wind, calm) to 29·757 inches at 9 a.m. of Saturday (wind, W.). The corrected mean temperature was 42·1°. The mean dry bulb reading at 9 a.m. and 9 p.m. was 44·7°. On Tuesday the screened thermometers fell to 27·8°; on Friday they rose to 53·0°. The prevailing winds were S.W. and W. Rain fell on four days to the amount of ·154 inch, ·082 inch being registered on Friday.

At first cyclonic in type, changeable and at times rainy, the weather of the closing period, 26th–31st, inclusive, became on Tuesday, the 28th, anticyclonic, quiet and fine, and so continued to the close of the month. For the third time in January, 1896, an anticyclone spread over the British Isles, and for the second time the barometric pressure reached a value of very abnormal and unusual intensity. At 11 p.m. of Wednesday the barometer rose to 30·96 inches at Roche's Point, Cork Harbour; and on the evening of this day as well as on Thursday morning the isobar of 30·90 inches enclosed the southern half of Ireland, Wales, and a great portion of the South of England. It will be remembered that the highest readings in the remarkable anticyclone of January 9th were reported from Scotland, and the northern parts of England and Ireland. After Thursday the barometer fell generally though gradually. During the anticyclonic period quiet, mild but not cold, often dull weather prevailed. The atmospheric humidity also varied very much—the mornings being damp, the evenings very dry. While the anticyclone hung over England and Ireland, large and deep depressions swept eastwards across Scandinavia, causing westerly gales and rainy, cool weather over in the extreme North of Europe. In Dublin the barometer ranged between [illegible] inches at 9 a.m. of Monday (wind, S.W.) and 30·322 inches at 4.10 p.m. of Wednesday (wind, W.N.W.). On Monday the screened thermometers rose to 55·5°; on Sunday, they fell to 36·5°. The prevailing wind was westerly. Rain fell on two days to the amount of ·133 inch, [illegible] inch being registered on Monday.

In Dublin the rainfall up to January 31st, 1896, amounted to only ·720 inch on 14 days, compared with 3·731 inches on 24 days in 1895, and with a twenty-five years' average (1865–1889) of [illegible] inches on 17·8 days.

At Knockdolian, Greystones, Co. Wicklow, the rainfall was only ·[illegible] inch on 7 days, compared with [illegible] inches of rain on 22 days in 1895. The heaviest falls in 24 hours were ·180 inch on the 24th, and ·100 inch on the 18th.

At Clonsilla, Killiney, Co. Dublin, the rainfall was ·780 inch on 9 days, ·31 inch being measured on the 24th. The average fall for the 10 years, 1885–1894, was 2·619 inches on 19·0 days. No snow fell. In 1895 the rainfall was 3·290 inches on 23 days, in 1893 it was 5·830 inches on 24 days. In 1891, only ·47 inch fell on, however, 11 days.

February.—A fine, dry, mild, often genial month—a complete contrast to February, 1895, which had been the coldest experienced for forty years. There was neither snow nor hail, and very little frost occurred in Ireland, scarcely any in or near Dublin. The mean temperature was not less than 11 degrees above that of February, 1895, while it was also 2·6° above the average. Absolute drought prevailed from the 9th to the 18th, inclusive, and three-eighths of the entire rainfall for the month was measured on the 25th.

In Dublin the mean temperature (45·2°) was 2·6° above the average (42·6°); the mean dry bulb readings at 9 a.m. and 9 p.m. were 44·3°. In the thirty-one years ending with 1895, February was coldest in 1895 (M. T. = 34·2°), and warmest in 1869 (M. T. = 46·7°).

The mean height of the barometer was 30·237 inches, or 0·387 inch above the average value for February—namely, 29·850 inches. The mercury rose to 30·648 inches at 9 a.m. of the 3rd, and fell to 29·420 inches at 9 p.m. of the 10th. The observed range of atmospheric pressure was, therefore, 1·228 inches—that is, a little less than an inch and a quarter.

The mean temperature deduced from daily readings of the dry bulb thermometer at 9 a.m. and 9 p.m. was 44·3°, or 10·7° above the value for February, 1895. Using the formula, *Mean Temp.* = *Min.* + (max.—min. × ·50), the M. T. is 45·5°, compared with a twenty-five years' average of 42·6°. On the 8th the thermometer in the screen rose to 56·7°—wind, W.S.W.; on the 18th the temperature fell to 31·9°—wind, calm. The minimum on the grass was 26·6°, also on the 18th.

The rainfall was only ·665 inch, distributed over 10 days. The average rainfall for February in the twenty-five years, 1865–89, inclusive, was 2·160 inches, and the average number of rainy days was 17·2. The rainfall, therefore, and also the rainy days, were much below the average. In 1866 the rainfall in February was large—3·759 inches on 17 days; in 1879, also, 3·703 inches fell on 22 days. On the other hand, in 1891, only ·042 inch was measured on but 2 days. The rainfall in 1891 was much the smallest recorded in February for very many years. The record is probably unparalleled in Dublin—·042 inch on 2 days. The nearest approach to this drought was in September, 1865, when only ·056 inch of rain was measured on but 3 days.

Neither hail, nor sleet or snow fell.

The atmosphere was foggy on 8 days—namely, the 1st, 2nd, 4th, 6th, 14th, 16th, 18th, and 21st. The amount of cloud—65·3 per cent.—was almost exactly the average—66 per cent. High winds were noted on 8 days, but never reached the force of a gale. A lunar halo was seen on the 24th. Faint aurora appeared on the 18th.

The temperature reached or exceeded 50° in the screen on 15 days, and it only once fell below 32°, compared with as many as 18 nights in 1895, only 2 nights in 1894, 5 nights in both 1893 and 1892, and 9 nights in 1891. The minima on the grass were 32°, or less, on 10 nights, compared with every night in 1895, 10 nights in 1894, 13 nights in 1893, 16 nights in 1892, and 17 nights in 1891. The thermometer never failed to rise to or above 40° in the screen during the daytime.

Generally fine and singularly mild and open weather prevailed during the week ended Saturday, the 8th, the mean temperature of which was in Dublin 47·2°, or 15·6° above that of the corresponding period of 1895, viz., 31·6°. The distribution of atmospheric pressure over North-western Europe was similar to that so persistently prevalent during the present season. An anticyclone held sway in France, Germany, and over the southern half of the United Kingdom. A series of Atlantic depressions moved eastwards across Scandinavia and Lapland. Only on Friday did the areas of low pressure encroach to a marked extent on the Irish and Scotch coasts. On Saturday, however, cyclonic conditions seemed fully established throughout the British Isles. As commonly happens, very frosty nights were observed within the central area of the anticyclone, and the period was decidedly cold in France and Germany. In England also sharp frosts were reported on the nights of Sunday and Monday—in Ireland the week was frostless, and on Friday temperature became remarkably high for the time of year. Rain fell freely on Saturday morning, but the afternoon was like April or the end of September. At 8 a.m. of Friday the thermometer ranged from—6° at Haparanda, on the Gulf of Bothnia, to 53° at Valentia Island. Twenty-four hours earlier, temperature had been 29° at Haparanda, or 37° higher. In Dublin the mean atmospheric pressure was 30·260 inches, the barometer rising to 30·643 inches at 9 a.m. of Monday (wind, S.S.E.), and falling to 29·523 inches at 9 a.m. of Saturday (wind, S.W.). The corrected mean temperature was 47·2°. The mean dry bulb temperature was 46·6°. On Tuesday the screened thermometers sank to 36·6°, on Saturday they rose to 56·7°. The rainfall amounted to ·214 inch, on three days, ·089 inch being registered on Friday and ·100 inch on Saturday. The prevailing winds were S.S.E. and S.W.

During the week ended Saturday, the 15th, the weather was very favourable—at first it was of the south-westerly type, warm and windy; afterwards it became more decidedly anticyclonic in character, quiet, gray, and cold, as well as dry. Until Thursday an area of high atmospheric pressure, with central readings of about 30·60 inches, lay directly over France; whereas the barometer was low over Scandinavia, and gradients for S.W. and W. winds were steep over Scotland, Ireland, and the North of England. In the districts named, mild, breezy weather prevailed, and the amount of cloud, after Sunday, was large. The week opened with warm, rainy weather in the S.E. of England, but this soon gave place to calm, foggy, and (at night) cold weather. On Thursday, the area of highest pressure—30·40 inches and upwards—embraced the United Kingdom and West of France, while a depression passed south-eastwards over Lapland to Russia, causing polar winds and a sudden and great fall of temperature in Norway and Sweden. This "chill" ultimately affected the British Isles, where the weather became seasonably cold, while it remained dry in most districts. On Friday and Saturday the anticyclone again gathered strength, and the week closed with a fully-established dry, cold, quiet, gray spell. In Dublin the mean atmospheric pressure was 30·363 inches, the barometer ranging from 30·093 inches at 9 a.m. of Sunday (wind, W.S.W.) to 30·564 inches at 9 p.m. of Saturday (wind, E.N.E.). The mean temperature was 46·2°. The mean dry bulb reading at 9 a.m. and 9 p.m. was 44·6°. On Tuesday the screened thermometers rose to 54·3°, on Friday they sank to 33·0°. The prevailing wind was S.W. No rain fell in or near Dublin. At 9.30 a.m. on Monday, a large meteor or aerolite burst in mid-air at a height of 20½ miles right over Madrid, the explosion shaking that city to its foundations and causing widespread consternation.

The record for the week ended Saturday, the 22nd, is again one of singularly favourable weather. Conditions remained anticyclonic until Wednesday, when a large depression approached the west coast of Ireland, causing changeable, showery, weather for a time. On Saturday there was a return to fair weather, as an anticyclone spread westward from the Continent over the British Isles. Tolerably steady frost held throughout the period in Central Europe, but only occasional night frosts occurred in the United Kingdom, where also the thermometer often rose above 50° during the day-time. In the earlier part of the week, the air was dry and keen, and the amount of cloud was extremely large. The daily range of temperature was consequently not great. On Tuesday, the maximum in Dublin was only 43·2°, at Oxford 38°, at Shields and York only 35°. As the depression approached Ireland, however, the southerly wind brought much more genial temperatures, and on Wednesday the shade thermometer rose to 58° at Cambridge, 57° at Loughborough, 55° in London and at Oxford, and 53·4° in Dublin. A well-marked secondary V-depression lay over St. George's Channel, Cornwall, and Wales on Thursday morning, producing a very general rainfall in Great Britain, but a beautiful, spring-like day in Ireland. Showers fell on Friday afternoon, and then the weather again took up, Saturday proving a very bright spring day. In Dublin, the mean height of the barometer was 30·004 inches, pressure ranging from 30·601 inches at 9 a.m. of Sunday (wind, E.), to 29·180 inches at 9 p.m. of Wednesday (wind, S.S.W.). The mean temperature was 45·5°. The mean dry bulb reading at 9 a.m. and 9 p.m. was 43·7°. The shade temperature fell to 31·9° on Tuesday, and rose to 53·4° on Wednesday. The prevailing wind was S.E. Rain fell on two days to the amount of 0·64 inch, ·050 inch being measured on Wednesday. Faint aurora appeared on Tuesday evening.

During the week ended Saturday, the 29th, at first cold and dry, with anticyclonic S.E. winds, the weather afterwards became mild, damp, cloudy, and often rainy, with fresh cyclonic W. winds. Until Tuesday a large anticyclone stretched south-westwards as far as Ireland from Finland and the Baltic. At 8 a.m. of Monday the barometer read 30·90 inches at Stockholm, and 31·00 to 31·02 inches over the S. of Finland and the neighbouring parts of the Baltic provinces. This system threw a cold easterly current upon Germany, France, and England, while the wind drew anticyclonically into S. over Ireland and S.S.W. over Scotland and Norway. Sharp frost held on the Continent and in Central England—the minima in the screen at Cambridge being 21° on Sunday and Monday nights, and 19° on Tuesday night. During Tuesday the barometer fell briskly in Ireland and Scotland, and towards evening a V-shaped depression had advanced over the former country, where it caused an abundant rainfall. At 6 p.m. the wind was S. in the east, but N. in the west of Ireland, and rain was falling in all parts of this island. The V-shaped system afterwards moved north-eastwards to Scotland and dispersed. Depressions now began to move across Northern Europe, while a new anticyclone appeared off the S.W. of Ireland. This distribution of pressure caused fresh westerly winds, clouded skies, a rapid rise of temperature, and more or less rain, followed by snow and hail in Scotland on Saturday. At Loughborough, the thermometer rose 22° (from 25° to 47°) in the 24 hours ending 9 a.m. of Friday. On the evening of this day a fine eclipse of the moon—87 out of 100 parts—was very well seen. In Dublin, the mean atmospheric pressure was 30·174 inches, the barometer rising to 30·329 inches at 9 a.m. of Monday (wind, S.S.E.), and falling to 29·855 inches at 9 p.m. of Tuesday (wind, S.S.E.). The mean temperature was 44·5°. The mean dry bulb temperature at 9 a.m. and 9 p.m. was 44·0°. On Monday the thermometer fell to 34·1°, on Friday it rose to 54·1°. The rainfall was ·160 inch on four days, ·080 inch being registered on Tuesday. The prevalent winds were S.E. and W.

In Dublin the rainfall up to February 29th, 1896, amounted to only 1·384 inches on 25 days compared with 6·280 inches on 52 days in 1895, 4·761 inches on 39 days in 1894, 4·004 inches on 41 days in 1893, 3·617 inches on 39 days in 1892, ·714 inch on 16 days in 1891, and a twenty-five years' (1865-1889) average of 4·350 inches on 34·3 days.

At Knockdolian, Greystones, Co. Wicklow, 1·455 inches of rain fell in February on 10 days. The heaviest fall in 24 hours was ·460 inch on the 25th. The total fall to February 29th inclusive was 1·940 inches on 17 days.

The rainfall in February at Cloneevin, Killiney, Co. Dublin, amounted to ·94 inch on 10 days. The average rainfall for February during 10 years (1885-94) at this station is 1·914 inches on 13·4 days. The greatest rainfall in 24 hours was ·35 inch on the 25th. Since January 1, the rainfall was 1·64 inches on 19 days.

MARCH.—A changeable, wild, and very rainy month. The general distribution of atmospheric pressure was cyclonic. Temperature, although on the whole decidedly above the average, was very unstable, and some sharp frosts were observed. The rainfall was rather more than 60 per cent. in excess of the average, but this did not make up for the deficiency in the two previous months, and the quarter closed with the rainfall still 23·3 per cent. short of the normal amount.

In Dublin the arithmetical mean temperature (45·1°) was three degrees above the average (42·1°); the mean dry bulb readings at 9 a.m. and 9 p.m. were 44·4°. In the thirty years ending with 1894, March was coldest in 1867 and 1883 (M. T. = 39·0°), and warmest in 1859 (M. T. = 46·1°), and in 1868 (M. T. = 47·2°). In 1896 the M. T. was 44·1°.

The mean height of the barometer was 29·710 inches, or 0·206 inch below the corrected average value for March—namely, 29·916 inches. The mercury rose to 30·242 inches at 9 a.m. of the 31st, and fell to 28·533 inches at 1 p.m. of the 3rd. The observed range of atmospheric pressure was, therefore, 1·709 inches—that is, almost an inch and seven-tenths.

The mean temperature deduced from daily readings of the dry bulb thermometer at 9 a.m. and 9 p.m. was 44·4°, or only 0·8° above the value for February, 1896. Using the formula, Mean Temp. = Min. + (max.—min. × ·476), the M.T. becomes 45·3°. The arithmetical mean of the maximal and minimal readings was 45·1°, compared with a twenty-five years' average of 43·1°. On the 26th the thermometer in the screen rose to 55·5°—wind, S.; on the 27th the temperature fell to 34·1°—wind, W. The minimum on the grass was 30·2° on the 19th.

The rainfall was 3·310 inches, distributed over 23 days. The average rainfall for March in the twenty-five years, 1865–89, inclusive, was 2·021 inches, and the average number of rainy days was 16·6. The rainfall, therefore, and also the rainy days, were considerably above the average. In 1867 the rainfall in March was very large—4·972 inches on 22 days. On the other hand, in 1871, only ·815 inch was measured on 13 days, and in 1893 only ·255 inch on 8 days. The smallest March rainfall was ·255 inch on 8 days in 1893. In 1895, 2·746 inches fell on 19 days.

The atmosphere was more or less foggy in the city on 6 days—viz., the 7th, 10th, 19th, 21st, 22nd, and 25th. High winds were noted on 17 days, reaching the force of a gale on four occasions—the 1st, 2nd, 3rd, 4th, 8th, 13th, 15th, 17th, 19th, and 26th. Snow or sleet occurred on the 3rd, 4th, and 28th; and hail fell on the 1st, 2nd, 3rd, and 28th. The temperature exceeded 50° in the screen on as many as 21 days, compared with 13 days in 1895, 22 days in 1894, 20 days in 1893, only 7 days in 1892, 9 days in 1891, and 19 days in 1890. It never fell to 32° in the screen. In March, 1892, frost was recorded in the shade on as many as 14 nights. The minima on the grass were 32°, or less on 4 nights, compared with 10 nights in 1895, 12 in 1894 and 1893, 25 in 1892, 20 in 1891, and 16 in 1890. The thermometer never rose to 60° in the screen, and never failed to reach 40°. In March, 1892, the thermometer did not rise to 40° in the screen on 9 days. A solar halo was seen on the 27th, and a lunar halo appeared on the 23rd. Brilliant aurora borealis occurred on the night of the 4th.

Exceedingly broken, wet, squally weather ushered in the month of March and held throughout the first week. On four days the wind reached gale force in Dublin, and rain, sleet, and hail fell freely. A brilliant display of aurora borealis was seen on the evening of Wednesday the 4th. Thunder and lightning occurred in several places in connection with a deep atmospheric depression on Tuesday and Wednesday. On Sunday morning a depression of some intensity (29·05 inches) was noticed in the Shetlands. It caused westerly gales and showers of rain and hail in most districts. A progressive reduction of pressure went on in the N. and N.W., so that by 8 a.m. of Tuesday the barometer fell to 28·18 inches at Wick and Sumburgh Head, to 28·20 inches at Malin Head, and to 28·42 inches at Holyhead. Even in Dublin the reading was as low as 28·53 inches at 1 p.m. In the afternoon, 28·20 inches was recorded at Sumburgh Head. Fresh westerly (between S.W. and N.W.) gales prevailed; wet rain, hail, sleet, and snow fell at intervals, the Dublin mountains being deeply snow-covered. Occasional thunder and lightning were at this time reported from various stations—particularly in the West of Ireland, the English Channel, and the South of England. In Dublin the barometer remained below 29 inches from 8 p.m. of Monday to 4 p.m. of Wednesday—that is, during 44 hours. With a brisk recovery of pressure during Wednesday night, temperature also rose fast, and rain took the place of hail and sleet. In Dublin the mean atmospheric pressure was 29·232 inches, or ·641 inch below the value for the previous week. The barometer fell to 28·533 inches at 1 p.m. of Tuesday (wind W.S.W.), and rose to 29·527 inches at 9 a.m. of Saturday (wind, S.E.). The corrected mean temperature was 41·7°. The mean dry bulb temperature at 9 a.m. and 9 p.m. was 42·4°. The screened thermometers fell to 34·3° on Tuesday and rose to 54·0° on Saturday. Westerly winds predominated. The rainfall was 1·073 inches on seven days, ·350 inch being measured on Saturday.

The week ended Saturday, the 14th, witnessed a continuance of the unsettled, dull, rainy weather which had prevailed from the beginning of the month. Both atmospheric pressure and air temperature were very unsteady, and the wind also was extremely variable in direction. The general tendency was for high barometer readings to develop in the extreme north and also over the Iberian Peninsula, while a succession of depressions of no great intensity moved slowly eastward or south-eastward across the intervening districts—the South of Scandinavia, the British Isles, and Central Europe. Hence the changeable weather of the period. On and after Wednesday a severe snowstorm prevailed in Sweden, while large quantities of rain had fallen in Southern Germany at the beginning of the week—at Munich, 1·78 inches of rain were measured on Sunday morning, 1·10 inches on Monday, and 0·79 inch on Tuesday at 8 a.m.—a total fall of 3·67 inches in 3 days. On Sunday the thermometer rose to 53° in Dublin, 61° at York and Cambridge, and 61° at Loughborough—60° was again reached at Loughborough and Oxford on Wednesday, but towards the close of the week a general reduction of temperature was taking place, consequent on the setting in of northerly and north-easterly winds. Very little sunshine was enjoyed. On Tuesday, however, 7 inches were registered at Cambridge and [illegible] at Eastbourne. In Dublin the mean height of the barometer was 29·879 inches, pressure ranging between 29·312 inches at 9 a.m. of Tuesday (wind, S.), and 29·791 inches at 9 p.m. of Friday (wind, N.N.W.). The corrected mean temperature was 47·1°. The mean dry bulb temperature at 9 a.m. and 9 p.m. was 46·1°. On Sunday the screened thermometers rose to 57·7°; on Tuesday they fell to 35·2°. The rainfall was ·[illegible] inch on two days, ·286 inch being measured on Monday.

Once more the record is of changeable, squally, rainy weather during the week ended Saturday, the 21st. The sky, however, was not so densely clouded as in previous weeks, and on Monday, Wednesday, and Thursday much bright sunshine was enjoyed. The distribution of atmospheric pressure was almost continuously cyclonic—on Wednesday night, indeed, "a wedge" of relatively high pressure did move eastward across Ireland, ushering in a spell of beautiful weather, but it was soon followed by another series of depressions. The most serious disturbance of the period lay off the North of Ireland on Monday morning, when the barometer was down to 28·79 inches at Malin Head, the reading at the same time (8 a.m.) being 29·70 inches at Valentia Island, and 29·07 inches at Roche's Point, Cork Harbour. Gradients for westerly to north-westerly winds were, therefore, very steep over Ireland and strong gales from the points named prevailed, with showers of rain and hail in some places, but a very dry air generally. Tuesday was wet owing to the arrival of new disturbances. On Wednesday the weather was bright in Ireland, but very wet in the South of England in connection with the passage eastward of a large V-shaped depression and several lesser cyclonic systems, in which singular contrasts of temperature were observed. On Thursday afternoon cirrus cloud spread over the sky from S.W. in Ireland, and the weather quickly fell again into an unsettled, rainy condition, so continuing to the end of the week. Thunder and lightning occurred in the N.W. and N. of Ireland on Friday. In Dublin the mean height of the barometer was 29·563 inches, pressure ranging between 28·830 inches at 7.15 a.m. of Monday (wind, W.) and 30·065 inches at 9 a.m. of Thursday (wind, S.W.). The corrected mean temperature was 46·6°. The mean dry bulb temperature at 9 a.m. and 9 p.m. was 44·1°. On Wednesday the screened thermometers fell to 34·9°; on Friday they rose to 58·6°. The rainfall was 1·011 inches on two days, ·906 inch being registered on Tuesday. The prevalent winds were W. and S.W.

"March many weathers"—thus may the week ended Saturday, the 28th, be most fitly described. At the beginning "the south wind blew softly," and fine summer-like weather was enjoyed. On Sunday the thermometer in the shade rose to 65° in London, and 67° at Cambridge. At the latter place a thunderstorm occurred in the evening. The weather was beautifully fine in Dublin also until Wednesday, at 6 p.m. of which day rain set in. Already on Tuesday a large, but shallow V-shaped depression had caused thunder and lightning in many parts of England and Wales. On Thursday morning the centre of a still larger and deeper depression was found lying over the north of Scotland. It caused strong, squally S.W. to N.W. winds and showers, or continuous rain in some places, especially Liverpool and its vicinity. The wind soon backed, and on Thursday afternoon a deep secondary cyclonic system travelled rapidly eastward over the middle of Ireland, afterwards crossing the Irish Sea, England, and the North Sea, with such speed that it was centred off the Helder at 8 a.m. of Friday. Its centre passed close to Dublin at 6 p.m. of Thursday, so that it travelled at the uniform rate of upwards of 30 miles an hour for 14 hours—the distance being some 440 miles in a direct line. The atmosphere remained in a very disturbed state to the close of the week, and on Saturday hail, sleet, and snow fell heavily at intervals. In Dublin the mean height of the barometer was 29·[illegible] inches, pressure ranging between 29·[illegible] inches at 6 p.m. of Thursday (wind, W.S.W.) and 30·094 inches at 9 a.m. of Friday (wind, W.). The corrected mean temperature was 46·5°. The mean dry bulb temperature at 9 a.m. and 9 p.m. was 45·8°. On Tuesday the shade maximum was 58·2°, on Friday the shade minimum was 34·1°. Rainfall was ·501 inch on four days, ·134 inch being registered on Friday. Hail, sleet, and snow fell on Saturday. The prevailing winds were S.W. and W.N.W. A lunar halo was seen on Monday, a solar halo on Friday.

Cloudy, cold, somewhat showery weather prevailed during the closing days of the month—29th to 31st, inclusive.

The rainfall in Dublin during the three months ending March 31st amounted to 4·[illegible] inches on 47 days, compared with 5·094 inches on 52 days in 1895, 6·025 inches on 51 days in 1894, 5·120 inches on 49 days in 1893, 4·808 inches on 46 days in 1892, only 1·930 inches on but 32 days in 1891, 7·470 inches on 45 days in 1890, and a twenty-five years' average of 6·411 inches on 51·[illegible] days (1865–1889, inclusive).

At Knockdolian, Greystones, Co. Wicklow, 2·791 inches of rain fell on 16 days during March; and the total rainfall since January 1, 1896, equals 4·750 inches on 42 days. The corresponding figures for 1895 are 2·140 inches on 20 days, the total rainfall since January 1 having been 10·085 inches on 54 days.

The rainfall in March at Cloneevin, Killiney, Co. Dublin, was 2·01 inches on 23 days, compared with 2·19 inches on 21 days in 1895, 1·11 inches on 14 days in 1894, ·36 inch on 8 days in 1893, ·86 inch on 10 days in 1892, and a ten years' average of 1·808 inches on 16·9 days. The maximum in the 10 years was 2·55 inches in 1888, the minimum was ·36 inch in 1893. At this station the total rainfall since January 1, was 4·23 inches on 41 days, compared with a fall of 9·08 inches on 52 days in the first quarter of 1895, and 8·16 inches on 55 days in that of 1894.

APRIL.—A very favourable, fine, and spring-like month. In Dublin rain fell on as many as 16 days, but it was almost entirely in the form of showers, and the total precipitation was slightly under nine-tenths of an inch. The steadiness of the barometer was a feature of the first ten days of the month. A relapse into winter took place on the 27th, from which day the weather remained cold to the end. Very little easterly wind was felt. The amount of cloud was small, particularly at 9 p.m., when it was only 41·7 per cent.

In Dublin the arithmetical mean temperature (50·6°) was 3·4° above the average (47·2°); the mean dry bulb readings at 9 a.m. and 9 p.m. were 50·7°. In the thirty-one years ending with 1895, April was coldest in 1879 (the cold year) (M. T. = 44·6°), and warmest in 1893 (M. T. = 51·4°). The month of April, 1893, was the warmest for at least 30 years, yet it was only half a degree warmer than the month now under discussion.

The mean height of the barometer was 30·179 inches, or 0·229 inch above the average value for April—namely, 29·950 inches. The mercury rose to 30·618 inches at 9 a.m. of the 19th, and fell to 29·891 inches at 9 p.m. of the 24th. The observed range of atmospheric pressure was, therefore, ·727 inch—that is, a little more than three-quarters of an inch.

The mean temperature deduced from daily readings of the dry bulb thermometer at 9 a.m. and 9 p.m. was 50·7°, or 8·1° above the value for March, 1896. Using the formula, Mean Temp. = min. + (max. − min. × ·476), the value is 50·6°, or 3·1° above the average mean temperature for April, calculated in the same way, in the twenty-five years, 1865–89, inclusive (47·5°). The arithmetical mean of the maximum and minimum readings was 50·9°, compared with a twenty-five years' (1865–1889, inclusive) average of 47·7°. On the 24th the thermometer in the screen rose to 66·0°—wind, S.W.; on the 3rd the temperature fell to 35·1°—wind, W.N.W. The minimum on the grass was 33·9°, also on the 3rd.

The rainfall was ·811 inch, distributed over 12 days. The average rainfall for April in the twenty-five years, 1865–89, inclusive, was 2·055 inches, and the average number of rainy days was 15·2. The rainfall, therefore, was considerably below the average, while the rainy days were slightly in defect. In 1877 the rainfall in April was very large—4·707 inches on 21 days; in 1882 also, 4·046 inches fell on 19 days; and in 1884, 3·128 inches on 20 days. On the other hand, in 1873, only ·498 inch was measured on 8 days; and in 1870, only ·635 inch fell, also on 8 days.

Solar halos were observed on the 20th and 21st. High winds were noted on 8 days, reaching the force of a gale on the 10th and 13th. Hail fell on the 10th, 11th, 13th, 24th, 25th, and 26th. The temperature exceeded 50° in the screen on every day except the 17th. It rose to or above 60° on 8 days, but never fell to 32° in screen, or even on the grass. The mean lowest temperature on the grass was 40·1°, compared with 37·9° in 1895, 39·6° in 1894, 38·2° in 1893, 32·4° in 1892, 34·1° in 1891 and 1890, 34·4° in 1889, 34·5° in 1888, and 31·6° in 1887. Thunder was heard on the afternoon of the 25th.

Clouded skies, light to moderate north-westerly winds and passing showers were the main features of the period ending Saturday, the 4th. An area of high atmospheric pressure remained almost stationary off the W. of Ireland throughout—the barometer standing a little above 30·30 inches. Meanwhile, a series of areas of relatively low pressure passed south-eastwards across the south of Scandinavia to Germany and Central Europe—hence the N.W. winds and changeable weather which prevailed. In Dublin the barometer ranged only from 30·110 inches at 9 p.m. of Wednesday, the 1st (wind N.E.), and also at 9 a.m. of Thursday, the 2nd (wind W.N.W.), to 30·288 inches at 9 a.m. of Good Friday, the 3rd (wind N. by W.). Rain fell on 2 out of the 4 days, the amount, however, of only ·017 inch. The shade thermometer fell to 39·1° on the 2nd, and rose to 58·8° on the 4th.

Quiet and fine though often cloudy, in the earlier part of the week ended Saturday, the 11th, the weather after Thursday fell into a showery, squally, and generally unsettled condition. Temperature also gave way rapidly. These changes were brought about by the appearance in the far North of a large area of low atmospheric pressure, which gradually spread east and southwards and south-eastwards across Scandinavia to Central Europe. The anticyclone, which had held its position over the West of Ireland from the closing days of March, was still found off the Kerry coast on Sunday and Monday. Its centre then moved in a south-easterly direction towards the Bay of Biscay and France, while the low pressure area in the North, already mentioned, encroached more and more on the British and Irish as well as the Norwegian coasts. The result was that the wind backed towards S.W. and freshened, with at first a rising temperature. On Wednesday the thermometer rose to 64° in [illegible] and [illegible], on Thursday to 62° in the east of Ireland, and to 60° or 63° in the east of Scotland. Showers began to fall on the last-named day, and a sharp decline in temperature followed at night. Friday and Saturday were rough and inclement, with squalls and heavy passing showers of cold rain and hail, alternating with fine, brighter intervals. Lightning was seen throughout Scotland on Friday night. In Dublin the mean height of the barometer was 30·113 inches, pressure ranging between 30·365 inches at 9 a.m. of Sunday (wind N.W.) and 29·928 inches at 9 a.m. of Saturday (wind W.N.W.). The corrected mean temperature was 51·0°. The mean dry bulb temperature at 9 a.m. and 9 p.m. was 50·9°. On Thursday the thermometer rose to 61·9° in the screen, on Friday it fell to 41·8°. The prevailing direction of the wind was W.N.W. Rainfall amounted to ·249 inch, on three days, ·151 inch being registered on Friday, and ·095 inch on Saturday.

The weather was changeable and showery throughout the week ended Saturday, the 18th. At first it was very rough, cold, and unsettled, a fresh to strong north-westerly gale being felt on Sunday. The wind afterwards moderated and became somewhat variable in direction, with weak cloud and frequent showers. At the end of the week an anticyclone of some intensity had formed over the British Isles, but it was accompanied with dull, damp weather and very light, variable winds. The gale of Sunday was caused by a depression with steep gradients for N.W. winds in its south-western quadrant, which travelled in a south-easterly direction from the Norwegian Sea to Denmark and the North of Germany. Hail and sleet fell in many places, and thunder and lightning occurred at Kew and Spurn Head. There was a brief spell of fine weather on Monday, but at night some shallow secondary disturbances, moving eastwards across Ireland and the South of England, led to a considerable fall of rain in those localities. On Thursday morning a new depression was noticed off the Hebrides, and the weather was again blustering and showery. This system threw out a well marked V-shaped "secondary" across England and the North Sea by Friday morning, while an area of high pressure formed over Ireland, England, and the Bay of Biscay. This latter change led to quiet, dull, damp weather on Saturday. In Dublin the mean height of the barometer was 30·151 inches, pressure ranging from [illegible] inches at 9 a.m. of Thursday (wind S.W.) to [illegible] inches at 9 p.m. of Saturday (wind W.S.W.). The corrected mean temperature was [illegible]. The mean dry bulb reading at 9 a.m. and 9 p.m. was [illegible]. On Monday the shade thermometers sank to [illegible], on Friday they rose to [illegible]. The rainfall was [illegible] inch on six days, [illegible] inch being measured on Monday. The prevailing wind was W.N.W.

Very favourable weather held throughout the week ended Saturday, 25th, particularly in Ireland, where the distribution of atmospheric pressure was steadily anticyclonic until Saturday. On this day, the barometer gave way decidedly in the North-west, as a large but not deep depression advanced to that region from the Atlantic. At the beginning of the period the barometer stood above 30·[illegible] inches in Munster, and gradients were slight throughout Ireland. Consequently, fine, quiet, hazy weather prevailed. During the following days, the weather remained fair and still. The diurnal range of temperature was considerable—bright sunny days being succeeded by hazy cold nights. This was especially the case in Central England, where some sharp ground frosts were felt. At Cambridge the thermometer fell to 30° even in the screen on the nights of both Monday and Thursday. On Wednesday a depression swept north-eastwards across Scandinavia, affecting the weather in Great Britain, but not in Ireland. Both in Scotland and in the east of England at this time the sky became overcast, temperature fell, and showers were reported from many stations. On Saturday a separate low pressure area reached the N. and N.W. of Ireland, causing showers in this country. In Dublin the mean atmospheric pressure was as high as 30·[illegible] inches, the barometer falling slowly from [illegible] inches at 9 a.m. of Sunday (wind W.S.W.) to [illegible] inches at 9 p.m. of Saturday (wind W.). The corrected mean temperature was [illegible]. The mean dry bulb reading at 9 a.m. and 9 p.m. was [illegible]. The screened thermometers rose to [illegible] on Friday, having fallen to [illegible] on Thursday. Rain was measured on Saturday to the amount of ·009 inch only. The prevailing winds were E. and W.

From Sunday, the 26th, the weather underwent an unfavourable change, and a distinctly cold, unsettled period occurred owing to the persistent presence of an area of low atmospheric pressure between Scotland and the Scandinavian Peninsula. In connection with this primary system a series of secondary depressions developed over the British Isles and the North Sea. Sunday was cloudy at times, and squally western winds blew, the weather being otherwise fine. Passing showers began to fall on Monday, and towards night a marked decline in temperature set in. During the three following days, more or less heavy showers of sleet, rain and hail broke in upon fair, bright intervals. In many places both in Ireland and in Great Britain thunder and lightning accompanied the showers and the wind blew gustily from N.W. or N. Towards nightfall the sky cleared, with the result that very low temperatures were recorded, frost occurring even in the screen at some inland stations on Thursday night, when the thermometer sank to [illegible] at Parsonstown, and to 32° at both Loughborough and Cambridge. In Dublin the barometer ranged during the period from [illegible] inches at 9 p.m. of Tuesday (wind W.) to [illegible] inches at 9 p.m. of Thursday (wind N.). On Sunday the screened thermometers rose to [illegible]; on Thursday they sank to [illegible]. Rain fell on four days to the amount of ·136 inch.

The rainfall in Dublin during the four months ending April 30th amounted to [illegible] inches on [illegible] days, compared with 10·[illegible] inches on [illegible] days in 1895, 9·[illegible] inches on [illegible] days in 1894, [illegible] inches on [illegible] days in 1893, [illegible] inches on [illegible] days in 1892, only [illegible] inches on [illegible] days in 1891, [illegible] inches on [illegible] days in 1890, and a twenty-five years' average of [illegible] inches on [illegible] days.

At Knockdolian, Greystones, Co. Wicklow, the rainfall amounted to [illegible] inch on [illegible] days. The heaviest falls in 24 hours were [illegible] inch on the 18th, and [illegible] inch on the 30th. The total rainfall in 1896 up to April 30, was [illegible] inches on [illegible] days, compared with [illegible] inches on [illegible] days in 1895, 17·[illegible] inches on [illegible] days in 1894, and [illegible] inches on [illegible] days in 1893.

At Cloneevin, Killiney, Co. Dublin, 1·[illegible] inches of rain fell on [illegible] days in April. The maximal fall in 24 hours was [illegible] inch on the [illegible]. The average rainfall in April of the ten years, [illegible]–1895, was 1·[illegible] inches on 13·2 days. Since January 1, 1896, [illegible] inches of rain fell at this station on [illegible] days, compared with [illegible] inches on [illegible] days in 1895, [illegible] inches on [illegible] days in 1894, and [illegible] inches on 57 days in 1893.

May.—A beautiful month, very similar to May, 1895—bright and dry, without any severe nipping night frosts. Persistent easterly sea breezes by day along the east coast of Ireland tempered the heat of an often unclouded sun. The amount of cloud was very low—only [illegible] per cent. At 9 a.m. it rose to [illegible] per cent., but at 9 p.m. it fell to [illegible] per cent. Rain fell in Dublin on only 7 days, and the total measurement was less than one-fifth of an inch, or about one-eleventh of the average rainfall for May.

In Dublin the arithmetical mean temperature ([illegible]°) was decidedly above the average ([illegible]°); the mean dry bulb readings at 9 a.m. and 9 p.m. were [illegible]°. In the thirty-one years ending with 1895, May was coldest in 1869 (M. T. = [illegible]°), and warmest in 1893 (M. T. = [illegible]°). In 1894 the M. T. was [illegible]°; in 1895 it was [illegible]°.

The mean height of the barometer was 30·[illegible] inches, or 0·[illegible] inch above the corrected average value for May—namely, 29·[illegible] inches. The mercury rose to 30·[illegible] inches at 9 a.m. of the [illegible], and fell to 29·[illegible] inches at 9 a.m. of the 23rd. The observed range of atmospheric pressure was, therefore, only 0·[illegible] inch.

The mean temperature deduced from daily readings of the dry bulb thermometer at 9 a.m. and 9 p.m. was [illegible]°, or [illegible]° above the value for April, 1896 ([illegible]°). Using the formula, *Mean Temp. = Min. + (max.—min. × ·47)*, the value was [illegible]°, or [illegible]° above the average. Mean temperature for May, calculated in the same way, in the twenty-five years, 1865–89, inclusive (53·6°). The arithmetical mean of the maximal and minimal readings was 55·2°, compared with a twenty-five years' average of 53·6°. On the 28th the thermometer in the screen rose to 71·6°—wind, E.; on the 1st the temperature fell to 36·2°—wind, N.N.W. The minimum on the grass was 32·2° on the 3rd.

The rainfall amounted to only ·880 inch, distributed over 7 days. The average rainfall for May in the twenty-five years, 1865–89, inclusive, was 2·032 inches, and the average number of rainy days was 15·4. The rainfall and the rainy days, therefore, were much below the average. In 1886 the rainfall in May was very large—5·473 inches on 21 days; in 1887, also, 3·414 inches fell on 15 days. On the other hand, in 1885, only ·777 inch was measured on but 9 days. In 1892 the large amount of 4·177 inches fell on 19 days. In 1893 the fall was 1·056 inches on 10 days; and in 1894, 3·589 inches on 17 days.

Solar halos were seen on the 13th, 21st, and 25th, lunar halos on the 19th, and an aurora on the 3rd. High winds were noted on but 3 days, attaining the force of a gale (from N.N.W.) on the 20th only. The atmosphere was slightly foggy on the 4th and 28th.

During the month the thermometer did not fall below 32° in the screen, but it indicated slight frost on the grass on the night of the 3rd. The mean minimal temperature on the grass was 42·4°, compared with 44·5° in 1895; 37·8° in 1894, 42·6° in 1893, 41·3° in 1892, 37·7° in 1891, 38·8° in 1890, 42·4° in 1889, 37·8° in 1888, and 37·2° in 1887.

On Friday, the 1st, an anticyclone was formed over Ireland, and this high-pressure system continued to develop until the close of the week, quiet, cool, dry, fine weather being the result. The screened thermometer sank to 36·2° on Friday. An aurora borealis was seen on Saturday night.

Favourable weather held throughout the week ended Saturday, the 9th. The type was chiefly anticyclonic, with westerly winds, dry and fine. At the beginning an extensive area of high pressure stretched across the British Islands, the North Sea and Scandinavia. The air was calm and the sky clear, so that the diurnal range of temperature was large, cold nights being followed at inland stations by warm days. On Monday the thermometer rose to 72° in London, while it fell to 34° during the ensuing night. Signs of a shallow depression at this time showed themselves off the N.W. of Ireland, so that the sky became cloudy over this country and rain fell, rather heavily in the N.W. At 8 a.m. of Tuesday ·36 inch of rain was registered at Malin Head and ·37 inch at Belmullet. Even in Dublin some slight showers occurred on Tuesday, both morning and evening; the measurement, however, was only ·013 inch. The anticyclone then began to develop again, and a spell of easterly winds set in. Sea fog accompanied the easterly current on Wednesday morning, but much bright sunshine was enjoyed daily until the end of the week, Friday being an especially genial day. On that day the thermometer rose to 72° in the shade at Parsonstown and Donaghadee, and to 71° at Belmullet. In Dublin the mean atmospheric pressure was 30·321 inches, the barometer ranging from 30·003 inches at 9 p.m. of Sunday (wind, S.E.), to 30·467 inches at 9 p.m. of Saturday (wind, E.). The corrected mean temperature was 53·1°. The mean dry bulb reading at 9 a.m. and 9 p.m. was 52·5°. On Sunday the thermometers in the screen fell to 37·8°, on Friday they rose to 66·5°. Easterly winds prevailed. The rainfall was ·013 inch on two days, ·008 inch being measured on Monday.

Throughout the week ended Saturday, the 16th, Ireland lay well within the central area of an anticyclone, so that the barometer readings were high and uniform, and the weather was fine and quiet. Winds from polar quarters predominated, but owing to the prevalence of bright sunshine, temperature rose even by night, and was very high on several occasions during the daytime. From Dublin not a cloud was to be seen in the sky until Tuesday afternoon. On Wednesday, however, a good deal of cirrus came up from N.W., producing a solar halo. There was also on this day some cumulus, which is a very uncommon cloud-formation. The last three days were rather cloudy, especially in the mornings, and a slight shower fell on Friday at an early hour. On Saturday, also, a few drops of rain fell at 9.15 a.m. While the weather was thus exceptionally fine in Ireland, less fair conditions prevailed in Scotland and also for a time in England. This was brought about by the passage of several depressions across Scandinavia in a south-easterly direction. On Tuesday the shade thermometer rose to 80° at York and Loughborough, to 77° in London and at Parsonstown and Oxford, and to 78° at Cambridge. Thunder and lightning followed very generally in the N.E. and E. of England, but scarcely any rain fell. In Dublin the mean height of the barometer was 30·305 inches, the pressure ranging from 30·444 inches at 9 a.m. of Tuesday (wind, E.), to 30·146 inches at 9 p.m. of Thursday (wind, N.W.). The corrected mean temperature was 57·8°. The mean dry bulb temperature at 9 a.m. and 9 p.m. was 57·4°. On Monday the screened thermometers fell to 43·8°; on Wednesday they rose to 71·2°. The rainfall was a mere trace—·002 inch on Thursday. The prevalent winds were E. and N.W.

Although not unfavourable, the weather for the week ended Saturday, the 23rd, was much less settled than that of past weeks, and grateful rain fell in frequent showers, abundantly in some parts of the kingdom, more sparingly in others. Speaking generally, the barometer stood high off the S.W. of Ireland, where an anticyclone held its position almost throughout, while a number of depressions formed over the Norwegian Sea, the southern half of Scandinavia and the North Sea, with a general tendency to drift south-eastwards to Central Europe. Hence N.W. winds prevailed in the British Isles, increasing in force to a moderate gale, at exposed stations, a strong gale on Wednesday. Temperature also gave way considerably after Monday, when the thermometer in the shade rose to 77° in London, 78° at Loughborough, 75° at Cambridge, and 69° in Dublin. On Wednesday night it fell to 34° at York, 35° at Parsonstown, 38° at Wick, Loughborough, Oxford, and Cambridge, 39° in London, and 40° in Dublin—the grass minimum at Loughborough was 26°. This chill has been preceded by thunder, lightning, and hail showers on Wednesday in several parts of England. Rain began to fall freely on Thursday, and the air, which had been dry and sparkling, became moist, soft, and warm. Fresh westerly to northerly winds continued to the close of the week. In Dublin the mean height of the barometer was 30·1[illegible] inches, pressure ranging between 30·[illegible] inches at [illegible] p.m. of Saturday (wind, N.W.) and 29·[illegible] inches at 3 a.m. of Friday (wind, S.W.). The corrected mean temperature was 56·[illegible]°, the mean dry bulb reading at 9 a.m. and 9 p.m. being [illegible]°. On Monday the screened thermometers rose to [illegible]°, on Thursday they fell to [illegible]°. The rainfall was [illegible] inch on five days, [illegible] inch being registered on Monday, on the afternoon of which day slight thunder and lightning occurred over the south-eastern suburbs of Dublin. The prevalent wind was N.W.

Anticyclonic conditions ruled in Ireland throughout the week ended Saturday, the [illegible]th, and the weather was very dry and fine, with continuous polar winds. At first the nights were cold, but as the week advanced a freshening breeze checked the nocturnal fall of temperature. By day the sun had great power, and on Friday, notwithstanding a fresh northerly wind, a shade maximum of 71·[illegible]° was recorded. The barometer stood at 30[illegible] inches or upwards over a great part of Ireland until Tuesday afternoon, when a somewhat decided fall in pressure spread southwards from Iceland, threatening to break up the fine weather. A recovery, however, soon followed. This in turn was succeeded by a brisk fall of the barometer in Scandinavia, so that by Friday morning the centre of a well-marked depression had advanced from the N.W. to the neighbourhood of Stockholm. This disturbance brought chilly rain to Norway, Sweden, and Denmark, showers to Scotland and to exposed places in the N.E. and E. of England, and fresh northerly winds in all parts of the British Islands. In Ireland (except in the extreme North) the weather remained rainless to the close of the week. Saturday broke overcast and cool, but the clouds soon dispersed and the afternoon was brilliant. Thunderstorms occurred on the Continent on and after Tuesday, and a terrific tornado devastated the city of St. Louis, Missouri, on Wednesday afternoon. In Dublin the mean height of the barometer was 30·[illegible] inches—highest, 30·[illegible] inches at 9 a.m. of Monday (wind, E.N.E.); lowest, 30·[illegible] inches at 1 p.m. of Friday (wind, N.). The corrected mean temperature was 56·0°, the mean dry bulb reading at 9 a.m. and 9 p.m. was 55·7°. The screened thermometers fell to 43·2° on Sunday, and rose to 71·3° on Friday. The prevalent wind was N.E. No rain fell.

Sunday, the 31st, was brilliantly fine.

The rainfall in Dublin during the five months ending May 31st amounted to only 5·971 inches on 70 days, compared with 10·430 inches on 68 days in 1895, 12·709 inches on 80 days in 1894, 7·[illegible] inches on 6[illegible] days in 1893, 10·0[illegible] inches on 80 days in 1892, only 5·[illegible] inches on 63 days in 1891, 11·[illegible] inches on 76 days in 1890, 10·476 inches on 81 days in 1889, 9·[illegible] inches on 63 days in 1888, 9·480 inches on 63 days in 1887, and a twenty-five years' average of 10·[illegible] inches on [illegible] days. The deficit so far in 1896 slightly exceeds [illegible] per cent.

At Knockdolian, Greystones, Co. Wicklow, the rainfall was 0·[illegible] inch, distributed over only 3 days, ·[illegible] inch falling on the 18th and the same quantity on the 19th. The total fall since January 1st, 1896, equals 5·718 inches on 52 days, compared with 12·[illegible] inches on [illegible] days in 1895, 1[illegible] inches on [illegible] days in 1894, and 9·[illegible] inches on 65 days in 1893.

The rainfall at Cloneevin, Killiney, Co. Dublin, was 0·[illegible] inch on 2 days—·0[illegible] inch falling on both the 18th and 19th. At this station the average rainfall in May in the ten years, 1885–1894, was 2·[illegible] inches on 15·2 days. May, 1895, was a very dry month, only 0·12 inch falling on 3 days, but the past month "beats the record." Since January 1, 1896, [illegible] inches of rain have fallen on 57 days at Cloneevin.

A more plentiful rainfall was recorded west and north of the city. The measurement at the Ordnance Survey Office, Phoenix Park, was ·[illegible] inch on 3 days; that at the Royal Botanic Gardens, Glasnevin, was ·[illegible] inch on 3 days.

JUNE.—A very favourable, warm, summer-like month. It is true that the rainfall and rainy days equalled or slightly exceeded the average, but 75 per cent. of the total precipitation occurred on 3 days, leaving only 25 per cent. to be distributed over the remaining 11 "rainy days." The month, therefore, was showery rather than wet. The heat on the 15th was very unusual for June in Ireland. The amount of cloud was large for so fine a month, and the strength and persistency of the N.W. winds of the closing period are noteworthy.

In Dublin the arithmetical mean temperature (61·[illegible]°) was above the average (57·[illegible]°) by [illegible]°; the mean dry bulb readings at 9 a.m. and 9 p.m. were 60·[illegible]°. In the thirty-one years ending with 1896, June was coldest in 1882 (M. T. = 5[illegible]°), and in 1879 (the "cold year") (M. T. = 5[illegible]°). It was warmest in 1887 (M. T. = 62·3°), in 1868 (M. T. = 62·0°), and in 18[illegible] (the "warm year") (M. T. = 60·5°). In 1895 the M. T. was 59·[illegible]°.

The mean height of the barometer was 30·[illegible] inches, or 0·[illegible] inch above the corrected average value for June—namely, 29·917 inches. The mercury rose to 30·276 inches at 9 p.m. of the 29th, and fell to 29·[illegible] inches at 9 a.m. of the 17th. The observed range of atmospheric pressure was, therefore, 0·[illegible] inch—that is, a little less than nine-tenths of an inch.

The mean temperature deduced from daily readings of the dry bulb thermometer at 9 a.m. and 9 p.m. was 60·[illegible]°, or 5·[illegible]° above the value for May, 1896. Using the formula, Mean Temp. = Min. + (max. − min. × ·4[illegible]), the value was 60·[illegible]°, or 2·7° above the average mean temperature for June, calculated in the same way, in the twenty-five years, 1865–89, inclusive (57·[illegible]°). The arithmetical mean of the maximal and minimal readings was 61·4°, compared with a twenty-five years' average of 57·[illegible]°. On the 15th the thermometer in the screen rose to [illegible]°—wind, E.S.E. to S.W.; on the 1st the temperature fell to [illegible]°—wind, E. The minimum on the grass was [illegible]°, also on the 1st.

The rainfall amounted to 1·[illegible] inches, distributed over 14 days. The average rainfall for June in the twenty-five years, 1865–89, inclusive, was 1·[illegible] inches, and the average number of rainy days was 13·[illegible]. The rainfall was, therefore, slightly above, while the rainy days were exactly the average. In 1878 the rainfall in June was very large—[illegible] inches on 1[illegible] days; in 1879 also [illegible] inches fell on 2[illegible] days. On the other hand, in 18[illegible], only ·[illegible] inch was measured on [illegible] days; in 1887, the rainfall was only ·262 inch, distributed over only [illegible] days; in 1895, 1·[illegible] inches fell on 12 days.

High winds were noted on 7 days, but the force of a gale was attained only on the 30th. Temperature reached or exceeded 70° in the screen on 9 days, compared with 17 days in 1897, only 1 day in 1896, and 7 days in 1895. Hail fell on the 24th. A thunderstorm occurred on the 25th, and thunder was heard on the 19th.

The period ended Saturday, the 6th, saw the disappearance of the anticyclonic conditions which had so long held sway over the British Islands, and the substitution for them of a cyclonic distribution of atmospheric pressure, with a consequent break in the fine weather. As usually happens, the change was accompanied by thunderstorms, which were particularly frequent and severe in France and Great Britain, less frequent and less severe in Ireland. In advance of the electrical disturbances very high day temperatures were recorded—the maxima up to Friday, for example, were—in Paris, 82°, 84°, 74°, and 79°; in London, 79°, 83°, 77°, and 81°. Dublin was much cooler because the prevailing easterly and north-easterly winds were off the sea—the corresponding values were—64°, 63°, 66°, and 67°. Monday, the 1st, was brilliantly fine. Showers fell on Tuesday afternoon and night, and the sky was cloudy. Wednesday was bright and warm in the east, showery inland. On Thursday evening rain fell in heavy showers. Friday was fine in Dublin, showery inland. On Saturday morning the S.E. wind freshened to a strong breeze and showery weather followed. In Dublin the barometer ranged from 30.071 inches at 9 a.m. of Monday (wind, E.) to 29.621 inches at 9 p.m. of Saturday (wind S.E.). On Monday the maximum thermometer fell to 60.1°; on Wednesday they rose to 68.9°. The rainfall was .155 inch on three days, .104 inch being measured on Thursday. The prevailing wind was S.E.

In the neighbourhood of Dublin especially the weather of the week ended Saturday, the 13th, was most favourable—fine and warm, only on Monday was there a moderate rainfall in or near the Irish capital. On the other hand, conditions were quite unsettled up to Friday in the S., S.E., and E. of England, where rain fell in abundance on Tuesday and Wednesday. This somewhat unequal distribution of weather was caused by the approach to the southern shores of the British Isles of two depressions—one on Sunday, the other on Tuesday. Of these the first hung off the extreme S.W. of Ireland during Sunday and Monday and then "filled up." It threw off various shallow subsidiaries, which brought thunderstorms and heavy hail (also local rains) in many parts of the United Kingdom. In Dublin on Monday afternoon the sky became hazy, cloudy and lowering, but only a few drops of rain fell—at Holyhead, on the contrary, the measurement was six-tenths of an inch. The second depression advanced across Brittany and the English Channel to England, Ireland almost escaping its influence. It caused abundant rains and thunderstorms in the S. and E. of Great Britain, as well as on the Continent. At Wimbledon 1.27 inches of rain fell in the 24 hours ending 8 a.m. of Wednesday. On Friday a large low pressure system lay off the W. of Ireland, but [illegible] and Saturday proved warm and bright. In Dublin the mean height of the barometer was 29.791 inches, pressure ranging from 29.671 inches at 9 p.m. of Sunday (wind, E.) to 30.061 inches at 9 p.m. of Saturday (wind, E. by S.). The corrected mean temperature was 60.6°. The mean dry bulb temperature at 9 a.m. and 9 p.m. was 60.5°. On Thursday the maximum in the shade was 68.4°; on Saturday the maximum was 72.0°. The wind was variable—chiefly W.N.W. and S.E. Rain fell on Monday to the amount of .020 inch.

Opening with a period of intense heat, the week ended Saturday, the 20th, proved changeable, and somewhat cool weather came back over Ireland, Scotland, and the North of England. In the south and [illegible] of the [illegible] the rainfall was steady—thus [illegible] the [illegible] of precipitation which had occurred in the previous week. Blazing sunshine prevailed throughout Sunday and Monday. On the latter day the thermometer rose in the shade to 84° in London, 86° at York, Liverpool, and Loughborough, 83° at Cambridge, 82° at Oxford and Parsonstown, and 81° in Dublin. This last reading was the highest recorded in Dublin in June for at least 36 years, and was higher than any maximum in this city observed since July 16, 1876, when the phenomenal reading (for Dublin), 87.2°, was recorded. On six occasions during the summer of 1887 the thermometer rose to 80° in the shade in Dublin, the highest readings of all being 84° on July 11 and 83° on July 22. On August 1, the maximum was 82°. After the great heat on Monday, temperature fell fast; a rather deep depression formed over Ireland and Scotland and a sudden downpour of rain occurred on Tuesday night. Afterwards the weather remained cool, breezy and showery to the end of the week. On Thursday very heavy electrical showers, accompanied by thunder, fell along the east coast of Ireland. They were due apparently to a great chill during the previous night, when the shade thermometer fell to 44° at Parsonstown, 40° at Donaghadee, and 49° in Dublin. In this city the mean pressure was 29.912 inches, the barometer falling to 29.453 inches at 6 p.m. of Wednesday (wind, W. by S.) and rising to 30.178 inches at 9 p.m. on Saturday (wind, W.N.W.). The corrected mean temperature was 62.2°. The mean dry bulb reading at 9 a.m. and 9 p.m. was 60.4°. On Monday the screened thermometers rose to 80.8°, on Friday they sank to 46.4°. The rainfall was 1.164 inches on four days, .760 inch being measured on Tuesday and .335 inch on Thursday, when thunder occurred. The prevailing winds were S.S.E. and W.S.W.

Another week of changeable but more favourable weather, closed on Saturday, the 27th. Except on Saturday the heat by day was moderate, while at times low temperatures by night were recorded. As a rule the barometer stood high in the S., but was relatively low in the N. or N.E. On Wednesday, when there was a decided tendency to thunderstorms, slight gradients for northerly winds became established over the British Isles, lasting until Friday. At the close of the week, a fall of the barometer in the N.W. brought W. and S.W. winds, a rapid rise of temperature and changeable, cloudy weather. In Dublin Sunday was fair to cloudy at times. On Monday some showers fell—a rather heavy one at 10 p.m. Tuesday also proved showery. Early on Wednesday dense electrical clouds were seen to form, and at noon a sharp thunderstorm, accompanied by heavy rain and hail, passed over Dublin. The rainfall resulting from the storm was three-tenths of an inch. Another heavy shower fell towards the evening. Thursday was cloudy and cool but fine. Friday was bright and warm or cloudy. Saturday was close and relaxing with much cloud—

K

between 2 and 3 p.m. heavy showers passed over the city. At this station the mean height of the barometer was 30·157 inches, the lowest reading being 30·004 inches at 7.15 a.m. of Tuesday (wind, W. by N.), the highest 30·297 inches at 9 a.m. of Friday (wind, N.N.W.). The corrected mean temperature was 61·0°. The mean dry bulb reading at 9 a.m. and 9 p.m. was 61·0°. On Sunday the screened thermometers fell to 51·1°, on Saturday they rose to 73·8°. Rainfall amounted to ·877 inch on five days, ·340 inch being measured on Wednesday. The prevailing wind was N.W. Thunder, lightning and hail were observed on Wednesday.

The last three days of the month were unsettled and windy, but for the most part dry. In Dublin only ·005 inch of rain fell on Tuesday morning, the 30th. The direction of the wind was chiefly N.W., so that temperature was not high, except on Monday afternoon, when the wind backed to W.S.W. On the 29th, a fresh N.W. gale prevailed—the squalls being of unusual severity for midsummer.

The rainfall in Dublin during the six months ending June 30th amounted to 7·634 inches on 84 days, compared with 12·202 inches on 89 days in 1895, 14·391 inches on 102 days in 1894, 9·034 inches on 78 days in 1893, 11·770 inches on 97 days in 1892, 8·745 inches on 77 days in 1891, 10·413 inches on 94 days in 1890, 10·376 inches on 87 days in 1889, 12·313 inches on 87 days in 1888, 6·761 inches on 67 days in 1887, and a twenty-five years' average of 12·913 inches on 95·4 days.

At Knockdolian, Greystones, Co. Wicklow, the rainfall was 1·640 inches, distributed over 9 days. Of this quantity ·960 inch fell on the 16th. The total fall since January 1 has been 7·350 inches on 61 days, compared with 14·270 inches on 67 days in the first six months of 1895, 17·281 inches on 96 days in 1894, and 11·776 inches on 75 days in 1893.

The rainfall at Cloneevin, Killiney, Co. Dublin, amounted to 1·65 inches on 13 days. The greatest fall in 24 hours was ·94 inch on the 16th. The average rainfall for June in the 10 years 1885-1894, was 1·460 inches on 11·6 days. In 1895, 1·94 inches fell on 12 days. Since January 1, 1896, 6·96 inches of rain have fallen at this station on 70 days.

the Iberian Peninsula. In this way steep gradients for W. winds were formed over the British Islands. On Wednesday, the hot, great heat set in over the North of Scandinavia, culminating in a temperature of 87° at Haparanda, on the Gulf of Bothnia, on Thursday and Friday. At 8 p.m. of Friday the thermometer read 79° at that station, but only 43° at Munich, some 17° further S. Saturday was a wild, blustering day, owing to the approach of a new depression to our N.W. coasts. In the afternoon heavy showers fell and caused a plague of dust. In Dublin the barometer ranged from 30·121 inches at 9 p.m. of Wednesday (wind, N.W.) to 29·774 inches at 4 p.m. of Friday (wind, W.). On Friday the screened thermometer rose to 69·5°, on Saturday they fell to 53·5°. The rainfall was ·366 inch on four days—·314 inch was measured on Thursday. The prevailing winds were N.W. and W.

The most noteworthy feature in the climatological record of the week ended Saturday, the 11th, was the rainstorm which affected Ireland and North Wales, and to a less extent the North of England and the South of Scotland on Wednesday and Thursday. At the beginning of the period the weather was fine and warm. On Monday a shift of wind to the northward, while the cloud-current was still south-westerly, caused a heavy rainfall at several Irish stations—1·25 inches at Donaghadee, [illegible] inch at Parsonstown, and ·36 inch in Dublin. The chill which led to the precipitation had already set in at Donaghadee at 8 a.m. on Monday, but did not reach Dublin until 8.44 p.m. In the course of the following day thunderstorms of great severity occurred in the midland and eastern counties of England. In London rain only threatened, and the thermometer rose to 88° in the shade. On Wednesday a complex depression advanced over Ireland from W. and rain fell in torrents, accompanied by sheet lightning at night and by thunder at Holyhead, Youghal, Liverpool, and Shields. Fog formed over the Irish Sea early on Thursday morning, while the rainstorm was at its worst. The wind soon shifted to N. and N.E. and towards evening of Thursday the weather became fair and bracing. At night the screened thermometers fell to 42° at Parsonstown, 42° at Nairn, 44° at Stornoway, and 47° at Wick and Valentia as well as in Dublin. The last two days of the week were very fine, and summer heat returned on Saturday. Marked "visibility" was observable on Saturday evening. In Dublin the mean height of the barometer was 30·023 inches, the extremes being—lowest, 29·715 inches at 9 p.m. of Wednesday (wind, S.E.); highest, 30·280 inches at 9 p.m. of Friday (wind, N.N.E.). The corrected mean temperature was 58·6°. The mean dry bulb temperature at 9 a.m. and 9 p.m. was 59·4°. On Saturday the screened thermometers rose to 74·1°, having fallen to 47·1° on Friday. The rainfall was 2·131 inches on three days, 1·563 inches being registered on Wednesday. The wind was very variable in direction. At Greystones, Co. Wicklow, the rainfall was 2·370 inches on three days, 1·085 inches falling on Wednesday, 1·075 inches on Thursday.

Changeable but favourable weather was recorded during the week ended Saturday, the 18th. At first an anticyclone embraced England, Belgium, and the North of France. It was attended by a great heat-wave, the thermometer rising to 89° in the shade on Monday in London and Paris and at Cambridge. Here in Dublin the maximum on that day was 77°. An irregular and shallow depression now moved in from the Atlantic, causing clouds, showers, and a fall of temperature. This system still had its centre over Holland on Friday morning when, however, it was filling up. In its rear an area of high atmospheric pressure advanced over Ireland from the Atlantic. This rendered the gradients for polar winds rather steep over the British Islands, and accordingly cold, squally northerly breezes set in, being accompanied by gloomy, chilly, rainy weather in the east and south-east of England. In London the maximal temperature for the 24 hours ending 8 a.m. of Friday was 63°, or 26° below the reading recorded on Monday. As the anticyclone moved southeastward on Friday, the wind backed towards W. in Ireland and moderated with a much higher temperature but very clouded skies. In Dublin the mean barometric reading was 30·219 inches, pressure ranging from 30·044 inches at 9 a.m. of Tuesday (wind, S.W.) to 30·375 inches at 9 a.m. of Friday (wind, N.). The corrected mean temperature was 61·4°. The mean dry bulb reading at 9 a.m. and 9 p.m. was 61·8°. On Monday the maximum in the screen was 78·7°, on Thursday the minimum was 47·2°. Rain fell on the first three days to the amount of ·048 inch only, ·030 inch being measured on Tuesday. The prevailing winds were S.W. and N.

As regards the week ended Saturday, the 25th, warm and summer-like at first, the weather soon fell into an unsettled rainy condition, so far as Ireland, Scotland, and the North of England were concerned. In the south and east of the last-named country the heat became almost tropical and very little rain fell until quite the close of the period. On Tuesday the thermometer rose to 88° in the shade in London and at Cambridge. During Sunday and Monday an anticyclone overlay the southern half of the British Isles. A warm S.W. wind prevailed in Ireland, sending the thermometer up to 72° at Donaghadee and Parsonstown, and to 73° in Dublin on Sunday, and to 75° in Dublin and at Parsonstown on Monday. A complex V-shaped depression spread eastward across Ireland on Monday night, causing rain, a shift of wind to N.W. and a brisk fall of temperature. Wednesday was a bright, bracing day, with a very dry atmosphere—at 2 p.m. the percentage of relative humidity fell to 46. Local showers occurred towards evening. On Thursday the barometer fell steadily as another complex depression came in from the Atlantic, momentarily growing deeper. The system continued to develop until Saturday afternoon, when the barometer read only 29·42 inches in Dublin. It caused torrential rains for the second time in the present month on the shores of the Irish Sea and St. George's Channel, which rains were, on Saturday afternoon, accompanied by thunder and lightning. In Dublin the mean height of the barometer was 29·925 inches, pressure ranging between 30·178 inches at 9 a.m. of Sunday (wind, W.S.W.) and 29·419 inches at 4 p.m. of Saturday (wind, S.W.). The corrected mean temperature was 61·7°. The mean dry bulb reading at 9 a.m. and 9 p.m. was 60·5°. On Sunday the screened thermometers rose to 75·0°; on Wednesday they fell to 52·4°. The rainfall was ·944 inches on five days, ·720 inches being measured on Friday. The prevailing winds were W.S.W. and N.W. A thunderstorm occurred on Saturday afternoon.

Although changeable in the middle of the period ending Friday, the 31st, the weather was much fairer and drier than that of the previous week. On Sunday the depression which had caused such heavy rains at the close of the preceding period, was still found off the W. of Scotland, while a "secondary" system was moving towards E.N.E. across the S. of England. Gusty N.W. winds and passing showers prevailed in Dublin, while a heavy fall of rain amounting to ·84 inch occurred in London, accompanied by thunder and lightning. By Monday morning the main depression had travelled eastward and lay between the N.E. of Scotland and S.W. of Norway. It was quickly filling up. N.W. winds and cool, cloudy weather were reported. Towards night the sky cleared and temperature fell fast, the minima in Dublin being 43° in the screen and 41°, on the grass. At Nairn 41° in the screen was recorded. On Tuesday night the thermometer sank to 39° on the grass at Oxford. At this time a new depression was showing off the N.W. of Ireland, its advent being heralded by the appearance of cirrus cloud in which parhelia developed. This disturbance suddenly changed its course and travelled in a south-easterly direction across Ireland. The wind was first S.W., afterwards N.E., but notwithstanding this abrupt change in direction rainfall was not heavy, except at Valentia Island (·71 inch), Donaghadee (·73 inch), Ardrossan (·63 inch), and in London (·39 inch). On Thursday in Dublin the weather was at first dull, but afterwards became fine and bright, and so continued to the end. The barometer in this city ranged between 30·139 inches at 9 a.m. of Tuesday (wind, N.W.), and 29·677 inches at 9 p.m. of Wednesday (wind, S.W.). On Tuesday the screened thermometer fell to 45·0°; on Wednesday they rose to 66·7°. Rain fell on three days to the amount of ·134 inch, ·070 inch being measured on Wednesday. The prevailing winds were N.W. and N.E.

The rainfall in Dublin during the seven months ending July 31st amounted to 13·438 inches on 108 days, compared with 10·783 inches on 96 days in 1895, 18·133 inches on 120 days in 1894, 11·866 inches on 98 days in 1893, 7·181 inches on 80 days in 1887, and a twenty-five years' average of 14·738 inches on 112·5 days.

At Knockdolian, Greystones, Co. Wicklow, the rainfall in July was 5·794 inches on 13 days, compared with 1·680 inches on 16 days in 1895, 2·805 inches on 19 days in 1894, and 1·890 inches on 15 days in 1893. Of the total rainfall 1·681 inches fell on the 24th, 1·075 inches on the 16th, and 1·020 inches on the 8th. The total fall since January 1 has been 12·482 inches on 77 days, compared with 17·850 inches on 83 days in 1895, 21·161 inches on 115 days in 1894, and 15·603 inches on 90 days in 1893.

At Cloncevin, Killiney, Co. Dublin, the rainfall in July was 4·72 inches on 20 days, compared with a nine years' average of 3·185 inches on 15·9 days. On the 24th the rainfall was 1·25 inches. In July, 1895, 2·56 inches fell on 17 days, in 1894 4·05 inches fell on 18 days. Since January 1, 1896, 15·10 inches of rain have fallen on 90 days at this station (Cloncevin), so that the rainfall in July nearly equalled that of the previous six months.

AUGUST.—A cool, breezy, showery month, with a remarkable prevalence of northerly and north-westerly winds. In Dublin rain fell in measurable amount on as many as 19 days, but the total precipitation fell short of the average by 1·689 inches. This was due to the fact that the rainfall was chiefly caused by showers—indeed, not a single continuously "wet day" occurred during the month. The amount of cloud was very large in the mornings—73·3 per cent., but the evening skies were much freer from cloud—54·2 per cent. only.

In Dublin the arithmetical mean temperature (57·8°) was decidedly below the average (59·7°); the mean dry bulb readings at 9 a.m. and 9 p.m. were 57·5°. In the thirty-one years ending with 1895, August was coldest in 1881 (M. T.=57·0°), and warmest in 1893 (M. T.=63·0°). In 1895 the M.T. was 60·0°; in 1879 (the "cold year"), it was 57·7°.

The mean height of the barometer was 30·073 inches, or 0·170 inch above the corrected average value for August—namely, 29·903 inches. The mercury marked 30·361 inches at 9 a.m. of the 10th, and fell to 29·570 inches at 11.30 p.m. of the 29th. The observed range of atmospheric pressure was, therefore, ·791 inch—that is, a little less than four-fifths of an inch.

The mean temperature deduced from daily readings of the dry bulb thermometer at 9 a.m. and 9 p.m. was 57·5°, or 1·3° below the value in August, 1895. It was also 2·3° below the value for July, 1896. Using the formula, *Mean Temp.* = *Min.* + (*max.*—*min.* × ·47), the mean temperature was 57·9°, or 1·4° below the average mean temperature for August, calculated in the same way, in the twenty-five years, 1865–89, inclusive (59·3°). The arithmetical mean of the maximal and minimal readings was 58·3°, compared with a twenty-five years' average of 59·7°. On the 23rd the thermometer in the screen rose to 71·1°—wind, W.S.W.; on the 28th the temperature fell to 46·6°—wind, N.W. The minimum on the grass was 42·0°, on the 24th and 30th.

The rainfall was 1·136 inches, distributed over 19 days. The average rainfall for August in the twenty-five years, 1865–89, inclusive, was 2·825 inches, and the average number of rainy days was 15·5. The rainfall, therefore, was much below, while the rainy days were considerably in excess of, the average. In 1874, the rainfall in August was very large—4·940 inches on 18 days; and in 1868, also 4·745 inches fell on, however, only 13 days; but the heaviest downpour in August occurred in 1882, when 5·717 inches were registered on 22 days. In 1883, 3·518 inches fell on 27 days. On the other hand, in 1884, only ·777 inch was measured on 8 days.

High winds were noted on as many as 13 days, and attained the force of a gale on three occasions in Dublin—the 13th, 24th, and 30th. Thunder occurred on the 26th. Lunar halos were seen on the 19th, 24th, and 27th. Temperature reached 70° in the screen on 2 days. Hail fell on the 20th.

The weather was very fine, bright, and summer-like on Saturday, the 1st.

Throughout the week ended Saturday, the 8th, an anticyclone, or area of high barometric pressure, lay over Ireland and upon the Atlantic to the westward of this country. It was of moderate intensity, the barometer never exceeding 30·4 inches. The weather may be described as cool and cloudy, with moderate to fresh northerly winds and scanty rainfall. On the Continent conditions were less favourable than in Ireland owing to the appearance of atmospheric depressions both over the Gulf of Bothnia and in the Mediterranean Basin. At times also secondary low-pressure systems moved across the North Sea in a southerly direction, bringing squally N. winds and cold showers to the eastern seaboard of Great Britain and even of Ireland, between Wednesday morning and Friday afternoon. No extreme heat was observed by day—the highest shade reading of the thermometer was 72° at Prawle Point (Devon) and Dungeness (Kent) on Tuesday—at Jersey a maximum of 73° was recorded on Monday. On the other hand, the nights were often very cool for the time of year. On Tuesday night the sheltered thermometer sank to 36° at Nairn and to 40° at Wick and Loughborough. At the last named station the thermometer fell to 32° on the grass. In Dublin the mean height of the barometer was 30·175 inches, pressure falling to 30·040 inches at 9 p.m. of Monday (wind, N.N.E.) and rising to 30·390 inches at 9 a.m. of Thursday (wind, N.). The corrected mean temperature was 57·1°. The mean dry bulb reading at 9 a.m. and 9 p.m. was 56·7°. On Monday the screened thermometers rose to 68·4°; on Wednesday they fell to 46·7°. Rainfall amounted to ·013 inch on two "rainy" days, ·011 inch being measured on Friday. An additional ·002 inch was recorded on Saturday. The prevailing winds were northerly (N.N.E. and N.N.W.).

Changeable, breezy, showery weather prevailed throughout the week ended Saturday, the 15th. As for some time past, so in this period an area of high atmospheric pressure existed over the Atlantic—at first to the N.W. and W. of Ireland, afterwards off the S.W. and S. of this country. On Sunday morning a large and irregular area of relatively low pressure—30 inches or slightly less—lay over France. It had caused heavy rain and thunder and lightning during the previous night in the S. and E. of England—even at Greystones, Co. Wicklow, a local heavy fall of rain, amounting to ·500 inch took place on Sunday morning. Only light showers fell at this time in Dublin, and the day proved fine and bright with a cool N.E. wind. On Monday afternoon the wind backed towards W., as a low pressure system approached Norway from W.N.W. This system caused higher temperatures, but at the same time showers in many districts. On Wednesday a deeper depression came in over Scotland, so that the wind freshened and showers continued to fall. At 8 a.m. of Friday the main depression was stationary near the Skagerrack, while secondaries lay over Denmark and also over the English Channel. On Saturday an anticyclone was again found off the West of Ireland, and northerly winds, cloudy skies, and lower temperatures prevailed. In Dublin the mean atmospheric pressure was 29·992 inches, the barometer varying from 30·311 inches at 9 a.m. of Monday (wind, N.N.E.) to 29·630 inches at 9 a.m. of Friday (wind, W.N.W.). The corrected mean temperature was 60·4°. The mean dry bulb temperature at 9 a.m. and 9 p.m. was 59·9°. On Monday the screened thermometers fell to 49·8°, on Wednesday they rose to 70·7°. The rainfall was ·280 inch on five days, ·140 inch being measured on Thursday. Northerly and westerly winds prevailed.

Although no atmospheric depressions of great importance were observed, yet the passage eastward or south-eastward across North-western Europe of numerous irregular and somewhat complex areas of relatively low barometer readings kept the weather in an unsettled, cloudy, showery condition all through the week ended Saturday, the 22nd. Sunday was a fine day in Ireland; the air was dry and temperature was low. A ridge of high pressure moved away eastward as the day advanced, so that by Monday morning gradients for southerly winds had developed, and the weather had become dull and threatening. A considerable fall of rain took place on Monday afternoon. Tuesday was fine, but some rain again fell at night. On Wednesday, southerly winds blew over Ireland, while the weather was kept in a rainy state in Great Britain by several shallow atmospheric depressions. The last three days of the week in Dublin began with cloudy and light falls of rain, but the afternoons and evenings were finer and brighter. Thunder and lightning occurred in London on Wednesday night. There was once more a tendency for the wind to draw into N.W. and N. In Dublin the mean height of the barometer was 30·017 inches, pressure ranging from 30·218 inches at 9 a.m. of Sunday (wind, N.) to 29·866 inches at 9 p.m. of Monday (wind, S.W.). The corrected mean temperature was 57·9°. The mean dry bulb reading at 9 a.m. and 9 p.m. was also 57·8°. On Sunday the screened thermometers fell to 46·3°; on Saturday they rose to 66·7°. The rainfall was ·321 inch, on six days, ·172 inch being measured on Monday. The prevailing winds were N. and W.N.W.

Throughout the week ended Saturday, the 29th, the weather remained in an unsettled state—with varying temperatures, much cloud, blustering winds, and frequent if not heavy falls of rain. The changeable conditions of the period were brought about by a succession of atmospheric depressions, which travelled eastwards or spread south-eastwards across the N.W. of Europe. At the beginning temperature was high, so that on Sunday the thermometer rose in the shade to 71° in Dublin and at Roche's Point, Co. Cork; to 73° at Birr Castle, 74° in London and at Prawle Point, Devon; and to 75° at Oxford. On Monday a decided "chill" occurred, which culminated in a spell of unusual cold for August on Tuesday, Wednesday, and Thursday. Within this period strong N. and N.W. winds prevailed, and heavy showers of rain and hail descended, accompanied in many places by thunder and lightning. On Tuesday night the thermometer in the screen fell to 37° at Aberdeen, 39° at Wick, and 40° at Nairn. Even in Dublin the minimum in the screen was 45·8, while 41° was recorded on the grass. Thursday and Friday were dry days, but the amount of cloud was large and the wind was fresh and gusty. On Saturday the wind was strong from S.W. and the weather again became very unsettled and showery. In Dublin the mean height of the barometer was 29·940 inches, the range being from 30·212 inches at 9 p.m. of Thursday (wind, N.W.) to 29·570 inches at 11.30 p.m. of Saturday (wind, S.S.W.). The corrected mean temperature was 57·6°. The mean dry bulb reading at 9 a.m. and 9 p.m. was 56·7°. On Sunday the screened thermometers rose to 71·1°, on Wednesday they fell to 45·4°. Rain fell on five days to the amount of ·456 inch, ·185 inch being registered on Sunday. Hail fell on Wednesday, when also thunder was heard. The prevailing winds were W., N.W., and N.

Sunday, the 30th, began with a gale of wind from S.W., but finally proved a very fine day. The sunset was of great beauty. Monday, the 31st, was at first cold, then fair and bright. A thunderstorm with heavy rain and hail passed across the centre of Ireland in the afternoon. At Parsonstown, ·41 inch of rain was measured after the storm.

The rainfall in Dublin during the eight months ending August 31st, amounted to 14·548 inches on 120 days, compared with 20·233 inches on 123 days in 1895, 9·443 inches on 96 days during the same period in 1887, and a twenty-five years' average of 17·356 inches on 128·1 days.

At Knockdolian, Greystones, Co. Wicklow, the rainfall in August, 1896, was 1·242 inches on 14 days, compared with 4·735 inches distributed over 24 days in 1895. Of this quantity ·350 inch fell on the 6th. The total fall since January 1 amounts to 14·237 inches on 81 days, compared with 22·188 inches on 117 days in 1895, 21·306 inches on 131 days in 1894, 16·811 inches on 106 days in 1893, and 21·386 inches on 103 days in 1892.

September.—Unlike the Septembers of 1893, 1894, and 1895—all of which were fine and summer-like—the month under review was throughout unsettled, stormy, and excessively wet. The rainfall was a record one—it amounted to 5·073 inches in Dublin, 5·78 inches at Clonsilla, Co. Dublin, and 7·358 inches at Greystones, Co. Wicklow. At the Ordnance Survey Office, Phoenix Park, it was 4·620 inches. The atmosphere was in a state of more unsettled equilibrium, and several very deep barometrical depressions passed across Western Europe. In Dublin, by a singular coincidence, the mean maximal and minimal temperatures, and the mean temperature derived from the daily extremes were all practically equal to the averages for September. The mean atmospheric pressure was, however, largely in defect.

In Dublin the arithmetical mean temperature (55·8°) was exactly the average (55·8°); the mean dry bulb readings at 9 a.m. and 9 p.m. were 54·4°. In the thirty-one years ending with 1896, September was coldest in 1886 and in 1882 (M. T. = 53·0°), and warmest in 1865 (M. T. = 61·4°). The three warmest Septembers experienced in Dublin of late years have been—1865 (M. T. = 61·4°), 1880 (M. T. = 58·6°), and 1894 (M. T. = 58·1°).

The mean height of the barometer was 29·707 inches, or 0·253 inch below the corrected average value for September—namely, 29·960 inches. The mercury rose to 30·449 inches at 9 p.m. of the 30th, and fell to 28·680 inches at 8.30 a.m. of the 25th. The observed range of atmospheric pressure was, therefore, 1·769 inches—that is, a little more than an inch and three-quarters.

The mean temperature deduced from daily readings of the dry bulb thermometer at 9 a.m. and 9 p.m. was 54·4°, or 3·1° below the value for August, 1896. Using the formula, Mean Temp. = Min. + (max. — min. × ·476), the mean temperature was 55·5°, or exactly equal to the average mean temperature for September, calculated in the same way, in the twenty-five years, 1865–89, inclusive (55·5°). The arithmetical mean of the maximal and minimal readings was 55·8°, compared with a twenty-five years' average of 55·8°. On the 17th the thermometer in the screen rose to 66·4°—wind, S.W.; on the 21st the temperature fell to 41·3°—wind, S.E. The minimum on the grass was 36·3°, also on the 21st.

The rainfall was 5·073 inches, distributed over 22 days. This was a record measurement, being more than double the average. The average rainfall for September in the twenty-five years, 1865–89, inclusive, was 2·175 inches, and the average number of rainy days was 14·7. In 1871, the rainfall was very large—4·048 inches on, however, only 15 days. On the other hand, in 1865, only ·056 inch was measured on but 2 days. In 1893, ·729 inch fell on 14 days; in 1894, only ·443 inch on 8 days; and in 1895, only ·541 inch on 7 days.

High winds were noted on fifteen days, and attained the force of a gale on seven occasions in Dublin—the 14th, 15th, 17th, 22nd, 23rd, 25th, and 27th. Lightning was seen on the 3rd, 10th, 12th, and 27th. The atmosphere was foggy on the 4th and 5th. Hail fell on the 15th. A lunar halo was seen on the 18th, a solar halo on the 19th.

During the period ended Saturday, the 5th, the weather was changeable and unsettled generally, but a very fine spell was enjoyed in and near Dublin up to the evening of Thursday, the 3rd, when heavy rain set in. At the beginning an area of relatively high pressure lay over the West of Ireland, while a depression moved across England, enlarging its borders and becoming both deeper and more complex. The result was that thunder and lightning and heavy rains occurred in many parts of Great Britain. On the morning of Thursday the 3rd, a new depression was found off the extreme N.W. of Ireland, so that the weather broke in this country also, and at night thunderstorms were reported from Roche's Point and Valentia Island, while ·480 inch of rain fell in Dublin and ·790 inch at Greystones. After a dull damp day the downpour was renewed on Friday evening and continued through the night—the measurement in Dublin on Saturday morning being ·940 inch. After 9 a.m. of Saturday the weather improved, becoming fine and bright and breezy. In Dublin the barometer ranged from 30·081 inches at 9 a.m. of Tuesday (wind, N.N.W.), to 29·756 inches at 9 p.m. of Friday (wind, N.E.). On Wednesday the screened thermometers fell to 39·7°, on Thursday they rose to 65·4°. The rainfall was 1·484 inches on two days, ·940 inch being registered on Friday. The prevailing winds were N.W. and N.E.

Very unsettled, thundery, and rainy weather prevailed during the greater part of the week ended Saturday, the 12th, over the British Islands, France, and Germany. At the beginning, however, a spell of fine weather was enjoyed, especially in Ireland, where moderate N.E. winds blew on Sunday, in connection with a high pressure system which stretched south-westwards to this country from the extreme N.W. of Norway. Already on Monday morning a disturbing element showed itself in the form of a large area of relatively low pressure, which was at that time moving northwards from the Peninsula. This system steadily advanced over the Bay of Biscay, grew deeper, and threw out various secondary areas of low pressure, in connection with which storms of thunder, lightning, rain and hail developed in many French and English districts. By Wednesday morning the centre of low pressure had reached Cornwall, whence it stretched across to Kerry. On Thursday morning it was passing out north-westwards over the Atlantic from Mayo and Donegal, but a new depression had reached the mouth of the English Channel travelling towards E.N.E. This caused a renewal of the electrical disturbances in France and England. At 3 p.m. of Thursday a violent and very destructive whirlwind passed over Paris, preceded by torrents of rain. In the course of the nights of both Thursday and Friday, further depressions crossed Ireland from the southward, accompanied by squally S.E. or S. winds and heavy rains. Sunny, warm intervals were enjoyed in the daytime—the changes from fair to foul weather and back again being unusually sudden and frequent. In Dublin the barometer ranged between [illegible] inches at 9 p.m. of Sunday (wind, N.E.) and 29·380 inches at 11.30 p.m. of Saturday (wind, S.E.). The mean atmospheric pressure was 29·710 inches. The corrected mean temperature was 57·1°. The mean dry bulb reading at 9 a.m. and 9 p.m. was 55·9°. On Sunday the screened thermometers fell to [illegible]°, on Saturday they rose to 67·7°. Rain fell on five days to the total amount of 1·372 inches, [illegible] inch being measured on Friday and [illegible] inch on Saturday. The prevalent wind was S.E. Lightning was seen on the evenings of Wednesday, Thursday, and Saturday.

The atmosphere over North-Western Europe was in a very perturbed state all through the week ended Saturday, the 18th. A series of large and deep depressions traversed the Atlantic and Norwegian Sea in a north-easterly direction, while secondary low pressure systems spread eastwards across the British Islands towards Central Europe. Connected with these barometric disturbances, copious rains fell from time to time in nearly all districts, and moderate to fresh or even strong gales blew from S., S.W., or N.W. at exposed points on the British and Irish coasts. On Tuesday and again on Friday morning the barometer sank below 29 inches—on the former occasion to [illegible] inches at Christiansund in Norway, on the latter to the same point at Sumburgh Head in the Shetlands. In Dublin the week was ushered in by strong southerly winds and torrents of rain early on Sunday morning. The day proved fine. Gales occurred on Monday, Wednesday, and Thursday—the last being the most severe. It was followed by a brisk decrease of temperature, so that on Friday the thermometer failed to reach 60° in the shade, whereas on Thursday it had risen to [illegible]° in front of the storm. Thunder and lightning occurred in the S.E. and E. of England on Sunday, and in some Scotch stations on Tuesday and Wednesday. A lunar halo appeared on Wednesday evening, and a solar halo on Friday afternoon. Heavy hail and rain showers fell on Saturday afternoon. In Dublin the mean atmospheric pressure was [illegible] inches, the barometer ranging between [illegible] inches at 1.30 p.m. of Monday (wind, S.W.) and [illegible] inches at 9 p.m. of Wednesday (wind, W.S.W.). The corrected mean temperature was [illegible]°. The mean dry bulb reading at 9 a.m. and 9 p.m. was [illegible]°. On Thursday the screened thermometers rose to [illegible]°; on both Friday and Saturday they fell to [illegible]°. The rainfall was [illegible] inch on six days, [illegible] inch being measured on Sunday. The prevalent winds were S.W., W., and W.N.W. Hail fell on Saturday.

As to the week ended Saturday, the 25th, yet another spell of storm and rain has to be recorded. In this period, besides other, small-scale disturbances, two storm-centres of great intensity passed rapidly across the British Isles in an easterly direction—the first on Monday night, the second on Thursday night. Both systems caused downpours of rain and violent gales from different quarters all over Western Europe, and even when the main disturbances had passed away the weather was kept in an unsettled, showery, squally condition by the arrival of secondary shallower depressions from the Atlantic. Sunday broke fair and cold, with N.W. winds. Heavy showers fell as the day advanced. A very cold night caused the thermometer falling in the shade to [illegible]° in Dublin, [illegible]° at Birmingham, [illegible]° at Parsonstown, [illegible]° in London, [illegible]° at Shields, York, and Cambridge, and [illegible]° at Loughborough. On Monday a general reduction of atmospheric pressure took place in advance of the deep depressions of Tuesday and Friday, and the weather became broken and rainy. At 1 p.m. of Tuesday the barometer was down to [illegible] inches in Dublin. In the evening the wind rose to a fresh or even a whole gale from W. and N.W. Squalls and heavy showers prevailed on Wednesday, but the weather improved in the afternoon. By 8 a.m. of Thursday the cyclonic centre had reached Copenhagen. On this day the sky became overcast with cirro-stratus, and at night another and still deeper depression swept eastwards across Ireland at the rate of some 30 miles an hour. The centre passed near Dublin about 3.30 a.m. (Irish time), reaching Liverpool at 5 a.m. (English time)—the barometer fell to [illegible] inches near the centre. A secondary depression followed on Saturday morning. In Dublin the mean height of the barometer was 29·517 inches, pressure ranging between [illegible] inches at 9 p.m. of Wednesday (wind, W. by N.) and [illegible] inches at 3.30 a.m. of Friday (wind, N. by W.). The corrected mean temperature was 51·8°. The mean dry bulb temperature at 9 a.m. and 9 p.m. was 51·7°. On Tuesday the screened thermometers rose to [illegible]°, having fallen to 41·1° on Monday. The rainfall was 1·60[illegible] inches on 7 days, [illegible] inch being registered on Thursday. The rainfall at Greystones, Co. Wicklow, was 3·070 inches, of which 1·[illegible] inches fell on Monday. The prevailing wind was W.N.W.

Changeable, showery, chilly weather continued to the 29th, when conditions temporarily improved owing to the formation of an anticyclone over the southern portion of the United Kingdom. On the 30th the barometer rose to about [illegible] inches near the centre of this high pressure system. On the morning of Sunday, the 25th, there was a S.W. gale, in front of which temperature rose to 64·6°. As the day advanced a brisk fall of the thermometer occurred, there were heavy showers, and lightning was seen in the evening over the Irish Sea. The 30th was the finest day enjoyed for several weeks.

The rainfall in Dublin during the nine months ending September 30th amounted to 14·687 inches on 148 days, compared with [illegible] inches on [illegible] days during the same period in 1897, [illegible] inches on 150 days in 1896, [illegible] inches on 130 days in 1895, and a twenty-five years' average of 19·734 inches on 152·6 days.

At Knockdolian, Greystones, Co. Wicklow, the rainfall was 7·565 inches distributed over 24 days. Of this quantity 1·000 inches fell on the 21st, and [illegible] inch on the 24th. At that station the rainfall from January 1, 1896, has been 21·812 inches on 115 days, compared with 21·583 inches on 125 days in the same nine months of 1892, 17·661 inches on 121 days in 1893, and 25·[illegible] inches on 137 days in 1894; and 21·565 inches on 117 days in 1895.

At Cloneevin, Killiney, Co. Dublin, the rainfall in August was 1·48 inches on 16 days (the maximal fall in 24 hours being ·47 inch on the 17th), compared with a ten years' average of 2·917 inches on 15·9 days. In September 7·17 inches fell at Cloneevin on 23 days. The maximal fall in 24 hours was ·87 inch on the 4th. On an average of ten years the September rainfall at this station has been 1·[illegible] inches on 11·6 days. Since January 1, 1896, 20·21 inches of rain have fallen at Cloneevin on 131 days. The rainfall in the first nine months of the year at Cloneevin was 20·12 inches on 150 days in 1894, 21·[illegible] inches on 140 days in 1895. Of the 20·[illegible] inches measured up to September 30 in 1896, 11·97 inches fell on 48 days in the two months July and September. The exceptional character of the rainfall in September, 1896, may be gathered from the fact that the greatest fall previously recorded in September at Cloneevin was 7·47 inches, on 17 days, in 1883.

At Brennanstown House, Cabinteely, Co. Dublin, the September rainfall was 5·15 inches; at Claremont, Carrickmines, it was 5·79 inches.

October.—As in 1892 and 1895, so in 1896, October proved a very cold month. It was also inclement in the matter of wind and rainfall. Had it not been for a few warm days at the beginning, the mean temperature would have been the lowest on record within recent years. As it was, it only exceeded the record-breaking value of 44·8° in 1892 by 0·7°, and was 4·7° below the average. The rainfall was excessive along the east coast of Dublin—6·025 inches at Greystones, 5·250 inches at Killiney. In Dublin not half this precipitation occurred. This result was brought about by a low temperature inland chilling the vapour-laden northerly winds along the coast. In Dublin the screened thermometer did not once reach 60° after the 17th. Sharp thunder and hailstorms occurred on the 20th near and in this city.

In Dublin the arithmetical mean temperature (45·5°) was much below the average (49·7°); the mean dry bulb readings at 9 a.m. and 9 p.m. were 44·8°. In the thirty-one years ending with 1896, October was coldest in 1892 (M. T. = 44·8°), in 1869 (M. T. = 44·9°), and in 1881 (M. T. = 45·5°). It was warmest in 1876 (M. T. = 53·1°). In 1886 the M. T. was only 46·2°. October, 1892, had the record for coldness, but was nearly approached by the month now under review.

The mean height of the barometer was 29·760 inches, or 0·050 inch below the corrected average value for October, namely, 29·840 inches. The mercury rose to 30·490 inches at 11.45 p.m. of the 15th, and fell to 28·790 inches at 7.15 a.m. of the 8th. The observed range of atmospheric pressure was, therefore, as much as 1·700 inches.

The mean temperature deduced from daily readings of the dry bulb thermometer at 9 a.m. and 9 p.m. was 44·8°, or 10·2° below the value for September. The arithmetical mean of the maximal and minimal readings was 45·5°, compared with a twenty-five years' average of 49·7°. Using the formula, Mean Temp. = Min. + (max. – min. × ·465), the value was 44·9°, or 4·7° below the average mean temperature for October, calculated in the same way, in the twenty-five years, 1865–89, inclusive (49·6°). On the 2nd the thermometer in the screen rose to 63·7°—wind, S.W.; on the 23rd, the temperature fell to 30·1°—wind, W.N.W. The minimum on the grass was 26·5°, also on the 23rd. On two nights the thermometer sank to or below 32° in the screen, and on thirteen nights frost occurred on the grass.

The rainfall was 2·113 inches, distributed over 22 days—the rainfall was below, while the rainy days were decidedly above, the average. The average rainfall for October in the twenty-five years, 1865–89, inclusive, was 3·106 inches, and the average number of rainy days was 17·6. In 1880 the rainfall in October was very large—7·330 inches on 13 days. In 1870, also, 7·034 inches fell on 20 days. On the other hand, in 1890, only ·480 inch fell on but 11 days; in 1884 only ·774 inch on but 14 days; and in 1888 only ·816 inch on 15 days. October, 1890, proved the driest on record for more than a quarter of a century at least.

There were thunderstorms on the evening of the 20th, and lightning was seen also on the night of the 23rd. High winds were noted on eleven days, but attained the force of a gale on only one occasion—the 8th. The atmosphere was more or less foggy in Dublin on the 7th, 13th, 26th, and 29th. Hail fell on the 8th, 24th, and 29th; sleet on the 11th, 24th, and 25th. A lunar halo appeared on the 18th. Solar halos were seen on the 7th, 19th, and 23rd. There was an aurora borealis on the evening of the 11th.

The period ended Saturday the 3rd, was favourable on the whole. On the morning of Thursday, the 1st, a broad band of high atmospheric pressure stretched from the Gulf of Finland south-westwards to the extreme S.W. of England and S. of Ireland. Depressions, however, had appeared both off the N.W. of Norway and over Italy and the Mediterranean. In the former country strong S.W. and W. gales set in, while rain fell heavily on the Riviera on both Thursday and Friday. In England quiet, cloudy weather was prevalent, and in Ireland the air became soft and genial although the tendency to showers continued, except on the east coast. Westerly (between S.W. and N.W.) winds prevailed.

Very unsettled weather prevailed over Western Europe during the week ended Saturday, the 10th. Atmospheric pressure was in a most unstable condition, and on Wednesday and Thursday an unusually deep depression passed across Ireland in a northerly direction, causing disastrous storms and heavy downpours of rain. The intensity of this cyclonic system was intensified by the presence of an area of high atmospheric pressure over Central Europe at the time. Early on Sunday morning a series of V-shaped depressions moved eastwards from Ireland to Wales and England. In their rear a brisk fall of temperature occurred, which lasted until Wednesday. On this day a very large and deep depression came in upon the Irish coasts from S.S.W. The wind first backed towards E. with squalls and heavy rain. Temperature then rose with a bound, so that at 9 p.m. the maximum of the day ([illegible]°) was recorded. Rain now fell in torrents—1·810 inches being measured at Greystones, Co. Wicklow, 1·14 inches at Killiney, Co. Dublin, 1·78 inches at Holyhead, 1·23 inches at Roche's Point, Co. Cork, and ·761 inch in Dublin. During the night the wind rose to a tempest from S.S.W., causing great damage along the S. and E. coasts of Ireland, in the S.W. of England, and in Wales. The gale continued to blow with lessened violence on Thursday, after which the weather improved, although remaining changeable to the end of the week. In Dublin the mean height of the barometer was [illegible] inches, pressure ranging between [illegible] inches at 7.1[illegible] a.m. of Thursday (wind, S.W.) and [illegible] inches at 9 p.m. of Saturday (wind, N.). The corrected mean temperature was [illegible]°. The mean dry bulb temperature at 9 a.m. and 9 p.m. was [illegible]°. On Sunday the screened thermometer rose to [illegible]°; on Monday they fell to [illegible]°. The rainfall was [illegible] inch on six days, ·761 inch being registered on Wednesday. Hail fell on Monday. Solar halos were observed on Wednesday and Saturday. There was a slight fog on Wednesday evening.

Although cold for the time of year, the weather of the week ended Saturday, the 17th, was chiefly fine in Ireland, but much less favourable in Great Britain and on the Continent. On Sunday a large but not deep depression lay over the North Sea, while an anticyclone was forming over Ireland. The result was a prevalence of cold northerly winds and showers of cold rain, hail or even snow in many places. In Dublin there was a slight snow-shower at 2.15 p.m., and hail fell heavily along the coast south of the city—in the evening an aurora borealis was seen. The anticyclone in the west continued to develop until Tuesday evening, when the barometer read [illegible] inches in Dublin. At this time a still larger system of high pressure was forming over Northern Europe, so that the barometer rose to [illegible] inches at Stockholm on Wednesday evening and to [illegible] inches at St. Petersburg on Thursday morning. Meanwhile, in rapid succession, two depressions formed over the Netherlands, causing very bad weather in the S.E. of England as well as in France and Germany. On Saturday, in addition, an area of low pressure approached Scotland from the north-westward. Under its influence, cold showery weather spread to Ireland, where a succession of dry days had been experienced earlier in the week. In Dublin the mean atmospheric pressure was 30·211 inches, the barometer ranging from [illegible] inches at 11.[illegible] p.m. of Tuesday (wind, N.N.E.) to 29·727 inches at 9 p.m. of Saturday (wind, N.N.W.). The corrected mean temperature was [illegible]°; the mean dry bulb reading at 9 a.m. and 9 p.m. was [illegible]°. The screened thermometer fell to [illegible]° on Sunday and rose to [illegible]° on Wednesday. The prevailing winds were N.W., N., and N.E. The rainfall was [illegible] inch on two days, ·019 inch falling on Saturday. Up to the morning of that day [illegible] inches of rain had fallen in the south of London (Brixton) on five days.

The most noteworthy feature in the weather of the week ended Saturday, the 24th, was the extreme coldness, considering the time of year. Atmospheric pressure was very unstable, and falls of cold rain or sleet and snow occurred in most districts from time to time. The rainfalls on the Continent were especially heavy and frequent, so that serious floods were produced in Italy, France, Germany, and Switzerland. During Sunday an irregular area of low pressure travelled southwards across Great Britain. It caused squally N.W. to N. winds in Scotland and Ireland, and cold rain or showers in all districts. Hail fell at several stations, and thunder and lightning were reported along the English coasts. By 8 a.m. of Monday the depression-centre had reached the Bristol Channel, whence it travelled towards E.N.E. across England, passing out to sea near Yarmouth on Tuesday morning. A secondary disturbance in the S. came in on Tuesday afternoon, when rain again fell copiously in Dublin. On Thursday morning a trough of low pressure stretched south-westward from England to the Bay of Biscay. It contained three minima, and caused thunder and hail showers over the Irish Sea and the English Channel. Sharp night frosts now set in at the Scotch, Irish, and inland English stations—the sheltered thermometer falling on Thursday night to [illegible]° at Nairn and Parsonstown; [illegible]° at Wick, Loughborough, and Ardrossan; [illegible]° at Leith, Shields, and in Dublin. On Friday a new disturbance approached Ireland from the Atlantic, temperature rose for a while and the wind backed to W. and freshened, with rain and passing showers. Sleet and hail fell on Saturday. In Dublin the mean height of the barometer was [illegible] inches, pressure varying from [illegible] inches at 9 a.m. of Friday (wind, W.N.W.) to [illegible] inches at [illegible] p.m. of Saturday (wind, W. by N.). The corrected mean temperature was [illegible]°. The mean dry bulb reading at 9 a.m. and 9 p.m. was [illegible]°. On Monday the screened thermometer rose to [illegible]°; on Friday they fell to [illegible]°. The rainfall was ·67[illegible] inch on five days, [illegible] inch being measured on Tuesday. Northerly winds prevailed.

A continuance of cold, unsettled, showery weather has to be recorded during the week ended Saturday, the 31st. The rainfall in the Dublin district, although frequent, was not heavy except on Thursday, when a succession of thunder and hail-storms passed over the metropolis and its neighbourhood. On the Continent downpours of rain again occurred, as much as [illegible] inches of rain being registered at [illegible] on Thursday morning. During the first three days irregular areas of low atmospheric pressure lay over Great Britain and the North Sea. Thunderstorms and hailstorms were very prevalent at coast stations, especially in the English Channel, while sharp night frosts were felt at inland stations both in Great Britain and in Ireland. On Sunday a minimum of [illegible]° was recorded in the screen at Nairn, in Scotland. On Wednesday the barometer gave way generally, and a deep depression travelled rapidly in a north-easterly direction from the N.W. of Spain towards Central Europe. At 8 a.m. of Thursday the centre of this disturbance had reached Wiesbaden. At the same time another depression formed off the mouth of the English Channel, causing a succession of thunder and hailstorms in the vicinity of Dublin on Thursday evening. Friday proved fine, but cold, rainy, dull weather prevailed on Saturday, when a depression was found over England. In Dublin the mean height of the barometer was [illegible] inches, pressure ranging from [illegible] inches at

9 a.m. of Sunday (wind, W.) and 29·911 inches at 9 a.m. of Friday (wind, N.E.). The corrected mean temperature was as low as 39·8°. The mean dry bulb reading at 9 a.m. and 9 p.m. was 39·9°. On Tuesday the screened thermometers rose to 47·0°; on Wednesday they fell to 30·0°. The rainfall was ·502 inch on seven days, ·417 inch being measured on Thursday. The prevalent winds were N.W. and N. Hail and sleet fell on Thursday, when also thunder and lightning occurred. The air was foggy on Wednesday and Thursday.

The rainfall in Dublin during the ten months ending October 31st amounted to 23·912 inches on 186 days, compared with 12·099 inches on 135 days during the same period in 1887 (the dry year), 20·268 inches on 179 days in 1894, 20·716 inches on 140 days in 1895, and a twenty-five years' average of 22·840 inches on 160·4 days.

At Knockdolian, Greystones, Co. Wicklow, the rainfall in October amounted to 4·923 inches on 20 days. Of this quantity 1·350 inches fell on the 7th, and 1·530 inches on the 29th. The rainfall at Greystones in October, 1882, was no less than 7·135 inches on 22 days, or more than 11 times as great as the fall in October, 1888, when only ·630 inch fell on 10 days. In 1886 7·509 inches fell on 18 days. From January 1st, 1896, up to October 31st, rain fell at Knockdolian on 137 days to the total amount of 27·637 inches. In 1895, the rainfall of the corresponding ten months was 22·228 inches on 140 days; in 1893, 17·601 inches on 118 days; in 1894, 25·221 inches on 144 days; in 1892, 25·870 inches on 131 days.

At Cloneevin, Killiney, Co. Dublin, the rainfall in October was 5·380 inches on 21 days, compared with ·714 inch on 14 days in 1888, 5·400 inches on 17 days in 1891, 2·630 inches on 14 days in 1895, and a ten years' average (1885–1894) of 3·378 inches on 16 days. On the 29th, 1·28 inches fell; on the 7th and also on the 29th, 1·18 inches fell. Since January 1, 1896, 25·53 inches of rain have fallen at this station on 130 days.

November.—A fine, quiet, rather cold month. The scanty rainfall in Dublin—only ·604 inch on 6 days—established a record for November. The barometer ruled high, and a large anticyclone embraced the British Islands, the North Sea and Central Europe, between the 21st and 30th. At first W. or S.W. winds, clouds, and warmth accompanied this system, but it moved northwards and the easterly winds of its southern face brought with them an unusually dry, cold, parching atmosphere, together with a clear sky.

In Dublin the arithmetical mean temperature (40·8°) was decidedly below the average (44·7°); the mean dry bulb readings at 9 a.m. and 9 p.m. were 42·6°. In the thirty-one years ending with 1895, November was coldest in 1878 (M. T. = 39·2°), and in 1879 (M. T. = 41·3°), warmest in 1881 (M. T. = 50·5°).

The mean height of the barometer was 30·153 inches, or 0·293 inch above the corrected average value for November—namely, 29·860 inches. The mercury rose to 30·518 inches at 9 p.m. of the 24th, having fallen to 29·137 inches at 3.30 p.m. of the 15th. The observed range of atmospheric pressure was, therefore, 1·436 inches—that is, slightly less than an inch and a half.

The mean temperature deduced from daily readings of the dry bulb thermometer at 9 a.m. and 9 p.m. was 42·3°, or 1·9° below the value for October, and 11·1° below that for September, 1896. The arithmetical mean of the maximal and minimal readings was 43·2°, compared with a twenty-five years' average of 44·7°. On the 22nd the thermometer in the screen rose to 56·4°—wind, S.W.; on the 6th the temperature fell to 25·3°—wind, W. The minimum on the grass was 22·1°, also on the 6th.

The rainfall was only ·604 inch, distributed over 6 days—the rainfall and the rainy days were considerably below the average, a record being established. The average rainfall for November in the twenty-five years, 1865–89, inclusive, was 2·443 inches, and the average number of rainy days was 17·0. In 1888, 6·430 inches fell on 26 days. On the other hand, the rainfall in 1883 was only ·990 inch on 8 days. In 1895, 3·593 inches fell on 21 days.

High winds were noted on 7 days, and attained the force of a gale on two occasions—the 13th and 20th. The atmosphere was more or less foggy in Dublin on the 4th, 5th, 6th, 9th, 10th, 17th, 22nd, and 24th.

Lunar halos were seen on the 15th and 19th; solar halos on the 4th and 5th.

During the week ended the 7th, cold but fine weather prevailed until Saturday, which was a dull, damp, rainy day. At the beginning of this period an anticyclone extended over Scotland and Ireland from the Atlantic, while various areas of relatively low pressure were found over Scandinavia and Central Europe, having a general trend towards S.E. Northerly winds with fine, but at times cloudy, weather held in Ireland, while rain fell in the E. and S.E. of England. On Tuesday a rather deep depression (29·4 inches and less) travelled eastwards across Central Europe from the Baltic. In its rear the weather became very cold, owing to a snow-covering in Scandinavia. A ridge of high pressure now developed over Ireland, England, and Germany, so that on Thursday morning the barometer read 30·63 inches at Berlin, 30·41 inches at York, and 30·38 inches at Loughborough, Liverpool, and Dublin. Calms, fogs, and very sharp night-frosts accompanied the high pressure. On Thursday night the screened thermometer sank to 23° at York, Loughborough and Parsonstown, 25° at Cambridge and 29° in Dublin. On Friday morning a vast depression was moving eastward across the North of Norway and extending southwards in the usual form. At 8 a.m. the barometer varied from 28·82 inches at Bodö in Norway to 30·53 at Berlin. Strong W. and S.W. winds accordingly set in, with clouds, rain, and a quickly rising temperature. Saturday was a very dull, damp day in Dublin, the change from the almost cloudless skies of the first period being very marked. The mean height of the barometer was 30·104 inches, the range being from 30·591 inches at 9 a.m. of Thursday (wind, W.) to 29·775 inches at 9 p.m. of Saturday (wind, W.N.W.). The mean temperature was 39·1°. The mean dry bulb temperature at 9 a.m. and 9 p.m. was 37·8°. On Friday the screened thermometers sank to 29·2°, on Saturday they rose to [illegible]. The prevailing winds were W.N.W. and W. Rain fell on two days to the amount of [illegible] inch, [illegible] inch being registered on Saturday. A solar halo was seen on Wednesday.

The earlier part of the week ended Saturday the 14th was fine but cold, with moderate northerly to westerly winds. A complete reversal of the conditions of distribution of atmospheric pressure over Western Europe took place in the period advanced. At first the barometer stood high in Ireland, where the conditions were favourable for northerly winds. Between Monday and Thursday an anticyclone moved slowly south-eastward from this country to Central France, the fall of the barometer in the W. and N.W. substituting southerly for northerly winds in the British Islands. On Friday morning a large V-shaped depression extended from the Hebrides to the Land's End, and on Saturday a still more important [illegible] system of low pressure passed across Ireland in a north-easterly direction, causing squally S. to W. winds and heavy rains or passing showers. Scandinavia, and the extreme North of Europe generally, experienced very intense cold for the time of the year. This was due to the fact that a good deal of snow lay on the ground in those regions. At Haparanda, on the Gulf of Bothnia, the minimum temperatures were daily below zero, namely: [illegible] respectively. At Karlstad in the south of Sweden the thermometer stood at [illegible] at 8 a.m. of Friday. In Dublin the mean height of the barometer was [illegible] inches, pressure ranging from [illegible] inches at 9 a.m. of Monday (wind, W.N.W.) to [illegible] inches at [illegible] p.m. of Saturday (wind, S.W.). The mean temperature was [illegible], or [illegible] above that of the previous week. The mean dry bulb reading at 9 a.m. and 9 p.m. was [illegible]. On Monday the screened thermometers fell to [illegible], on Friday they rose to [illegible]. The rainfall was [illegible] inch on two days, [illegible] inch being measured on Saturday. The prevailing winds were first N.W., then S. to W.

Although changeable, the weather of the week ended Saturday, the 21st, was generally favourable, and no extremes were recorded. On Sunday cyclonic conditions prevailed. A depression in which the barometer read [illegible] inches or less lay off the Norfolk coast at 8 a.m., while another and deeper low pressure system ([illegible] inches and less) was found over the N.W. of Scotland, travelling north-eastwards. N.W. to W. winds of considerable strength blew in Ireland, where also rain fell in the forenoon. By 8 a.m. of Monday the Scottish centre of low pressure had reached Norway, and the barometer had risen in all parts of the British Isles, with improving weather. On Tuesday morning a tongue of relatively high atmospheric pressure stretched south-westward from the S. of Sweden to the S.E. of Ireland. Frost prevailed in Dublin, as well as fog. A complex depression quickly came in from the Atlantic as the day advanced, and rain fell at night, the thermometer rising to [illegible] in Dublin, with S.W. to W. winds. The remainder of the week was chiefly fine, but rain unsettled. During Friday and Saturday an anticyclone spread over the British Islands from S.W., and temperature became high for the time of year with a good deal of cloud and but little rain. In Dublin the mean height of the barometer was [illegible] inches, pressure ranging between [illegible] inches at 9 a.m. of Sunday (wind, W. by N.), and [illegible] inches at 9 p.m. of Saturday (wind, W.S.W.). The mean temperature was [illegible]. The mean dry bulb temperature at 9 a.m. and 9 p.m. was [illegible]. On Tuesday the screened thermometers sank to [illegible], on Wednesday they rose to [illegible]. Rain fell on three days to the amount of [illegible] inch, [illegible] inch being registered on Tuesday. There was a moderate gale on Sunday. Fog prevailed on Monday and Tuesday. A lunar corona was seen on Wednesday and a lunar halo on Thursday.

Anticyclonic weather was experienced throughout the greater part of the week ended Saturday, the 28th. A broad band of high atmospheric pressure stretched across Central Europe early in the period, and afterwards slowly drifted northwards in front of a succession of depressions which formed in the Mediterranean Basin and over the Peninsula. The distribution of pressure just described caused S.W. and W. winds and remarkably high temperatures in Ireland, Scotland, and Scandinavia, E. and N.E. winds and much lower temperatures in Austria, Germany, France, and the S.E. and E. of England. On Sunday the thermometer in the screen rose to [illegible] in Dublin, [illegible] at Leith and [illegible], and [illegible] at Fraserburgh, Aberdeen, and Nairn—even as far north as Christiansund in Norway (lat. [illegible]) the maximum on that day was [illegible]. Slight rain fell at various points in the British Isles between Monday and Thursday, but the weather was generally dry although overcast, dull and misty or foggy. The ridge of high barometer gradually moved northward, so that easterly winds took the place of the westerly winds of the beginning, and the calms of the middle, of the week. With the easterly winds came a considerable reduction of temperature in the Continent and the southern half of the United Kingdom. On Friday the anticyclone showed a remarkable lessening of its intensity. Its centre was then found over Scotland, where the barometer began to rise while it continued to fall over France and the Bay of Biscay. Steep gradients for easterly winds were in this way formed, so that the wind freshened to a gale from E. on Saturday with cold showers at exposed east coast stations. In Dublin the mean height of the barometer was [illegible] inches, pressure ranging from [illegible] inches at 9 p.m. of Tuesday (wind, S.S.E.) to [illegible] inches at 9 a.m. of Saturday (wind, E.N.E.). The mean temperature was [illegible]. The mean dry bulb temperature at 9 a.m. and 9 p.m. was [illegible]. On Sunday the screened thermometers rose to [illegible], on Thursday they fell to [illegible]. Rain fell on two days to the amount of [illegible] inch, [illegible] inch being measured on Tuesday. The prevailing winds were W.S.W. and E.N.E.

The last two days were bright, cold, and very dry. Severe frost occurred in England on Monday, the 30th, when the thermometer read [illegible] in the screen at Loughborough at 8 a.m.

The rainfall in Dublin during the eleven months ending November 30th amounted to [illegible] inches on [illegible] days, compared with [illegible] inches on [illegible] days during the same period in [illegible], [illegible] inches on [illegible] days in [illegible], [illegible] inches on [illegible] days in [illegible], and a twenty-five years' average of [illegible] inches on [illegible] days.

At Knockdolian, Greystones, Co. Wicklow, the rainfall in November was [illegible] inch distributed over [illegible] days. Of this quantity [illegible] inch fell on the 14th, and [illegible] inch fell on the 13th. From January 1st, 1896, up to November 30th, rain fell at that station on 147 days, and to the total amount of 23·042 inches. The corresponding figures for 1893 were 19·448 inches on 150 days, for 1894, 25·716 inches on 188 days, and for 1895, 21·715 inches on 151 days.

At Cloneevin, Killiney, Co. Dublin, ·56 inch of rain fell on 8 days, compared with a ten years' average of 2·737 inches on 17·8 days. The maximal fall in 24 hours was ·23 inch on the 14th. Since January 1st, 1896, 26·81 inches of rain have fallen at this station on 159 days.

DECEMBER.—A generally unsettled, open, rainy month. The only severe frost experienced in the British Islands occurred between the 19th and 20th. It was most severe in Central Ireland, where the thermometer in the screen sank, on the morning of Sunday, the 20th, to 18° at Markree Castle, Co. Sligo, 16° at Parsonstown, King's Co., and 14° at Edenfel, Omagh, Co. Tyrone. The distribution of atmospheric pressure was almost exclusively cyclonic, and the variations in the height of the barometer were abrupt and rapid. The chief depressions observed appeared at the mouth of the English Channel, up which they usually travelled in an irregular fashion, causing downpours of rain and violent gales in the South of England and North of France. In the closing period of the month, vast depressions skirted our extreme N.W. and N. coasts on their way to Northern Europe, and, as in 1882, a remarkable wave of warmth passed over Western Europe.

In Dublin the arithmetical mean temperature (41·4°) was a shade above the average (41·3°); the mean dry bulb readings at 9 a.m. and 9 p.m. were 40·8°. In the thirty-one years ending with 1896, December was coldest in 1878 (M. T. = 32·8°), and in 1874 (M. T. = 36·6°), and warmest in 1865 (M. T. = 45·3°). In 1895, the M. T. was 41·6°.

The mean height of the barometer was 29·702 inches, or 0·173 inch below the corrected average value for December—namely, 29·875 inches. The mercury rose to 30·301 inches at 9 a.m. of the 27th, and fell to 28·784 inches at 9 a.m. of the 5th. The observed range of atmospheric pressure was, therefore, 1·517 inches—that is, a little more than one inch and a half.

The mean temperature deduced from daily readings of the dry bulb thermometer at 9 a.m. and 9 p.m. was 40·8°, or 1·5° below the value for November, and 8·0° below that for October, 1896. Using the formula, *Mean Temp.* = *Min.* + (*max.*—*min.* × ·52), the value was 41·6°, or 0·1° above the average mean temperature for December, calculated in the same way, in the twenty-five years, 1865–89, inclusive (41·5°). The arithmetical mean of the maximal and minimal readings was 41·4°, compared with a twenty-five years' average of 41·3°. On the 26th the thermometer in the screen rose to 57·2°—wind, S.W.; on the 19th and again on the 20th the temperature fell to 27·0°—wind, W.N.W. The minimum on the grass was 20·1°, on the 19th. There were only 5 days of frost in the screen, but 22 days of frost on the grass.

The rainfall was 4·185 inches, distributed over as many as 30 days. The average rainfall for December in the twenty-five years, 1865–89, was 2·404 inches, and the average number of rainy days was 18·0. Both rainfall, therefore, and rainy days were considerably above the average. In 1876 the rainfall in December was very large—7·566 inches on 22 days. In 1872, 4·[illegible] inches fell on as many as 24 days, and in 1868 (which was otherwise a fine and dry year) 4·740 inches fell on as many as 17 days. On the other hand, in 1867, only ·771 inch was measured on 13 days; in 1885, only ·795 inch on 10 days; and in 1871, only ·777 inch on 14 days. In 1888, only ·748 inch of rain was measured on but 10 days; but in 1895 the rainfall was 3·844 inches on 27 days.

Solar halos appeared on the 4th, 13th, and 14th; a lunar halo on the 23rd. High winds were noted on 13 days, but attained the force of a gale on only 2 occasions—the 26th and 31st. The atmosphere was more or less foggy in Dublin on the 4th, 9th, 11th, 15th, 20th, 22nd, and 23rd. No snow or sleet fell in Dublin. Hail fell on the 9th and 13th. Aurora borealis was seen on the 3rd.

A succession of very large and deep depressions began to approach the S.W. of both Ireland and England from the Atlantic on Tuesday, the 1st. The sky became densely clouded, temperature rose, and squally S.E. and S. winds set in accompanied by heavy falls of rain in all districts. At 8 a.m. of Friday the centre of a depression lay near the Scilly Isles, where the barometer was down to 28·60 inches. In the evening of this day the reading at Jersey was 28·52 inches. On Saturday pressure remained very low, but as gradients became less steep, the gales died down. Bright aurora borealis was seen on Thursday evening in Scotland and Ireland. In Dublin the barometer fell to 28·823 inches at 9 p.m. of Saturday (wind calm). The shaded thermometer rose to 51·4° on Thursday, and fell to 35·1 on Friday. The prevailing wind was S.E. Rainfall amounted to 1·153 inches on four days, ·780 inch being registered on Friday.

The weather was very unsettled during the greater part of the week ended Saturday, the 12th, and rain fell in large quantities—the downpour in the night of Tuesday, the 8th, being particularly heavy on the east coast of Ireland near Dublin. On Sunday morning the centre of a large and deep depression lay at the entrance to the English Channel, the barometer reading only 28·45 inches in the Scilly Isles and 28·40 inches at Brest. At Kilkenny Castle the reading was 28·83 inches. Light northerly winds blew over Ireland, where temperature was rather low. Monday was fine and bright, but cold in Dublin. In the afternoon a beautiful conjunction of the moon and the planet Venus was well seen in a cloudless sky. On Tuesday there was a complete change in the weather owing to the arrival off the West Coast of Ireland of a new area of low pressure. This was quickly followed by another depression, which moved up St. George's Channel at night, producing the downpour of rain on the East Coast of Ireland, of which mention is made above. In Dublin the measurement on Wednesday morning was 1·388 inches. The depression reached Anglesea at 8 a.m., but then changed its course and travelled eastwards across central England to Holland. Thursday was a gloomy wet day, caused by another and a complex depression, in the wake of which came a bright day on Friday. This improvement was only temporary, for Saturday broke dull and wet with the barometer down half an inch from Friday's reading. In the afternoon the wind shifted to N.W. and the sky cleared, with a falling temperature. In Dublin the mean barometric pressure was [illegible] inches, pressure ranging between 29.[illegible] inches at [illegible] a.m. of Sunday (wind, N.) and 30.[illegible] inches at [illegible] p.m. of Friday (wind, W.S.W.). The corrected mean temperature was [illegible]°. The mean dry bulb reading at 9 a.m. and 9 p.m. was [illegible]°. On Sunday the screened thermometers fell to [illegible]°, on Thursday they rose to [illegible]°. Rain fell on two days to the amount of 1.721 inches, [illegible] inches being registered on Tuesday. The wind was very variable.

A change from the mild weather of the preceding week to cold and dry weather was observed early in the week ended Saturday, the 19th. On Sunday, however, a considerable fall of rain occurred, in connection with a deep depression which arrived off the South of Ireland in the afternoon and subsequently travelled eastward to Central Germany, where its centre was found on Tuesday morning. At 8 a.m. of Monday the barometer was as low as 28.[illegible] inches at Dungeness in Kent. At both Valentia Island and Roche's Point, Cork, more than an inch of rain fell between 8 a.m. of Sunday and the same hour on Monday. While this depression was passing, an anticyclonic area extended south-westward across Scandinavia from Lapland, and this system ultimately caused a polar air current to pass over the British Islands. A number of shallow depressions formed over Great Britain and the North Sea on Wednesday, and with the coming of the N. wind temperature gave way and frost set in at many inland stations. On Thursday night the frost was severe in Central Ireland, Parsonstown registering a minimum of 21°. Even in Dublin the thermometer sank to [illegible]° in the screen and to [illegible]° on the grass. About midday of Friday light hail showers fell in this city. The weather remained dry and frosty to the close of the week, although an increase of cloud interfered with radiation to a great extent. At Parsonstown a minimum of 20° was recorded on Friday night. Mention should be made of an earthquake which occurred in England, Wales, and the east of Ireland at 5.3[illegible] a.m. (West European time) on Thursday; also of a thunderstorm with rain and snow which passed over Liverpool in the early morning of the same day. In Dublin the mean height of the barometer was 29.7[illegible] inches, pressure ranging between [illegible] inches at [illegible] p.m. of Sunday (wind, S.E.) and 30.[illegible] inches at 9 p.m. of Saturday (wind, N.W.). The corrected mean temperature was [illegible]°. The mean dry bulb reading at 9 a.m. and 9 p.m. was [illegible]°. On Sunday the screened thermometers rose to [illegible]°, on Friday they fell to 27.0°. The rainfall was [illegible] inch on two days, [illegible] inch being registered on Sunday. The prevailing wind was N.W.

At first cold, and at times frosty and foggy, the weather of the week ended Saturday, the 26th, finally became singularly open and warm for the time of year—on Saturday the thermometer rose to [illegible]° in the shade, and the corrected mean temperature of the day was [illegible]°, or 12° above the average. At the beginning of the period an anticyclone lay over Sweden and Norway, whence it stretched south-westwards to Scotland and the northern half of both England and Ireland. Frost then held in the central districts of the last-named country—the thermometer falling to 1[illegible]° in the screen at Parsonstown and to 2[illegible]° even in the city of Dublin early on Sunday morning. In the afternoon a south-easterly breeze sprang up, causing a brisk rise of temperature and a thaw. At 9 p.m. of Sunday the thermometer read [illegible]° at Parsonstown, or [illegible]° above its reading [illegible] hours previously. Tuesday was a gloomy, cold, wet day in Dublin owing to a depression over St. George's Channel. An anticyclone [illegible] and [illegible] temperature again fell [illegible], so that Wednesday was frosty throughout in Dublin, with a good deal of [illegible] fog still existing. A [illegible] at night heralded a complete change of weather. Depressions began to move north-east along our extreme western coasts, and their S.W. winds brought cloudy, showery, mild weather. Saturday, the 26th, was the warmest St. Stephen's Day experienced for many years—in the afternoon the S.W. wind freshened to a gale. In Dublin the mean height of the barometer was [illegible] inches, pressure ranging between [illegible] inches at 9 a.m. of Wednesday (wind, W. by N.) and [illegible] inches at [illegible] p.m. of Thursday (wind, S.W.). The corrected mean temperature was [illegible]°, as was also the mean dry bulb reading at 9 a.m. and 9 p.m. On Sunday the screened thermometers fell to [illegible]°, on Saturday they rose to [illegible]°. The prevailing winds were first S.E., afterwards S.W. Rain fell on four days to the amount of [illegible] inch, [illegible] inch being registered on Thursday.

The last five days of the month and of the year 1896 were unseasonably mild, but very changeable, cloudy and showery or rainy. On Wednesday, the 30th, the thermometer rose to [illegible]° in the screen, and there was a S.W. gale in the afternoon.

The rainfall in Dublin during 1896 amounted to [illegible] inches on [illegible] days, compared with [illegible] inches on [illegible] days in 1895, [illegible] inches on [illegible] days in 1894, only [illegible] inches on 174 days in 1893, [illegible] inches on [illegible] days in 1892, [illegible] inches on [illegible] days in 1891, [illegible] inches on [illegible] days in 1890, [illegible] inches on [illegible] days in 1889, [illegible] inches on [illegible] days in 1888, [illegible] inches on [illegible] days in 1887, and a twenty-five years' average of [illegible] inches on [illegible] days.

At Knockdolian, Greystones, Co. Wicklow, the rainfall in December, 1896, was [illegible] inches, distributed over [illegible] days. Of this quantity [illegible] inches fell on the 1st, and [illegible] inches on the [illegible]. From January 1st to December 31st, 1896, rain fell at Knockdolian on [illegible] days, and to the total amount of [illegible] inches. The corresponding figures for 1893 were [illegible] inches on [illegible] days; for 1894, [illegible] inches on [illegible] days; and for 1895, [illegible] inches on [illegible] days.

Mr. Robert O'Brien Furlong, M.A., writes:—

The rainfall at [illegible], Killiney, in December, 1896, was [illegible] inches on [illegible] days. The maximal fall in 24 hours was [illegible] inches on the [illegible]. The average December rainfall of the ten years, 1885–94, was [illegible] inches on [illegible] days. In the year 1896 the total rainfall amounted to [illegible] inches on [illegible] days. The maximal daily fall was [illegible] inches on July [illegible]. The rainfall for 1896, though less than that of [illegible] (= [illegible] inches) or 1894 (= [illegible] inches), was largely in excess of the average of the eleven years, 1885–95, viz., [illegible] inches. Rain measuring .01 inch and upwards fell on [illegible] days, the average of eleven years being 177. During the first six months only [illegible] inches fell on 70 days.

There was a period of absolute drought from April [illegible] to May [illegible], and of partial drought from April [illegible] to June [illegible], during which only [illegible] inch was recorded. On July [illegible] there was a thunderstorm between [illegible] and [illegible] p.m., and during these [illegible] minutes [illegible] inches fell. The fall for July—[illegible] inches—is the highest recorded in any one month since the observations were begun. That of May is the lowest, with the exception of February, [illegible], during which month only [illegible] inch fell. Snow fell on three days only—March [illegible] and [illegible], and December [illegible]—but did not lie for any time. The winter months of the year were exceptionally mild.

RAINFALL IN 18[illegible],

At 40, Fitzwilliam-square, West, Dublin.

Rain Gauge:—Diameter of funnel, 8 in. Height of top—Above ground, 1 ft. 1 in.; above sea level, 50 ft.

Month.	Total Depth.	Greatest Fall in 24 hours.		Number of Days on which ·01 or more fell.	Month.	Total Depth.	Greatest Fall in 24 hours.		Number of Days on which ·01 or more fell.
	Inches.	Depth.	Date.			Inches.	Depth.	Date.	
January,	[illegible]	[illegible]	[illegible]	[illegible]	August,	[illegible]	[illegible]	[illegible]	[illegible]
February,	[illegible]	[illegible]	[illegible]	[illegible]	September,	[illegible]	[illegible]	[illegible]	[illegible]
March,	[illegible]	[illegible]	[illegible]	[illegible]	October,	[illegible]	[illegible]	[illegible]	[illegible]
April,	[illegible]	[illegible]	[illegible]	[illegible]	November,	[illegible]	[illegible]	[illegible]	[illegible]
May,	[illegible]	[illegible]	[illegible]	[illegible]	December,	[illegible]	[illegible]	[illegible]	[illegible]
June,	[illegible]	[illegible]	[illegible]	[illegible]					
July,	[illegible]	[illegible]	[illegible]	[illegible]	Total,	[illegible]	[illegible]	July [illegible]	[illegible]

The rainfall was [illegible] inch in defect of the average annual measurement of the twenty-five years, [illegible], inclusive—viz., 27·[illegible] inches.

If it be remembered that the rainfall in 18[illegible] was very exceptionally small—[illegible] inches, the only approach to this measurement in Dublin being in 18[illegible], when only [illegible] inches fell, in [illegible], when the measurement was [illegible] inches, and in [illegible] with its rainfall of [illegible] inches. In [illegible] of the twenty-five years in question, the rainfall was less than [illegible] inches.

The scanty rainfall in 18[illegible] was in marked contrast to the abundant downpour in [illegible], when [illegible] inches—or as nearly as possible double the fall of 18[illegible]—fell on [illegible] days. Only [illegible] times since records commenced has the rainfall in Dublin exceeded that of [illegible]—namely, in [illegible], when [illegible] inches fell on [illegible] days, and in [illegible], when [illegible] inches were measured on, however, only [illegible] days.

In [illegible], there were [illegible] rainy days, or days upon which not less than ·01 inch of rain (one hundredth of an inch) was measured. This was almost exactly equal to the average number of rainy days, which was [illegible] in the twenty-five years, [illegible], inclusive. In [illegible] and [illegible]—the [illegible] dry years of recent times—the rainy days were only [illegible], and in [illegible] they were only [illegible].

The rainfall in 24 hours from 9 a.m. to 9 a.m. exceeded one inch on two occasions in [illegible]—viz., May [illegible] ([illegible] inches) and August [illegible] ([illegible] inches). On no occasion in [illegible] did one inch of rain fall on a given day in Dublin. In [illegible] falls of upwards of an inch of rain in 24 hours were recorded on four occasions, viz., May [illegible] ([illegible] inches); July [illegible] ([illegible] inches); August [illegible] ([illegible] inches); and October [illegible] ([illegible] inches). In [illegible], [illegible] inches fell on January [illegible]; [illegible] inches on July [illegible]; and [illegible] inches on July [illegible]. In [illegible], [illegible] inches fell on July [illegible]; [illegible] inches on July [illegible]; and [illegible] inches on December [illegible].

Included in the [illegible] rainy days in [illegible] are [illegible] on which snow or sleet fell, and [illegible] on which there was hail. In [illegible] hail was observed on [illegible] days, in April on [illegible] days, in June, August, and September on 1 day, in October on [illegible] days, and on [illegible] days in December. Snow or sleet fell on [illegible] day in January, on [illegible] days in March, and also on [illegible] days in October. Thunder occurred on [illegible] occasions during the year—once in April, twice in June, once in July, August, and October. Lightning was also seen on [illegible] occasions in September, and once in July and October.

The rainfall in the first six months was [illegible] inches, on [illegible] days. The rainfall exceeded [illegible] inches in March ([illegible]), July ([illegible]), September ([illegible]), and December ([illegible]). In May it was only [illegible] inch on [illegible] days.

The rainfall was distributed as follows:—[illegible] inches fell on [illegible] days in the first quarter, [illegible] inches on [illegible] days in the second, [illegible] inches on [illegible] days in the third, [illegible] inches on [illegible] days in the fourth and last quarter.

Aurora borealis was observed on five occasions—namely, on February [illegible], March [illegible], May [illegible], October [illegible], and December [illegible]. More or less fog prevailed on [illegible] occasions—[illegible] in January, [illegible] in February, [illegible] in March, [illegible] in April, May, July, and September, [illegible] in October, [illegible] in November, and [illegible] in December. High winds were noted on [illegible] days—[illegible] in January, [illegible] in February, [illegible] in March, [illegible] in April, [illegible] in May, [illegible] in June, [illegible] in July, [illegible] in August, [illegible] in September, [illegible] in October, [illegible] in November, and [illegible] in December. The high winds amounted to gales (force 7 or upwards according to the Beaufort scale) on [illegible] occasions—[illegible] in January, [illegible] in March, [illegible] in April, [illegible] in May, June, and July, [illegible] in August, [illegible] in September, [illegible] in October, [illegible] in November and December.

For Abstracts of Meteorological Observations, 18[illegible]–[illegible], see pages [illegible].

ANNUAL ABSTRACTS

OF

MARRIAGES, BIRTHS, AND DEATHS,

1890.

ABSTRACT OF MARRIAGES.—Marriages registered in Ireland, pursuant to the

No.	PROVINCES AND COUNTIES.	Area in Statute Acres, exclusive of the larger Rivers, Lakes, and Tideways.	Population, 1871.	TOTAL MARRIAGES.	MARRIAGES: Registered under the Act: According to the Rites of the Church of Ireland: Special Licence.	Licence.	Banns.	Registrar's Certificate.	[illegible]	Total.	[illegible] Presbyterian [illegible]	In Registered Buildings.	In the Registrar's Office.	Society of Friends.	Jews.	TOTAL Registered under the Act.	[illegible]
	IRELAND,	[illegible]	[illegible]	[illegible]	[illegible]	[illegible]	[illegible]	[illegible]	[illegible]	[illegible]	[illegible]	[illegible]	[illegible]	[illegible]	[illegible]	[illegible]	[illegible]
	PROVINCES.																
I.	LEINSTER,	[illegible]	[illegible]	[illegible]	[illegible]	[illegible]	[illegible]	[illegible]	[illegible]	[illegible]	[illegible]	[illegible]	[illegible]	[illegible]	[illegible]	[illegible]	[illegible]
II.	MUNSTER,	[illegible]	[illegible]	[illegible]	[illegible]	[illegible]	[illegible]	[illegible]	[illegible]	[illegible]	[illegible]	[illegible]	[illegible]	[illegible]	[illegible]	[illegible]	[illegible]
III.	ULSTER,	[illegible]	[illegible]	[illegible]	[illegible]	[illegible]	[illegible]	[illegible]	[illegible]	[illegible]	[illegible]	[illegible]	[illegible]	[illegible]	[illegible]	[illegible]	[illegible]
IV.	CONNAUGHT,	[illegible]	[illegible]	[illegible]	[illegible]	[illegible]	[illegible]	[illegible]	[illegible]	[illegible]	[illegible]	[illegible]	[illegible]	[illegible]	[illegible]	[illegible]	[illegible]
	I.—PROVINCE OF LEINSTER.—																
1	Carlow,	[illegible]	[illegible]	[illegible]	[illegible]	[illegible]	[illegible]	[illegible]	[illegible]	[illegible]	[illegible]	[illegible]	[illegible]	[illegible]	[illegible]	[illegible]	[illegible]
2	Dublin,	[illegible]	[illegible]	[illegible]	[illegible]	[illegible]	[illegible]	[illegible]	[illegible]	[illegible]	[illegible]	[illegible]	[illegible]	[illegible]	[illegible]	[illegible]	[illegible]
3	Kildare,	[illegible]	[illegible]	[illegible]	[illegible]	[illegible]	[illegible]	[illegible]	[illegible]	[illegible]	[illegible]	[illegible]	[illegible]	[illegible]	[illegible]	[illegible]	[illegible]
4	Kilkenny,	[illegible]	[illegible]	[illegible]	[illegible]	[illegible]	[illegible]	[illegible]	[illegible]	[illegible]	[illegible]	[illegible]	[illegible]	[illegible]	[illegible]	[illegible]	[illegible]
5	King's,	[illegible]	[illegible]	[illegible]	[illegible]	[illegible]	[illegible]	[illegible]	[illegible]	[illegible]	[illegible]	[illegible]	[illegible]	[illegible]	[illegible]	[illegible]	[illegible]
6	Longford,	[illegible]	[illegible]	[illegible]	[illegible]	[illegible]	[illegible]	[illegible]	[illegible]	[illegible]	[illegible]	[illegible]	[illegible]	[illegible]	[illegible]	[illegible]	[illegible]
7	Louth, and Co. of the Town of Drogheda,	[illegible]	[illegible]	[illegible]	[illegible]	[illegible]	[illegible]	[illegible]	[illegible]	[illegible]	[illegible]	[illegible]	[illegible]	[illegible]	[illegible]	[illegible]	[illegible]
8	Meath,	[illegible]	[illegible]	[illegible]	[illegible]	[illegible]	[illegible]	[illegible]	[illegible]	[illegible]	[illegible]	[illegible]	[illegible]	[illegible]	[illegible]	[illegible]	[illegible]
9	Queen's,	[illegible]	[illegible]	[illegible]	[illegible]	[illegible]	[illegible]	[illegible]	[illegible]	[illegible]	[illegible]	[illegible]	[illegible]	[illegible]	[illegible]	[illegible]	[illegible]
10	Westmeath,	[illegible]	[illegible]	[illegible]	[illegible]	[illegible]	[illegible]	[illegible]	[illegible]	[illegible]	[illegible]	[illegible]	[illegible]	[illegible]	[illegible]	[illegible]	[illegible]
11	Wexford,	[illegible]	[illegible]	[illegible]	[illegible]	[illegible]	[illegible]	[illegible]	[illegible]	[illegible]	[illegible]	[illegible]	[illegible]	[illegible]	[illegible]	[illegible]	[illegible]
12	Wicklow,	[illegible]	[illegible]	[illegible]	[illegible]	[illegible]	[illegible]	[illegible]	[illegible]	[illegible]	[illegible]	[illegible]	[illegible]	[illegible]	[illegible]	[illegible]	[illegible]
	II.—PROVINCE OF MUNSTER.—																
13	Clare,	[illegible]	[illegible]	[illegible]	[illegible]	[illegible]	[illegible]	[illegible]	[illegible]	[illegible]	[illegible]	[illegible]	[illegible]	[illegible]	[illegible]	[illegible]	[illegible]
14	Cork,	[illegible]	[illegible]	[illegible]	[illegible]	[illegible]	[illegible]	[illegible]	[illegible]	[illegible]	[illegible]	[illegible]	[illegible]	[illegible]	[illegible]	[illegible]	[illegible]
15	Kerry,	[illegible]	[illegible]	[illegible]	[illegible]	[illegible]	[illegible]	[illegible]	[illegible]	[illegible]	[illegible]	[illegible]	[illegible]	[illegible]	[illegible]	[illegible]	[illegible]
16	Limerick,	[illegible]	[illegible]	[illegible]	[illegible]	[illegible]	[illegible]	[illegible]	[illegible]	[illegible]	[illegible]	[illegible]	[illegible]	[illegible]	[illegible]	[illegible]	[illegible]
17	Tipperary,	[illegible]	[illegible]	[illegible]	[illegible]	[illegible]	[illegible]	[illegible]	[illegible]	[illegible]	[illegible]	[illegible]	[illegible]	[illegible]	[illegible]	[illegible]	[illegible]
18	Waterford,	[illegible]	[illegible]	[illegible]	[illegible]	[illegible]	[illegible]	[illegible]	[illegible]	[illegible]	[illegible]	[illegible]	[illegible]	[illegible]	[illegible]	[illegible]	[illegible]
	III.—PROVINCE OF ULSTER.—																
19	Antrim,	[illegible]	[illegible]	[illegible]	[illegible]	[illegible]	[illegible]	[illegible]	[illegible]	[illegible]	[illegible]	[illegible]	[illegible]	[illegible]	[illegible]	[illegible]	[illegible]
20	Armagh,	[illegible]	[illegible]	[illegible]	[illegible]	[illegible]	[illegible]	[illegible]	[illegible]	[illegible]	[illegible]	[illegible]	[illegible]	[illegible]	[illegible]	[illegible]	[illegible]
21	Cavan,	[illegible]	[illegible]	[illegible]	[illegible]	[illegible]	[illegible]	[illegible]	[illegible]	[illegible]	[illegible]	[illegible]	[illegible]	[illegible]	[illegible]	[illegible]	[illegible]
22	Donegal,	[illegible]	[illegible]	[illegible]	[illegible]	[illegible]	[illegible]	[illegible]	[illegible]	[illegible]	[illegible]	[illegible]	[illegible]	[illegible]	[illegible]	[illegible]	[illegible]
23	Down,	[illegible]	[illegible]	[illegible]	[illegible]	[illegible]	[illegible]	[illegible]	[illegible]	[illegible]	[illegible]	[illegible]	[illegible]	[illegible]	[illegible]	[illegible]	[illegible]
24	Fermanagh,	[illegible]	[illegible]	[illegible]	[illegible]	[illegible]	[illegible]	[illegible]	[illegible]	[illegible]	[illegible]	[illegible]	[illegible]	[illegible]	[illegible]	[illegible]	[illegible]
25	Londonderry,	[illegible]	[illegible]	[illegible]	[illegible]	[illegible]	[illegible]	[illegible]	[illegible]	[illegible]	[illegible]	[illegible]	[illegible]	[illegible]	[illegible]	[illegible]	[illegible]
26	Monaghan,	[illegible]	[illegible]	[illegible]	[illegible]	[illegible]	[illegible]	[illegible]	[illegible]	[illegible]	[illegible]	[illegible]	[illegible]	[illegible]	[illegible]	[illegible]	[illegible]
27	Tyrone,	[illegible]	[illegible]	[illegible]	[illegible]	[illegible]	[illegible]	[illegible]	[illegible]	[illegible]	[illegible]	[illegible]	[illegible]	[illegible]	[illegible]	[illegible]	[illegible]
	IV.—PROVINCE OF CONNAUGHT.—																
28	Galway,	[illegible]	[illegible]	[illegible]	[illegible]	[illegible]	[illegible]	[illegible]	[illegible]	[illegible]	[illegible]	[illegible]	[illegible]	[illegible]	[illegible]	[illegible]	[illegible]
29	Leitrim,	[illegible]	[illegible]	[illegible]	[illegible]	[illegible]	[illegible]	[illegible]	[illegible]	[illegible]	[illegible]	[illegible]	[illegible]	[illegible]	[illegible]	[illegible]	[illegible]
30	Mayo,	[illegible]	[illegible]	[illegible]	[illegible]	[illegible]	[illegible]	[illegible]	[illegible]	[illegible]	[illegible]	[illegible]	[illegible]	[illegible]	[illegible]	[illegible]	[illegible]
31	Roscommon,	[illegible]	[illegible]	[illegible]	[illegible]	[illegible]	[illegible]	[illegible]	[illegible]	[illegible]	[illegible]	[illegible]	[illegible]	[illegible]	[illegible]	[illegible]	[illegible]
32	Sligo,	[illegible]	[illegible]	[illegible]	[illegible]	[illegible]	[illegible]	[illegible]	[illegible]	[illegible]	[illegible]	[illegible]	[illegible]	[illegible]	[illegible]	[illegible]	[illegible]

Acts 7 & 8 Vic., c. 81, and 26 & 27 Vic., c. 90, in the year ending 31st December, 1896.

[illegible]																		PROVINCES AND COUNTIES.
[illegible]	[illegible]	[illegible]	[illegible]	[illegible]	[illegible]	[illegible]	[illegible]	[illegible]	[illegible]	[illegible]	[illegible]	[illegible]	[illegible]	[illegible]	[illegible]	[illegible]	[illegible]	
[illegible]	[illegible]	[illegible]	[illegible]	[illegible]	[illegible]	[illegible]	[illegible]	[illegible]	[illegible]	[illegible]	[illegible]	[illegible]	[illegible]	[illegible]	[illegible]	[illegible]	[illegible]	IRELAND.
																		PROVINCES.
[illegible]	[illegible]	[illegible]	[illegible]	[illegible]	[illegible]	[illegible]	[illegible]	[illegible]	[illegible]	[illegible]	[illegible]	[illegible]	[illegible]	[illegible]	[illegible]	[illegible]	[illegible]	LEINSTER.
[illegible]	[illegible]	[illegible]	[illegible]	[illegible]	[illegible]	[illegible]	[illegible]	[illegible]	[illegible]	[illegible]	[illegible]	[illegible]	[illegible]	[illegible]	[illegible]	[illegible]	[illegible]	MUNSTER.
[illegible]	[illegible]	[illegible]	[illegible]	[illegible]	[illegible]	[illegible]	[illegible]	[illegible]	[illegible]	[illegible]	[illegible]	[illegible]	[illegible]	[illegible]	[illegible]	[illegible]	[illegible]	ULSTER.
[illegible]	[illegible]	[illegible]	[illegible]	[illegible]	[illegible]	[illegible]	[illegible]	[illegible]	[illegible]	[illegible]	[illegible]	[illegible]	[illegible]	[illegible]	[illegible]	[illegible]	[illegible]	CONNAUGHT.

MARRIAGES in the Year 1896—in Counties.

[illegible]	[illegible]	[illegible]	[illegible]	[illegible]	[illegible]	[illegible]	[illegible]	[illegible]	[illegible]	[illegible]	[illegible]	[illegible]	[illegible]	[illegible]	[illegible]	[illegible]	[illegible]	Carlow.
[illegible]	[illegible]	[illegible]	[illegible]	[illegible]	[illegible]	[illegible]	[illegible]	[illegible]	[illegible]	[illegible]	[illegible]	[illegible]	[illegible]	[illegible]	[illegible]	[illegible]	[illegible]	Dublin.
[illegible]	[illegible]	[illegible]	[illegible]	[illegible]	[illegible]	[illegible]	[illegible]	[illegible]	[illegible]	[illegible]	[illegible]	[illegible]	[illegible]	[illegible]	[illegible]	[illegible]	[illegible]	Kildare.
[illegible]	[illegible]	[illegible]	[illegible]	[illegible]	[illegible]	[illegible]	[illegible]	[illegible]	[illegible]	[illegible]	[illegible]	[illegible]	[illegible]	[illegible]	[illegible]	[illegible]	[illegible]	Kilkenny.
[illegible]	[illegible]	[illegible]	[illegible]	[illegible]	[illegible]	[illegible]	[illegible]	[illegible]	[illegible]	[illegible]	[illegible]	[illegible]	[illegible]	[illegible]	[illegible]	[illegible]	[illegible]	King's.
[illegible]	[illegible]	[illegible]	[illegible]	[illegible]	[illegible]	[illegible]	[illegible]	[illegible]	[illegible]	[illegible]	[illegible]	[illegible]	[illegible]	[illegible]	[illegible]	[illegible]	[illegible]	Longford.
[illegible]	[illegible]	[illegible]	[illegible]	[illegible]	[illegible]	[illegible]	[illegible]	[illegible]	[illegible]	[illegible]	[illegible]	[illegible]	[illegible]	[illegible]	[illegible]	[illegible]	[illegible]	Louth, and Co. of the Town of Drogheda.
[illegible]	[illegible]	[illegible]	[illegible]	[illegible]	[illegible]	[illegible]	[illegible]	[illegible]	[illegible]	[illegible]	[illegible]	[illegible]	[illegible]	[illegible]	[illegible]	[illegible]	[illegible]	Meath.
[illegible]	[illegible]	[illegible]	[illegible]	[illegible]	[illegible]	[illegible]	[illegible]	[illegible]	[illegible]	[illegible]	[illegible]	[illegible]	[illegible]	[illegible]	[illegible]	[illegible]	[illegible]	Queen's.
[illegible]	[illegible]	[illegible]	[illegible]	[illegible]	[illegible]	[illegible]	[illegible]	[illegible]	[illegible]	[illegible]	[illegible]	[illegible]	[illegible]	[illegible]	[illegible]	[illegible]	[illegible]	Westmeath.
[illegible]	[illegible]	[illegible]	[illegible]	[illegible]	[illegible]	[illegible]	[illegible]	[illegible]	[illegible]	[illegible]	[illegible]	[illegible]	[illegible]	[illegible]	[illegible]	[illegible]	[illegible]	Wexford.
[illegible]	[illegible]	[illegible]	[illegible]	[illegible]	[illegible]	[illegible]	[illegible]	[illegible]	[illegible]	[illegible]	[illegible]	[illegible]	[illegible]	[illegible]	[illegible]	[illegible]	[illegible]	Wicklow.

MARRIAGES in the Year 1896—in Counties.

[illegible]	[illegible]	[illegible]	[illegible]	[illegible]	[illegible]	[illegible]	[illegible]	[illegible]	[illegible]	[illegible]	[illegible]	[illegible]	[illegible]	[illegible]	[illegible]	[illegible]	[illegible]	Clare.
[illegible]	[illegible]	[illegible]	[illegible]	[illegible]	[illegible]	[illegible]	[illegible]	[illegible]	[illegible]	[illegible]	[illegible]	[illegible]	[illegible]	[illegible]	[illegible]	[illegible]	[illegible]	Cork.
[illegible]	[illegible]	[illegible]	[illegible]	[illegible]	[illegible]	[illegible]	[illegible]	[illegible]	[illegible]	[illegible]	[illegible]	[illegible]	[illegible]	[illegible]	[illegible]	[illegible]	[illegible]	Kerry.
[illegible]	[illegible]	[illegible]	[illegible]	[illegible]	[illegible]	[illegible]	[illegible]	[illegible]	[illegible]	[illegible]	[illegible]	[illegible]	[illegible]	[illegible]	[illegible]	[illegible]	[illegible]	Limerick.
[illegible]	[illegible]	[illegible]	[illegible]	[illegible]	[illegible]	[illegible]	[illegible]	[illegible]	[illegible]	[illegible]	[illegible]	[illegible]	[illegible]	[illegible]	[illegible]	[illegible]	[illegible]	Tipperary.
[illegible]	[illegible]	[illegible]	[illegible]	[illegible]	[illegible]	[illegible]	[illegible]	[illegible]	[illegible]	[illegible]	[illegible]	[illegible]	[illegible]	[illegible]	[illegible]	[illegible]	[illegible]	Waterford.

MARRIAGES in the Year 1896—in Counties.

[illegible]	[illegible]	[illegible]	[illegible]	[illegible]	[illegible]	[illegible]	[illegible]	[illegible]	[illegible]	[illegible]	[illegible]	[illegible]	[illegible]	[illegible]	[illegible]	[illegible]	[illegible]	Antrim.
[illegible]	[illegible]	[illegible]	[illegible]	[illegible]	[illegible]	[illegible]	[illegible]	[illegible]	[illegible]	[illegible]	[illegible]	[illegible]	[illegible]	[illegible]	[illegible]	[illegible]	[illegible]	Armagh.
[illegible]	[illegible]	[illegible]	[illegible]	[illegible]	[illegible]	[illegible]	[illegible]	[illegible]	[illegible]	[illegible]	[illegible]	[illegible]	[illegible]	[illegible]	[illegible]	[illegible]	[illegible]	Cavan.
[illegible]	[illegible]	[illegible]	[illegible]	[illegible]	[illegible]	[illegible]	[illegible]	[illegible]	[illegible]	[illegible]	[illegible]	[illegible]	[illegible]	[illegible]	[illegible]	[illegible]	[illegible]	Donegal.
[illegible]	[illegible]	[illegible]	[illegible]	[illegible]	[illegible]	[illegible]	[illegible]	[illegible]	[illegible]	[illegible]	[illegible]	[illegible]	[illegible]	[illegible]	[illegible]	[illegible]	[illegible]	Down.
[illegible]	[illegible]	[illegible]	[illegible]	[illegible]	[illegible]	[illegible]	[illegible]	[illegible]	[illegible]	[illegible]	[illegible]	[illegible]	[illegible]	[illegible]	[illegible]	[illegible]	[illegible]	Fermanagh.
[illegible]	[illegible]	[illegible]	[illegible]	[illegible]	[illegible]	[illegible]	[illegible]	[illegible]	[illegible]	[illegible]	[illegible]	[illegible]	[illegible]	[illegible]	[illegible]	[illegible]	[illegible]	Londonderry.
[illegible]	[illegible]	[illegible]	[illegible]	[illegible]	[illegible]	[illegible]	[illegible]	[illegible]	[illegible]	[illegible]	[illegible]	[illegible]	[illegible]	[illegible]	[illegible]	[illegible]	[illegible]	Monaghan.
[illegible]	[illegible]	[illegible]	[illegible]	[illegible]	[illegible]	[illegible]	[illegible]	[illegible]	[illegible]	[illegible]	[illegible]	[illegible]	[illegible]	[illegible]	[illegible]	[illegible]	[illegible]	Tyrone.

MARRIAGES in the Year 1896—in Counties.

[illegible]	[illegible]	[illegible]	[illegible]	[illegible]	[illegible]	[illegible]	[illegible]	[illegible]	[illegible]	[illegible]	[illegible]	[illegible]	[illegible]	[illegible]	[illegible]	[illegible]	[illegible]	Galway.
[illegible]	[illegible]	[illegible]	[illegible]	[illegible]	[illegible]	[illegible]	[illegible]	[illegible]	[illegible]	[illegible]	[illegible]	[illegible]	[illegible]	[illegible]	[illegible]	[illegible]	[illegible]	Leitrim.
[illegible]	[illegible]	[illegible]	[illegible]	[illegible]	[illegible]	[illegible]	[illegible]	[illegible]	[illegible]	[illegible]	[illegible]	[illegible]	[illegible]	[illegible]	[illegible]	[illegible]	[illegible]	Mayo.
[illegible]	[illegible]	[illegible]	[illegible]	[illegible]	[illegible]	[illegible]	[illegible]	[illegible]	[illegible]	[illegible]	[illegible]	[illegible]	[illegible]	[illegible]	[illegible]	[illegible]	[illegible]	Roscommon.
[illegible]	[illegible]	[illegible]	[illegible]	[illegible]	[illegible]	[illegible]	[illegible]	[illegible]	[illegible]	[illegible]	[illegible]	[illegible]	[illegible]	[illegible]	[illegible]	[illegible]	[illegible]	Sligo.

ABSTRACT OF MARRIAGES.—Marriages registered in Ireland, pursuant to the

1.—PROVINCE OF LEINSTER.—

No.	Superintendent Registrars' Districts.	Area in Statute Acres	Population	Total Marriages	Marriages (by denomination and form)
	1. Carlow Co.				
1	[illegible]	[illegible]	[illegible]	[illegible]	[illegible]
2	[illegible]	[illegible]	[illegible]	[illegible]	[illegible]
3	[illegible]	[illegible]	[illegible]	[illegible]	[illegible]
4	[illegible]	[illegible]	[illegible]	[illegible]	[illegible]
5	[illegible]	[illegible]	[illegible]	[illegible]	[illegible]
	2. Dublin Co.				
6	[illegible]	[illegible]	[illegible]	[illegible]	[illegible]
7	[illegible]	[illegible]	[illegible]	[illegible]	[illegible]
8	[illegible]	[illegible]	[illegible]	[illegible]	[illegible]
9	[illegible]	[illegible]	[illegible]	[illegible]	[illegible]
10	[illegible]	[illegible]	[illegible]	[illegible]	[illegible]
11	[illegible]	[illegible]	[illegible]	[illegible]	[illegible]
	3. Kildare Co.				
12	[illegible]	[illegible]	[illegible]	[illegible]	[illegible]
13	[illegible]	[illegible]	[illegible]	[illegible]	[illegible]
14	[illegible]	[illegible]	[illegible]	[illegible]	[illegible]
15	[illegible]	[illegible]	[illegible]	[illegible]	[illegible]
16	[illegible]	[illegible]	[illegible]	[illegible]	[illegible]
	4. Kilkenny Co.				
17	[illegible]	[illegible]	[illegible]	[illegible]	[illegible]
18	[illegible]	[illegible]	[illegible]	[illegible]	[illegible]
19	[illegible]	[illegible]	[illegible]	[illegible]	[illegible]
20	[illegible]	[illegible]	[illegible]	[illegible]	[illegible]
21	[illegible]	[illegible]	[illegible]	[illegible]	[illegible]
22	[illegible]	[illegible]	[illegible]	[illegible]	[illegible]
23	[illegible]	[illegible]	[illegible]	[illegible]	[illegible]
24	[illegible]	[illegible]	[illegible]	[illegible]	[illegible]
	5. King's Co.				
25	[illegible]	[illegible]	[illegible]	[illegible]	[illegible]
26	[illegible]	[illegible]	[illegible]	[illegible]	[illegible]
27	[illegible]	[illegible]	[illegible]	[illegible]	[illegible]
28	[illegible]	[illegible]	[illegible]	[illegible]	[illegible]
29	[illegible]	[illegible]	[illegible]	[illegible]	[illegible]
	6. Longford Co.				
30	[illegible]	[illegible]	[illegible]	[illegible]	[illegible]
31	[illegible]	[illegible]	[illegible]	[illegible]	[illegible]
32	[illegible]	[illegible]	[illegible]	[illegible]	[illegible]
	7. Louth and Co. of Town of Drogheda.				
33	[illegible]	[illegible]	[illegible]	[illegible]	[illegible]
34	[illegible]	[illegible]	[illegible]	[illegible]	[illegible]
35	[illegible]	[illegible]	[illegible]	[illegible]	[illegible]

Acts 7 & 8 Vict., c. 81, and 26 & 27 Vict., c. 90, in the year ending 31st December, 1866.

MARRIAGES in the Year 1866—in the SUPERINTENDENT REGISTRARS' DISTRICTS in each County.

MARRIAGES: Registered in Quarters ending the last day of — March	June	September	December	Condition of Parties — Bachelors and Spinsters	Bachelors and Widows	Widowers and Spinsters	Widowers and Widows	Of — [illegible]	[illegible]	[illegible] — Men	Women	Signed the Marriage Register with Marks — Men	Women	Cases in which — Both parties	One party	SUPERINTENDENT REGISTRARS' DISTRICTS
																1. Carlow Co.
[illegible]	[illegible]	[illegible]	[illegible]	[illegible]	[illegible]	[illegible]	[illegible]	[illegible]	[illegible]	[illegible]	[illegible]	[illegible]	[illegible]	[illegible]	[illegible]	[illegible], part of
[illegible]	[illegible]	[illegible]	[illegible]	[illegible]	[illegible]	[illegible]	[illegible]	[illegible]	[illegible]	[illegible]	[illegible]	[illegible]	[illegible]	[illegible]	[illegible]	[illegible], do.
[illegible]	[illegible]	[illegible]	[illegible]	[illegible]	[illegible]	[illegible]	[illegible]	[illegible]	[illegible]	[illegible]	[illegible]	[illegible]	[illegible]	[illegible]	[illegible]	[illegible], do.
[illegible]	[illegible]	[illegible]	[illegible]	[illegible]	[illegible]	[illegible]	[illegible]	[illegible]	[illegible]	[illegible]	[illegible]	[illegible]	[illegible]	[illegible]	[illegible]	[illegible], do.
[illegible]	[illegible]	[illegible]	[illegible]	[illegible]	[illegible]	[illegible]	[illegible]	[illegible]	[illegible]	[illegible]	[illegible]	[illegible]	[illegible]	[illegible]	[illegible]	[illegible], do.
																2. Dublin Co.
[illegible]	[illegible]	[illegible]	[illegible]	[illegible]	[illegible]	[illegible]	[illegible]	[illegible]	[illegible]	[illegible]	[illegible]	[illegible]	[illegible]	[illegible]	[illegible]	[illegible]
[illegible]	[illegible]	[illegible]	[illegible]	[illegible]	[illegible]	[illegible]	[illegible]	[illegible]	[illegible]	[illegible]	[illegible]	[illegible]	[illegible]	[illegible]	[illegible]	[illegible]
[illegible]	[illegible]	[illegible]	[illegible]	[illegible]	[illegible]	[illegible]	[illegible]	[illegible]	[illegible]	[illegible]	[illegible]	[illegible]	[illegible]	[illegible]	[illegible]	[illegible]
[illegible]	[illegible]	[illegible]	[illegible]	[illegible]	[illegible]	[illegible]	[illegible]	[illegible]	[illegible]	[illegible]	[illegible]	[illegible]	[illegible]	[illegible]	[illegible]	[illegible]
[illegible]	[illegible]	[illegible]	[illegible]	[illegible]	[illegible]	[illegible]	[illegible]	[illegible]	[illegible]	[illegible]	[illegible]	[illegible]	[illegible]	[illegible]	[illegible]	[illegible], part of
[illegible]	[illegible]	[illegible]	[illegible]	[illegible]	[illegible]	[illegible]	[illegible]	[illegible]	[illegible]	[illegible]	[illegible]	[illegible]	[illegible]	[illegible]	[illegible]	[illegible], do.
																3. Kildare Co.
[illegible]	[illegible]	[illegible]	[illegible]	[illegible]	[illegible]	[illegible]	[illegible]	[illegible]	[illegible]	[illegible]	[illegible]	[illegible]	[illegible]	[illegible]	[illegible]	[illegible], part of
[illegible]	[illegible]	[illegible]	[illegible]	[illegible]	[illegible]	[illegible]	[illegible]	[illegible]	[illegible]	[illegible]	[illegible]	[illegible]	[illegible]	[illegible]	[illegible]	[illegible], do.
[illegible]	[illegible]	[illegible]	[illegible]	[illegible]	[illegible]	[illegible]	[illegible]	[illegible]	[illegible]	[illegible]	[illegible]	[illegible]	[illegible]	[illegible]	[illegible]	[illegible], do.
[illegible]	[illegible]	[illegible]	[illegible]	[illegible]	[illegible]	[illegible]	[illegible]	[illegible]	[illegible]	[illegible]	[illegible]	[illegible]	[illegible]	[illegible]	[illegible]	[illegible], do.
[illegible]	[illegible]	[illegible]	[illegible]	[illegible]	[illegible]	[illegible]	[illegible]	[illegible]	[illegible]	[illegible]	[illegible]	[illegible]	[illegible]	[illegible]	[illegible]	[illegible], do.
																4. Kilkenny Co.
[illegible]	[illegible]	[illegible]	[illegible]	[illegible]	[illegible]	[illegible]	[illegible]	[illegible]	[illegible]	[illegible]	[illegible]	[illegible]	[illegible]	[illegible]	[illegible]	[illegible], part of
[illegible]	[illegible]	[illegible]	[illegible]	[illegible]	[illegible]	[illegible]	[illegible]	[illegible]	[illegible]	[illegible]	[illegible]	[illegible]	[illegible]	[illegible]	[illegible]	[illegible], do.
[illegible]	[illegible]	[illegible]	[illegible]	[illegible]	[illegible]	[illegible]	[illegible]	[illegible]	[illegible]	[illegible]	[illegible]	[illegible]	[illegible]	[illegible]	[illegible]	[illegible]
[illegible]	[illegible]	[illegible]	[illegible]	[illegible]	[illegible]	[illegible]	[illegible]	[illegible]	[illegible]	[illegible]	[illegible]	[illegible]	[illegible]	[illegible]	[illegible]	Kilkenny
[illegible]	[illegible]	[illegible]	[illegible]	[illegible]	[illegible]	[illegible]	[illegible]	[illegible]	[illegible]	[illegible]	[illegible]	[illegible]	[illegible]	[illegible]	[illegible]	[illegible], part of
[illegible]	[illegible]	[illegible]	[illegible]	[illegible]	[illegible]	[illegible]	[illegible]	[illegible]	[illegible]	[illegible]	[illegible]	[illegible]	[illegible]	[illegible]	[illegible]	[illegible]
[illegible]	[illegible]	[illegible]	[illegible]	[illegible]	[illegible]	[illegible]	[illegible]	[illegible]	[illegible]	[illegible]	[illegible]	[illegible]	[illegible]	[illegible]	[illegible]	[illegible], part of
[illegible]	[illegible]	[illegible]	[illegible]	[illegible]	[illegible]	[illegible]	[illegible]	[illegible]	[illegible]	[illegible]	[illegible]	[illegible]	[illegible]	[illegible]	[illegible]	[illegible], do.
																5. King's Co.
[illegible]	[illegible]	[illegible]	[illegible]	[illegible]	[illegible]	[illegible]	[illegible]	[illegible]	[illegible]	[illegible]	[illegible]	[illegible]	[illegible]	[illegible]	[illegible]	[illegible], part of
[illegible]	[illegible]	[illegible]	[illegible]	[illegible]	[illegible]	[illegible]	[illegible]	[illegible]	[illegible]	[illegible]	[illegible]	[illegible]	[illegible]	[illegible]	[illegible]	[illegible], do.
[illegible]	[illegible]	[illegible]	[illegible]	[illegible]	[illegible]	[illegible]	[illegible]	[illegible]	[illegible]	[illegible]	[illegible]	[illegible]	[illegible]	[illegible]	[illegible]	[illegible], do.
[illegible]	[illegible]	[illegible]	[illegible]	[illegible]	[illegible]	[illegible]	[illegible]	[illegible]	[illegible]	[illegible]	[illegible]	[illegible]	[illegible]	[illegible]	[illegible]	[illegible], do.
[illegible]	[illegible]	[illegible]	[illegible]	[illegible]	[illegible]	[illegible]	[illegible]	[illegible]	[illegible]	[illegible]	[illegible]	[illegible]	[illegible]	[illegible]	[illegible]	[illegible], do.
																6. Longford Co.
[illegible]	[illegible]	[illegible]	[illegible]	[illegible]	[illegible]	[illegible]	[illegible]	[illegible]	[illegible]	[illegible]	[illegible]	[illegible]	[illegible]	[illegible]	[illegible]	[illegible], part of
[illegible]	[illegible]	[illegible]	[illegible]	[illegible]	[illegible]	[illegible]	[illegible]	[illegible]	[illegible]	[illegible]	[illegible]	[illegible]	[illegible]	[illegible]	[illegible]	[illegible], do.
[illegible]	[illegible]	[illegible]	[illegible]	[illegible]	[illegible]	[illegible]	[illegible]	[illegible]	[illegible]	[illegible]	[illegible]	[illegible]	[illegible]	[illegible]	[illegible]	[illegible]
																7. County of the Town of Drogheda.
[illegible]	[illegible]	[illegible]	[illegible]	[illegible]	[illegible]	[illegible]	[illegible]	[illegible]	[illegible]	[illegible]	[illegible]	[illegible]	[illegible]	[illegible]	[illegible]	[illegible], part of
[illegible]	[illegible]	[illegible]	[illegible]	[illegible]	[illegible]	[illegible]	[illegible]	[illegible]	[illegible]	[illegible]	[illegible]	[illegible]	[illegible]	[illegible]	[illegible]	[illegible], do.
[illegible]	[illegible]	[illegible]	[illegible]	[illegible]	[illegible]	[illegible]	[illegible]	[illegible]	[illegible]	[illegible]	[illegible]	[illegible]	[illegible]	[illegible]	[illegible]	[illegible], do.

[illegible]

I.—PROVINCE OF LEINSTER—*continued.*

No.	Superintendent Registrars' Districts.	Area in Statute Acres, exclusive of the Tideway, Lakes, and Drainage.	Population, 1871.	Total Marriages.	Marriages: Registered under the 7 & 8 Vic., c. 81 — According to the Rites of the Church of Ireland: Special Licence.	Licence.	Banns.	Registrar's Certificate.	Not stated by which of the foregoing forms.	Total.	In Registered Presbyterian Meeting Houses.	In Registered Buildings.	In the Registrar's Office.	Society of Friends.	Jews.	Total Registered under the Act 7 & 8 Vic., c. 81.	Roman Catholic Marriages Registered under the 26 Vic., c. 27.
	8. Meath Co.																
36	Ardee, part of,	[illegible]	[illegible]	[illegible]	[illegible]	[illegible]	[illegible]	[illegible]	[illegible]	[illegible]	[illegible]	[illegible]	[illegible]	[illegible]	[illegible]	[illegible]	[illegible]
37	Celbridge, do.	[illegible]	[illegible]	[illegible]	[illegible]	[illegible]	[illegible]	[illegible]	[illegible]	[illegible]	[illegible]	[illegible]	[illegible]	[illegible]	[illegible]	[illegible]	[illegible]
38	Drogheda, do.	[illegible]	[illegible]	[illegible]	[illegible]	[illegible]	[illegible]	[illegible]	[illegible]	[illegible]	[illegible]	[illegible]	[illegible]	[illegible]	[illegible]	[illegible]	[illegible]
39	Dunshaughlin, do.	[illegible]	[illegible]	[illegible]	[illegible]	[illegible]	[illegible]	[illegible]	[illegible]	[illegible]	[illegible]	[illegible]	[illegible]	[illegible]	[illegible]	[illegible]	[illegible]
40	Edenderry, do.	[illegible]	[illegible]	[illegible]	[illegible]	[illegible]	[illegible]	[illegible]	[illegible]	[illegible]	[illegible]	[illegible]	[illegible]	[illegible]	[illegible]	[illegible]	[illegible]
41	Kells, do.	[illegible]	[illegible]	[illegible]	[illegible]	[illegible]	[illegible]	[illegible]	[illegible]	[illegible]	[illegible]	[illegible]	[illegible]	[illegible]	[illegible]	[illegible]	[illegible]
42	Navan,	[illegible]	[illegible]	[illegible]	[illegible]	[illegible]	[illegible]	[illegible]	[illegible]	[illegible]	[illegible]	[illegible]	[illegible]	[illegible]	[illegible]	[illegible]	[illegible]
43	Oldcastle, part of,	[illegible]	[illegible]	[illegible]	[illegible]	[illegible]	[illegible]	[illegible]	[illegible]	[illegible]	[illegible]	[illegible]	[illegible]	[illegible]	[illegible]	[illegible]	[illegible]
44	Trim,	[illegible]	[illegible]	[illegible]	[illegible]	[illegible]	[illegible]	[illegible]	[illegible]	[illegible]	[illegible]	[illegible]	[illegible]	[illegible]	[illegible]	[illegible]	[illegible]
	9. Queen's Co.																
45	Abbeyleix,	[illegible]	[illegible]	[illegible]	[illegible]	[illegible]	[illegible]	[illegible]	[illegible]	[illegible]	[illegible]	[illegible]	[illegible]	[illegible]	[illegible]	[illegible]	[illegible]
46	Athy, part of,	[illegible]	[illegible]	[illegible]	[illegible]	[illegible]	[illegible]	[illegible]	[illegible]	[illegible]	[illegible]	[illegible]	[illegible]	[illegible]	[illegible]	[illegible]	[illegible]
47	Carlow, do.	[illegible]	[illegible]	[illegible]	[illegible]	[illegible]	[illegible]	[illegible]	[illegible]	[illegible]	[illegible]	[illegible]	[illegible]	[illegible]	[illegible]	[illegible]	[illegible]
48	Mountmellick, do.	[illegible]	[illegible]	[illegible]	[illegible]	[illegible]	[illegible]	[illegible]	[illegible]	[illegible]	[illegible]	[illegible]	[illegible]	[illegible]	[illegible]	[illegible]	[illegible]
49	Roscrea, do.	[illegible]	[illegible]	[illegible]	[illegible]	[illegible]	[illegible]	[illegible]	[illegible]	[illegible]	[illegible]	[illegible]	[illegible]	[illegible]	[illegible]	[illegible]	[illegible]
50	Donaghmore, do.	[illegible]	[illegible]	[illegible]	[illegible]	[illegible]	[illegible]	[illegible]	[illegible]	[illegible]	[illegible]	[illegible]	[illegible]	[illegible]	[illegible]	[illegible]	[illegible]
	10. Westmeath Co.																
51	Athlone, part of,	[illegible]	[illegible]	[illegible]	[illegible]	[illegible]	[illegible]	[illegible]	[illegible]	[illegible]	[illegible]	[illegible]	[illegible]	[illegible]	[illegible]	[illegible]	[illegible]
52	Ballymahon, do.	[illegible]	[illegible]	[illegible]	[illegible]	[illegible]	[illegible]	[illegible]	[illegible]	[illegible]	[illegible]	[illegible]	[illegible]	[illegible]	[illegible]	[illegible]	[illegible]
53	Delvin,	[illegible]	[illegible]	[illegible]	[illegible]	[illegible]	[illegible]	[illegible]	[illegible]	[illegible]	[illegible]	[illegible]	[illegible]	[illegible]	[illegible]	[illegible]	[illegible]
54	Oldcastle, part of,	[illegible]	[illegible]	[illegible]	[illegible]	[illegible]	[illegible]	[illegible]	[illegible]	[illegible]	[illegible]	[illegible]	[illegible]	[illegible]	[illegible]	[illegible]	[illegible]
55	Mullingar,	[illegible]	[illegible]	[illegible]	[illegible]	[illegible]	[illegible]	[illegible]	[illegible]	[illegible]	[illegible]	[illegible]	[illegible]	[illegible]	[illegible]	[illegible]	[illegible]
56	Tullamore, part of,	[illegible]	[illegible]	[illegible]	[illegible]	[illegible]	[illegible]	[illegible]	[illegible]	[illegible]	[illegible]	[illegible]	[illegible]	[illegible]	[illegible]	[illegible]	[illegible]
	11. Wexford Co.																
57	Enniscorthy, part of,	[illegible]	[illegible]	[illegible]	[illegible]	[illegible]	[illegible]	[illegible]	[illegible]	[illegible]	[illegible]	[illegible]	[illegible]	[illegible]	[illegible]	[illegible]	[illegible]
58	Gorey,	[illegible]	[illegible]	[illegible]	[illegible]	[illegible]	[illegible]	[illegible]	[illegible]	[illegible]	[illegible]	[illegible]	[illegible]	[illegible]	[illegible]	[illegible]	[illegible]
59	New Ross, part of,	[illegible]	[illegible]	[illegible]	[illegible]	[illegible]	[illegible]	[illegible]	[illegible]	[illegible]	[illegible]	[illegible]	[illegible]	[illegible]	[illegible]	[illegible]	[illegible]
60	Shillelagh, do.	[illegible]	[illegible]	[illegible]	[illegible]	[illegible]	[illegible]	[illegible]	[illegible]	[illegible]	[illegible]	[illegible]	[illegible]	[illegible]	[illegible]	[illegible]	[illegible]
61	Wexford,	[illegible]	[illegible]	[illegible]	[illegible]	[illegible]	[illegible]	[illegible]	[illegible]	[illegible]	[illegible]	[illegible]	[illegible]	[illegible]	[illegible]	[illegible]	[illegible]
	12. Wicklow Co.																
62	Baltinglass, part of,	[illegible]	[illegible]	[illegible]	[illegible]	[illegible]	[illegible]	[illegible]	[illegible]	[illegible]	[illegible]	[illegible]	[illegible]	[illegible]	[illegible]	[illegible]	[illegible]
63	Naas, do.	[illegible]	[illegible]	[illegible]	[illegible]	[illegible]	[illegible]	[illegible]	[illegible]	[illegible]	[illegible]	[illegible]	[illegible]	[illegible]	[illegible]	[illegible]	[illegible]
64	Rathdown, do.	[illegible]	[illegible]	[illegible]	[illegible]	[illegible]	[illegible]	[illegible]	[illegible]	[illegible]	[illegible]	[illegible]	[illegible]	[illegible]	[illegible]	[illegible]	[illegible]
65	Rathdrum,	[illegible]	[illegible]	[illegible]	[illegible]	[illegible]	[illegible]	[illegible]	[illegible]	[illegible]	[illegible]	[illegible]	[illegible]	[illegible]	[illegible]	[illegible]	[illegible]
66	Shillelagh, part of,	[illegible]	[illegible]	[illegible]	[illegible]	[illegible]	[illegible]	[illegible]	[illegible]	[illegible]	[illegible]	[illegible]	[illegible]	[illegible]	[illegible]	[illegible]	[illegible]

II.—PROVINCE OF MUNSTER.

No.	Superintendent Registrars' Districts.	Area	Population	Total Marriages	Special Licence	Licence	Banns	Registrar's Certificate	Not stated	Total	Presbyterian Meeting Houses	Registered Buildings	Registrar's Office	Society of Friends	Jews	Total Registered under 7 & 8 Vic., c. 81	Roman Catholic Marriages
	13. Clare Co.																
67	Ballyvaghan,	[illegible]	[illegible]	[illegible]	[illegible]	[illegible]	[illegible]	[illegible]	[illegible]	[illegible]	[illegible]	[illegible]	[illegible]	[illegible]	[illegible]	[illegible]	[illegible]
68	Corrofin,	[illegible]	[illegible]	[illegible]	[illegible]	[illegible]	[illegible]	[illegible]	[illegible]	[illegible]	[illegible]	[illegible]	[illegible]	[illegible]	[illegible]	[illegible]	[illegible]
69	Ennis,	[illegible]	[illegible]	[illegible]	[illegible]	[illegible]	[illegible]	[illegible]	[illegible]	[illegible]	[illegible]	[illegible]	[illegible]	[illegible]	[illegible]	[illegible]	[illegible]
70	Ennistymon,	[illegible]	[illegible]	[illegible]	[illegible]	[illegible]	[illegible]	[illegible]	[illegible]	[illegible]	[illegible]	[illegible]	[illegible]	[illegible]	[illegible]	[illegible]	[illegible]
71	Killadysert,	[illegible]	[illegible]	[illegible]	[illegible]	[illegible]	[illegible]	[illegible]	[illegible]	[illegible]	[illegible]	[illegible]	[illegible]	[illegible]	[illegible]	[illegible]	[illegible]
72	[illegible],	[illegible]	[illegible]	[illegible]	[illegible]	[illegible]	[illegible]	[illegible]	[illegible]	[illegible]	[illegible]	[illegible]	[illegible]	[illegible]	[illegible]	[illegible]	[illegible]
73	Limerick, part of,	[illegible]	[illegible]	[illegible]	[illegible]	[illegible]	[illegible]	[illegible]	[illegible]	[illegible]	[illegible]	[illegible]	[illegible]	[illegible]	[illegible]	[illegible]	[illegible]
74	Scarriff, do.	[illegible]	[illegible]	[illegible]	[illegible]	[illegible]	[illegible]	[illegible]	[illegible]	[illegible]	[illegible]	[illegible]	[illegible]	[illegible]	[illegible]	[illegible]	[illegible]
75	Tulla,	[illegible]	[illegible]	[illegible]	[illegible]	[illegible]	[illegible]	[illegible]	[illegible]	[illegible]	[illegible]	[illegible]	[illegible]	[illegible]	[illegible]	[illegible]	[illegible]

MARRIAGES in the Year 1896—in the Superintendent Registrars' Districts in each County.

MARRIAGES: Registered in the Quarter ending the last day of				Contracted between				Of		Of Persons under full Age		Signed the Marriage Register with Marks				SUPERINTENDENT REGISTRARS' DISTRICTS.
[illegible]	[illegible]	[illegible]	[illegible]	[illegible]	[illegible]	[illegible]	[illegible]	[illegible]	[illegible]	[illegible]	[illegible]	[illegible]	[illegible]	[illegible]	[illegible]	
																[illegible] Co.
[illegible]	[illegible]	[illegible]	[illegible]	[illegible]	[illegible]	[illegible]	[illegible]	[illegible]	[illegible]	[illegible]	[illegible]	[illegible]	[illegible]	[illegible]	[illegible]	[illegible]
[illegible]	[illegible]	[illegible]	[illegible]	[illegible]	[illegible]	[illegible]	[illegible]	[illegible]	[illegible]	[illegible]	[illegible]	[illegible]	[illegible]	[illegible]	[illegible]	[illegible]
[illegible]	[illegible]	[illegible]	[illegible]	[illegible]	[illegible]	[illegible]	[illegible]	[illegible]	[illegible]	[illegible]	[illegible]	[illegible]	[illegible]	[illegible]	[illegible]	[illegible]
[illegible]	[illegible]	[illegible]	[illegible]	[illegible]	[illegible]	[illegible]	[illegible]	[illegible]	[illegible]	[illegible]	[illegible]	[illegible]	[illegible]	[illegible]	[illegible]	[illegible]
[illegible]	[illegible]	[illegible]	[illegible]	[illegible]	[illegible]	[illegible]	[illegible]	[illegible]	[illegible]	[illegible]	[illegible]	[illegible]	[illegible]	[illegible]	[illegible]	[illegible]
[illegible]	[illegible]	[illegible]	[illegible]	[illegible]	[illegible]	[illegible]	[illegible]	[illegible]	[illegible]	[illegible]	[illegible]	[illegible]	[illegible]	[illegible]	[illegible]	[illegible]
[illegible]	[illegible]	[illegible]	[illegible]	[illegible]	[illegible]	[illegible]	[illegible]	[illegible]	[illegible]	[illegible]	[illegible]	[illegible]	[illegible]	[illegible]	[illegible]	[illegible]
[illegible]	[illegible]	[illegible]	[illegible]	[illegible]	[illegible]	[illegible]	[illegible]	[illegible]	[illegible]	[illegible]	[illegible]	[illegible]	[illegible]	[illegible]	[illegible]	[illegible]
[illegible]	[illegible]	[illegible]	[illegible]	[illegible]	[illegible]	[illegible]	[illegible]	[illegible]	[illegible]	[illegible]	[illegible]	[illegible]	[illegible]	[illegible]	[illegible]	[illegible]
																[illegible] Co.
[illegible]	[illegible]	[illegible]	[illegible]	[illegible]	[illegible]	[illegible]	[illegible]	[illegible]	[illegible]	[illegible]	[illegible]	[illegible]	[illegible]	[illegible]	[illegible]	[illegible]
[illegible]	[illegible]	[illegible]	[illegible]	[illegible]	[illegible]	[illegible]	[illegible]	[illegible]	[illegible]	[illegible]	[illegible]	[illegible]	[illegible]	[illegible]	[illegible]	[illegible]
[illegible]	[illegible]	[illegible]	[illegible]	[illegible]	[illegible]	[illegible]	[illegible]	[illegible]	[illegible]	[illegible]	[illegible]	[illegible]	[illegible]	[illegible]	[illegible]	[illegible]
[illegible]	[illegible]	[illegible]	[illegible]	[illegible]	[illegible]	[illegible]	[illegible]	[illegible]	[illegible]	[illegible]	[illegible]	[illegible]	[illegible]	[illegible]	[illegible]	[illegible]
[illegible]	[illegible]	[illegible]	[illegible]	[illegible]	[illegible]	[illegible]	[illegible]	[illegible]	[illegible]	[illegible]	[illegible]	[illegible]	[illegible]	[illegible]	[illegible]	[illegible]
[illegible]	[illegible]	[illegible]	[illegible]	[illegible]	[illegible]	[illegible]	[illegible]	[illegible]	[illegible]	[illegible]	[illegible]	[illegible]	[illegible]	[illegible]	[illegible]	[illegible]
																[illegible] Co.
[illegible]	[illegible]	[illegible]	[illegible]	[illegible]	[illegible]	[illegible]	[illegible]	[illegible]	[illegible]	[illegible]	[illegible]	[illegible]	[illegible]	[illegible]	[illegible]	[illegible]
[illegible]	[illegible]	[illegible]	[illegible]	[illegible]	[illegible]	[illegible]	[illegible]	[illegible]	[illegible]	[illegible]	[illegible]	[illegible]	[illegible]	[illegible]	[illegible]	[illegible]
[illegible]	[illegible]	[illegible]	[illegible]	[illegible]	[illegible]	[illegible]	[illegible]	[illegible]	[illegible]	[illegible]	[illegible]	[illegible]	[illegible]	[illegible]	[illegible]	[illegible]
[illegible]	[illegible]	[illegible]	[illegible]	[illegible]	[illegible]	[illegible]	[illegible]	[illegible]	[illegible]	[illegible]	[illegible]	[illegible]	[illegible]	[illegible]	[illegible]	[illegible]
[illegible]	[illegible]	[illegible]	[illegible]	[illegible]	[illegible]	[illegible]	[illegible]	[illegible]	[illegible]	[illegible]	[illegible]	[illegible]	[illegible]	[illegible]	[illegible]	[illegible]
[illegible]	[illegible]	[illegible]	[illegible]	[illegible]	[illegible]	[illegible]	[illegible]	[illegible]	[illegible]	[illegible]	[illegible]	[illegible]	[illegible]	[illegible]	[illegible]	[illegible]
																[illegible] Co.
[illegible]	[illegible]	[illegible]	[illegible]	[illegible]	[illegible]	[illegible]	[illegible]	[illegible]	[illegible]	[illegible]	[illegible]	[illegible]	[illegible]	[illegible]	[illegible]	[illegible]
[illegible]	[illegible]	[illegible]	[illegible]	[illegible]	[illegible]	[illegible]	[illegible]	[illegible]	[illegible]	[illegible]	[illegible]	[illegible]	[illegible]	[illegible]	[illegible]	[illegible]
[illegible]	[illegible]	[illegible]	[illegible]	[illegible]	[illegible]	[illegible]	[illegible]	[illegible]	[illegible]	[illegible]	[illegible]	[illegible]	[illegible]	[illegible]	[illegible]	[illegible]
[illegible]	[illegible]	[illegible]	[illegible]	[illegible]	[illegible]	[illegible]	[illegible]	[illegible]	[illegible]	[illegible]	[illegible]	[illegible]	[illegible]	[illegible]	[illegible]	[illegible]
[illegible]	[illegible]	[illegible]	[illegible]	[illegible]	[illegible]	[illegible]	[illegible]	[illegible]	[illegible]	[illegible]	[illegible]	[illegible]	[illegible]	[illegible]	[illegible]	[illegible]
																[illegible] Co.
[illegible]	[illegible]	[illegible]	[illegible]	[illegible]	[illegible]	[illegible]	[illegible]	[illegible]	[illegible]	[illegible]	[illegible]	[illegible]	[illegible]	[illegible]	[illegible]	[illegible]
[illegible]	[illegible]	[illegible]	[illegible]	[illegible]	[illegible]	[illegible]	[illegible]	[illegible]	[illegible]	[illegible]	[illegible]	[illegible]	[illegible]	[illegible]	[illegible]	[illegible]
[illegible]	[illegible]	[illegible]	[illegible]	[illegible]	[illegible]	[illegible]	[illegible]	[illegible]	[illegible]	[illegible]	[illegible]	[illegible]	[illegible]	[illegible]	[illegible]	[illegible]
[illegible]	[illegible]	[illegible]	[illegible]	[illegible]	[illegible]	[illegible]	[illegible]	[illegible]	[illegible]	[illegible]	[illegible]	[illegible]	[illegible]	[illegible]	[illegible]	[illegible]
[illegible]	[illegible]	[illegible]	[illegible]	[illegible]	[illegible]	[illegible]	[illegible]	[illegible]	[illegible]	[illegible]	[illegible]	[illegible]	[illegible]	[illegible]	[illegible]	[illegible]

MARRIAGES in the Year 1896—in the Superintendent Registrars' Districts in each County.

																[illegible] Co.
[illegible]	[illegible]	[illegible]	[illegible]	[illegible]	[illegible]	[illegible]	[illegible]	[illegible]	[illegible]	[illegible]	[illegible]	[illegible]	[illegible]	[illegible]	[illegible]	[illegible]
[illegible]	[illegible]	[illegible]	[illegible]	[illegible]	[illegible]	[illegible]	[illegible]	[illegible]	[illegible]	[illegible]	[illegible]	[illegible]	[illegible]	[illegible]	[illegible]	[illegible]
[illegible]	[illegible]	[illegible]	[illegible]	[illegible]	[illegible]	[illegible]	[illegible]	[illegible]	[illegible]	[illegible]	[illegible]	[illegible]	[illegible]	[illegible]	[illegible]	[illegible]
[illegible]	[illegible]	[illegible]	[illegible]	[illegible]	[illegible]	[illegible]	[illegible]	[illegible]	[illegible]	[illegible]	[illegible]	[illegible]	[illegible]	[illegible]	[illegible]	[illegible]
[illegible]	[illegible]	[illegible]	[illegible]	[illegible]	[illegible]	[illegible]	[illegible]	[illegible]	[illegible]	[illegible]	[illegible]	[illegible]	[illegible]	[illegible]	[illegible]	[illegible]
[illegible]	[illegible]	[illegible]	[illegible]	[illegible]	[illegible]	[illegible]	[illegible]	[illegible]	[illegible]	[illegible]	[illegible]	[illegible]	[illegible]	[illegible]	[illegible]	[illegible]
[illegible]	[illegible]	[illegible]	[illegible]	[illegible]	[illegible]	[illegible]	[illegible]	[illegible]	[illegible]	[illegible]	[illegible]	[illegible]	[illegible]	[illegible]	[illegible]	[illegible]
[illegible]	[illegible]	[illegible]	[illegible]	[illegible]	[illegible]	[illegible]	[illegible]	[illegible]	[illegible]	[illegible]	[illegible]	[illegible]	[illegible]	[illegible]	[illegible]	[illegible]
[illegible]	[illegible]	[illegible]	[illegible]	[illegible]	[illegible]	[illegible]	[illegible]	[illegible]	[illegible]	[illegible]	[illegible]	[illegible]	[illegible]	[illegible]	[illegible]	[illegible]

II.—PROVINCE OF MUNSTER—continued.

No.	Superintendent Registrars' Districts	Area in Statute Acres, inclusive of the larger Towns, Loughs, and Rivers	Population, 1861	Total Marriages	Special Licence	Licence	Banns	Registrar's Certificate	Not stated by whom or the Licensing Formula	Total	In Registered Presbyterian Meeting Houses	In Registered Buildings	In the Registrar's Office	Society of Friends	Jews	Total Registered under the …
	14. Cork Co.															
[illegible]	Bandon,	[illegible]	[illegible]	[illegible]	[illegible]	[illegible]	[illegible]	[illegible]	[illegible]	[illegible]	[illegible]	[illegible]	[illegible]	[illegible]	[illegible]	[illegible]
[illegible]	Bantry,	[illegible]	[illegible]	[illegible]	[illegible]	[illegible]	[illegible]	[illegible]	[illegible]	[illegible]	[illegible]	[illegible]	[illegible]	[illegible]	[illegible]	[illegible]
[illegible]	Castletown,	[illegible]	[illegible]	[illegible]	[illegible]	[illegible]	[illegible]	[illegible]	[illegible]	[illegible]	[illegible]	[illegible]	[illegible]	[illegible]	[illegible]	[illegible]
[illegible]	Clonakilty,	[illegible]	[illegible]	[illegible]	[illegible]	[illegible]	[illegible]	[illegible]	[illegible]	[illegible]	[illegible]	[illegible]	[illegible]	[illegible]	[illegible]	[illegible]
[illegible]	Cork,	[illegible]	[illegible]	[illegible]	[illegible]	[illegible]	[illegible]	[illegible]	[illegible]	[illegible]	[illegible]	[illegible]	[illegible]	[illegible]	[illegible]	[illegible]
[illegible]	Dunmanway,	[illegible]	[illegible]	[illegible]	[illegible]	[illegible]	[illegible]	[illegible]	[illegible]	[illegible]	[illegible]	[illegible]	[illegible]	[illegible]	[illegible]	[illegible]
[illegible]	Fermoy,	[illegible]	[illegible]	[illegible]	[illegible]	[illegible]	[illegible]	[illegible]	[illegible]	[illegible]	[illegible]	[illegible]	[illegible]	[illegible]	[illegible]	[illegible]
[illegible]	Kanturk,	[illegible]	[illegible]	[illegible]	[illegible]	[illegible]	[illegible]	[illegible]	[illegible]	[illegible]	[illegible]	[illegible]	[illegible]	[illegible]	[illegible]	[illegible]
[illegible]	Kilmallock, part of,	[illegible]	[illegible]	[illegible]	[illegible]	[illegible]	[illegible]	[illegible]	[illegible]	[illegible]	[illegible]	[illegible]	[illegible]	[illegible]	[illegible]	[illegible]
[illegible]	Kinsale,	[illegible]	[illegible]	[illegible]	[illegible]	[illegible]	[illegible]	[illegible]	[illegible]	[illegible]	[illegible]	[illegible]	[illegible]	[illegible]	[illegible]	[illegible]
[illegible]	Macroom,	[illegible]	[illegible]	[illegible]	[illegible]	[illegible]	[illegible]	[illegible]	[illegible]	[illegible]	[illegible]	[illegible]	[illegible]	[illegible]	[illegible]	[illegible]
[illegible]	Mallow,	[illegible]	[illegible]	[illegible]	[illegible]	[illegible]	[illegible]	[illegible]	[illegible]	[illegible]	[illegible]	[illegible]	[illegible]	[illegible]	[illegible]	[illegible]
[illegible]	Midleton,	[illegible]	[illegible]	[illegible]	[illegible]	[illegible]	[illegible]	[illegible]	[illegible]	[illegible]	[illegible]	[illegible]	[illegible]	[illegible]	[illegible]	[illegible]
[illegible]	Millstreet,	[illegible]	[illegible]	[illegible]	[illegible]	[illegible]	[illegible]	[illegible]	[illegible]	[illegible]	[illegible]	[illegible]	[illegible]	[illegible]	[illegible]	[illegible]
[illegible]	Mitchelstown, part of,	[illegible]	[illegible]	[illegible]	[illegible]	[illegible]	[illegible]	[illegible]	[illegible]	[illegible]	[illegible]	[illegible]	[illegible]	[illegible]	[illegible]	[illegible]
[illegible]	Skibbereen,	[illegible]	[illegible]	[illegible]	[illegible]	[illegible]	[illegible]	[illegible]	[illegible]	[illegible]	[illegible]	[illegible]	[illegible]	[illegible]	[illegible]	[illegible]
[illegible]	Skull,	[illegible]	[illegible]	[illegible]	[illegible]	[illegible]	[illegible]	[illegible]	[illegible]	[illegible]	[illegible]	[illegible]	[illegible]	[illegible]	[illegible]	[illegible]
[illegible]	Youghal, part of,	[illegible]	[illegible]	[illegible]	[illegible]	[illegible]	[illegible]	[illegible]	[illegible]	[illegible]	[illegible]	[illegible]	[illegible]	[illegible]	[illegible]	[illegible]
	15. Kerry Co.															
[illegible]	Cahersiveen,	[illegible]	[illegible]	[illegible]	[illegible]	[illegible]	[illegible]	[illegible]	[illegible]	[illegible]	[illegible]	[illegible]	[illegible]	[illegible]	[illegible]	[illegible]
[illegible]	Dingle,	[illegible]	[illegible]	[illegible]	[illegible]	[illegible]	[illegible]	[illegible]	[illegible]	[illegible]	[illegible]	[illegible]	[illegible]	[illegible]	[illegible]	[illegible]
[illegible]	Kenmare,	[illegible]	[illegible]	[illegible]	[illegible]	[illegible]	[illegible]	[illegible]	[illegible]	[illegible]	[illegible]	[illegible]	[illegible]	[illegible]	[illegible]	[illegible]
[illegible]	Killarney,	[illegible]	[illegible]	[illegible]	[illegible]	[illegible]	[illegible]	[illegible]	[illegible]	[illegible]	[illegible]	[illegible]	[illegible]	[illegible]	[illegible]	[illegible]
[illegible]	Listowel, part of,	[illegible]	[illegible]	[illegible]	[illegible]	[illegible]	[illegible]	[illegible]	[illegible]	[illegible]	[illegible]	[illegible]	[illegible]	[illegible]	[illegible]	[illegible]
[illegible]	Tralee,	[illegible]	[illegible]	[illegible]	[illegible]	[illegible]	[illegible]	[illegible]	[illegible]	[illegible]	[illegible]	[illegible]	[illegible]	[illegible]	[illegible]	[illegible]
	16. Limerick Co.															
[illegible]	Croom,	[illegible]	[illegible]	[illegible]	[illegible]	[illegible]	[illegible]	[illegible]	[illegible]	[illegible]	[illegible]	[illegible]	[illegible]	[illegible]	[illegible]	[illegible]
[illegible]	Kilmallock, part of,	[illegible]	[illegible]	[illegible]	[illegible]	[illegible]	[illegible]	[illegible]	[illegible]	[illegible]	[illegible]	[illegible]	[illegible]	[illegible]	[illegible]	[illegible]
[illegible]	Limerick, do.	[illegible]	[illegible]	[illegible]	[illegible]	[illegible]	[illegible]	[illegible]	[illegible]	[illegible]	[illegible]	[illegible]	[illegible]	[illegible]	[illegible]	[illegible]
[illegible]	Listowel, do.	[illegible]	[illegible]	[illegible]	[illegible]	[illegible]	[illegible]	[illegible]	[illegible]	[illegible]	[illegible]	[illegible]	[illegible]	[illegible]	[illegible]	[illegible]
[illegible]	Mitchelstown, do.	[illegible]	[illegible]	[illegible]	[illegible]	[illegible]	[illegible]	[illegible]	[illegible]	[illegible]	[illegible]	[illegible]	[illegible]	[illegible]	[illegible]	[illegible]
[illegible]	Newcastle,	[illegible]	[illegible]	[illegible]	[illegible]	[illegible]	[illegible]	[illegible]	[illegible]	[illegible]	[illegible]	[illegible]	[illegible]	[illegible]	[illegible]	[illegible]
[illegible]	Rathkeale,	[illegible]	[illegible]	[illegible]	[illegible]	[illegible]	[illegible]	[illegible]	[illegible]	[illegible]	[illegible]	[illegible]	[illegible]	[illegible]	[illegible]	[illegible]
[illegible]	Tipperary, part of,	[illegible]	[illegible]	[illegible]	[illegible]	[illegible]	[illegible]	[illegible]	[illegible]	[illegible]	[illegible]	[illegible]	[illegible]	[illegible]	[illegible]	[illegible]
	17. Tipperary Co.															

MARRIAGES in the Year 1836—in the SUPERINTENDENT REGISTRARS' DISTRICTS in each County.

II.—PROVINCE OF MUNSTER—continued.

No.	Superintendent Registrars' Districts.	Area in Statute Acres	Population 1861.	Total Marriages.	[illegible]	[illegible]	[illegible]	[illegible]	[illegible]	Total.	[illegible]	[illegible]	[illegible]	[illegible]	[illegible]	Total [illegible]	[illegible]
	[illegible]																
[illegible]	[illegible]	[illegible]	[illegible]	[illegible]	[illegible]	[illegible]	[illegible]	[illegible]	[illegible]	[illegible]	[illegible]	[illegible]	[illegible]	[illegible]	[illegible]	[illegible]	[illegible]
[illegible]	[illegible]	[illegible]	[illegible]	[illegible]	[illegible]	[illegible]	[illegible]	[illegible]	[illegible]	[illegible]	[illegible]	[illegible]	[illegible]	[illegible]	[illegible]	[illegible]	[illegible]
[illegible]	[illegible]	[illegible]	[illegible]	[illegible]	[illegible]	[illegible]	[illegible]	[illegible]	[illegible]	[illegible]	[illegible]	[illegible]	[illegible]	[illegible]	[illegible]	[illegible]	[illegible]
[illegible]	[illegible]	[illegible]	[illegible]	[illegible]	[illegible]	[illegible]	[illegible]	[illegible]	[illegible]	[illegible]	[illegible]	[illegible]	[illegible]	[illegible]	[illegible]	[illegible]	[illegible]
[illegible]	[illegible]	[illegible]	[illegible]	[illegible]	[illegible]	[illegible]	[illegible]	[illegible]	[illegible]	[illegible]	[illegible]	[illegible]	[illegible]	[illegible]	[illegible]	[illegible]	[illegible]
[illegible]	[illegible]	[illegible]	[illegible]	[illegible]	[illegible]	[illegible]	[illegible]	[illegible]	[illegible]	[illegible]	[illegible]	[illegible]	[illegible]	[illegible]	[illegible]	[illegible]	[illegible]
[illegible]	[illegible]	[illegible]	[illegible]	[illegible]	[illegible]	[illegible]	[illegible]	[illegible]	[illegible]	[illegible]	[illegible]	[illegible]	[illegible]	[illegible]	[illegible]	[illegible]	[illegible]

III.—PROVINCE OF ULSTER.

No.	Superintendent Registrars' Districts.	Area in Statute Acres	Population 1861.	Total Marriages.	[illegible]	[illegible]	[illegible]	[illegible]	[illegible]	Total.	[illegible]	[illegible]	[illegible]	[illegible]	[illegible]	Total [illegible]	[illegible]
	[illegible] Co.																
[illegible]	[illegible]	[illegible]	[illegible]	[illegible]	[illegible]	[illegible]	[illegible]	[illegible]	[illegible]	[illegible]	[illegible]	[illegible]	[illegible]	[illegible]	[illegible]	[illegible]	[illegible]
[illegible]	[illegible]	[illegible]	[illegible]	[illegible]	[illegible]	[illegible]	[illegible]	[illegible]	[illegible]	[illegible]	[illegible]	[illegible]	[illegible]	[illegible]	[illegible]	[illegible]	[illegible]
[illegible]	[illegible]	[illegible]	[illegible]	[illegible]	[illegible]	[illegible]	[illegible]	[illegible]	[illegible]	[illegible]	[illegible]	[illegible]	[illegible]	[illegible]	[illegible]	[illegible]	[illegible]
[illegible]	[illegible]	[illegible]	[illegible]	[illegible]	[illegible]	[illegible]	[illegible]	[illegible]	[illegible]	[illegible]	[illegible]	[illegible]	[illegible]	[illegible]	[illegible]	[illegible]	[illegible]
[illegible]	[illegible]	[illegible]	[illegible]	[illegible]	[illegible]	[illegible]	[illegible]	[illegible]	[illegible]	[illegible]	[illegible]	[illegible]	[illegible]	[illegible]	[illegible]	[illegible]	[illegible]
[illegible]	[illegible]	[illegible]	[illegible]	[illegible]	[illegible]	[illegible]	[illegible]	[illegible]	[illegible]	[illegible]	[illegible]	[illegible]	[illegible]	[illegible]	[illegible]	[illegible]	[illegible]
[illegible]	[illegible]	[illegible]	[illegible]	[illegible]	[illegible]	[illegible]	[illegible]	[illegible]	[illegible]	[illegible]	[illegible]	[illegible]	[illegible]	[illegible]	[illegible]	[illegible]	[illegible]
[illegible]	[illegible]	[illegible]	[illegible]	[illegible]	[illegible]	[illegible]	[illegible]	[illegible]	[illegible]	[illegible]	[illegible]	[illegible]	[illegible]	[illegible]	[illegible]	[illegible]	[illegible]
[illegible]	[illegible]	[illegible]	[illegible]	[illegible]	[illegible]	[illegible]	[illegible]	[illegible]	[illegible]	[illegible]	[illegible]	[illegible]	[illegible]	[illegible]	[illegible]	[illegible]	[illegible]
	[illegible] Co.																
[illegible]	[illegible]	[illegible]	[illegible]	[illegible]	[illegible]	[illegible]	[illegible]	[illegible]	[illegible]	[illegible]	[illegible]	[illegible]	[illegible]	[illegible]	[illegible]	[illegible]	[illegible]
[illegible]	[illegible]	[illegible]	[illegible]	[illegible]	[illegible]	[illegible]	[illegible]	[illegible]	[illegible]	[illegible]	[illegible]	[illegible]	[illegible]	[illegible]	[illegible]	[illegible]	[illegible]
[illegible]	[illegible]	[illegible]	[illegible]	[illegible]	[illegible]	[illegible]	[illegible]	[illegible]	[illegible]	[illegible]	[illegible]	[illegible]	[illegible]	[illegible]	[illegible]	[illegible]	[illegible]
[illegible]	[illegible]	[illegible]	[illegible]	[illegible]	[illegible]	[illegible]	[illegible]	[illegible]	[illegible]	[illegible]	[illegible]	[illegible]	[illegible]	[illegible]	[illegible]	[illegible]	[illegible]
[illegible]	[illegible]	[illegible]	[illegible]	[illegible]	[illegible]	[illegible]	[illegible]	[illegible]	[illegible]	[illegible]	[illegible]	[illegible]	[illegible]	[illegible]	[illegible]	[illegible]	[illegible]
[illegible]	[illegible]	[illegible]	[illegible]	[illegible]	[illegible]	[illegible]	[illegible]	[illegible]	[illegible]	[illegible]	[illegible]	[illegible]	[illegible]	[illegible]	[illegible]	[illegible]	[illegible]
	[illegible] Co.																
[illegible]	[illegible]	[illegible]	[illegible]	[illegible]	[illegible]	[illegible]	[illegible]	[illegible]	[illegible]	[illegible]	[illegible]	[illegible]	[illegible]	[illegible]	[illegible]	[illegible]	[illegible]
[illegible]	[illegible]	[illegible]	[illegible]	[illegible]	[illegible]	[illegible]	[illegible]	[illegible]	[illegible]	[illegible]	[illegible]	[illegible]	[illegible]	[illegible]	[illegible]	[illegible]	[illegible]
[illegible]	[illegible]	[illegible]	[illegible]	[illegible]	[illegible]	[illegible]	[illegible]	[illegible]	[illegible]	[illegible]	[illegible]	[illegible]	[illegible]	[illegible]	[illegible]	[illegible]	[illegible]
[illegible]	[illegible]	[illegible]	[illegible]	[illegible]	[illegible]	[illegible]	[illegible]	[illegible]	[illegible]	[illegible]	[illegible]	[illegible]	[illegible]	[illegible]	[illegible]	[illegible]	[illegible]
[illegible]	[illegible]	[illegible]	[illegible]	[illegible]	[illegible]	[illegible]	[illegible]	[illegible]	[illegible]	[illegible]	[illegible]	[illegible]	[illegible]	[illegible]	[illegible]	[illegible]	[illegible]
[illegible]	[illegible]	[illegible]	[illegible]	[illegible]	[illegible]	[illegible]	[illegible]	[illegible]	[illegible]	[illegible]	[illegible]	[illegible]	[illegible]	[illegible]	[illegible]	[illegible]	[illegible]
[illegible]	[illegible]	[illegible]	[illegible]	[illegible]	[illegible]	[illegible]	[illegible]	[illegible]	[illegible]	[illegible]	[illegible]	[illegible]	[illegible]	[illegible]	[illegible]	[illegible]	[illegible]
[illegible]	[illegible]	[illegible]	[illegible]	[illegible]	[illegible]	[illegible]	[illegible]	[illegible]	[illegible]	[illegible]	[illegible]	[illegible]	[illegible]	[illegible]	[illegible]	[illegible]	[illegible]
	[illegible] Co.																
[illegible]	[illegible]	[illegible]	[illegible]	[illegible]	[illegible]	[illegible]	[illegible]	[illegible]	[illegible]	[illegible]	[illegible]	[illegible]	[illegible]	[illegible]	[illegible]	[illegible]	[illegible]
[illegible]	[illegible]	[illegible]	[illegible]	[illegible]	[illegible]	[illegible]	[illegible]	[illegible]	[illegible]	[illegible]	[illegible]	[illegible]	[illegible]	[illegible]	[illegible]	[illegible]	[illegible]
[illegible]	[illegible]	[illegible]	[illegible]	[illegible]	[illegible]	[illegible]	[illegible]	[illegible]	[illegible]	[illegible]	[illegible]	[illegible]	[illegible]	[illegible]	[illegible]	[illegible]	[illegible]
[illegible]	[illegible]	[illegible]	[illegible]	[illegible]	[illegible]	[illegible]	[illegible]	[illegible]	[illegible]	[illegible]	[illegible]	[illegible]	[illegible]	[illegible]	[illegible]	[illegible]	[illegible]
[illegible]	[illegible]	[illegible]	[illegible]	[illegible]	[illegible]	[illegible]	[illegible]	[illegible]	[illegible]	[illegible]	[illegible]	[illegible]	[illegible]	[illegible]	[illegible]	[illegible]	[illegible]
[illegible]	[illegible]	[illegible]	[illegible]	[illegible]	[illegible]	[illegible]	[illegible]	[illegible]	[illegible]	[illegible]	[illegible]	[illegible]	[illegible]	[illegible]	[illegible]	[illegible]	[illegible]
[illegible]	[illegible]	[illegible]	[illegible]	[illegible]	[illegible]	[illegible]	[illegible]	[illegible]	[illegible]	[illegible]	[illegible]	[illegible]	[illegible]	[illegible]	[illegible]	[illegible]	[illegible]
[illegible]	[illegible]	[illegible]	[illegible]	[illegible]	[illegible]	[illegible]	[illegible]	[illegible]	[illegible]	[illegible]	[illegible]	[illegible]	[illegible]	[illegible]	[illegible]	[illegible]	[illegible]
[illegible]	[illegible]	[illegible]	[illegible]	[illegible]	[illegible]	[illegible]	[illegible]	[illegible]	[illegible]	[illegible]	[illegible]	[illegible]	[illegible]	[illegible]	[illegible]	[illegible]	[illegible]
[illegible]	[illegible]	[illegible]	[illegible]	[illegible]	[illegible]	[illegible]	[illegible]	[illegible]	[illegible]	[illegible]	[illegible]	[illegible]	[illegible]	[illegible]	[illegible]	[illegible]	[illegible]

MARRIAGES in the Year 1866—in the SUPERINTENDENT REGISTRARS' DISTRICTS in each County.

Registered in the Quarter ending the last day of: March	June	September	December	Contracted between: Bachelors and Spinsters	Bachelors and Widows	Widowers and Spinsters	Widowers and Widows	By: Males	Females	Of Persons not of Full Age: Males	Females	Signed the Marriage Register with Marks: Men	Women	Cases in which: both signed	one signed	SUPERINTENDENT REGISTRARS' DISTRICTS
																25. Westmeath Co.
[illegible]	[illegible]	[illegible]	[illegible]	[illegible]	[illegible]	[illegible]	[illegible]	[illegible]	[illegible]	[illegible]	[illegible]	[illegible]	[illegible]	[illegible]	[illegible]	Castletowndelvin, part of
[illegible]	[illegible]	[illegible]	[illegible]	[illegible]	[illegible]	[illegible]	[illegible]	[illegible]	[illegible]	[illegible]	[illegible]	[illegible]	[illegible]	[illegible]	[illegible]	Granard, do.
[illegible]	[illegible]	[illegible]	[illegible]	[illegible]	[illegible]	[illegible]	[illegible]	[illegible]	[illegible]	[illegible]	[illegible]	[illegible]	[illegible]	[illegible]	[illegible]	Mullingar.
[illegible]	[illegible]	[illegible]	[illegible]	[illegible]	[illegible]	[illegible]	[illegible]	[illegible]	[illegible]	[illegible]	[illegible]	[illegible]	[illegible]	[illegible]	[illegible]	Kilbeggan.
[illegible]	[illegible]	[illegible]	[illegible]	[illegible]	[illegible]	[illegible]	[illegible]	[illegible]	[illegible]	[illegible]	[illegible]	[illegible]	[illegible]	[illegible]	[illegible]	Athlone.
[illegible]	[illegible]	[illegible]	[illegible]	[illegible]	[illegible]	[illegible]	[illegible]	[illegible]	[illegible]	[illegible]	[illegible]	[illegible]	[illegible]	[illegible]	[illegible]	[illegible], part of
[illegible]	[illegible]	[illegible]	[illegible]	[illegible]	[illegible]	[illegible]	[illegible]	[illegible]	[illegible]	[illegible]	[illegible]	[illegible]	[illegible]	[illegible]	[illegible]	Trim, part of

MARRIAGES in the Year 1866—in the SUPERINTENDENT REGISTRARS' DISTRICTS in each County.

Registered in the Quarter ending the last day of: March	June	September	December	Contracted between: Bachelors and Spinsters	Bachelors and Widows	Widowers and Spinsters	Widowers and Widows	By: Males	Females	Of Persons not of Full Age: Males	Females	Signed the Marriage Register with Marks: Men	Women	Cases in which: both signed	one signed	SUPERINTENDENT REGISTRARS' DISTRICTS
																29. Antrim Co.
[illegible]	[illegible]	[illegible]	[illegible]	[illegible]	[illegible]	[illegible]	[illegible]	[illegible]	[illegible]	[illegible]	[illegible]	[illegible]	[illegible]	[illegible]	[illegible]	Antrim.
[illegible]	[illegible]	[illegible]	[illegible]	[illegible]	[illegible]	[illegible]	[illegible]	[illegible]	[illegible]	[illegible]	[illegible]	[illegible]	[illegible]	[illegible]	[illegible]	Ballycastle.
[illegible]	[illegible]	[illegible]	[illegible]	[illegible]	[illegible]	[illegible]	[illegible]	[illegible]	[illegible]	[illegible]	[illegible]	[illegible]	[illegible]	[illegible]	[illegible]	Ballymena.
[illegible]	[illegible]	[illegible]	[illegible]	[illegible]	[illegible]	[illegible]	[illegible]	[illegible]	[illegible]	[illegible]	[illegible]	[illegible]	[illegible]	[illegible]	[illegible]	Ballymoney, part of
[illegible]	[illegible]	[illegible]	[illegible]	[illegible]	[illegible]	[illegible]	[illegible]	[illegible]	[illegible]	[illegible]	[illegible]	[illegible]	[illegible]	[illegible]	[illegible]	Belfast, do.
[illegible]	[illegible]	[illegible]	[illegible]	[illegible]	[illegible]	[illegible]	[illegible]	[illegible]	[illegible]	[illegible]	[illegible]	[illegible]	[illegible]	[illegible]	[illegible]	[illegible], do.
[illegible]	[illegible]	[illegible]	[illegible]	[illegible]	[illegible]	[illegible]	[illegible]	[illegible]	[illegible]	[illegible]	[illegible]	[illegible]	[illegible]	[illegible]	[illegible]	Larne.
[illegible]	[illegible]	[illegible]	[illegible]	[illegible]	[illegible]	[illegible]	[illegible]	[illegible]	[illegible]	[illegible]	[illegible]	[illegible]	[illegible]	[illegible]	[illegible]	Lisburn, part of
[illegible]	[illegible]	[illegible]	[illegible]	[illegible]	[illegible]	[illegible]	[illegible]	[illegible]	[illegible]	[illegible]	[illegible]	[illegible]	[illegible]	[illegible]	[illegible]	Lurgan, do.
																30. Armagh Co.
[illegible]	[illegible]	[illegible]	[illegible]	[illegible]	[illegible]	[illegible]	[illegible]	[illegible]	[illegible]	[illegible]	[illegible]	[illegible]	[illegible]	[illegible]	[illegible]	Armagh, part of
[illegible]	[illegible]	[illegible]	[illegible]	[illegible]	[illegible]	[illegible]	[illegible]	[illegible]	[illegible]	[illegible]	[illegible]	[illegible]	[illegible]	[illegible]	[illegible]	Banbridge, do.
[illegible]	[illegible]	[illegible]	[illegible]	[illegible]	[illegible]	[illegible]	[illegible]	[illegible]	[illegible]	[illegible]	[illegible]	[illegible]	[illegible]	[illegible]	[illegible]	Castleblayney, do.
[illegible]	[illegible]	[illegible]	[illegible]	[illegible]	[illegible]	[illegible]	[illegible]	[illegible]	[illegible]	[illegible]	[illegible]	[illegible]	[illegible]	[illegible]	[illegible]	Dundalk, do.
[illegible]	[illegible]	[illegible]	[illegible]	[illegible]	[illegible]	[illegible]	[illegible]	[illegible]	[illegible]	[illegible]	[illegible]	[illegible]	[illegible]	[illegible]	[illegible]	Lurgan, do.
[illegible]	[illegible]	[illegible]	[illegible]	[illegible]	[illegible]	[illegible]	[illegible]	[illegible]	[illegible]	[illegible]	[illegible]	[illegible]	[illegible]	[illegible]	[illegible]	Newry, do.
																31. Cavan Co.
[illegible]	[illegible]	[illegible]	[illegible]	[illegible]	[illegible]	[illegible]	[illegible]	[illegible]	[illegible]	[illegible]	[illegible]	[illegible]	[illegible]	[illegible]	[illegible]	Bailieborough.
[illegible]	[illegible]	[illegible]	[illegible]	[illegible]	[illegible]	[illegible]	[illegible]	[illegible]	[illegible]	[illegible]	[illegible]	[illegible]	[illegible]	[illegible]	[illegible]	[illegible], part of
[illegible]	[illegible]	[illegible]	[illegible]	[illegible]	[illegible]	[illegible]	[illegible]	[illegible]	[illegible]	[illegible]	[illegible]	[illegible]	[illegible]	[illegible]	[illegible]	Cavan.
[illegible]	[illegible]	[illegible]	[illegible]	[illegible]	[illegible]	[illegible]	[illegible]	[illegible]	[illegible]	[illegible]	[illegible]	[illegible]	[illegible]	[illegible]	[illegible]	Cootehill, part of
[illegible]	[illegible]	[illegible]	[illegible]	[illegible]	[illegible]	[illegible]	[illegible]	[illegible]	[illegible]	[illegible]	[illegible]	[illegible]	[illegible]	[illegible]	[illegible]	Enniskillen, do.
[illegible]	[illegible]	[illegible]	[illegible]	[illegible]	[illegible]	[illegible]	[illegible]	[illegible]	[illegible]	[illegible]	[illegible]	[illegible]	[illegible]	[illegible]	[illegible]	Oldcastle, do.
[illegible]	[illegible]	[illegible]	[illegible]	[illegible]	[illegible]	[illegible]	[illegible]	[illegible]	[illegible]	[illegible]	[illegible]	[illegible]	[illegible]	[illegible]	[illegible]	Kells, do.
[illegible]	[illegible]	[illegible]	[illegible]	[illegible]	[illegible]	[illegible]	[illegible]	[illegible]	[illegible]	[illegible]	[illegible]	[illegible]	[illegible]	[illegible]	[illegible]	[illegible], do.
																32. Donegal Co.
[illegible]	[illegible]	[illegible]	[illegible]	[illegible]	[illegible]	[illegible]	[illegible]	[illegible]	[illegible]	[illegible]	[illegible]	[illegible]	[illegible]	[illegible]	[illegible]	Ballyshannon, part of
[illegible]	[illegible]	[illegible]	[illegible]	[illegible]	[illegible]	[illegible]	[illegible]	[illegible]	[illegible]	[illegible]	[illegible]	[illegible]	[illegible]	[illegible]	[illegible]	Donegal.
[illegible]	[illegible]	[illegible]	[illegible]	[illegible]	[illegible]	[illegible]	[illegible]	[illegible]	[illegible]	[illegible]	[illegible]	[illegible]	[illegible]	[illegible]	[illegible]	Dunfanaghy.
[illegible]	[illegible]	[illegible]	[illegible]	[illegible]	[illegible]	[illegible]	[illegible]	[illegible]	[illegible]	[illegible]	[illegible]	[illegible]	[illegible]	[illegible]	[illegible]	Glenties.
[illegible]	[illegible]	[illegible]	[illegible]	[illegible]	[illegible]	[illegible]	[illegible]	[illegible]	[illegible]	[illegible]	[illegible]	[illegible]	[illegible]	[illegible]	[illegible]	Inishowen.
[illegible]	[illegible]	[illegible]	[illegible]	[illegible]	[illegible]	[illegible]	[illegible]	[illegible]	[illegible]	[illegible]	[illegible]	[illegible]	[illegible]	[illegible]	[illegible]	Letterkenny.
[illegible]	[illegible]	[illegible]	[illegible]	[illegible]	[illegible]	[illegible]	[illegible]	[illegible]	[illegible]	[illegible]	[illegible]	[illegible]	[illegible]	[illegible]	[illegible]	Londonderry, part of
[illegible]	[illegible]	[illegible]	[illegible]	[illegible]	[illegible]	[illegible]	[illegible]	[illegible]	[illegible]	[illegible]	[illegible]	[illegible]	[illegible]	[illegible]	[illegible]	Milford.
[illegible]	[illegible]	[illegible]	[illegible]	[illegible]	[illegible]	[illegible]	[illegible]	[illegible]	[illegible]	[illegible]	[illegible]	[illegible]	[illegible]	[illegible]	[illegible]	Strabane, part of
[illegible]	[illegible]	[illegible]	[illegible]	[illegible]	[illegible]	[illegible]	[illegible]	[illegible]	[illegible]	[illegible]	[illegible]	[illegible]	[illegible]	[illegible]	[illegible]	Stranorlar.

II.—PROVINCE OF ULSTER—continued.

No.	Superintendent Registrars' Districts	Area in Statute Acres	Population	Total Marriages	[illegible]	[illegible]	[illegible]	[illegible]	[illegible]	Total	[illegible]	[illegible]	[illegible]	[illegible]	[illegible]	[illegible]	[illegible]
	Down Co.																
[illegible]	[illegible]	[illegible]	[illegible]	[illegible]	[illegible]	[illegible]	[illegible]	[illegible]	[illegible]	[illegible]	[illegible]	[illegible]	[illegible]	[illegible]	[illegible]	[illegible]	[illegible]
[illegible]	[illegible]	[illegible]	[illegible]	[illegible]	[illegible]	[illegible]	[illegible]	[illegible]	[illegible]	[illegible]	[illegible]	[illegible]	[illegible]	[illegible]	[illegible]	[illegible]	[illegible]
[illegible]	[illegible]	[illegible]	[illegible]	[illegible]	[illegible]	[illegible]	[illegible]	[illegible]	[illegible]	[illegible]	[illegible]	[illegible]	[illegible]	[illegible]	[illegible]	[illegible]	[illegible]
[illegible]	[illegible]	[illegible]	[illegible]	[illegible]	[illegible]	[illegible]	[illegible]	[illegible]	[illegible]	[illegible]	[illegible]	[illegible]	[illegible]	[illegible]	[illegible]	[illegible]	[illegible]
[illegible]	[illegible]	[illegible]	[illegible]	[illegible]	[illegible]	[illegible]	[illegible]	[illegible]	[illegible]	[illegible]	[illegible]	[illegible]	[illegible]	[illegible]	[illegible]	[illegible]	[illegible]
[illegible]	[illegible]	[illegible]	[illegible]	[illegible]	[illegible]	[illegible]	[illegible]	[illegible]	[illegible]	[illegible]	[illegible]	[illegible]	[illegible]	[illegible]	[illegible]	[illegible]	[illegible]
[illegible]	[illegible]	[illegible]	[illegible]	[illegible]	[illegible]	[illegible]	[illegible]	[illegible]	[illegible]	[illegible]	[illegible]	[illegible]	[illegible]	[illegible]	[illegible]	[illegible]	[illegible]
[illegible]	[illegible]	[illegible]	[illegible]	[illegible]	[illegible]	[illegible]	[illegible]	[illegible]	[illegible]	[illegible]	[illegible]	[illegible]	[illegible]	[illegible]	[illegible]	[illegible]	[illegible]
	Fermanagh Co.																
[illegible]	[illegible]	[illegible]	[illegible]	[illegible]	[illegible]	[illegible]	[illegible]	[illegible]	[illegible]	[illegible]	[illegible]	[illegible]	[illegible]	[illegible]	[illegible]	[illegible]	[illegible]
[illegible]	[illegible]	[illegible]	[illegible]	[illegible]	[illegible]	[illegible]	[illegible]	[illegible]	[illegible]	[illegible]	[illegible]	[illegible]	[illegible]	[illegible]	[illegible]	[illegible]	[illegible]
[illegible]	[illegible]	[illegible]	[illegible]	[illegible]	[illegible]	[illegible]	[illegible]	[illegible]	[illegible]	[illegible]	[illegible]	[illegible]	[illegible]	[illegible]	[illegible]	[illegible]	[illegible]
[illegible]	[illegible]	[illegible]	[illegible]	[illegible]	[illegible]	[illegible]	[illegible]	[illegible]	[illegible]	[illegible]	[illegible]	[illegible]	[illegible]	[illegible]	[illegible]	[illegible]	[illegible]
[illegible]	[illegible]	[illegible]	[illegible]	[illegible]	[illegible]	[illegible]	[illegible]	[illegible]	[illegible]	[illegible]	[illegible]	[illegible]	[illegible]	[illegible]	[illegible]	[illegible]	[illegible]
	Londonderry Co.																
[illegible]	[illegible]	[illegible]	[illegible]	[illegible]	[illegible]	[illegible]	[illegible]	[illegible]	[illegible]	[illegible]	[illegible]	[illegible]	[illegible]	[illegible]	[illegible]	[illegible]	[illegible]
[illegible]	[illegible]	[illegible]	[illegible]	[illegible]	[illegible]	[illegible]	[illegible]	[illegible]	[illegible]	[illegible]	[illegible]	[illegible]	[illegible]	[illegible]	[illegible]	[illegible]	[illegible]
[illegible]	[illegible]	[illegible]	[illegible]	[illegible]	[illegible]	[illegible]	[illegible]	[illegible]	[illegible]	[illegible]	[illegible]	[illegible]	[illegible]	[illegible]	[illegible]	[illegible]	[illegible]
[illegible]	[illegible]	[illegible]	[illegible]	[illegible]	[illegible]	[illegible]	[illegible]	[illegible]	[illegible]	[illegible]	[illegible]	[illegible]	[illegible]	[illegible]	[illegible]	[illegible]	[illegible]
[illegible]	[illegible]	[illegible]	[illegible]	[illegible]	[illegible]	[illegible]	[illegible]	[illegible]	[illegible]	[illegible]	[illegible]	[illegible]	[illegible]	[illegible]	[illegible]	[illegible]	[illegible]
	Monaghan Co.																
[illegible]	[illegible]	[illegible]	[illegible]	[illegible]	[illegible]	[illegible]	[illegible]	[illegible]	[illegible]	[illegible]	[illegible]	[illegible]	[illegible]	[illegible]	[illegible]	[illegible]	[illegible]
[illegible]	[illegible]	[illegible]	[illegible]	[illegible]	[illegible]	[illegible]	[illegible]	[illegible]	[illegible]	[illegible]	[illegible]	[illegible]	[illegible]	[illegible]	[illegible]	[illegible]	[illegible]
[illegible]	[illegible]	[illegible]	[illegible]	[illegible]	[illegible]	[illegible]	[illegible]	[illegible]	[illegible]	[illegible]	[illegible]	[illegible]	[illegible]	[illegible]	[illegible]	[illegible]	[illegible]
[illegible]	[illegible]	[illegible]	[illegible]	[illegible]	[illegible]	[illegible]	[illegible]	[illegible]	[illegible]	[illegible]	[illegible]	[illegible]	[illegible]	[illegible]	[illegible]	[illegible]	[illegible]
[illegible]	[illegible]	[illegible]	[illegible]	[illegible]	[illegible]	[illegible]	[illegible]	[illegible]	[illegible]	[illegible]	[illegible]	[illegible]	[illegible]	[illegible]	[illegible]	[illegible]	[illegible]
[illegible]	[illegible]	[illegible]	[illegible]	[illegible]	[illegible]	[illegible]	[illegible]	[illegible]	[illegible]	[illegible]	[illegible]	[illegible]	[illegible]	[illegible]	[illegible]	[illegible]	[illegible]
[illegible]	[illegible]	[illegible]	[illegible]	[illegible]	[illegible]	[illegible]	[illegible]	[illegible]	[illegible]	[illegible]	[illegible]	[illegible]	[illegible]	[illegible]	[illegible]	[illegible]	[illegible]
	Tyrone Co.																
[illegible]	[illegible]	[illegible]	[illegible]	[illegible]	[illegible]	[illegible]	[illegible]	[illegible]	[illegible]	[illegible]	[illegible]	[illegible]	[illegible]	[illegible]	[illegible]	[illegible]	[illegible]
[illegible]	[illegible]	[illegible]	[illegible]	[illegible]	[illegible]	[illegible]	[illegible]	[illegible]	[illegible]	[illegible]	[illegible]	[illegible]	[illegible]	[illegible]	[illegible]	[illegible]	[illegible]
[illegible]	[illegible]	[illegible]	[illegible]	[illegible]	[illegible]	[illegible]	[illegible]	[illegible]	[illegible]	[illegible]	[illegible]	[illegible]	[illegible]	[illegible]	[illegible]	[illegible]	[illegible]
[illegible]	[illegible]	[illegible]	[illegible]	[illegible]	[illegible]	[illegible]	[illegible]	[illegible]	[illegible]	[illegible]	[illegible]	[illegible]	[illegible]	[illegible]	[illegible]	[illegible]	[illegible]
[illegible]	[illegible]	[illegible]	[illegible]	[illegible]	[illegible]	[illegible]	[illegible]	[illegible]	[illegible]	[illegible]	[illegible]	[illegible]	[illegible]	[illegible]	[illegible]	[illegible]	[illegible]
[illegible]	[illegible]	[illegible]	[illegible]	[illegible]	[illegible]	[illegible]	[illegible]	[illegible]	[illegible]	[illegible]	[illegible]	[illegible]	[illegible]	[illegible]	[illegible]	[illegible]	[illegible]
[illegible]	[illegible]	[illegible]	[illegible]	[illegible]	[illegible]	[illegible]	[illegible]	[illegible]	[illegible]	[illegible]	[illegible]	[illegible]	[illegible]	[illegible]	[illegible]	[illegible]	[illegible]
[illegible]	[illegible]	[illegible]	[illegible]	[illegible]	[illegible]	[illegible]	[illegible]	[illegible]	[illegible]	[illegible]	[illegible]	[illegible]	[illegible]	[illegible]	[illegible]	[illegible]	[illegible]
[illegible]	[illegible]	[illegible]	[illegible]	[illegible]	[illegible]	[illegible]	[illegible]	[illegible]	[illegible]	[illegible]	[illegible]	[illegible]	[illegible]	[illegible]	[illegible]	[illegible]	[illegible]

MARRIAGES in the Year 1896—in the SUPERINTENDENT REGISTRARS' DISTRICTS in each County.

MARRIAGES.																	
Registered in the Quarter ending the last day of				Contracted between				[illegible]		Of Persons under 21 years of age.		Signed the Marriage Register with Marks.					SUPERINTENDENT REGISTRARS' DISTRICTS.
														Cases in which			
March.	June.	September.	December.	Bachelors and Spinsters.	Bachelors and Widows.	Widowers and Spinsters.	Widowers and Widows.	[illegible]	[illegible]	Men.	Women.	Men.	Women.	Both signed.	One signed.		
																	63. Down Co.
[illegible]	[illegible]	[illegible]	[illegible]	[illegible]	[illegible]	[illegible]	[illegible]	[illegible]	[illegible]	[illegible]	[illegible]	[illegible]	[illegible]	[illegible]	[illegible]		Banbridge, part of
[illegible]	[illegible]	[illegible]	[illegible]	[illegible]	[illegible]	[illegible]	[illegible]	[illegible]	[illegible]	[illegible]	[illegible]	[illegible]	[illegible]	[illegible]	[illegible]		Belfast, do.
[illegible]	[illegible]	[illegible]	[illegible]	[illegible]	[illegible]	[illegible]	[illegible]	[illegible]	[illegible]	[illegible]	[illegible]	[illegible]	[illegible]	[illegible]	[illegible]		Downpatrick.
[illegible]	[illegible]	[illegible]	[illegible]	[illegible]	[illegible]	[illegible]	[illegible]	[illegible]	[illegible]	[illegible]	[illegible]	[illegible]	[illegible]	[illegible]	[illegible]		Kilkeel.
[illegible]	[illegible]	[illegible]	[illegible]	[illegible]	[illegible]	[illegible]	[illegible]	[illegible]	[illegible]	[illegible]	[illegible]	[illegible]	[illegible]	[illegible]	[illegible]		Lisburn, part of
[illegible]	[illegible]	[illegible]	[illegible]	[illegible]	[illegible]	[illegible]	[illegible]	[illegible]	[illegible]	[illegible]	[illegible]	[illegible]	[illegible]	[illegible]	[illegible]		Lurgan, do.
[illegible]	[illegible]	[illegible]	[illegible]	[illegible]	[illegible]	[illegible]	[illegible]	[illegible]	[illegible]	[illegible]	[illegible]	[illegible]	[illegible]	[illegible]	[illegible]		Newry, do.
[illegible]	[illegible]	[illegible]	[illegible]	[illegible]	[illegible]	[illegible]	[illegible]	[illegible]	[illegible]	[illegible]	[illegible]	[illegible]	[illegible]	[illegible]	[illegible]		Newtownards.
																	64. Fermanagh Co.
[illegible]	[illegible]	[illegible]	[illegible]	[illegible]	[illegible]	[illegible]	[illegible]	[illegible]	[illegible]	[illegible]	[illegible]	[illegible]	[illegible]	[illegible]	[illegible]		Ballyshannon, part of
[illegible]	[illegible]	[illegible]	[illegible]	[illegible]	[illegible]	[illegible]	[illegible]	[illegible]	[illegible]	[illegible]	[illegible]	[illegible]	[illegible]	[illegible]	[illegible]		Clones, do.
[illegible]	[illegible]	[illegible]	[illegible]	[illegible]	[illegible]	[illegible]	[illegible]	[illegible]	[illegible]	[illegible]	[illegible]	[illegible]	[illegible]	[illegible]	[illegible]		Enniskillen, do.
[illegible]	[illegible]	[illegible]	[illegible]	[illegible]	[illegible]	[illegible]	[illegible]	[illegible]	[illegible]	[illegible]	[illegible]	[illegible]	[illegible]	[illegible]	[illegible]		Irvinestown, do.
[illegible]	[illegible]	[illegible]	[illegible]	[illegible]	[illegible]	[illegible]	[illegible]	[illegible]	[illegible]	[illegible]	[illegible]	[illegible]	[illegible]	[illegible]	[illegible]		Lisnaskea.
																	65. Londonderry Co.
[illegible]	[illegible]	[illegible]	[illegible]	[illegible]	[illegible]	[illegible]	[illegible]	[illegible]	[illegible]	[illegible]	[illegible]	[illegible]	[illegible]	[illegible]	[illegible]		Ballymoney, part of
[illegible]	[illegible]	[illegible]	[illegible]	[illegible]	[illegible]	[illegible]	[illegible]	[illegible]	[illegible]	[illegible]	[illegible]	[illegible]	[illegible]	[illegible]	[illegible]		Coleraine, do.
[illegible]	[illegible]	[illegible]	[illegible]	[illegible]	[illegible]	[illegible]	[illegible]	[illegible]	[illegible]	[illegible]	[illegible]	[illegible]	[illegible]	[illegible]	[illegible]		Limavady.
[illegible]	[illegible]	[illegible]	[illegible]	[illegible]	[illegible]	[illegible]	[illegible]	[illegible]	[illegible]	[illegible]	[illegible]	[illegible]	[illegible]	[illegible]	[illegible]		Londonderry, part of
[illegible]	[illegible]	[illegible]	[illegible]	[illegible]	[illegible]	[illegible]	[illegible]	[illegible]	[illegible]	[illegible]	[illegible]	[illegible]	[illegible]	[illegible]	[illegible]		Magherafelt.
																	66. Monaghan Co.
[illegible]	[illegible]	[illegible]	[illegible]	[illegible]	[illegible]	[illegible]	[illegible]	[illegible]	[illegible]	[illegible]	[illegible]	[illegible]	[illegible]	[illegible]	[illegible]		Carrickmacross.
[illegible]	[illegible]	[illegible]	[illegible]	[illegible]	[illegible]	[illegible]	[illegible]	[illegible]	[illegible]	[illegible]	[illegible]	[illegible]	[illegible]	[illegible]	[illegible]		Castleblayney, part of
[illegible]	[illegible]	[illegible]	[illegible]	[illegible]	[illegible]	[illegible]	[illegible]	[illegible]	[illegible]	[illegible]	[illegible]	[illegible]	[illegible]	[illegible]	[illegible]		Clogher, do.
[illegible]	[illegible]	[illegible]	[illegible]	[illegible]	[illegible]	[illegible]	[illegible]	[illegible]	[illegible]	[illegible]	[illegible]	[illegible]	[illegible]	[illegible]	[illegible]		Clones, do.
[illegible]	[illegible]	[illegible]	[illegible]	[illegible]	[illegible]	[illegible]	[illegible]	[illegible]	[illegible]	[illegible]	[illegible]	[illegible]	[illegible]	[illegible]	[illegible]		Cootehill, do.
[illegible]	[illegible]	[illegible]	[illegible]	[illegible]	[illegible]	[illegible]	[illegible]	[illegible]	[illegible]	[illegible]	[illegible]	[illegible]	[illegible]	[illegible]	[illegible]		Dundalk, do.
[illegible]	[illegible]	[illegible]	[illegible]	[illegible]	[illegible]	[illegible]	[illegible]	[illegible]	[illegible]	[illegible]	[illegible]	[illegible]	[illegible]	[illegible]	[illegible]		Monaghan.
																	67. Tyrone Co.
[illegible]	[illegible]	[illegible]	[illegible]	[illegible]	[illegible]	[illegible]	[illegible]	[illegible]	[illegible]	[illegible]	[illegible]	[illegible]	[illegible]	[illegible]	[illegible]		Armagh, part of
[illegible]	[illegible]	[illegible]	[illegible]	[illegible]	[illegible]	[illegible]	[illegible]	[illegible]	[illegible]	[illegible]	[illegible]	[illegible]	[illegible]	[illegible]	[illegible]		Castlederg.
[illegible]	[illegible]	[illegible]	[illegible]	[illegible]	[illegible]	[illegible]	[illegible]	[illegible]	[illegible]	[illegible]	[illegible]	[illegible]	[illegible]	[illegible]	[illegible]		Clogher, part of
[illegible]	[illegible]	[illegible]	[illegible]	[illegible]	[illegible]	[illegible]	[illegible]	[illegible]	[illegible]	[illegible]	[illegible]	[illegible]	[illegible]	[illegible]	[illegible]		Cookstown.
[illegible]	[illegible]	[illegible]	[illegible]	[illegible]	[illegible]	[illegible]	[illegible]	[illegible]	[illegible]	[illegible]	[illegible]	[illegible]	[illegible]	[illegible]	[illegible]		[illegible]
[illegible]	[illegible]	[illegible]	[illegible]	[illegible]	[illegible]	[illegible]	[illegible]	[illegible]	[illegible]	[illegible]	[illegible]	[illegible]	[illegible]	[illegible]	[illegible]		Enniskillen, part of
[illegible]	[illegible]	[illegible]	[illegible]	[illegible]	[illegible]	[illegible]	[illegible]	[illegible]	[illegible]	[illegible]	[illegible]	[illegible]	[illegible]	[illegible]	[illegible]		[illegible], do.
[illegible]	[illegible]	[illegible]	[illegible]	[illegible]	[illegible]	[illegible]	[illegible]	[illegible]	[illegible]	[illegible]	[illegible]	[illegible]	[illegible]	[illegible]	[illegible]		Omagh.
[illegible]	[illegible]	[illegible]	[illegible]	[illegible]	[illegible]	[illegible]	[illegible]	[illegible]	[illegible]	[illegible]	[illegible]	[illegible]	[illegible]	[illegible]	[illegible]		Strabane, part of

IV.—PROVINCE OF CONNAUGHT.—

MARRIAGES

No.	District	Area	Population	TOTAL MARRIAGES
	[illegible] Co.			
[illegible]	[illegible]	[illegible]	[illegible]	[illegible]
[illegible]	[illegible]	[illegible]	[illegible]	[illegible]
[illegible]	[illegible]	[illegible]	[illegible]	[illegible]
[illegible]	[illegible]	[illegible]	[illegible]	[illegible]
[illegible]	[illegible]	[illegible]	[illegible]	[illegible]
[illegible]	[illegible]	[illegible]	[illegible]	[illegible]
[illegible]	[illegible]	[illegible]	[illegible]	[illegible]
[illegible]	[illegible]	[illegible]	[illegible]	[illegible]
[illegible]	[illegible]	[illegible]	[illegible]	[illegible]
[illegible]	[illegible]	[illegible]	[illegible]	[illegible]
[illegible]	[illegible]	[illegible]	[illegible]	[illegible]
[illegible]	[illegible]	[illegible]	[illegible]	[illegible]
[illegible]	[illegible]	[illegible]	[illegible]	[illegible]
	[illegible] Co.			
[illegible]	[illegible]	[illegible]	[illegible]	[illegible]
[illegible]	[illegible]	[illegible]	[illegible]	[illegible]
[illegible]	[illegible]	[illegible]	[illegible]	[illegible]
[illegible]	[illegible]	[illegible]	[illegible]	[illegible]
[illegible]	[illegible]	[illegible]	[illegible]	[illegible]
	[illegible]. Mayo Co.			
[illegible]	[illegible]	[illegible]	[illegible]	[illegible]
[illegible]	[illegible]	[illegible]	[illegible]	[illegible]
[illegible]	[illegible]	[illegible]	[illegible]	[illegible]
[illegible]	[illegible]	[illegible]	[illegible]	[illegible]
[illegible]	[illegible]	[illegible]	[illegible]	[illegible]
[illegible]	[illegible]	[illegible]	[illegible]	[illegible]
[illegible]	[illegible]	[illegible]	[illegible]	[illegible]
[illegible]	[illegible]	[illegible]	[illegible]	[illegible]
[illegible]	[illegible]	[illegible]	[illegible]	[illegible]
	[illegible]. Roscommon Co.			
[illegible]	[illegible]	[illegible]	[illegible]	[illegible]
[illegible]	[illegible]	[illegible]	[illegible]	[illegible]
[illegible]	[illegible]	[illegible]	[illegible]	[illegible]
[illegible]	[illegible]	[illegible]	[illegible]	[illegible]
[illegible]	[illegible]	[illegible]	[illegible]	[illegible]

MARRIAGES in the Year 1896—in the SUPERINTENDENT REGISTRARS' DISTRICTS in each County.

MARRIAGES.																
Registered in the Quarter ending the last day of				Contracted between				Of [illegible]		Of Persons not of full Age		Signed the Marriage Register with marks				SUPERINTENDENT REGISTRARS' DISTRICTS.
[illegible]	[illegible]	[illegible]	[illegible]	[illegible]	[illegible]	[illegible]	[illegible]	[illegible]	[illegible]	[illegible]	[illegible]	[illegible]	[illegible]	Cases in which [illegible]	[illegible]	
																28. Galway Co.
[illegible]	[illegible]	[illegible]	[illegible]	[illegible]	[illegible]	[illegible]	[illegible]	[illegible]	[illegible]	[illegible]	[illegible]	[illegible]	[illegible]	[illegible]	[illegible]	Ballinasloe, part of
.	.	.	.	.	.	.	.	.	.	.	.	.	.	.	.	Ballinrobe, do.
[illegible]	[illegible]	[illegible]	[illegible]	[illegible]	[illegible]	[illegible]	[illegible]	[illegible]	[illegible]	[illegible]	[illegible]	[illegible]	[illegible]	[illegible]	[illegible]	Clifden.
[illegible]	[illegible]	[illegible]	[illegible]	[illegible]	[illegible]	[illegible]	[illegible]	[illegible]	[illegible]	[illegible]	[illegible]	[illegible]	[illegible]	[illegible]	[illegible]	Galway.
[illegible]	[illegible]	[illegible]	[illegible]	[illegible]	[illegible]	[illegible]	[illegible]	[illegible]	[illegible]	[illegible]	[illegible]	[illegible]	[illegible]	[illegible]	[illegible]	Glennamaddy.
[illegible]	[illegible]	[illegible]	[illegible]	[illegible]	[illegible]	[illegible]	[illegible]	[illegible]	[illegible]	[illegible]	[illegible]	[illegible]	[illegible]	[illegible]	[illegible]	Gort.
[illegible]	[illegible]	[illegible]	[illegible]	[illegible]	[illegible]	[illegible]	[illegible]	[illegible]	[illegible]	[illegible]	[illegible]	[illegible]	[illegible]	[illegible]	[illegible]	Loughrea.
[illegible]	[illegible]	[illegible]	[illegible]	[illegible]	[illegible]	[illegible]	[illegible]	[illegible]	[illegible]	[illegible]	[illegible]	[illegible]	[illegible]	[illegible]	[illegible]	Mountbellew.
[illegible]	[illegible]	[illegible]	[illegible]	[illegible]	[illegible]	[illegible]	[illegible]	[illegible]	[illegible]	[illegible]	[illegible]	[illegible]	[illegible]	[illegible]	[illegible]	Oughterard.
[illegible]	[illegible]	[illegible]	[illegible]	[illegible]	[illegible]	[illegible]	[illegible]	[illegible]	[illegible]	[illegible]	[illegible]	[illegible]	[illegible]	[illegible]	[illegible]	Portumna.
[illegible]	[illegible]	[illegible]	[illegible]	[illegible]	[illegible]	[illegible]	[illegible]	[illegible]	[illegible]	[illegible]	[illegible]	[illegible]	[illegible]	[illegible]	[illegible]	Roscommon, part of
[illegible]	[illegible]	[illegible]	[illegible]	[illegible]	[illegible]	[illegible]	[illegible]	[illegible]	[illegible]	[illegible]	[illegible]	[illegible]	[illegible]	[illegible]	[illegible]	Scarriff, do.
[illegible]	[illegible]	[illegible]	[illegible]	[illegible]	[illegible]	[illegible]	[illegible]	[illegible]	[illegible]	[illegible]	[illegible]	[illegible]	[illegible]	[illegible]	[illegible]	Tuam.
																29. Leitrim Co.
[illegible]	[illegible]	[illegible]	[illegible]	[illegible]	[illegible]	[illegible]	[illegible]	[illegible]	[illegible]	[illegible]	[illegible]	[illegible]	[illegible]	[illegible]	[illegible]	Ballyshannon, part of
[illegible]	[illegible]	[illegible]	[illegible]	[illegible]	[illegible]	[illegible]	[illegible]	[illegible]	[illegible]	[illegible]	[illegible]	[illegible]	[illegible]	[illegible]	[illegible]	Bawnboy, do.
[illegible]	[illegible]	[illegible]	[illegible]	[illegible]	[illegible]	[illegible]	[illegible]	[illegible]	[illegible]	[illegible]	[illegible]	[illegible]	[illegible]	[illegible]	[illegible]	Carrick-on-Shannon, do.
[illegible]	[illegible]	[illegible]	[illegible]	[illegible]	[illegible]	[illegible]	[illegible]	[illegible]	[illegible]	[illegible]	[illegible]	[illegible]	[illegible]	[illegible]	[illegible]	Manorhamilton.
[illegible]	[illegible]	[illegible]	[illegible]	[illegible]	[illegible]	[illegible]	[illegible]	[illegible]	[illegible]	[illegible]	[illegible]	[illegible]	[illegible]	[illegible]	[illegible]	Mohill.
																30. Mayo Co.
[illegible]	[illegible]	[illegible]	[illegible]	[illegible]	[illegible]	[illegible]	[illegible]	[illegible]	[illegible]	[illegible]	[illegible]	[illegible]	[illegible]	[illegible]	[illegible]	Ballina, part of
[illegible]	[illegible]	[illegible]	[illegible]	[illegible]	[illegible]	[illegible]	[illegible]	[illegible]	[illegible]	[illegible]	[illegible]	[illegible]	[illegible]	[illegible]	[illegible]	Ballinrobe, do.
[illegible]	[illegible]	[illegible]	[illegible]	[illegible]	[illegible]	[illegible]	[illegible]	[illegible]	[illegible]	[illegible]	[illegible]	[illegible]	[illegible]	[illegible]	[illegible]	Belmullet.
[illegible]	[illegible]	[illegible]	[illegible]	[illegible]	[illegible]	[illegible]	[illegible]	[illegible]	[illegible]	[illegible]	[illegible]	[illegible]	[illegible]	[illegible]	[illegible]	Castlebar.
[illegible]	[illegible]	[illegible]	[illegible]	[illegible]	[illegible]	[illegible]	[illegible]	[illegible]	[illegible]	[illegible]	[illegible]	[illegible]	[illegible]	[illegible]	[illegible]	Castlerea, part of
[illegible]	[illegible]	[illegible]	[illegible]	[illegible]	[illegible]	[illegible]	[illegible]	[illegible]	[illegible]	[illegible]	[illegible]	[illegible]	[illegible]	[illegible]	[illegible]	Claremorris.
[illegible]	[illegible]	[illegible]	[illegible]	[illegible]	[illegible]	[illegible]	[illegible]	[illegible]	[illegible]	[illegible]	[illegible]	[illegible]	[illegible]	[illegible]	[illegible]	Killala.
[illegible]	[illegible]	[illegible]	[illegible]	[illegible]	[illegible]	[illegible]	[illegible]	[illegible]	[illegible]	[illegible]	[illegible]	[illegible]	[illegible]	[illegible]	[illegible]	Swineford.
[illegible]	[illegible]	[illegible]	[illegible]	[illegible]	[illegible]	[illegible]	[illegible]	[illegible]	[illegible]	[illegible]	[illegible]	[illegible]	[illegible]	[illegible]	[illegible]	Westport.
																31. Roscommon Co.
[illegible]	[illegible]	[illegible]	[illegible]	[illegible]	[illegible]	[illegible]	[illegible]	[illegible]	[illegible]	[illegible]	[illegible]	[illegible]	[illegible]	[illegible]	[illegible]	Athlone, part of
[illegible]	[illegible]	[illegible]	[illegible]	[illegible]	[illegible]	[illegible]	[illegible]	[illegible]	[illegible]	[illegible]	[illegible]	[illegible]	[illegible]	[illegible]	[illegible]	Ballinasloe, do.
[illegible]	[illegible]	[illegible]	[illegible]	[illegible]	[illegible]	[illegible]	[illegible]	[illegible]	[illegible]	[illegible]	[illegible]	[illegible]	[illegible]	[illegible]	[illegible]	Boyle, do.
[illegible]	[illegible]	[illegible]	[illegible]	[illegible]	[illegible]	[illegible]	[illegible]	[illegible]	[illegible]	[illegible]	[illegible]	[illegible]	[illegible]	[illegible]	[illegible]	Carrick-on-Shannon, do.
[illegible]	[illegible]	[illegible]	[illegible]	[illegible]	[illegible]	[illegible]	[illegible]	[illegible]	[illegible]	[illegible]	[illegible]	[illegible]	[illegible]	[illegible]	[illegible]	Castlerea, do.
[illegible]	[illegible]	[illegible]	[illegible]	[illegible]	[illegible]	[illegible]	[illegible]	[illegible]	[illegible]	[illegible]	[illegible]	[illegible]	[illegible]	[illegible]	[illegible]	Roscommon, do.
[illegible]	[illegible]	[illegible]	[illegible]	[illegible]	[illegible]	[illegible]	[illegible]	[illegible]	[illegible]	[illegible]	[illegible]	[illegible]	[illegible]	[illegible]	[illegible]	Strokestown.
																32. Sligo Co.
[illegible]	[illegible]	[illegible]	[illegible]	[illegible]	[illegible]	[illegible]	[illegible]	[illegible]	[illegible]	[illegible]	[illegible]	[illegible]	[illegible]	[illegible]	[illegible]	Ballina, part of
[illegible]	[illegible]	[illegible]	[illegible]	[illegible]	[illegible]	[illegible]	[illegible]	[illegible]	[illegible]	[illegible]	[illegible]	[illegible]	[illegible]	[illegible]	[illegible]	Boyle, do.
[illegible]	[illegible]	[illegible]	[illegible]	[illegible]	[illegible]	[illegible]	[illegible]	[illegible]	[illegible]	[illegible]	[illegible]	[illegible]	[illegible]	[illegible]	[illegible]	Dromore West.
[illegible]	[illegible]	[illegible]	[illegible]	[illegible]	[illegible]	[illegible]	[illegible]	[illegible]	[illegible]	[illegible]	[illegible]	[illegible]	[illegible]	[illegible]	[illegible]	Sligo.
[illegible]	[illegible]	[illegible]	[illegible]	[illegible]	[illegible]	[illegible]	[illegible]	[illegible]	[illegible]	[illegible]	[illegible]	[illegible]	[illegible]	[illegible]	[illegible]	Tobercurry.

Ages of 8,450 Persons who were Married in Ireland in the Year 1866.

The Total Number of Marriages registered in Ireland in the Year 1866 was [illegible]; the precise Ages of both Parties were specified in 4,225 instances.

Ages of 4,225 Men and 4,225 Women married in Ireland in the Year 1866.

—	[illegible]	Total
Men,	[illegible]	[illegible]
Women,	[illegible]	[illegible]

Ages of 3,882 Bachelors and 4,072 Spinsters married in 1866.

—	[illegible]	Total
Bachelors,	[illegible]	[illegible]
Spinsters,	[illegible]	[illegible]

Ages of 343 Widowers and 153 Widows married in 1866.

—	[illegible]	Total
Widowers,	[illegible]	[illegible]
Widows,	[illegible]	[illegible]

Ages of 4,225 Husbands and their Wives in combination in 1866.

YEARS.	AGES OF WIVES.	Total	
AGES OF HUSBANDS.	[illegible]	[illegible]	AGES OF HUSBANDS.
		[illegible]	Husbands.
Total Wives,	[illegible]	[illegible]	Wives.

[illegible]

Ages of 67 Bachelors and 67 Widows who intermarried in the year 1806.

Years	Ages of Widows																				Total
Ages of Bachelors	[illegible]	[illegible]	[illegible]	[illegible]	[illegible]	[illegible]	[illegible]	[illegible]	[illegible]	[illegible]	[illegible]	[illegible]	[illegible]	[illegible]	[illegible]	[illegible]	[illegible]	[illegible]	[illegible]	[illegible]	[illegible]
Total Bachelors																					[illegible]
Total Widows	[illegible]	[illegible]	[illegible]	[illegible]	[illegible]	[illegible]	[illegible]	[illegible]	[illegible]	[illegible]	[illegible]	[illegible]	[illegible]	[illegible]	[illegible]	[illegible]	[illegible]	[illegible]	[illegible]	[illegible]	[illegible]

Ages of 277 Widowers and 277 Spinsters who intermarried in the year 1896.

Years	Ages of Spinsters																				Total
Ages of Widowers	[illegible]	[illegible]	[illegible]	[illegible]	[illegible]	[illegible]	[illegible]	[illegible]	[illegible]	[illegible]	[illegible]	[illegible]	[illegible]	[illegible]	[illegible]	[illegible]	[illegible]	[illegible]	[illegible]	[illegible]	[illegible]
Total Widowers																					[illegible]
Total Spinsters	[illegible]	[illegible]	[illegible]	[illegible]	[illegible]	[illegible]	[illegible]	[illegible]	[illegible]	[illegible]	[illegible]	[illegible]	[illegible]	[illegible]	[illegible]	[illegible]	[illegible]	[illegible]	[illegible]	[illegible]	[illegible]

MARRIAGES, BIRTHS, AND DEATHS in each PROVINCE and COUNTY in IRELAND, registered in the year 1896.

No.	PROVINCES AND COUNTIES	Area in Statute Acres, exclusive of the Larger Rivers, Lakes, and Tideways	Population, 1891	TOTAL: MARRIAGES	TOTAL: BIRTHS	TOTAL: DEATHS	BIRTHS: Legitimate Children: Males	BIRTHS: Legitimate Children: Females	BIRTHS: Illegitimate Children: Males	BIRTHS: Illegitimate Children: Females	DEATHS: Males	DEATHS: Females	Excess of Births over Deaths
	IRELAND,	[illegible]	[illegible]	[illegible]	[illegible]	[illegible]	[illegible]	[illegible]	[illegible]	[illegible]	[illegible]	[illegible]	[illegible]
No.	PROVINCES.												
I.	LEINSTER,	[illegible]	[illegible]	[illegible]	[illegible]	[illegible]	[illegible]	[illegible]	[illegible]	[illegible]	[illegible]	[illegible]	[illegible]
II.	MUNSTER,	[illegible]	[illegible]	[illegible]	[illegible]	[illegible]	[illegible]	[illegible]	[illegible]	[illegible]	[illegible]	[illegible]	[illegible]
III.	ULSTER,	[illegible]	[illegible]	[illegible]	[illegible]	[illegible]	[illegible]	[illegible]	[illegible]	[illegible]	[illegible]	[illegible]	[illegible]
IV.	CONNAUGHT,	[illegible]	[illegible]	[illegible]	[illegible]	[illegible]	[illegible]	[illegible]	[illegible]	[illegible]	[illegible]	[illegible]	[illegible]
	I.—PROVINCE OF LEINSTER.—MARRIAGES, BIRTHS, AND DEATHS, 1896—COUNTIES.												
No.													
1	Carlow,	[illegible]	[illegible]	[illegible]	[illegible]	[illegible]	[illegible]	[illegible]	[illegible]	[illegible]	[illegible]	[illegible]	[illegible]
2	Dublin,	[illegible]	[illegible]	[illegible]	[illegible]	[illegible]	[illegible]	[illegible]	[illegible]	[illegible]	[illegible]	[illegible]	[illegible]
3	Kildare,	[illegible]	[illegible]	[illegible]	[illegible]	[illegible]	[illegible]	[illegible]	[illegible]	[illegible]	[illegible]	[illegible]	[illegible]
4	Kilkenny,	[illegible]	[illegible]	[illegible]	[illegible]	[illegible]	[illegible]	[illegible]	[illegible]	[illegible]	[illegible]	[illegible]	[illegible]
5	King's,	[illegible]	[illegible]	[illegible]	[illegible]	[illegible]	[illegible]	[illegible]	[illegible]	[illegible]	[illegible]	[illegible]	[illegible]
6	Longford,	[illegible]	[illegible]	[illegible]	[illegible]	[illegible]	[illegible]	[illegible]	[illegible]	[illegible]	[illegible]	[illegible]	[illegible]
7	Louth, and Co. of the Town of Drogheda,	[illegible]	[illegible]	[illegible]	[illegible]	[illegible]	[illegible]	[illegible]	[illegible]	[illegible]	[illegible]	[illegible]	[illegible]
8	Meath,	[illegible]	[illegible]	[illegible]	[illegible]	[illegible]	[illegible]	[illegible]	[illegible]	[illegible]	[illegible]	[illegible]	[illegible]
9	Queen's,	[illegible]	[illegible]	[illegible]	[illegible]	[illegible]	[illegible]	[illegible]	[illegible]	[illegible]	[illegible]	[illegible]	[illegible]
10	Westmeath,	[illegible]	[illegible]	[illegible]	[illegible]	[illegible]	[illegible]	[illegible]	[illegible]	[illegible]	[illegible]	[illegible]	[illegible]
11	Wexford,	[illegible]	[illegible]	[illegible]	[illegible]	[illegible]	[illegible]	[illegible]	[illegible]	[illegible]	[illegible]	[illegible]	[illegible]
12	Wicklow,	[illegible]	[illegible]	[illegible]	[illegible]	[illegible]	[illegible]	[illegible]	[illegible]	[illegible]	[illegible]	[illegible]	[illegible]
	II.—PROVINCE OF MUNSTER.—MARRIAGES, BIRTHS, AND DEATHS, 1896—COUNTIES.												
13	Clare,	[illegible]	[illegible]	[illegible]	[illegible]	[illegible]	[illegible]	[illegible]	[illegible]	[illegible]	[illegible]	[illegible]	[illegible]
14	Cork,	[illegible]	[illegible]	[illegible]	[illegible]	[illegible]	[illegible]	[illegible]	[illegible]	[illegible]	[illegible]	[illegible]	[illegible]
15	Kerry,	[illegible]	[illegible]	[illegible]	[illegible]	[illegible]	[illegible]	[illegible]	[illegible]	[illegible]	[illegible]	[illegible]	[illegible]
16	Limerick,	[illegible]	[illegible]	[illegible]	[illegible]	[illegible]	[illegible]	[illegible]	[illegible]	[illegible]	[illegible]	[illegible]	[illegible]
17	Tipperary,	[illegible]	[illegible]	[illegible]	[illegible]	[illegible]	[illegible]	[illegible]	[illegible]	[illegible]	[illegible]	[illegible]	[illegible]
18	Waterford,	[illegible]	[illegible]	[illegible]	[illegible]	[illegible]	[illegible]	[illegible]	[illegible]	[illegible]	[illegible]	[illegible]	[illegible]
	III.—PROVINCE OF ULSTER.—MARRIAGES, BIRTHS, AND DEATHS, 1896—COUNTIES.												
19	Antrim,	[illegible]	[illegible]	[illegible]	[illegible]	[illegible]	[illegible]	[illegible]	[illegible]	[illegible]	[illegible]	[illegible]	[illegible]
20	Armagh,	[illegible]	[illegible]	[illegible]	[illegible]	[illegible]	[illegible]	[illegible]	[illegible]	[illegible]	[illegible]	[illegible]	[illegible]
21	Cavan,	[illegible]	[illegible]	[illegible]	[illegible]	[illegible]	[illegible]	[illegible]	[illegible]	[illegible]	[illegible]	[illegible]	[illegible]
22	Donegal,	[illegible]	[illegible]	[illegible]	[illegible]	[illegible]	[illegible]	[illegible]	[illegible]	[illegible]	[illegible]	[illegible]	[illegible]
23	Down,	[illegible]	[illegible]	[illegible]	[illegible]	[illegible]	[illegible]	[illegible]	[illegible]	[illegible]	[illegible]	[illegible]	[illegible]
24	Fermanagh,	[illegible]	[illegible]	[illegible]	[illegible]	[illegible]	[illegible]	[illegible]	[illegible]	[illegible]	[illegible]	[illegible]	[illegible]
25	Londonderry,	[illegible]	[illegible]	[illegible]	[illegible]	[illegible]	[illegible]	[illegible]	[illegible]	[illegible]	[illegible]	[illegible]	[illegible]
26	Monaghan,	[illegible]	[illegible]	[illegible]	[illegible]	[illegible]	[illegible]	[illegible]	[illegible]	[illegible]	[illegible]	[illegible]	[illegible]
27	Tyrone,	[illegible]	[illegible]	[illegible]	[illegible]	[illegible]	[illegible]	[illegible]	[illegible]	[illegible]	[illegible]	[illegible]	[illegible]
	IV.—PROVINCE OF CONNAUGHT.—MARRIAGES, BIRTHS, AND DEATHS, 1896—COUNTIES.												
28	Galway,	[illegible]	[illegible]	[illegible]	[illegible]	[illegible]	[illegible]	[illegible]	[illegible]	[illegible]	[illegible]	[illegible]	[illegible]
29	Leitrim,	[illegible]	[illegible]	[illegible]	[illegible]	[illegible]	[illegible]	[illegible]	[illegible]	[illegible]	[illegible]	[illegible]	[illegible]
30	Mayo,	[illegible]	[illegible]	[illegible]	[illegible]	[illegible]	[illegible]	[illegible]	[illegible]	[illegible]	[illegible]	[illegible]	[illegible]
31	Roscommon,	[illegible]	[illegible]	[illegible]	[illegible]	[illegible]	[illegible]	[illegible]	[illegible]	[illegible]	[illegible]	[illegible]	[illegible]
32	Sligo,	[illegible]	[illegible]	[illegible]	[illegible]	[illegible]	[illegible]	[illegible]	[illegible]	[illegible]	[illegible]	[illegible]	[illegible]

MARRIAGES, BIRTHS, and DEATHS registered in the Year 1896.

I.—PROVINCE OF LEINSTER.—MARRIAGES, BIRTHS, AND DEATHS, 1896.

SUPERINTENDENT REGISTRARS' DISTRICTS, ARRANGED BY COUNTIES.*

[illegible]

No.	SUPERINTENDENT REGISTRARS' DISTRICTS	Area in Statute Acres.	Population, 1891.	TOTAL: MARRIAGES	TOTAL: BIRTHS	TOTAL: DEATHS	BIRTHS: Including Illegitimate Births: Males	BIRTHS: Including Illegitimate Births: Females	BIRTHS: Illegitimate Births: Males	BIRTHS: Illegitimate Births: Females	DEATHS: Males	DEATHS: Females	Excess of Births over Deaths
	1. Carlow Co.*												
1	[illegible], part of	[illegible]	[illegible]	[illegible]	[illegible]	[illegible]	[illegible]	[illegible]	[illegible]	[illegible]	[illegible]	[illegible]	[illegible]
2	Carlow, do.	[illegible]	[illegible]	[illegible]	[illegible]	[illegible]	[illegible]	[illegible]	[illegible]	[illegible]	[illegible]	[illegible]	[illegible]
3	[illegible], do.	[illegible]	[illegible]	[illegible]	[illegible]	[illegible]	[illegible]	[illegible]	[illegible]	[illegible]	[illegible]	[illegible]	[illegible]
4	[illegible], do.	[illegible]	[illegible]	[illegible]	[illegible]	[illegible]	[illegible]	[illegible]	[illegible]	[illegible]	[illegible]	[illegible]	[illegible]
5	[illegible], do.	[illegible]	[illegible]	[illegible]	[illegible]	[illegible]	[illegible]	[illegible]	[illegible]	[illegible]	[illegible]	[illegible]	[illegible]
	2. Dublin Co.												
6	Balrothery,	[illegible]	[illegible]	[illegible]	[illegible]	[illegible]	[illegible]	[illegible]	[illegible]	[illegible]	[illegible]	[illegible]	[illegible]
7	[illegible], part of	[illegible]	[illegible]	[illegible]	[illegible]	[illegible]	[illegible]	[illegible]	[illegible]	[illegible]	[illegible]	[illegible]	[illegible]
8	Dublin, North,	[illegible]	[illegible]	[illegible]	[illegible]	[illegible]	[illegible]	[illegible]	[illegible]	[illegible]	[illegible]	[illegible]	[illegible]
9	Dublin, South,	[illegible]	[illegible]	[illegible]	[illegible]	[illegible]	[illegible]	[illegible]	[illegible]	[illegible]	[illegible]	[illegible]	[illegible]
10	[illegible], part of	[illegible]	[illegible]	[illegible]	[illegible]	[illegible]	[illegible]	[illegible]	[illegible]	[illegible]	[illegible]	[illegible]	[illegible]
11	Rathdown, do.	[illegible]	[illegible]	[illegible]	[illegible]	[illegible]	[illegible]	[illegible]	[illegible]	[illegible]	[illegible]	[illegible]	[illegible]
	3. Kildare Co.												
12	Athy, part of	[illegible]	[illegible]	[illegible]	[illegible]	[illegible]	[illegible]	[illegible]	[illegible]	[illegible]	[illegible]	[illegible]	[illegible]
13	[illegible], do.	[illegible]	[illegible]	[illegible]	[illegible]	[illegible]	[illegible]	[illegible]	[illegible]	[illegible]	[illegible]	[illegible]	[illegible]
14	[illegible], do.	[illegible]	[illegible]	[illegible]	[illegible]	[illegible]	[illegible]	[illegible]	[illegible]	[illegible]	[illegible]	[illegible]	[illegible]
15	[illegible], do.	[illegible]	[illegible]	[illegible]	[illegible]	[illegible]	[illegible]	[illegible]	[illegible]	[illegible]	[illegible]	[illegible]	[illegible]
16	Naas, do.	[illegible]	[illegible]	[illegible]	[illegible]	[illegible]	[illegible]	[illegible]	[illegible]	[illegible]	[illegible]	[illegible]	[illegible]
	4. Kilkenny Co.												
17	[illegible], part of	[illegible]	[illegible]	[illegible]	[illegible]	[illegible]	[illegible]	[illegible]	[illegible]	[illegible]	[illegible]	[illegible]	[illegible]
18	[illegible], do.	[illegible]	[illegible]	[illegible]	[illegible]	[illegible]	[illegible]	[illegible]	[illegible]	[illegible]	[illegible]	[illegible]	[illegible]
19	Castlecomer,	[illegible]	[illegible]	[illegible]	[illegible]	[illegible]	[illegible]	[illegible]	[illegible]	[illegible]	[illegible]	[illegible]	[illegible]
20	Kilkenny,	[illegible]	[illegible]	[illegible]	[illegible]	[illegible]	[illegible]	[illegible]	[illegible]	[illegible]	[illegible]	[illegible]	[illegible]
21	New Ross, part of	[illegible]	[illegible]	[illegible]	[illegible]	[illegible]	[illegible]	[illegible]	[illegible]	[illegible]	[illegible]	[illegible]	[illegible]
22	Thomastown,	[illegible]	[illegible]	[illegible]	[illegible]	[illegible]	[illegible]	[illegible]	[illegible]	[illegible]	[illegible]	[illegible]	[illegible]
23	[illegible], part of	[illegible]	[illegible]	[illegible]	[illegible]	[illegible]	[illegible]	[illegible]	[illegible]	[illegible]	[illegible]	[illegible]	[illegible]
24	Waterford, do.	[illegible]	[illegible]	[illegible]	[illegible]	[illegible]	[illegible]	[illegible]	[illegible]	[illegible]	[illegible]	[illegible]	[illegible]
	5. King's Co.												
25	[illegible], part of	[illegible]	[illegible]	[illegible]	[illegible]	[illegible]	[illegible]	[illegible]	[illegible]	[illegible]	[illegible]	[illegible]	[illegible]
26	[illegible], do.	[illegible]	[illegible]	[illegible]	[illegible]	[illegible]	[illegible]	[illegible]	[illegible]	[illegible]	[illegible]	[illegible]	[illegible]
27	[illegible], do.	[illegible]	[illegible]	[illegible]	[illegible]	[illegible]	[illegible]	[illegible]	[illegible]	[illegible]	[illegible]	[illegible]	[illegible]
28	[illegible], do.	[illegible]	[illegible]	[illegible]	[illegible]	[illegible]	[illegible]	[illegible]	[illegible]	[illegible]	[illegible]	[illegible]	[illegible]
29	Tullamore, do.	[illegible]	[illegible]	[illegible]	[illegible]	[illegible]	[illegible]	[illegible]	[illegible]	[illegible]	[illegible]	[illegible]	[illegible]
	6. Longford Co.												
30	[illegible], part of	[illegible]	[illegible]	[illegible]	[illegible]	[illegible]	[illegible]	[illegible]	[illegible]	[illegible]	[illegible]	[illegible]	[illegible]
31	[illegible], do.	[illegible]	[illegible]	[illegible]	[illegible]	[illegible]	[illegible]	[illegible]	[illegible]	[illegible]	[illegible]	[illegible]	[illegible]
32	Longford,	[illegible]	[illegible]	[illegible]	[illegible]	[illegible]	[illegible]	[illegible]	[illegible]	[illegible]	[illegible]	[illegible]	[illegible]
	7. Louth Co. and Co. of Town of Drogheda.												
33	Ardee, part of	[illegible]	[illegible]	[illegible]	[illegible]	[illegible]	[illegible]	[illegible]	[illegible]	[illegible]	[illegible]	[illegible]	[illegible]
34	Drogheda, do.	[illegible]	[illegible]	[illegible]	[illegible]	[illegible]	[illegible]	[illegible]	[illegible]	[illegible]	[illegible]	[illegible]	[illegible]
35	Dundalk, do.	[illegible]	[illegible]	[illegible]	[illegible]	[illegible]	[illegible]	[illegible]	[illegible]	[illegible]	[illegible]	[illegible]	[illegible]

* [illegible]

I.—PROVINCE OF LEINSTER.—MARRIAGES, BIRTHS, AND DEATHS, 1896—
SUPERINTENDENT REGISTRARS' DISTRICTS by Counties—continued.

No.	Superintendent Registrars' Districts.	Area in Statute Acres.	Population, 1891.	Total: Marriages	Total: Births	Total: Deaths	Births: Legitimate: Males	Births: Legitimate: Females	Births: Illegitimate: Males	Births: Illegitimate: Females	Deaths: Males	Deaths: Females	[illegible]
	9. Meath Co.												
[illegible]	Ardee, part of	[illegible]	[illegible]	[illegible]	[illegible]	[illegible]	[illegible]	[illegible]	[illegible]	[illegible]	[illegible]	[illegible]	[illegible]
[illegible]	[illegible], do.	[illegible]	[illegible]	[illegible]	[illegible]	[illegible]	[illegible]	[illegible]	[illegible]	[illegible]	[illegible]	[illegible]	[illegible]
[illegible]	[illegible], do.	[illegible]	[illegible]	[illegible]	[illegible]	[illegible]	[illegible]	[illegible]	[illegible]	[illegible]	[illegible]	[illegible]	[illegible]
[illegible]	[illegible], do.	[illegible]	[illegible]	[illegible]	[illegible]	[illegible]	[illegible]	[illegible]	[illegible]	[illegible]	[illegible]	[illegible]	[illegible]
[illegible]	[illegible], do.	[illegible]	[illegible]	[illegible]	[illegible]	[illegible]	[illegible]	[illegible]	[illegible]	[illegible]	[illegible]	[illegible]	[illegible]
[illegible]	Kells, do.	[illegible]	[illegible]	[illegible]	[illegible]	[illegible]	[illegible]	[illegible]	[illegible]	[illegible]	[illegible]	[illegible]	[illegible]
[illegible]	Navan,	[illegible]	[illegible]	[illegible]	[illegible]	[illegible]	[illegible]	[illegible]	[illegible]	[illegible]	[illegible]	[illegible]	[illegible]
[illegible]	Oldcastle, part of,	[illegible]	[illegible]	[illegible]	[illegible]	[illegible]	[illegible]	[illegible]	[illegible]	[illegible]	[illegible]	[illegible]	[illegible]
[illegible]	Trim,	[illegible]	[illegible]	[illegible]	[illegible]	[illegible]	[illegible]	[illegible]	[illegible]	[illegible]	[illegible]	[illegible]	[illegible]
	10. Queen's Co.												
[illegible]	Abbeyleix,	[illegible]	[illegible]	[illegible]	[illegible]	[illegible]	[illegible]	[illegible]	[illegible]	[illegible]	[illegible]	[illegible]	[illegible]
[illegible]	Athy, part of,	[illegible]	[illegible]	[illegible]	[illegible]	[illegible]	[illegible]	[illegible]	[illegible]	[illegible]	[illegible]	[illegible]	[illegible]
[illegible]	Carlow, do.	[illegible]	[illegible]	[illegible]	[illegible]	[illegible]	[illegible]	[illegible]	[illegible]	[illegible]	[illegible]	[illegible]	[illegible]
[illegible]	Mountmellick, do.	[illegible]	[illegible]	[illegible]	[illegible]	[illegible]	[illegible]	[illegible]	[illegible]	[illegible]	[illegible]	[illegible]	[illegible]
[illegible]	Roscrea, do.	[illegible]	[illegible]	[illegible]	[illegible]	[illegible]	[illegible]	[illegible]	[illegible]	[illegible]	[illegible]	[illegible]	[illegible]
[illegible]	Donaghmore, do.	[illegible]	[illegible]	[illegible]	[illegible]	[illegible]	[illegible]	[illegible]	[illegible]	[illegible]	[illegible]	[illegible]	[illegible]
	11. Westmeath Co.												
[illegible]	Athlone, part of,	[illegible]	[illegible]	[illegible]	[illegible]	[illegible]	[illegible]	[illegible]	[illegible]	[illegible]	[illegible]	[illegible]	[illegible]
[illegible]	Ballymahon, do.	[illegible]	[illegible]	[illegible]	[illegible]	[illegible]	[illegible]	[illegible]	[illegible]	[illegible]	[illegible]	[illegible]	[illegible]
[illegible]	Delvin,	[illegible]	[illegible]	[illegible]	[illegible]	[illegible]	[illegible]	[illegible]	[illegible]	[illegible]	[illegible]	[illegible]	[illegible]
[illegible]	Granard, part of,	[illegible]	[illegible]	[illegible]	[illegible]	[illegible]	[illegible]	[illegible]	[illegible]	[illegible]	[illegible]	[illegible]	[illegible]
[illegible]	Mullingar,	[illegible]	[illegible]	[illegible]	[illegible]	[illegible]	[illegible]	[illegible]	[illegible]	[illegible]	[illegible]	[illegible]	[illegible]
[illegible]	Tullamore, part of,	[illegible]	[illegible]	[illegible]	[illegible]	[illegible]	[illegible]	[illegible]	[illegible]	[illegible]	[illegible]	[illegible]	[illegible]
	12. Wexford Co.												
[illegible]	Enniscorthy, part of,	[illegible]	[illegible]	[illegible]	[illegible]	[illegible]	[illegible]	[illegible]	[illegible]	[illegible]	[illegible]	[illegible]	[illegible]
[illegible]	Gorey,	[illegible]	[illegible]	[illegible]	[illegible]	[illegible]	[illegible]	[illegible]	[illegible]	[illegible]	[illegible]	[illegible]	[illegible]
[illegible]	New Ross, part of,	[illegible]	[illegible]	[illegible]	[illegible]	[illegible]	[illegible]	[illegible]	[illegible]	[illegible]	[illegible]	[illegible]	[illegible]
[illegible]	Shillelagh, do.	[illegible]	[illegible]	[illegible]	[illegible]	[illegible]	[illegible]	[illegible]	[illegible]	[illegible]	[illegible]	[illegible]	[illegible]
[illegible]	Wexford,	[illegible]	[illegible]	[illegible]	[illegible]	[illegible]	[illegible]	[illegible]	[illegible]	[illegible]	[illegible]	[illegible]	[illegible]
	13. Wicklow Co.												
[illegible]	Baltinglass, part of,	[illegible]	[illegible]	[illegible]	[illegible]	[illegible]	[illegible]	[illegible]	[illegible]	[illegible]	[illegible]	[illegible]	[illegible]
[illegible]	Naas, do.	[illegible]	[illegible]	[illegible]	[illegible]	[illegible]	[illegible]	[illegible]	[illegible]	[illegible]	[illegible]	[illegible]	[illegible]
[illegible]	Rathdown, do.	[illegible]	[illegible]	[illegible]	[illegible]	[illegible]	[illegible]	[illegible]	[illegible]	[illegible]	[illegible]	[illegible]	[illegible]
[illegible]	Rathdrum,	[illegible]	[illegible]	[illegible]	[illegible]	[illegible]	[illegible]	[illegible]	[illegible]	[illegible]	[illegible]	[illegible]	[illegible]
[illegible]	Shillelagh, part of,	[illegible]	[illegible]	[illegible]	[illegible]	[illegible]	[illegible]	[illegible]	[illegible]	[illegible]	[illegible]	[illegible]	[illegible]

II.—PROVINCE OF MUNSTER.—MARRIAGES, BIRTHS, AND DEATHS, 1896—
SUPERINTENDENT REGISTRARS' DISTRICTS by Counties.

No.	Superintendent Registrars' Districts.	Area in Statute Acres.	Population, 1891.	Total: Marriages	Total: Births	Total: Deaths	Births: Legitimate: Males	Births: Legitimate: Females	Births: Illegitimate: Males	Births: Illegitimate: Females	Deaths: Males	Deaths: Females	[illegible]
	14. Clare Co.												
[illegible]	Ballyvaghan,	[illegible]	[illegible]	[illegible]	[illegible]	[illegible]	[illegible]	[illegible]	[illegible]	[illegible]	[illegible]	[illegible]	[illegible]
[illegible]	Corrofin,	[illegible]	[illegible]	[illegible]	[illegible]	[illegible]	[illegible]	[illegible]	[illegible]	[illegible]	[illegible]	[illegible]	[illegible]
[illegible]	Ennis,	[illegible]	[illegible]	[illegible]	[illegible]	[illegible]	[illegible]	[illegible]	[illegible]	[illegible]	[illegible]	[illegible]	[illegible]
[illegible]	Ennistimon,	[illegible]	[illegible]	[illegible]	[illegible]	[illegible]	[illegible]	[illegible]	[illegible]	[illegible]	[illegible]	[illegible]	[illegible]
[illegible]	Kildysart,	[illegible]	[illegible]	[illegible]	[illegible]	[illegible]	[illegible]	[illegible]	[illegible]	[illegible]	[illegible]	[illegible]	[illegible]
[illegible]	Kilrush,	[illegible]	[illegible]	[illegible]	[illegible]	[illegible]	[illegible]	[illegible]	[illegible]	[illegible]	[illegible]	[illegible]	[illegible]
[illegible]	Limerick, part of,	[illegible]	[illegible]	[illegible]	[illegible]	[illegible]	[illegible]	[illegible]	[illegible]	[illegible]	[illegible]	[illegible]	[illegible]
[illegible]	Scarriff, do.	[illegible]	[illegible]	[illegible]	[illegible]	[illegible]	[illegible]	[illegible]	[illegible]	[illegible]	[illegible]	[illegible]	[illegible]
[illegible]	Tulla,	[illegible]	[illegible]	[illegible]	[illegible]	[illegible]	[illegible]	[illegible]	[illegible]	[illegible]	[illegible]	[illegible]	[illegible]

III.—PROVINCE OF MUNSTER.—MARRIAGES, BIRTHS, AND DEATHS, 1896—
SUPERINTENDENT REGISTRARS' DISTRICTS by Counties—*continued*.

No.	Superintendent Registrars' Districts	Area in Statute Acres	Population, 1891	Total: Marriages	Total: Births	Total: Deaths	Births: Legitimate Males	Births: Legitimate Females	Births: Illegitimate Males	Births: Illegitimate Females	Deaths: Males	Deaths: Females	[illegible]
	[illegible] Cork Co.												
76	[illegible]	[illegible]	[illegible]	[illegible]	[illegible]	[illegible]	[illegible]	[illegible]	[illegible]	[illegible]	[illegible]	[illegible]	[illegible]
77	[illegible]	[illegible]	[illegible]	[illegible]	[illegible]	[illegible]	[illegible]	[illegible]	[illegible]	[illegible]	[illegible]	[illegible]	[illegible]
[illegible]	[illegible]	[illegible]	[illegible]	[illegible]	[illegible]	[illegible]	[illegible]	[illegible]	[illegible]	[illegible]	[illegible]	[illegible]	[illegible]
79	[illegible]	[illegible]	[illegible]	[illegible]	[illegible]	[illegible]	[illegible]	[illegible]	[illegible]	[illegible]	[illegible]	[illegible]	[illegible]
[illegible]	Cork,	[illegible]	[illegible]	[illegible]	[illegible]	[illegible]	[illegible]	[illegible]	[illegible]	[illegible]	[illegible]	[illegible]	[illegible]
[illegible]	[illegible]	[illegible]	[illegible]	[illegible]	[illegible]	[illegible]	[illegible]	[illegible]	[illegible]	[illegible]	[illegible]	[illegible]	[illegible]
[illegible]	[illegible]	[illegible]	[illegible]	[illegible]	[illegible]	[illegible]	[illegible]	[illegible]	[illegible]	[illegible]	[illegible]	[illegible]	[illegible]
[illegible]	[illegible]	[illegible]	[illegible]	[illegible]	[illegible]	[illegible]	[illegible]	[illegible]	[illegible]	[illegible]	[illegible]	[illegible]	[illegible]
[illegible]	[illegible], part of,	[illegible]	[illegible]	[illegible]	[illegible]	[illegible]	[illegible]	[illegible]	[illegible]	[illegible]	[illegible]	[illegible]	[illegible]
[illegible]	[illegible]	[illegible]	[illegible]	[illegible]	[illegible]	[illegible]	[illegible]	[illegible]	[illegible]	[illegible]	[illegible]	[illegible]	[illegible]
[illegible]	[illegible]	[illegible]	[illegible]	[illegible]	[illegible]	[illegible]	[illegible]	[illegible]	[illegible]	[illegible]	[illegible]	[illegible]	[illegible]
[illegible]	[illegible]	[illegible]	[illegible]	[illegible]	[illegible]	[illegible]	[illegible]	[illegible]	[illegible]	[illegible]	[illegible]	[illegible]	[illegible]
[illegible]	[illegible]	[illegible]	[illegible]	[illegible]	[illegible]	[illegible]	[illegible]	[illegible]	[illegible]	[illegible]	[illegible]	[illegible]	[illegible]
[illegible]	[illegible]	[illegible]	[illegible]	[illegible]	[illegible]	[illegible]	[illegible]	[illegible]	[illegible]	[illegible]	[illegible]	[illegible]	[illegible]
[illegible]	[illegible], part of,	[illegible]	[illegible]	[illegible]	[illegible]	[illegible]	[illegible]	[illegible]	[illegible]	[illegible]	[illegible]	[illegible]	[illegible]
[illegible]	[illegible]	[illegible]	[illegible]	[illegible]	[illegible]	[illegible]	[illegible]	[illegible]	[illegible]	[illegible]	[illegible]	[illegible]	[illegible]
[illegible]	[illegible]	[illegible]	[illegible]	[illegible]	[illegible]	[illegible]	[illegible]	[illegible]	[illegible]	[illegible]	[illegible]	[illegible]	[illegible]
[illegible]	[illegible], part of,	[illegible]	[illegible]	[illegible]	[illegible]	[illegible]	[illegible]	[illegible]	[illegible]	[illegible]	[illegible]	[illegible]	[illegible]
	[illegible] Kerry Co.												
[illegible]	[illegible]	[illegible]	[illegible]	[illegible]	[illegible]	[illegible]	[illegible]	[illegible]	[illegible]	[illegible]	[illegible]	[illegible]	[illegible]
[illegible]	[illegible]	[illegible]	[illegible]	[illegible]	[illegible]	[illegible]	[illegible]	[illegible]	[illegible]	[illegible]	[illegible]	[illegible]	[illegible]
[illegible]	[illegible]	[illegible]	[illegible]	[illegible]	[illegible]	[illegible]	[illegible]	[illegible]	[illegible]	[illegible]	[illegible]	[illegible]	[illegible]
[illegible]	[illegible]	[illegible]	[illegible]	[illegible]	[illegible]	[illegible]	[illegible]	[illegible]	[illegible]	[illegible]	[illegible]	[illegible]	[illegible]
[illegible]	[illegible], part of,	[illegible]	[illegible]	[illegible]	[illegible]	[illegible]	[illegible]	[illegible]	[illegible]	[illegible]	[illegible]	[illegible]	[illegible]
[illegible]	[illegible]	[illegible]	[illegible]	[illegible]	[illegible]	[illegible]	[illegible]	[illegible]	[illegible]	[illegible]	[illegible]	[illegible]	[illegible]
	[illegible] Limerick Co.												
[illegible]	[illegible]	[illegible]	[illegible]	[illegible]	[illegible]	[illegible]	[illegible]	[illegible]	[illegible]	[illegible]	[illegible]	[illegible]	[illegible]
[illegible]	[illegible], part of,	[illegible]	[illegible]	[illegible]	[illegible]	[illegible]	[illegible]	[illegible]	[illegible]	[illegible]	[illegible]	[illegible]	[illegible]
[illegible]	[illegible], do.	[illegible]	[illegible]	[illegible]	[illegible]	[illegible]	[illegible]	[illegible]	[illegible]	[illegible]	[illegible]	[illegible]	[illegible]
[illegible]	[illegible], do.	[illegible]	[illegible]	[illegible]	[illegible]	[illegible]	[illegible]	[illegible]	[illegible]	[illegible]	[illegible]	[illegible]	[illegible]
[illegible]	[illegible], do.	[illegible]	[illegible]	[illegible]	[illegible]	[illegible]	[illegible]	[illegible]	[illegible]	[illegible]	[illegible]	[illegible]	[illegible]
[illegible]	[illegible]	[illegible]	[illegible]	[illegible]	[illegible]	[illegible]	[illegible]	[illegible]	[illegible]	[illegible]	[illegible]	[illegible]	[illegible]
[illegible]	[illegible]	[illegible]	[illegible]	[illegible]	[illegible]	[illegible]	[illegible]	[illegible]	[illegible]	[illegible]	[illegible]	[illegible]	[illegible]
[illegible]	[illegible], part of,	[illegible]	[illegible]	[illegible]	[illegible]	[illegible]	[illegible]	[illegible]	[illegible]	[illegible]	[illegible]	[illegible]	[illegible]
	[illegible] Tipperary Co.												
[illegible]	[illegible]	[illegible]	[illegible]	[illegible]	[illegible]	[illegible]	[illegible]	[illegible]	[illegible]	[illegible]	[illegible]	[illegible]	[illegible]
[illegible]	[illegible], part of,	[illegible]	[illegible]	[illegible]	[illegible]	[illegible]	[illegible]	[illegible]	[illegible]	[illegible]	[illegible]	[illegible]	[illegible]
[illegible]	[illegible], do.	[illegible]	[illegible]	[illegible]	[illegible]	[illegible]	[illegible]	[illegible]	[illegible]	[illegible]	[illegible]	[illegible]	[illegible]
[illegible]	[illegible]	[illegible]	[illegible]	[illegible]	[illegible]	[illegible]	[illegible]	[illegible]	[illegible]	[illegible]	[illegible]	[illegible]	[illegible]
[illegible]	[illegible]	[illegible]	[illegible]	[illegible]	[illegible]	[illegible]	[illegible]	[illegible]	[illegible]	[illegible]	[illegible]	[illegible]	[illegible]
[illegible]	[illegible], part of,	[illegible]	[illegible]	[illegible]	[illegible]	[illegible]	[illegible]	[illegible]	[illegible]	[illegible]	[illegible]	[illegible]	[illegible]
[illegible]	[illegible]	[illegible]	[illegible]	[illegible]	[illegible]	[illegible]	[illegible]	[illegible]	[illegible]	[illegible]	[illegible]	[illegible]	[illegible]
[illegible]	[illegible], part of,	[illegible]	[illegible]	[illegible]	[illegible]	[illegible]	[illegible]	[illegible]	[illegible]	[illegible]	[illegible]	[illegible]	[illegible]
[illegible]	[illegible], do.	[illegible]	[illegible]	[illegible]	[illegible]	[illegible]	[illegible]	[illegible]	[illegible]	[illegible]	[illegible]	[illegible]	[illegible]
[illegible]	[illegible]	[illegible]	[illegible]	[illegible]	[illegible]	[illegible]	[illegible]	[illegible]	[illegible]	[illegible]	[illegible]	[illegible]	[illegible]
[illegible]	[illegible], part of,	[illegible]	[illegible]	[illegible]	[illegible]	[illegible]	[illegible]	[illegible]	[illegible]	[illegible]	[illegible]	[illegible]	[illegible]
[illegible]	[illegible], do.	[illegible]	[illegible]	[illegible]	[illegible]	[illegible]	[illegible]	[illegible]	[illegible]	[illegible]	[illegible]	[illegible]	[illegible]

XI.—PROVINCE OF MUNSTER.—MARRIAGES, BIRTHS, AND DEATHS, 1896—Superintendent Registrars' Districts by Counties—continued.

No.	Superintendent Registrars' Districts.	Area in Statute Acres.	Population, 1891.	Total: Marriages.	Total: Births.	Total: Deaths.	Births: Legitimate: Males.	Births: Legitimate: Females.	Births: Illegitimate: Males.	Births: Illegitimate: Females.	Deaths: Males.	Deaths: Females.	[illegible]
	[illegible] Waterford Co.												
[illegible]	Carrick-on-Suir, part of	[illegible]	[illegible]	[illegible]	[illegible]	[illegible]	[illegible]	[illegible]	[illegible]	[illegible]	[illegible]	[illegible]	[illegible]
[illegible]	Clonmel, do.	[illegible]	[illegible]	[illegible]	[illegible]	[illegible]	[illegible]	[illegible]	[illegible]	[illegible]	[illegible]	[illegible]	[illegible]
[illegible]	Dungarvan,	[illegible]	[illegible]	[illegible]	[illegible]	[illegible]	[illegible]	[illegible]	[illegible]	[illegible]	[illegible]	[illegible]	[illegible]
[illegible]	Kilmacthomas,	[illegible]	[illegible]	[illegible]	[illegible]	[illegible]	[illegible]	[illegible]	[illegible]	[illegible]	[illegible]	[illegible]	[illegible]
[illegible]	Lismore,	[illegible]	[illegible]	[illegible]	[illegible]	[illegible]	[illegible]	[illegible]	[illegible]	[illegible]	[illegible]	[illegible]	[illegible]
[illegible]	Waterford, part of	[illegible]	[illegible]	[illegible]	[illegible]	[illegible]	[illegible]	[illegible]	[illegible]	[illegible]	[illegible]	[illegible]	[illegible]
[illegible]	Youghal, do.	[illegible]	[illegible]	[illegible]	[illegible]	[illegible]	[illegible]	[illegible]	[illegible]	[illegible]	[illegible]	[illegible]	[illegible]

XII.—PROVINCE OF ULSTER.—MARRIAGES, BIRTHS, AND DEATHS, 1896—Superintendent Registrars' Districts by Counties.

No.	Superintendent Registrars' Districts.	Area in Statute Acres.	Population, 1891.	Total: Marriages.	Total: Births.	Total: Deaths.	Births: Legitimate: Males.	Births: Legitimate: Females.	Births: Illegitimate: Males.	Births: Illegitimate: Females.	Deaths: Males.	Deaths: Females.	[illegible]
	[illegible] Antrim Co.												
[illegible]	Antrim,	[illegible]	[illegible]	[illegible]	[illegible]	[illegible]	[illegible]	[illegible]	[illegible]	[illegible]	[illegible]	[illegible]	[illegible]
[illegible]	Ballycastle,	[illegible]	[illegible]	[illegible]	[illegible]	[illegible]	[illegible]	[illegible]	[illegible]	[illegible]	[illegible]	[illegible]	[illegible]
[illegible]	Ballymena,	[illegible]	[illegible]	[illegible]	[illegible]	[illegible]	[illegible]	[illegible]	[illegible]	[illegible]	[illegible]	[illegible]	[illegible]
[illegible]	Ballymoney, part of	[illegible]	[illegible]	[illegible]	[illegible]	[illegible]	[illegible]	[illegible]	[illegible]	[illegible]	[illegible]	[illegible]	[illegible]
[illegible]	Belfast, do.	[illegible]	[illegible]	[illegible]	[illegible]	[illegible]	[illegible]	[illegible]	[illegible]	[illegible]	[illegible]	[illegible]	[illegible]
[illegible]	Coleraine, do.	[illegible]	[illegible]	[illegible]	[illegible]	[illegible]	[illegible]	[illegible]	[illegible]	[illegible]	[illegible]	[illegible]	[illegible]
[illegible]	Larne,	[illegible]	[illegible]	[illegible]	[illegible]	[illegible]	[illegible]	[illegible]	[illegible]	[illegible]	[illegible]	[illegible]	[illegible]
[illegible]	Lisburn, part of	[illegible]	[illegible]	[illegible]	[illegible]	[illegible]	[illegible]	[illegible]	[illegible]	[illegible]	[illegible]	[illegible]	[illegible]
[illegible]	Lurgan, do.	[illegible]	[illegible]	[illegible]	[illegible]	[illegible]	[illegible]	[illegible]	[illegible]	[illegible]	[illegible]	[illegible]	[illegible]
	[illegible] Armagh Co.												
[illegible]	Armagh, part of	[illegible]	[illegible]	[illegible]	[illegible]	[illegible]	[illegible]	[illegible]	[illegible]	[illegible]	[illegible]	[illegible]	[illegible]
[illegible]	Banbridge, do.	[illegible]	[illegible]	[illegible]	[illegible]	[illegible]	[illegible]	[illegible]	[illegible]	[illegible]	[illegible]	[illegible]	[illegible]
[illegible]	Castleblayney, do.	[illegible]	[illegible]	[illegible]	[illegible]	[illegible]	[illegible]	[illegible]	[illegible]	[illegible]	[illegible]	[illegible]	[illegible]
[illegible]	Dundalk, do.	[illegible]	[illegible]	[illegible]	[illegible]	[illegible]	[illegible]	[illegible]	[illegible]	[illegible]	[illegible]	[illegible]	[illegible]
[illegible]	Lurgan, do.	[illegible]	[illegible]	[illegible]	[illegible]	[illegible]	[illegible]	[illegible]	[illegible]	[illegible]	[illegible]	[illegible]	[illegible]
[illegible]	Newry, do.	[illegible]	[illegible]	[illegible]	[illegible]	[illegible]	[illegible]	[illegible]	[illegible]	[illegible]	[illegible]	[illegible]	[illegible]
	[illegible] Cavan Co.												
[illegible]	Bailieborough,	[illegible]	[illegible]	[illegible]	[illegible]	[illegible]	[illegible]	[illegible]	[illegible]	[illegible]	[illegible]	[illegible]	[illegible]
[illegible]	Bawnboy, part of	[illegible]	[illegible]	[illegible]	[illegible]	[illegible]	[illegible]	[illegible]	[illegible]	[illegible]	[illegible]	[illegible]	[illegible]
[illegible]	Cavan,	[illegible]	[illegible]	[illegible]	[illegible]	[illegible]	[illegible]	[illegible]	[illegible]	[illegible]	[illegible]	[illegible]	[illegible]
[illegible]	Cootehill, part of	[illegible]	[illegible]	[illegible]	[illegible]	[illegible]	[illegible]	[illegible]	[illegible]	[illegible]	[illegible]	[illegible]	[illegible]
[illegible]	Enniskillen, do.	[illegible]	[illegible]	[illegible]	[illegible]	[illegible]	[illegible]	[illegible]	[illegible]	[illegible]	[illegible]	[illegible]	[illegible]
[illegible]	Granard, do.	[illegible]	[illegible]	[illegible]	[illegible]	[illegible]	[illegible]	[illegible]	[illegible]	[illegible]	[illegible]	[illegible]	[illegible]
[illegible]	Kells, do.	[illegible]	[illegible]	[illegible]	[illegible]	[illegible]	[illegible]	[illegible]	[illegible]	[illegible]	[illegible]	[illegible]	[illegible]
[illegible]	Oldcastle, do.	[illegible]	[illegible]	[illegible]	[illegible]	[illegible]	[illegible]	[illegible]	[illegible]	[illegible]	[illegible]	[illegible]	[illegible]
	[illegible] Donegal Co.												
[illegible]	Ballyshannon, part of	[illegible]	[illegible]	[illegible]	[illegible]	[illegible]	[illegible]	[illegible]	[illegible]	[illegible]	[illegible]	[illegible]	[illegible]
[illegible]	Donegal,	[illegible]	[illegible]	[illegible]	[illegible]	[illegible]	[illegible]	[illegible]	[illegible]	[illegible]	[illegible]	[illegible]	[illegible]
[illegible]	Dunfanaghy,	[illegible]	[illegible]	[illegible]	[illegible]	[illegible]	[illegible]	[illegible]	[illegible]	[illegible]	[illegible]	[illegible]	[illegible]
[illegible]	Glenties,	[illegible]	[illegible]	[illegible]	[illegible]	[illegible]	[illegible]	[illegible]	[illegible]	[illegible]	[illegible]	[illegible]	[illegible]
[illegible]	Inishowen,	[illegible]	[illegible]	[illegible]	[illegible]	[illegible]	[illegible]	[illegible]	[illegible]	[illegible]	[illegible]	[illegible]	[illegible]
[illegible]	Letterkenny,	[illegible]	[illegible]	[illegible]	[illegible]	[illegible]	[illegible]	[illegible]	[illegible]	[illegible]	[illegible]	[illegible]	[illegible]
[illegible]	Londonderry, part of	[illegible]	[illegible]	[illegible]	[illegible]	[illegible]	[illegible]	[illegible]	[illegible]	[illegible]	[illegible]	[illegible]	[illegible]
[illegible]	Milford,	[illegible]	[illegible]	[illegible]	[illegible]	[illegible]	[illegible]	[illegible]	[illegible]	[illegible]	[illegible]	[illegible]	[illegible]
[illegible]	Strabane, part of	[illegible]	[illegible]	[illegible]	[illegible]	[illegible]	[illegible]	[illegible]	[illegible]	[illegible]	[illegible]	[illegible]	[illegible]
[illegible]	Stranorlar,	[illegible]	[illegible]	[illegible]	[illegible]	[illegible]	[illegible]	[illegible]	[illegible]	[illegible]	[illegible]	[illegible]	[illegible]

III.—PROVINCE OF ULSTER.—MARRIAGES, BIRTHS, AND DEATHS, 1896.—
SUPERINTENDENT REGISTRARS' DISTRICTS by Counties—*continued.*

No.	Superintendent Registrars' Districts	Area in Statute Acres	Population 1891	Total: Marriages	Total: Births	Total: Deaths	Births including Illegitimate: Males	Births including Illegitimate: Females	Illegitimate Births: Males	Illegitimate Births: Females	Deaths: Males	Deaths: Females	Excess of Births over Deaths
	23. Down Co.												
[illegible]	Banbridge, part of	[illegible]	[illegible]	[illegible]	[illegible]	[illegible]	[illegible]	[illegible]	[illegible]	[illegible]	[illegible]	[illegible]	[illegible]
[illegible]	Belfast, do.	[illegible]	[illegible]	[illegible]	[illegible]	[illegible]	[illegible]	[illegible]	[illegible]	[illegible]	[illegible]	[illegible]	[illegible]
[illegible]	Downpatrick,	[illegible]	[illegible]	[illegible]	[illegible]	[illegible]	[illegible]	[illegible]	[illegible]	[illegible]	[illegible]	[illegible]	[illegible]
[illegible]	Kilkeel,	[illegible]	[illegible]	[illegible]	[illegible]	[illegible]	[illegible]	[illegible]	[illegible]	[illegible]	[illegible]	[illegible]	[illegible]
[illegible]	Lisburn, part of,	[illegible]	[illegible]	[illegible]	[illegible]	[illegible]	[illegible]	[illegible]	[illegible]	[illegible]	[illegible]	[illegible]	[illegible]
[illegible]	Lurgan, do.	[illegible]	[illegible]	[illegible]	[illegible]	[illegible]	[illegible]	[illegible]	[illegible]	[illegible]	[illegible]	[illegible]	[illegible]
[illegible]	Newry, do.	[illegible]	[illegible]	[illegible]	[illegible]	[illegible]	[illegible]	[illegible]	[illegible]	[illegible]	[illegible]	[illegible]	[illegible]
[illegible]	Newtownards,	[illegible]	[illegible]	[illegible]	[illegible]	[illegible]	[illegible]	[illegible]	[illegible]	[illegible]	[illegible]	[illegible]	[illegible]
	24. Fermanagh Co.												
[illegible]	Ballyshannon, part of,	[illegible]	[illegible]	[illegible]	[illegible]	[illegible]	[illegible]	[illegible]	[illegible]	[illegible]	[illegible]	[illegible]	[illegible]
[illegible]	Clones, do.	[illegible]	[illegible]	[illegible]	[illegible]	[illegible]	[illegible]	[illegible]	[illegible]	[illegible]	[illegible]	[illegible]	[illegible]
[illegible]	Enniskillen, do.	[illegible]	[illegible]	[illegible]	[illegible]	[illegible]	[illegible]	[illegible]	[illegible]	[illegible]	[illegible]	[illegible]	[illegible]
[illegible]	Irvinestown, do.	[illegible]	[illegible]	[illegible]	[illegible]	[illegible]	[illegible]	[illegible]	[illegible]	[illegible]	[illegible]	[illegible]	[illegible]
[illegible]	Lisnaskea,	[illegible]	[illegible]	[illegible]	[illegible]	[illegible]	[illegible]	[illegible]	[illegible]	[illegible]	[illegible]	[illegible]	[illegible]
	25. Londonderry Co.												
[illegible]	Ballymoney, part of,	[illegible]	[illegible]	[illegible]	[illegible]	[illegible]	[illegible]	[illegible]	[illegible]	[illegible]	[illegible]	[illegible]	[illegible]
[illegible]	Coleraine, do.	[illegible]	[illegible]	[illegible]	[illegible]	[illegible]	[illegible]	[illegible]	[illegible]	[illegible]	[illegible]	[illegible]	[illegible]
[illegible]	Limavady,	[illegible]	[illegible]	[illegible]	[illegible]	[illegible]	[illegible]	[illegible]	[illegible]	[illegible]	[illegible]	[illegible]	[illegible]
[illegible]	Londonderry, part of,	[illegible]	[illegible]	[illegible]	[illegible]	[illegible]	[illegible]	[illegible]	[illegible]	[illegible]	[illegible]	[illegible]	[illegible]
[illegible]	Magherafelt,	[illegible]	[illegible]	[illegible]	[illegible]	[illegible]	[illegible]	[illegible]	[illegible]	[illegible]	[illegible]	[illegible]	[illegible]
	26. Monaghan Co.												
[illegible]	Carrickmacross,	[illegible]	[illegible]	[illegible]	[illegible]	[illegible]	[illegible]	[illegible]	[illegible]	[illegible]	[illegible]	[illegible]	[illegible]
[illegible]	Castleblayney, part of,	[illegible]	[illegible]	[illegible]	[illegible]	[illegible]	[illegible]	[illegible]	[illegible]	[illegible]	[illegible]	[illegible]	[illegible]
[illegible]	Clones, do.	[illegible]	[illegible]	[illegible]	[illegible]	[illegible]	[illegible]	[illegible]	[illegible]	[illegible]	[illegible]	[illegible]	[illegible]
[illegible]	Dundalk, do.	[illegible]	[illegible]	[illegible]	[illegible]	[illegible]	[illegible]	[illegible]	[illegible]	[illegible]	[illegible]	[illegible]	[illegible]
[illegible]	[illegible], do.	[illegible]	[illegible]	[illegible]	[illegible]	[illegible]	[illegible]	[illegible]	[illegible]	[illegible]	[illegible]	[illegible]	[illegible]
[illegible]	[illegible], do.	[illegible]	[illegible]	[illegible]	[illegible]	[illegible]	[illegible]	[illegible]	[illegible]	[illegible]	[illegible]	[illegible]	[illegible]
[illegible]	Monaghan,	[illegible]	[illegible]	[illegible]	[illegible]	[illegible]	[illegible]	[illegible]	[illegible]	[illegible]	[illegible]	[illegible]	[illegible]
	27. Tyrone Co.												
[illegible]	Armagh, part of,	[illegible]	[illegible]	[illegible]	[illegible]	[illegible]	[illegible]	[illegible]	[illegible]	[illegible]	[illegible]	[illegible]	[illegible]
[illegible]	Castlederg,	[illegible]	[illegible]	[illegible]	[illegible]	[illegible]	[illegible]	[illegible]	[illegible]	[illegible]	[illegible]	[illegible]	[illegible]
[illegible]	Clogher, part of,	[illegible]	[illegible]	[illegible]	[illegible]	[illegible]	[illegible]	[illegible]	[illegible]	[illegible]	[illegible]	[illegible]	[illegible]
[illegible]	Cookstown,	[illegible]	[illegible]	[illegible]	[illegible]	[illegible]	[illegible]	[illegible]	[illegible]	[illegible]	[illegible]	[illegible]	[illegible]
[illegible]	Dungannon,	[illegible]	[illegible]	[illegible]	[illegible]	[illegible]	[illegible]	[illegible]	[illegible]	[illegible]	[illegible]	[illegible]	[illegible]
[illegible]	Enniskillen, part of,	[illegible]	[illegible]	[illegible]	[illegible]	[illegible]	[illegible]	[illegible]	[illegible]	[illegible]	[illegible]	[illegible]	[illegible]
[illegible]	[illegible], do.	[illegible]	[illegible]	[illegible]	[illegible]	[illegible]	[illegible]	[illegible]	[illegible]	[illegible]	[illegible]	[illegible]	[illegible]
[illegible]	Omagh,	[illegible]	[illegible]	[illegible]	[illegible]	[illegible]	[illegible]	[illegible]	[illegible]	[illegible]	[illegible]	[illegible]	[illegible]
[illegible]	Strabane, part of,	[illegible]	[illegible]	[illegible]	[illegible]	[illegible]	[illegible]	[illegible]	[illegible]	[illegible]	[illegible]	[illegible]	[illegible]

IV.—[illegible]—MARRIAGES, BIRTHS, AND DEATHS, 18[illegible]—
Superintendent Registrars' Districts by Counties.

No.	Superintendent Registrars' Districts	Area in Statute Acres	Population, [illegible]	Total: Marriages	Total: Births	Total: Deaths	Births: Including [illegible]: Males	Births: Including [illegible]: Females	Births: Illegitimate: Males	Births: Illegitimate: Females	Deaths: Males	Deaths: Females	[illegible]
	[illegible] Galway Co.												
[illegible]	[illegible], part of,	[illegible]	[illegible]	[illegible]	[illegible]	[illegible]	[illegible]	[illegible]	[illegible]	[illegible]	[illegible]	[illegible]	[illegible]
[illegible]	[illegible], do.	[illegible]	[illegible]	[illegible]	[illegible]	[illegible]	[illegible]	[illegible]	[illegible]	[illegible]	[illegible]	[illegible]	[illegible]
[illegible]	[illegible]	[illegible]	[illegible]	[illegible]	[illegible]	[illegible]	[illegible]	[illegible]	[illegible]	[illegible]	[illegible]	[illegible]	[illegible]
[illegible]	[illegible]	[illegible]	[illegible]	[illegible]	[illegible]	[illegible]	[illegible]	[illegible]	[illegible]	[illegible]	[illegible]	[illegible]	[illegible]
[illegible]	[illegible]	[illegible]	[illegible]	[illegible]	[illegible]	[illegible]	[illegible]	[illegible]	[illegible]	[illegible]	[illegible]	[illegible]	[illegible]
[illegible]	[illegible]	[illegible]	[illegible]	[illegible]	[illegible]	[illegible]	[illegible]	[illegible]	[illegible]	[illegible]	[illegible]	[illegible]	[illegible]
[illegible]	[illegible]	[illegible]	[illegible]	[illegible]	[illegible]	[illegible]	[illegible]	[illegible]	[illegible]	[illegible]	[illegible]	[illegible]	[illegible]
[illegible]	[illegible]	[illegible]	[illegible]	[illegible]	[illegible]	[illegible]	[illegible]	[illegible]	[illegible]	[illegible]	[illegible]	[illegible]	[illegible]
[illegible]	[illegible]	[illegible]	[illegible]	[illegible]	[illegible]	[illegible]	[illegible]	[illegible]	[illegible]	[illegible]	[illegible]	[illegible]	[illegible]
[illegible]	[illegible]	[illegible]	[illegible]	[illegible]	[illegible]	[illegible]	[illegible]	[illegible]	[illegible]	[illegible]	[illegible]	[illegible]	[illegible]
[illegible]	[illegible], part of,	[illegible]	[illegible]	[illegible]	[illegible]	[illegible]	[illegible]	[illegible]	[illegible]	[illegible]	[illegible]	[illegible]	[illegible]
[illegible]	[illegible], do.	[illegible]	[illegible]	[illegible]	[illegible]	[illegible]	[illegible]	[illegible]	[illegible]	[illegible]	[illegible]	[illegible]	[illegible]
[illegible]	[illegible]	[illegible]	[illegible]	[illegible]	[illegible]	[illegible]	[illegible]	[illegible]	[illegible]	[illegible]	[illegible]	[illegible]	[illegible]
	[illegible] Leitrim Co.												
[illegible]	[illegible], part of,	[illegible]	[illegible]	[illegible]	[illegible]	[illegible]	[illegible]	[illegible]	[illegible]	[illegible]	[illegible]	[illegible]	[illegible]
[illegible]	[illegible], do.	[illegible]	[illegible]	[illegible]	[illegible]	[illegible]	[illegible]	[illegible]	[illegible]	[illegible]	[illegible]	[illegible]	[illegible]
[illegible]	[illegible], do.	[illegible]	[illegible]	[illegible]	[illegible]	[illegible]	[illegible]	[illegible]	[illegible]	[illegible]	[illegible]	[illegible]	[illegible]
[illegible]	[illegible]	[illegible]	[illegible]	[illegible]	[illegible]	[illegible]	[illegible]	[illegible]	[illegible]	[illegible]	[illegible]	[illegible]	[illegible]
[illegible]	[illegible]	[illegible]	[illegible]	[illegible]	[illegible]	[illegible]	[illegible]	[illegible]	[illegible]	[illegible]	[illegible]	[illegible]	[illegible]
	[illegible] Mayo Co.												
[illegible]	[illegible], part of,	[illegible]	[illegible]	[illegible]	[illegible]	[illegible]	[illegible]	[illegible]	[illegible]	[illegible]	[illegible]	[illegible]	[illegible]
[illegible]	[illegible], do.	[illegible]	[illegible]	[illegible]	[illegible]	[illegible]	[illegible]	[illegible]	[illegible]	[illegible]	[illegible]	[illegible]	[illegible]
[illegible]	[illegible]	[illegible]	[illegible]	[illegible]	[illegible]	[illegible]	[illegible]	[illegible]	[illegible]	[illegible]	[illegible]	[illegible]	[illegible]
[illegible]	[illegible]	[illegible]	[illegible]	[illegible]	[illegible]	[illegible]	[illegible]	[illegible]	[illegible]	[illegible]	[illegible]	[illegible]	[illegible]
[illegible]	[illegible], part of,	[illegible]	[illegible]	[illegible]	[illegible]	[illegible]	[illegible]	[illegible]	[illegible]	[illegible]	[illegible]	[illegible]	[illegible]
[illegible]	[illegible]	[illegible]	[illegible]	[illegible]	[illegible]	[illegible]	[illegible]	[illegible]	[illegible]	[illegible]	[illegible]	[illegible]	[illegible]
[illegible]	[illegible]	[illegible]	[illegible]	[illegible]	[illegible]	[illegible]	[illegible]	[illegible]	[illegible]	[illegible]	[illegible]	[illegible]	[illegible]
[illegible]	[illegible]	[illegible]	[illegible]	[illegible]	[illegible]	[illegible]	[illegible]	[illegible]	[illegible]	[illegible]	[illegible]	[illegible]	[illegible]
[illegible]	[illegible]	[illegible]	[illegible]	[illegible]	[illegible]	[illegible]	[illegible]	[illegible]	[illegible]	[illegible]	[illegible]	[illegible]	[illegible]
	[illegible] Roscommon Co.												
[illegible]	[illegible], part of,	[illegible]	[illegible]	[illegible]	[illegible]	[illegible]	[illegible]	[illegible]	[illegible]	[illegible]	[illegible]	[illegible]	[illegible]
[illegible]	[illegible], do.	[illegible]	[illegible]	[illegible]	[illegible]	[illegible]	[illegible]	[illegible]	[illegible]	[illegible]	[illegible]	[illegible]	[illegible]
[illegible]	[illegible], do.	[illegible]	[illegible]	[illegible]	[illegible]	[illegible]	[illegible]	[illegible]	[illegible]	[illegible]	[illegible]	[illegible]	[illegible]
[illegible]	[illegible], do.	[illegible]	[illegible]	[illegible]	[illegible]	[illegible]	[illegible]	[illegible]	[illegible]	[illegible]	[illegible]	[illegible]	[illegible]
[illegible]	[illegible], do.	[illegible]	[illegible]	[illegible]	[illegible]	[illegible]	[illegible]	[illegible]	[illegible]	[illegible]	[illegible]	[illegible]	[illegible]
[illegible]	[illegible], do.	[illegible]	[illegible]	[illegible]	[illegible]	[illegible]	[illegible]	[illegible]	[illegible]	[illegible]	[illegible]	[illegible]	[illegible]
[illegible]	[illegible]	[illegible]	[illegible]	[illegible]	[illegible]	[illegible]	[illegible]	[illegible]	[illegible]	[illegible]	[illegible]	[illegible]	[illegible]
	[illegible] Sligo Co.												
[illegible]	[illegible], part of,	[illegible]	[illegible]	[illegible]	[illegible]	[illegible]	[illegible]	[illegible]	[illegible]	[illegible]	[illegible]	[illegible]	[illegible]
[illegible]	[illegible], do.	[illegible]	[illegible]	[illegible]	[illegible]	[illegible]	[illegible]	[illegible]	[illegible]	[illegible]	[illegible]	[illegible]	[illegible]
[illegible]	[illegible]	[illegible]	[illegible]	[illegible]	[illegible]	[illegible]	[illegible]	[illegible]	[illegible]	[illegible]	[illegible]	[illegible]	[illegible]
[illegible]	[illegible]	[illegible]	[illegible]	[illegible]	[illegible]	[illegible]	[illegible]	[illegible]	[illegible]	[illegible]	[illegible]	[illegible]	[illegible]
[illegible]	[illegible]	[illegible]	[illegible]	[illegible]	[illegible]	[illegible]	[illegible]	[illegible]	[illegible]	[illegible]	[illegible]	[illegible]	[illegible]

MARRIAGES, BIRTHS, AND DEATHS, REGISTERED IN THE YEAR 1896.

SUPERINTENDENT REGISTRARS' DISTRICTS OR POOR LAW UNIONS, ARRANGED ALPHABETICALLY.

[illegible]	Superintendent Registrars' Districts or Poor Law Unions.	Area in Statute Acres.	Population, [illegible]	TOTAL.			BIRTHS.				DEATHS.		[illegible]
				Marriages.	Births.	Deaths.	Legitimate Males.	Legitimate Females.	Illegitimate Males.	Illegitimate Females.	Males.	Females.	
[illegible]	[illegible]	[illegible]	[illegible]	[illegible]	[illegible]	[illegible]	[illegible]	[illegible]	[illegible]	[illegible]	[illegible]	[illegible]	[illegible]
[illegible]	[illegible]	[illegible]	[illegible]	[illegible]	[illegible]	[illegible]	[illegible]	[illegible]	[illegible]	[illegible]	[illegible]	[illegible]	[illegible]
[illegible]	[illegible]	[illegible]	[illegible]	[illegible]	[illegible]	[illegible]	[illegible]	[illegible]	[illegible]	[illegible]	[illegible]	[illegible]	[illegible]
[illegible]	[illegible]	[illegible]	[illegible]	[illegible]	[illegible]	[illegible]	[illegible]	[illegible]	[illegible]	[illegible]	[illegible]	[illegible]	[illegible]
[illegible]	[illegible]	[illegible]	[illegible]	[illegible]	[illegible]	[illegible]	[illegible]	[illegible]	[illegible]	[illegible]	[illegible]	[illegible]	[illegible]
[illegible]	[illegible]	[illegible]	[illegible]	[illegible]	[illegible]	[illegible]	[illegible]	[illegible]	[illegible]	[illegible]	[illegible]	[illegible]	[illegible]
[illegible]	[illegible]	[illegible]	[illegible]	[illegible]	[illegible]	[illegible]	[illegible]	[illegible]	[illegible]	[illegible]	[illegible]	[illegible]	[illegible]
[illegible]	[illegible]	[illegible]	[illegible]	[illegible]	[illegible]	[illegible]	[illegible]	[illegible]	[illegible]	[illegible]	[illegible]	[illegible]	[illegible]
[illegible]	[illegible]	[illegible]	[illegible]	[illegible]	[illegible]	[illegible]	[illegible]	[illegible]	[illegible]	[illegible]	[illegible]	[illegible]	[illegible]
[illegible]	[illegible]	[illegible]	[illegible]	[illegible]	[illegible]	[illegible]	[illegible]	[illegible]	[illegible]	[illegible]	[illegible]	[illegible]	[illegible]
[illegible]	[illegible]	[illegible]	[illegible]	[illegible]	[illegible]	[illegible]	[illegible]	[illegible]	[illegible]	[illegible]	[illegible]	[illegible]	[illegible]
[illegible]	[illegible]	[illegible]	[illegible]	[illegible]	[illegible]	[illegible]	[illegible]	[illegible]	[illegible]	[illegible]	[illegible]	[illegible]	[illegible]
[illegible]	[illegible]	[illegible]	[illegible]	[illegible]	[illegible]	[illegible]	[illegible]	[illegible]	[illegible]	[illegible]	[illegible]	[illegible]	[illegible]
[illegible]	[illegible]	[illegible]	[illegible]	[illegible]	[illegible]	[illegible]	[illegible]	[illegible]	[illegible]	[illegible]	[illegible]	[illegible]	[illegible]
[illegible]	[illegible]	[illegible]	[illegible]	[illegible]	[illegible]	[illegible]	[illegible]	[illegible]	[illegible]	[illegible]	[illegible]	[illegible]	[illegible]
[illegible]	[illegible]	[illegible]	[illegible]	[illegible]	[illegible]	[illegible]	[illegible]	[illegible]	[illegible]	[illegible]	[illegible]	[illegible]	[illegible]
[illegible]	[illegible]	[illegible]	[illegible]	[illegible]	[illegible]	[illegible]	[illegible]	[illegible]	[illegible]	[illegible]	[illegible]	[illegible]	[illegible]
[illegible]	[illegible]	[illegible]	[illegible]	[illegible]	[illegible]	[illegible]	[illegible]	[illegible]	[illegible]	[illegible]	[illegible]	[illegible]	[illegible]
[illegible]	[illegible]	[illegible]	[illegible]	[illegible]	[illegible]	[illegible]	[illegible]	[illegible]	[illegible]	[illegible]	[illegible]	[illegible]	[illegible]
[illegible]	[illegible]	[illegible]	[illegible]	[illegible]	[illegible]	[illegible]	[illegible]	[illegible]	[illegible]	[illegible]	[illegible]	[illegible]	[illegible]
[illegible]	[illegible]	[illegible]	[illegible]	[illegible]	[illegible]	[illegible]	[illegible]	[illegible]	[illegible]	[illegible]	[illegible]	[illegible]	[illegible]
[illegible]	[illegible]	[illegible]	[illegible]	[illegible]	[illegible]	[illegible]	[illegible]	[illegible]	[illegible]	[illegible]	[illegible]	[illegible]	[illegible]
[illegible]	[illegible]	[illegible]	[illegible]	[illegible]	[illegible]	[illegible]	[illegible]	[illegible]	[illegible]	[illegible]	[illegible]	[illegible]	[illegible]
[illegible]	[illegible]	[illegible]	[illegible]	[illegible]	[illegible]	[illegible]	[illegible]	[illegible]	[illegible]	[illegible]	[illegible]	[illegible]	[illegible]
[illegible]	[illegible]	[illegible]	[illegible]	[illegible]	[illegible]	[illegible]	[illegible]	[illegible]	[illegible]	[illegible]	[illegible]	[illegible]	[illegible]
[illegible]	[illegible]	[illegible]	[illegible]	[illegible]	[illegible]	[illegible]	[illegible]	[illegible]	[illegible]	[illegible]	[illegible]	[illegible]	[illegible]
[illegible]	[illegible]	[illegible]	[illegible]	[illegible]	[illegible]	[illegible]	[illegible]	[illegible]	[illegible]	[illegible]	[illegible]	[illegible]	[illegible]
[illegible]	[illegible]	[illegible]	[illegible]	[illegible]	[illegible]	[illegible]	[illegible]	[illegible]	[illegible]	[illegible]	[illegible]	[illegible]	[illegible]
[illegible]	[illegible]	[illegible]	[illegible]	[illegible]	[illegible]	[illegible]	[illegible]	[illegible]	[illegible]	[illegible]	[illegible]	[illegible]	[illegible]
[illegible]	[illegible]	[illegible]	[illegible]	[illegible]	[illegible]	[illegible]	[illegible]	[illegible]	[illegible]	[illegible]	[illegible]	[illegible]	[illegible]
[illegible]	[illegible]	[illegible]	[illegible]	[illegible]	[illegible]	[illegible]	[illegible]	[illegible]	[illegible]	[illegible]	[illegible]	[illegible]	[illegible]
[illegible]	[illegible]	[illegible]	[illegible]	[illegible]	[illegible]	[illegible]	[illegible]	[illegible]	[illegible]	[illegible]	[illegible]	[illegible]	[illegible]
[illegible]	[illegible]	[illegible]	[illegible]	[illegible]	[illegible]	[illegible]	[illegible]	[illegible]	[illegible]	[illegible]	[illegible]	[illegible]	[illegible]
[illegible]	[illegible]	[illegible]	[illegible]	[illegible]	[illegible]	[illegible]	[illegible]	[illegible]	[illegible]	[illegible]	[illegible]	[illegible]	[illegible]
[illegible]	[illegible]	[illegible]	[illegible]	[illegible]	[illegible]	[illegible]	[illegible]	[illegible]	[illegible]	[illegible]	[illegible]	[illegible]	[illegible]
[illegible]	[illegible]	[illegible]	[illegible]	[illegible]	[illegible]	[illegible]	[illegible]	[illegible]	[illegible]	[illegible]	[illegible]	[illegible]	[illegible]
[illegible]	[illegible]	[illegible]	[illegible]	[illegible]	[illegible]	[illegible]	[illegible]	[illegible]	[illegible]	[illegible]	[illegible]	[illegible]	[illegible]
[illegible]	[illegible]	[illegible]	[illegible]	[illegible]	[illegible]	[illegible]	[illegible]	[illegible]	[illegible]	[illegible]	[illegible]	[illegible]	[illegible]
[illegible]	[illegible]	[illegible]	[illegible]	[illegible]	[illegible]	[illegible]	[illegible]	[illegible]	[illegible]	[illegible]	[illegible]	[illegible]	[illegible]
[illegible]	[illegible]	[illegible]	[illegible]	[illegible]	[illegible]	[illegible]	[illegible]	[illegible]	[illegible]	[illegible]	[illegible]	[illegible]	[illegible]
[illegible]	[illegible]	[illegible]	[illegible]	[illegible]	[illegible]	[illegible]	[illegible]	[illegible]	[illegible]	[illegible]	[illegible]	[illegible]	[illegible]
[illegible]	[illegible]	[illegible]	[illegible]	[illegible]	[illegible]	[illegible]	[illegible]	[illegible]	[illegible]	[illegible]	[illegible]	[illegible]	[illegible]
[illegible]	[illegible]	[illegible]	[illegible]	[illegible]	[illegible]	[illegible]	[illegible]	[illegible]	[illegible]	[illegible]	[illegible]	[illegible]	[illegible]
[illegible]	[illegible]	[illegible]	[illegible]	[illegible]	[illegible]	[illegible]	[illegible]	[illegible]	[illegible]	[illegible]	[illegible]	[illegible]	[illegible]
[illegible]	[illegible]	[illegible]	[illegible]	[illegible]	[illegible]	[illegible]	[illegible]	[illegible]	[illegible]	[illegible]	[illegible]	[illegible]	[illegible]
[illegible]	[illegible]	[illegible]	[illegible]	[illegible]	[illegible]	[illegible]	[illegible]	[illegible]	[illegible]	[illegible]	[illegible]	[illegible]	[illegible]
[illegible]	[illegible]	[illegible]	[illegible]	[illegible]	[illegible]	[illegible]	[illegible]	[illegible]	[illegible]	[illegible]	[illegible]	[illegible]	[illegible]
[illegible]	[illegible]	[illegible]	[illegible]	[illegible]	[illegible]	[illegible]	[illegible]	[illegible]	[illegible]	[illegible]	[illegible]	[illegible]	[illegible]
[illegible]	[illegible]	[illegible]	[illegible]	[illegible]	[illegible]	[illegible]	[illegible]	[illegible]	[illegible]	[illegible]	[illegible]	[illegible]	[illegible]
[illegible]	[illegible]	[illegible]	[illegible]	[illegible]	[illegible]	[illegible]	[illegible]	[illegible]	[illegible]	[illegible]	[illegible]	[illegible]	[illegible]
[illegible]	[illegible]	[illegible]	[illegible]	[illegible]	[illegible]	[illegible]	[illegible]	[illegible]	[illegible]	[illegible]	[illegible]	[illegible]	[illegible]
[illegible]	[illegible]	[illegible]	[illegible]	[illegible]	[illegible]	[illegible]	[illegible]	[illegible]	[illegible]	[illegible]	[illegible]	[illegible]	[illegible]
[illegible]	[illegible]	[illegible]	[illegible]	[illegible]	[illegible]	[illegible]	[illegible]	[illegible]	[illegible]	[illegible]	[illegible]	[illegible]	[illegible]

MARRIAGES, BIRTHS, AND DEATHS, REGISTERED IN THE YEAR [illegible].

SUPERINTENDENT REGISTRARS' DISTRICTS OR POOR LAW UNIONS, ARRANGED ALPHABETICALLY—*con.*

Number or Numbers of Union in preceding Abstract.	Superintendent Registrars' Districts or Poor Law Unions.	Area in Statute Acres.	Population, [illegible].	TOTAL. Marriages.	TOTAL. Births.	TOTAL. Deaths.	Births. Legitimate. Males.	Births. Legitimate. Females.	Births. Illegitimate. Males.	Births. Illegitimate. Females.	Deaths. Males.	Deaths. Females.	Excess of Births over Deaths.
[illegible]	Croom,	[illegible]	[illegible]	[illegible]	[illegible]	[illegible]	[illegible]	[illegible]	[illegible]	[illegible]	[illegible]	[illegible]	[illegible]
[illegible]	[illegible]	[illegible]	[illegible]	[illegible]	[illegible]	[illegible]	[illegible]	[illegible]	[illegible]	[illegible]	[illegible]	[illegible]	[illegible]
[illegible]	Dingle,	[illegible]	[illegible]	[illegible]	[illegible]	[illegible]	[illegible]	[illegible]	[illegible]	[illegible]	[illegible]	[illegible]	[illegible]
[illegible]	Donegal,	[illegible]	[illegible]	[illegible]	[illegible]	[illegible]	[illegible]	[illegible]	[illegible]	[illegible]	[illegible]	[illegible]	[illegible]
[illegible]	Downpatrick,	[illegible]	[illegible]	[illegible]	[illegible]	[illegible]	[illegible]	[illegible]	[illegible]	[illegible]	[illegible]	[illegible]	[illegible]
[illegible]	Drogheda,	[illegible]	[illegible]	[illegible]	[illegible]	[illegible]	[illegible]	[illegible]	[illegible]	[illegible]	[illegible]	[illegible]	[illegible]
[illegible]	Dromore West,	[illegible]	[illegible]	[illegible]	[illegible]	[illegible]	[illegible]	[illegible]	[illegible]	[illegible]	[illegible]	[illegible]	[illegible]
[illegible]	Dublin, North,	[illegible]	[illegible]	[illegible]	[illegible]	[illegible]	[illegible]	[illegible]	[illegible]	[illegible]	[illegible]	[illegible]	[illegible]
[illegible]	Dublin, South,	[illegible]	[illegible]	[illegible]	[illegible]	[illegible]	[illegible]	[illegible]	[illegible]	[illegible]	[illegible]	[illegible]	[illegible]
[illegible]	Dundalk,	[illegible]	[illegible]	[illegible]	[illegible]	[illegible]	[illegible]	[illegible]	[illegible]	[illegible]	[illegible]	[illegible]	[illegible]
[illegible]	Dunfanaghy,	[illegible]	[illegible]	[illegible]	[illegible]	[illegible]	[illegible]	[illegible]	[illegible]	[illegible]	[illegible]	[illegible]	[illegible]
[illegible]	Dungannon,	[illegible]	[illegible]	[illegible]	[illegible]	[illegible]	[illegible]	[illegible]	[illegible]	[illegible]	[illegible]	[illegible]	[illegible]
[illegible]	Dungarvan,	[illegible]	[illegible]	[illegible]	[illegible]	[illegible]	[illegible]	[illegible]	[illegible]	[illegible]	[illegible]	[illegible]	[illegible]
[illegible]	Dunmanway,	[illegible]	[illegible]	[illegible]	[illegible]	[illegible]	[illegible]	[illegible]	[illegible]	[illegible]	[illegible]	[illegible]	[illegible]
[illegible]	Dunshaughlin,	[illegible]	[illegible]	[illegible]	[illegible]	[illegible]	[illegible]	[illegible]	[illegible]	[illegible]	[illegible]	[illegible]	[illegible]
[illegible]	Edenderry,	[illegible]	[illegible]	[illegible]	[illegible]	[illegible]	[illegible]	[illegible]	[illegible]	[illegible]	[illegible]	[illegible]	[illegible]
[illegible]	Ennis,	[illegible]	[illegible]	[illegible]	[illegible]	[illegible]	[illegible]	[illegible]	[illegible]	[illegible]	[illegible]	[illegible]	[illegible]
[illegible]	Enniscorthy,	[illegible]	[illegible]	[illegible]	[illegible]	[illegible]	[illegible]	[illegible]	[illegible]	[illegible]	[illegible]	[illegible]	[illegible]
[illegible]	Enniskillen,	[illegible]	[illegible]	[illegible]	[illegible]	[illegible]	[illegible]	[illegible]	[illegible]	[illegible]	[illegible]	[illegible]	[illegible]
[illegible]	Ennistimon,	[illegible]	[illegible]	[illegible]	[illegible]	[illegible]	[illegible]	[illegible]	[illegible]	[illegible]	[illegible]	[illegible]	[illegible]
[illegible]	Fermoy,	[illegible]	[illegible]	[illegible]	[illegible]	[illegible]	[illegible]	[illegible]	[illegible]	[illegible]	[illegible]	[illegible]	[illegible]
[illegible]	Galway,	[illegible]	[illegible]	[illegible]	[illegible]	[illegible]	[illegible]	[illegible]	[illegible]	[illegible]	[illegible]	[illegible]	[illegible]
[illegible]	Glenamaddy,	[illegible]	[illegible]	[illegible]	[illegible]	[illegible]	[illegible]	[illegible]	[illegible]	[illegible]	[illegible]	[illegible]	[illegible]
[illegible]	Glenties,	[illegible]	[illegible]	[illegible]	[illegible]	[illegible]	[illegible]	[illegible]	[illegible]	[illegible]	[illegible]	[illegible]	[illegible]
[illegible]	Gorey,	[illegible]	[illegible]	[illegible]	[illegible]	[illegible]	[illegible]	[illegible]	[illegible]	[illegible]	[illegible]	[illegible]	[illegible]
[illegible]	Gort,	[illegible]	[illegible]	[illegible]	[illegible]	[illegible]	[illegible]	[illegible]	[illegible]	[illegible]	[illegible]	[illegible]	[illegible]
[illegible]	Granard,	[illegible]	[illegible]	[illegible]	[illegible]	[illegible]	[illegible]	[illegible]	[illegible]	[illegible]	[illegible]	[illegible]	[illegible]
[illegible]	Inishowen,	[illegible]	[illegible]	[illegible]	[illegible]	[illegible]	[illegible]	[illegible]	[illegible]	[illegible]	[illegible]	[illegible]	[illegible]
[illegible]	Irvinestown,	[illegible]	[illegible]	[illegible]	[illegible]	[illegible]	[illegible]	[illegible]	[illegible]	[illegible]	[illegible]	[illegible]	[illegible]
[illegible]	Kanturk,	[illegible]	[illegible]	[illegible]	[illegible]	[illegible]	[illegible]	[illegible]	[illegible]	[illegible]	[illegible]	[illegible]	[illegible]
[illegible]	Kells,	[illegible]	[illegible]	[illegible]	[illegible]	[illegible]	[illegible]	[illegible]	[illegible]	[illegible]	[illegible]	[illegible]	[illegible]
[illegible]	Kenmare,	[illegible]	[illegible]	[illegible]	[illegible]	[illegible]	[illegible]	[illegible]	[illegible]	[illegible]	[illegible]	[illegible]	[illegible]
[illegible]	Kilkeel,	[illegible]	[illegible]	[illegible]	[illegible]	[illegible]	[illegible]	[illegible]	[illegible]	[illegible]	[illegible]	[illegible]	[illegible]
[illegible]	Kilkenny,	[illegible]	[illegible]	[illegible]	[illegible]	[illegible]	[illegible]	[illegible]	[illegible]	[illegible]	[illegible]	[illegible]	[illegible]
[illegible]	Killadysert,	[illegible]	[illegible]	[illegible]	[illegible]	[illegible]	[illegible]	[illegible]	[illegible]	[illegible]	[illegible]	[illegible]	[illegible]
[illegible]	Killala,	[illegible]	[illegible]	[illegible]	[illegible]	[illegible]	[illegible]	[illegible]	[illegible]	[illegible]	[illegible]	[illegible]	[illegible]
[illegible]	Killarney,	[illegible]	[illegible]	[illegible]	[illegible]	[illegible]	[illegible]	[illegible]	[illegible]	[illegible]	[illegible]	[illegible]	[illegible]
[illegible]	Kilmacthomas,	[illegible]	[illegible]	[illegible]	[illegible]	[illegible]	[illegible]	[illegible]	[illegible]	[illegible]	[illegible]	[illegible]	[illegible]
[illegible]	Kilmallock,	[illegible]	[illegible]	[illegible]	[illegible]	[illegible]	[illegible]	[illegible]	[illegible]	[illegible]	[illegible]	[illegible]	[illegible]
[illegible]	Kilrush,	[illegible]	[illegible]	[illegible]	[illegible]	[illegible]	[illegible]	[illegible]	[illegible]	[illegible]	[illegible]	[illegible]	[illegible]
[illegible]	Kinsale,	[illegible]	[illegible]	[illegible]	[illegible]	[illegible]	[illegible]	[illegible]	[illegible]	[illegible]	[illegible]	[illegible]	[illegible]
[illegible]	Larne,	[illegible]	[illegible]	[illegible]	[illegible]	[illegible]	[illegible]	[illegible]	[illegible]	[illegible]	[illegible]	[illegible]	[illegible]
[illegible]	Letterkenny,	[illegible]	[illegible]	[illegible]	[illegible]	[illegible]	[illegible]	[illegible]	[illegible]	[illegible]	[illegible]	[illegible]	[illegible]
[illegible]	Limavady,	[illegible]	[illegible]	[illegible]	[illegible]	[illegible]	[illegible]	[illegible]	[illegible]	[illegible]	[illegible]	[illegible]	[illegible]
[illegible]	Limerick,	[illegible]	[illegible]	[illegible]	[illegible]	[illegible]	[illegible]	[illegible]	[illegible]	[illegible]	[illegible]	[illegible]	[illegible]
[illegible]	Lisburn,	[illegible]	[illegible]	[illegible]	[illegible]	[illegible]	[illegible]	[illegible]	[illegible]	[illegible]	[illegible]	[illegible]	[illegible]
[illegible]	Lismore,	[illegible]	[illegible]	[illegible]	[illegible]	[illegible]	[illegible]	[illegible]	[illegible]	[illegible]	[illegible]	[illegible]	[illegible]
[illegible]	Lisnaskea,	[illegible]	[illegible]	[illegible]	[illegible]	[illegible]	[illegible]	[illegible]	[illegible]	[illegible]	[illegible]	[illegible]	[illegible]
[illegible]	Listowel,	[illegible]	[illegible]	[illegible]	[illegible]	[illegible]	[illegible]	[illegible]	[illegible]	[illegible]	[illegible]	[illegible]	[illegible]
[illegible]	Londonderry,	[illegible]	[illegible]	[illegible]	[illegible]	[illegible]	[illegible]	[illegible]	[illegible]	[illegible]	[illegible]	[illegible]	[illegible]

MARRIAGES, BIRTHS, AND DEATHS, REGISTERED IN THE YEAR 1896

SUPERINTENDENT REGISTRARS' DISTRICTS OR POOR LAW UNIONS, ARRANGED ALPHABETICALLY—*con.*

Number or Numbers of Union in preceding Abstract	Superintendent Registrars' Districts or Poor Law Unions	Area in Statute Acres	Population, 1891	Total: Marriages	Total: Births	Total: Deaths	Legitimate Births: Males	Legitimate Births: Females	Illegitimate Births: Males	Illegitimate Births: Females	Deaths: Males	Deaths: Females	Excess of Births over Deaths
[illegible]	Longford,	[illegible]	[illegible]	[illegible]	[illegible]	[illegible]	[illegible]	[illegible]	[illegible]	[illegible]	[illegible]	[illegible]	[illegible]
[illegible]	Loughrea,	[illegible]	[illegible]	[illegible]	[illegible]	[illegible]	[illegible]	[illegible]	[illegible]	[illegible]	[illegible]	[illegible]	[illegible]
[illegible]	Lurgan,	[illegible]	[illegible]	[illegible]	[illegible]	[illegible]	[illegible]	[illegible]	[illegible]	[illegible]	[illegible]	[illegible]	[illegible]
[illegible]	Macroom,	[illegible]	[illegible]	[illegible]	[illegible]	[illegible]	[illegible]	[illegible]	[illegible]	[illegible]	[illegible]	[illegible]	[illegible]
[illegible]	Magherafelt,	[illegible]	[illegible]	[illegible]	[illegible]	[illegible]	[illegible]	[illegible]	[illegible]	[illegible]	[illegible]	[illegible]	[illegible]
[illegible]	Mallow,	[illegible]	[illegible]	[illegible]	[illegible]	[illegible]	[illegible]	[illegible]	[illegible]	[illegible]	[illegible]	[illegible]	[illegible]
[illegible]	Manorhamilton,	[illegible]	[illegible]	[illegible]	[illegible]	[illegible]	[illegible]	[illegible]	[illegible]	[illegible]	[illegible]	[illegible]	[illegible]
[illegible]	Middleton,	[illegible]	[illegible]	[illegible]	[illegible]	[illegible]	[illegible]	[illegible]	[illegible]	[illegible]	[illegible]	[illegible]	[illegible]
[illegible]	Millford,	[illegible]	[illegible]	[illegible]	[illegible]	[illegible]	[illegible]	[illegible]	[illegible]	[illegible]	[illegible]	[illegible]	[illegible]
[illegible]	Millstreet,	[illegible]	[illegible]	[illegible]	[illegible]	[illegible]	[illegible]	[illegible]	[illegible]	[illegible]	[illegible]	[illegible]	[illegible]
[illegible]	Mitchelstown,	[illegible]	[illegible]	[illegible]	[illegible]	[illegible]	[illegible]	[illegible]	[illegible]	[illegible]	[illegible]	[illegible]	[illegible]
[illegible]	Mohill,	[illegible]	[illegible]	[illegible]	[illegible]	[illegible]	[illegible]	[illegible]	[illegible]	[illegible]	[illegible]	[illegible]	[illegible]
[illegible]	Monaghan,	[illegible]	[illegible]	[illegible]	[illegible]	[illegible]	[illegible]	[illegible]	[illegible]	[illegible]	[illegible]	[illegible]	[illegible]
[illegible]	Mountbellew,	[illegible]	[illegible]	[illegible]	[illegible]	[illegible]	[illegible]	[illegible]	[illegible]	[illegible]	[illegible]	[illegible]	[illegible]
[illegible]	Mountmellick,	[illegible]	[illegible]	[illegible]	[illegible]	[illegible]	[illegible]	[illegible]	[illegible]	[illegible]	[illegible]	[illegible]	[illegible]
[illegible]	Mullingar,	[illegible]	[illegible]	[illegible]	[illegible]	[illegible]	[illegible]	[illegible]	[illegible]	[illegible]	[illegible]	[illegible]	[illegible]
[illegible]	Naas,	[illegible]	[illegible]	[illegible]	[illegible]	[illegible]	[illegible]	[illegible]	[illegible]	[illegible]	[illegible]	[illegible]	[illegible]
[illegible]	Navan,	[illegible]	[illegible]	[illegible]	[illegible]	[illegible]	[illegible]	[illegible]	[illegible]	[illegible]	[illegible]	[illegible]	[illegible]
[illegible]	Nenagh,	[illegible]	[illegible]	[illegible]	[illegible]	[illegible]	[illegible]	[illegible]	[illegible]	[illegible]	[illegible]	[illegible]	[illegible]
[illegible]	Newcastle,	[illegible]	[illegible]	[illegible]	[illegible]	[illegible]	[illegible]	[illegible]	[illegible]	[illegible]	[illegible]	[illegible]	[illegible]
[illegible]	New Ross,	[illegible]	[illegible]	[illegible]	[illegible]	[illegible]	[illegible]	[illegible]	[illegible]	[illegible]	[illegible]	[illegible]	[illegible]
[illegible]	Newry,	[illegible]	[illegible]	[illegible]	[illegible]	[illegible]	[illegible]	[illegible]	[illegible]	[illegible]	[illegible]	[illegible]	[illegible]
[illegible]	Newtownards,	[illegible]	[illegible]	[illegible]	[illegible]	[illegible]	[illegible]	[illegible]	[illegible]	[illegible]	[illegible]	[illegible]	[illegible]
[illegible]	Oldcastle,	[illegible]	[illegible]	[illegible]	[illegible]	[illegible]	[illegible]	[illegible]	[illegible]	[illegible]	[illegible]	[illegible]	[illegible]
[illegible]	Omagh,	[illegible]	[illegible]	[illegible]	[illegible]	[illegible]	[illegible]	[illegible]	[illegible]	[illegible]	[illegible]	[illegible]	[illegible]
[illegible]	Oughterard,	[illegible]	[illegible]	[illegible]	[illegible]	[illegible]	[illegible]	[illegible]	[illegible]	[illegible]	[illegible]	[illegible]	[illegible]
[illegible]	Parsonstown,	[illegible]	[illegible]	[illegible]	[illegible]	[illegible]	[illegible]	[illegible]	[illegible]	[illegible]	[illegible]	[illegible]	[illegible]
[illegible]	Rathdown,	[illegible]	[illegible]	[illegible]	[illegible]	[illegible]	[illegible]	[illegible]	[illegible]	[illegible]	[illegible]	[illegible]	[illegible]
[illegible]	Rathdrum,	[illegible]	[illegible]	[illegible]	[illegible]	[illegible]	[illegible]	[illegible]	[illegible]	[illegible]	[illegible]	[illegible]	[illegible]
[illegible]	Rathkeale,	[illegible]	[illegible]	[illegible]	[illegible]	[illegible]	[illegible]	[illegible]	[illegible]	[illegible]	[illegible]	[illegible]	[illegible]
[illegible]	[illegible]	[illegible]	[illegible]	[illegible]	[illegible]	[illegible]	[illegible]	[illegible]	[illegible]	[illegible]	[illegible]	[illegible]	[illegible]
[illegible]	[illegible]	[illegible]	[illegible]	[illegible]	[illegible]	[illegible]	[illegible]	[illegible]	[illegible]	[illegible]	[illegible]	[illegible]	[illegible]
[illegible]	[illegible]	[illegible]	[illegible]	[illegible]	[illegible]	[illegible]	[illegible]	[illegible]	[illegible]	[illegible]	[illegible]	[illegible]	[illegible]
[illegible]	[illegible]	[illegible]	[illegible]	[illegible]	[illegible]	[illegible]	[illegible]	[illegible]	[illegible]	[illegible]	[illegible]	[illegible]	[illegible]
[illegible]	Shillelagh,	[illegible]	[illegible]	[illegible]	[illegible]	[illegible]	[illegible]	[illegible]	[illegible]	[illegible]	[illegible]	[illegible]	[illegible]
[illegible]	Skibbereen,	[illegible]	[illegible]	[illegible]	[illegible]	[illegible]	[illegible]	[illegible]	[illegible]	[illegible]	[illegible]	[illegible]	[illegible]
[illegible]	Skull,	[illegible]	[illegible]	[illegible]	[illegible]	[illegible]	[illegible]	[illegible]	[illegible]	[illegible]	[illegible]	[illegible]	[illegible]
[illegible]	Sligo,	[illegible]	[illegible]	[illegible]	[illegible]	[illegible]	[illegible]	[illegible]	[illegible]	[illegible]	[illegible]	[illegible]	[illegible]
[illegible]	Strabane,	[illegible]	[illegible]	[illegible]	[illegible]	[illegible]	[illegible]	[illegible]	[illegible]	[illegible]	[illegible]	[illegible]	[illegible]
[illegible]	Stranorlar,	[illegible]	[illegible]	[illegible]	[illegible]	[illegible]	[illegible]	[illegible]	[illegible]	[illegible]	[illegible]	[illegible]	[illegible]
[illegible]	Strokestown,	[illegible]	[illegible]	[illegible]	[illegible]	[illegible]	[illegible]	[illegible]	[illegible]	[illegible]	[illegible]	[illegible]	[illegible]
[illegible]	Swineford,	[illegible]	[illegible]	[illegible]	[illegible]	[illegible]	[illegible]	[illegible]	[illegible]	[illegible]	[illegible]	[illegible]	[illegible]
[illegible]	Thomastown,	[illegible]	[illegible]	[illegible]	[illegible]	[illegible]	[illegible]	[illegible]	[illegible]	[illegible]	[illegible]	[illegible]	[illegible]
[illegible]	Thurles,	[illegible]	[illegible]	[illegible]	[illegible]	[illegible]	[illegible]	[illegible]	[illegible]	[illegible]	[illegible]	[illegible]	[illegible]
[illegible]	Tipperary,	[illegible]	[illegible]	[illegible]	[illegible]	[illegible]	[illegible]	[illegible]	[illegible]	[illegible]	[illegible]	[illegible]	[illegible]
[illegible]	Tobercurry,	[illegible]	[illegible]	[illegible]	[illegible]	[illegible]	[illegible]	[illegible]	[illegible]	[illegible]	[illegible]	[illegible]	[illegible]
[illegible]	Tralee,	[illegible]	[illegible]	[illegible]	[illegible]	[illegible]	[illegible]	[illegible]	[illegible]	[illegible]	[illegible]	[illegible]	[illegible]
[illegible]	Trim,	[illegible]	[illegible]	[illegible]	[illegible]	[illegible]	[illegible]	[illegible]	[illegible]	[illegible]	[illegible]	[illegible]	[illegible]
[illegible]	Tuam,	[illegible]	[illegible]	[illegible]	[illegible]	[illegible]	[illegible]	[illegible]	[illegible]	[illegible]	[illegible]	[illegible]	[illegible]
[illegible]	Tulla,	[illegible]	[illegible]	[illegible]	[illegible]	[illegible]	[illegible]	[illegible]	[illegible]	[illegible]	[illegible]	[illegible]	[illegible]
[illegible]	Tullamore,	[illegible]	[illegible]	[illegible]	[illegible]	[illegible]	[illegible]	[illegible]	[illegible]	[illegible]	[illegible]	[illegible]	[illegible]
[illegible]	Urlingford,	[illegible]	[illegible]	[illegible]	[illegible]	[illegible]	[illegible]	[illegible]	[illegible]	[illegible]	[illegible]	[illegible]	[illegible]
[illegible]	Waterford,	[illegible]	[illegible]	[illegible]	[illegible]	[illegible]	[illegible]	[illegible]	[illegible]	[illegible]	[illegible]	[illegible]	[illegible]
[illegible]	Westport,	[illegible]	[illegible]	[illegible]	[illegible]	[illegible]	[illegible]	[illegible]	[illegible]	[illegible]	[illegible]	[illegible]	[illegible]
[illegible]	Wexford,	[illegible]	[illegible]	[illegible]	[illegible]	[illegible]	[illegible]	[illegible]	[illegible]	[illegible]	[illegible]	[illegible]	[illegible]
[illegible]	Youghal,	[illegible]	[illegible]	[illegible]	[illegible]	[illegible]	[illegible]	[illegible]	[illegible]	[illegible]	[illegible]	[illegible]	[illegible]

BIRTHS AND DEATHS Registered in the Year [illegible]—Registrars' Districts, [illegible]

[illegible]

Registrars' Districts	[illegible]	[illegible]	Births		Deaths			
			[illegible]	[illegible]	[illegible]	[illegible]	[illegible]	[illegible]
I.—PROVINCE OF LEINSTER.								
[illegible] Co.								
1. [illegible], part of.								
[illegible]	[illegible]	[illegible]	[illegible]	[illegible]	[illegible]	[illegible]	[illegible]	[illegible]
[illegible]	[illegible]	[illegible]	[illegible]	[illegible]	[illegible]	[illegible]	[illegible]	[illegible]
2. [illegible], part of.								
[illegible]	[illegible]	[illegible]	[illegible]	[illegible]	[illegible]	[illegible]	[illegible]	[illegible]
[illegible]	[illegible]	[illegible]	[illegible]	[illegible]	[illegible]	[illegible]	[illegible]	[illegible]
[illegible]	[illegible]	[illegible]	[illegible]	[illegible]	[illegible]	[illegible]	[illegible]	[illegible]
[illegible]	[illegible]	[illegible]	[illegible]	[illegible]	[illegible]	[illegible]	[illegible]	[illegible]
[illegible]	[illegible]	[illegible]	[illegible]	[illegible]	[illegible]	[illegible]	[illegible]	[illegible]
[illegible]	[illegible]	[illegible]	[illegible]	[illegible]	[illegible]	[illegible]	[illegible]	[illegible]
3. [illegible], part of.								
[illegible]	[illegible]	[illegible]	[illegible]	[illegible]	[illegible]	[illegible]	[illegible]	[illegible]
4. [illegible], part of.								
[illegible]	[illegible]	[illegible]	[illegible]	[illegible]	[illegible]	[illegible]	[illegible]	[illegible]
5. [illegible], part of.								
[illegible]	[illegible]	[illegible]	[illegible]	[illegible]	[illegible]	[illegible]	[illegible]	[illegible]
[illegible]	[illegible]	[illegible]	[illegible]	[illegible]	[illegible]	[illegible]	[illegible]	[illegible]
[illegible] Co.								
6. [illegible]								
[illegible]	[illegible]	[illegible]	[illegible]	[illegible]	[illegible]	[illegible]	[illegible]	[illegible]
[illegible]	[illegible]	[illegible]	[illegible]	[illegible]	[illegible]	[illegible]	[illegible]	[illegible]
[illegible]	[illegible]	[illegible]	[illegible]	[illegible]	[illegible]	[illegible]	[illegible]	[illegible]
[illegible]	[illegible]	[illegible]	[illegible]	[illegible]	[illegible]	[illegible]	[illegible]	[illegible]
[illegible]	[illegible]	[illegible]	[illegible]	[illegible]	[illegible]	[illegible]	[illegible]	[illegible]
[illegible]	[illegible]	[illegible]	[illegible]	[illegible]	[illegible]	[illegible]	[illegible]	[illegible]
7. [illegible], part of.								
[illegible]	[illegible]	[illegible]	[illegible]	[illegible]	[illegible]	[illegible]	[illegible]	[illegible]
[illegible]	[illegible]	[illegible]	[illegible]	[illegible]	[illegible]	[illegible]	[illegible]	[illegible]
8. [illegible]								
[illegible]	[illegible]	[illegible]	[illegible]	[illegible]	[illegible]	[illegible]	[illegible]	[illegible]
[illegible]	[illegible]	[illegible]	[illegible]	[illegible]	[illegible]	[illegible]	[illegible]	[illegible]
[illegible]	[illegible]	[illegible]	[illegible]	[illegible]	[illegible]	[illegible]	[illegible]	[illegible]
[illegible]	[illegible]	[illegible]	[illegible]	[illegible]	[illegible]	[illegible]	[illegible]	[illegible]
[illegible]	[illegible]	[illegible]	[illegible]	[illegible]	[illegible]	[illegible]	[illegible]	[illegible]
[illegible]	[illegible]	[illegible]	[illegible]	[illegible]	[illegible]	[illegible]	[illegible]	[illegible]
[illegible]	[illegible]	[illegible]	[illegible]	[illegible]	[illegible]	[illegible]	[illegible]	[illegible]
[illegible]		[illegible]	[illegible]	[illegible]	[illegible]	[illegible]	[illegible]	[illegible]
[illegible]		[illegible]	[illegible]	[illegible]	[illegible]	[illegible]	[illegible]	[illegible]
[illegible]		[illegible]	[illegible]	[illegible]	[illegible]	[illegible]	[illegible]	[illegible]
9. [illegible]								
[illegible]	[illegible]	[illegible]	[illegible]	[illegible]	[illegible]	[illegible]	[illegible]	[illegible]
[illegible]	[illegible]	[illegible]	[illegible]	[illegible]	[illegible]	[illegible]	[illegible]	[illegible]
[illegible]	[illegible]	[illegible]	[illegible]	[illegible]	[illegible]	[illegible]	[illegible]	[illegible]
[illegible]	[illegible]	[illegible]	[illegible]	[illegible]	[illegible]	[illegible]	[illegible]	[illegible]
[illegible]	[illegible]	[illegible]	[illegible]	[illegible]	[illegible]	[illegible]	[illegible]	[illegible]
[illegible]	[illegible]	[illegible]	[illegible]	[illegible]	[illegible]	[illegible]	[illegible]	[illegible]
[illegible]		[illegible]	[illegible]	[illegible]	[illegible]	[illegible]	[illegible]	[illegible]
[illegible]		[illegible]	[illegible]	[illegible]	[illegible]	[illegible]	[illegible]	[illegible]
[illegible]		[illegible]	[illegible]	[illegible]	[illegible]	[illegible]	[illegible]	[illegible]
[illegible]	[illegible]	[illegible]	[illegible]	[illegible]	[illegible]	[illegible]	[illegible]	[illegible]

BIRTHS and DEATHS Registered in the Year 188[illegible].—Registrars' Districts, arranged by Counties and Superintendent Registrars' Districts—continued.

[illegible]	[illegible]	[illegible]	[illegible]	[illegible]	[illegible]	[illegible]	[illegible]	[illegible]	[illegible]	[illegible]	[illegible]	[illegible]	[illegible]

BIRTHS AND DEATHS Registered in the Year 1856—REGISTRARS' DISTRICTS, arranged by COUNTIES and SUPERINTENDENT REGISTRARS' DISTRICTS—*continued.*

No.	Registrars' Districts.	Area in Statute Acres.	Population in 1851.	Total Births.	Total Deaths.	Births: Legitimate Males	Births: Legitimate Females	Births: Illegitimate Males	Births: Illegitimate Females	Deaths: Males	Deaths: Females	Excess of Births over Deaths.
	I.—PROVINCE OF LEINSTER—*contd.*											
	20. KILKENNY.											
1	Freshford,	[illegible]	[illegible]	[illegible]	[illegible]	[illegible]	[illegible]	.	1	[illegible]	[illegible]	[illegible]
2	Gowran,	[illegible]	[illegible]	[illegible]	[illegible]	[illegible]	[illegible]	1	.	[illegible]	[illegible]	[illegible]
3	Kilkenny, No. 1, W.,	[illegible]	[illegible]	[illegible]	[illegible]	[illegible]	[illegible]	[illegible]	[illegible]	[illegible]	[illegible]	[illegible]
4	" 2,	[illegible]	[illegible]	[illegible]	[illegible]	[illegible]	[illegible]	1	1	[illegible]	[illegible]	[illegible]
5	Thomastown,	[illegible]	[illegible]	[illegible]	[illegible]	[illegible]	[illegible]	1	.	[illegible]	[illegible]	[illegible]
6	Tullaroan,	[illegible]	[illegible]	[illegible]	[illegible]	[illegible]	[illegible]	.	.	[illegible]	[illegible]	[illegible]
	21. NEW ROSS, part of											
1	[illegible],	[illegible]	[illegible]	[illegible]	[illegible]	[illegible]	[illegible]	.	1	[illegible]	[illegible]	[illegible]
	22. THOMASTOWN.											
1	Graigue,	[illegible]	[illegible]	[illegible]	[illegible]	[illegible]	[illegible]	1	3	[illegible]	[illegible]	[illegible]
2	Inistioge,	[illegible]	[illegible]	[illegible]	[illegible]	[illegible]	[illegible]	1	1	[illegible]	[illegible]	.
3	Knocktopher,	[illegible]	[illegible]	[illegible]	[illegible]	[illegible]	[illegible]	.	.	[illegible]	[illegible]	[illegible]
4	Thomastown, W.,	[illegible]	[illegible]	[illegible]	[illegible]	[illegible]	[illegible]	3	1	[illegible]	[illegible]	[illegible]
	23. URLINGFORD, part of											
1	Balleen,	17,301	[illegible]	[illegible]	[illegible]	[illegible]	[illegible]	1	.	[illegible]	[illegible]	[illegible]
2	Johnstown, part of,	[illegible]	[illegible]	[illegible]	[illegible]	[illegible]	[illegible]	.	.	[illegible]	[illegible]	[illegible]
3	[illegible], do., W.,	16,4[illegible]	[illegible]	[illegible]	[illegible]	[illegible]	[illegible]	[illegible]	1	[illegible]	[illegible]	−6
	24. WATERFORD, part of											
1	[illegible],	[illegible]	[illegible]	[illegible]	[illegible]	[illegible]	[illegible]	1	.	[illegible]	[illegible]	[illegible]
2	[illegible],	[illegible]	[illegible]	[illegible]	[illegible]	[illegible]	[illegible]	1	1	[illegible]	[illegible]	[illegible]
	King's Co.											
	25. EDENDERRY, part of											
1	Edenderry, W.,	[illegible]	[illegible]	[illegible]	[illegible]	[illegible]	[illegible]	.	1	[illegible]	[illegible]	[illegible]
2	[illegible], part of,	[illegible]	[illegible]	[illegible]	[illegible]	[illegible]	[illegible]	.	.	7	[illegible]	[illegible]
3	[illegible],	[illegible]	[illegible]	[illegible]	[illegible]	[illegible]	[illegible]	1	.	[illegible]	[illegible]	7
	26. MOUNTMELLICK, part of											
1	Clonygowan, part of,	[illegible]	[illegible]	[illegible]	[illegible]	[illegible]	[illegible]	.	[illegible]	[illegible]	[illegible]	[illegible]
	27. PARSONSTOWN, part of											
1	[illegible],	[illegible]	[illegible]	[illegible]	[illegible]	[illegible]	[illegible]	.	1	[illegible]	[illegible]	[illegible]
2	[illegible],	[illegible]	[illegible]	[illegible]	[illegible]	[illegible]	[illegible]	.	.	[illegible]	[illegible]	[illegible]
3	[illegible],	[illegible]	[illegible]	[illegible]	[illegible]	[illegible]	[illegible]	.	.	[illegible]	[illegible]	[illegible]
4	[illegible],	[illegible]	[illegible]	[illegible]	[illegible]	[illegible]	[illegible]	.	.	[illegible]	[illegible]	[illegible]
5	[illegible],	[illegible]	[illegible]	[illegible]	[illegible]	[illegible]	[illegible]	.	.	[illegible]	[illegible]	[illegible]
6	Parsonstown, W.,	[illegible]	[illegible]	[illegible]	[illegible]	[illegible]	[illegible]	[illegible]	[illegible]	[illegible]	[illegible]	[illegible]
	28. ROSCREA, part of											
1	Roscrea, No. 1, part of,	[illegible]	[illegible]	[illegible]	[illegible]	[illegible]	[illegible]	.	.	[illegible]	[illegible]	[illegible]
2	" 2,	[illegible]	[illegible]	[illegible]	[illegible]	[illegible]	[illegible]	.	.	[illegible]	[illegible]	[illegible]
3	Shinrone,	[illegible]	[illegible]	[illegible]	[illegible]	[illegible]	[illegible]	1	.	[illegible]	[illegible]	[illegible]
	29. TULLAMORE, part of											
1	Clara,	[illegible]	[illegible]	[illegible]	[illegible]	[illegible]	[illegible]	.	.	[illegible]	[illegible]	[illegible]
2	Kilbeggan, part of,	[illegible]	[illegible]	[illegible]	[illegible]	[illegible]	[illegible]	1	.	[illegible]	[illegible]	[illegible]
3	Kilcormac,	[illegible]	[illegible]	[illegible]	[illegible]	[illegible]	[illegible]	.	.	[illegible]	[illegible]	[illegible]
4	Philipstown,	[illegible]	[illegible]	[illegible]	[illegible]	[illegible]	[illegible]	.	.	[illegible]	[illegible]	[illegible]
5	Tullamore, W.,	[illegible]	[illegible]	[illegible]	[illegible]	[illegible]	[illegible]	[illegible]	[illegible]	[illegible]	[illegible]	[illegible]

[illegible]

BIRTHS AND DEATHS Registered in the Year 1896—REGISTRARS' DISTRICTS, arranged by COUNTIES and SUPERINTENDENT REGISTRARS' DISTRICTS—*continued*.

No.	REGISTRARS' DISTRICTS.	Area in Statute Acres.	Population in 1891.	TOTAL: Births.	TOTAL: Deaths.	Births: Including Illegitimate Births: Males.	Births: Including Illegitimate Births: Females.	Illegitimate Births: Males.	Illegitimate Births: Females.	Deaths: Males.	Deaths: Females.	Number of Workhouse Deaths.
	I.—PROVINCE OF LEINSTER.—*con.*											
	Longford Co.											
	32. BALLYMAHON, part of.											
1	Abbeyshrule,	[illegible]	[illegible]	[illegible]	[illegible]	[illegible]	[illegible]	1	-	[illegible]	[illegible]	[illegible]
2	Ballymahon, E.	[illegible]	[illegible]	[illegible]	[illegible]	[illegible]	[illegible]	[illegible]	[illegible]	[illegible]	[illegible]	[illegible]
	31. GRANARD, part of.											
1	Ballinalee,	[illegible]	[illegible]	[illegible]	[illegible]	[illegible]	[illegible]	-	-	[illegible]	[illegible]	[illegible]
2	Granard, E.,	[illegible]	[illegible]	[illegible]	[illegible]	[illegible]	[illegible]	[illegible]	[illegible]	[illegible]	[illegible]	[illegible]
3	Scrabby, part of,	[illegible]	[illegible]	[illegible]	[illegible]	[illegible]	[illegible]	-	-	[illegible]	[illegible]	[illegible]
4	Streete, do.,	[illegible]	[illegible]	[illegible]	[illegible]	[illegible]	[illegible]	1	1	[illegible]	[illegible]	[illegible]
	33. LONGFORD.											
1	Drumlish,	[illegible]	[illegible]	[illegible]	[illegible]	[illegible]	[illegible]	[illegible]	-	[illegible]	[illegible]	[illegible]
2	Killashee,	[illegible]	[illegible]	[illegible]	[illegible]	[illegible]	[illegible]	-	-	[illegible]	[illegible]	[illegible]
3	Longford, E.,	[illegible]	[illegible]	[illegible]	[illegible]	[illegible]	[illegible]	-	1	[illegible]	[illegible]	[illegible]
	Louth Co., and Co. of Town of Drogheda.											
	15. ARDEE, part of.											
1	Ardee, E.,	[illegible]	[illegible]	[illegible]	[illegible]	[illegible]	[illegible]	[illegible]	[illegible]	[illegible]	[illegible]	1
2	Castlebellingham,	[illegible]	[illegible]	[illegible]	[illegible]	[illegible]	[illegible]	-	-	[illegible]	[illegible]	[illegible]
3	Collon, part of,	[illegible]	[illegible]	[illegible]	[illegible]	[illegible]	[illegible]	-	-	[illegible]	[illegible]	[illegible]
4	Louth,	[illegible]	[illegible]	[illegible]	[illegible]	[illegible]	[illegible]	-	-	[illegible]	[illegible]	[illegible]
	34. DUNDALK, part of.											
1	Dundalk, No. 1,	[illegible]	[illegible]	[illegible]	[illegible]	[illegible]	[illegible]	-	-	[illegible]	[illegible]	[illegible]
2	" 2,	[illegible]	[illegible]	[illegible]	[illegible]	[illegible]	[illegible]	-	[illegible]	[illegible]	[illegible]	[illegible]
3	[illegible], part of,	[illegible]	[illegible]	[illegible]	[illegible]	[illegible]	16	1	-	[illegible]	[illegible]	[illegible]
4	St. Mary's, do.,	[illegible]	[illegible]	[illegible]	[illegible]	[illegible]	[illegible]	1	1	[illegible]	[illegible]	[illegible]
5	[illegible],	[illegible]	[illegible]	[illegible]	[illegible]	[illegible]	[illegible]	-	-	[illegible]	[illegible]	[illegible]
	35. DROGHEDA, part of.											
1	[illegible], part of,	[illegible]	[illegible]	[illegible]	[illegible]	[illegible]	[illegible]	-	1	[illegible]	[illegible]	-
2	[illegible],	[illegible]	[illegible]	[illegible]	[illegible]	[illegible]	[illegible]	[illegible]	-	[illegible]	[illegible]	[illegible]
3	[illegible],	[illegible]	[illegible]	[illegible]	[illegible]	[illegible]	[illegible]	-	-	[illegible]	[illegible]	[illegible]
4	Drogheda, W.,	[illegible]	[illegible]	[illegible]	[illegible]	[illegible]	[illegible]	[illegible]	[illegible]	[illegible]	[illegible]	[illegible]
5	Louth, part of,	[illegible]	[illegible]	[illegible]	[illegible]	[illegible]	[illegible]	-	1	[illegible]	[illegible]	[illegible]
6	[illegible],	[illegible]	[illegible]	[illegible]	[illegible]	[illegible]	[illegible]	-	-	[illegible]	[illegible]	[illegible]
	Meath Co.											
	15. ARDEE, part of.											
1	Collon, part of,	[illegible]	[illegible]	[illegible]	[illegible]	[illegible]	[illegible]	-	-	[illegible]	[illegible]	[illegible]
2	[illegible],	[illegible]	[illegible]	[illegible]	[illegible]	[illegible]	[illegible]	-	-	[illegible]	[illegible]	[illegible]
	37. CELBRIDGE, part of.											
1	Maynooth, part of,	[illegible]	[illegible]	[illegible]	7	-	[illegible]	-	-	[illegible]	[illegible]	[illegible]
	38. [illegible], part of.					[illegible]				[illegible]	[illegible]	[illegible]

[illegible]

[illegible], part of.

[illegible]

[illegible], part of

[illegible]

[illegible]

[illegible]

[illegible]

[illegible]

[illegible]

[illegible]

[illegible]

[illegible], part of.

[illegible]

[illegible]

[illegible]

[illegible]

[illegible]

[illegible]

[illegible]

[illegible]

[illegible]

[illegible]

[illegible]

[illegible]

[illegible]

[illegible]

[illegible]

[illegible]

BIRTHS AND DEATHS Registered in the Year 1896.—Registrars' Districts, arranged by Counties and Superintendent Registrars' Districts—*continued.*

No.	Registrars' Districts	Area in Statute Acres	Population in 1891	Total Births	Total Deaths	Births, Including Illegitimate Births: Males	Births, Including Illegitimate Births: Females	Illegitimate Births: Males	Illegitimate Births: Females	Deaths: Males	Deaths: Females	Excess of Births over Deaths
	II.—PROVINCE OF LEINSTER—*con.*											
	Westmeath Co.											
	11. Athlone, part of.											
1	Athlone, No. 1, W.,	16,277	4,778	[illegible]	114	[illegible]	56	[illegible]	1	67	[illegible]	1
2	[illegible]	14,571	[illegible]	73	57	40	[illegible]	1	.	[illegible]	15	[illegible]
3	[illegible]	22,540	4,444	[illegible]	[illegible]	35	57	1	.	[illegible]	10	[illegible]
	12. Ballymahon, part of.											
1	Ballymore,	[illegible]	[illegible]	[illegible]	44	[illegible]	[illegible]	.	.	[illegible]	[illegible]	[illegible]
	13. Delvin.											
1	Castlepollard,	[illegible]	[illegible]	81	34	41	40	.	.	[illegible]	[illegible]	47
2	[illegible]	[illegible]	[illegible]	40	44	[illegible]	[illegible]	.	1	[illegible]	[illegible]	7
3	Delvin, W.,	27,574	[illegible]	[illegible]	[illegible]	[illegible]	[illegible]	.	[illegible]	[illegible]	31	—[illegible]
	14. Granard, part of.											
1	[illegible]	11,[illegible]	1,5[illegible]	[illegible]	[illegible]	15	6	.	1	4	4	[illegible]
2	[illegible], part of,	[illegible]	[illegible]	[illegible]	[illegible]	10	13	.	.	[illegible]	[illegible]	[illegible]
3	[illegible], do.	[illegible]	[illegible]	[illegible]	17	10	19	.	.	9	7	[illegible]
	15. Mullingar.											
1	[illegible]	[illegible]	[illegible]	77	[illegible]	[illegible]	41	.	1	[illegible]	[illegible]	[illegible]
2	Castletown Geoghegan,	[illegible]	[illegible]	71	[illegible]	[illegible]	[illegible]	.	2	[illegible]	[illegible]	9
3	Kilbeggan,	[illegible]	[illegible]	[illegible]	[illegible]	[illegible]	[illegible]	.	.	71	[illegible]	14
4	[illegible]	[illegible]	[illegible]	[illegible]	[illegible]	[illegible]	18	.	.	13	17	[illegible]
5	Mullingar, W.,	[illegible]	[illegible]	[illegible]	[illegible]	1[illegible]	[illegible]	[illegible]	7	[illegible]	[illegible]	[illegible]
6	[illegible]	[illegible]	2,7[illegible]	[illegible]	41	[illegible]	[illegible]	.	1	[illegible]	[illegible]	[illegible]
7	[illegible]	[illegible]	3,[illegible]	[illegible]	[illegible]	[illegible]	[illegible]	[illegible]	.	[illegible]	[illegible]	[illegible]
	23. Tullamore, part of.											
1	[illegible], part of,	[illegible]	[illegible]	[illegible]	[illegible]	[illegible]	[illegible]	[illegible]	.	[illegible]	[illegible]	4
	Wexford Co.											
	27. Enniscorthy, part of.											
1	[illegible]	[illegible]	[illegible]	[illegible]	54	47	[illegible]	.	1	[illegible]	[illegible]	[illegible]
2	Enniscorthy, No. 1,	[illegible]	[illegible]	[illegible]	64	[illegible]	[illegible]	1	1	[illegible]	[illegible]	1
3	" " 2, W.,	[illegible]	[illegible]	[illegible]	[illegible]	75	[illegible]	[illegible]	[illegible]	[illegible]	[illegible]	[illegible]
4	Ferns,	[illegible]	2,1[illegible]	73	[illegible]	[illegible]	[illegible]	.	.	[illegible]	[illegible]	[illegible]
5	[illegible]	[illegible]	[illegible]	[illegible]	[illegible]	[illegible]	[illegible]	.	1	[illegible]	[illegible]	[illegible]
6	Newtownbarry, part of,	[illegible]	[illegible]	[illegible]	46	[illegible]	[illegible]	.	.	[illegible]	[illegible]	[illegible]
7	Oylegate,	[illegible]	3,1[illegible]	[illegible]	[illegible]	[illegible]	[illegible]	[illegible]	.	46	[illegible]	[illegible]
	28. Gorey.											
1	[illegible]	[illegible]	[illegible]	79	75	[illegible]	[illegible]	.	1	64	[illegible]	1
2	[illegible]	[illegible]	[illegible]	[illegible]	[illegible]	[illegible]	[illegible]	1	.	[illegible]	77	[illegible]
3	Gorey, W.,	51,[illegible]	[illegible]	1[illegible]	[illegible]	[illegible]	72	[illegible]	[illegible]	[illegible]	[illegible]	—[illegible]
4	[illegible] and [illegible],	[illegible]	4,[illegible]	[illegible]	[illegible]	31	45	.	1	[illegible]	[illegible]	[illegible]
	33. New Ross, part of.											
1	[illegible]	[illegible]	4,77[illegible]	[illegible]	[illegible]	41	31	[illegible]	.	[illegible]	41	[illegible]
2	Fethard, No. 1,	[illegible]	[illegible]	[illegible]	[illegible]	[illegible]	[illegible]	.	.	[illegible]	41	[illegible]
3	" " 2,	16,[illegible]	[illegible]	[illegible]	[illegible]	[illegible]	[illegible]	[illegible]	1	[illegible]	[illegible]	15
4	New Ross, W.,	4,[illegible]	[illegible]	[illegible]	[illegible]	[illegible]	[illegible]	[illegible]	[illegible]	74	[illegible]	[illegible]
5	Old Ross,	[illegible]	4,[illegible]	[illegible]	[illegible]	41	[illegible]	.	1	17	[illegible]	[illegible]
6	Templeludigan,	17,[illegible]	[illegible]	[illegible]	[illegible]	[illegible]	14	.	1	13	[illegible]	[illegible]
	36. Shillelagh, part of.											
1	[illegible] and [illegible], part of,	[illegible]	[illegible]	4	4	[illegible]	[illegible]	1	.	.	[illegible]	[illegible]

BIRTHS AND DEATHS Registered in the Year [illegible]—Registrars' Districts, arranged by Counties and Superintendent Registrars' Districts—continued.

No.	Registrars' Districts.	Area in Statute Acres.	Population in [illegible]	Total: Births.	Total: Deaths.	Births, including Illegitimate Births: Males.	Births, including Illegitimate Births: Females.	Illegitimate Births: Males.	Illegitimate Births: Females.	Deaths: Males.	Deaths: Females.	Excess of Births over Deaths.
	I.—Province of Leinster—con.											
	51. Wexford.											
1	Bannow,	[illegible]	[illegible]	[illegible]	[illegible]	[illegible]	[illegible]	[illegible]		[illegible]	[illegible]	[illegible]
2	Bridgetown,	[illegible]	[illegible]	[illegible]	[illegible]	[illegible]	[illegible]	[illegible]	[illegible]	[illegible]	[illegible]	[illegible]
3	Broadway,	[illegible]	[illegible]	[illegible]	[illegible]	[illegible]	[illegible]		[illegible]	[illegible]	[illegible]	[illegible]
4	[illegible],	[illegible]	[illegible]	[illegible]	[illegible]	[illegible]	[illegible]		[illegible]	[illegible]	[illegible]	[illegible]
5	Taghmon and [illegible],	[illegible]	[illegible]	[illegible]	[illegible]	[illegible]	[illegible]	[illegible]		[illegible]	[illegible]	[illegible]
6	Wexford, W.,	[illegible]	[illegible]	[illegible]	[illegible]	[illegible]	[illegible]	[illegible]	[illegible]	[illegible]	[illegible]	[illegible]
	Wicklow Co.											
	52. [illegible], part of.											
1	[illegible], part of, W.,	[illegible]	[illegible]	[illegible]	[illegible]	[illegible]	[illegible]		[illegible]	[illegible]	[illegible]	[illegible]
2	[illegible],	[illegible]	[illegible]	[illegible]	[illegible]	[illegible]	[illegible]			[illegible]	[illegible]	[illegible]
3	[illegible], part of,	[illegible]	[illegible]	[illegible]	[illegible]	[illegible]	[illegible]			[illegible]	[illegible]	[illegible]
	53. Naas, part of.											
1	[illegible] & [illegible], pt. of,	[illegible]	[illegible]	[illegible]	[illegible]	[illegible]	[illegible]			[illegible]	[illegible]	[illegible]
	54. Rathdown, part of.											
1	Bray and Rathmichael, No. 1, part of,	[illegible]	[illegible]	[illegible]	[illegible]	[illegible]	[illegible]			[illegible]	[illegible]	[illegible]
2	" " No. 2, do.,		[illegible]	[illegible]	[illegible]	[illegible]	[illegible]			[illegible]	[illegible]	[illegible]
3	Delgany,	[illegible]	[illegible]	[illegible]	[illegible]	[illegible]	[illegible]	[illegible]		[illegible]	[illegible]	[illegible]
4	Powerscourt,	[illegible]	[illegible]	[illegible]	[illegible]	[illegible]	[illegible]	[illegible]		[illegible]	[illegible]	[illegible]
	55. Rathdrum.											
1	Annamoe,	[illegible]	[illegible]	[illegible]	[illegible]	[illegible]	[illegible]	[illegible]	[illegible]	[illegible]	[illegible]	[illegible]
2	Arklow,	[illegible]	[illegible]	[illegible]	[illegible]	[illegible]	[illegible]	[illegible]	[illegible]	[illegible]	[illegible]	[illegible]
3	Aughrim,	[illegible]	[illegible]	[illegible]	[illegible]	[illegible]	[illegible]		[illegible]	[illegible]	[illegible]	[illegible]
4	[illegible],	[illegible]	[illegible]	[illegible]	[illegible]	[illegible]	[illegible]		[illegible]	[illegible]	[illegible]	[illegible]
5	[illegible],	[illegible]	[illegible]	[illegible]	[illegible]	[illegible]	[illegible]	[illegible]	[illegible]	[illegible]	[illegible]	[illegible]
6	[illegible],	[illegible]	[illegible]	[illegible]	[illegible]	[illegible]	[illegible]	[illegible]	[illegible]	[illegible]	[illegible]	[illegible]
7	Rathdrum, W.,	[illegible]	[illegible]	[illegible]	[illegible]	[illegible]	[illegible]	[illegible]	[illegible]	[illegible]	[illegible]	[illegible]
8	Wicklow,	[illegible]	[illegible]	[illegible]	[illegible]	[illegible]	[illegible]	[illegible]	[illegible]	[illegible]	[illegible]	[illegible]
	56. Shillelagh, part of.											
1	[illegible] & [illegible], pt. of, W.,	[illegible]	[illegible]	[illegible]	[illegible]	[illegible]	[illegible]	[illegible]		[illegible]	[illegible]	[illegible]
2	[illegible] and Shillelagh, part of,	[illegible]	[illegible]	[illegible]	[illegible]	[illegible]	[illegible]			[illegible]	[illegible]	[illegible]
3	Tinahely,	[illegible]	[illegible]	[illegible]	[illegible]	[illegible]	[illegible]			[illegible]	[illegible]	[illegible]
	II.—Province of Munster.											
	Clare Co.											
	57. Ballyvaghan.											
1	Ballyvaghan, W.,	[illegible]	[illegible]	[illegible]	[illegible]	[illegible]	[illegible]	[illegible]		[illegible]	[illegible]	[illegible]

BIRTHS AND DEATHS Registered in the Year 1896?—Registrars' Districts, arranged by Counties and Superintendent Registrars' Districts—*continued*.

	Registrars' Districts.	Area in Statute Acres.	Population in 1891.	Total?		Births?				Deaths?		Deaths?
						Excluding Illegitimate Births?		Illegitimate Births?				
				Males?	Females?	Males?	Females?	Males?	Females?	Males?	Females?	
	[illegible]											
	[illegible]											
1	[illegible]	[illegible]	[illegible]	[illegible]	[illegible]	[illegible]	[illegible]	[illegible]	[illegible]	[illegible]	[illegible]	[illegible]
2	[illegible]	[illegible]	[illegible]	[illegible]	[illegible]	[illegible]	[illegible]	[illegible]	[illegible]	[illegible]	[illegible]	[illegible]
3	[illegible]	[illegible]	[illegible]	[illegible]	[illegible]	[illegible]	[illegible]	[illegible]	[illegible]	[illegible]	[illegible]	[illegible]
	[illegible]											
1	[illegible]	[illegible]	[illegible]	[illegible]	[illegible]	[illegible]	[illegible]	[illegible]	[illegible]	[illegible]	[illegible]	[illegible]
2	[illegible]	[illegible]	[illegible]	[illegible]	[illegible]	[illegible]	[illegible]	[illegible]	[illegible]	[illegible]	[illegible]	[illegible]
	[illegible]											
1	[illegible]	[illegible]	[illegible]	[illegible]	[illegible]	[illegible]	[illegible]	[illegible]	[illegible]	[illegible]	[illegible]	[illegible]
2	[illegible]	[illegible]	[illegible]	[illegible]	[illegible]	[illegible]	[illegible]	[illegible]	[illegible]	[illegible]	[illegible]	[illegible]
3	[illegible]	[illegible]	[illegible]	[illegible]	[illegible]	[illegible]	[illegible]	[illegible]	[illegible]	[illegible]	[illegible]	[illegible]
4	[illegible]	[illegible]	[illegible]	[illegible]	[illegible]	[illegible]	[illegible]	[illegible]	[illegible]	[illegible]	[illegible]	[illegible]
5	[illegible]	[illegible]	[illegible]	[illegible]	[illegible]	[illegible]	[illegible]	[illegible]	[illegible]	[illegible]	[illegible]	[illegible]
	[illegible]											
1	[illegible]	[illegible]	[illegible]	[illegible]	[illegible]	[illegible]	[illegible]	[illegible]	[illegible]	[illegible]	[illegible]	[illegible]
2	[illegible]	[illegible]	[illegible]	[illegible]	[illegible]	[illegible]	[illegible]	[illegible]	[illegible]	[illegible]	[illegible]	[illegible]
	[illegible]											
1	[illegible]	[illegible]	[illegible]	[illegible]	[illegible]	[illegible]	[illegible]	[illegible]	[illegible]	[illegible]	[illegible]	[illegible]
2	[illegible]	[illegible]	[illegible]	[illegible]	[illegible]	[illegible]	[illegible]	[illegible]	[illegible]	[illegible]	[illegible]	[illegible]
3	[illegible]	[illegible]	[illegible]	[illegible]	[illegible]	[illegible]	[illegible]	[illegible]	[illegible]	[illegible]	[illegible]	[illegible]
	[illegible]											
1	[illegible]	[illegible]	[illegible]	[illegible]	[illegible]	[illegible]	[illegible]	[illegible]	[illegible]	[illegible]	[illegible]	[illegible]
2	[illegible]	[illegible]	[illegible]	[illegible]	[illegible]	[illegible]	[illegible]	[illegible]	[illegible]	[illegible]	[illegible]	[illegible]
3	[illegible]	[illegible]	[illegible]	[illegible]	[illegible]	[illegible]	[illegible]	[illegible]	[illegible]	[illegible]	[illegible]	[illegible]
	[illegible]											
	[illegible]											
1	[illegible]	[illegible]	[illegible]	[illegible]	[illegible]	[illegible]	[illegible]	[illegible]	[illegible]	[illegible]	[illegible]	[illegible]
2	[illegible]	[illegible]	[illegible]	[illegible]	[illegible]	[illegible]	[illegible]	[illegible]	[illegible]	[illegible]	[illegible]	[illegible]
3	[illegible]	[illegible]	[illegible]	[illegible]	[illegible]	[illegible]	[illegible]	[illegible]	[illegible]	[illegible]	[illegible]	[illegible]
4	[illegible]	[illegible]	[illegible]	[illegible]	[illegible]	[illegible]	[illegible]	[illegible]	[illegible]	[illegible]	[illegible]	[illegible]
5	[illegible]	[illegible]	[illegible]	[illegible]	[illegible]	[illegible]	[illegible]	[illegible]	[illegible]	[illegible]	[illegible]	[illegible]
	[illegible]											
1	[illegible]	[illegible]	[illegible]	[illegible]	[illegible]	[illegible]	[illegible]	[illegible]	[illegible]	[illegible]	[illegible]	[illegible]
2	[illegible]	[illegible]	[illegible]	[illegible]	[illegible]	[illegible]	[illegible]	[illegible]	[illegible]	[illegible]	[illegible]	[illegible]
3	[illegible]	[illegible]	[illegible]	[illegible]	[illegible]	[illegible]	[illegible]	[illegible]	[illegible]	[illegible]	[illegible]	[illegible]
4	[illegible]	[illegible]	[illegible]	[illegible]	[illegible]	[illegible]	[illegible]	[illegible]	[illegible]	[illegible]	[illegible]	[illegible]
	[illegible]											

BIRTHS AND DEATHS Registered in the year 1896—Registrars' Districts, arranged by Counties and Superintendent Registrars' Districts—continued.

No.	Registrars' Districts.	Area in Statute Acres.	Population in 1891.	Total: Births.	Total: Deaths.	Births: Legitimate: Males.	Births: Legitimate: Females.	Births: Illegitimate: Males.	Births: Illegitimate: Females.	Deaths: Males.	Deaths: Females.	Excess of Births over Deaths.
	II.—PROVINCE OF MUNSTER—con.											
	60 Cork.											
1	Ballincollig, . . .	17,718	4,184	73	48	[illegible]	41	.	1	[illegible]	[illegible]	[illegible]
2	Ballygarvan, . . .	13,[illegible]	1,641	[illegible]	[illegible]	17	14	.	1	17	11	1
3	Blarney, . . .	[illegible]	2,772	[illegible]	43	[illegible]	45	.	.	[illegible]	18	[illegible]
4	Carrigaline, No. 1, . .	[illegible]	3,074	[illegible]	[illegible]	[illegible]	18	4	.	16	19	[illegible]
5	" No. 2, . .	2,765	[illegible]	[illegible]	47	[illegible]	[illegible]	.	.	[illegible]	[illegible]	[illegible]
6	Carrigrohane, No. 1, . .	10,[illegible]	[illegible]	[illegible]	[illegible]	[illegible]	27	.	.	[illegible]	[illegible]	[illegible]
7	" No. 2, . .	[illegible]	2,[illegible]	45	[illegible]	[illegible]	[illegible]	.	.	19	14	11
8	Cork, No. 1, . .	18,416	11,[illegible]	347	[illegible]	[illegible]	[illegible]	1	1	[illegible]	[illegible]	[illegible]
9	" No. 2, . .		10,410	[illegible]	[illegible]	[illegible]	117	.	.	[illegible]	[illegible]	[illegible]
10	" No. 3, . .		[illegible]	[illegible]	[illegible]	41	111	.	.	[illegible]	49	[illegible]
11	" No. 4, . .		[illegible]	[illegible]	149	[illegible]	[illegible]	.	.	[illegible]	[illegible]	[illegible]
12	" No. 5, . .		13,[illegible]	[illegible]	[illegible]	[illegible]	[illegible]	1	.	[illegible]	[illegible]	[illegible]
13	" No. 6, . .		12,[illegible]	417	[illegible]	[illegible]	[illegible]	1	.	179	119	[illegible]
14	" No. 7, . .		8,870	[illegible]	110	110	[illegible]	.	.	[illegible]	[illegible]	[illegible]
15	" No. 8, W., .		10,[illegible]	[illegible]	777	[illegible]	[illegible]	[illegible]	[illegible]	[illegible]	[illegible]	[illegible]
16	" No. 9, . .		3,818	[illegible]	[illegible]	73	76	.	.	[illegible]	79	3
17	Douglas, . .	10,[illegible]	[illegible]	[illegible]	[illegible]	[illegible]	[illegible]	.	.	[illegible]	12	[illegible]
18	Dripsey, . .	16,733	[illegible]	[illegible]	[illegible]	[illegible]	[illegible]	.	1	[illegible]	14	[illegible]
19	Queenstown, No. 1, .	7,818	[illegible]	[illegible]	61	47	[illegible]	.	.	[illegible]	[illegible]	[illegible]
20	" No. 2, .		4,127	[illegible]	[illegible]	[illegible]	[illegible]	.	.	[illegible]	75	61
21	Whitechurch, . .	15,341	4,376	[illegible]	[illegible]	[illegible]	[illegible]	.	.	[illegible]	37	[illegible]
	61. Dunmanway.											
1	Ballineen, . .	29,193	[illegible]	109	[illegible]	[illegible]	[illegible]	1	.	[illegible]	[illegible]	[illegible]
2	Coolmountain, . .	[illegible]	6,615	[illegible]	[illegible]	[illegible]	[illegible]	.	.	[illegible]	[illegible]	[illegible]
3	Dunmanway, W., . .	[illegible]	[illegible]	[illegible]	[illegible]	[illegible]	[illegible]	.	1	[illegible]	[illegible]	[illegible]
	62. Fermoy.											
1	Ballyhooly, . .	[illegible]	[illegible]	41	[illegible]	[illegible]	[illegible]	1	[illegible]	[illegible]	[illegible]	[illegible]
2	Ballynoe, . .	14,[illegible]	[illegible]	[illegible]	[illegible]	[illegible]	[illegible]	1	.	[illegible]	[illegible]	[illegible]
3	Fermoy, W., . .	18,[illegible]	[illegible]	[illegible]	[illegible]	[illegible]	[illegible]	1	[illegible]	[illegible]	[illegible]	[illegible]
4	Kilworth, . .	[illegible]	[illegible]	[illegible]	[illegible]	[illegible]	[illegible]	1	1	[illegible]	[illegible]	[illegible]
5	Rathcormack, . .	[illegible]	[illegible]	[illegible]	[illegible]	[illegible]	[illegible]	.	.	[illegible]	[illegible]	[illegible]
	63. Kanturk.											
1	Boherbue, . .	[illegible]	[illegible]	[illegible]	[illegible]	81	77	.	.	37	[illegible]	[illegible]
2	Kanturk, W., . .	47,[illegible]	7,[illegible]	[illegible]	[illegible]	[illegible]	[illegible]	[illegible]	4	[illegible]	72	[illegible]
3	Millstreet, . .	[illegible]	[illegible]	[illegible]	[illegible]	[illegible]	44	.	[illegible]	[illegible]	[illegible]	[illegible]
4	Newmarket, . .	[illegible]	7,101	[illegible]	[illegible]	[illegible]	[illegible]	.	.	[illegible]	[illegible]	[illegible]
	64. Kilmallock, part of.											
1	Charleville, part of, . .	[illegible]	[illegible]	[illegible]	[illegible]	71	[illegible]	1	1	[illegible]	[illegible]	[illegible]
	65. Kinsale.											
1	Ballyfeard, . .	[illegible]	[illegible]	[illegible]	[illegible]	[illegible]	[illegible]	.	.	[illegible]	[illegible]	[illegible]
2	Ballymartle, . .	10,170	2,[illegible]	[illegible]	[illegible]	[illegible]	14	.	.	11	[illegible]	[illegible]
3	Carrigaline, . .	[illegible]	[illegible]	[illegible]	[illegible]	[illegible]	[illegible]	.	.	17	[illegible]	[illegible]

2	[illegible],	[illegible]
1	[illegible],	[illegible]
2	[illegible], W.,	[illegible]
3	[illegible],	[illegible]

[illegible]

1	[illegible],	[illegible]
2	[illegible],	[illegible]
3	[illegible],	[illegible]
4	[illegible], No. 1, W.,	[illegible]
5	„ 2,	[illegible]
6	[illegible], East,	[illegible]

[illegible]

1	[illegible],	[illegible]
2	[illegible], W.,	[illegible]

[illegible], part of.

1	[illegible].	[illegible]
2	[illegible], part of, W.,	[illegible]

[illegible]

1	[illegible],	[illegible]
2	[illegible], W.,	[illegible]
3	[illegible],	[illegible]
4	[illegible],	[illegible]

[illegible]

1	[illegible].	[illegible]
2	[illegible], W.,	[illegible]

[illegible], part of.

1	[illegible].	[illegible]
2	[illegible], part of.	[illegible]
3	[illegible], W.,	[illegible]

Kerry Co.

[illegible]

BIRTHS AND DEATHS Registered in the Year 18[illegible]—Registrars' Districts, arranged by Counties and Superintendent Registrars' Districts—continued.

No.	[illegible] Districts	Area in [illegible]	[illegible] in 18[illegible]	Births: [illegible]	Births: [illegible]	Deaths: [illegible]: Males	Deaths: [illegible]: Females	Deaths: [illegible]: Males	Deaths: [illegible]: Females	[illegible]: Males	[illegible]: Females	[illegible]
	[illegible]											
	[illegible]											
1	[illegible]	[illegible]	[illegible]	[illegible]	[illegible]	[illegible]	[illegible]			[illegible]	[illegible]	[illegible]
2	[illegible]	[illegible]	[illegible]	[illegible]	[illegible]	[illegible]	[illegible]			[illegible]	[illegible]	[illegible]
3	[illegible]	[illegible]	[illegible]	[illegible]	[illegible]	[illegible]	[illegible]		[illegible]	[illegible]	[illegible]	[illegible]
4	[illegible]	[illegible]	[illegible]	[illegible]	[illegible]	[illegible]	[illegible]			[illegible]	[illegible]	[illegible]
	[illegible]											
1	[illegible]	[illegible]	[illegible]	[illegible]	[illegible]	[illegible]	[illegible]			[illegible]	[illegible]	[illegible]
2	[illegible]	[illegible]	[illegible]	[illegible]	[illegible]	[illegible]	[illegible]	[illegible]	[illegible]	[illegible]	[illegible]	[illegible]
3	[illegible]	[illegible]	[illegible]	[illegible]	[illegible]	[illegible]	[illegible]			[illegible]	[illegible]	[illegible]
4	[illegible]	[illegible]	[illegible]	[illegible]	[illegible]	[illegible]	[illegible]	[illegible]	[illegible]	[illegible]	[illegible]	[illegible]
5	[illegible]	[illegible]	[illegible]	[illegible]	[illegible]	[illegible]	[illegible]		[illegible]	[illegible]	[illegible]	[illegible]
6	[illegible]	[illegible]	[illegible]	[illegible]	[illegible]	[illegible]	[illegible]			[illegible]	[illegible]	[illegible]
	[illegible], part of											
1	[illegible]	[illegible]	[illegible]	[illegible]	[illegible]	[illegible]	[illegible]	[illegible]		[illegible]	[illegible]	[illegible]
2	[illegible]	[illegible]	[illegible]	[illegible]	[illegible]	[illegible]	[illegible]	[illegible]	[illegible]	[illegible]	[illegible]	[illegible]
3	[illegible]	[illegible]	[illegible]	[illegible]	[illegible]	[illegible]	[illegible]	[illegible]	[illegible]	[illegible]	[illegible]	[illegible]
4	[illegible]	[illegible]	[illegible]	[illegible]	[illegible]	[illegible]	[illegible]	[illegible]	[illegible]	[illegible]	[illegible]	[illegible]
5	[illegible], No. 1, part of	[illegible]	[illegible]	[illegible]	[illegible]	[illegible]	[illegible]			[illegible]	[illegible]	[illegible]
	[illegible]											
1	[illegible]	[illegible]	[illegible]	[illegible]	[illegible]	[illegible]	[illegible]	[illegible]		[illegible]	[illegible]	[illegible]
2	[illegible], No. 1	[illegible]	[illegible]	[illegible]	[illegible]	[illegible]	[illegible]	[illegible]		[illegible]	[illegible]	[illegible]
3	[illegible]	[illegible]	[illegible]	[illegible]	[illegible]	[illegible]	[illegible]	[illegible]	[illegible]	[illegible]	[illegible]	[illegible]
4	[illegible]	[illegible]	[illegible]	[illegible]	[illegible]	[illegible]	[illegible]	[illegible]		[illegible]	[illegible]	[illegible]
5	[illegible]	[illegible]	[illegible]	[illegible]	[illegible]	[illegible]	[illegible]	[illegible]		[illegible]	[illegible]	[illegible]
6	[illegible]	[illegible]	[illegible]	[illegible]	[illegible]	[illegible]	[illegible]	[illegible]		[illegible]	[illegible]	[illegible]
7	[illegible], No. 1	[illegible]	[illegible]	[illegible]	[illegible]	[illegible]	[illegible]	[illegible]		[illegible]	[illegible]	[illegible]
8	[illegible]	[illegible]	[illegible]	[illegible]	[illegible]	[illegible]	[illegible]	[illegible]	[illegible]	[illegible]	[illegible]	[illegible]
	[illegible]											
	[illegible]											
1	[illegible]	[illegible]	[illegible]	[illegible]	[illegible]	[illegible]	[illegible]	[illegible]		[illegible]	[illegible]	[illegible]
2	[illegible]	[illegible]	[illegible]	[illegible]	[illegible]	[illegible]	[illegible]	[illegible]	[illegible]	[illegible]	[illegible]	[illegible]
3	[illegible]	[illegible]	[illegible]	[illegible]	[illegible]	[illegible]	[illegible]	[illegible]	[illegible]	[illegible]	[illegible]	[illegible]
	[illegible], part of											
1	[illegible]	[illegible]	[illegible]	[illegible]	[illegible]	[illegible]	[illegible]	[illegible]		[illegible]	[illegible]	[illegible]
2	[illegible]	[illegible]	[illegible]	[illegible]	[illegible]	[illegible]	[illegible]		[illegible]	[illegible]	[illegible]	[illegible]
3	[illegible], part of	[illegible]	[illegible]	[illegible]	[illegible]	[illegible]	[illegible]		[illegible]	[illegible]	[illegible]	[illegible]
4	[illegible]	[illegible]	[illegible]	[illegible]	[illegible]	[illegible]	[illegible]			[illegible]	[illegible]	[illegible]
5	[illegible]	[illegible]	[illegible]	[illegible]	[illegible]	[illegible]	[illegible]		[illegible]	[illegible]	[illegible]	[illegible]
6	[illegible]	[illegible]	[illegible]	[illegible]	[illegible]	[illegible]	[illegible]	[illegible]	[illegible]	[illegible]	[illegible]	[illegible]
	[illegible], part of											
1	[illegible]	[illegible]	[illegible]	[illegible]	[illegible]	[illegible]	[illegible]	[illegible]		[illegible]	[illegible]	[illegible]
2	[illegible]	[illegible]	[illegible]	[illegible]	[illegible]	[illegible]	[illegible]		[illegible]	[illegible]	[illegible]	[illegible]

BIRTHS AND DEATHS Registered in the Year 1896—REGISTRARS' DISTRICTS, arranged by COUNTIES and SUPERINTENDENT REGISTRARS' DISTRICTS—*continued.*

No.	REGISTRARS' DISTRICTS.	Area in Statute Acres.	Population in 1891.	TOTAL: Births.	TOTAL: Deaths.	BIRTHS: Including Illegitimate Births: Males.	BIRTHS: Including Illegitimate Births: Females.	BIRTHS: Illegitimate Births: Males.	BIRTHS: Illegitimate Births: Females.	Deaths: Males.	Deaths: Females.	Excess of Births over Deaths.
	II.—PROVINCE OF MUNSTER—cont.											
	102. [illegible], part of.											
1	Galbally,	[illegible]	4,?91	111	[illegible]	61	[illegible]	1	-	[illegible]	[illegible]	[illegible]
2	Mitchelstown, part of.	[illegible]	[illegible]	[illegible]	18	13	18	-	-	5	3	10
	103. NEWCASTLE.											
1	Abbeyfeale,	[illegible]	[illegible]	[illegible]	[illegible]	119	[illegible]	-	4	[illegible]	84	[illegible]
2	Ardagh,	[illegible]	[illegible]	107	41	[illegible]	44	1	-	[illegible]	21	[illegible]
3	[illegible]	[illegible]	[illegible]	116	61	[illegible]	[illegible]	2	-	[illegible]	[illegible]	[illegible]
4	[illegible]	[illegible]	[illegible]	[illegible]	47	[illegible]	[illegible]	-	-	77	[illegible]	14
5	Newcastle, W.	[illegible]	[illegible]	[illegible]	[illegible]	[illegible]	[illegible]	[illegible]	1	41	43	[illegible]
	104. RATHKEALE.											
1	Askeaton,	[illegible]	[illegible]	[illegible]	[illegible]	[illegible]	27	-	-	[illegible]	[illegible]	[illegible]
2	Pallaskenry,	[illegible]	3,?14	[illegible]	[illegible]	[illegible]	31	-	-	[illegible]	[illegible]	[illegible]
3	Rathkeale, No. 1, W.	[illegible]	[illegible]	[illegible]	[illegible]	[illegible]	[illegible]	[illegible]	[illegible]	[illegible]	[illegible]	[illegible]
4	" No. 2,	[illegible]	[illegible]	[illegible]	[illegible]	19	[illegible]	-	-	[illegible]	14	[illegible]
5	Shanagolden,	[illegible]	[illegible]	[illegible]	[illegible]	[illegible]	[illegible]	[illegible]	-	17	18	[illegible]
	107. TIPPERARY, part of.											
1	[illegible], part of,	[illegible]	[illegible]	47	[illegible]	23	[illegible]	-	[illegible]	17	[illegible]	[illegible]
2	[illegible], do.,	[illegible]	[illegible]	[illegible]	[illegible]	[illegible]	[illegible]	1	-	[illegible]	[illegible]	[illegible]
	Tipperary Co.											
	108. BORRISOKANE.											
1	Borrisokane, W.	[illegible]	[illegible]	[illegible]	[illegible]	[illegible]	[illegible]	-	1	17	14	[illegible]
2	Cloughjordan,	[illegible]	[illegible]	[illegible]	[illegible]	[illegible]	[illegible]	-	-	[illegible]	11	[illegible]
3	Terryglass,	[illegible]	[illegible]	[illegible]	[illegible]	31	17	-	-	17	[illegible]	[illegible]
	109. CALLAN, part of.											
1	Ballingarry,	[illegible]	[illegible]	71	[illegible]	[illegible]	[illegible]	-	1	[illegible]	[illegible]	47
2	Mullinahone,	[illegible]	[illegible]	[illegible]	[illegible]	[illegible]	21	-	-	17	[illegible]	1
	110. CARRICK-ON-SUIR, part of.											
1	Carrick-on-Suir, part of, W.	[illegible]	4,?17	[illegible]	[illegible]	[illegible]	[illegible]	4	[illegible]	[illegible]	[illegible]	[illegible]
2	[illegible],	[illegible]	[illegible]	47	[illegible]	33	[illegible]	[illegible]	1	[illegible]	17	[illegible]
	111. CASHEL.											
1	Cashel, W.	[illegible]	[illegible]	[illegible]	[illegible]	[illegible]	[illegible]	4	[illegible]	[illegible]	[illegible]	[illegible]
2	Fethard,	[illegible]	[illegible]	[illegible]	[illegible]	[illegible]	47	1	-	[illegible]	[illegible]	[illegible]
3	Killenaule,	[illegible]	[illegible]	[illegible]	[illegible]	[illegible]	[illegible]	1	-	[illegible]	17	16
4	[illegible],	[illegible]	[illegible]	[illegible]	[illegible]	41	[illegible]	1	1	13	37	[illegible]
5	[illegible],	[illegible]	[illegible]	[illegible]	[illegible]	[illegible]	[illegible]	-	-	[illegible]	[illegible]	[illegible]
	112. CLOGHEEN.											
1	Ardfinnan,	[illegible]	[illegible]	[illegible]	[illegible]	47	[illegible]	1	-	[illegible]	[illegible]	[illegible]
2	Cahir,	[illegible]	[illegible]	[illegible]	[illegible]	[illegible]	77	2	1	[illegible]	[illegible]	[illegible]
3	Clogheen, W.	[illegible]	[illegible]	[illegible]	[illegible]	[illegible]	[illegible]	1	1	47	[illegible]	17
	113. CLONMEL, part of.											
1	Clonmel, W.	[illegible]	[illegible]	[illegible]	[illegible]	[illegible]	[illegible]	[illegible]	[illegible]	[illegible]	114	[illegible]
2	Kilsheelan, part of.	[illegible]	[illegible]	[illegible]	[illegible]	[illegible]	[illegible]	[illegible]	1	[illegible]	14	18
3	[illegible],	[illegible]	[illegible]	18	[illegible]	[illegible]	[illegible]	-	-	[illegible]	[illegible]	[illegible]
4	Marlfield,	[illegible]	[illegible]	[illegible]	15	[illegible]	12	-	-	[illegible]	[illegible]	[illegible]

BIRTHS and DEATHS Registered in the Year [illegible].—REGISTRARS' DISTRICTS, arranged by COUNTIES and SUPERINTENDENT REGISTRARS' DISTRICTS—continued.

No.	REGISTRARS' DISTRICTS.	Area in Statute Acres.	Population in 1861.	Total: Births	Total: Deaths	Births including illegitimate Births: Male	Births including illegitimate Births: Female	Illegitimate Births: Male	Illegitimate Births: Female	Deaths: Male	Deaths: Female	[illegible]
	[illegible]—con.											
	[illegible], part of											
1	[illegible]	[illegible]	[illegible]	[illegible]	[illegible]	[illegible]	[illegible]			[illegible]	[illegible]	[illegible]
2	[illegible], part of, W.	[illegible]	[illegible]	[illegible]	[illegible]	[illegible]	[illegible]	[illegible]		[illegible]	[illegible]	[illegible]
	[illegible]											
1	[illegible]	[illegible]	[illegible]	[illegible]	[illegible]	[illegible]	[illegible]			[illegible]	[illegible]	[illegible]
2	[illegible]	[illegible]	[illegible]	[illegible]	[illegible]	[illegible]	[illegible]	[illegible]		[illegible]	[illegible]	[illegible]
3	[illegible]	[illegible]	[illegible]	[illegible]	[illegible]	[illegible]	[illegible]			[illegible]	[illegible]	[illegible]
4	[illegible]	[illegible]	[illegible]	[illegible]	[illegible]	[illegible]	[illegible]		[illegible]	[illegible]	[illegible]	[illegible]
5	[illegible]	[illegible]	[illegible]	[illegible]	[illegible]	[illegible]	[illegible]		[illegible]	[illegible]	[illegible]	[illegible]
6	[illegible], W.	[illegible]	[illegible]	[illegible]	[illegible]	[illegible]	[illegible]	[illegible]	[illegible]	[illegible]	[illegible]	[illegible]
	[illegible], part of											
1	[illegible]	[illegible]	[illegible]	[illegible]	[illegible]	[illegible]	[illegible]			[illegible]	[illegible]	[illegible]
2	[illegible], part of	[illegible]	[illegible]	[illegible]	[illegible]	[illegible]	[illegible]	[illegible]		[illegible]	[illegible]	[illegible]
3	[illegible]	[illegible]	[illegible]	[illegible]	[illegible]	[illegible]	[illegible]	[illegible]	[illegible]	[illegible]	[illegible]	[illegible]
4	[illegible]	[illegible]	[illegible]	[illegible]	[illegible]	[illegible]	[illegible]			[illegible]	[illegible]	[illegible]
5	[illegible], part of	[illegible]	[illegible]	[illegible]	[illegible]	[illegible]	[illegible]		[illegible]	[illegible]	[illegible]	[illegible]
6	[illegible], W.	[illegible]	[illegible]	[illegible]	[illegible]	[illegible]	[illegible]	[illegible]	[illegible]	[illegible]	[illegible]	[illegible]
	[illegible], part of											
1	[illegible]	[illegible]	[illegible]	[illegible]	[illegible]	[illegible]	[illegible]			[illegible]	[illegible]	[illegible]
2	[illegible], part of	[illegible]	[illegible]	[illegible]	[illegible]	[illegible]	[illegible]			[illegible]	[illegible]	[illegible]
	Waterford Co.											
	[illegible], part of											
1	[illegible], part of	[illegible]	[illegible]	[illegible]	[illegible]	[illegible]	[illegible]			[illegible]	[illegible]	[illegible]
2	[illegible]	[illegible]	[illegible]	[illegible]	[illegible]	[illegible]	[illegible]	[illegible]	[illegible]	[illegible]	[illegible]	[illegible]
3	[illegible]	[illegible]	[illegible]	[illegible]	[illegible]	[illegible]	[illegible]			[illegible]	[illegible]	[illegible]
	[illegible], part of											
1	[illegible]	[illegible]	[illegible]	[illegible]	[illegible]	[illegible]	[illegible]	[illegible]		[illegible]	[illegible]	[illegible]
2	[illegible], part of	[illegible]	[illegible]	[illegible]	[illegible]	[illegible]	[illegible]		[illegible]	[illegible]	[illegible]	[illegible]
3	[illegible]	[illegible]	[illegible]	[illegible]	[illegible]	[illegible]	[illegible]	[illegible]	[illegible]	[illegible]	[illegible]	[illegible]
	[illegible]											
1	[illegible], W.	[illegible]	[illegible]	[illegible]	[illegible]	[illegible]	[illegible]	[illegible]	[illegible]	[illegible]	[illegible]	[illegible]
2	[illegible]	[illegible]	[illegible]	[illegible]	[illegible]	[illegible]	[illegible]		[illegible]	[illegible]	[illegible]	[illegible]
3	[illegible]	[illegible]	[illegible]	[illegible]	[illegible]	[illegible]	[illegible]	[illegible]		[illegible]	[illegible]	[illegible]
4	[illegible]	[illegible]	[illegible]	[illegible]	[illegible]	[illegible]	[illegible]	[illegible]		[illegible]	[illegible]	[illegible]
	[illegible]											
1	[illegible]	[illegible]	[illegible]	[illegible]	[illegible]	[illegible]	[illegible]	[illegible]	[illegible]	[illegible]	[illegible]	[illegible]
2	[illegible], W.	[illegible]	[illegible]	[illegible]	[illegible]	[illegible]	[illegible]	[illegible]	[illegible]	[illegible]	[illegible]	[illegible]
	[illegible]											
1	[illegible]	[illegible]	[illegible]	[illegible]	[illegible]	[illegible]	[illegible]	[illegible]		[illegible]	[illegible]	[illegible]
2	[illegible]	[illegible]	[illegible]	[illegible]	[illegible]	[illegible]	[illegible]	[illegible]	[illegible]	[illegible]	[illegible]	[illegible]
3	[illegible], W.	[illegible]	[illegible]	[illegible]	[illegible]	[illegible]	[illegible]	[illegible]	[illegible]	[illegible]	[illegible]	[illegible]
4	[illegible]	[illegible]	[illegible]	[illegible]	[illegible]	[illegible]	[illegible]		[illegible]	[illegible]	[illegible]	[illegible]
	[illegible], part of											
1	[illegible]	[illegible]	[illegible]	[illegible]	[illegible]	[illegible]	[illegible]	[illegible]	[illegible]	[illegible]	[illegible]	[illegible]
2	[illegible]	[illegible]	[illegible]	[illegible]	[illegible]	[illegible]	[illegible]	[illegible]	[illegible]	[illegible]	[illegible]	[illegible]
3	[illegible], No. 1, W.	[illegible]	[illegible]	[illegible]	[illegible]	[illegible]	[illegible]	[illegible]	[illegible]	[illegible]	[illegible]	[illegible]
4	„ No. 2.	[illegible]	[illegible]	[illegible]	[illegible]	[illegible]	[illegible]			[illegible]	[illegible]	[illegible]
5	[illegible]	[illegible]	[illegible]	[illegible]	[illegible]	[illegible]	[illegible]	[illegible]	[illegible]	[illegible]	[illegible]	[illegible]
	[illegible], part of											
1	[illegible]	[illegible]	[illegible]	[illegible]	[illegible]	[illegible]	[illegible]	[illegible]		[illegible]	[illegible]	[illegible]
2	[illegible]	[illegible]	[illegible]	[illegible]	[illegible]	[illegible]	[illegible]	[illegible]	[illegible]	[illegible]	[illegible]	[illegible]
3	[illegible], part of	[illegible]	[illegible]	[illegible]	[illegible]	[illegible]	[illegible]			[illegible]	[illegible]	[illegible]

BIRTHS AND DEATHS Registered in the Year 1896—REGISTRARS' DISTRICTS, arranged by COUNTIES and SUPERINTENDENT REGISTRARS' DISTRICTS—*continued*.

No.	REGISTRARS' DISTRICTS.	Area in Statute Acres.	Population in 1891	TOTAL [illegible]	TOTAL [illegible]	BIRTHS [illegible] [illegible]	BIRTHS [illegible] [illegible]	BIRTHS [illegible] [illegible]	BIRTHS [illegible] [illegible]	DEATHS [illegible]	DEATHS [illegible]	[illegible]
	III.—PROVINCE OF ULSTER.											
	ANTRIM CO.											
	127. ANTRIM.											
1	Antrim, W.,	14,379	[illegible]	[illegible]	112	72	67	[illegible]	4	44	[illegible]	27
2	[illegible]	21,[illegible]	4,174	[illegible]	79	[illegible]	[illegible]	[illegible]	[illegible]	23	[illegible]	[illegible]
3	Crumlin,	[illegible]	[illegible]	105	[illegible]	[illegible]	[illegible]	[illegible]	[illegible]	[illegible]	[illegible]	[illegible]
4	Dough,	[illegible]	[illegible]	[illegible]	118	[illegible]	104	[illegible]	[illegible]	[illegible]	[illegible]	[illegible]
5	[illegible]	[illegible]	[illegible]	[illegible]	[illegible]	[illegible]	[illegible]	[illegible]		[illegible]	[illegible]	[illegible]
6	[illegible]	21,172	[illegible]	107	73	[illegible]	[illegible]	3	[illegible]	[illegible]	[illegible]	[illegible]
	128. BALLYCASTLE.											
1	Ballycastle, W.,	[illegible]	[illegible]	[illegible]	[illegible]	[illegible]	[illegible]	[illegible]	3	[illegible]	[illegible]	[illegible]
2	[illegible]	[illegible]	4,[illegible]	[illegible]	[illegible]	[illegible]	[illegible]	[illegible]	[illegible]	[illegible]	[illegible]	[illegible]
3	[illegible]	[illegible]	[illegible]	[illegible]	[illegible]	41	[illegible]	1		[illegible]	[illegible]	10
	129. BALLYMENA.											
1	[illegible]	[illegible]	7,[illegible]	170	[illegible]	94	[illegible]	[illegible]	[illegible]	[illegible]	[illegible]	44
2	Ballymena, W.	[illegible]	12,[illegible]	[illegible]	[illegible]	[illegible]	173	11	[illegible]	[illegible]	[illegible]	[illegible]
3	[illegible]	[illegible]	[illegible]	125	[illegible]	[illegible]	47	[illegible]	[illegible]	[illegible]	41	[illegible]
4	Clogh,	[illegible]	[illegible]	[illegible]	[illegible]	[illegible]	71	[illegible]	[illegible]	[illegible]	[illegible]	[illegible]
5	[illegible]	10,[illegible]	[illegible]	[illegible]	[illegible]	[illegible]	[illegible]	[illegible]	[illegible]	[illegible]	[illegible]	[illegible]
6	[illegible]	[illegible]	[illegible]	[illegible]	[illegible]	[illegible]	[illegible]	[illegible]	[illegible]	[illegible]	[illegible]	[illegible]
7	[illegible]	17,[illegible]	7,[illegible]	[illegible]	[illegible]	[illegible]	[illegible]	[illegible]	[illegible]	[illegible]	[illegible]	[illegible]
8	[illegible]	[illegible]	[illegible]	114	[illegible]	[illegible]	[illegible]	[illegible]	[illegible]	[illegible]	[illegible]	[illegible]
	130. BALLYMONEY, part of.											
1	Ballymoney, W.	[illegible]	[illegible]	[illegible]	[illegible]	[illegible]	[illegible]	[illegible]	[illegible]	[illegible]	[illegible]	[illegible]
2	[illegible]	[illegible]	[illegible]	[illegible]	[illegible]	[illegible]	[illegible]	[illegible]	[illegible]	[illegible]	[illegible]	[illegible]
3	[illegible]	[illegible]	[illegible]	[illegible]	[illegible]	[illegible]	[illegible]	[illegible]	[illegible]	[illegible]	[illegible]	[illegible]
4	[illegible]	[illegible]	7,[illegible]	[illegible]	[illegible]	[illegible]	[illegible]	1	[illegible]	[illegible]	[illegible]	[illegible]
	131. BELFAST, part of.											
1	Belfast, No. 1,	[illegible]	[illegible]	479	[illegible]	[illegible]	[illegible]	[illegible]	[illegible]	[illegible]	[illegible]	[illegible]
2	" No. 2,		[illegible]	1,[illegible]	[illegible]	[illegible]	[illegible]	[illegible]	[illegible]	[illegible]	616	[illegible]
3	" No. 3,		[illegible]	1,[illegible]	[illegible]	[illegible]	777	[illegible]	[illegible]	[illegible]	[illegible]	[illegible]
4	" No. 4, W.		[illegible]	1,[illegible]	1,[illegible]	[illegible]	[illegible]	[illegible]	[illegible]	742	[illegible]	[illegible]
5	" No. 5,		[illegible]	[illegible]	[illegible]	[illegible]	[illegible]	[illegible]	[illegible]	[illegible]	[illegible]	[illegible]
6	" No. 6,		[illegible]	[illegible]	[illegible]	[illegible]	[illegible]	[illegible]	[illegible]	[illegible]	[illegible]	[illegible]
7	" No. 7,		[illegible]	[illegible]	[illegible]	[illegible]	[illegible]	[illegible]	1	41	[illegible]	[illegible]
8	" No. 8,		[illegible]	[illegible]	[illegible]	[illegible]	41	1	[illegible]	[illegible]	[illegible]	[illegible]
9	" No. 9,		[illegible]	[illegible]	[illegible]	[illegible]	[illegible]	[illegible]	[illegible]	[illegible]	[illegible]	[illegible]
10	" No. 10,		[illegible]	[illegible]	[illegible]	[illegible]	[illegible]	[illegible]	[illegible]	119	[illegible]	[illegible]
11	" No. 11,		[illegible]	[illegible]	[illegible]	[illegible]	[illegible]	[illegible]	[illegible]	[illegible]	[illegible]	[illegible]
	132. CARRICKFERGUS, part of.											
1	[illegible]	[illegible]	[illegible]	[illegible]	[illegible]	[illegible]	[illegible]	4	[illegible]	14	[illegible]	[illegible]
2	[illegible], part of,	[illegible]	[illegible]	[illegible]	41	[illegible]	[illegible]	[illegible]	1	[illegible]	[illegible]	[illegible]
	133. LARNE.											
1	[illegible]	[illegible]	[illegible]	[illegible]	[illegible]	[illegible]	[illegible]	1	1	[illegible]	[illegible]	[illegible]
2	[illegible]	[illegible]	4,[illegible]	[illegible]	[illegible]	[illegible]	[illegible]	1	[illegible]	[illegible]	[illegible]	[illegible]
3	[illegible]	[illegible]	[illegible]	[illegible]	[illegible]	117	[illegible]	[illegible]	14	[illegible]	[illegible]	[illegible]
4	Glenarm,	[illegible]	4,[illegible]	[illegible]	[illegible]	[illegible]	[illegible]	[illegible]	4	[illegible]	[illegible]	81
[illegible]	[illegible]	[illegible]	[illegible]	[illegible]	[illegible]	[illegible]	[illegible]	[illegible]	[illegible]	[illegible]	[illegible]	[illegible]

BIRTHS AND DEATHS Registered in the Year 1896—Registrars' Districts, arranged by Counties and Superintendent Registrars' Districts—continued.

No.	Registrars' Districts.	Area in Statute Acres.	Population in 1891.	Total: Births.	Total: Deaths.	Births: Legitimate: Males.	Births: Legitimate: Females.	Births: Illegitimate: Males.	Births: Illegitimate: Females.	Deaths: Males.	Deaths: Females.
	III.—PROVINCE OF ULSTER—con.										
	Armagh Co.										
	135. Armagh, part of.										
1	Armagh W.,	[illegible]	[illegible]	[illegible]	[illegible]	[illegible]	[illegible]	[illegible]	11	[illegible]	[illegible]
2	Blackwatertown,	[illegible]	[illegible]	[illegible]	[illegible]	[illegible]	[illegible]	[illegible]	-	[illegible]	[illegible]
3	Keady,	[illegible]	[illegible]	[illegible]	[illegible]	[illegible]	[illegible]	[illegible]	[illegible]	[illegible]	[illegible]
4	Loughgall,	[illegible]	[illegible]	[illegible]	[illegible]	[illegible]	[illegible]	[illegible]	[illegible]	[illegible]	[illegible]
5	Markethill,	[illegible]	[illegible]	[illegible]	[illegible]	[illegible]	[illegible]	[illegible]	[illegible]	[illegible]	[illegible]
6	Rich Hill,	[illegible]	[illegible]	[illegible]	[illegible]	[illegible]	[illegible]	[illegible]	[illegible]	[illegible]	[illegible]
7	Tynan,	[illegible]	[illegible]	[illegible]	[illegible]	[illegible]	[illegible]	-	-	[illegible]	[illegible]
	137. Banbridge, part of.										
1	Tandragee,	[illegible]	[illegible]	[illegible]	[illegible]	[illegible]	[illegible]	[illegible]	[illegible]	[illegible]	[illegible]
	138. Castleblayney, part of.										
1	Crossmaglen, part of,	[illegible]	[illegible]	[illegible]	[illegible]	[illegible]	[illegible]	[illegible]	-	[illegible]	[illegible]
2	Newtownhamilton, do.,	[illegible]	[illegible]	[illegible]	[illegible]	[illegible]	[illegible]	[illegible]	[illegible]	[illegible]	[illegible]
	139. Dundalk, part of.										
1	[illegible], part of.,	[illegible]	[illegible]	[illegible]	[illegible]	[illegible]	[illegible]	-	-	[illegible]	[illegible]
	140. Lurgan, part of.										
1	Lurgan, No. 1, part of, W.,	[illegible]	[illegible]	[illegible]	[illegible]	[illegible]	[illegible]	[illegible]	[illegible]	[illegible]	[illegible]
2	" No. 2,	[illegible]	[illegible]	[illegible]	[illegible]	[illegible]	[illegible]	1	[illegible]	[illegible]	[illegible]
3	Portadown,	[illegible]	[illegible]	[illegible]	[illegible]	[illegible]	[illegible]	[illegible]	[illegible]	[illegible]	[illegible]
4	Tartaraghan,	[illegible]	[illegible]	[illegible]	[illegible]	[illegible]	[illegible]	[illegible]	[illegible]	[illegible]	[illegible]
	141. Newry, part of.										
1	Forkhill,	[illegible]	[illegible]	[illegible]	[illegible]	[illegible]	[illegible]	[illegible]	-	[illegible]	[illegible]
2	Meigh,	[illegible]	[illegible]	[illegible]	[illegible]	[illegible]	[illegible]	[illegible]	[illegible]	[illegible]	[illegible]
3	Mountnorris,	[illegible]	[illegible]	[illegible]	[illegible]	[illegible]	[illegible]	[illegible]	-	[illegible]	[illegible]
4	Mullaghglass,	[illegible]	[illegible]	[illegible]	[illegible]	[illegible]	[illegible]	[illegible]	[illegible]	[illegible]	[illegible]
5	Newry, No. 1, part of, W.,	[illegible]	[illegible]	[illegible]	[illegible]	[illegible]	[illegible]	[illegible]	[illegible]	[illegible]	[illegible]
6	Poyntzpass,	[illegible]	[illegible]	[illegible]	[illegible]	[illegible]	[illegible]	-	-	[illegible]	[illegible]
	Cavan Co.										
	142. Bailieborough.										
1	Bailieborough, W.,	[illegible]	[illegible]	[illegible]	[illegible]	[illegible]	[illegible]	[illegible]	[illegible]	[illegible]	[illegible]
2	Canningstown,	[illegible]	[illegible]	[illegible]	[illegible]	[illegible]	[illegible]	1	-	[illegible]	[illegible]
3	Kingscourt,	[illegible]	[illegible]	[illegible]	[illegible]	[illegible]	[illegible]	1	[illegible]	[illegible]	[illegible]

BIRTHS AND DEATHS Registered in the Year 1896—REGISTRARS' DISTRICTS, arranged by COUNTIES and SUPERINTENDENT REGISTRARS' DISTRICTS—*continued*.

No.	Registrars' Districts	Area in Statute Acres	Population in 1891	Total Births	Total Deaths	Births, including Illegitimate: Males	Births, including Illegitimate: Females	Illegitimate: Males	Illegitimate: Females	Deaths: Males	Deaths: Females	Excess of Births over Deaths
	III.—PROVINCE OF ULSTER—*con.*											
	145. COOTEHILL, part of.											
1	Cootehill, part of, W.	71,3?6	[illegible]	[illegible]	[illegible]	[illegible]	[illegible]	[illegible]	[illegible]	[illegible]	[illegible]	[illegible]
2	Drum, part of,	71,?1?	[illegible]	[illegible]	[illegible]	[illegible]	[illegible]	.	.	[illegible]	[illegible]	[illegible]
3	Tullyvin,	[illegible]	[illegible]	[illegible]	[illegible]	[illegible]	[illegible]	.	2	[illegible]	[illegible]	[illegible]
	146. [illegible], part of.											
1	[illegible], part of,	[illegible]	[illegible]	[illegible]	[illegible]	[illegible]	[illegible]	.	.	[illegible]	[illegible]	[illegible]
	147. [illegible], part of.											
1	[illegible], part of,	[illegible]	[illegible]	[illegible]	[illegible]	[illegible]	[illegible]	.	.	[illegible]	[illegible]	[illegible]
2	[illegible], &c.,	7,?43	[illegible]	[illegible]	[illegible]	1?	[illegible]	.	.	[illegible]	[illegible]	[illegible]
	148. KELLS, part of.											
1	Moynalty, part of,	[illegible]	[illegible]	[illegible]	[illegible]	[illegible]	1?	.	.	[illegible]	[illegible]	[illegible]
	149. OLDCASTLE, part of.											
1	Ballyjamesduff,	[illegible]	[illegible]	[illegible]	[illegible]	[illegible]	[illegible]	.	1	[illegible]	[illegible]	[illegible]
2	Virginia,	[illegible]	[illegible]	[illegible]	[illegible]	[illegible]	[illegible]	.	1	[illegible]	[illegible]	[illegible]
	DONEGAL CO.											
	150. BALLYSHANNON, part of.											
1	[illegible],	[illegible]	[illegible]	[illegible]	[illegible]	[illegible]	[illegible]	.	1	[illegible]	[illegible]	[illegible]
2	[illegible], W.,	[illegible]	[illegible]	[illegible]	[illegible]	[illegible]	[illegible]	1	.	[illegible]	[illegible]	[illegible]
	151. DONEGAL.											
1	[illegible], W.,	[illegible]	[illegible]	[illegible]	[illegible]	[illegible]	[illegible]	1	.	[illegible]	[illegible]	[illegible]
2	[illegible],	[illegible]	[illegible]	[illegible]	[illegible]	[illegible]	[illegible]	1	.	[illegible]	[illegible]	[illegible]
3	Laghy,	[illegible]	[illegible]	[illegible]	[illegible]	[illegible]	[illegible]	1	.	[illegible]	[illegible]	[illegible]
4	[illegible],	[illegible]	[illegible]	[illegible]	[illegible]	[illegible]	[illegible]	.	1	[illegible]	[illegible]	[illegible]
5	Pettigo,	[illegible]	[illegible]	[illegible]	[illegible]	[illegible]	[illegible]	.	.	[illegible]	[illegible]	[illegible]
	152. DUNFANAGHY.											
1	[illegible],	[illegible]	[illegible]	[illegible]	[illegible]	[illegible]	[illegible]	.	[illegible]	[illegible]	[illegible]	[illegible]
2	[illegible], W.,	[illegible]	[illegible]	[illegible]	[illegible]	[illegible]	[illegible]	1	.	[illegible]	[illegible]	[illegible]
3	[illegible],	[illegible]	[illegible]	[illegible]	[illegible]	[illegible]	47	[illegible]	.	[illegible]	[illegible]	[illegible]
4	Tory Island,	[illegible]	[illegible]	[illegible]	[illegible]	[illegible]	[illegible]	.	.	[illegible]	[illegible]	.
	153. GLENTIES.											
1	[illegible],	[illegible]	[illegible]	[illegible]	[illegible]	[illegible]	[illegible]	.	.	[illegible]	[illegible]	[illegible]
2	[illegible],	[illegible]	[illegible]	[illegible]	[illegible]	[illegible]	[illegible]	1	.	[illegible]	[illegible]	[illegible]
3	[illegible],	[illegible]	[illegible]	[illegible]	[illegible]	[illegible]	[illegible]	.	.	[illegible]	[illegible]	[illegible]
4	[illegible], No. 1,	[illegible]	[illegible]	[illegible]	[illegible]	[illegible]	[illegible]	.	.	[illegible]	[illegible]	[illegible]
5	„ No. 2,	[illegible]	[illegible]	[illegible]	[illegible]	[illegible]	[illegible]	[illegible]	.	[illegible]	[illegible]	[illegible]
6	[illegible], W.,	[illegible]	[illegible]	[illegible]	[illegible]	[illegible]	[illegible]	[illegible]	.	[illegible]	[illegible]	[illegible]
7	Killybegs,	[illegible]	[illegible]	[illegible]	[illegible]	[illegible]	[illegible]	.	.	[illegible]	[illegible]	[illegible]
	154. [illegible].											
1	[illegible],	[illegible]	[illegible]	[illegible]	[illegible]	[illegible]	[illegible]	.	.	[illegible]	[illegible]	[illegible]

BIRTHS AND DEATHS Registered in the Year 18[illegible]—REGISTRARS' DISTRICTS, arranged by COUNTIES and SUPERINTENDENT REGISTRARS' DISTRICTS—*continued.*

No.	REGISTRARS' DISTRICTS.	Area in Statute Acres.	Population in 18[illegible].	TOTAL. Births.	TOTAL. Deaths.	BIRTHS. Including Illegitimate Births. Males.	Females.	Illegitimate Births. Males.	Females.	DEATHS. Males.	Females.	Excess of Births over Deaths.
	III.—PROVINCE OF ULSTER—*con.*											
	156. [illegible], part of.											
1	Burt,	[illegible]	[illegible]	73	[illegible]	37	36	-	-	15	14	[illegible]
2	[illegible], part of,	[illegible]	[illegible]	[illegible]	43	[illegible]	[illegible]	2	-	[illegible]	[illegible]	13
3	[illegible],	15,145	[illegible]	[illegible]	41	[illegible]	[illegible]	1	4	[illegible]	[illegible]	[illegible]
	157. MILFORD.											
1	Fanad,	[illegible]	[illegible]	[illegible]	[illegible]	47	[illegible]	-	-	[illegible]	41	[illegible]
2	[illegible] and [illegible],	[illegible]	[illegible]	[illegible]	[illegible]	[illegible]	[illegible]	1	1	[illegible]	[illegible]	[illegible]
3	Rathmullan,	[illegible]	[illegible]	[illegible]	[illegible]	[illegible]	[illegible]	3	3	[illegible]	[illegible]	16
4	[illegible],	[illegible]	[illegible]	[illegible]	[illegible]	[illegible]	[illegible]	-	-	15	[illegible]	[illegible]
5	[illegible],	[illegible]	[illegible]	[illegible]	41	[illegible]	[illegible]	-	-	[illegible]	[illegible]	[illegible]
	158. STRABANE, part of.											
1	Castlefinn,	[illegible]	[illegible]	[illegible]	[illegible]	[illegible]	[illegible]	-	9	[illegible]	[illegible]	[illegible]
2	Raphoe,	[illegible]	[illegible]	[illegible]	[illegible]	[illegible]	[illegible]	1	7	[illegible]	[illegible]	[illegible]
	159. STRANORLAR.											
1	Cloghan,	[illegible]	[illegible]	[illegible]	[illegible]	[illegible]	[illegible]	-	-	[illegible]	[illegible]	[illegible]
2	Killygordon,	[illegible]	[illegible]	[illegible]	[illegible]	[illegible]	[illegible]	-	1	[illegible]	[illegible]	[illegible]
3	Stranorlar, W.	[illegible]	[illegible]	117	[illegible]	[illegible]	[illegible]	1	4	[illegible]	[illegible]	[illegible]
	DOWN CO.											
	160. BANBRIDGE, part of.											
1	Ballyward,	[illegible]	[illegible]	[illegible]	[illegible]	[illegible]	[illegible]	1	-	[illegible]	[illegible]	[illegible]
2	Banbridge, W.	[illegible]	[illegible]	[illegible]	[illegible]	[illegible]	[illegible]	10	11	[illegible]	[illegible]	[illegible]
3	[illegible],	[illegible]	[illegible]	[illegible]	[illegible]	[illegible]	[illegible]	1	-	[illegible]	[illegible]	[illegible]
4	Dromore,	[illegible]	[illegible]	[illegible]	[illegible]	[illegible]	[illegible]	4	7	[illegible]	[illegible]	[illegible]
5	Loughbrickland,	[illegible]	[illegible]	[illegible]	[illegible]	[illegible]	[illegible]	7	5	[illegible]	[illegible]	[illegible]
	161. BELFAST, part of.											
1	Castlereagh, No. 1,	17,[illegible]	[illegible]	[illegible]	[illegible]	[illegible]	[illegible]	3	6	[illegible]	[illegible]	[illegible]
2	" " 2,		[illegible]	[illegible]	[illegible]	[illegible]	[illegible]	[illegible]	1	[illegible]	[illegible]	41
3	" " 3,		[illegible]	[illegible]	[illegible]	[illegible]	[illegible]	[illegible]	5	[illegible]	[illegible]	[illegible]
4	" " 4,		[illegible]	[illegible]	[illegible]	[illegible]	[illegible]	14	5	[illegible]	[illegible]	[illegible]
	162. DOWNPATRICK.											
1	Ballynahinch,	[illegible]	[illegible]	[illegible]	[illegible]	[illegible]	[illegible]	[illegible]	3	[illegible]	[illegible]	[illegible]
2	Clough,	[illegible]	[illegible]	[illegible]	[illegible]	[illegible]	[illegible]	[illegible]	3	[illegible]	[illegible]	[illegible]
3	Downpatrick, W.	[illegible]	[illegible]	[illegible]	[illegible]	[illegible]	[illegible]	[illegible]	4	[illegible]	[illegible]	[illegible]
4	Killough,	17,[illegible]	[illegible]	[illegible]	[illegible]	[illegible]	47	4	[illegible]	[illegible]	[illegible]	[illegible]
5	Killyleagh,	[illegible]	[illegible]	[illegible]	[illegible]	[illegible]	[illegible]	[illegible]	3	[illegible]	[illegible]	[illegible]
6	Portaferry,	[illegible]	[illegible]	[illegible]	[illegible]	[illegible]	[illegible]		1	[illegible]	[illegible]	[illegible]
7	Saintfield,	17,[illegible]	[illegible]	[illegible]	[illegible]	[illegible]	[illegible]	-	1	[illegible]	41	[illegible]
	163. KILKEEL.											
1	[illegible],	[illegible]	[illegible]	[illegible]	[illegible]	[illegible]	[illegible]	[illegible]	1	[illegible]	[illegible]	[illegible]
2	Kilkeel, No. 1,	[illegible]	[illegible]	[illegible]	[illegible]	[illegible]	[illegible]	[illegible]	-	[illegible]	[illegible]	[illegible]

BIRTHS AND DEATHS Registered in the year 1896—REGISTRARS' DISTRICTS, arranged by COUNTIES and SUPERINTENDENT REGISTRARS' DISTRICTS—*continued.*

REGISTRARS' DISTRICTS.	Area in Statute Acres.	Population in 1891.	TOTAL Births.	TOTAL Deaths.	BIRTHS Including Illegitimate Births: Males	Females	Illegitimate Births: Males	Females	DEATHS: Males	Females	[illegible]
III.—PROVINCE OF ULSTER—con.											
165. Lurgan, part of.											
Lurgan, No. 1, part of,	1,341	47[illegible]	14	8	8	7	1	.	1	4	10
Moira,	[illegible]	[illegible]	116	78	[illegible]	[illegible]	2	1	[illegible]	[illegible]	[illegible]
Waringstown,	11,4[illegible]	[illegible]	171	[illegible]	[illegible]	[illegible]	6	1	[illegible]	[illegible]	[illegible]
166. Newry, part of.											
[illegible],	13,[illegible]	[illegible]	[illegible]	44	[illegible]	[illegible]	4	.	[illegible]	11	[illegible]
Newry, No. 1, part of,	2,[illegible]	[illegible]	[illegible]	[illegible]	14	[illegible]	.	.	17	[illegible]	[illegible]
" " 2,	5,441	[illegible]	[illegible]	[illegible]	[illegible]	[illegible]	[illegible]	1	[illegible]	116	40
Rathfriland,	[illegible]	[illegible]	1[illegible]	[illegible]	[illegible]	[illegible]	5	[illegible]	[illegible]	[illegible]	[illegible]
Warrenpoint,	[illegible]	[illegible]	1[illegible]	7[illegible]	[illegible]	[illegible]	.	1	[illegible]	[illegible]	[illegible]
167. Newtownards.											
Bangor,	[illegible]	7,[illegible]	[illegible]	[illegible]	[illegible]	171	4	7	[illegible]	[illegible]	116
Comber,	[illegible]	[illegible]	1[illegible]	[illegible]	71	[illegible]	3	3	[illegible]	[illegible]	[illegible]
Donaghadee,	6,[illegible]	4,[illegible]	[illegible]	7[illegible]	[illegible]	[illegible]	.	[illegible]	[illegible]	[illegible]	[illegible]
Greyabbey,	20,47[illegible]	6,[illegible]	1[illegible]	[illegible]	41	77	[illegible]	[illegible]	[illegible]	[illegible]	[illegible]
Kilmood,	14,[illegible]	[illegible]	[illegible]	44	[illegible]	[illegible]	.	.	[illegible]	[illegible]	[illegible]
Newtownards, W.,	17,[illegible]	12,37[illegible]	[illegible]	[illegible]	[illegible]	17[illegible]	16	[illegible]	[illegible]	11[illegible]	76
Fermanagh Co.											
168. Ballyshannon, part of.											
Belleek,	40,[illegible]	3,[illegible]	[illegible]	[illegible]	[illegible]	[illegible]	.	1	[illegible]	[illegible]	[illegible]
Church Hill,	[illegible]	2,[illegible]	[illegible]	[illegible]	16	14	.	.	14	[illegible]	[illegible]
169. Clones, part of.											
[illegible], part of,	71,7[illegible]	[illegible]	[illegible]	[illegible]	[illegible]	[illegible]	.	.	[illegible]	[illegible]	70
[illegible], do.,	[illegible]	4,[illegible]	[illegible]	[illegible]	[illegible]	[illegible]	.	.	[illegible]	[illegible]	14
170. Enniskillen, part of.											
Ely,	40,[illegible]	4,[illegible]	[illegible]	[illegible]	[illegible]	[illegible]	.	5	[illegible]	[illegible]	[illegible]
Enniskillen, W.,	[illegible]	[illegible]	[illegible]	[illegible]	[illegible]	11[illegible]	6	6	[illegible]	[illegible]	[illegible]
Florencecourt,	41,[illegible]	4,[illegible]	[illegible]	[illegible]	[illegible]	[illegible]	1	3	[illegible]	[illegible]	[illegible]
[illegible], part of,	8,[illegible]	[illegible]	[illegible]	[illegible]	16	11	.	6	6	7	[illegible]
Lisbellaw,	[illegible]	[illegible]	[illegible]	[illegible]	[illegible]	[illegible]	9	.	[illegible]	[illegible]	6
Tempo, part of,	[illegible]	4,[illegible]	[illegible]	[illegible]	[illegible]	[illegible]	1	.	17	[illegible]	[illegible]
171. Irvinestown, part of.											
[illegible],	7,[illegible]	1,[illegible]	[illegible]	[illegible]	7	6	.	.	19	[illegible]	[illegible]
[illegible],	[illegible]	[illegible]	[illegible]	[illegible]	[illegible]	[illegible]	4	.	[illegible]	[illegible]	11
Irvinestown, No. 1, part of, W.,	[illegible]	[illegible]	[illegible]	[illegible]	[illegible]	[illegible]	2	6	[illegible]	[illegible]	10
" No. 2, do.,	1,7[illegible]	[illegible]	[illegible]	[illegible]	4	6	1	2	7	[illegible]	2
172. Lisnaskea.											
[illegible],	[illegible]	[illegible]	[illegible]	[illegible]	[illegible]	[illegible]	1	6	[illegible]	[illegible]	[illegible]
[illegible],	[illegible]	[illegible]	7[illegible]	[illegible]	[illegible]	[illegible]	.	1	41	[illegible]	11
Lisnaskea, W.	[illegible]	4,[illegible]	[illegible]	[illegible]	[illegible]	[illegible]	8	4	[illegible]	[illegible]	16
[illegible],	11,1[illegible]	[illegible]	[illegible]	41	[illegible]	[illegible]	5	1	[illegible]	[illegible]	7

BIRTHS and DEATHS Registered in the Year [illegible].—Registrars' Districts arranged by Counties and Superintendent Registrars' Districts—continued.

No.	Registrars' Districts.	Area in Statute Acres.	Population in [illegible].	Births.	Deaths.	[illegible] Males	[illegible] Females	[illegible] Males	[illegible] Females	[illegible] Males	[illegible] Females
	[illegible]										
	[illegible]										
1	[illegible]	[illegible]	[illegible]	[illegible]	[illegible]	[illegible]	[illegible]	[illegible]	[illegible]	[illegible]	[illegible]
2	[illegible]	[illegible]	[illegible]	[illegible]	[illegible]	[illegible]	[illegible]	[illegible]	[illegible]	[illegible]	[illegible]
3	[illegible]	[illegible]	[illegible]	[illegible]	[illegible]	[illegible]	[illegible]	[illegible]	[illegible]	[illegible]	[illegible]
4	[illegible]	[illegible]	[illegible]	[illegible]	[illegible]	[illegible]	[illegible]	[illegible]	[illegible]	[illegible]	[illegible]
5	[illegible]	[illegible]	[illegible]	[illegible]	[illegible]	[illegible]	[illegible]	[illegible]	[illegible]	[illegible]	[illegible]
	[illegible], part of.										
1	[illegible]	[illegible]	[illegible]	[illegible]	[illegible]	[illegible]	[illegible]	[illegible]	[illegible]	[illegible]	[illegible]
2	City of Derry, No. 1,	[illegible]	[illegible]	[illegible]	[illegible]	[illegible]	[illegible]	[illegible]	[illegible]	[illegible]	[illegible]
3	" No. 2,	[illegible]	[illegible]	[illegible]	[illegible]	[illegible]	[illegible]	[illegible]	[illegible]	[illegible]	[illegible]
4	[illegible]	[illegible]	[illegible]	[illegible]	[illegible]	[illegible]	[illegible]	[illegible]	[illegible]	[illegible]	[illegible]
5	[illegible]	[illegible]	[illegible]	[illegible]	[illegible]	[illegible]	[illegible]	[illegible]	[illegible]	[illegible]	[illegible]
6	[illegible], part of,	[illegible]	[illegible]	[illegible]	[illegible]	[illegible]	[illegible]	[illegible]	[illegible]	[illegible]	[illegible]
	[illegible]										
1	[illegible]	[illegible]	[illegible]	[illegible]	[illegible]	[illegible]	[illegible]	[illegible]	[illegible]	[illegible]	[illegible]
2	[illegible]	[illegible]	[illegible]	[illegible]	[illegible]	[illegible]	[illegible]	[illegible]	[illegible]	[illegible]	[illegible]
3	[illegible]	[illegible]	[illegible]	[illegible]	[illegible]	[illegible]	[illegible]	[illegible]	[illegible]	[illegible]	[illegible]
4	[illegible]	[illegible]	[illegible]	[illegible]	[illegible]	[illegible]	[illegible]	[illegible]	[illegible]	[illegible]	[illegible]
5	[illegible]	[illegible]	[illegible]	[illegible]	[illegible]	[illegible]	[illegible]	[illegible]	[illegible]	[illegible]	[illegible]
	[illegible] Co.										
	[illegible]										
1	[illegible]	[illegible]	[illegible]	[illegible]	[illegible]	[illegible]	[illegible]	[illegible]	[illegible]	[illegible]	[illegible]
2	[illegible]	[illegible]	[illegible]	[illegible]	[illegible]	[illegible]	[illegible]	[illegible]	[illegible]	[illegible]	[illegible]
3	[illegible]	[illegible]	[illegible]	[illegible]	[illegible]	[illegible]	[illegible]	[illegible]	[illegible]	[illegible]	[illegible]
	[illegible], part of.										
1	[illegible]	[illegible]	[illegible]	[illegible]	[illegible]	[illegible]	[illegible]	[illegible]	[illegible]	[illegible]	[illegible]
2	[illegible]	[illegible]	[illegible]	[illegible]	[illegible]	[illegible]	[illegible]	[illegible]	[illegible]	[illegible]	[illegible]
3	[illegible], part of,	[illegible]	[illegible]	[illegible]	[illegible]	[illegible]	[illegible]	[illegible]	[illegible]	[illegible]	[illegible]
4	[illegible]	[illegible]	[illegible]	[illegible]	[illegible]	[illegible]	[illegible]	[illegible]	[illegible]	[illegible]	[illegible]
	[illegible], part of.										
1	[illegible], part of,	[illegible]	[illegible]	[illegible]	[illegible]	[illegible]	[illegible]	[illegible]	[illegible]	[illegible]	[illegible]
	[illegible], part of.										
1	[illegible]	[illegible]	[illegible]	[illegible]	[illegible]	[illegible]	[illegible]	[illegible]	[illegible]	[illegible]	[illegible]
2	[illegible], part of,	[illegible]	[illegible]	[illegible]	[illegible]	[illegible]	[illegible]	[illegible]	[illegible]	[illegible]	[illegible]
3	[illegible]	[illegible]	[illegible]	[illegible]	[illegible]	[illegible]	[illegible]	[illegible]	[illegible]	[illegible]	[illegible]
	[illegible], part of.										
1	[illegible], part of,	[illegible]	[illegible]	[illegible]	[illegible]	[illegible]	[illegible]	[illegible]	[illegible]	[illegible]	[illegible]
2	[illegible]	[illegible]	[illegible]	[illegible]	[illegible]	[illegible]	[illegible]	[illegible]	[illegible]	[illegible]	[illegible]
3	[illegible], part of,	[illegible]	[illegible]	[illegible]	[illegible]	[illegible]	[illegible]	[illegible]	[illegible]	[illegible]	[illegible]
	[illegible], part of.										
1	[illegible], part of,	[illegible]	[illegible]	[illegible]	[illegible]	[illegible]	[illegible]	[illegible]	[illegible]	[illegible]	[illegible]
	[illegible]										
1	[illegible]	[illegible]	[illegible]	[illegible]	[illegible]	[illegible]	[illegible]	[illegible]	[illegible]	[illegible]	[illegible]
2	[illegible]	[illegible]	[illegible]	[illegible]	[illegible]	[illegible]	[illegible]	[illegible]	[illegible]	[illegible]	[illegible]
3	[illegible]	[illegible]	[illegible]	[illegible]	[illegible]	[illegible]	[illegible]	[illegible]	[illegible]	[illegible]	[illegible]
4	[illegible]	[illegible]	[illegible]	[illegible]	[illegible]	[illegible]	[illegible]	[illegible]	[illegible]	[illegible]	[illegible]
5	[illegible]	[illegible]	[illegible]	[illegible]	[illegible]	[illegible]	[illegible]	[illegible]	[illegible]	[illegible]	[illegible]

[illegible] AND DEATHS Registered in the Year 1896—[illegible] DISTRICTS, arranged by [illegible] and [illegible] DISTRICTS—continued.

No.	REGISTRARS' DISTRICTS.	Area in Statute Acres.	[illegible] in 189[illegible].	[illegible]	[illegible]	[illegible]	[illegible]	[illegible]	[illegible]	[illegible]	[illegible]	[illegible]
	[illegible] PROVINCE OF [illegible]—con.											
	[illegible]											
	[illegible]											
1	[illegible]	[illegible]	[illegible]	[illegible]	[illegible]	[illegible]	[illegible]	[illegible]	[illegible]	[illegible]	[illegible]	[illegible]
	[illegible]											
1	[illegible]	[illegible]	[illegible]	[illegible]	[illegible]	[illegible]	[illegible]	[illegible]	[illegible]	[illegible]	[illegible]	[illegible]
2	[illegible]	[illegible]	[illegible]	[illegible]	[illegible]	[illegible]	[illegible]	[illegible]	[illegible]	[illegible]	[illegible]	[illegible]
3	[illegible]	[illegible]	[illegible]	[illegible]	[illegible]	[illegible]	[illegible]	[illegible]	[illegible]	[illegible]	[illegible]	[illegible]
	[illegible], part of											
1	[illegible], part of	[illegible]	[illegible]	[illegible]	[illegible]	[illegible]	[illegible]	[illegible]	[illegible]	[illegible]	[illegible]	[illegible]
2	[illegible]	[illegible]	[illegible]	[illegible]	[illegible]	[illegible]	[illegible]	[illegible]	[illegible]	[illegible]	[illegible]	[illegible]
3	[illegible]	[illegible]	[illegible]	[illegible]	[illegible]	[illegible]	[illegible]	[illegible]	[illegible]	[illegible]	[illegible]	[illegible]
4	[illegible]	[illegible]	[illegible]	[illegible]	[illegible]	[illegible]	[illegible]	[illegible]	[illegible]	[illegible]	[illegible]	[illegible]
	[illegible]											
1	[illegible]	[illegible]	[illegible]	[illegible]	[illegible]	[illegible]	[illegible]	[illegible]	[illegible]	[illegible]	[illegible]	[illegible]
2	[illegible]	[illegible]	[illegible]	[illegible]	[illegible]	[illegible]	[illegible]	[illegible]	[illegible]	[illegible]	[illegible]	[illegible]
3	[illegible]	[illegible]	[illegible]	[illegible]	[illegible]	[illegible]	[illegible]	[illegible]	[illegible]	[illegible]	[illegible]	[illegible]
4	[illegible]	[illegible]	[illegible]	[illegible]	[illegible]	[illegible]	[illegible]	[illegible]	[illegible]	[illegible]	[illegible]	[illegible]
	[illegible]											
1	[illegible]	[illegible]	[illegible]	[illegible]	[illegible]	[illegible]	[illegible]	[illegible]	[illegible]	[illegible]	[illegible]	[illegible]
2	[illegible]	[illegible]	[illegible]	[illegible]	[illegible]	[illegible]	[illegible]	[illegible]	[illegible]	[illegible]	[illegible]	[illegible]
3	[illegible]	[illegible]	[illegible]	[illegible]	[illegible]	[illegible]	[illegible]	[illegible]	[illegible]	[illegible]	[illegible]	[illegible]
4	[illegible]	[illegible]	[illegible]	[illegible]	[illegible]	[illegible]	[illegible]	[illegible]	[illegible]	[illegible]	[illegible]	[illegible]
5	[illegible]	[illegible]	[illegible]	[illegible]	[illegible]	[illegible]	[illegible]	[illegible]	[illegible]	[illegible]	[illegible]	[illegible]
	[illegible], part of											
1	[illegible], part of	[illegible]	[illegible]	[illegible]	[illegible]	[illegible]	[illegible]	[illegible]	[illegible]	[illegible]	[illegible]	[illegible]
	[illegible], part of											
1	[illegible] No. 1, part of	[illegible]	[illegible]	[illegible]	[illegible]	[illegible]	[illegible]	[illegible]	[illegible]	[illegible]	[illegible]	[illegible]
2	" No. 2, do.	[illegible]	[illegible]	[illegible]	[illegible]	[illegible]	[illegible]	[illegible]	[illegible]	[illegible]	[illegible]	[illegible]
	[illegible]											
1	[illegible]	[illegible]	[illegible]	[illegible]	[illegible]	[illegible]	[illegible]	[illegible]	[illegible]	[illegible]	[illegible]	[illegible]
2	[illegible]	[illegible]	[illegible]	[illegible]	[illegible]	[illegible]	[illegible]	[illegible]	[illegible]	[illegible]	[illegible]	[illegible]
3	[illegible]	[illegible]	[illegible]	[illegible]	[illegible]	[illegible]	[illegible]	[illegible]	[illegible]	[illegible]	[illegible]	[illegible]
4	[illegible]	[illegible]	[illegible]	[illegible]	[illegible]	[illegible]	[illegible]	[illegible]	[illegible]	[illegible]	[illegible]	[illegible]
5	[illegible] No. 1	[illegible]	[illegible]	[illegible]	[illegible]	[illegible]	[illegible]	[illegible]	[illegible]	[illegible]	[illegible]	[illegible]
6	" No. 2	[illegible]	[illegible]	[illegible]	[illegible]	[illegible]	[illegible]	[illegible]	[illegible]	[illegible]	[illegible]	[illegible]
7	[illegible]	[illegible]	[illegible]	[illegible]	[illegible]	[illegible]	[illegible]	[illegible]	[illegible]	[illegible]	[illegible]	[illegible]
	[illegible], part of											
1	[illegible]	[illegible]	[illegible]	[illegible]	[illegible]	[illegible]	[illegible]	[illegible]	[illegible]	[illegible]	[illegible]	[illegible]
2	[illegible]	[illegible]	[illegible]	[illegible]	[illegible]	[illegible]	[illegible]	[illegible]	[illegible]	[illegible]	[illegible]	[illegible]
3	[illegible]	[illegible]	[illegible]	[illegible]	[illegible]	[illegible]	[illegible]	[illegible]	[illegible]	[illegible]	[illegible]	[illegible]
4	[illegible]	[illegible]	[illegible]	[illegible]	[illegible]	[illegible]	[illegible]	[illegible]	[illegible]	[illegible]	[illegible]	[illegible]

BIRTHS AND DEATHS Registered in the Year 18[illegible]—Registrars' Districts, arranged by Counties and Superintendent Registrars' Districts—continued.

No.	Registrars' Districts.	Area in Statute Acres.	Population in 18[illegible].	[illegible]	[illegible]	[illegible]	[illegible]	[illegible]	[illegible]	[illegible]	[illegible]	[illegible]
	XV.—[illegible]											
	[illegible] Co.											
	[illegible], part of											
1	[illegible]	27,202	3,208	64	56	[illegible]	10	-	-	[illegible]	[illegible]	
2	[illegible], W.	[illegible]	[illegible]	[illegible]	[illegible]	[illegible]	[illegible]	[illegible]	[illegible]	[illegible]	[illegible]	
3	Kil[illegible]	[illegible]	[illegible]	[illegible]	[illegible]	[illegible]	[illegible]	-	-	[illegible]	[illegible]	
4	[illegible]	[illegible]	[illegible]	[illegible]	[illegible]	[illegible]	[illegible]	-	-	[illegible]	[illegible]	
5	[illegible]	[illegible]	[illegible]	[illegible]	[illegible]	[illegible]	[illegible]	[illegible]	[illegible]	[illegible]	[illegible]	
	[illegible], part of											
1	[illegible], part of	[illegible]	[illegible]	[illegible]	[illegible]	[illegible]	[illegible]			[illegible]	[illegible]	
	[illegible]											
1	[illegible], W.	[illegible]	[illegible]	[illegible]	[illegible]	[illegible]	[illegible]	[illegible]		[illegible]	[illegible]	
2	[illegible]	[illegible]	[illegible]	[illegible]	[illegible]	[illegible]	[illegible]	[illegible]		[illegible]	[illegible]	
3	[illegible]	[illegible]	[illegible]	140	[illegible]	[illegible]	[illegible]	[illegible]		[illegible]	[illegible]	
4	[illegible], No. 1	[illegible]	[illegible]	[illegible]	[illegible]	[illegible]	[illegible]	[illegible]		[illegible]	[illegible]	
5	" No. 2	[illegible]	[illegible]	[illegible]	[illegible]	[illegible]	[illegible]			[illegible]	[illegible]	
	[illegible]											
1	Galway, No. 1	[illegible]	[illegible]	[illegible]	[illegible]	[illegible]	[illegible]	1	[illegible]	[illegible]	[illegible]	
2	" No. 2, [illegible]	[illegible]	[illegible]	[illegible]	[illegible]	[illegible]	[illegible]	[illegible]	[illegible]	[illegible]	[illegible]	
3	" No. 3 [illegible]	[illegible]	[illegible]	[illegible]	[illegible]	[illegible]	[illegible]	-		[illegible]	[illegible]	
4	[illegible]	[illegible]	[illegible]	[illegible]	[illegible]	[illegible]	[illegible]	-		[illegible]	[illegible]	
5	[illegible]	[illegible]	[illegible]	[illegible]	[illegible]	[illegible]	[illegible]	-		[illegible]	[illegible]	
6	[illegible]	[illegible]	[illegible]	[illegible]	[illegible]	72	[illegible]	1	[illegible]	[illegible]	[illegible]	
7	[illegible]	[illegible]	[illegible]	[illegible]	[illegible]	[illegible]	[illegible]	-		[illegible]	[illegible]	
	[illegible]											
1	[illegible]	[illegible]	[illegible]	[illegible]	[illegible]	[illegible]	[illegible]	[illegible]	-	[illegible]	[illegible]	
2	[illegible], W.	[illegible]	[illegible]	[illegible]	[illegible]	[illegible]	[illegible]	[illegible]	-	[illegible]	[illegible]	
3	[illegible]	[illegible]	[illegible]	[illegible]	[illegible]	[illegible]	[illegible]	-	-	[illegible]	[illegible]	
	[illegible]											
1	[illegible]	[illegible]	[illegible]	[illegible]	[illegible]	[illegible]	[illegible]			[illegible]	[illegible]	
2	[illegible], W.	[illegible]	[illegible]	[illegible]	[illegible]	[illegible]	[illegible]			[illegible]	[illegible]	
3	[illegible]	[illegible]	[illegible]	72	[illegible]	[illegible]	[illegible]			[illegible]	[illegible]	
	[illegible]											
1	[illegible]	[illegible]	[illegible]	[illegible]	[illegible]	[illegible]	[illegible]	-	-	[illegible]	[illegible]	
2	[illegible]	[illegible]	[illegible]	[illegible]	[illegible]	[illegible]	[illegible]	-	-	[illegible]	[illegible]	
3	[illegible], W.	[illegible]	[illegible]	[illegible]	[illegible]	[illegible]	[illegible]	1	1	[illegible]	[illegible]	
4	[illegible]	[illegible]	[illegible]	[illegible]	[illegible]	[illegible]	[illegible]	-	-	[illegible]	[illegible]	

BIRTHS AND DEATHS Registered in the Year 1896—REGISTRARS' DISTRICTS, arranged by COUNTIES and SUPERINTENDENT REGISTRARS' DISTRICTS—*continued.*

No.	REGISTRARS' DISTRICTS.	Area in Statute Acres.	Population in 1891.	TOTAL Births.	TOTAL Deaths.	BIRTHS Legitimate Males	BIRTHS Legitimate Females	BIRTHS Illegitimate Males	BIRTHS Illegitimate Females	DEATHS Males	DEATHS Females	[illegible]
	IV.—PROVINCE OF CONNAUGHT—continued.											
	201. [illegible], part of.											
1	Athleague, part of,	4,996	435	5	6	1	4	.	1	.	6	5
	205. [illegible], part of.											
1	[illegible], part of,	26,391	1,791	30	18	11	11	.	.	8	7	77
	206. TUAM.											
1	Abbey,	34,581	4,815	85	40	53	43	.	.	35	31	47
2	Dunmore,	26,483	8,354	172	88	73	50	.	1	47	54	84
3	Headford,	43,458	6,772	124	88	61	34	.	1	60	67	68
4	Tuam, No. 1, W.	34,601	7,871	153	79	79	75	1	2	75	60	30
5	" No. 2,	34,841	7,308	140	73	68	70	.	.	38	37	79
	Leitrim Co.											
	207. BALLYSHANNON, part of.											
1	Kinlough,	23,425	3,878	64	40	30	27	1	.	27	13	[illegible]
	208. BAWNBOY, part of.											
1	[illegible],	28,045	6,026	100	73	50	51	.	.	40	33	23
2	[illegible], part of,	26,310	5,423	63	58	37	28	.	.	18	26	18
	209. CARRICK-ON-SHANNON, part of											
1	[illegible],	33,740	6,440	109	74	51	50	.	.	43	41	35
2	Jamestown, part of, W.	13,416	4,481	80	79	45	44	1	2	41	37	4
3	Leitrim, part of,	16,026	5,237	75	47	43	32	.	.	14	23	38
	210. MANORHAMILTON.											
1	[illegible],	33,873	6,407	177	85	66	71	.	.	39	49	43
2	[illegible],	37,423	4,780	120	58	67	65	.	.	39	37	25
3	Lurganboy,	44,873	6,200	114	40	60	46	1	.	33	30	16
4	Manorhamilton, W.	35,741	7,083	160	64	80	73	.	2	43	47	67
	211. MOHILL.											
1	Carrigallen,	18,143	4,800	74	43	31	43	.	.	39	35	71
2	Mohill, W.	30,383	7,443	142	69	46	38	1	2	67	35	80
3	[illegible],	33,423	5,467	103	74	73	60	.	.	43	33	40
4	[illegible],	16,084	4,329	74	40	47	27	.	.	30	19	34
	Mayo Co.											
	212. BALLINA, part of.											
1	Ballina, part of, W.	64,231	11,087	275	130	141	130	3	.	63	64	100
2	[illegible],	78,447	7,115	136	88	73	64	.	.	67	38	38
	213. BALLINROBE, part of.											
1	Ballinrobe, W.	33,090	5,880	100	114	50	56	.	.	38	44	68
2	[illegible], part of,	18,777	1,785	40	30	18	27	.	.	15	14	11
3	Cong,	33,107	4,480	121	70	60	44	1	.	31	40	21
4	Hollymount,	41,083	5,026	100	42	50	56	.	1	31	30	43
	214. BELMULLET.											
1	Bangor,	79,483	4,441	122	40	56	60	.	.	35	30	75
2	[illegible], W.	33,493	5,530	138	60	73	82	.	1	33	26	67
3	[illegible],	67,380	4,443	111	43	56	38	3	.	33	33	30

BIRTHS AND DEATHS Registered in the Year 18[illegible]—REGISTRARS' DISTRICTS, arranged by COUNTIES and SUPERINTENDENT REGISTRARS' DISTRICTS—*continued.*

No.	REGISTRARS' DISTRICTS.	Area in Statute Acres.	Population in 1871.	TOTAL BIRTHS.	TOTAL DEATHS.	[illegible] Males	[illegible] Females	[illegible] Males	[illegible] Females	[illegible] Males	[illegible] Females
	IV.—PROVINCE OF CONNAUGHT—*continued.*										
	712. CASTLEBAR.										
1	Balla,	[illegible]	[illegible]	[illegible]	[illegible]	[illegible]	[illegible]	–	1	[illegible]	[illegible]
2	Castlebar, No. 1, W.	[illegible]	[illegible]	[illegible]	[illegible]	[illegible]	[illegible]	.	.	[illegible]	[illegible]
3	„ No. 2,	[illegible]	[illegible]	[illegible]	[illegible]	[illegible]	[illegible]	.	.	[illegible]	[illegible]
	714. CASTLEREAGH, part of.										
1	Ballaghaderreen, part of,	[illegible]	[illegible]	[illegible]	[illegible]	[illegible]	[illegible]	.	1	[illegible]	[illegible]
	717. CLAREMORRIS.										
1	Ballindine,	[illegible]	[illegible]	[illegible]	[illegible]	[illegible]	[illegible]	.	.	[illegible]	[illegible]
2	Ballyhaunis,	[illegible]	[illegible]	[illegible]	[illegible]	[illegible]	[illegible]	.	1	[illegible]	[illegible]
3	Claremorris, W.	[illegible]	[illegible]	[illegible]	[illegible]	[illegible]	[illegible]	.	1	[illegible]	[illegible]
	718. KILLALA.										
1	Ballycastle,	[illegible]	[illegible]	[illegible]	[illegible]	[illegible]	[illegible]	.	.	[illegible]	[illegible]
2	Killala, W.	[illegible]	[illegible]	[illegible]	[illegible]	[illegible]	[illegible]	3	.	[illegible]	[illegible]
	729. SWINEFORD.										
1	Foxford,	[illegible]	[illegible]	[illegible]	[illegible]	[illegible]	[illegible]	.	.	[illegible]	[illegible]
2	Kilkelly,	[illegible]	[illegible]	[illegible]	[illegible]	[illegible]	[illegible]	.	.	[illegible]	[illegible]
3	Kiltimagh,	[illegible]	[illegible]	[illegible]	[illegible]	[illegible]	[illegible]	.	.	[illegible]	[illegible]
4	Leogart,	[illegible]	[illegible]	[illegible]	[illegible]	[illegible]	[illegible]	.	.	[illegible]	[illegible]
5	Swineford, W.	[illegible]	[illegible]	[illegible]	[illegible]	[illegible]	[illegible]	.	.	[illegible]	[illegible]
	730. WESTPORT.										
1	Achill,	[illegible]	[illegible]	[illegible]	[illegible]	[illegible]	[illegible]	.	.	[illegible]	[illegible]
2	Ballycroy,	[illegible]	[illegible]	[illegible]	[illegible]	[illegible]	[illegible]	[illegible]	.	[illegible]	[illegible]
3	Islandeady,	[illegible]	[illegible]	[illegible]	[illegible]	[illegible]	[illegible]	[illegible]	.	[illegible]	[illegible]
4	Louisburgh, No. 1,	[illegible]	[illegible]	[illegible]	[illegible]	[illegible]	[illegible]	.	.	[illegible]	[illegible]
5	„ No. 2,	[illegible]	[illegible]	2	[illegible]	[illegible]	[illegible]	.	.	1	[illegible]

BIRTHS AND DEATHS Registered in the Year 1896—REGISTRARS' DISTRICTS, arranged by COUNTIES and SUPERINTENDENT REGISTRARS' DISTRICTS—continued.

No.	REGISTRARS' DISTRICTS.	Area in Statute Acres.	Population in 1891.	TOTAL: Births.	TOTAL: Deaths.	Births: Legitimate: Males	Births: Legitimate: Females	Births: Illegitimate: Males	Births: Illegitimate: Females	Deaths: Males	Deaths: Females	[illegible]
	IV.—PROVINCE OF CONNAUGHT—continued.											
	224. CASTLEREA, part of.											
1	Ballaghaderreen, part of,	28,431	7,259	171	[illegible]	71	97	.	.	67	[illegible]	47
2	[illegible]	20,[illegible]	6,11[illegible]	83	47	[illegible]	[illegible]	.	.	14	[illegible]	[illegible]
3	Castlerea, W.,	44,671	13,[illegible]	[illegible]	110	1[illegible]	[illegible]	2	1	84	[illegible]	[illegible]
4	Frenchpark,	[illegible]	7,741	[illegible]	1[illegible]	91	79	.	.	[illegible]	64	[illegible]
	225. ROSCOMMON, part of.											
1	Athleague, part of	[illegible]	4,1[illegible]	74	[illegible]	75	[illegible]	.	.	[illegible]	[illegible]	[illegible]
2	[illegible]	41,[illegible]	[illegible]	1[illegible]	[illegible]	79	[illegible]	.	.	[illegible]	[illegible]	47
3	Roscommon, W.	56,[illegible]	[illegible]	110	[illegible]	[illegible]	[illegible]	2	3	[illegible]	[illegible]	17
	227. STROKESTOWN.											
1	Elphin,	[illegible]	4,[illegible]	[illegible]	74	4[illegible]	[illegible]	.	.	[illegible]	[illegible]	[illegible]
2	Rooskey,	[illegible]	[illegible]	114	71	[illegible]	54	.	.	[illegible]	[illegible]	[illegible]
3	Strokestown, W.	51,[illegible]	7,1[illegible]	[illegible]	[illegible]	41	47	1	1	[illegible]	57	[illegible]
	SLIGO CO.											
	228. BALLINA, part of.											
1	[illegible], part of,	9,[illegible]	[illegible]	44	11	[illegible]	[illegible]	.	.	4	1[illegible]	[illegible]
	229. BOYLE, part of.											
1	Ballyfarnon, part of,	23,[illegible]	[illegible]	71	[illegible]	44	[illegible]	.	.	[illegible]	17	[illegible]
2	Boyle, do.,	19,[illegible]	4,[illegible]	66	[illegible]	[illegible]	[illegible]	.	.	[illegible]	18	[illegible]
3	Gurteen,	23,[illegible]	4,[illegible]	1[illegible]	1[illegible]	[illegible]	70	.	.	[illegible]	15	[illegible]
	230. DROMORE WEST.											
1	[illegible],	21,[illegible]	[illegible]	94	[illegible]	50	44	1	.	[illegible]	[illegible]	[illegible]
2	Easky, W.,	43,[illegible]	[illegible]	1[illegible]	[illegible]	[illegible]	[illegible]	.	.	[illegible]	[illegible]	[illegible]
3	Skreen,	[illegible]	[illegible]	[illegible]	41	[illegible]	[illegible]	.	.	[illegible]	16	17
	231. SLIGO.											
1	Ballymote,	15,[illegible]	4,[illegible]	[illegible]	[illegible]	[illegible]	[illegible]	.	.	[illegible]	[illegible]	[illegible]
2	Collooney, No. 1,	[illegible]	[illegible]	94	[illegible]	47	[illegible]	1	2	[illegible]	91	[illegible]
3	,, No. 2,	[illegible]	4,7[illegible]	[illegible]	[illegible]	[illegible]	[illegible]	.	.	[illegible]	[illegible]	[illegible]
4	[illegible],	[illegible]	4,[illegible]	97	77	42	44	.	.	[illegible]	[illegible]	[illegible]
5	[illegible],	23,[illegible]	4,[illegible]	[illegible]	47	[illegible]	[illegible]	.	.	[illegible]	[illegible]	[illegible]
6	Sligo, No. 1, W.,	16,[illegible]	[illegible]	[illegible]	[illegible]	[illegible]	64	1	5	[illegible]	70	[illegible]
7	,, No. 2,	14,[illegible]	14,[illegible]	[illegible]	1[illegible]	1[illegible]	11[illegible]	.	1	[illegible]	[illegible]	[illegible]
	232. TOBERCURRY.											
1	Achonry,	45,[illegible]	[illegible]	[illegible]	[illegible]	51	1[illegible]	.	.	[illegible]	41	1[illegible]
2	Coolaney,	[illegible]	4,[illegible]	[illegible]	[illegible]	91	[illegible]	.	.	[illegible]	[illegible]	11
3	Tobercurry, W.,	[illegible]	[illegible]	1[illegible]	[illegible]	[illegible]	[illegible]	.	1	[illegible]	[illegible]	[illegible]

BIRTHS AND DEATHS Registered in the Year [illegible], in those Superintendent Registrars' Districts in Ireland which extend into more than one County.

[illegible]	Registrars' Districts.	Area in Statute Acres.	Population in [illegible].	TOTALS. Births.	TOTALS. Deaths.	Births. Legitimate. Males.	Births. Legitimate. Females.	Births. Illegitimate. Males.	Births. Illegitimate. Females.	Deaths. Males.	Deaths. Females.	[illegible]
[illegible]	[illegible]	[illegible]	[illegible]	[illegible]	[illegible]	[illegible]	[illegible]	[illegible]	[illegible]	[illegible]	[illegible]	[illegible]

TABLES SHOWING THE NUMBER

OF

BIRTHS

AND

DEATHS

REGISTERED IN EACH OF THE FOUR QUARTERS OF THE YEAR.

ALSO

DEATHS AT DIFFERENT AGES,

AND

CAUSES OF DEATH,

IN 1896.

Note.—The Number of Marriages Registered in each Quarter of the Year [illegible] will be found stated in the Abstract of Marriages commencing at Page [illegible].

DEATHS registered in Ireland in the Four Quarters ending
(Exclusive of

No.	Provinces and Counties.	Area in Statute Acres.	Population in 1891.	Males and Females: Total.	Registered in the Quarter ending the last day of March.	June.	Sept.	Dec.
	IRELAND,	[illegible]	4,704,750	[illegible]	[illegible]	[illegible]	[illegible]	[illegible]
	Provinces.							
I.	LEINSTER,	[illegible]	1,187,760	27,411	[illegible]	[illegible]	[illegible]	[illegible]
II.	MUNSTER,	[illegible]	1,172,402	[illegible]	[illegible]	[illegible]	[illegible]	[illegible]
III.	ULSTER,	[illegible]	1,619,814	[illegible]	[illegible]	[illegible]	[illegible]	[illegible]
IV.	CONNAUGHT,	[illegible]	724,774	[illegible]	[illegible]	[illegible]	[illegible]	[illegible]
	I.—PROVINCE OF							
1	Carlow,	[illegible]	40,936	774	[illegible]	[illegible]	[illegible]	[illegible]
2	Dublin,	[illegible]	419,216	[illegible]	[illegible]	[illegible]	[illegible]	[illegible]
3	Kildare,	[illegible]	70,206	[illegible]	[illegible]	[illegible]	[illegible]	[illegible]
4	Kilkenny,	[illegible]	87,261	[illegible]	[illegible]	[illegible]	[illegible]	[illegible]
5	King's,	[illegible]	65,563	[illegible]	[illegible]	[illegible]	[illegible]	[illegible]
6	Longford,	[illegible]	52,647	[illegible]	[illegible]	[illegible]	[illegible]	[illegible]
7	Louth, and county of the town of Drogheda,	[illegible]	71,038	[illegible]	[illegible]	[illegible]	[illegible]	[illegible]
8	Meath,	[illegible]	76,987	[illegible]	[illegible]	[illegible]	[illegible]	[illegible]
9	Queen's,	[illegible]	64,883	[illegible]	[illegible]	[illegible]	[illegible]	[illegible]
10	Westmeath,	[illegible]	65,109	[illegible]	[illegible]	[illegible]	[illegible]	[illegible]
11	Wexford,	[illegible]	111,778	[illegible]	[illegible]	[illegible]	[illegible]	[illegible]
12	Wicklow,	[illegible]	62,136	[illegible]	[illegible]	[illegible]	[illegible]	[illegible]
	II.—PROVINCE OF							
13	Clare,	[illegible]	124,483	[illegible]	[illegible]	[illegible]	[illegible]	[illegible]
14	Cork,	[illegible]	438,432	[illegible]	[illegible]	[illegible]	[illegible]	[illegible]
15	Kerry,	[illegible]	179,136	[illegible]	[illegible]	[illegible]	[illegible]	[illegible]
16	Limerick,	[illegible]	158,912	[illegible]	[illegible]	[illegible]	[illegible]	[illegible]
17	Tipperary,	[illegible]	173,188	[illegible]	[illegible]	[illegible]	[illegible]	[illegible]
18	Waterford,	[illegible]	98,251	[illegible]	[illegible]	[illegible]	[illegible]	[illegible]
	III.—PROVINCE OF							
19	Antrim,	[illegible]	428,128	[illegible]	[illegible]	[illegible]	[illegible]	[illegible]
20	Armagh,	[illegible]	143,289	[illegible]	[illegible]	[illegible]	[illegible]	[illegible]
21	Cavan,	[illegible]	111,917	[illegible]	[illegible]	[illegible]	[illegible]	477
22	Donegal,	[illegible]	185,635	[illegible]	[illegible]	[illegible]	[illegible]	[illegible]
23	Down,	[illegible]	267,059	[illegible]	[illegible]	[illegible]	[illegible]	[illegible]
24	Fermanagh,	[illegible]	74,170	[illegible]	[illegible]	[illegible]	[illegible]	[illegible]
25	Londonderry,	[illegible]	152,009	[illegible]	[illegible]	[illegible]	[illegible]	[illegible]
26	Monaghan,	[illegible]	86,206	[illegible]	[illegible]	[illegible]	[illegible]	[illegible]
27	Tyrone,	[illegible]	171,401	[illegible]	[illegible]	[illegible]	[illegible]	[illegible]
	IV.—PROVINCE OF							
28	Galway,	[illegible]	214,712	[illegible]	[illegible]	[illegible]	[illegible]	[illegible]
29	Leitrim,	[illegible]	78,618	[illegible]	[illegible]	[illegible]	[illegible]	[illegible]
30	Mayo,	[illegible]	219,034	[illegible]	[illegible]	[illegible]	[illegible]	[illegible]
31	Roscommon,	[illegible]	114,397	[illegible]	[illegible]	[illegible]	[illegible]	[illegible]
32	Sligo,	[illegible]	98,013	[illegible]	[illegible]	[illegible]	[illegible]	[illegible]

March 31st, June 30th, September 30th, and December 31st, 189[illegible] (still-born).

MALES.					FEMALES.					PROVINCES AND COUNTIES.
Registered in the Quarter ending the last day of				Total.	Total.	Registered in the Quarter ending the last day of				
March.	June.	Sept.	Dec.			March.	June.	Sept.	Dec.	
[illegible]	[illegible]	[illegible]	[illegible]	[illegible]	[illegible]	[illegible]	[illegible]	[illegible]	[illegible]	IRELAND.
										Provinces.
[illegible]	[illegible]	[illegible]	[illegible]	[illegible]	[illegible]	[illegible]	[illegible]	[illegible]	[illegible]	LEINSTER.
[illegible]	[illegible]	[illegible]	[illegible]	[illegible]	[illegible]	[illegible]	[illegible]	[illegible]	[illegible]	MUNSTER.
[illegible]	[illegible]	[illegible]	[illegible]	[illegible]	[illegible]	[illegible]	[illegible]	[illegible]	[illegible]	ULSTER.
[illegible]	[illegible]	[illegible]	[illegible]	[illegible]	[illegible]	[illegible]	[illegible]	[illegible]	[illegible]	CONNAUGHT.

LEINSTER.

[illegible]	[illegible]	[illegible]	[illegible]	[illegible]	[illegible]	[illegible]	[illegible]	[illegible]	[illegible]	Carlow.
[illegible]	[illegible]	[illegible]	[illegible]	[illegible]	[illegible]	[illegible]	[illegible]	[illegible]	[illegible]	Dublin.
[illegible]	[illegible]	[illegible]	[illegible]	[illegible]	[illegible]	[illegible]	[illegible]	[illegible]	[illegible]	Kildare.
[illegible]	[illegible]	[illegible]	[illegible]	[illegible]	[illegible]	[illegible]	[illegible]	[illegible]	[illegible]	Kilkenny.
[illegible]	[illegible]	[illegible]	[illegible]	[illegible]	[illegible]	[illegible]	[illegible]	[illegible]	[illegible]	King's.
[illegible]	[illegible]	[illegible]	[illegible]	[illegible]	[illegible]	[illegible]	[illegible]	[illegible]	[illegible]	Longford.
[illegible]	[illegible]	[illegible]	[illegible]	[illegible]	[illegible]	[illegible]	[illegible]	[illegible]	[illegible]	Louth, and county of the town of Drogheda.
[illegible]	[illegible]	[illegible]	[illegible]	[illegible]	[illegible]	[illegible]	[illegible]	[illegible]	[illegible]	Meath.
[illegible]	[illegible]	[illegible]	[illegible]	[illegible]	[illegible]	[illegible]	[illegible]	[illegible]	[illegible]	Queen's.
[illegible]	[illegible]	[illegible]	[illegible]	[illegible]	[illegible]	[illegible]	[illegible]	[illegible]	[illegible]	Westmeath.
[illegible]	[illegible]	[illegible]	[illegible]	[illegible]	[illegible]	[illegible]	[illegible]	[illegible]	[illegible]	Wexford.
[illegible]	[illegible]	[illegible]	[illegible]	[illegible]	[illegible]	[illegible]	[illegible]	[illegible]	[illegible]	Wicklow.

MUNSTER.

[illegible]	[illegible]	[illegible]	[illegible]	[illegible]	[illegible]	[illegible]	[illegible]	[illegible]	[illegible]	Clare.
[illegible]	[illegible]	[illegible]	[illegible]	[illegible]	[illegible]	[illegible]	[illegible]	[illegible]	[illegible]	Cork.
[illegible]	[illegible]	[illegible]	[illegible]	[illegible]	[illegible]	[illegible]	[illegible]	[illegible]	[illegible]	Kerry.
[illegible]	[illegible]	[illegible]	[illegible]	[illegible]	[illegible]	[illegible]	[illegible]	[illegible]	[illegible]	Limerick.
[illegible]	[illegible]	[illegible]	[illegible]	[illegible]	[illegible]	[illegible]	[illegible]	[illegible]	[illegible]	Tipperary.
[illegible]	[illegible]	[illegible]	[illegible]	[illegible]	[illegible]	[illegible]	[illegible]	[illegible]	[illegible]	Waterford.

ULSTER.

[illegible]	[illegible]	[illegible]	[illegible]	[illegible]	[illegible]	[illegible]	[illegible]	[illegible]	[illegible]	Antrim.
[illegible]	[illegible]	[illegible]	[illegible]	[illegible]	[illegible]	[illegible]	[illegible]	[illegible]	[illegible]	Armagh.
[illegible]	[illegible]	[illegible]	[illegible]	[illegible]	[illegible]	[illegible]	[illegible]	[illegible]	[illegible]	Cavan.
[illegible]	[illegible]	[illegible]	[illegible]	[illegible]	[illegible]	[illegible]	[illegible]	[illegible]	[illegible]	Donegal.
[illegible]	[illegible]	[illegible]	[illegible]	[illegible]	[illegible]	[illegible]	[illegible]	[illegible]	[illegible]	Down.
[illegible]	[illegible]	[illegible]	[illegible]	[illegible]	[illegible]	[illegible]	[illegible]	[illegible]	[illegible]	Fermanagh.
[illegible]	[illegible]	[illegible]	[illegible]	[illegible]	[illegible]	[illegible]	[illegible]	[illegible]	[illegible]	Londonderry.
[illegible]	[illegible]	[illegible]	[illegible]	[illegible]	[illegible]	[illegible]	[illegible]	[illegible]	[illegible]	Monaghan.
[illegible]	[illegible]	[illegible]	[illegible]	[illegible]	[illegible]	[illegible]	[illegible]	[illegible]	[illegible]	Tyrone.

CONNAUGHT.

[illegible]	[illegible]	[illegible]	[illegible]	[illegible]	[illegible]	[illegible]	[illegible]	[illegible]	[illegible]	Galway.
[illegible]	[illegible]	[illegible]	[illegible]	[illegible]	[illegible]	[illegible]	[illegible]	[illegible]	[illegible]	Leitrim.
[illegible]	[illegible]	[illegible]	[illegible]	[illegible]	[illegible]	[illegible]	[illegible]	[illegible]	[illegible]	Mayo.
[illegible]	[illegible]	[illegible]	[illegible]	[illegible]	[illegible]	[illegible]	[illegible]	[illegible]	[illegible]	Roscommon.
[illegible]	[illegible]	[illegible]	[illegible]	[illegible]	[illegible]	[illegible]	[illegible]	[illegible]	[illegible]	Sligo.

DEATHS registered in Ireland in the Four Quarters ending [illegible]

B.—[illegible]

No.	Superintendent Registrars' Districts	Area in Statute Acres.	Population in 1861.	Deaths. (Males and Females)	Registered in the Four Quarters ending: March.	June.	Sept.	Dec.
	Carlow Co.							
1	Baltinglass, part of,	[illegible]	[illegible]	[illegible]	[illegible]	[illegible]	[illegible]	[illegible]
2	Carlow, do.	[illegible]	[illegible]	[illegible]	[illegible]	[illegible]	[illegible]	[illegible]
3	[illegible] do.	[illegible]	[illegible]	[illegible]	[illegible]	[illegible]	[illegible]	[illegible]
4	New Ross, do.	[illegible]	[illegible]	[illegible]	[illegible]	[illegible]	[illegible]	[illegible]
5	Shillelagh, do.	[illegible]	[illegible]	[illegible]	[illegible]	[illegible]	[illegible]	[illegible]
	Dublin Co.							
6	Balrothery,	[illegible]	[illegible]	[illegible]	[illegible]	[illegible]	[illegible]	[illegible]
7	Celbridge, part of,	[illegible]	[illegible]	[illegible]	[illegible]	[illegible]	[illegible]	[illegible]
8	Dublin, North,	[illegible]	[illegible]	[illegible]	[illegible]	[illegible]	[illegible]	[illegible]
9	Dublin, South,	[illegible]	[illegible]	[illegible]	[illegible]	[illegible]	[illegible]	[illegible]
10	Dunshaughlin, part of,	[illegible]	[illegible]	[illegible]	[illegible]	[illegible]	[illegible]	[illegible]
11	Rathdown, do.	[illegible]	[illegible]	[illegible]	[illegible]	[illegible]	[illegible]	[illegible]
	Kildare Co.							
12	Athy, part of,	[illegible]	[illegible]	[illegible]	[illegible]	[illegible]	[illegible]	[illegible]
13	Baltinglass, do.	[illegible]	[illegible]	[illegible]	[illegible]	[illegible]	[illegible]	[illegible]
14	Celbridge, do.	[illegible]	[illegible]	[illegible]	[illegible]	[illegible]	[illegible]	[illegible]
15	Edenderry, do.	[illegible]	[illegible]	[illegible]	[illegible]	[illegible]	[illegible]	[illegible]
16	Naas, do.	[illegible]	[illegible]	[illegible]	[illegible]	[illegible]	[illegible]	[illegible]
	Kilkenny Co.							
17	Callan, part of,	[illegible]	[illegible]	[illegible]	[illegible]	[illegible]	[illegible]	[illegible]
18	Carrick-on-Suir, do.	[illegible]	[illegible]	[illegible]	[illegible]	[illegible]	[illegible]	[illegible]
19	Castlecomer,	[illegible]	[illegible]	[illegible]	[illegible]	[illegible]	[illegible]	[illegible]
20	Kilkenny,	[illegible]	[illegible]	[illegible]	[illegible]	[illegible]	[illegible]	[illegible]
21	New Ross, part of,	[illegible]	[illegible]	[illegible]	[illegible]	[illegible]	[illegible]	[illegible]
22	Thomastown,	[illegible]	[illegible]	[illegible]	[illegible]	[illegible]	[illegible]	[illegible]
23	Urlingford, part of,	[illegible]	[illegible]	[illegible]	[illegible]	[illegible]	[illegible]	[illegible]
24	Waterford, do.	[illegible]	[illegible]	[illegible]	[illegible]	[illegible]	[illegible]	[illegible]
	King's Co.							
25	[illegible] part of,	[illegible]	[illegible]	[illegible]	[illegible]	[illegible]	[illegible]	[illegible]
26	Mountmellick, do.	[illegible]	[illegible]	[illegible]	[illegible]	[illegible]	[illegible]	[illegible]
27	Parsonstown, do.	[illegible]	[illegible]	[illegible]	[illegible]	[illegible]	[illegible]	[illegible]
28	Roscrea, do.	[illegible]	[illegible]	[illegible]	[illegible]	[illegible]	[illegible]	[illegible]
29	Tullamore, do.	[illegible]	[illegible]	[illegible]	[illegible]	[illegible]	[illegible]	[illegible]
	Longford Co.							
30	Ballymahon, part of,	[illegible]	[illegible]	[illegible]	[illegible]	[illegible]	[illegible]	[illegible]
31	Granard, do.	[illegible]	[illegible]	[illegible]	[illegible]	[illegible]	[illegible]	[illegible]
32	Longford,	[illegible]	[illegible]	[illegible]	[illegible]	[illegible]	[illegible]	[illegible]
	Louth Co. and Co. of Town of Drogheda.							
33	Ardee, part of,	[illegible]	[illegible]	[illegible]	[illegible]	[illegible]	[illegible]	[illegible]
34	Drogheda, do.	[illegible]	[illegible]	[illegible]	[illegible]	[illegible]	[illegible]	[illegible]
35	Dundalk, do.	[illegible]	[illegible]	[illegible]	[illegible]	[illegible]	[illegible]	[illegible]
	Meath Co.							
36	Ardee, part of,	[illegible]	[illegible]	[illegible]	[illegible]	[illegible]	[illegible]	[illegible]
37	[illegible] do.	[illegible]	[illegible]	[illegible]	[illegible]	[illegible]	[illegible]	[illegible]
38	[illegible] do.	[illegible]	[illegible]	[illegible]	[illegible]	[illegible]	[illegible]	[illegible]
39	[illegible] do.	[illegible]	[illegible]	[illegible]	[illegible]	[illegible]	[illegible]	[illegible]
40	Edenderry, do.	[illegible]	[illegible]	[illegible]	[illegible]	[illegible]	[illegible]	[illegible]
41	Kells, do.	[illegible]	[illegible]	[illegible]	[illegible]	[illegible]	[illegible]	[illegible]
42	Navan,	[illegible]	[illegible]	[illegible]	[illegible]	[illegible]	[illegible]	[illegible]
43	Oldcastle, part of,	[illegible]	[illegible]	[illegible]	[illegible]	[illegible]	[illegible]	[illegible]
44	Trim,	[illegible]	[illegible]	[illegible]	[illegible]	[illegible]	[illegible]	[illegible]

March 31st, June 30th, September 30th, and December 31st, 1866—*continued.*

LEINSTER.

MALES.					FEMALES.					SUPERINTENDENT REGISTRARS' DISTRICTS.
Registered in the Quarter ending the last day of				Total.	Total.	Registered in the Quarter ending the last day of				
March.	June.	Sept.	Dec.			March.	June.	Sept.	Dec.	
										Carlow Co.
[illegible]	4	1	10	[illegible]	[illegible]	[illegible]	4	[illegible]	7	Baltinglass, part of
[illegible]	71	61	71	[illegible]	277	75	79	[illegible]	44	Carlow, do.
1	3	-	5	[illegible]	7		1	1	4	Enniscorthy, do.
19	7	4	[illegible]	[illegible]	[illegible]	10	4	5	5	New Ross, do.
[illegible]	14	11	7	[illegible]	[illegible]	6	11	[illegible]	13	Shillelagh, do.
										Dublin Co.
[illegible]	66	61	57	[illegible]	177	[illegible]	61	41	40	Balrothery.
12	10	11	8	[illegible]	[illegible]	14	13	21	9	Celbridge, part of
[illegible]	672	611	[illegible]	[illegible]	2,416	[illegible]	[illegible]	[illegible]	641	Dublin, North.
[illegible]	[illegible]	[illegible]	[illegible]	[illegible]	2,770	[illegible]	[illegible]	716	[illegible]	Dublin, South.
-	6	1	4	14	[illegible]	1	4	[illegible]	7	Dunshaughlin, part of
[illegible]	164	151	[illegible]	[illegible]	[illegible]	152	149	[illegible]	127	Rathdown, do.
										Kildare Co.
[illegible]	[illegible]	[illegible]	64	[illegible]	212	47	57	53	61	Athy, part of
4	1	4	8	17	[illegible]	6	6	4	7	Baltinglass, do.
17	18	[illegible]	27	61	87	[illegible]	21	24	[illegible]	Celbridge, do.
17	[illegible]	14	16	64	58	12	18	16	[illegible]	Edenderry, do.
71	[illegible]	[illegible]	64	[illegible]	[illegible]	[illegible]	67	111	61	Naas, do.
										Kilkenny Co.
[illegible]	[illegible]	[illegible]	[illegible]	[illegible]	[illegible]	[illegible]	[illegible]	[illegible]	23	Callan, part of
[illegible]	16	11	9	64	[illegible]	4	[illegible]	6	6	Carrick-on-Suir, do.
[illegible]	[illegible]	[illegible]	[illegible]	[illegible]	[illegible]	[illegible]	[illegible]	[illegible]	[illegible]	Castlecomer.
[illegible]	[illegible]	73	[illegible]	[illegible]	[illegible]	42	[illegible]	[illegible]	[illegible]	Kilkenny.
6	11	[illegible]	[illegible]	[illegible]	43	9	4	14	13	New Ross, part of
[illegible]	63	35	[illegible]	[illegible]	[illegible]	[illegible]	53	[illegible]	[illegible]	Thomastown.
[illegible]	17	14	[illegible]	74	[illegible]	[illegible]	16	[illegible]	[illegible]	Urlingford, part of
[illegible]	[illegible]	27	[illegible]	[illegible]	[illegible]	19	[illegible]	[illegible]	[illegible]	Waterford, do.
										King's Co.
[illegible]	17	[illegible]	12	[illegible]	[illegible]	[illegible]	[illegible]	[illegible]	[illegible]	Edenderry, part of
[illegible]	7	6	5	[illegible]	[illegible]	[illegible]	6	[illegible]	6	Mountmellick, do.
[illegible]	[illegible]	36	[illegible]	[illegible]	[illegible]	[illegible]	40	[illegible]	71	Parsonstown, do.
[illegible]	[illegible]	15	6	[illegible]	[illegible]	16	13	[illegible]	15	Roscrea, do.
[illegible]	[illegible]	[illegible]	[illegible]	[illegible]	[illegible]	[illegible]	78	71	16	Tullamore, do.
										Longford Co.
[illegible]	[illegible]	34	19	[illegible]	73	[illegible]	17	[illegible]	[illegible]	Ballymahon, part of
[illegible]	[illegible]	[illegible]	[illegible]	152	[illegible]	67	[illegible]	[illegible]	[illegible]	Granard, do.
[illegible]	[illegible]	[illegible]	[illegible]	[illegible]	[illegible]	[illegible]	[illegible]	[illegible]	[illegible]	Longford.
										Louth Co. and Co. of Town of Drogheda.
[illegible]	[illegible]	[illegible]	41	[illegible]	[illegible]	[illegible]	[illegible]	[illegible]	61	Ardee, part of
71	[illegible]	65	[illegible]	[illegible]	[illegible]	[illegible]	[illegible]	[illegible]	[illegible]	Drogheda, do.
[illegible]	[illegible]	94	[illegible]	[illegible]	444	[illegible]	[illegible]	117	[illegible]	Dundalk, do.
										Meath Co.
[illegible]	8	6	4	[illegible]	[illegible]	6	6	5	7	Ardee, part of
					4		9	1	[illegible]	Celbridge, do.
13	[illegible]	21	[illegible]	[illegible]	74	22	18	[illegible]	17	Drogheda, do.
[illegible]	19	14	10	[illegible]	77	[illegible]	[illegible]	[illegible]	11	Dunshaughlin, do.
6	9	4	6	[illegible]	15	6	3	4	4	Edenderry, do.
[illegible]	43	41	47	[illegible]	[illegible]	[illegible]	[illegible]	[illegible]	[illegible]	Kells, do.
[illegible]	47	[illegible]	[illegible]	175	157	44	[illegible]	[illegible]	[illegible]	Navan.
[illegible]	18	1	19	[illegible]	47	11	11	14	11	Oldcastle, part of
[illegible]	43	[illegible]	[illegible]	[illegible]	147	47	84	27	41	Trim.

[illegible] registered in Ireland in the Four Quarters ending

I.—PROVINCE OF

No.	Superintendent Registrars' Districts.	Area in Statute Acres.	[illegible]	Totals.	[illegible]	[illegible]	[illegible]	[illegible]
	Queen's Co.							
42	Abbeyleix,	[illegible]	[illegible]	[illegible]	[illegible]	[illegible]	[illegible]	[illegible]
43	Athy, part of,	[illegible]	[illegible]	[illegible]	[illegible]	[illegible]	[illegible]	[illegible]
44	Carlow, do.,	[illegible]	[illegible]	[illegible]	[illegible]	[illegible]	[illegible]	[illegible]
45	Mountmellick, part of,	[illegible]	[illegible]	[illegible]	[illegible]	[illegible]	[illegible]	[illegible]
46	Roscrea, do.,	[illegible]	[illegible]	[illegible]	[illegible]	[illegible]	[illegible]	[illegible]
47	Tullamore, do.,	[illegible]	[illegible]	[illegible]	[illegible]	[illegible]	[illegible]	[illegible]
	Westmeath Co.							
48	Athlone, part of,	[illegible]	[illegible]	[illegible]	[illegible]	[illegible]	[illegible]	[illegible]
49	Ballymahon, do.,	[illegible]	[illegible]	[illegible]	[illegible]	[illegible]	[illegible]	[illegible]
50	Delvin,	[illegible]	[illegible]	[illegible]	[illegible]	[illegible]	[illegible]	[illegible]
51	Granard, part of,	[illegible]	[illegible]	[illegible]	[illegible]	[illegible]	[illegible]	[illegible]
52	Mullingar,	[illegible]	[illegible]	[illegible]	[illegible]	[illegible]	[illegible]	[illegible]
53	Tullamore, part of,	[illegible]	[illegible]	[illegible]	[illegible]	[illegible]	[illegible]	[illegible]
	Wexford Co.							
54	Enniscorthy, part of,	[illegible]	[illegible]	[illegible]	[illegible]	[illegible]	[illegible]	[illegible]
55	Gorey,	[illegible]	[illegible]	[illegible]	[illegible]	[illegible]	[illegible]	[illegible]
56	New Ross, part of,	[illegible]	[illegible]	[illegible]	[illegible]	[illegible]	[illegible]	[illegible]
57	Shillelagh, do.,	[illegible]	[illegible]	[illegible]	[illegible]	[illegible]	[illegible]	[illegible]
58	Wexford,	[illegible]	[illegible]	[illegible]	[illegible]	[illegible]	[illegible]	[illegible]
	Wicklow Co.							
59	Baltinglass, part of,	[illegible]	[illegible]	[illegible]	[illegible]	[illegible]	[illegible]	[illegible]
60	Naas, do.,	[illegible]	[illegible]	[illegible]	[illegible]	[illegible]	[illegible]	[illegible]
61	Rathdown, do.,	[illegible]	[illegible]	[illegible]	[illegible]	[illegible]	[illegible]	[illegible]
62	Rathdrum,	[illegible]	[illegible]	[illegible]	[illegible]	[illegible]	[illegible]	[illegible]
63	Shillelagh, part of,	[illegible]	[illegible]	[illegible]	[illegible]	[illegible]	[illegible]	[illegible]

II.—PROVINCE OF

No.	Superintendent Registrars' Districts.	Area in Statute Acres.	[illegible]	Totals.	[illegible]	[illegible]	[illegible]	[illegible]
	Clare Co.							
67	Ballyvaghan,	[illegible]	[illegible]	[illegible]	[illegible]	[illegible]	[illegible]	[illegible]
68	Corrofin,	[illegible]	[illegible]	[illegible]	[illegible]	[illegible]	[illegible]	[illegible]
69	Ennis,	[illegible]	[illegible]	[illegible]	[illegible]	[illegible]	[illegible]	[illegible]
70	Ennistymon,	[illegible]	[illegible]	[illegible]	[illegible]	[illegible]	[illegible]	[illegible]
71	Kildysart,	[illegible]	[illegible]	[illegible]	[illegible]	[illegible]	[illegible]	[illegible]
72	Kilrush,	[illegible]	[illegible]	[illegible]	[illegible]	[illegible]	[illegible]	[illegible]
73	Limerick, part of,	[illegible]	[illegible]	[illegible]	[illegible]	[illegible]	[illegible]	[illegible]
74	Scariff, do.,	[illegible]	[illegible]	[illegible]	[illegible]	[illegible]	[illegible]	[illegible]
75	Tulla,	[illegible]	[illegible]	[illegible]	[illegible]	[illegible]	[illegible]	[illegible]
	Cork Co.							
76	Bandon,	[illegible]	[illegible]	[illegible]	[illegible]	[illegible]	[illegible]	[illegible]
77	Bantry,	[illegible]	[illegible]	[illegible]	[illegible]	[illegible]	[illegible]	[illegible]
78	Castletown,	[illegible]	[illegible]	[illegible]	[illegible]	[illegible]	[illegible]	[illegible]
79	Clonakilty,	[illegible]	[illegible]	[illegible]	[illegible]	[illegible]	[illegible]	[illegible]
80	Cork,	[illegible]	[illegible]	[illegible]	[illegible]	[illegible]	[illegible]	[illegible]
81	Dunmanway,	[illegible]	[illegible]	[illegible]	[illegible]	[illegible]	[illegible]	[illegible]

March 31st, June 30th, September 30th, and December 31st, 1896—*continued.*

LEINSTER—*continued.*

MALES. Registered in the Quarter ending the last day of March.	June.	Sept.	Dec.	Total.	FEMALES. Total.	Registered in the Quarter ending the last day of March.	June.	Sept.	Dec.	SUPERINTENDENT REGISTRARS' DISTRICTS.
										Queen's Co.
[illegible]	[illegible]	[illegible]	[illegible]	[illegible]	[illegible]	[illegible]	[illegible]	[illegible]	[illegible]	Abbeyleix.
[illegible]	[illegible]	17	[illegible]	[illegible]	[illegible]	[illegible]	[illegible]	[illegible]	[illegible]	Athy, part of.
16	[illegible]	[illegible]	[illegible]	[illegible]	[illegible]	[illegible]	[illegible]	[illegible]	[illegible]	Carlow, do.
[illegible]	[illegible]	[illegible]	[illegible]	[illegible]	[illegible]	[illegible]	[illegible]	[illegible]	[illegible]	Mountmellick, part of.
[illegible]	1	[illegible]	[illegible]	[illegible]	[illegible]	[illegible]	[illegible]	1	[illegible]	Roscrea, do.
3	1	1	1	7	[illegible]	.	[illegible]	1	[illegible]	[illegible], do.
										Westmeath Co.
[illegible]	[illegible]	[illegible]	[illegible]	[illegible]	[illegible]	[illegible]	[illegible]	[illegible]	[illegible]	Athlone, part of.
[illegible]	[illegible]	[illegible]	[illegible]	[illegible]	[illegible]	[illegible]	[illegible]	[illegible]	[illegible]	Ballymahon, do.
[illegible]	[illegible]	[illegible]	17	[illegible]	[illegible]	[illegible]	[illegible]	[illegible]	[illegible]	Delvin.
[illegible]	[illegible]	[illegible]	[illegible]	[illegible]	[illegible]	[illegible]	[illegible]	[illegible]	[illegible]	Granard, part of.
[illegible]	[illegible]	[illegible]	[illegible]	[illegible]	[illegible]	[illegible]	[illegible]	[illegible]	[illegible]	Mullingar.
[illegible]	[illegible]	[illegible]	3	[illegible]	[illegible]	[illegible]	[illegible]	[illegible]	[illegible]	Tullamore, part of.
										Wexford Co.
[illegible]	[illegible]	[illegible]	[illegible]	[illegible]	[illegible]	71	[illegible]	[illegible]	[illegible]	Enniscorthy, part of.
[illegible]	[illegible]	[illegible]	[illegible]	[illegible]	[illegible]	[illegible]	[illegible]	[illegible]	[illegible]	Gorey.
[illegible]	[illegible]	[illegible]	[illegible]	[illegible]	[illegible]	[illegible]	77	[illegible]	[illegible]	New Ross, part of.
1	.	.	1	2	[illegible]	.	.	1	1	Shillelagh, do.
[illegible]	[illegible]	[illegible]	[illegible]	[illegible]	[illegible]	[illegible]	[illegible]	[illegible]	[illegible]	Wexford.
										Wicklow Co.
[illegible]	[illegible]	[illegible]	[illegible]	[illegible]	118	[illegible]	[illegible]	[illegible]	[illegible]	Baltinglass, part of.
[illegible]	[illegible]	[illegible]	[illegible]	[illegible]	[illegible]	7	[illegible]	[illegible]	[illegible]	Naas, do.
[illegible]	[illegible]	[illegible]	[illegible]	[illegible]	[illegible]	[illegible]	[illegible]	[illegible]	17	Rathdown, do.
[illegible]	[illegible]	[illegible]	[illegible]	[illegible]	[illegible]	[illegible]	[illegible]	[illegible]	[illegible]	Rathdrum.
[illegible]	[illegible]	[illegible]	[illegible]	[illegible]	[illegible]	17	[illegible]	[illegible]	[illegible]	Shillelagh, part of.

MUNSTER.

MALES. March.	June.	Sept.	Dec.	Total.	FEMALES. Total.	March.	June.	Sept.	Dec.	SUPERINTENDENT REGISTRARS' DISTRICTS.
										Clare Co.
[illegible]	[illegible]	[illegible]	[illegible]	[illegible]	[illegible]	[illegible]	[illegible]	[illegible]	[illegible]	Ballyvaghan.
[illegible]	[illegible]	[illegible]	[illegible]	[illegible]	[illegible]	[illegible]	[illegible]	[illegible]	[illegible]	Corofin.
[illegible]	[illegible]	[illegible]	[illegible]	[illegible]	[illegible]	[illegible]	[illegible]	[illegible]	[illegible]	Ennis.
[illegible]	[illegible]	[illegible]	[illegible]	[illegible]	[illegible]	[illegible]	[illegible]	[illegible]	[illegible]	Ennistymon.
[illegible]	[illegible]	[illegible]	17	[illegible]	114	[illegible]	[illegible]	[illegible]	[illegible]	Kildysart.
[illegible]	[illegible]	[illegible]	[illegible]	[illegible]	[illegible]	[illegible]	[illegible]	[illegible]	[illegible]	Kilrush.
[illegible]	[illegible]	[illegible]	[illegible]	[illegible]	[illegible]	[illegible]	11	[illegible]	[illegible]	Limerick, part of.
[illegible]	[illegible]	[illegible]	[illegible]	[illegible]	[illegible]	[illegible]	[illegible]	[illegible]	[illegible]	Scarriff, do.
[illegible]	[illegible]	[illegible]	[illegible]	[illegible]	[illegible]	[illegible]	[illegible]	[illegible]	[illegible]	Tulla.
										Cork Co.
[illegible]	[illegible]	[illegible]	[illegible]	[illegible]	[illegible]	[illegible]	[illegible]	[illegible]	[illegible]	Bandon.
[illegible]	[illegible]	[illegible]	[illegible]	[illegible]	[illegible]	[illegible]	[illegible]	[illegible]	[illegible]	Bantry.
[illegible]	[illegible]	[illegible]	[illegible]	[illegible]	[illegible]	[illegible]	[illegible]	[illegible]	[illegible]	Castletown.
[illegible]	[illegible]	[illegible]	[illegible]	[illegible]	[illegible]	[illegible]	[illegible]	[illegible]	41	Clonakilty.
[illegible]	[illegible]	[illegible]	[illegible]	[illegible]	[illegible]	[illegible]	[illegible]	[illegible]	[illegible]	Cork.
[illegible]	[illegible]	[illegible]	[illegible]	[illegible]	[illegible]	[illegible]	[illegible]	[illegible]	[illegible]	Dunmanway.

[illegible] registered in Ireland in the Four Quarters ending

IX.—PROVINCE OF [illegible]

No.	Superintendent Registrars' Districts	Area in Statute Acres	Population in 1861	Males and Females: Total	Registered in the Quarters ending the last day of: March	June	Sept.	Dec.
	Cork Co.—continued.							
82	Fermoy,	[illegible]	[illegible]	[illegible]	[illegible]	[illegible]	[illegible]	[illegible]
83	Kanturk,	[illegible]	[illegible]	[illegible]	[illegible]	[illegible]	[illegible]	[illegible]
84	Kilmallock, part of,	[illegible]	[illegible]	[illegible]	[illegible]	[illegible]	[illegible]	[illegible]
85	Kinsale,	[illegible]	[illegible]	[illegible]	[illegible]	[illegible]	[illegible]	[illegible]
86	Macroom,	[illegible]	[illegible]	[illegible]	[illegible]	[illegible]	[illegible]	[illegible]
87	Mallow,	[illegible]	[illegible]	[illegible]	[illegible]	[illegible]	[illegible]	[illegible]
88	Midleton,	[illegible]	[illegible]	[illegible]	[illegible]	[illegible]	[illegible]	[illegible]
89	Millstreet,	[illegible]	[illegible]	[illegible]	[illegible]	[illegible]	[illegible]	[illegible]
90	Mitchelstown, part of,	[illegible]	[illegible]	[illegible]	[illegible]	[illegible]	[illegible]	[illegible]
91	Skibbereen,	[illegible]	[illegible]	[illegible]	[illegible]	[illegible]	[illegible]	[illegible]
92	Skull,	[illegible]	[illegible]	[illegible]	[illegible]	[illegible]	[illegible]	[illegible]
93	Youghal, part of,	[illegible]	[illegible]	[illegible]	[illegible]	[illegible]	[illegible]	[illegible]
	Kerry Co.							
94	Cahersiveen,	[illegible]	[illegible]	[illegible]	[illegible]	[illegible]	[illegible]	[illegible]
95	Dingle,	[illegible]	[illegible]	[illegible]	[illegible]	[illegible]	[illegible]	[illegible]
96	Kenmare,	[illegible]	[illegible]	[illegible]	[illegible]	[illegible]	[illegible]	[illegible]
97	Killarney,	[illegible]	[illegible]	[illegible]	[illegible]	[illegible]	[illegible]	[illegible]
98	Listowel, part of,	[illegible]	[illegible]	[illegible]	[illegible]	[illegible]	[illegible]	[illegible]
99	Tralee,	[illegible]	[illegible]	[illegible]	[illegible]	[illegible]	[illegible]	[illegible]
	Limerick Co.							
100	Croom,	[illegible]	[illegible]	[illegible]	[illegible]	[illegible]	[illegible]	[illegible]
101	Kilmallock, part of,	[illegible]	[illegible]	[illegible]	[illegible]	[illegible]	[illegible]	[illegible]
102	Limerick, do.,	[illegible]	[illegible]	[illegible]	[illegible]	[illegible]	[illegible]	[illegible]
103	[illegible], do.,	[illegible]	[illegible]	[illegible]	[illegible]	[illegible]	[illegible]	[illegible]
104	[illegible], do.,	[illegible]	[illegible]	[illegible]	[illegible]	[illegible]	[illegible]	[illegible]
105	Newcastle,	[illegible]	[illegible]	[illegible]	[illegible]	[illegible]	[illegible]	[illegible]
106	Rathkeale,	[illegible]	[illegible]	[illegible]	[illegible]	[illegible]	[illegible]	[illegible]
107	[illegible], part of,	[illegible]	[illegible]	[illegible]	[illegible]	[illegible]	[illegible]	[illegible]
	Tipperary Co.							
108	Borrisokane,	[illegible]	[illegible]	[illegible]	[illegible]	[illegible]	[illegible]	[illegible]
109	Callan, part of,	[illegible]	[illegible]	[illegible]	[illegible]	[illegible]	[illegible]	[illegible]
110	Carrick-on-Suir, do.,	[illegible]	[illegible]	[illegible]	[illegible]	[illegible]	[illegible]	[illegible]
111	Cashel,	[illegible]	[illegible]	[illegible]	[illegible]	[illegible]	[illegible]	[illegible]
112	Clogheen,	[illegible]	[illegible]	[illegible]	[illegible]	[illegible]	[illegible]	[illegible]
113	Clonmel, part of,	[illegible]	[illegible]	[illegible]	[illegible]	[illegible]	[illegible]	[illegible]
114	Nenagh,	[illegible]	[illegible]	[illegible]	[illegible]	[illegible]	[illegible]	[illegible]
115	Roscrea, part of,	[illegible]	[illegible]	[illegible]	[illegible]	[illegible]	[illegible]	[illegible]
116	Thurles, do.,	[illegible]	[illegible]	[illegible]	[illegible]	[illegible]	[illegible]	[illegible]
117	Tipperary,	[illegible]	[illegible]	[illegible]	[illegible]	[illegible]	[illegible]	[illegible]
118	[illegible], part of,	[illegible]	[illegible]	[illegible]	[illegible]	[illegible]	[illegible]	[illegible]
119	Urlingford, do.,	[illegible]	[illegible]	[illegible]	[illegible]	[illegible]	[illegible]	[illegible]
	Waterford Co.							

March 31st, June 30th, September 30th, and December 31st, 1896—*continued.*

[illegible]—*continued.*

Males: Registered in the Quarter ending the last day of March	June	Sept.	Dec.	Total.	Females: Total.	Registered in the Quarter ending the last day of March	June	Sept.	Dec.	Superintendent Registrars' Districts
										Cork Co.—continued.
[illegible]	[illegible]	[illegible]	[illegible]	[illegible]	[illegible]	[illegible]	[illegible]	[illegible]	[illegible]	Fermoy.
[illegible]	[illegible]	[illegible]	[illegible]	[illegible]	[illegible]	[illegible]	[illegible]	[illegible]	[illegible]	Kanturk.
[illegible]	[illegible]	[illegible]	[illegible]	[illegible]	[illegible]	[illegible]	[illegible]	[illegible]	[illegible]	Kilmallock, part of.
[illegible]	[illegible]	[illegible]	[illegible]	[illegible]	[illegible]	[illegible]	[illegible]	[illegible]	[illegible]	Kinsale.
[illegible]	[illegible]	[illegible]	[illegible]	[illegible]	[illegible]	[illegible]	[illegible]	[illegible]	[illegible]	Macroom.
[illegible]	[illegible]	[illegible]	[illegible]	[illegible]	[illegible]	[illegible]	[illegible]	[illegible]	[illegible]	Mallow.
[illegible]	[illegible]	[illegible]	[illegible]	[illegible]	[illegible]	[illegible]	[illegible]	[illegible]	[illegible]	Midleton.
[illegible]	[illegible]	[illegible]	[illegible]	[illegible]	[illegible]	[illegible]	[illegible]	[illegible]	[illegible]	Millstreet.
[illegible]	[illegible]	[illegible]	[illegible]	[illegible]	[illegible]	[illegible]	[illegible]	[illegible]	[illegible]	Mitchelstown, part of.
[illegible]	[illegible]	[illegible]	[illegible]	[illegible]	[illegible]	[illegible]	[illegible]	[illegible]	[illegible]	Skibbereen.
[illegible]	[illegible]	[illegible]	[illegible]	[illegible]	[illegible]	[illegible]	[illegible]	[illegible]	[illegible]	Skull.
[illegible]	[illegible]	[illegible]	[illegible]	[illegible]	[illegible]	[illegible]	[illegible]	[illegible]	[illegible]	Youghal, part of.
										Kerry Co.
[illegible]	[illegible]	[illegible]	[illegible]	[illegible]	[illegible]	[illegible]	[illegible]	[illegible]	[illegible]	Cahirciveen.
[illegible]	[illegible]	[illegible]	[illegible]	[illegible]	[illegible]	[illegible]	[illegible]	[illegible]	[illegible]	Dingle.
[illegible]	[illegible]	[illegible]	[illegible]	[illegible]	[illegible]	[illegible]	[illegible]	[illegible]	[illegible]	Kenmare.
[illegible]	[illegible]	[illegible]	[illegible]	[illegible]	[illegible]	[illegible]	[illegible]	[illegible]	[illegible]	Killarney.
[illegible]	[illegible]	[illegible]	[illegible]	[illegible]	[illegible]	[illegible]	[illegible]	[illegible]	[illegible]	Listowel, part of.
[illegible]	[illegible]	[illegible]	[illegible]	[illegible]	[illegible]	[illegible]	[illegible]	[illegible]	[illegible]	Tralee.
										Limerick Co.
[illegible]	[illegible]	[illegible]	[illegible]	[illegible]	[illegible]	[illegible]	[illegible]	[illegible]	[illegible]	Croom.
[illegible]	[illegible]	[illegible]	[illegible]	[illegible]	[illegible]	[illegible]	[illegible]	[illegible]	[illegible]	Kilmallock, part of.
[illegible]	[illegible]	[illegible]	[illegible]	[illegible]	[illegible]	[illegible]	[illegible]	[illegible]	[illegible]	Limerick, do.
[illegible]	[illegible]	[illegible]	[illegible]	[illegible]	[illegible]	[illegible]	[illegible]	[illegible]	[illegible]	Listowel, do.
[illegible]	[illegible]	[illegible]	[illegible]	[illegible]	[illegible]	[illegible]	[illegible]	[illegible]	[illegible]	Mitchelstown, do.
[illegible]	[illegible]	[illegible]	[illegible]	[illegible]	[illegible]	[illegible]	[illegible]	[illegible]	[illegible]	Newcastle.
[illegible]	[illegible]	[illegible]	[illegible]	[illegible]	[illegible]	[illegible]	[illegible]	[illegible]	[illegible]	Rathkeale.
[illegible]	[illegible]	[illegible]	[illegible]	[illegible]	[illegible]	[illegible]	[illegible]	[illegible]	[illegible]	Tipperary, part of.
										Tipperary Co.
[illegible]	[illegible]	[illegible]	[illegible]	[illegible]	[illegible]	[illegible]	[illegible]	[illegible]	[illegible]	Borrisokane.
[illegible]	[illegible]	[illegible]	[illegible]	[illegible]	[illegible]	[illegible]	[illegible]	[illegible]	[illegible]	Callan, part of.
[illegible]	[illegible]	[illegible]	[illegible]	[illegible]	[illegible]	[illegible]	[illegible]	[illegible]	[illegible]	Carrick-on-Suir, do.
[illegible]	[illegible]	[illegible]	[illegible]	[illegible]	[illegible]	[illegible]	[illegible]	[illegible]	[illegible]	Cashel.
[illegible]	[illegible]	[illegible]	[illegible]	[illegible]	[illegible]	[illegible]	[illegible]	[illegible]	[illegible]	Clogheen.
[illegible]	[illegible]	[illegible]	[illegible]	[illegible]	[illegible]	[illegible]	[illegible]	[illegible]	[illegible]	Clonmel, part of.
[illegible]	[illegible]	[illegible]	[illegible]	[illegible]	[illegible]	[illegible]	[illegible]	[illegible]	[illegible]	Nenagh.
[illegible]	[illegible]	[illegible]	[illegible]	[illegible]	[illegible]	[illegible]	[illegible]	[illegible]	[illegible]	Parsonstown, part of.
[illegible]	[illegible]	[illegible]	[illegible]	[illegible]	[illegible]	[illegible]	[illegible]	[illegible]	[illegible]	Roscrea, do.
[illegible]	[illegible]	[illegible]	[illegible]	[illegible]	[illegible]	[illegible]	[illegible]	[illegible]	[illegible]	Thurles.
[illegible]	[illegible]	[illegible]	[illegible]	[illegible]	[illegible]	[illegible]	[illegible]	[illegible]	[illegible]	Tipperary, part of.
[illegible]	[illegible]	[illegible]	[illegible]	[illegible]	[illegible]	[illegible]	[illegible]	[illegible]	[illegible]	Urlingford, do.
										Waterford Co.
[illegible]	[illegible]	[illegible]	[illegible]	[illegible]	[illegible]	[illegible]	[illegible]	[illegible]	[illegible]	Carrick-on-Suir, pt. of.
[illegible]	[illegible]	[illegible]	[illegible]	[illegible]	[illegible]	[illegible]	[illegible]	[illegible]	[illegible]	Clonmel, do.
[illegible]	[illegible]	[illegible]	[illegible]	[illegible]	[illegible]	[illegible]	[illegible]	[illegible]	[illegible]	Dungarvan.
[illegible]	[illegible]	[illegible]	[illegible]	[illegible]	[illegible]	[illegible]	[illegible]	[illegible]	[illegible]	Kilmacthomas.
[illegible]	[illegible]	[illegible]	[illegible]	[illegible]	[illegible]	[illegible]	[illegible]	[illegible]	[illegible]	Lismore.
[illegible]	[illegible]	[illegible]	[illegible]	[illegible]	[illegible]	[illegible]	[illegible]	[illegible]	[illegible]	Waterford, part of.
[illegible]	[illegible]	[illegible]	[illegible]	[illegible]	[illegible]	[illegible]	[illegible]	[illegible]	[illegible]	Youghal, do.

Births registered in Ireland in the Four Quarters ending

III.—Province of

No.	Superintendent Registrars' Districts.	Area in Statute Acres.	Population in 1861.	Males and Females. Total.	Registered in the Quarter ending the last day of March.	June.	Sept.	Dec.
	Antrim Co.							
127	Antrim,	157,727	23,4[illegible]	7[illegible]	1[illegible]	[illegible]	1[illegible]	1[illegible]
128	Ballycastle,	[illegible]	14,4[illegible]	[illegible]	[illegible]	[illegible]	[illegible]	[illegible]
129	Ballymena,	[illegible]	[illegible]	1,[illegible]	[illegible]	[illegible]	[illegible]	[illegible]
130	Ballymoney, part of,	[illegible]	[illegible]	[illegible]	142	[illegible]	1[illegible]	1[illegible]
131	Belfast, do.,	[illegible]	[illegible]	[illegible]	[illegible]	[illegible]	2,1[illegible]	[illegible]
132	Coleraine, do.,	10,[illegible]	[illegible]	16[illegible]	44	[illegible]	4[illegible]	[illegible]
133	Larne,	117,[illegible]	[illegible]	[illegible]	[illegible]	711	[illegible]	[illegible]
134	Lisburn, part of,	[illegible]	[illegible]	[illegible]	[illegible]	[illegible]	[illegible]	[illegible]
135	Lurgan, do.,	13,[illegible]	[illegible]	[illegible]	17	24	[illegible]	[illegible]
	Armagh Co.							
136	Armagh, part of,	141,[illegible]	[illegible]	1,[illegible]	[illegible]	[illegible]	[illegible]	[illegible]
137	Banbridge, do.,	18,[illegible]	[illegible]	1[illegible]	[illegible]	[illegible]	[illegible]	[illegible]
138	Castleblayney, do.,	[illegible]	10,[illegible]	[illegible]	[illegible]	[illegible]	[illegible]	[illegible]
139	Dundalk, do.,	[illegible]	1,[illegible]	[illegible]	[illegible]	[illegible]	[illegible]	1[illegible]
140	Lurgan, do.,	[illegible]	41,[illegible]	1,[illegible]	[illegible]	1[illegible]	[illegible]	2[illegible]
141	Newry, do.,	[illegible]	[illegible]	[illegible]	[illegible]	[illegible]	1[illegible]	1[illegible]
	Cavan Co.							
142	Bailieborough,	[illegible]	[illegible]	[illegible]	[illegible]	[illegible]	[illegible]	71
143	Bawnboy, part of,	[illegible]	1[illegible]	1[illegible]	[illegible]	44	41	[illegible]
144	Cavan,	[illegible]	[illegible]	[illegible]	1[illegible]	[illegible]	[illegible]	[illegible]
145	Cootehill, part of,	[illegible]	[illegible]	[illegible]	[illegible]	[illegible]	77	[illegible]
146	Enniskillen, do.,	[illegible]	[illegible]	1[illegible]	[illegible]	[illegible]	[illegible]	[illegible]
147	Granard, do.,	[illegible]	[illegible]	[illegible]	[illegible]	[illegible]	[illegible]	[illegible]
148	Kells, do.,	[illegible]	1,[illegible]	[illegible]	[illegible]	[illegible]	[illegible]	[illegible]
149	Oldcastle, do.,	[illegible]	[illegible]	[illegible]	[illegible]	[illegible]	[illegible]	[illegible]
	Donegal Co.							
150	Ballyshannon, part of,	[illegible]	[illegible]	[illegible]	[illegible]	[illegible]	41	[illegible]
151	Donegal,	[illegible]	[illegible]	[illegible]	[illegible]	[illegible]	[illegible]	[illegible]
152	Dunfanaghy,	[illegible]	[illegible]	[illegible]	1[illegible]	[illegible]	[illegible]	[illegible]
153	Glenties,	[illegible]	[illegible]	[illegible]	[illegible]	1[illegible]	1[illegible]	[illegible]
154	Inishowen,	[illegible]	[illegible]	[illegible]	1[illegible]	1[illegible]	[illegible]	[illegible]
155	Letterkenny,	[illegible]	[illegible]	[illegible]	[illegible]	[illegible]	[illegible]	[illegible]
156	Londonderry, part of,	[illegible]	[illegible]	[illegible]	[illegible]	[illegible]	[illegible]	[illegible]
157	Milford,	[illegible]	[illegible]	[illegible]	[illegible]	[illegible]	[illegible]	[illegible]
158	Strabane, part of,	[illegible]	11,[illegible]	[illegible]	[illegible]	[illegible]	[illegible]	[illegible]
159	Stranorlar,	[illegible]	[illegible]	[illegible]	[illegible]	[illegible]	[illegible]	[illegible]
	Down Co.							
160	Banbridge, part of,	[illegible]	[illegible]	[illegible]	[illegible]	[illegible]	[illegible]	[illegible]
161	Belfast, do.,	[illegible]	[illegible]	2,[illegible]	[illegible]	[illegible]	[illegible]	[illegible]
162	Downpatrick,	[illegible]	[illegible]	[illegible]	[illegible]	[illegible]	[illegible]	[illegible]
163	Kilkeel,	[illegible]	1[illegible]	[illegible]	[illegible]	[illegible]	114	1[illegible]
164	Lisburn, part of,	[illegible]	[illegible]	[illegible]	1[illegible]	1[illegible]	[illegible]	[illegible]
165	Lurgan, do.,	[illegible]	[illegible]	[illegible]	[illegible]	[illegible]	41	[illegible]
166	Newry, do.,	[illegible]	[illegible]	[illegible]	1[illegible]	1[illegible]	1[illegible]	1[illegible]
167	Newtownards,	[illegible]	[illegible]	1,[illegible]	[illegible]	[illegible]	[illegible]	[illegible]
	Fermanagh Co.							
168	Ballyshannon, part of,	[illegible]	7,1[illegible]	1[illegible]	[illegible]	[illegible]	[illegible]	[illegible]
169	Clones, do.,	[illegible]	[illegible]	1[illegible]	[illegible]	[illegible]	4[illegible]	4[illegible]
170	Enniskillen, do.,	1[illegible]	[illegible]	[illegible]	1[illegible]	1[illegible]	1[illegible]	[illegible]
171	Irvinestown, do.,	[illegible]	11,[illegible]	1[illegible]	[illegible]	[illegible]	[illegible]	[illegible]
172	Lisnaskea,	[illegible]	[illegible]	[illegible]	[illegible]	[illegible]	[illegible]	77

March 31st, June 30th, September 30th, and December 31st, 1896—*continued.*

ULSTER.

MALES.					FEMALES.					SUPERINTENDENT REGISTRARS' DISTRICTS.
Registered in the Quarter ending the last day of				Total.	Total.	Registered in the Quarter ending the last day of				
March.	June.	Sept.	Dec.			March.	June.	Sept.	Dec.	
										ANTRIM CO.
[illegible]	[illegible]	[illegible]	[illegible]	[illegible]	[illegible]	[illegible]	[illegible]	[illegible]	[illegible]	ANTRIM.
[illegible]	[illegible]	[illegible]	[illegible]	[illegible]	[illegible]	[illegible]	[illegible]	[illegible]	[illegible]	[illegible]
[illegible]	[illegible]	[illegible]	[illegible]	[illegible]	[illegible]	[illegible]	[illegible]	[illegible]	[illegible]	BALLYMENA.
[illegible]	[illegible]	[illegible]	[illegible]	[illegible]	[illegible]	[illegible]	[illegible]	[illegible]	[illegible]	BALLYMONEY, part of
[illegible]	[illegible]	[illegible]	[illegible]	[illegible]	[illegible]	[illegible]	[illegible]	[illegible]	[illegible]	BELFAST, do.
[illegible]	[illegible]	[illegible]	[illegible]	[illegible]	[illegible]	[illegible]	[illegible]	[illegible]	[illegible]	COLERAINE, do.
[illegible]	[illegible]	[illegible]	[illegible]	[illegible]	[illegible]	[illegible]	[illegible]	[illegible]	[illegible]	LARNE.
[illegible]	[illegible]	[illegible]	[illegible]	[illegible]	[illegible]	[illegible]	[illegible]	[illegible]	[illegible]	LISBURN, part of
[illegible]	[illegible]	[illegible]	[illegible]	[illegible]	[illegible]	[illegible]	[illegible]	[illegible]	[illegible]	LURGAN, do.
										ARMAGH CO.
[illegible]	[illegible]	[illegible]	[illegible]	[illegible]	[illegible]	[illegible]	[illegible]	[illegible]	[illegible]	ARMAGH, part of
[illegible]	[illegible]	[illegible]	[illegible]	[illegible]	[illegible]	[illegible]	[illegible]	[illegible]	[illegible]	BANBRIDGE, do.
[illegible]	[illegible]	[illegible]	[illegible]	[illegible]	[illegible]	[illegible]	[illegible]	[illegible]	[illegible]	CASTLEBLAYNEY, do.
[illegible]	[illegible]	[illegible]	[illegible]	[illegible]	[illegible]	[illegible]	[illegible]	[illegible]	[illegible]	DUNDALK, do.
[illegible]	[illegible]	[illegible]	[illegible]	[illegible]	[illegible]	[illegible]	[illegible]	[illegible]	[illegible]	LURGAN, do.
[illegible]	[illegible]	[illegible]	[illegible]	[illegible]	[illegible]	[illegible]	[illegible]	[illegible]	[illegible]	NEWRY, do.
										CAVAN CO.
[illegible]	[illegible]	[illegible]	[illegible]	[illegible]	[illegible]	[illegible]	[illegible]	[illegible]	[illegible]	BAILIEBOROUGH.
[illegible]	[illegible]	[illegible]	[illegible]	[illegible]	[illegible]	[illegible]	[illegible]	[illegible]	[illegible]	BAWNBOY, part of
[illegible]	[illegible]	[illegible]	[illegible]	[illegible]	[illegible]	[illegible]	[illegible]	[illegible]	[illegible]	CAVAN.
[illegible]	[illegible]	[illegible]	[illegible]	[illegible]	[illegible]	[illegible]	[illegible]	[illegible]	[illegible]	COOTEHILL, part of
[illegible]	[illegible]	[illegible]	[illegible]	[illegible]	[illegible]	[illegible]	[illegible]	[illegible]	[illegible]	ENNISKILLEN, do.
[illegible]	[illegible]	[illegible]	[illegible]	[illegible]	[illegible]	[illegible]	[illegible]	[illegible]	[illegible]	GRANARD, do.
[illegible]	[illegible]	[illegible]	[illegible]	[illegible]	[illegible]	[illegible]	[illegible]	[illegible]	[illegible]	KELLS, do.
[illegible]	[illegible]	[illegible]	[illegible]	[illegible]	[illegible]	[illegible]	[illegible]	[illegible]	[illegible]	OLDCASTLE, do.
										DONEGAL CO.
[illegible]	[illegible]	[illegible]	[illegible]	[illegible]	[illegible]	[illegible]	[illegible]	[illegible]	[illegible]	BALLYSHANNON, part of
[illegible]	[illegible]	[illegible]	[illegible]	[illegible]	[illegible]	[illegible]	[illegible]	[illegible]	[illegible]	DONEGAL.
[illegible]	[illegible]	[illegible]	[illegible]	[illegible]	[illegible]	[illegible]	[illegible]	[illegible]	[illegible]	DUNFANAGHY.
[illegible]	[illegible]	[illegible]	[illegible]	[illegible]	[illegible]	[illegible]	[illegible]	[illegible]	[illegible]	GLENTIES.
[illegible]	[illegible]	[illegible]	[illegible]	[illegible]	[illegible]	[illegible]	[illegible]	[illegible]	[illegible]	INISHOWEN.
[illegible]	[illegible]	[illegible]	[illegible]	[illegible]	[illegible]	[illegible]	[illegible]	[illegible]	[illegible]	LETTERKENNY.
[illegible]	[illegible]	[illegible]	[illegible]	[illegible]	[illegible]	[illegible]	[illegible]	[illegible]	[illegible]	LONDONDERRY, part of
[illegible]	[illegible]	[illegible]	[illegible]	[illegible]	[illegible]	[illegible]	[illegible]	[illegible]	[illegible]	MILFORD.
[illegible]	[illegible]	[illegible]	[illegible]	[illegible]	[illegible]	[illegible]	[illegible]	[illegible]	[illegible]	STRABANE, part of
[illegible]	[illegible]	[illegible]	[illegible]	[illegible]	[illegible]	[illegible]	[illegible]	[illegible]	[illegible]	STRANORLAR.
										DOWN CO.
[illegible]	[illegible]	[illegible]	[illegible]	[illegible]	[illegible]	[illegible]	[illegible]	[illegible]	[illegible]	BANBRIDGE, part of
[illegible]	[illegible]	[illegible]	[illegible]	[illegible]	[illegible]	[illegible]	[illegible]	[illegible]	[illegible]	BELFAST, do.
[illegible]	[illegible]	[illegible]	[illegible]	[illegible]	[illegible]	[illegible]	[illegible]	[illegible]	[illegible]	DOWNPATRICK.
[illegible]	[illegible]	[illegible]	[illegible]	[illegible]	[illegible]	[illegible]	[illegible]	[illegible]	[illegible]	KILKEEL.
[illegible]	[illegible]	[illegible]	[illegible]	[illegible]	[illegible]	[illegible]	[illegible]	[illegible]	[illegible]	LISBURN, part of
[illegible]	[illegible]	[illegible]	[illegible]	[illegible]	[illegible]	[illegible]	[illegible]	[illegible]	[illegible]	LURGAN, do.
[illegible]	[illegible]	[illegible]	[illegible]	[illegible]	[illegible]	[illegible]	[illegible]	[illegible]	[illegible]	NEWRY, do.
[illegible]	[illegible]	[illegible]	[illegible]	[illegible]	[illegible]	[illegible]	[illegible]	[illegible]	[illegible]	NEWTOWNARDS.
										FERMANAGH CO.
[illegible]	[illegible]	[illegible]	[illegible]	[illegible]	[illegible]	[illegible]	[illegible]	[illegible]	[illegible]	BALLYSHANNON, part of
[illegible]	[illegible]	[illegible]	[illegible]	[illegible]	[illegible]	[illegible]	[illegible]	[illegible]	[illegible]	CLONES, do.
[illegible]	[illegible]	[illegible]	[illegible]	[illegible]	[illegible]	[illegible]	[illegible]	[illegible]	[illegible]	ENNISKILLEN, do.
[illegible]	[illegible]	[illegible]	[illegible]	[illegible]	[illegible]	[illegible]	[illegible]	[illegible]	[illegible]	IRVINESTOWN, do.
[illegible]	[illegible]	[illegible]	[illegible]	[illegible]	[illegible]	[illegible]	[illegible]	[illegible]	[illegible]	LISNASKEA.

P

[illegible] registered in Ireland in the Four Quarters ending

III.—PROVINCE OF

No.	Superintendent Registrars' Districts	Area in Statute Acres	Population in	Males and Females: Total	Registered in the Quarters ending the last day of: March	June	Sept.	Dec.
	Londonderry Co.							
174	Ballymoney, part of,	[illegible]	[illegible]	[illegible]	[illegible]	[illegible]	[illegible]	31
175	Coleraine, do.,	94,[illegible]	[illegible]	[illegible]	174	144	[illegible]	115
175	Limavady,	[illegible]	[illegible]	[illegible]	[illegible]	136	119	[illegible]
176	Londonderry, part of,	[illegible]	[illegible]	1,[illegible]	[illegible]	[illegible]	[illegible]	[illegible]
177	Magherafelt,	1[illegible],779	[illegible]	[illegible]	[illegible]	[illegible]	[illegible]	[illegible]
	Monaghan Co.							
178	Carrickmacross,	[illegible]	[illegible]	[illegible]	[illegible]	[illegible]	[illegible]	[illegible]
179	Castleblayney, part of,	[illegible]	[illegible]	[illegible]	[illegible]	[illegible]	[illegible]	[illegible]
180	Clogher, do.,	[illegible]	1,[illegible]	[illegible]	[illegible]	[illegible]	[illegible]	[illegible]
181	Clones, do.,	[illegible]	[illegible]	[illegible]	[illegible]	[illegible]	[illegible]	[illegible]
182	Cootehill, do.,	[illegible]	7,[illegible]	[illegible]	[illegible]	[illegible]	[illegible]	[illegible]
183	Dundalk, do.,	[illegible]	[illegible]	[illegible]	[illegible]	[illegible]	11	[illegible]
184	Monaghan,	[illegible]	[illegible]	[illegible]	[illegible]	[illegible]	[illegible]	[illegible]
	Tyrone Co.							
185	Armagh, part of,	7,[illegible]	[illegible]	[illegible]	[illegible]	7	[illegible]	[illegible]
186	Castlederg,	[illegible]	[illegible]	[illegible]	[illegible]	[illegible]	[illegible]	71
187	Clogher, part of,	[illegible]	[illegible]	[illegible]	[illegible]	[illegible]	[illegible]	[illegible]
188	Cookstown,	[illegible]	[illegible]	[illegible]	[illegible]	119	110	[illegible]
189	Dungannon,	[illegible]	[illegible]	[illegible]	[illegible]	[illegible]	[illegible]	[illegible]
190	Enniskillen, part of,	[illegible]	1,[illegible]	[illegible]	[illegible]	[illegible]	[illegible]	11
191	Irvinestown, do.,	[illegible]	[illegible]	[illegible]	[illegible]	[illegible]	[illegible]	[illegible]
192	Omagh,	[illegible]	[illegible]	[illegible]	[illegible]	[illegible]	[illegible]	[illegible]
193	Strabane, part of,	[illegible]	[illegible]	[illegible]	[illegible]	[illegible]	[illegible]	[illegible]

IV.—PROVINCE OF

No.	Superintendent Registrars' Districts	Area in Statute Acres	Population in	Males and Females: Total	March	June	Sept.	Dec.
	Galway Co.							
194	Ballinasloe, part of,	[illegible]	[illegible]	[illegible]	[illegible]	[illegible]	[illegible]	[illegible]
195	Ballinrobe, do.,	[illegible]	2,[illegible]	[illegible]	14	[illegible]	31	13
196	Clifden,	[illegible]	[illegible]	[illegible]	119	[illegible]	114	[illegible]
197	Galway,	[illegible]	[illegible]	[illegible]	[illegible]	[illegible]	[illegible]	[illegible]
198	Glenamaddy,	[illegible]	[illegible]	[illegible]	[illegible]	[illegible]	[illegible]	75
199	Gort,	[illegible]	14,[illegible]	[illegible]	[illegible]	[illegible]	[illegible]	[illegible]
200	Loughrea,	[illegible]	[illegible]	[illegible]	[illegible]	[illegible]	[illegible]	[illegible]
201	Mountbellew,	[illegible]	14,[illegible]	[illegible]	[illegible]	[illegible]	[illegible]	77
202	Oughterard,	[illegible]	[illegible]	[illegible]	[illegible]	[illegible]	[illegible]	115
203	Portumna,	[illegible]	[illegible]	184	[illegible]	[illegible]	[illegible]	[illegible]
204	Roscommon, part of,	[illegible]	[illegible]	7	[illegible]	[illegible]	[illegible]	[illegible]
205	Scarriff, do.,	[illegible]	[illegible]	[illegible]	[illegible]	[illegible]	[illegible]	7
206	Tuam,	[illegible]	[illegible]	[illegible]	[illegible]	[illegible]	[illegible]	[illegible]
	Leitrim Co.							
207	Ballyshannon, part of,	[illegible]	[illegible]	[illegible]	[illegible]	[illegible]	[illegible]	[illegible]
208	Bawnboy, do.,	[illegible]	[illegible]	177	[illegible]	[illegible]	[illegible]	[illegible]
209	Carrick-on-Shannon, do.,	[illegible]	[illegible]	[illegible]	[illegible]	[illegible]	[illegible]	[illegible]
210	Manorhamilton,	144,[illegible]	[illegible]	[illegible]	[illegible]	[illegible]	[illegible]	104
211	Mohill,	[illegible]	[illegible]	[illegible]	117	[illegible]	[illegible]	[illegible]

March 31st, June 30th, September 30th, and December 31st, 1866—continued.

ULSTER—continued.

MALES. Registered in the Quarter ending the last day of March	June	Sept.	Dec.	Total.	FEMALES. Total.	Registered in the Quarter ending the last day of March	June	Sept.	Dec.	SUPERINTENDENT REGISTRARS' DISTRICTS.
										Londonderry Co.
[illegible]	17	[illegible]	[illegible]	78	41	13	19	[illegible]	6	Ballymoney, part of.
[illegible]	79	[illegible]	73	341	[illegible]	[illegible]	[illegible]	87	77	Coleraine, do.
[illegible]	77	[illegible]	[illegible]	[illegible]	[illegible]	[illegible]	[illegible]	84	[illegible]	Limavady.
171	190	171	[illegible]	[illegible]	644	150	187	149	176	Londonderry, part of.
[illegible]	112	[illegible]	116	[illegible]	[illegible]	[illegible]	[illegible]	[illegible]	[illegible]	Magherafelt.
										Monaghan Co.
[illegible]	[illegible]	[illegible]	[illegible]	[illegible]	[illegible]	34	47	[illegible]	[illegible]	Carrickmacross.
[illegible]	[illegible]	[illegible]	[illegible]	[illegible]	[illegible]	[illegible]	[illegible]	[illegible]	[illegible]	Castleblayney, part of.
7	4	6	[illegible]	[illegible]	[illegible]	1	4	6	4	Clones, do.
[illegible]	[illegible]	[illegible]	[illegible]	[illegible]	[illegible]	17	[illegible]	14	[illegible]	Clogher, do.
24	[illegible]	27	16	84	[illegible]	[illegible]	17	14	14	Cootehill, do.
1	4	7	4	17	13	4	4	4	1	Dundalk, do.
[illegible]	[illegible]	73	[illegible]	[illegible]	[illegible]	[illegible]	[illegible]	70	[illegible]	Monaghan.
										Tyrone Co.
9	3	2	1	[illegible]	17	[illegible]	6	7	3	Armagh, part of.
34	[illegible]	[illegible]	[illegible]	137	[illegible]	[illegible]	[illegible]	[illegible]	[illegible]	Castlederg.
47	[illegible]	31	[illegible]	[illegible]	[illegible]	[illegible]	[illegible]	[illegible]	[illegible]	Clogher, part of.
[illegible]	73	87	73	[illegible]	[illegible]	72	47	[illegible]	75	Cookstown.
[illegible]	44	[illegible]	67	[illegible]	[illegible]	71	[illegible]	77	[illegible]	Dungannon.
4		6	4	11	[illegible]	9	[illegible]	4	4	Enniskillen, part of.
6	4	14	[illegible]	[illegible]	[illegible]	6	10	4	6	Newtownstewart, part of.
[illegible]	[illegible]	[illegible]	[illegible]	311	[illegible]	[illegible]	91	[illegible]	[illegible]	Omagh.
47	[illegible]	75	[illegible]	[illegible]	[illegible]	[illegible]	[illegible]	74	73	Strabane, part of.

CONNAUGHT.

MALES. March	June	Sept.	Dec.	Total.	FEMALES. Total.	March	June	Sept.	Dec.	SUPERINTENDENT REGISTRARS' DISTRICTS.
										Galway Co.
41	[illegible]	57	[illegible]	[illegible]	[illegible]	40	40	[illegible]	[illegible]	Ballinasloe, part of.
4	9	11	8	37	[illegible]	10	9	[illegible]	14	Ballinrobe, do.
[illegible]	[illegible]	75	72	[illegible]	[illegible]	64	[illegible]	[illegible]	[illegible]	Clifden.
114	[illegible]	116	[illegible]	[illegible]	[illegible]	[illegible]	118	110	[illegible]	Galway.
[illegible]	[illegible]	[illegible]	54	[illegible]	[illegible]	46	[illegible]	[illegible]	41	Glennamaddy.
91	31	[illegible]	[illegible]	[illegible]	[illegible]	[illegible]	[illegible]	[illegible]	[illegible]	Gort.
[illegible]	44	74	[illegible]	[illegible]	[illegible]	47	74	[illegible]	[illegible]	Loughrea.
[illegible]	[illegible]	[illegible]	[illegible]	[illegible]	[illegible]	[illegible]	[illegible]	41	[illegible]	Mountbellew.
[illegible]	[illegible]	[illegible]	[illegible]	[illegible]	[illegible]	[illegible]	[illegible]	[illegible]	[illegible]	Oughterard.
[illegible]	[illegible]	[illegible]	[illegible]	[illegible]	[illegible]	[illegible]	[illegible]	[illegible]	[illegible]	Portumna.
1	1		1	8	4	1		1	3	Roscommon, part of.
4	6	8	4	13	17	7	4	3	4	Scariff, do.
[illegible]	[illegible]	[illegible]	[illegible]	[illegible]	[illegible]	103	[illegible]	74	[illegible]	Tuam.
										Leitrim Co.
[illegible]	4	7	[illegible]	[illegible]	17	[illegible]	8	5	6	Ballyshannon, part of.
31	[illegible]	[illegible]	[illegible]	[illegible]	[illegible]	[illegible]	19	[illegible]	14	Bawnboy, do.
17	34	[illegible]	[illegible]	[illegible]	[illegible]	[illegible]	[illegible]	[illegible]	[illegible]	Carrick-on-Shannon, do.
[illegible]	[illegible]	[illegible]	[illegible]	[illegible]	154	[illegible]	[illegible]	77	[illegible]	Manorhamilton.
[illegible]	87	[illegible]	51	[illegible]	[illegible]	[illegible]	[illegible]	[illegible]	67	Mohill.

[illegible] registered in Ireland in the Four Quarters ending

IV. PROVINCE OF

No.	Superintendent Registrars' Districts.	Area in Statute Acres.	Population in [illegible].	Males and Females. Total.	Registered in the Quarter ending the last day of March.	June.	Sept.	Dec.
	Mayo Co.							
212	Ballina, part of,	[illegible]	[illegible]	[illegible]	[illegible]	[illegible]	116	73
213	Ballinrobe, do.	[illegible]	[illegible]	[illegible]	[illegible]	[illegible]	111	[illegible]
214	Belmullet,	[illegible]	[illegible]	[illegible]	[illegible]	[illegible]	[illegible]	[illegible]
215	Castlebar,	[illegible]	[illegible]	[illegible]	[illegible]	[illegible]	[illegible]	[illegible]
216	Castlerea, part of,	[illegible]	[illegible]	[illegible]	[illegible]	[illegible]	[illegible]	[illegible]
217	Claremorris,	[illegible]	[illegible]	[illegible]	[illegible]	[illegible]	[illegible]	[illegible]
218	Killala,	[illegible]	[illegible]	[illegible]	[illegible]	[illegible]	[illegible]	[illegible]
219	Swineford,	[illegible]	[illegible]	[illegible]	[illegible]	[illegible]	[illegible]	[illegible]
220	Westport,	[illegible]	[illegible]	[illegible]	[illegible]	[illegible]	[illegible]	[illegible]
	Roscommon Co.							
221	Athlone, part of,	[illegible]	[illegible]	[illegible]	[illegible]	[illegible]	[illegible]	71
222	Ballinasloe, do.	[illegible]	[illegible]	[illegible]	[illegible]	[illegible]	13	[illegible]
223	Boyle, do.	[illegible]	[illegible]	[illegible]	[illegible]	[illegible]	[illegible]	[illegible]
224	Carrick-on-Shannon, do.	[illegible]	[illegible]	[illegible]	[illegible]	61	[illegible]	[illegible]
225	Castlerea, do.	[illegible]	[illegible]	[illegible]	[illegible]	[illegible]	[illegible]	[illegible]
226	Roscommon, do.	[illegible]	[illegible]	[illegible]	[illegible]	[illegible]	[illegible]	[illegible]
227	Strokestown,	[illegible]	[illegible]	[illegible]	[illegible]	[illegible]	[illegible]	[illegible]
	Sligo Co.							
228	Ballina, part of,	[illegible]	[illegible]	[illegible]	11	16	18	[illegible]
229	Boyle, do.	[illegible]	[illegible]	[illegible]	[illegible]	[illegible]	[illegible]	[illegible]
230	Dromore West,	[illegible]	[illegible]	[illegible]	[illegible]	[illegible]	[illegible]	[illegible]
231	Sligo,	[illegible]	[illegible]	[illegible]	[illegible]	[illegible]	[illegible]	[illegible]
232	Tobercurry,	[illegible]	[illegible]	[illegible]	[illegible]	[illegible]	[illegible]	[illegible]

March 31st, June 30th, September 30th, and December 31st, 1896—*continued.*

CONNAUGHT—*continued.*

MALES.					FEMALES.					SUPERINTENDENT REGISTRARS' DISTRICTS.
Registered in the Quarter ending the last day of				Total.	Total.	Registered in the Quarter ending the last day of				
March.	June.	Sept.	Dec.			March.	June.	Sept.	Dec.	
										Mayo Co.
[illegible]	[illegible]	[illegible]	[illegible]	[illegible]	[illegible]	[illegible]	[illegible]	[illegible]	[illegible]	Ballina, part of.
[illegible]	[illegible]	[illegible]	[illegible]	[illegible]	[illegible]	[illegible]	[illegible]	[illegible]	[illegible]	Ballinrobe, do.
[illegible]	[illegible]	[illegible]	[illegible]	[illegible]	[illegible]	[illegible]	[illegible]	[illegible]	[illegible]	Belmullet.
[illegible]	[illegible]	[illegible]	[illegible]	[illegible]	[illegible]	[illegible]	[illegible]	[illegible]	[illegible]	Castlebar.
[illegible]	[illegible]	[illegible]	[illegible]	[illegible]	[illegible]	[illegible]	[illegible]	[illegible]	[illegible]	Castlereagh, part of.
[illegible]	[illegible]	[illegible]	[illegible]	[illegible]	[illegible]	[illegible]	[illegible]	[illegible]	[illegible]	Claremorris.
[illegible]	[illegible]	[illegible]	[illegible]	[illegible]	[illegible]	[illegible]	[illegible]	[illegible]	[illegible]	Killala.
[illegible]	[illegible]	[illegible]	[illegible]	[illegible]	[illegible]	[illegible]	[illegible]	[illegible]	[illegible]	Swinford.
[illegible]	[illegible]	[illegible]	[illegible]	[illegible]	[illegible]	[illegible]	161	114	[illegible]	Westport.
										Roscommon Co.
[illegible]	[illegible]	[illegible]	[illegible]	[illegible]	[illegible]	41	[illegible]	[illegible]	[illegible]	Athlone, part of.
[illegible]	[illegible]	4	7	[illegible]	[illegible]	[illegible]	14	8	[illegible]	Ballinasloe, do.
[illegible]	[illegible]	[illegible]	[illegible]	[illegible]	[illegible]	[illegible]	[illegible]	[illegible]	[illegible]	Boyle, do.
10	[illegible]	11	14	[illegible]	[illegible]	[illegible]	[illegible]	14	4	Carrick-on-Shannon, do.
[illegible]	[illegible]	[illegible]	[illegible]	[illegible]	[illegible]	74	[illegible]	[illegible]	[illegible]	Castlereagh, do.
[illegible]	[illegible]	[illegible]	[illegible]	[illegible]	[illegible]	[illegible]	[illegible]	[illegible]	[illegible]	Roscommon, do.
[illegible]	[illegible]	[illegible]	[illegible]	[illegible]	[illegible]	[illegible]	[illegible]	[illegible]	[illegible]	Strokestown.
										Sligo Co.
4	4	11	6	[illegible]	[illegible]	4	[illegible]	7	8	Ballina, part of.
51	41	[illegible]	[illegible]	[illegible]	[illegible]	[illegible]	[illegible]	[illegible]	[illegible]	Boyle, do.
[illegible]	[illegible]	[illegible]	[illegible]	[illegible]	[illegible]	[illegible]	[illegible]	[illegible]	[illegible]	Dromore West.
[illegible]	[illegible]	[illegible]	[illegible]	[illegible]	[illegible]	[illegible]	111	[illegible]	[illegible]	Sligo.
[illegible]	[illegible]	[illegible]	[illegible]	[illegible]	[illegible]	[illegible]	[illegible]	[illegible]	[illegible]	Tobercurry.

BIRTHS Registered in Ireland in the Four Quarters ending March 31st, June 30th, September 30th, and December 31st, 1886, in each Superintendent Registrar's District or Poor Law Union.

Number of Counties ...	Superintendent Registrars' Districts or Poor Law Unions.	Area in Statute Acres.	Population in 1881.	Males and Females: Total.	Males and Females: Registered in the Quarter ending the last day of Mar.	June.	Sept.	Dec.	Males: Registered in the Quarter ending the last day of Mar.	June.	Sept.	Dec.	Males: Total.	Females: Total.	Females: Registered in the Quarter ending the last day of Mar.	June.	Sept.	Dec.
[illegible]	Abbeyleix,	[illegible]	[illegible]	[illegible]	[illegible]	[illegible]	[illegible]	[illegible]	[illegible]	[illegible]	[illegible]	[illegible]	[illegible]	[illegible]	[illegible]	[illegible]	[illegible]	[illegible]
[illegible]	Antrim,	[illegible]	[illegible]	[illegible]	[illegible]	[illegible]	[illegible]	[illegible]	[illegible]	[illegible]	[illegible]	[illegible]	[illegible]	[illegible]	[illegible]	[illegible]	[illegible]	[illegible]
[illegible]	Ardee,	[illegible]	[illegible]	[illegible]	[illegible]	[illegible]	[illegible]	[illegible]	[illegible]	[illegible]	[illegible]	[illegible]	[illegible]	[illegible]	[illegible]	[illegible]	[illegible]	[illegible]
[illegible]	Armagh,	[illegible]	[illegible]	[illegible]	[illegible]	[illegible]	[illegible]	[illegible]	[illegible]	[illegible]	[illegible]	[illegible]	[illegible]	[illegible]	[illegible]	[illegible]	[illegible]	[illegible]
[illegible]	Athlone,	[illegible]	[illegible]	[illegible]	[illegible]	[illegible]	[illegible]	[illegible]	[illegible]	[illegible]	[illegible]	[illegible]	[illegible]	[illegible]	[illegible]	[illegible]	[illegible]	[illegible]
[illegible]	Athy,	[illegible]	[illegible]	[illegible]	[illegible]	[illegible]	[illegible]	[illegible]	[illegible]	[illegible]	[illegible]	[illegible]	[illegible]	[illegible]	[illegible]	[illegible]	[illegible]	[illegible]
[illegible]	Bailieborough,	[illegible]	[illegible]	[illegible]	[illegible]	[illegible]	[illegible]	[illegible]	[illegible]	[illegible]	[illegible]	[illegible]	[illegible]	[illegible]	[illegible]	[illegible]	[illegible]	[illegible]
[illegible]	Ballina,	[illegible]	[illegible]	[illegible]	[illegible]	[illegible]	[illegible]	[illegible]	[illegible]	[illegible]	[illegible]	[illegible]	[illegible]	[illegible]	[illegible]	[illegible]	[illegible]	[illegible]
[illegible]	Ballinasloe,	[illegible]	[illegible]	[illegible]	[illegible]	[illegible]	[illegible]	[illegible]	[illegible]	[illegible]	[illegible]	[illegible]	[illegible]	[illegible]	[illegible]	[illegible]	[illegible]	[illegible]
[illegible]	Ballinrobe,	[illegible]	[illegible]	[illegible]	[illegible]	[illegible]	[illegible]	[illegible]	[illegible]	[illegible]	[illegible]	[illegible]	[illegible]	[illegible]	[illegible]	[illegible]	[illegible]	[illegible]
[illegible]	Ballycastle,	[illegible]	[illegible]	[illegible]	[illegible]	[illegible]	[illegible]	[illegible]	[illegible]	[illegible]	[illegible]	[illegible]	[illegible]	[illegible]	[illegible]	[illegible]	[illegible]	[illegible]
[illegible]	Ballymahon,	[illegible]	[illegible]	[illegible]	[illegible]	[illegible]	[illegible]	[illegible]	[illegible]	[illegible]	[illegible]	[illegible]	[illegible]	[illegible]	[illegible]	[illegible]	[illegible]	[illegible]
[illegible]	Ballymena,	[illegible]	[illegible]	[illegible]	[illegible]	[illegible]	[illegible]	[illegible]	[illegible]	[illegible]	[illegible]	[illegible]	[illegible]	[illegible]	[illegible]	[illegible]	[illegible]	[illegible]
[illegible]	Ballymoney,	[illegible]	[illegible]	[illegible]	[illegible]	[illegible]	[illegible]	[illegible]	[illegible]	[illegible]	[illegible]	[illegible]	[illegible]	[illegible]	[illegible]	[illegible]	[illegible]	[illegible]
[illegible]	Ballyshannon,	[illegible]	[illegible]	[illegible]	[illegible]	[illegible]	[illegible]	[illegible]	[illegible]	[illegible]	[illegible]	[illegible]	[illegible]	[illegible]	[illegible]	[illegible]	[illegible]	[illegible]
[illegible]	Ballyvaughan,	[illegible]	[illegible]	[illegible]	[illegible]	[illegible]	[illegible]	[illegible]	[illegible]	[illegible]	[illegible]	[illegible]	[illegible]	[illegible]	[illegible]	[illegible]	[illegible]	[illegible]
[illegible]	Balrothery,	[illegible]	[illegible]	[illegible]	[illegible]	[illegible]	[illegible]	[illegible]	[illegible]	[illegible]	[illegible]	[illegible]	[illegible]	[illegible]	[illegible]	[illegible]	[illegible]	[illegible]
[illegible]	Baltinglass,	[illegible]	[illegible]	[illegible]	[illegible]	[illegible]	[illegible]	[illegible]	[illegible]	[illegible]	[illegible]	[illegible]	[illegible]	[illegible]	[illegible]	[illegible]	[illegible]	[illegible]
[illegible]	Banbridge,	[illegible]	[illegible]	[illegible]	[illegible]	[illegible]	[illegible]	[illegible]	[illegible]	[illegible]	[illegible]	[illegible]	[illegible]	[illegible]	[illegible]	[illegible]	[illegible]	[illegible]
[illegible]	Bandon,	[illegible]	[illegible]	[illegible]	[illegible]	[illegible]	[illegible]	[illegible]	[illegible]	[illegible]	[illegible]	[illegible]	[illegible]	[illegible]	[illegible]	[illegible]	[illegible]	[illegible]
[illegible]	Bantry,	[illegible]	[illegible]	[illegible]	[illegible]	[illegible]	[illegible]	[illegible]	[illegible]	[illegible]	[illegible]	[illegible]	[illegible]	[illegible]	[illegible]	[illegible]	[illegible]	[illegible]
[illegible]	Bawnboy,	[illegible]	[illegible]	[illegible]	[illegible]	[illegible]	[illegible]	[illegible]	[illegible]	[illegible]	[illegible]	[illegible]	[illegible]	[illegible]	[illegible]	[illegible]	[illegible]	[illegible]
[illegible]	Belfast,	[illegible]	[illegible]	[illegible]	[illegible]	[illegible]	[illegible]	[illegible]	[illegible]	[illegible]	[illegible]	[illegible]	[illegible]	[illegible]	[illegible]	[illegible]	[illegible]	[illegible]
[illegible]	Belmullet,	[illegible]	[illegible]	[illegible]	[illegible]	[illegible]	[illegible]	[illegible]	[illegible]	[illegible]	[illegible]	[illegible]	[illegible]	[illegible]	[illegible]	[illegible]	[illegible]	[illegible]
[illegible]	Borrisokane,	[illegible]	[illegible]	[illegible]	[illegible]	[illegible]	[illegible]	[illegible]	[illegible]	[illegible]	[illegible]	[illegible]	[illegible]	[illegible]	[illegible]	[illegible]	[illegible]	[illegible]
[illegible]	Boyle,	[illegible]	[illegible]	[illegible]	[illegible]	[illegible]	[illegible]	[illegible]	[illegible]	[illegible]	[illegible]	[illegible]	[illegible]	[illegible]	[illegible]	[illegible]	[illegible]	[illegible]
[illegible]	Cahersiveen,	[illegible]	[illegible]	[illegible]	[illegible]	[illegible]	[illegible]	[illegible]	[illegible]	[illegible]	[illegible]	[illegible]	[illegible]	[illegible]	[illegible]	[illegible]	[illegible]	[illegible]
[illegible]	Callan,	[illegible]	[illegible]	[illegible]	[illegible]	[illegible]	[illegible]	[illegible]	[illegible]	[illegible]	[illegible]	[illegible]	[illegible]	[illegible]	[illegible]	[illegible]	[illegible]	[illegible]
[illegible]	Carlow,	[illegible]	[illegible]	[illegible]	[illegible]	[illegible]	[illegible]	[illegible]	[illegible]	[illegible]	[illegible]	[illegible]	[illegible]	[illegible]	[illegible]	[illegible]	[illegible]	[illegible]
[illegible]	Carrickmacross,	[illegible]	[illegible]	[illegible]	[illegible]	[illegible]	[illegible]	[illegible]	[illegible]	[illegible]	[illegible]	[illegible]	[illegible]	[illegible]	[illegible]	[illegible]	[illegible]	[illegible]
[illegible]	Carrick-on-Shannon,	[illegible]	[illegible]	[illegible]	[illegible]	[illegible]	[illegible]	[illegible]	[illegible]	[illegible]	[illegible]	[illegible]	[illegible]	[illegible]	[illegible]	[illegible]	[illegible]	[illegible]
[illegible]	Carrick-on-Suir,	[illegible]	[illegible]	[illegible]	[illegible]	[illegible]	[illegible]	[illegible]	[illegible]	[illegible]	[illegible]	[illegible]	[illegible]	[illegible]	[illegible]	[illegible]	[illegible]	[illegible]
[illegible]	Cashel,	[illegible]	[illegible]	[illegible]	[illegible]	[illegible]	[illegible]	[illegible]	[illegible]	[illegible]	[illegible]	[illegible]	[illegible]	[illegible]	[illegible]	[illegible]	[illegible]	[illegible]
[illegible]	Castlebar,	[illegible]	[illegible]	[illegible]	[illegible]	[illegible]	[illegible]	[illegible]	[illegible]	[illegible]	[illegible]	[illegible]	[illegible]	[illegible]	[illegible]	[illegible]	[illegible]	[illegible]
[illegible]	Castleblayney,	[illegible]	[illegible]	[illegible]	[illegible]	[illegible]	[illegible]	[illegible]	[illegible]	[illegible]	[illegible]	[illegible]	[illegible]	[illegible]	[illegible]	[illegible]	[illegible]	[illegible]
[illegible]	Castlecomer,	[illegible]	[illegible]	[illegible]	[illegible]	[illegible]	[illegible]	[illegible]	[illegible]	[illegible]	[illegible]	[illegible]	[illegible]	[illegible]	[illegible]	[illegible]	[illegible]	[illegible]
[illegible]	Castlederg,	[illegible]	[illegible]	[illegible]	[illegible]	[illegible]	[illegible]	[illegible]	[illegible]	[illegible]	[illegible]	[illegible]	[illegible]	[illegible]	[illegible]	[illegible]	[illegible]	[illegible]
[illegible]	Castlereagh,	[illegible]	[illegible]	[illegible]	[illegible]	[illegible]	[illegible]	[illegible]	[illegible]	[illegible]	[illegible]	[illegible]	[illegible]	[illegible]	[illegible]	[illegible]	[illegible]	[illegible]
[illegible]	Castletown,	[illegible]	[illegible]	[illegible]	[illegible]	[illegible]	[illegible]	[illegible]	[illegible]	[illegible]	[illegible]	[illegible]	[illegible]	[illegible]	[illegible]	[illegible]	[illegible]	[illegible]
[illegible]	Cavan,	[illegible]	[illegible]	[illegible]	[illegible]	[illegible]	[illegible]	[illegible]	[illegible]	[illegible]	[illegible]	[illegible]	[illegible]	[illegible]	[illegible]	[illegible]	[illegible]	[illegible]
[illegible]	Celbridge,	[illegible]	[illegible]	[illegible]	[illegible]	[illegible]	[illegible]	[illegible]	[illegible]	[illegible]	[illegible]	[illegible]	[illegible]	[illegible]	[illegible]	[illegible]	[illegible]	[illegible]
[illegible]	Claremorris,	[illegible]	[illegible]	[illegible]	[illegible]	[illegible]	[illegible]	[illegible]	[illegible]	[illegible]	[illegible]	[illegible]	[illegible]	[illegible]	[illegible]	[illegible]	[illegible]	[illegible]
[illegible]	Clifden,	[illegible]	[illegible]	[illegible]	[illegible]	[illegible]	[illegible]	[illegible]	[illegible]	[illegible]	[illegible]	[illegible]	[illegible]	[illegible]	[illegible]	[illegible]	[illegible]	[illegible]
[illegible]	Clogheen,	[illegible]	[illegible]	[illegible]	[illegible]	[illegible]	[illegible]	[illegible]	[illegible]	[illegible]	[illegible]	[illegible]	[illegible]	[illegible]	[illegible]	[illegible]	[illegible]	[illegible]
[illegible]	Clogher,	[illegible]	[illegible]	[illegible]	[illegible]	[illegible]	[illegible]	[illegible]	[illegible]	[illegible]	[illegible]	[illegible]	[illegible]	[illegible]	[illegible]	[illegible]	[illegible]	[illegible]
[illegible]	Clonakilty,	[illegible]	[illegible]	[illegible]	[illegible]	[illegible]	[illegible]	[illegible]	[illegible]	[illegible]	[illegible]	[illegible]	[illegible]	[illegible]	[illegible]	[illegible]	[illegible]	[illegible]
[illegible]	Clones,	[illegible]	[illegible]	[illegible]	[illegible]	[illegible]	[illegible]	[illegible]	[illegible]	[illegible]	[illegible]	[illegible]	[illegible]	[illegible]	[illegible]	[illegible]	[illegible]	[illegible]
[illegible]	Clonmel,	[illegible]	[illegible]	[illegible]	[illegible]	[illegible]	[illegible]	[illegible]	[illegible]	[illegible]	[illegible]	[illegible]	[illegible]	[illegible]	[illegible]	[illegible]	[illegible]	[illegible]
[illegible]	Coleraine,	[illegible]	[illegible]	[illegible]	[illegible]	[illegible]	[illegible]	[illegible]	[illegible]	[illegible]	[illegible]	[illegible]	[illegible]	[illegible]	[illegible]	[illegible]	[illegible]	[illegible]
[illegible]	Cookstown,	[illegible]	[illegible]	[illegible]	[illegible]	[illegible]	[illegible]	[illegible]	[illegible]	[illegible]	[illegible]	[illegible]	[illegible]	[illegible]	[illegible]	[illegible]	[illegible]	[illegible]
[illegible]	Cootehill,	[illegible]	[illegible]	[illegible]	[illegible]	[illegible]	[illegible]	[illegible]	[illegible]	[illegible]	[illegible]	[illegible]	[illegible]	[illegible]	[illegible]	[illegible]	[illegible]	[illegible]
[illegible]	Cork,	[illegible]	[illegible]	[illegible]	[illegible]	[illegible]	[illegible]	[illegible]	[illegible]	[illegible]	[illegible]	[illegible]	[illegible]	[illegible]	[illegible]	[illegible]	[illegible]	[illegible]
[illegible]	Corofin,	[illegible]	[illegible]	[illegible]	[illegible]	[illegible]	[illegible]	[illegible]	[illegible]	[illegible]	[illegible]	[illegible]	[illegible]	[illegible]	[illegible]	[illegible]	[illegible]	[illegible]
[illegible]	Croom,	[illegible]	[illegible]	[illegible]	[illegible]	[illegible]	[illegible]	[illegible]	[illegible]	[illegible]	[illegible]	[illegible]	[illegible]	[illegible]	[illegible]	[illegible]	[illegible]	[illegible]
[illegible]	Dingle,	[illegible]	[illegible]	[illegible]	[illegible]	[illegible]	[illegible]	[illegible]	[illegible]	[illegible]	[illegible]	[illegible]	[illegible]	[illegible]	[illegible]	[illegible]	[illegible]	[illegible]

BIRTHS Registered in Ireland in the Four Quarters ending March 31st, June 30th, September 30th, and December 31st, 1896, in each Superintendent Registrar's District or Poor Law Union—*continued.*

[illegible]	Superintendent Registrars' Districts or Poor Law Unions	Area in Statute Acres	Population 1891	Males and Females					Males					Females				
				Total	Registered in the Quarters ending the last day of				Registered in the Quarters ending the last day of				Total	Total	Registered in the Quarters ending the last day of			
					Mar.	June	Sept.	Dec.	Mar.	June	Sept.	Dec.			Mar.	June	Sept.	Dec.
[illegible]	[illegible]	[illegible]	[illegible]	[illegible]	[illegible]	[illegible]	[illegible]	[illegible]	[illegible]	[illegible]	[illegible]	[illegible]	[illegible]	[illegible]	[illegible]	[illegible]	[illegible]	[illegible]
[illegible]	[illegible]	[illegible]	[illegible]	[illegible]	[illegible]	[illegible]	[illegible]	[illegible]	[illegible]	[illegible]	[illegible]	[illegible]	[illegible]	[illegible]	[illegible]	[illegible]	[illegible]	[illegible]
[illegible]	[illegible]	[illegible]	[illegible]	[illegible]	[illegible]	[illegible]	[illegible]	[illegible]	[illegible]	[illegible]	[illegible]	[illegible]	[illegible]	[illegible]	[illegible]	[illegible]	[illegible]	[illegible]
[illegible]	[illegible]	[illegible]	[illegible]	[illegible]	[illegible]	[illegible]	[illegible]	[illegible]	[illegible]	[illegible]	[illegible]	[illegible]	[illegible]	[illegible]	[illegible]	[illegible]	[illegible]	[illegible]
[illegible]	[illegible]	[illegible]	[illegible]	[illegible]	[illegible]	[illegible]	[illegible]	[illegible]	[illegible]	[illegible]	[illegible]	[illegible]	[illegible]	[illegible]	[illegible]	[illegible]	[illegible]	[illegible]
[illegible]	[illegible]	[illegible]	[illegible]	[illegible]	[illegible]	[illegible]	[illegible]	[illegible]	[illegible]	[illegible]	[illegible]	[illegible]	[illegible]	[illegible]	[illegible]	[illegible]	[illegible]	[illegible]
[illegible]	[illegible]	[illegible]	[illegible]	[illegible]	[illegible]	[illegible]	[illegible]	[illegible]	[illegible]	[illegible]	[illegible]	[illegible]	[illegible]	[illegible]	[illegible]	[illegible]	[illegible]	[illegible]
[illegible]	[illegible]	[illegible]	[illegible]	[illegible]	[illegible]	[illegible]	[illegible]	[illegible]	[illegible]	[illegible]	[illegible]	[illegible]	[illegible]	[illegible]	[illegible]	[illegible]	[illegible]	[illegible]
[illegible]	[illegible]	[illegible]	[illegible]	[illegible]	[illegible]	[illegible]	[illegible]	[illegible]	[illegible]	[illegible]	[illegible]	[illegible]	[illegible]	[illegible]	[illegible]	[illegible]	[illegible]	[illegible]
[illegible]	[illegible]	[illegible]	[illegible]	[illegible]	[illegible]	[illegible]	[illegible]	[illegible]	[illegible]	[illegible]	[illegible]	[illegible]	[illegible]	[illegible]	[illegible]	[illegible]	[illegible]	[illegible]
[illegible]	[illegible]	[illegible]	[illegible]	[illegible]	[illegible]	[illegible]	[illegible]	[illegible]	[illegible]	[illegible]	[illegible]	[illegible]	[illegible]	[illegible]	[illegible]	[illegible]	[illegible]	[illegible]
[illegible]	[illegible]	[illegible]	[illegible]	[illegible]	[illegible]	[illegible]	[illegible]	[illegible]	[illegible]	[illegible]	[illegible]	[illegible]	[illegible]	[illegible]	[illegible]	[illegible]	[illegible]	[illegible]
[illegible]	[illegible]	[illegible]	[illegible]	[illegible]	[illegible]	[illegible]	[illegible]	[illegible]	[illegible]	[illegible]	[illegible]	[illegible]	[illegible]	[illegible]	[illegible]	[illegible]	[illegible]	[illegible]
[illegible]	[illegible]	[illegible]	[illegible]	[illegible]	[illegible]	[illegible]	[illegible]	[illegible]	[illegible]	[illegible]	[illegible]	[illegible]	[illegible]	[illegible]	[illegible]	[illegible]	[illegible]	[illegible]
[illegible]	[illegible]	[illegible]	[illegible]	[illegible]	[illegible]	[illegible]	[illegible]	[illegible]	[illegible]	[illegible]	[illegible]	[illegible]	[illegible]	[illegible]	[illegible]	[illegible]	[illegible]	[illegible]
[illegible]	[illegible]	[illegible]	[illegible]	[illegible]	[illegible]	[illegible]	[illegible]	[illegible]	[illegible]	[illegible]	[illegible]	[illegible]	[illegible]	[illegible]	[illegible]	[illegible]	[illegible]	[illegible]
[illegible]	[illegible]	[illegible]	[illegible]	[illegible]	[illegible]	[illegible]	[illegible]	[illegible]	[illegible]	[illegible]	[illegible]	[illegible]	[illegible]	[illegible]	[illegible]	[illegible]	[illegible]	[illegible]
[illegible]	[illegible]	[illegible]	[illegible]	[illegible]	[illegible]	[illegible]	[illegible]	[illegible]	[illegible]	[illegible]	[illegible]	[illegible]	[illegible]	[illegible]	[illegible]	[illegible]	[illegible]	[illegible]
[illegible]	[illegible]	[illegible]	[illegible]	[illegible]	[illegible]	[illegible]	[illegible]	[illegible]	[illegible]	[illegible]	[illegible]	[illegible]	[illegible]	[illegible]	[illegible]	[illegible]	[illegible]	[illegible]
[illegible]	[illegible]	[illegible]	[illegible]	[illegible]	[illegible]	[illegible]	[illegible]	[illegible]	[illegible]	[illegible]	[illegible]	[illegible]	[illegible]	[illegible]	[illegible]	[illegible]	[illegible]	[illegible]
[illegible]	[illegible]	[illegible]	[illegible]	[illegible]	[illegible]	[illegible]	[illegible]	[illegible]	[illegible]	[illegible]	[illegible]	[illegible]	[illegible]	[illegible]	[illegible]	[illegible]	[illegible]	[illegible]
[illegible]	[illegible]	[illegible]	[illegible]	[illegible]	[illegible]	[illegible]	[illegible]	[illegible]	[illegible]	[illegible]	[illegible]	[illegible]	[illegible]	[illegible]	[illegible]	[illegible]	[illegible]	[illegible]
[illegible]	[illegible]	[illegible]	[illegible]	[illegible]	[illegible]	[illegible]	[illegible]	[illegible]	[illegible]	[illegible]	[illegible]	[illegible]	[illegible]	[illegible]	[illegible]	[illegible]	[illegible]	[illegible]
[illegible]	[illegible]	[illegible]	[illegible]	[illegible]	[illegible]	[illegible]	[illegible]	[illegible]	[illegible]	[illegible]	[illegible]	[illegible]	[illegible]	[illegible]	[illegible]	[illegible]	[illegible]	[illegible]
[illegible]	[illegible]	[illegible]	[illegible]	[illegible]	[illegible]	[illegible]	[illegible]	[illegible]	[illegible]	[illegible]	[illegible]	[illegible]	[illegible]	[illegible]	[illegible]	[illegible]	[illegible]	[illegible]
[illegible]	[illegible]	[illegible]	[illegible]	[illegible]	[illegible]	[illegible]	[illegible]	[illegible]	[illegible]	[illegible]	[illegible]	[illegible]	[illegible]	[illegible]	[illegible]	[illegible]	[illegible]	[illegible]
[illegible]	[illegible]	[illegible]	[illegible]	[illegible]	[illegible]	[illegible]	[illegible]	[illegible]	[illegible]	[illegible]	[illegible]	[illegible]	[illegible]	[illegible]	[illegible]	[illegible]	[illegible]	[illegible]
[illegible]	[illegible]	[illegible]	[illegible]	[illegible]	[illegible]	[illegible]	[illegible]	[illegible]	[illegible]	[illegible]	[illegible]	[illegible]	[illegible]	[illegible]	[illegible]	[illegible]	[illegible]	[illegible]
[illegible]	[illegible]	[illegible]	[illegible]	[illegible]	[illegible]	[illegible]	[illegible]	[illegible]	[illegible]	[illegible]	[illegible]	[illegible]	[illegible]	[illegible]	[illegible]	[illegible]	[illegible]	[illegible]
[illegible]	[illegible]	[illegible]	[illegible]	[illegible]	[illegible]	[illegible]	[illegible]	[illegible]	[illegible]	[illegible]	[illegible]	[illegible]	[illegible]	[illegible]	[illegible]	[illegible]	[illegible]	[illegible]
[illegible]	[illegible]	[illegible]	[illegible]	[illegible]	[illegible]	[illegible]	[illegible]	[illegible]	[illegible]	[illegible]	[illegible]	[illegible]	[illegible]	[illegible]	[illegible]	[illegible]	[illegible]	[illegible]
[illegible]	[illegible]	[illegible]	[illegible]	[illegible]	[illegible]	[illegible]	[illegible]	[illegible]	[illegible]	[illegible]	[illegible]	[illegible]	[illegible]	[illegible]	[illegible]	[illegible]	[illegible]	[illegible]
[illegible]	[illegible]	[illegible]	[illegible]	[illegible]	[illegible]	[illegible]	[illegible]	[illegible]	[illegible]	[illegible]	[illegible]	[illegible]	[illegible]	[illegible]	[illegible]	[illegible]	[illegible]	[illegible]
[illegible]	[illegible]	[illegible]	[illegible]	[illegible]	[illegible]	[illegible]	[illegible]	[illegible]	[illegible]	[illegible]	[illegible]	[illegible]	[illegible]	[illegible]	[illegible]	[illegible]	[illegible]	[illegible]
[illegible]	[illegible]	[illegible]	[illegible]	[illegible]	[illegible]	[illegible]	[illegible]	[illegible]	[illegible]	[illegible]	[illegible]	[illegible]	[illegible]	[illegible]	[illegible]	[illegible]	[illegible]	[illegible]
[illegible]	[illegible]	[illegible]	[illegible]	[illegible]	[illegible]	[illegible]	[illegible]	[illegible]	[illegible]	[illegible]	[illegible]	[illegible]	[illegible]	[illegible]	[illegible]	[illegible]	[illegible]	[illegible]
[illegible]	[illegible]	[illegible]	[illegible]	[illegible]	[illegible]	[illegible]	[illegible]	[illegible]	[illegible]	[illegible]	[illegible]	[illegible]	[illegible]	[illegible]	[illegible]	[illegible]	[illegible]	[illegible]
[illegible]	[illegible]	[illegible]	[illegible]	[illegible]	[illegible]	[illegible]	[illegible]	[illegible]	[illegible]	[illegible]	[illegible]	[illegible]	[illegible]	[illegible]	[illegible]	[illegible]	[illegible]	[illegible]
[illegible]	[illegible]	[illegible]	[illegible]	[illegible]	[illegible]	[illegible]	[illegible]	[illegible]	[illegible]	[illegible]	[illegible]	[illegible]	[illegible]	[illegible]	[illegible]	[illegible]	[illegible]	[illegible]
[illegible]	[illegible]	[illegible]	[illegible]	[illegible]	[illegible]	[illegible]	[illegible]	[illegible]	[illegible]	[illegible]	[illegible]	[illegible]	[illegible]	[illegible]	[illegible]	[illegible]	[illegible]	[illegible]
[illegible]	[illegible]	[illegible]	[illegible]	[illegible]	[illegible]	[illegible]	[illegible]	[illegible]	[illegible]	[illegible]	[illegible]	[illegible]	[illegible]	[illegible]	[illegible]	[illegible]	[illegible]	[illegible]
[illegible]	[illegible]	[illegible]	[illegible]	[illegible]	[illegible]	[illegible]	[illegible]	[illegible]	[illegible]	[illegible]	[illegible]	[illegible]	[illegible]	[illegible]	[illegible]	[illegible]	[illegible]	[illegible]
[illegible]	[illegible]	[illegible]	[illegible]	[illegible]	[illegible]	[illegible]	[illegible]	[illegible]	[illegible]	[illegible]	[illegible]	[illegible]	[illegible]	[illegible]	[illegible]	[illegible]	[illegible]	[illegible]
[illegible]	[illegible]	[illegible]	[illegible]	[illegible]	[illegible]	[illegible]	[illegible]	[illegible]	[illegible]	[illegible]	[illegible]	[illegible]	[illegible]	[illegible]	[illegible]	[illegible]	[illegible]	[illegible]
[illegible]	[illegible]	[illegible]	[illegible]	[illegible]	[illegible]	[illegible]	[illegible]	[illegible]	[illegible]	[illegible]	[illegible]	[illegible]	[illegible]	[illegible]	[illegible]	[illegible]	[illegible]	[illegible]
[illegible]	[illegible]	[illegible]	[illegible]	[illegible]	[illegible]	[illegible]	[illegible]	[illegible]	[illegible]	[illegible]	[illegible]	[illegible]	[illegible]	[illegible]	[illegible]	[illegible]	[illegible]	[illegible]
[illegible]	[illegible]	[illegible]	[illegible]	[illegible]	[illegible]	[illegible]	[illegible]	[illegible]	[illegible]	[illegible]	[illegible]	[illegible]	[illegible]	[illegible]	[illegible]	[illegible]	[illegible]	[illegible]
[illegible]	[illegible]	[illegible]	[illegible]	[illegible]	[illegible]	[illegible]	[illegible]	[illegible]	[illegible]	[illegible]	[illegible]	[illegible]	[illegible]	[illegible]	[illegible]	[illegible]	[illegible]	[illegible]
[illegible]	[illegible]	[illegible]	[illegible]	[illegible]	[illegible]	[illegible]	[illegible]	[illegible]	[illegible]	[illegible]	[illegible]	[illegible]	[illegible]	[illegible]	[illegible]	[illegible]	[illegible]	[illegible]
[illegible]	[illegible]	[illegible]	[illegible]	[illegible]	[illegible]	[illegible]	[illegible]	[illegible]	[illegible]	[illegible]	[illegible]	[illegible]	[illegible]	[illegible]	[illegible]	[illegible]	[illegible]	[illegible]
[illegible]	[illegible]	[illegible]	[illegible]	[illegible]	[illegible]	[illegible]	[illegible]	[illegible]	[illegible]	[illegible]	[illegible]	[illegible]	[illegible]	[illegible]	[illegible]	[illegible]	[illegible]	[illegible]
[illegible]	[illegible]	[illegible]	[illegible]	[illegible]	[illegible]	[illegible]	[illegible]	[illegible]	[illegible]	[illegible]	[illegible]	[illegible]	[illegible]	[illegible]	[illegible]	[illegible]	[illegible]	[illegible]
[illegible]	[illegible]	[illegible]	[illegible]	[illegible]	[illegible]	[illegible]	[illegible]	[illegible]	[illegible]	[illegible]	[illegible]	[illegible]	[illegible]	[illegible]	[illegible]	[illegible]	[illegible]	[illegible]
[illegible]	[illegible]	[illegible]	[illegible]	[illegible]	[illegible]	[illegible]	[illegible]	[illegible]	[illegible]	[illegible]	[illegible]	[illegible]	[illegible]	[illegible]	[illegible]	[illegible]	[illegible]	[illegible]
[illegible]	[illegible]	[illegible]	[illegible]	[illegible]	[illegible]	[illegible]	[illegible]	[illegible]	[illegible]	[illegible]	[illegible]	[illegible]	[illegible]	[illegible]	[illegible]	[illegible]	[illegible]	[illegible]
[illegible]	[illegible]	[illegible]	[illegible]	[illegible]	[illegible]	[illegible]	[illegible]	[illegible]	[illegible]	[illegible]	[illegible]	[illegible]	[illegible]	[illegible]	[illegible]	[illegible]	[illegible]	[illegible]
[illegible]	[illegible]	[illegible]	[illegible]	[illegible]	[illegible]	[illegible]	[illegible]	[illegible]	[illegible]	[illegible]	[illegible]	[illegible]	[illegible]	[illegible]	[illegible]	[illegible]	[illegible]	[illegible]
[illegible]	[illegible]	[illegible]	[illegible]	[illegible]	[illegible]	[illegible]	[illegible]	[illegible]	[illegible]	[illegible]	[illegible]	[illegible]	[illegible]	[illegible]	[illegible]	[illegible]	[illegible]	[illegible]
[illegible]	[illegible]	[illegible]	[illegible]	[illegible]	[illegible]	[illegible]	[illegible]	[illegible]	[illegible]	[illegible]	[illegible]	[illegible]	[illegible]	[illegible]	[illegible]	[illegible]	[illegible]	[illegible]
[illegible]	[illegible]	[illegible]	[illegible]	[illegible]	[illegible]	[illegible]	[illegible]	[illegible]	[illegible]	[illegible]	[illegible]	[illegible]	[illegible]	[illegible]	[illegible]	[illegible]	[illegible]	[illegible]
[illegible]	[illegible]	[illegible]	[illegible]	[illegible]	[illegible]	[illegible]	[illegible]	[illegible]	[illegible]	[illegible]	[illegible]	[illegible]	[illegible]	[illegible]	[illegible]	[illegible]	[illegible]	[illegible]
[illegible]	[illegible]	[illegible]	[illegible]	[illegible]	[illegible]	[illegible]	[illegible]	[illegible]	[illegible]	[illegible]	[illegible]	[illegible]	[illegible]	[illegible]	[illegible]	[illegible]	[illegible]	[illegible]
[illegible]	[illegible]	[illegible]	[illegible]	[illegible]	[illegible]	[illegible]	[illegible]	[illegible]	[illegible]	[illegible]	[illegible]	[illegible]	[illegible]	[illegible]	[illegible]	[illegible]	[illegible]	[illegible]
[illegible]	[illegible]	[illegible]	[illegible]	[illegible]	[illegible]	[illegible]	[illegible]	[illegible]	[illegible]	[illegible]	[illegible]	[illegible]	[illegible]	[illegible]	[illegible]	[illegible]	[illegible]	[illegible]
[illegible]	[illegible]	[illegible]	[illegible]	[illegible]	[illegible]	[illegible]	[illegible]	[illegible]	[illegible]	[illegible]	[illegible]	[illegible]	[illegible]	[illegible]	[illegible]	[illegible]	[illegible]	[illegible]
[illegible]	[illegible]	[illegible]	[illegible]	[illegible]	[illegible]	[illegible]	[illegible]	[illegible]	[illegible]	[illegible]	[illegible]	[illegible]	[illegible]	[illegible]	[illegible]	[illegible]	[illegible]	[illegible]

BIRTHS Registered in Ireland in the Four Quarters ending March 31st, June 30th, September 30th, and December 31st, [illegible], in each Superintendent Registrar's District or Poor Law Union—continued.

Number of Districts of Unions	Superintendent Registrars' Districts or Poor Law Unions	Area in Statute Acres	Population in 1881	Males and Females: Total	Mar.	June	Sept.	Dec.	Males: Mar.	June	Sept.	Dec.	Total	Females: Total	Mar.	June	Sept.	Dec.
[illegible]	Magherafelt,	[illegible]	[illegible]	[illegible]	[illegible]	[illegible]	[illegible]	[illegible]	[illegible]	[illegible]	[illegible]	[illegible]	[illegible]	[illegible]	[illegible]	[illegible]	[illegible]	[illegible]
[illegible]	Mallow,	[illegible]	[illegible]	[illegible]	[illegible]	[illegible]	[illegible]	[illegible]	[illegible]	[illegible]	[illegible]	[illegible]	[illegible]	[illegible]	[illegible]	[illegible]	[illegible]	[illegible]
[illegible]	Manorhamilton,	[illegible]	[illegible]	[illegible]	[illegible]	[illegible]	[illegible]	[illegible]	[illegible]	[illegible]	[illegible]	[illegible]	[illegible]	[illegible]	[illegible]	[illegible]	[illegible]	[illegible]
[illegible]	Midleton,	[illegible]	[illegible]	[illegible]	[illegible]	[illegible]	[illegible]	[illegible]	[illegible]	[illegible]	[illegible]	[illegible]	[illegible]	[illegible]	[illegible]	[illegible]	[illegible]	[illegible]
[illegible]	Milford,	[illegible]	[illegible]	[illegible]	[illegible]	[illegible]	[illegible]	[illegible]	[illegible]	[illegible]	[illegible]	[illegible]	[illegible]	[illegible]	[illegible]	[illegible]	[illegible]	[illegible]
[illegible]	Millstreet,	[illegible]	[illegible]	[illegible]	[illegible]	[illegible]	[illegible]	[illegible]	[illegible]	[illegible]	[illegible]	[illegible]	[illegible]	[illegible]	[illegible]	[illegible]	[illegible]	[illegible]
[illegible]	Mitchelstown,	[illegible]	[illegible]	[illegible]	[illegible]	[illegible]	[illegible]	[illegible]	[illegible]	[illegible]	[illegible]	[illegible]	[illegible]	[illegible]	[illegible]	[illegible]	[illegible]	[illegible]
[illegible]	Mohill,	[illegible]	[illegible]	[illegible]	[illegible]	[illegible]	[illegible]	[illegible]	[illegible]	[illegible]	[illegible]	[illegible]	[illegible]	[illegible]	[illegible]	[illegible]	[illegible]	[illegible]
[illegible]	Monaghan,	[illegible]	[illegible]	[illegible]	[illegible]	[illegible]	[illegible]	[illegible]	[illegible]	[illegible]	[illegible]	[illegible]	[illegible]	[illegible]	[illegible]	[illegible]	[illegible]	[illegible]
[illegible]	Mountbellew,	[illegible]	[illegible]	[illegible]	[illegible]	[illegible]	[illegible]	[illegible]	[illegible]	[illegible]	[illegible]	[illegible]	[illegible]	[illegible]	[illegible]	[illegible]	[illegible]	[illegible]
[illegible]	Mountmellick,	[illegible]	[illegible]	[illegible]	[illegible]	[illegible]	[illegible]	[illegible]	[illegible]	[illegible]	[illegible]	[illegible]	[illegible]	[illegible]	[illegible]	[illegible]	[illegible]	[illegible]
[illegible]	Mullingar,	[illegible]	[illegible]	[illegible]	[illegible]	[illegible]	[illegible]	[illegible]	[illegible]	[illegible]	[illegible]	[illegible]	[illegible]	[illegible]	[illegible]	[illegible]	[illegible]	[illegible]
[illegible]	Naas,	[illegible]	[illegible]	[illegible]	[illegible]	[illegible]	[illegible]	[illegible]	[illegible]	[illegible]	[illegible]	[illegible]	[illegible]	[illegible]	[illegible]	[illegible]	[illegible]	[illegible]
[illegible]	Navan,	[illegible]	[illegible]	[illegible]	[illegible]	[illegible]	[illegible]	[illegible]	[illegible]	[illegible]	[illegible]	[illegible]	[illegible]	[illegible]	[illegible]	[illegible]	[illegible]	[illegible]
[illegible]	Nenagh,	[illegible]	[illegible]	[illegible]	[illegible]	[illegible]	[illegible]	[illegible]	[illegible]	[illegible]	[illegible]	[illegible]	[illegible]	[illegible]	[illegible]	[illegible]	[illegible]	[illegible]
[illegible]	Newcastle,	[illegible]	[illegible]	[illegible]	[illegible]	[illegible]	[illegible]	[illegible]	[illegible]	[illegible]	[illegible]	[illegible]	[illegible]	[illegible]	[illegible]	[illegible]	[illegible]	[illegible]
[illegible]	New Ross,	[illegible]	[illegible]	[illegible]	[illegible]	[illegible]	[illegible]	[illegible]	[illegible]	[illegible]	[illegible]	[illegible]	[illegible]	[illegible]	[illegible]	[illegible]	[illegible]	[illegible]
[illegible]	Newry,	[illegible]	[illegible]	[illegible]	[illegible]	[illegible]	[illegible]	[illegible]	[illegible]	[illegible]	[illegible]	[illegible]	[illegible]	[illegible]	[illegible]	[illegible]	[illegible]	[illegible]
[illegible]	Newtownards,	[illegible]	[illegible]	[illegible]	[illegible]	[illegible]	[illegible]	[illegible]	[illegible]	[illegible]	[illegible]	[illegible]	[illegible]	[illegible]	[illegible]	[illegible]	[illegible]	[illegible]
[illegible]	Oldcastle,	[illegible]	[illegible]	[illegible]	[illegible]	[illegible]	[illegible]	[illegible]	[illegible]	[illegible]	[illegible]	[illegible]	[illegible]	[illegible]	[illegible]	[illegible]	[illegible]	[illegible]
[illegible]	Omagh,	[illegible]	[illegible]	[illegible]	[illegible]	[illegible]	[illegible]	[illegible]	[illegible]	[illegible]	[illegible]	[illegible]	[illegible]	[illegible]	[illegible]	[illegible]	[illegible]	[illegible]
[illegible]	Oughterard,	[illegible]	[illegible]	[illegible]	[illegible]	[illegible]	[illegible]	[illegible]	[illegible]	[illegible]	[illegible]	[illegible]	[illegible]	[illegible]	[illegible]	[illegible]	[illegible]	[illegible]
[illegible]	Parsonstown,	[illegible]	[illegible]	[illegible]	[illegible]	[illegible]	[illegible]	[illegible]	[illegible]	[illegible]	[illegible]	[illegible]	[illegible]	[illegible]	[illegible]	[illegible]	[illegible]	[illegible]
[illegible]	Portumna,	[illegible]	[illegible]	[illegible]	[illegible]	[illegible]	[illegible]	[illegible]	[illegible]	[illegible]	[illegible]	[illegible]	[illegible]	[illegible]	[illegible]	[illegible]	[illegible]	[illegible]
[illegible]	Rathdown,	[illegible]	[illegible]	[illegible]	[illegible]	[illegible]	[illegible]	[illegible]	[illegible]	[illegible]	[illegible]	[illegible]	[illegible]	[illegible]	[illegible]	[illegible]	[illegible]	[illegible]
[illegible]	Rathdrum,	[illegible]	[illegible]	[illegible]	[illegible]	[illegible]	[illegible]	[illegible]	[illegible]	[illegible]	[illegible]	[illegible]	[illegible]	[illegible]	[illegible]	[illegible]	[illegible]	[illegible]
[illegible]	Rathkeale,	[illegible]	[illegible]	[illegible]	[illegible]	[illegible]	[illegible]	[illegible]	[illegible]	[illegible]	[illegible]	[illegible]	[illegible]	[illegible]	[illegible]	[illegible]	[illegible]	[illegible]
[illegible]	Roscommon,	[illegible]	[illegible]	[illegible]	[illegible]	[illegible]	[illegible]	[illegible]	[illegible]	[illegible]	[illegible]	[illegible]	[illegible]	[illegible]	[illegible]	[illegible]	[illegible]	[illegible]
[illegible]	Roscrea,	[illegible]	[illegible]	[illegible]	[illegible]	[illegible]	[illegible]	[illegible]	[illegible]	[illegible]	[illegible]	[illegible]	[illegible]	[illegible]	[illegible]	[illegible]	[illegible]	[illegible]
[illegible]	Scarriff,	[illegible]	[illegible]	[illegible]	[illegible]	[illegible]	[illegible]	[illegible]	[illegible]	[illegible]	[illegible]	[illegible]	[illegible]	[illegible]	[illegible]	[illegible]	[illegible]	[illegible]
[illegible]	Shillelagh,	[illegible]	[illegible]	[illegible]	[illegible]	[illegible]	[illegible]	[illegible]	[illegible]	[illegible]	[illegible]	[illegible]	[illegible]	[illegible]	[illegible]	[illegible]	[illegible]	[illegible]
[illegible]	Skibbereen,	[illegible]	[illegible]	[illegible]	[illegible]	[illegible]	[illegible]	[illegible]	[illegible]	[illegible]	[illegible]	[illegible]	[illegible]	[illegible]	[illegible]	[illegible]	[illegible]	[illegible]
[illegible]	Skull,	[illegible]	[illegible]	[illegible]	[illegible]	[illegible]	[illegible]	[illegible]	[illegible]	[illegible]	[illegible]	[illegible]	[illegible]	[illegible]	[illegible]	[illegible]	[illegible]	[illegible]
[illegible]	Sligo,	[illegible]	[illegible]	[illegible]	[illegible]	[illegible]	[illegible]	[illegible]	[illegible]	[illegible]	[illegible]	[illegible]	[illegible]	[illegible]	[illegible]	[illegible]	[illegible]	[illegible]
[illegible]	Strabane,	[illegible]	[illegible]	[illegible]	[illegible]	[illegible]	[illegible]	[illegible]	[illegible]	[illegible]	[illegible]	[illegible]	[illegible]	[illegible]	[illegible]	[illegible]	[illegible]	[illegible]
[illegible]	Stranorlar,	[illegible]	[illegible]	[illegible]	[illegible]	[illegible]	[illegible]	[illegible]	[illegible]	[illegible]	[illegible]	[illegible]	[illegible]	[illegible]	[illegible]	[illegible]	[illegible]	[illegible]
[illegible]	Strokestown,	[illegible]	[illegible]	[illegible]	[illegible]	[illegible]	[illegible]	[illegible]	[illegible]	[illegible]	[illegible]	[illegible]	[illegible]	[illegible]	[illegible]	[illegible]	[illegible]	[illegible]
[illegible]	Swineford,	[illegible]	[illegible]	[illegible]	[illegible]	[illegible]	[illegible]	[illegible]	[illegible]	[illegible]	[illegible]	[illegible]	[illegible]	[illegible]	[illegible]	[illegible]	[illegible]	[illegible]
[illegible]	Thomastown,	[illegible]	[illegible]	[illegible]	[illegible]	[illegible]	[illegible]	[illegible]	[illegible]	[illegible]	[illegible]	[illegible]	[illegible]	[illegible]	[illegible]	[illegible]	[illegible]	[illegible]
[illegible]	Thurles,	[illegible]	[illegible]	[illegible]	[illegible]	[illegible]	[illegible]	[illegible]	[illegible]	[illegible]	[illegible]	[illegible]	[illegible]	[illegible]	[illegible]	[illegible]	[illegible]	[illegible]
[illegible]	Tipperary,	[illegible]	[illegible]	[illegible]	[illegible]	[illegible]	[illegible]	[illegible]	[illegible]	[illegible]	[illegible]	[illegible]	[illegible]	[illegible]	[illegible]	[illegible]	[illegible]	[illegible]
[illegible]	Tobercurry,	[illegible]	[illegible]	[illegible]	[illegible]	[illegible]	[illegible]	[illegible]	[illegible]	[illegible]	[illegible]	[illegible]	[illegible]	[illegible]	[illegible]	[illegible]	[illegible]	[illegible]
[illegible]	Tralee,	[illegible]	[illegible]	[illegible]	[illegible]	[illegible]	[illegible]	[illegible]	[illegible]	[illegible]	[illegible]	[illegible]	[illegible]	[illegible]	[illegible]	[illegible]	[illegible]	[illegible]
[illegible]	Trim,	[illegible]	[illegible]	[illegible]	[illegible]	[illegible]	[illegible]	[illegible]	[illegible]	[illegible]	[illegible]	[illegible]	[illegible]	[illegible]	[illegible]	[illegible]	[illegible]	[illegible]
[illegible]	Tuam,	[illegible]	[illegible]	[illegible]	[illegible]	[illegible]	[illegible]	[illegible]	[illegible]	[illegible]	[illegible]	[illegible]	[illegible]	[illegible]	[illegible]	[illegible]	[illegible]	[illegible]
[illegible]	Tulla,	[illegible]	[illegible]	[illegible]	[illegible]	[illegible]	[illegible]	[illegible]	[illegible]	[illegible]	[illegible]	[illegible]	[illegible]	[illegible]	[illegible]	[illegible]	[illegible]	[illegible]
[illegible]	Tullamore,	[illegible]	[illegible]	[illegible]	[illegible]	[illegible]	[illegible]	[illegible]	[illegible]	[illegible]	[illegible]	[illegible]	[illegible]	[illegible]	[illegible]	[illegible]	[illegible]	[illegible]
[illegible]	Urlingford,	[illegible]	[illegible]	[illegible]	[illegible]	[illegible]	[illegible]	[illegible]	[illegible]	[illegible]	[illegible]	[illegible]	[illegible]	[illegible]	[illegible]	[illegible]	[illegible]	[illegible]
[illegible]	Waterford,	[illegible]	[illegible]	[illegible]	[illegible]	[illegible]	[illegible]	[illegible]	[illegible]	[illegible]	[illegible]	[illegible]	[illegible]	[illegible]	[illegible]	[illegible]	[illegible]	[illegible]
[illegible]	Westport,	[illegible]	[illegible]	[illegible]	[illegible]	[illegible]	[illegible]	[illegible]	[illegible]	[illegible]	[illegible]	[illegible]	[illegible]	[illegible]	[illegible]	[illegible]	[illegible]	[illegible]
[illegible]	Wexford,	[illegible]	[illegible]	[illegible]	[illegible]	[illegible]	[illegible]	[illegible]	[illegible]	[illegible]	[illegible]	[illegible]	[illegible]	[illegible]	[illegible]	[illegible]	[illegible]	[illegible]
[illegible]	Youghal,	[illegible]	[illegible]	[illegible]	[illegible]	[illegible]	[illegible]	[illegible]	[illegible]	[illegible]	[illegible]	[illegible]	[illegible]	[illegible]	[illegible]	[illegible]	[illegible]	[illegible]

DEATHS registered in each Province and County in Ireland in the Four Quarters ending March 31st, June 30th, September 30th, and December 31st, 1896.

No.	PROVINCES AND COUNTIES.	Area in Statute Acres.	Population in [illegible]	MALES AND FEMALES: Total.	Registered in the Quarter ending the last day of: March.	June.	Sept.	Dec.	MALES: Registered in the Quarter ending the last day of: March.	June.	Sept.	Dec.	Total.	FEMALES: Total.	Registered in the Quarter ending the last day of: March.	June.	Sept.	Dec.
	IRELAND,	[illegible]	[illegible]	[illegible]	[illegible]	[illegible]	[illegible]	[illegible]	[illegible]	[illegible]	[illegible]	[illegible]	[illegible]	[illegible]	[illegible]	[illegible]	[illegible]	[illegible]
	PROVINCES.																	
I.	LEINSTER,	[illegible]	[illegible]	[illegible]	[illegible]	[illegible]	[illegible]	[illegible]	[illegible]	[illegible]	[illegible]	[illegible]	[illegible]	[illegible]	[illegible]	[illegible]	[illegible]	[illegible]
II.	MUNSTER,	[illegible]	[illegible]	[illegible]	[illegible]	[illegible]	[illegible]	[illegible]	[illegible]	[illegible]	[illegible]	[illegible]	[illegible]	[illegible]	[illegible]	[illegible]	[illegible]	[illegible]
III.	ULSTER,	[illegible]	[illegible]	[illegible]	[illegible]	[illegible]	[illegible]	[illegible]	[illegible]	[illegible]	[illegible]	[illegible]	[illegible]	[illegible]	[illegible]	[illegible]	[illegible]	[illegible]
IV.	CONNAUGHT,	[illegible]	[illegible]	[illegible]	[illegible]	[illegible]	[illegible]	[illegible]	[illegible]	[illegible]	[illegible]	[illegible]	[illegible]	[illegible]	[illegible]	[illegible]	[illegible]	[illegible]
	I.—PROVINCE OF LEINSTER.—COUNTIES.																	
1	Carlow,	[illegible]	[illegible]	[illegible]	[illegible]	[illegible]	[illegible]	[illegible]	[illegible]	[illegible]	[illegible]	[illegible]	[illegible]	[illegible]	[illegible]	[illegible]	[illegible]	[illegible]
2	Dublin,	[illegible]	[illegible]	[illegible]	[illegible]	[illegible]	[illegible]	[illegible]	[illegible]	[illegible]	[illegible]	[illegible]	[illegible]	[illegible]	[illegible]	[illegible]	[illegible]	[illegible]
3	Kildare,	[illegible]	[illegible]	[illegible]	[illegible]	[illegible]	[illegible]	[illegible]	[illegible]	[illegible]	[illegible]	[illegible]	[illegible]	[illegible]	[illegible]	[illegible]	[illegible]	[illegible]
4	Kilkenny,	[illegible]	[illegible]	[illegible]	[illegible]	[illegible]	[illegible]	[illegible]	[illegible]	[illegible]	[illegible]	[illegible]	[illegible]	[illegible]	[illegible]	[illegible]	[illegible]	[illegible]
5	King's,	[illegible]	[illegible]	[illegible]	[illegible]	[illegible]	[illegible]	[illegible]	[illegible]	[illegible]	[illegible]	[illegible]	[illegible]	[illegible]	[illegible]	[illegible]	[illegible]	[illegible]
6	Longford,	[illegible]	[illegible]	[illegible]	[illegible]	[illegible]	[illegible]	[illegible]	[illegible]	[illegible]	[illegible]	[illegible]	[illegible]	[illegible]	[illegible]	[illegible]	[illegible]	[illegible]
7	Louth, and Co. of the Town of Drogheda,	[illegible]	[illegible]	[illegible]	[illegible]	[illegible]	[illegible]	[illegible]	[illegible]	[illegible]	[illegible]	[illegible]	[illegible]	[illegible]	[illegible]	[illegible]	[illegible]	[illegible]
8	Meath,	[illegible]	[illegible]	[illegible]	[illegible]	[illegible]	[illegible]	[illegible]	[illegible]	[illegible]	[illegible]	[illegible]	[illegible]	[illegible]	[illegible]	[illegible]	[illegible]	[illegible]
9	Queen's,	[illegible]	[illegible]	[illegible]	[illegible]	[illegible]	[illegible]	[illegible]	[illegible]	[illegible]	[illegible]	[illegible]	[illegible]	[illegible]	[illegible]	[illegible]	[illegible]	[illegible]
10	Westmeath,	[illegible]	[illegible]	[illegible]	[illegible]	[illegible]	[illegible]	[illegible]	[illegible]	[illegible]	[illegible]	[illegible]	[illegible]	[illegible]	[illegible]	[illegible]	[illegible]	[illegible]
11	Wexford,	[illegible]	[illegible]	[illegible]	[illegible]	[illegible]	[illegible]	[illegible]	[illegible]	[illegible]	[illegible]	[illegible]	[illegible]	[illegible]	[illegible]	[illegible]	[illegible]	[illegible]
12	Wicklow,	[illegible]	[illegible]	[illegible]	[illegible]	[illegible]	[illegible]	[illegible]	[illegible]	[illegible]	[illegible]	[illegible]	[illegible]	[illegible]	[illegible]	[illegible]	[illegible]	[illegible]
	II.—PROVINCE OF MUNSTER.—COUNTIES.																	
13	Clare,	[illegible]	[illegible]	[illegible]	[illegible]	[illegible]	[illegible]	[illegible]	[illegible]	[illegible]	[illegible]	[illegible]	[illegible]	[illegible]	[illegible]	[illegible]	[illegible]	[illegible]
14	Cork,	[illegible]	[illegible]	[illegible]	[illegible]	[illegible]	[illegible]	[illegible]	[illegible]	[illegible]	[illegible]	[illegible]	[illegible]	[illegible]	[illegible]	[illegible]	[illegible]	[illegible]
15	Kerry,	[illegible]	[illegible]	[illegible]	[illegible]	[illegible]	[illegible]	[illegible]	[illegible]	[illegible]	[illegible]	[illegible]	[illegible]	[illegible]	[illegible]	[illegible]	[illegible]	[illegible]
16	Limerick,	[illegible]	[illegible]	[illegible]	[illegible]	[illegible]	[illegible]	[illegible]	[illegible]	[illegible]	[illegible]	[illegible]	[illegible]	[illegible]	[illegible]	[illegible]	[illegible]	[illegible]
17	Tipperary,	[illegible]	[illegible]	[illegible]	[illegible]	[illegible]	[illegible]	[illegible]	[illegible]	[illegible]	[illegible]	[illegible]	[illegible]	[illegible]	[illegible]	[illegible]	[illegible]	[illegible]
18	Waterford,	[illegible]	[illegible]	[illegible]	[illegible]	[illegible]	[illegible]	[illegible]	[illegible]	[illegible]	[illegible]	[illegible]	[illegible]	[illegible]	[illegible]	[illegible]	[illegible]	[illegible]
	III.—PROVINCE OF ULSTER.—COUNTIES.																	
19	Antrim,	[illegible]	[illegible]	[illegible]	[illegible]	[illegible]	[illegible]	[illegible]	[illegible]	[illegible]	[illegible]	[illegible]	[illegible]	[illegible]	[illegible]	[illegible]	[illegible]	[illegible]
20	Armagh,	[illegible]	[illegible]	[illegible]	[illegible]	[illegible]	[illegible]	[illegible]	[illegible]	[illegible]	[illegible]	[illegible]	[illegible]	[illegible]	[illegible]	[illegible]	[illegible]	[illegible]
21	Cavan,	[illegible]	[illegible]	[illegible]	[illegible]	[illegible]	[illegible]	[illegible]	[illegible]	[illegible]	[illegible]	[illegible]	[illegible]	[illegible]	[illegible]	[illegible]	[illegible]	[illegible]
22	Donegal,	[illegible]	[illegible]	[illegible]	[illegible]	[illegible]	[illegible]	[illegible]	[illegible]	[illegible]	[illegible]	[illegible]	[illegible]	[illegible]	[illegible]	[illegible]	[illegible]	[illegible]
23	Down,	[illegible]	[illegible]	[illegible]	[illegible]	[illegible]	[illegible]	[illegible]	[illegible]	[illegible]	[illegible]	[illegible]	[illegible]	[illegible]	[illegible]	[illegible]	[illegible]	[illegible]
24	Fermanagh,	[illegible]	[illegible]	[illegible]	[illegible]	[illegible]	[illegible]	[illegible]	[illegible]	[illegible]	[illegible]	[illegible]	[illegible]	[illegible]	[illegible]	[illegible]	[illegible]	[illegible]
25	Londonderry,	[illegible]	[illegible]	[illegible]	[illegible]	[illegible]	[illegible]	[illegible]	[illegible]	[illegible]	[illegible]	[illegible]	[illegible]	[illegible]	[illegible]	[illegible]	[illegible]	[illegible]
26	Monaghan,	[illegible]	[illegible]	[illegible]	[illegible]	[illegible]	[illegible]	[illegible]	[illegible]	[illegible]	[illegible]	[illegible]	[illegible]	[illegible]	[illegible]	[illegible]	[illegible]	[illegible]
27	Tyrone,	[illegible]	[illegible]	[illegible]	[illegible]	[illegible]	[illegible]	[illegible]	[illegible]	[illegible]	[illegible]	[illegible]	[illegible]	[illegible]	[illegible]	[illegible]	[illegible]	[illegible]
	IV.—PROVINCE OF CONNAUGHT.—COUNTIES.																	
28	Galway,	[illegible]	[illegible]	[illegible]	[illegible]	[illegible]	[illegible]	[illegible]	[illegible]	[illegible]	[illegible]	[illegible]	[illegible]	[illegible]	[illegible]	[illegible]	[illegible]	[illegible]
29	Leitrim,	[illegible]	[illegible]	[illegible]	[illegible]	[illegible]	[illegible]	[illegible]	[illegible]	[illegible]	[illegible]	[illegible]	[illegible]	[illegible]	[illegible]	[illegible]	[illegible]	[illegible]
30	Mayo,	[illegible]	[illegible]	[illegible]	[illegible]	[illegible]	[illegible]	[illegible]	[illegible]	[illegible]	[illegible]	[illegible]	[illegible]	[illegible]	[illegible]	[illegible]	[illegible]	[illegible]
31	Roscommon,	[illegible]	[illegible]	[illegible]	[illegible]	[illegible]	[illegible]	[illegible]	[illegible]	[illegible]	[illegible]	[illegible]	[illegible]	[illegible]	[illegible]	[illegible]	[illegible]	[illegible]
32	Sligo,	[illegible]	[illegible]	[illegible]	[illegible]	[illegible]	[illegible]	[illegible]	[illegible]	[illegible]	[illegible]	[illegible]	[illegible]	[illegible]	[illegible]	[illegible]	[illegible]	[illegible]

[illegible] registered in Ireland in the Four Quarters ending [illegible]

No.	Provinces, and Superintendent Registrars' Districts	Area in Statute Acres	Population in 1861	Total	March	June	Sept.	Dec.
	Carlow Co.							
1	Baltinglass, part of,	[illegible]	[illegible]	[illegible]	[illegible]	[illegible]	[illegible]	[illegible]
2	Carlow, do.	[illegible]	[illegible]	[illegible]	[illegible]	[illegible]	[illegible]	[illegible]
3	Enniscorthy, do.	[illegible]	[illegible]	[illegible]	[illegible]	[illegible]	[illegible]	[illegible]
4	New Ross, do.	[illegible]	[illegible]	[illegible]	[illegible]	[illegible]	[illegible]	[illegible]
5	Shillelagh, do.	[illegible]	[illegible]	[illegible]	[illegible]	[illegible]	[illegible]	[illegible]
	Dublin Co.							
6	Balrothery,	[illegible]	[illegible]	[illegible]	[illegible]	[illegible]	[illegible]	[illegible]
7	Celbridge, part of,	[illegible]	[illegible]	[illegible]	[illegible]	[illegible]	[illegible]	[illegible]
8	Dublin, North,	[illegible]	[illegible]	[illegible]	[illegible]	[illegible]	[illegible]	[illegible]
9	Dublin, South,	[illegible]	[illegible]	[illegible]	[illegible]	[illegible]	[illegible]	[illegible]
10	Edenderry, part of,	[illegible]	[illegible]	[illegible]	[illegible]	[illegible]	[illegible]	[illegible]
11	Rathdown, do.	[illegible]	[illegible]	[illegible]	[illegible]	[illegible]	[illegible]	[illegible]
	Kildare Co.							
12	Athy, part of,	[illegible]	[illegible]	[illegible]	[illegible]	[illegible]	[illegible]	[illegible]
13	Baltinglass, do.	[illegible]	[illegible]	[illegible]	[illegible]	[illegible]	[illegible]	[illegible]
14	Celbridge, do.	[illegible]	[illegible]	[illegible]	[illegible]	[illegible]	[illegible]	[illegible]
15	Edenderry, do.	[illegible]	[illegible]	[illegible]	[illegible]	[illegible]	[illegible]	[illegible]
16	Naas, do.	[illegible]	[illegible]	[illegible]	[illegible]	[illegible]	[illegible]	[illegible]
	Kilkenny Co.							
17	Callan, part of,	[illegible]	[illegible]	[illegible]	[illegible]	[illegible]	[illegible]	[illegible]
18	Carrick-on-Suir, do.	[illegible]	[illegible]	[illegible]	[illegible]	[illegible]	[illegible]	[illegible]
19	Castlecomer,	[illegible]	[illegible]	[illegible]	[illegible]	[illegible]	[illegible]	[illegible]
20	Kilkenny,	[illegible]	[illegible]	[illegible]	[illegible]	[illegible]	[illegible]	[illegible]
21	New Ross, part of,	[illegible]	[illegible]	[illegible]	[illegible]	[illegible]	[illegible]	[illegible]
22	Thomastown,	[illegible]	[illegible]	[illegible]	[illegible]	[illegible]	[illegible]	[illegible]
23	Urlingford, part of,	[illegible]	[illegible]	[illegible]	[illegible]	[illegible]	[illegible]	[illegible]
24	Waterford, do.	[illegible]	[illegible]	[illegible]	[illegible]	[illegible]	[illegible]	[illegible]
	King's Co.							
25	Edenderry, part of,	[illegible]	[illegible]	[illegible]	[illegible]	[illegible]	[illegible]	[illegible]
26	Mountmellick, do.	[illegible]	[illegible]	[illegible]	[illegible]	[illegible]	[illegible]	[illegible]
27	Parsonstown, do.	[illegible]	[illegible]	[illegible]	[illegible]	[illegible]	[illegible]	[illegible]
28	Roscrea, do.	[illegible]	[illegible]	[illegible]	[illegible]	[illegible]	[illegible]	[illegible]
29	Tullamore, do.	[illegible]	[illegible]	[illegible]	[illegible]	[illegible]	[illegible]	[illegible]
	Longford Co.							
30	Ballymahon, part of,	[illegible]	[illegible]	[illegible]	[illegible]	[illegible]	[illegible]	[illegible]
31	Granard, do.	[illegible]	[illegible]	[illegible]	[illegible]	[illegible]	[illegible]	[illegible]
32	Longford,	[illegible]	[illegible]	[illegible]	[illegible]	[illegible]	[illegible]	[illegible]
	Louth Co., and Co. of Town of Drogheda.							
33	Ardee, part of,	[illegible]	[illegible]	[illegible]	[illegible]	[illegible]	[illegible]	[illegible]
34	Drogheda, do.	[illegible]	[illegible]	[illegible]	[illegible]	[illegible]	[illegible]	[illegible]
35	Dundalk, do.	[illegible]	[illegible]	[illegible]	[illegible]	[illegible]	[illegible]	[illegible]
	Meath Co.							
36	Ardee, part of,	[illegible]	[illegible]	[illegible]	[illegible]	[illegible]	[illegible]	[illegible]
37	Celbridge, do.	[illegible]	[illegible]	[illegible]	[illegible]	[illegible]	[illegible]	[illegible]
38	Drogheda, do.	[illegible]	[illegible]	[illegible]	[illegible]	[illegible]	[illegible]	[illegible]
39	Dunshaughlin, do.	[illegible]	[illegible]	[illegible]	[illegible]	[illegible]	[illegible]	[illegible]
40	Edenderry, do.	[illegible]	[illegible]	[illegible]	[illegible]	[illegible]	[illegible]	[illegible]
41	Kells, do.	[illegible]	[illegible]	[illegible]	[illegible]	[illegible]	[illegible]	[illegible]
42	Navan,	[illegible]	[illegible]	[illegible]	[illegible]	[illegible]	[illegible]	[illegible]
43	Oldcastle, part of,	[illegible]	[illegible]	[illegible]	[illegible]	[illegible]	[illegible]	[illegible]
44	Trim,	[illegible]	[illegible]	[illegible]	[illegible]	[illegible]	[illegible]	[illegible]

March 31st, June 30th, September 30th, and December 31st, 1896.

LEINSTER.

MALES.					FEMALES.					SUPERINTENDENT REGISTRARS' DISTRICTS.
Registered in the Quarter ending the last day of				Total.	Total.	Registered in the Quarter ending the last day of				
March.	June.	Sept.	Dec.			March.	June.	Sept.	Dec.	
										Carlow Co.
[illegible]	[illegible]	[illegible]	[illegible]	[illegible]	[illegible]	[illegible]	7	[illegible]	[illegible]	Baltinglass, part of.
[illegible]	[illegible]	[illegible]	[illegible]	[illegible]	[illegible]	[illegible]	[illegible]	[illegible]	[illegible]	Carlow, do.
[illegible]	[illegible]	1	1	[illegible]	[illegible]	[illegible]	1	[illegible]	[illegible]	Enniscorthy, do.
[illegible]	[illegible]	[illegible]	[illegible]	[illegible]	[illegible]	[illegible]	[illegible]	[illegible]	[illegible]	New Ross, do.
[illegible]	[illegible]	[illegible]	[illegible]	[illegible]	[illegible]	[illegible]	[illegible]	[illegible]	[illegible]	Shillelagh, do.
										Dublin Co.
[illegible]	[illegible]	[illegible]	[illegible]	[illegible]	[illegible]	[illegible]	[illegible]	[illegible]	[illegible]	Balrothery.
[illegible]	[illegible]	[illegible]	[illegible]	[illegible]	[illegible]	[illegible]	[illegible]	[illegible]	[illegible]	Celbridge, part of.
[illegible]	[illegible]	[illegible]	[illegible]	[illegible]	[illegible]	[illegible]	[illegible]	[illegible]	[illegible]	Dublin, North.
[illegible]	[illegible]	[illegible]	[illegible]	[illegible]	[illegible]	[illegible]	[illegible]	[illegible]	[illegible]	Dublin, South.
[illegible]	1	[illegible]	3	[illegible]	[illegible]	[illegible]	1	1	1	Dunshaughlin, part of.
[illegible]	[illegible]	[illegible]	[illegible]	[illegible]	[illegible]	[illegible]	[illegible]	[illegible]	[illegible]	Rathdown, do.
										Kildare Co.
[illegible]	[illegible]	[illegible]	[illegible]	[illegible]	[illegible]	[illegible]	[illegible]	[illegible]	[illegible]	Athy, part of.
[illegible]	[illegible]	1	[illegible]	[illegible]	[illegible]	[illegible]	[illegible]	[illegible]	[illegible]	Baltinglass, do.
[illegible]	[illegible]	[illegible]	[illegible]	[illegible]	[illegible]	[illegible]	[illegible]	[illegible]	[illegible]	Celbridge, do.
[illegible]	[illegible]	[illegible]	[illegible]	[illegible]	[illegible]	[illegible]	[illegible]	[illegible]	[illegible]	Edenderry, do.
[illegible]	[illegible]	[illegible]	[illegible]	[illegible]	[illegible]	[illegible]	[illegible]	[illegible]	[illegible]	Naas, do.
										Kilkenny Co.
[illegible]	[illegible]	[illegible]	[illegible]	[illegible]	[illegible]	[illegible]	[illegible]	[illegible]	[illegible]	Callan, part of.
[illegible]	[illegible]	[illegible]	[illegible]	[illegible]	[illegible]	[illegible]	[illegible]	[illegible]	[illegible]	Carrick-on-Suir, do.
[illegible]	[illegible]	[illegible]	[illegible]	[illegible]	[illegible]	[illegible]	[illegible]	[illegible]	[illegible]	Castlecomer do.
[illegible]	[illegible]	[illegible]	[illegible]	[illegible]	[illegible]	[illegible]	[illegible]	[illegible]	[illegible]	Kilkenny.
[illegible]	[illegible]	[illegible]	[illegible]	[illegible]	[illegible]	[illegible]	[illegible]	[illegible]	[illegible]	New Ross, part of.
[illegible]	[illegible]	[illegible]	[illegible]	[illegible]	[illegible]	[illegible]	[illegible]	[illegible]	[illegible]	Thomastown.
[illegible]	[illegible]	[illegible]	[illegible]	[illegible]	[illegible]	[illegible]	[illegible]	[illegible]	[illegible]	Urlingford, part of.
[illegible]	[illegible]	[illegible]	[illegible]	[illegible]	[illegible]	[illegible]	[illegible]	[illegible]	[illegible]	Waterford, do.
										King's Co.
[illegible]	[illegible]	[illegible]	[illegible]	[illegible]	[illegible]	[illegible]	[illegible]	[illegible]	[illegible]	Edenderry, part of.
[illegible]	[illegible]	[illegible]	[illegible]	[illegible]	[illegible]	[illegible]	[illegible]	[illegible]	[illegible]	Mountmellick, do.
[illegible]	[illegible]	[illegible]	[illegible]	[illegible]	[illegible]	[illegible]	[illegible]	[illegible]	[illegible]	Parsonstown, do.
[illegible]	[illegible]	[illegible]	[illegible]	[illegible]	[illegible]	[illegible]	[illegible]	[illegible]	[illegible]	Roscrea, do.
[illegible]	[illegible]	[illegible]	[illegible]	[illegible]	[illegible]	[illegible]	[illegible]	[illegible]	[illegible]	Tullamore, do.
										Longford Co.
[illegible]	[illegible]	[illegible]	[illegible]	[illegible]	[illegible]	[illegible]	[illegible]	[illegible]	[illegible]	Ballymahon, part of.
[illegible]	[illegible]	[illegible]	[illegible]	[illegible]	[illegible]	[illegible]	[illegible]	[illegible]	[illegible]	Granard, do.
[illegible]	[illegible]	[illegible]	[illegible]	[illegible]	[illegible]	[illegible]	[illegible]	[illegible]	[illegible]	Longford.
										Louth Co. and part of Town of Drogheda.
[illegible]	[illegible]	[illegible]	[illegible]	[illegible]	[illegible]	[illegible]	[illegible]	[illegible]	[illegible]	Ardee, part of.
[illegible]	[illegible]	[illegible]	[illegible]	[illegible]	[illegible]	[illegible]	[illegible]	[illegible]	[illegible]	Dundalk, do.
[illegible]	[illegible]	[illegible]	[illegible]	[illegible]	[illegible]	[illegible]	[illegible]	[illegible]	[illegible]	Drogheda, do.
										Meath Co.
[illegible]	[illegible]	[illegible]	[illegible]	[illegible]	[illegible]	[illegible]	3	[illegible]	[illegible]	Ardee, part of.
[illegible]	[illegible]	1	1	[illegible]	[illegible]	1	[illegible]	[illegible]	[illegible]	Celbridge, do.
[illegible]	[illegible]	[illegible]	[illegible]	[illegible]	[illegible]	[illegible]	[illegible]	[illegible]	[illegible]	Drogheda, do.
[illegible]	[illegible]	[illegible]	[illegible]	[illegible]	[illegible]	[illegible]	[illegible]	[illegible]	[illegible]	Dunshaughlin, do.
[illegible]	[illegible]	[illegible]	[illegible]	[illegible]	[illegible]	[illegible]	[illegible]	[illegible]	[illegible]	Edenderry, do.
[illegible]	[illegible]	[illegible]	[illegible]	[illegible]	[illegible]	[illegible]	[illegible]	[illegible]	[illegible]	Kells, do.
[illegible]	[illegible]	[illegible]	[illegible]	[illegible]	[illegible]	[illegible]	[illegible]	[illegible]	[illegible]	Navan.
[illegible]	[illegible]	[illegible]	[illegible]	[illegible]	[illegible]	[illegible]	[illegible]	[illegible]	[illegible]	Oldcastle, part of.
[illegible]	[illegible]	[illegible]	[illegible]	[illegible]	[illegible]	[illegible]	[illegible]	[illegible]	[illegible]	Trim.

DEATHS registered in Ireland in the Four Quarters ending

X.—PROVINCE OF

No.	Superintendent Registrars' Districts	Area in Statute Acres	Population in 1861	Males and Females: Total	Registered in the Quarter ending the 31st day of: March	June	Sept.	Dec.
	Queen's Co.							
[illegible]	Abbeyleix,	[illegible]	[illegible]	[illegible]	[illegible]	[illegible]	[illegible]	[illegible]
[illegible]	Athy, part of,	[illegible]	[illegible]	[illegible]	[illegible]	[illegible]	[illegible]	[illegible]
[illegible]	Carlow, do.	[illegible]	[illegible]	[illegible]	[illegible]	[illegible]	[illegible]	[illegible]
[illegible]	Mountmellick, part of,	[illegible]	[illegible]	[illegible]	122	[illegible]	[illegible]	[illegible]
[illegible]	Roscrea, do.	[illegible]	[illegible]	[illegible]	[illegible]	[illegible]	[illegible]	[illegible]
[illegible]	[illegible], do.	[illegible]	[illegible]	[illegible]		[illegible]	[illegible]	[illegible]
	Westmeath Co.							
[illegible]	Athlone, part of,	[illegible]	[illegible]	[illegible]	[illegible]	[illegible]	[illegible]	[illegible]
[illegible]	Ballymahon, do.	[illegible]	[illegible]	[illegible]	[illegible]	[illegible]	[illegible]	[illegible]
[illegible]	Delvin,	[illegible]	[illegible]	[illegible]	[illegible]	[illegible]	[illegible]	[illegible]
[illegible]	Granard, part of,	[illegible]	[illegible]	[illegible]	[illegible]	[illegible]	[illegible]	[illegible]
[illegible]	Mullingar,	[illegible]	[illegible]	[illegible]	[illegible]	[illegible]	[illegible]	[illegible]
[illegible]	Tullamore, part of,	[illegible]	[illegible]	[illegible]	[illegible]	[illegible]	[illegible]	[illegible]
	Wexford Co.							
[illegible]	Enniscorthy, part of,	[illegible]	[illegible]	[illegible]	[illegible]	[illegible]	[illegible]	[illegible]
[illegible]	Gorey,	[illegible]	[illegible]	[illegible]	[illegible]	[illegible]	[illegible]	[illegible]
[illegible]	New Ross, part of,	[illegible]	[illegible]	[illegible]	[illegible]	[illegible]	[illegible]	[illegible]
[illegible]	[illegible], do.	[illegible]	[illegible]	[illegible]	[illegible]	[illegible]	[illegible]	
[illegible]	Wexford,	[illegible]	[illegible]	[illegible]	[illegible]	[illegible]	[illegible]	[illegible]
	Wicklow Co.							
[illegible]	Baltinglass, part of,	[illegible]	[illegible]	[illegible]	[illegible]	[illegible]	[illegible]	[illegible]
[illegible]	Naas, do.	[illegible]	[illegible]	[illegible]	[illegible]	[illegible]	[illegible]	[illegible]
[illegible]	Rathdown, do.	[illegible]	[illegible]	[illegible]	[illegible]	[illegible]	[illegible]	[illegible]
[illegible]	Rathdrum,	[illegible]	[illegible]	[illegible]	[illegible]	[illegible]	[illegible]	[illegible]
[illegible]	Shillelagh, part of,	[illegible]	[illegible]	[illegible]	[illegible]	[illegible]	[illegible]	[illegible]

March 31st, June 30th, September 30th, and December 31st, 1896—*continued.*

LEINSTER—*continued.*

MALES. Registered in the Quarter ending the last day of March.	June.	Sept.	Dec.	Total.	FEMALES. Total.	Registered in the Quarter ending the last day of March.	June.	Sept.	Dec.	SUPERINTENDENT REGISTRARS' DISTRICTS.
										Queen's Co.
[illegible]	[illegible]	[illegible]	[illegible]	147	[illegible]	[illegible]	[illegible]	[illegible]	[illegible]	Abbeyleix.
10	[illegible]	11	[illegible]	[illegible]	47	[illegible]	[illegible]	[illegible]	11	Athy, part of.
[illegible]	[illegible]	[illegible]	14	[illegible]	[illegible]	[illegible]	[illegible]	[illegible]	[illegible]	Carlow, do.
[illegible]	[illegible]	[illegible]	[illegible]	[illegible]	[illegible]	[illegible]	[illegible]	44	[illegible]	Mountmellick, part of.
[illegible]	[illegible]	[illegible]	[illegible]	[illegible]	[illegible]	[illegible]	[illegible]	[illegible]	[illegible]	Roscrea, do.
-	1	-	-	1	4	-	-	-	4	Urlingford, do.
										Westmeath Co.
[illegible]	[illegible]	[illegible]	[illegible]	111	[illegible]	[illegible]	[illegible]	14	[illegible]	Athlone, part of.
[illegible]	[illegible]	[illegible]	4	[illegible]	[illegible]	[illegible]	[illegible]	[illegible]	[illegible]	Ballymahon do.
[illegible]	[illegible]	14	14	[illegible]	[illegible]	[illegible]	[illegible]	11	[illegible]	Delvin.
[illegible]	[illegible]	[illegible]	[illegible]	[illegible]	[illegible]	[illegible]	[illegible]	[illegible]	[illegible]	Granard, part of.
[illegible]	[illegible]	[illegible]	[illegible]	[illegible]	[illegible]	[illegible]	[illegible]	[illegible]	[illegible]	Mullingar.
[illegible]	[illegible]	4	11	[illegible]	[illegible]	[illegible]	[illegible]	[illegible]	[illegible]	Tullamore, part of.
										Wexford Co.
[illegible]	[illegible]	[illegible]	[illegible]	[illegible]	[illegible]	[illegible]	[illegible]	[illegible]	[illegible]	Enniscorthy, part of.
[illegible]	[illegible]	[illegible]	[illegible]	[illegible]	[illegible]	[illegible]	[illegible]	[illegible]	[illegible]	Gorey.
[illegible]	[illegible]	[illegible]	[illegible]	[illegible]	[illegible]	[illegible]	[illegible]	[illegible]	[illegible]	New Ross, part of.
-	-	-	-	-	4	1	1	[illegible]	-	Shillelagh, do.
[illegible]	[illegible]	[illegible]	[illegible]	[illegible]	[illegible]	[illegible]	[illegible]	[illegible]	[illegible]	Wexford.
										Wicklow Co.
[illegible]	[illegible]	[illegible]	[illegible]	[illegible]	[illegible]	[illegible]	[illegible]	[illegible]	[illegible]	Baltinglass, part of.
[illegible]	4	[illegible]	4	[illegible]	[illegible]	[illegible]	[illegible]	[illegible]	7	Naas, do.
[illegible]	[illegible]	[illegible]	[illegible]	[illegible]	[illegible]	[illegible]	[illegible]	[illegible]	[illegible]	Rathdown, do.
[illegible]	[illegible]	[illegible]	[illegible]	[illegible]	[illegible]	[illegible]	[illegible]	[illegible]	[illegible]	Rathdrum.
[illegible]	14	[illegible]	[illegible]	[illegible]	[illegible]	[illegible]	[illegible]	[illegible]	14	Shillelagh, part of.

MUNSTER.

MALES. March.	June.	Sept.	Dec.	Total.	FEMALES. Total.	March.	June.	Sept.	Dec.	SUPERINTENDENT REGISTRARS' DISTRICTS.
										Clare Co.
[illegible]	[illegible]	[illegible]	[illegible]	[illegible]	[illegible]	[illegible]	[illegible]	[illegible]	11	Ballyvaghan.
[illegible]	[illegible]	[illegible]	[illegible]	[illegible]	[illegible]	[illegible]	[illegible]	[illegible]	[illegible]	Corrofin.
[illegible]	[illegible]	[illegible]	[illegible]	[illegible]	[illegible]	[illegible]	[illegible]	[illegible]	[illegible]	Ennis.
[illegible]	[illegible]	[illegible]	[illegible]	[illegible]	[illegible]	[illegible]	[illegible]	[illegible]	[illegible]	Ennistymon.
[illegible]	[illegible]	[illegible]	[illegible]	[illegible]	[illegible]	[illegible]	[illegible]	[illegible]	[illegible]	Killadysert.
[illegible]	[illegible]	[illegible]	[illegible]	[illegible]	[illegible]	[illegible]	[illegible]	[illegible]	[illegible]	Kilrush.
[illegible]	[illegible]	[illegible]	[illegible]	[illegible]	[illegible]	[illegible]	[illegible]	[illegible]	[illegible]	Limerick, part of.
11	[illegible]	[illegible]	[illegible]	[illegible]	[illegible]	[illegible]	[illegible]	11	[illegible]	Scarriff, do.
[illegible]	[illegible]	[illegible]	[illegible]	[illegible]	74	[illegible]	[illegible]	14	[illegible]	Tulla.
										Cork Co.
[illegible]	[illegible]	[illegible]	[illegible]	[illegible]	[illegible]	[illegible]	[illegible]	[illegible]	[illegible]	Bandon.
[illegible]	[illegible]	[illegible]	[illegible]	[illegible]	[illegible]	[illegible]	[illegible]	17	[illegible]	Bantry.
[illegible]	[illegible]	[illegible]	[illegible]	[illegible]	[illegible]	[illegible]	[illegible]	[illegible]	[illegible]	Castletown.
[illegible]	[illegible]	[illegible]	[illegible]	[illegible]	[illegible]	[illegible]	[illegible]	[illegible]	[illegible]	Clonakilty.
[illegible]	[illegible]	[illegible]	[illegible]	[illegible]	[illegible]	[illegible]	[illegible]	[illegible]	[illegible]	Cork.
[illegible]	[illegible]	[illegible]	[illegible]	[illegible]	[illegible]	[illegible]	[illegible]	[illegible]	[illegible]	Dunmanway.
[illegible]	[illegible]	[illegible]	[illegible]	[illegible]	[illegible]	[illegible]	[illegible]	[illegible]	[illegible]	Fermoy.
[illegible]	[illegible]	[illegible]	[illegible]	[illegible]	[illegible]	[illegible]	[illegible]	[illegible]	[illegible]	Kanturk.
4	[illegible]	[illegible]	[illegible]	[illegible]	[illegible]	[illegible]	[illegible]	[illegible]	[illegible]	Kilmallock, part of.
[illegible]	[illegible]	[illegible]	[illegible]	[illegible]	[illegible]	[illegible]	[illegible]	[illegible]	[illegible]	Kinsale.
[illegible]	[illegible]	[illegible]	[illegible]	[illegible]	[illegible]	[illegible]	[illegible]	[illegible]	[illegible]	Macroom.
[illegible]	[illegible]	[illegible]	[illegible]	[illegible]	[illegible]	[illegible]	[illegible]	[illegible]	[illegible]	Mallow.

DEATHS registered in Ireland in the Four Quarters ending

II.—PROVINCE OF

No.	SUPERINTENDENT REGISTRAR'S DISTRICTS.	Area in Statute Acres.	Population in 1871.	MALES AND FEMALES. Total.	Quarters ending the last day of March.	June.	Sept.	Dec.
	Cork Co.—continued.							
[illegible]	Macroom,	[illegible]	[illegible]	[illegible]	[illegible]	[illegible]	[illegible]	[illegible]
[illegible]	Millstreet,	[illegible]	[illegible]	[illegible]	[illegible]	[illegible]	[illegible]	[illegible]
[illegible]	Mitchelstown, part of,	[illegible]	[illegible]	[illegible]	[illegible]	[illegible]	[illegible]	[illegible]
[illegible]	Skibbereen,	[illegible]	[illegible]	[illegible]	[illegible]	[illegible]	[illegible]	[illegible]
[illegible]	Skull,	[illegible]	[illegible]	[illegible]	[illegible]	[illegible]	[illegible]	[illegible]
[illegible]	Youghal, part of,	[illegible]	[illegible]	[illegible]	[illegible]	[illegible]	[illegible]	[illegible]
	Kerry Co.							
[illegible]	Cahersiveen,	[illegible]	[illegible]	[illegible]	[illegible]	[illegible]	[illegible]	[illegible]
[illegible]	Dingle,	[illegible]	[illegible]	[illegible]	[illegible]	[illegible]	[illegible]	[illegible]
[illegible]	Kenmare,	[illegible]	[illegible]	[illegible]	[illegible]	41	31	41
97	Killarney,	[illegible]	[illegible]	[illegible]	[illegible]	[illegible]	[illegible]	[illegible]
[illegible]	Listowel, part of,	[illegible]	[illegible]	477	[illegible]	[illegible]	115	[illegible]
[illegible]	Tralee,	[illegible]	[illegible]	[illegible]	[illegible]	[illegible]	[illegible]	[illegible]
	Limerick Co.							
[illegible]	Croom,	[illegible]	[illegible]	[illegible]	[illegible]	[illegible]	[illegible]	[illegible]
101	Kilmallock, part of	[illegible]	[illegible]	[illegible]	[illegible]	[illegible]	[illegible]	[illegible]
102	Limerick, do.	[illegible]	[illegible]	[illegible]	[illegible]	[illegible]	[illegible]	[illegible]
103	[illegible], do.	[illegible]	[illegible]	[illegible]	[illegible]	[illegible]	[illegible]	11
104	Mitchelstown, do.	[illegible]	[illegible]	[illegible]	[illegible]	[illegible]	11	11
105	Newcastle,	[illegible]	[illegible]	[illegible]	[illegible]	[illegible]	71	[illegible]
106	Rathkeale,	[illegible]	[illegible]	[illegible]	[illegible]	[illegible]	[illegible]	[illegible]
107	Tipperary, part of,	[illegible]	[illegible]	[illegible]	[illegible]	[illegible]	[illegible]	14
	Tipperary Co.							
[illegible]	Borrisokane,	[illegible]	[illegible]	[illegible]	[illegible]	[illegible]	[illegible]	[illegible]
[illegible]	Callan, part of,	[illegible]	[illegible]	[illegible]	[illegible]	[illegible]	[illegible]	[illegible]
170	Carrick-on-Suir, do.	[illegible]	[illegible]	[illegible]	[illegible]	[illegible]	[illegible]	[illegible]
171	Cashel,	[illegible]	[illegible]	[illegible]	[illegible]	[illegible]	[illegible]	[illegible]
172	Clogheen,	[illegible]	[illegible]	[illegible]	[illegible]	[illegible]	[illegible]	[illegible]
173	Clonmel, part of,	[illegible]	[illegible]	[illegible]	[illegible]	[illegible]	[illegible]	[illegible]
174	Nenagh,	[illegible]	[illegible]	[illegible]	[illegible]	[illegible]	[illegible]	[illegible]
175	Parsonstown, part of,	[illegible]	[illegible]	[illegible]	4	6	4	4
176	Roscrea, do.	[illegible]	[illegible]	[illegible]	[illegible]	[illegible]	[illegible]	[illegible]
177	Thurles,	[illegible]	[illegible]	[illegible]	[illegible]	[illegible]	[illegible]	[illegible]
178	Tipperary, part of,	[illegible]	[illegible]	[illegible]	111	[illegible]	[illegible]	[illegible]
179	Urlingford, do.	[illegible]	[illegible]	[illegible]	8	[illegible]	14	11
	Waterford Co.							
[illegible]	Carrick-on-Suir, part of,	[illegible]	[illegible]	[illegible]	[illegible]	14	[illegible]	[illegible]
[illegible]	Clonmel, do.	[illegible]	[illegible]	[illegible]	[illegible]	[illegible]	[illegible]	[illegible]
[illegible]	Dungarvan,	[illegible]	[illegible]	[illegible]	[illegible]	[illegible]	[illegible]	[illegible]
[illegible]	Kilmacthomas,	[illegible]	[illegible]	[illegible]	[illegible]	[illegible]	[illegible]	[illegible]
[illegible]	Lismore,	[illegible]	[illegible]	[illegible]	[illegible]	73	[illegible]	[illegible]
[illegible]	Waterford, part of,	[illegible]	[illegible]	[illegible]	[illegible]	[illegible]	[illegible]	144
[illegible]	Youghal, do.	[illegible]	[illegible]	73	17	[illegible]	[illegible]	[illegible]

March 31st, June 30th, September 30th, and December 31st, 1896—*continued.*

MUNSTER—*continued.*

MALES.					FEMALES.					SUPERINTENDENT REGISTRARS' DISTRICTS.
Registered in the Quarters ending the last day of				Total.	Total.	Registered in the Quarters ending the last day of				
March.	June.	Sept.	Dec.			March.	June.	Sept.	Dec.	
										Cork Co.—*continued.*
[illegible]	[illegible]	[illegible]	[illegible]	[illegible]	[illegible]	[illegible]	[illegible]	[illegible]	[illegible]	[illegible]
[illegible]	[illegible]	[illegible]	[illegible]	[illegible]	[illegible]	[illegible]	[illegible]	[illegible]	[illegible]	[illegible]
[illegible]	[illegible]	[illegible]	[illegible]	[illegible]	[illegible]	[illegible]	[illegible]	[illegible]	[illegible]	Mitchelstown, part of.
[illegible]	[illegible]	[illegible]	[illegible]	[illegible]	[illegible]	[illegible]	[illegible]	[illegible]	[illegible]	Skibbereen.
[illegible]	[illegible]	[illegible]	[illegible]	[illegible]	[illegible]	[illegible]	[illegible]	[illegible]	[illegible]	Skull.
[illegible]	[illegible]	[illegible]	[illegible]	[illegible]	[illegible]	[illegible]	[illegible]	[illegible]	[illegible]	Youghal, part of.
										Kerry Co.
[illegible]	[illegible]	[illegible]	[illegible]	[illegible]	[illegible]	[illegible]	[illegible]	[illegible]	[illegible]	Cahersiveen.
[illegible]	[illegible]	[illegible]	[illegible]	[illegible]	[illegible]	[illegible]	[illegible]	[illegible]	[illegible]	Dingle.
[illegible]	[illegible]	[illegible]	[illegible]	[illegible]	[illegible]	[illegible]	[illegible]	[illegible]	[illegible]	Kenmare.
[illegible]	[illegible]	[illegible]	[illegible]	[illegible]	[illegible]	[illegible]	[illegible]	[illegible]	[illegible]	Killarney.
[illegible]	[illegible]	[illegible]	[illegible]	[illegible]	[illegible]	[illegible]	[illegible]	[illegible]	[illegible]	Listowel, part of.
[illegible]	[illegible]	[illegible]	[illegible]	[illegible]	[illegible]	[illegible]	[illegible]	[illegible]	[illegible]	Tralee.
										Limerick Co.
[illegible]	[illegible]	[illegible]	[illegible]	[illegible]	[illegible]	[illegible]	[illegible]	[illegible]	[illegible]	Croom.
[illegible]	[illegible]	[illegible]	[illegible]	[illegible]	[illegible]	[illegible]	[illegible]	[illegible]	[illegible]	Kilmallock, part of.
[illegible]	[illegible]	[illegible]	[illegible]	[illegible]	[illegible]	[illegible]	[illegible]	[illegible]	[illegible]	Limerick, do.
[illegible]	[illegible]	[illegible]	[illegible]	[illegible]	[illegible]	[illegible]	[illegible]	[illegible]	[illegible]	Listowel, do.
[illegible]	[illegible]	[illegible]	[illegible]	[illegible]	[illegible]	[illegible]	[illegible]	[illegible]	[illegible]	Mitchelstown, do.
[illegible]	[illegible]	[illegible]	[illegible]	[illegible]	[illegible]	[illegible]	[illegible]	[illegible]	[illegible]	Newcastle.
[illegible]	[illegible]	[illegible]	[illegible]	[illegible]	[illegible]	[illegible]	[illegible]	[illegible]	[illegible]	Rathkeale.
[illegible]	[illegible]	[illegible]	[illegible]	[illegible]	[illegible]	[illegible]	[illegible]	[illegible]	[illegible]	Tipperary, part of.
										Tipperary Co.
[illegible]	[illegible]	[illegible]	[illegible]	[illegible]	[illegible]	[illegible]	[illegible]	[illegible]	[illegible]	Borrisokane.
[illegible]	[illegible]	[illegible]	[illegible]	[illegible]	[illegible]	[illegible]	[illegible]	[illegible]	[illegible]	Callan, part of.
[illegible]	[illegible]	[illegible]	[illegible]	[illegible]	[illegible]	[illegible]	[illegible]	[illegible]	[illegible]	Carrick-on-Suir, do.
[illegible]	[illegible]	[illegible]	[illegible]	[illegible]	[illegible]	[illegible]	[illegible]	[illegible]	[illegible]	Cashel.
[illegible]	[illegible]	[illegible]	[illegible]	[illegible]	[illegible]	[illegible]	[illegible]	[illegible]	[illegible]	Clogheen.
[illegible]	[illegible]	[illegible]	[illegible]	[illegible]	[illegible]	[illegible]	[illegible]	[illegible]	[illegible]	Clonmel, part of.
[illegible]	[illegible]	[illegible]	[illegible]	[illegible]	[illegible]	[illegible]	[illegible]	[illegible]	[illegible]	Nenagh.
[illegible]	[illegible]	[illegible]	[illegible]	[illegible]	[illegible]	[illegible]	[illegible]	[illegible]	[illegible]	Parsonstown, part of.
[illegible]	[illegible]	[illegible]	[illegible]	[illegible]	[illegible]	[illegible]	[illegible]	[illegible]	[illegible]	Roscrea, do.
[illegible]	[illegible]	[illegible]	[illegible]	[illegible]	[illegible]	[illegible]	[illegible]	[illegible]	[illegible]	Thurles.
[illegible]	[illegible]	[illegible]	[illegible]	[illegible]	[illegible]	[illegible]	[illegible]	[illegible]	[illegible]	Tipperary, part of.
[illegible]	[illegible]	[illegible]	[illegible]	[illegible]	[illegible]	[illegible]	[illegible]	[illegible]	[illegible]	Urlingford, do.
										Waterford Co.
[illegible]	[illegible]	[illegible]	[illegible]	[illegible]	[illegible]	[illegible]	[illegible]	[illegible]	[illegible]	Carrick-on-Suir, part of.
[illegible]	[illegible]	[illegible]	[illegible]	[illegible]	[illegible]	[illegible]	[illegible]	[illegible]	[illegible]	Clonmel, do.
[illegible]	[illegible]	[illegible]	[illegible]	[illegible]	[illegible]	[illegible]	[illegible]	[illegible]	[illegible]	Dungarvan.
[illegible]	[illegible]	[illegible]	[illegible]	[illegible]	[illegible]	[illegible]	[illegible]	[illegible]	[illegible]	Kilmacthomas.
[illegible]	[illegible]	[illegible]	[illegible]	[illegible]	[illegible]	[illegible]	[illegible]	[illegible]	[illegible]	Lismore.
[illegible]	[illegible]	[illegible]	[illegible]	[illegible]	[illegible]	[illegible]	[illegible]	[illegible]	[illegible]	Waterford, part of.
[illegible]	[illegible]	[illegible]	[illegible]	[illegible]	[illegible]	[illegible]	[illegible]	[illegible]	[illegible]	Youghal, do.

DEATHS registered in Ireland in the Four Quarters ending

III.—PROVINCE OF

No.	Superintendent Registrars' Districts.	Area in Statute Acres.	Population in [illegible].	Males and Females. Total.	Registered in the Quarter ending the last day of March.	June.	Sept.	Dec.
	Antrim Co.							
127	Antrim,	[illegible]	[illegible]	[illegible]	[illegible]	[illegible]	[illegible]	[illegible]
128	Ballycastle,	[illegible]	[illegible]	[illegible]	[illegible]	[illegible]	[illegible]	[illegible]
129	Ballymena,	[illegible]	[illegible]	[illegible]	[illegible]	[illegible]	[illegible]	[illegible]
130	Ballymoney, part of,	[illegible]	[illegible]	[illegible]	[illegible]	[illegible]	[illegible]	[illegible]
131	Belfast, do.	[illegible]	[illegible]	[illegible]	[illegible]	[illegible]	[illegible]	[illegible]
132	Coleraine, do.	[illegible]	[illegible]	[illegible]	[illegible]	17	[illegible]	[illegible]
133	Larne,	[illegible]	[illegible]	[illegible]	[illegible]	[illegible]	91	[illegible]
134	Lisburn, part of,	[illegible]	[illegible]	[illegible]	[illegible]	[illegible]	[illegible]	[illegible]
135	Lurgan, do.	[illegible]	[illegible]	79	[illegible]	[illegible]	[illegible]	[illegible]
	Armagh Co.							
136	Armagh, part of,	[illegible]	[illegible]	[illegible]	[illegible]	[illegible]	[illegible]	211
137	Banbridge, do.	[illegible]	[illegible]	[illegible]	[illegible]	[illegible]	23	[illegible]
138	Castleblayney, do.	[illegible]	[illegible]	[illegible]	44	44	70	[illegible]
139	Dundalk, do.	[illegible]	[illegible]	[illegible]	8	7	11	7
140	Lurgan, do.	[illegible]	[illegible]	[illegible]	[illegible]	[illegible]	[illegible]	[illegible]
141	Newry do.	[illegible]	[illegible]	[illegible]	[illegible]	[illegible]	[illegible]	[illegible]
	Cavan Co.							
142	Bailieborough,	[illegible]	[illegible]	[illegible]	[illegible]	[illegible]	[illegible]	[illegible]
143	Bawnboy, part of,	[illegible]	[illegible]	[illegible]	[illegible]	[illegible]	[illegible]	[illegible]
144	Cavan,	[illegible]	[illegible]	[illegible]	[illegible]	[illegible]	[illegible]	[illegible]
145	Cootehill, part of,	[illegible]	[illegible]	[illegible]	[illegible]	[illegible]	[illegible]	[illegible]
146	Enniskillen, do.	[illegible]	[illegible]	[illegible]	[illegible]	[illegible]	[illegible]	[illegible]
147	Granard, do.	[illegible]	[illegible]	[illegible]	[illegible]	14	[illegible]	[illegible]
148	Kells, do.	[illegible]	[illegible]	18	[illegible]	[illegible]	7	7
149	Oldcastle, do.	[illegible]	[illegible]	114	[illegible]	[illegible]	[illegible]	[illegible]
	Donegal Co.							
150	Ballyshannon, part of,	[illegible]	[illegible]	[illegible]	[illegible]	[illegible]	[illegible]	41
151	Donegal,	[illegible]	[illegible]	[illegible]	[illegible]	[illegible]	[illegible]	[illegible]
152	Dunfanaghy,	[illegible]	[illegible]	[illegible]	[illegible]	[illegible]	[illegible]	[illegible]
153	Glenties,	[illegible]	[illegible]	[illegible]	[illegible]	[illegible]	[illegible]	[illegible]
154	Inishowen,	[illegible]	[illegible]	[illegible]	[illegible]	[illegible]	[illegible]	[illegible]
155	Letterkenny,	[illegible]	[illegible]	[illegible]	[illegible]	[illegible]	[illegible]	[illegible]
156	Londonderry, part of,	[illegible]	[illegible]	[illegible]	[illegible]	[illegible]	[illegible]	[illegible]
157	Millford,	[illegible]	[illegible]	[illegible]	[illegible]	[illegible]	[illegible]	[illegible]
158	Strabane, part of,	[illegible]	[illegible]	[illegible]	[illegible]	[illegible]	[illegible]	[illegible]
159	Stranorlar,	[illegible]	[illegible]	[illegible]	[illegible]	[illegible]	[illegible]	[illegible]
	Down Co.							
160	Banbridge, part of,	[illegible]	[illegible]	[illegible]	[illegible]	[illegible]	[illegible]	171
161	Belfast, do.	[illegible]	[illegible]	[illegible]	[illegible]	[illegible]	[illegible]	[illegible]
162	Downpatrick,	[illegible]	[illegible]	[illegible]	[illegible]	[illegible]	[illegible]	[illegible]
163	Kilkeel,	[illegible]	[illegible]	[illegible]	[illegible]	71	[illegible]	[illegible]
164	Lisburn, part of,	[illegible]	[illegible]	[illegible]	[illegible]	[illegible]	[illegible]	[illegible]
165	Lurgan, do.	[illegible]	[illegible]	[illegible]	[illegible]	[illegible]	[illegible]	[illegible]
166	Newry, do.	[illegible]	[illegible]	[illegible]	[illegible]	[illegible]	[illegible]	[illegible]
167	Newtownards,	[illegible]	[illegible]	[illegible]	[illegible]	[illegible]	[illegible]	[illegible]
	Fermanagh Co.							
168	Ballyshannon, part of,	[illegible]	[illegible]	[illegible]	[illegible]	17	[illegible]	27
169	Clones, do.	[illegible]	[illegible]	[illegible]	[illegible]	[illegible]	[illegible]	[illegible]
170	Enniskillen, do.	[illegible]	[illegible]	[illegible]	[illegible]	[illegible]	114	[illegible]
171	Irvinestown, do.	[illegible]	[illegible]	[illegible]	[illegible]	[illegible]	[illegible]	[illegible]
172	Lisnaskea,	[illegible]	[illegible]	[illegible]	[illegible]	[illegible]	[illegible]	[illegible]

March 31st, June 30th, September 30th, and December 31st, 1896—*continued.*

ULSTER.

MALES. Registered in the Quarter ending the last day of — March.	June.	Sept.	Dec.	Total.	FEMALES. Total.	Registered in the Quarter ending the last day of — March.	June.	Sept.	Dec.	SUPERINTENDENT REGISTRARS' DISTRICTS.
										Antrim Co.
[illegible]	[illegible]	[illegible]	[illegible]	[illegible]	[illegible]	[illegible]	[illegible]	[illegible]	[illegible]	Antrim.
[illegible]	[illegible]	[illegible]	[illegible]	[illegible]	[illegible]	[illegible]	[illegible]	[illegible]	[illegible]	Ballycastle.
[illegible]	[illegible]	[illegible]	[illegible]	[illegible]	[illegible]	[illegible]	[illegible]	[illegible]	[illegible]	Ballymena.
[illegible]	[illegible]	[illegible]	[illegible]	[illegible]	[illegible]	[illegible]	[illegible]	[illegible]	[illegible]	Ballymoney, part of.
[illegible]	[illegible]	[illegible]	[illegible]	[illegible]	[illegible]	[illegible]	[illegible]	[illegible]	[illegible]	Belfast, do.
[illegible]	[illegible]	[illegible]	[illegible]	[illegible]	[illegible]	[illegible]	[illegible]	[illegible]	[illegible]	Coleraine, do.
[illegible]	[illegible]	[illegible]	[illegible]	[illegible]	[illegible]	[illegible]	[illegible]	[illegible]	[illegible]	Larne.
[illegible]	[illegible]	[illegible]	[illegible]	[illegible]	[illegible]	[illegible]	[illegible]	[illegible]	[illegible]	Lisburn, part of.
[illegible]	[illegible]	[illegible]	[illegible]	[illegible]	[illegible]	[illegible]	[illegible]	[illegible]	[illegible]	Lurgan, do.
										Armagh Co.
[illegible]	[illegible]	[illegible]	[illegible]	[illegible]	[illegible]	[illegible]	[illegible]	[illegible]	[illegible]	Armagh, part of.
[illegible]	[illegible]	[illegible]	[illegible]	[illegible]	[illegible]	[illegible]	[illegible]	[illegible]	[illegible]	Banbridge, do.
[illegible]	[illegible]	[illegible]	[illegible]	[illegible]	[illegible]	[illegible]	[illegible]	[illegible]	[illegible]	Castleblayney, do.
[illegible]	[illegible]	[illegible]	[illegible]	[illegible]	[illegible]	[illegible]	[illegible]	[illegible]	[illegible]	Dundalk, do.
[illegible]	[illegible]	[illegible]	[illegible]	[illegible]	[illegible]	[illegible]	[illegible]	[illegible]	[illegible]	Lurgan, do.
[illegible]	[illegible]	[illegible]	[illegible]	[illegible]	[illegible]	[illegible]	[illegible]	[illegible]	[illegible]	Newry, do.
										Cavan Co.
[illegible]	[illegible]	[illegible]	[illegible]	[illegible]	[illegible]	[illegible]	[illegible]	[illegible]	[illegible]	Bailieborough.
[illegible]	[illegible]	[illegible]	[illegible]	[illegible]	[illegible]	[illegible]	[illegible]	[illegible]	[illegible]	Belturbet, part of.
[illegible]	[illegible]	[illegible]	[illegible]	[illegible]	[illegible]	[illegible]	[illegible]	[illegible]	[illegible]	Cavan.
[illegible]	[illegible]	[illegible]	[illegible]	[illegible]	[illegible]	[illegible]	[illegible]	[illegible]	[illegible]	Cootehill, part of.
[illegible]	[illegible]	[illegible]	[illegible]	[illegible]	[illegible]	[illegible]	[illegible]	[illegible]	[illegible]	Enniskillen, do.
[illegible]	[illegible]	[illegible]	[illegible]	[illegible]	[illegible]	[illegible]	[illegible]	[illegible]	[illegible]	Kells, do.
[illegible]	[illegible]	[illegible]	[illegible]	[illegible]	[illegible]	[illegible]	[illegible]	[illegible]	[illegible]	[illegible], do.
[illegible]	[illegible]	[illegible]	[illegible]	[illegible]	[illegible]	[illegible]	[illegible]	[illegible]	[illegible]	[illegible], do.
										Donegal Co.
[illegible]	[illegible]	[illegible]	[illegible]	[illegible]	[illegible]	[illegible]	[illegible]	[illegible]	[illegible]	Ballyshannon, part of.
[illegible]	[illegible]	[illegible]	[illegible]	[illegible]	[illegible]	[illegible]	[illegible]	[illegible]	[illegible]	Donegal.
[illegible]	[illegible]	[illegible]	[illegible]	[illegible]	[illegible]	[illegible]	[illegible]	[illegible]	[illegible]	Dunfanaghy.
[illegible]	[illegible]	[illegible]	[illegible]	[illegible]	[illegible]	[illegible]	[illegible]	[illegible]	[illegible]	Glenties.
[illegible]	[illegible]	[illegible]	[illegible]	[illegible]	[illegible]	[illegible]	[illegible]	[illegible]	[illegible]	Inishowen.
[illegible]	[illegible]	[illegible]	[illegible]	[illegible]	[illegible]	[illegible]	[illegible]	[illegible]	[illegible]	Letterkenny.
[illegible]	[illegible]	[illegible]	[illegible]	[illegible]	[illegible]	[illegible]	[illegible]	[illegible]	[illegible]	Londonderry, part of.
[illegible]	[illegible]	[illegible]	[illegible]	[illegible]	[illegible]	[illegible]	[illegible]	[illegible]	[illegible]	Milford.
[illegible]	[illegible]	[illegible]	[illegible]	[illegible]	[illegible]	[illegible]	[illegible]	[illegible]	[illegible]	Strabane, part of.
[illegible]	[illegible]	[illegible]	[illegible]	[illegible]	[illegible]	[illegible]	[illegible]	[illegible]	[illegible]	Stranorlar.
										Down Co.
[illegible]	[illegible]	[illegible]	[illegible]	[illegible]	[illegible]	[illegible]	[illegible]	[illegible]	[illegible]	Banbridge, part of.
[illegible]	[illegible]	[illegible]	[illegible]	[illegible]	[illegible]	[illegible]	[illegible]	[illegible]	[illegible]	Belfast, do.
[illegible]	[illegible]	[illegible]	[illegible]	[illegible]	[illegible]	[illegible]	[illegible]	[illegible]	[illegible]	Downpatrick.
[illegible]	[illegible]	[illegible]	[illegible]	[illegible]	[illegible]	[illegible]	[illegible]	[illegible]	[illegible]	Kilkeel.
[illegible]	[illegible]	[illegible]	[illegible]	[illegible]	[illegible]	[illegible]	[illegible]	[illegible]	[illegible]	Lisburn, part of.
[illegible]	[illegible]	[illegible]	[illegible]	[illegible]	[illegible]	[illegible]	[illegible]	[illegible]	[illegible]	Lurgan, do.
[illegible]	[illegible]	[illegible]	[illegible]	[illegible]	[illegible]	[illegible]	[illegible]	[illegible]	[illegible]	Newry, do.
[illegible]	[illegible]	[illegible]	[illegible]	[illegible]	[illegible]	[illegible]	[illegible]	[illegible]	[illegible]	Newtownards.
										Fermanagh Co.
[illegible]	[illegible]	[illegible]	[illegible]	[illegible]	[illegible]	[illegible]	[illegible]	[illegible]	[illegible]	Ballyshannon, part of.
[illegible]	[illegible]	[illegible]	[illegible]	[illegible]	[illegible]	[illegible]	[illegible]	[illegible]	[illegible]	Clones, do.
[illegible]	[illegible]	[illegible]	[illegible]	[illegible]	[illegible]	[illegible]	[illegible]	[illegible]	[illegible]	Enniskillen, do.
[illegible]	[illegible]	[illegible]	[illegible]	[illegible]	[illegible]	[illegible]	[illegible]	[illegible]	[illegible]	Irvinestown, do.
[illegible]	[illegible]	[illegible]	[illegible]	[illegible]	[illegible]	[illegible]	[illegible]	[illegible]	[illegible]	Lisnaskea.

Registration of Marriages, Births, and Deaths, Ireland.

[illegible] registered in Ireland in the Four Quarters ending

[illegible]

SUPERINTENDENT REGISTRARS' DISTRICTS.	Area in Statute Acres.	Population in 1861.	Marriages Registered.				
			Total.	Registered in the Quarters ending on the last day of			
				March.	June.	Sept.	Dec.
Londonderry Co.							
[illegible], part of,	[illegible]	[illegible]	[illegible]	[illegible]	[illegible]	[illegible]	[illegible]
Coleraine, do.	[illegible]	[illegible]	[illegible]	[illegible]	[illegible]	[illegible]	[illegible]
Limavady,	[illegible]	[illegible]	[illegible]	[illegible]	[illegible]	[illegible]	[illegible]
Londonderry, part of,	[illegible]	[illegible]	[illegible]	[illegible]	[illegible]	[illegible]	[illegible]
Magherafelt,	[illegible]	[illegible]	[illegible]	[illegible]	[illegible]	[illegible]	[illegible]
Monaghan Co.							
Carrickmacross,	[illegible]	[illegible]	[illegible]	[illegible]	[illegible]	[illegible]	[illegible]
Castleblayney, part of,	[illegible]	[illegible]	[illegible]	[illegible]	[illegible]	[illegible]	[illegible]
Clones, do.	[illegible]	[illegible]	[illegible]	[illegible]	[illegible]	[illegible]	[illegible]
Cootehill, do.	[illegible]	[illegible]	[illegible]	[illegible]	[illegible]	[illegible]	[illegible]
Dundalk, do.	[illegible]	[illegible]	[illegible]	[illegible]	[illegible]	[illegible]	[illegible]
Enniskillen, do.	[illegible]	[illegible]	[illegible]	[illegible]	[illegible]	[illegible]	[illegible]
Monaghan,	[illegible]	[illegible]	[illegible]	[illegible]	[illegible]	[illegible]	[illegible]
Tyrone Co.							
Armagh, part of,	[illegible]	[illegible]	[illegible]	[illegible]	[illegible]	[illegible]	[illegible]
[illegible],	[illegible]	[illegible]	[illegible]	[illegible]	[illegible]	[illegible]	[illegible]
Clogher, part of,	[illegible]	[illegible]	[illegible]	[illegible]	[illegible]	[illegible]	[illegible]
Cookstown,	[illegible]	[illegible]	[illegible]	[illegible]	[illegible]	[illegible]	[illegible]
Dungannon,	[illegible]	[illegible]	[illegible]	[illegible]	[illegible]	[illegible]	[illegible]
Enniskillen, part of,	[illegible]	[illegible]	[illegible]	[illegible]	[illegible]	[illegible]	[illegible]
[illegible], do.	[illegible]	[illegible]	[illegible]	[illegible]	[illegible]	[illegible]	[illegible]
Omagh,	[illegible]	[illegible]	[illegible]	[illegible]	[illegible]	[illegible]	[illegible]
Strabane, part of,	[illegible]	[illegible]	[illegible]	[illegible]	[illegible]	[illegible]	[illegible]

March 31st, June 30th, September 30th, and December 31st, 1896—*continued.*

ULSTER—*continued.*

Males: Registered in the Quarter ending the last day of March	June	Sept.	Dec.	Total	Females: Total	Registered in the Quarter ending the last day of March	June	Sept.	Dec.	Superintendent Registrars' Districts
										Londonderry Co.
[illegible]	[illegible]	[illegible]	[illegible]	[illegible]	[illegible]	12	[illegible]	11	[illegible]	Ballymoney, part of.
[illegible]	[illegible]	[illegible]	[illegible]	[illegible]	[illegible]	[illegible]	[illegible]	[illegible]	[illegible]	Coleraine, do.
[illegible]	[illegible]	[illegible]	[illegible]	[illegible]	[illegible]	[illegible]	[illegible]	[illegible]	[illegible]	Limavady.
[illegible]	[illegible]	[illegible]	112	[illegible]	[illegible]	[illegible]	[illegible]	[illegible]	[illegible]	Londonderry, part of.
[illegible]	[illegible]	[illegible]	[illegible]	[illegible]	[illegible]	[illegible]	[illegible]	[illegible]	[illegible]	Magherafelt.
										Monaghan Co.
33	37	[illegible]	[illegible]	[illegible]	[illegible]	[illegible]	[illegible]	[illegible]	31	Castleblayney.
[illegible]	35	[illegible]	[illegible]	[illegible]	[illegible]	[illegible]	[illegible]	[illegible]	[illegible]	Carrickmacross, part of.
5	5	1	5	11	[illegible]	[illegible]	[illegible]	1	4	Clones, do.
19	15	[illegible]	[illegible]	[illegible]	[illegible]	[illegible]	16	[illegible]	17	Cavan, do.
[illegible]	[illegible]	11	[illegible]	[illegible]	[illegible]	[illegible]	14	11	[illegible]	Cootehill, do.
5	[illegible]	4	8	30	[illegible]	7	3	6	1	Dundalk, do.
[illegible]	[illegible]	[illegible]	[illegible]	[illegible]	[illegible]	[illegible]	[illegible]	[illegible]	[illegible]	Monaghan.
										Tyrone Co.
4	6	[illegible]	[illegible]	14	[illegible]	[illegible]	1	3	7	Antrim, part of.
[illegible]	[illegible]	[illegible]	[illegible]	[illegible]	[illegible]	[illegible]	[illegible]	16	[illegible]	Castlederg.
[illegible]	[illegible]	[illegible]	[illegible]	[illegible]	[illegible]	[illegible]	[illegible]	[illegible]	[illegible]	Clogher, part of.
[illegible]	[illegible]	[illegible]	[illegible]	[illegible]	[illegible]	[illegible]	[illegible]	[illegible]	[illegible]	Cookstown.
[illegible]	[illegible]	[illegible]	[illegible]	[illegible]	[illegible]	[illegible]	[illegible]	[illegible]	[illegible]	Dungannon.
[illegible]	[illegible]	[illegible]	[illegible]	16	[illegible]	[illegible]	1	[illegible]	–	Enniskillen, part of.
[illegible]	[illegible]	[illegible]	[illegible]	[illegible]	[illegible]	6	2	[illegible]	[illegible]	Letterkenny, do.
[illegible]	[illegible]	[illegible]	[illegible]	[illegible]	[illegible]	[illegible]	[illegible]	[illegible]	[illegible]	Omagh.
[illegible]	[illegible]	[illegible]	[illegible]	[illegible]	[illegible]	[illegible]	[illegible]	[illegible]	[illegible]	Strabane, part of.

OF CONNAUGHT.

Males: March	June	Sept.	Dec.	Total	Females: Total	March	June	Sept.	Dec.	Superintendent Registrars' Districts
										Galway Co.
[illegible]	[illegible]	[illegible]	[illegible]	[illegible]	[illegible]	[illegible]	[illegible]	[illegible]	[illegible]	Ballinasloe, part of.
[illegible]	[illegible]	[illegible]	[illegible]	17	[illegible]	8	7	7	3	Ballinrobe, do.
[illegible]	[illegible]	[illegible]	[illegible]	[illegible]	[illegible]	[illegible]	[illegible]	[illegible]	[illegible]	Clifden.
[illegible]	[illegible]	[illegible]	[illegible]	[illegible]	[illegible]	[illegible]	[illegible]	[illegible]	[illegible]	Galway.
[illegible]	[illegible]	[illegible]	[illegible]	[illegible]	[illegible]	[illegible]	[illegible]	[illegible]	[illegible]	Glenamaddy.
[illegible]	[illegible]	[illegible]	[illegible]	[illegible]	[illegible]	[illegible]	[illegible]	[illegible]	[illegible]	Gort.
[illegible]	[illegible]	[illegible]	[illegible]	[illegible]	[illegible]	[illegible]	[illegible]	[illegible]	[illegible]	Loughrea.
[illegible]	[illegible]	[illegible]	[illegible]	[illegible]	[illegible]	[illegible]	[illegible]	[illegible]	[illegible]	Mountbellew.
[illegible]	[illegible]	[illegible]	[illegible]	[illegible]	[illegible]	[illegible]	[illegible]	[illegible]	[illegible]	Oughterard.
[illegible]	[illegible]	[illegible]	[illegible]	[illegible]	[illegible]	[illegible]	[illegible]	[illegible]	[illegible]	Portumna.
[illegible]	[illegible]	[illegible]	[illegible]	[illegible]	[illegible]	[illegible]	[illegible]	[illegible]	1	Roscommon, part of.
[illegible]	[illegible]	[illegible]	[illegible]	[illegible]	7	[illegible]	1	1	[illegible]	Scarriff, do.
[illegible]	[illegible]	[illegible]	[illegible]	[illegible]	[illegible]	[illegible]	[illegible]	[illegible]	[illegible]	Tuam.
										Leitrim Co.
[illegible]	[illegible]	[illegible]	[illegible]	[illegible]	[illegible]	[illegible]	[illegible]	6	[illegible]	Ballyshannon, part of.
[illegible]	[illegible]	[illegible]	[illegible]	[illegible]	[illegible]	14	14	[illegible]	[illegible]	Bawnboy, do.
[illegible]	[illegible]	[illegible]	[illegible]	[illegible]	[illegible]	[illegible]	[illegible]	[illegible]	[illegible]	Carrick-on-Shannon, do.
[illegible]	[illegible]	[illegible]	[illegible]	[illegible]	[illegible]	[illegible]	[illegible]	[illegible]	[illegible]	Manorhamilton.
[illegible]	[illegible]	[illegible]	[illegible]	[illegible]	[illegible]	[illegible]	[illegible]	[illegible]	[illegible]	Mohill.

[illegible] registered in Ireland in the Four Quarters ending

[illegible]

No.	Superintendent Registrar's Districts.	Area in Statute Acres.	Population in 1861.	Males and Females. Total.	Registered in the Quarter ending the last day of March.	June.	Sept.	Dec.
	Mayo Co.							
[illegible]	Ballina, part of,	[illegible]	[illegible]	[illegible]	[illegible]	[illegible]	[illegible]	[illegible]
[illegible]	Ballinrobe, do.	[illegible]	[illegible]	[illegible]	[illegible]	[illegible]	[illegible]	[illegible]
[illegible]	Belmullet,	[illegible]	[illegible]	[illegible]	[illegible]	[illegible]	[illegible]	[illegible]
[illegible]	Castlebar,	[illegible]	[illegible]	[illegible]	[illegible]	[illegible]	[illegible]	[illegible]
[illegible]	[illegible], part of,	[illegible]	[illegible]	[illegible]	[illegible]	[illegible]	[illegible]	[illegible]
[illegible]	Claremorris,	[illegible]	[illegible]	[illegible]	[illegible]	[illegible]	[illegible]	[illegible]
[illegible]	Killala,	[illegible]	[illegible]	[illegible]	[illegible]	[illegible]	[illegible]	[illegible]
[illegible]	[illegible],	[illegible]	[illegible]	[illegible]	[illegible]	[illegible]	[illegible]	[illegible]
[illegible]	Westport,	[illegible]	[illegible]	[illegible]	[illegible]	[illegible]	[illegible]	[illegible]
	Roscommon Co.							
[illegible]	Athlone, part of,	[illegible]	[illegible]	[illegible]	[illegible]	[illegible]	[illegible]	[illegible]
[illegible]	Ballinasloe, do.	[illegible]	[illegible]	[illegible]	[illegible]	[illegible]	[illegible]	[illegible]
[illegible]	Boyle, do.	[illegible]	[illegible]	[illegible]	[illegible]	[illegible]	[illegible]	[illegible]
[illegible]	Carrick-on-Shannon, do.	[illegible]	[illegible]	[illegible]	[illegible]	[illegible]	[illegible]	[illegible]
[illegible]	Castlerea, do.	[illegible]	[illegible]	[illegible]	[illegible]	[illegible]	[illegible]	[illegible]
[illegible]	Roscommon, do.	[illegible]	[illegible]	[illegible]	[illegible]	[illegible]	[illegible]	[illegible]
[illegible]	Strokestown,	[illegible]	[illegible]	[illegible]	[illegible]	[illegible]	[illegible]	[illegible]
	Sligo Co.							
[illegible]	Ballina, part of,	[illegible]	[illegible]	17	[illegible]	3	3	3
[illegible]	Boyle, do.	[illegible]	[illegible]	[illegible]	[illegible]	[illegible]	[illegible]	[illegible]
[illegible]	Dromore West,	[illegible]	[illegible]	[illegible]	[illegible]	[illegible]	[illegible]	[illegible]
[illegible]	Sligo,	[illegible]	[illegible]	[illegible]	[illegible]	[illegible]	[illegible]	[illegible]
[illegible]	Tobercurry,	[illegible]	[illegible]	[illegible]	[illegible]	[illegible]	[illegible]	[illegible]

DEATHS Registered in Ireland in the Four Quarters ending March 31st, June 30th, September 30th, and December 31st, [illegible], in each Superintendent Registrar's District or Poor Law Union.

Number on Map of Union in preceding Abstracts.	Superintendent Registrar's Districts or Poor Law Unions.	Area in Statute Acres.	Population in 1861.	Males and Females. Total.	Registered in the Quarter ending the last day of March.	June.	Sept.	Dec.	Males. Registered in Qr. ending the last day of Mar.	June.	Sept.	Dec.	Total.	Females. Total.	Registered in Qr. ending the last day of Mar.	June.	Sept.	Dec.
[illegible]	Abbeyleix,	[illegible]	[illegible]	[illegible]	[illegible]	[illegible]	[illegible]	[illegible]	[illegible]	[illegible]	[illegible]	[illegible]	[illegible]	[illegible]	[illegible]	[illegible]	[illegible]	[illegible]
[illegible]	Antrim,	[illegible]	[illegible]	[illegible]	[illegible]	[illegible]	[illegible]	[illegible]	[illegible]	[illegible]	[illegible]	[illegible]	[illegible]	[illegible]	[illegible]	[illegible]	[illegible]	[illegible]
[illegible]	Ardee,	[illegible]	[illegible]	[illegible]	[illegible]	[illegible]	[illegible]	[illegible]	[illegible]	[illegible]	[illegible]	[illegible]	[illegible]	[illegible]	[illegible]	[illegible]	[illegible]	[illegible]
[illegible]	Armagh,	[illegible]	[illegible]	[illegible]	[illegible]	[illegible]	[illegible]	[illegible]	[illegible]	[illegible]	[illegible]	[illegible]	[illegible]	[illegible]	[illegible]	[illegible]	[illegible]	[illegible]
[illegible]	Athlone,	[illegible]	[illegible]	[illegible]	[illegible]	[illegible]	[illegible]	[illegible]	[illegible]	[illegible]	[illegible]	[illegible]	[illegible]	[illegible]	[illegible]	[illegible]	[illegible]	[illegible]
[illegible]	Athy,	[illegible]	[illegible]	[illegible]	[illegible]	[illegible]	[illegible]	[illegible]	[illegible]	[illegible]	[illegible]	[illegible]	[illegible]	[illegible]	[illegible]	[illegible]	[illegible]	[illegible]
[illegible]	[illegible]	[illegible]	[illegible]	[illegible]	[illegible]	[illegible]	[illegible]	[illegible]	[illegible]	[illegible]	[illegible]	[illegible]	[illegible]	[illegible]	[illegible]	[illegible]	[illegible]	[illegible]
[illegible]	[illegible]	[illegible]	[illegible]	[illegible]	[illegible]	[illegible]	[illegible]	[illegible]	[illegible]	[illegible]	[illegible]	[illegible]	[illegible]	[illegible]	[illegible]	[illegible]	[illegible]	[illegible]
[illegible]	[illegible]	[illegible]	[illegible]	[illegible]	[illegible]	[illegible]	[illegible]	[illegible]	[illegible]	[illegible]	[illegible]	[illegible]	[illegible]	[illegible]	[illegible]	[illegible]	[illegible]	[illegible]
[illegible]	[illegible]	[illegible]	[illegible]	[illegible]	[illegible]	[illegible]	[illegible]	[illegible]	[illegible]	[illegible]	[illegible]	[illegible]	[illegible]	[illegible]	[illegible]	[illegible]	[illegible]	[illegible]
[illegible]	[illegible]	[illegible]	[illegible]	[illegible]	[illegible]	[illegible]	[illegible]	[illegible]	[illegible]	[illegible]	[illegible]	[illegible]	[illegible]	[illegible]	[illegible]	[illegible]	[illegible]	[illegible]
[illegible]	[illegible]	[illegible]	[illegible]	[illegible]	[illegible]	[illegible]	[illegible]	[illegible]	[illegible]	[illegible]	[illegible]	[illegible]	[illegible]	[illegible]	[illegible]	[illegible]	[illegible]	[illegible]
[illegible]	[illegible]	[illegible]	[illegible]	[illegible]	[illegible]	[illegible]	[illegible]	[illegible]	[illegible]	[illegible]	[illegible]	[illegible]	[illegible]	[illegible]	[illegible]	[illegible]	[illegible]	[illegible]
[illegible]	[illegible]	[illegible]	[illegible]	[illegible]	[illegible]	[illegible]	[illegible]	[illegible]	[illegible]	[illegible]	[illegible]	[illegible]	[illegible]	[illegible]	[illegible]	[illegible]	[illegible]	[illegible]
[illegible]	[illegible]	[illegible]	[illegible]	[illegible]	[illegible]	[illegible]	[illegible]	[illegible]	[illegible]	[illegible]	[illegible]	[illegible]	[illegible]	[illegible]	[illegible]	[illegible]	[illegible]	[illegible]
[illegible]	[illegible]	[illegible]	[illegible]	[illegible]	[illegible]	[illegible]	[illegible]	[illegible]	[illegible]	[illegible]	[illegible]	[illegible]	[illegible]	[illegible]	[illegible]	[illegible]	[illegible]	[illegible]
[illegible]	[illegible]	[illegible]	[illegible]	[illegible]	[illegible]	[illegible]	[illegible]	[illegible]	[illegible]	[illegible]	[illegible]	[illegible]	[illegible]	[illegible]	[illegible]	[illegible]	[illegible]	[illegible]
[illegible]	[illegible]	[illegible]	[illegible]	[illegible]	[illegible]	[illegible]	[illegible]	[illegible]	[illegible]	[illegible]	[illegible]	[illegible]	[illegible]	[illegible]	[illegible]	[illegible]	[illegible]	[illegible]
[illegible]	[illegible]	[illegible]	[illegible]	[illegible]	[illegible]	[illegible]	[illegible]	[illegible]	[illegible]	[illegible]	[illegible]	[illegible]	[illegible]	[illegible]	[illegible]	[illegible]	[illegible]	[illegible]
[illegible]	[illegible]	[illegible]	[illegible]	[illegible]	[illegible]	[illegible]	[illegible]	[illegible]	[illegible]	[illegible]	[illegible]	[illegible]	[illegible]	[illegible]	[illegible]	[illegible]	[illegible]	[illegible]

March 31st, June 30th, September 30th, and December 31st, 1896—*continued.*

CONNAUGHT—*continued.*

MALES. Registered in the Quarter ending the last day of March	June	Sept.	Dec.	Total	FEMALES. Total	Registered in the Quarter ending the last day of March	June	Sept.	Dec.	SUPERINTENDENT REGISTRARS' DISTRICTS.
										Mayo Co.
[illegible]	[illegible]	[illegible]	[illegible]	[illegible]	[illegible]	[illegible]	[illegible]	[illegible]	16	Ballina, part of.
[illegible]	[illegible]	[illegible]	[illegible]	[illegible]	[illegible]	[illegible]	[illegible]	[illegible]	[illegible]	Ballinrobe, do.
[illegible]	[illegible]	[illegible]	[illegible]	[illegible]	[illegible]	[illegible]	[illegible]	[illegible]	[illegible]	Belmullet.
[illegible]	[illegible]	[illegible]	[illegible]	[illegible]	[illegible]	[illegible]	[illegible]	[illegible]	[illegible]	Castlebar.
[illegible]	[illegible]	[illegible]	[illegible]	[illegible]	[illegible]	[illegible]	[illegible]	[illegible]	[illegible]	Castlerea, part of.
[illegible]	[illegible]	[illegible]	[illegible]	[illegible]	[illegible]	[illegible]	[illegible]	[illegible]	[illegible]	Claremorris.
[illegible]	[illegible]	[illegible]	[illegible]	[illegible]	[illegible]	[illegible]	[illegible]	[illegible]	[illegible]	Killala.
[illegible]	[illegible]	[illegible]	[illegible]	[illegible]	[illegible]	[illegible]	[illegible]	[illegible]	[illegible]	Swinford.
[illegible]	[illegible]	[illegible]	[illegible]	[illegible]	[illegible]	[illegible]	[illegible]	[illegible]	[illegible]	Westport.
										Roscommon Co.
[illegible]	[illegible]	[illegible]	[illegible]	[illegible]	[illegible]	[illegible]	[illegible]	[illegible]	[illegible]	Athlone, part of.
[illegible]	[illegible]	[illegible]	[illegible]	[illegible]	[illegible]	[illegible]	[illegible]	[illegible]	[illegible]	Ballinasloe, do.
[illegible]	[illegible]	[illegible]	[illegible]	[illegible]	[illegible]	[illegible]	[illegible]	[illegible]	[illegible]	Boyle, do.
[illegible]	[illegible]	[illegible]	[illegible]	[illegible]	[illegible]	[illegible]	[illegible]	[illegible]	11	Carrick-on-Shannon, do.
[illegible]	[illegible]	[illegible]	[illegible]	[illegible]	[illegible]	[illegible]	[illegible]	[illegible]	41	Castlerea, do.
[illegible]	[illegible]	[illegible]	[illegible]	[illegible]	[illegible]	[illegible]	[illegible]	[illegible]	[illegible]	Roscommon, do.
[illegible]	[illegible]	[illegible]	[illegible]	[illegible]	[illegible]	[illegible]	[illegible]	[illegible]	[illegible]	Strokestown.
										Sligo Co.
1	[illegible]	[illegible]	[illegible]	[illegible]	[illegible]	[illegible]	[illegible]	[illegible]	[illegible]	Ballina, part of.
[illegible]	[illegible]	[illegible]	[illegible]	[illegible]	[illegible]	[illegible]	[illegible]	[illegible]	[illegible]	Boyle, do.
[illegible]	[illegible]	[illegible]	[illegible]	[illegible]	[illegible]	[illegible]	[illegible]	[illegible]	[illegible]	Dromore West.
[illegible]	[illegible]	[illegible]	71	[illegible]	[illegible]	[illegible]	[illegible]	[illegible]	[illegible]	Sligo.
[illegible]	[illegible]	[illegible]	[illegible]	[illegible]	[illegible]	[illegible]	[illegible]	[illegible]	[illegible]	Tobercurry.

DEATHS Registered in Ireland in the Four Quarters ending March 31st, June 30th, September 30th, and December 31st, 1896, in each SUPERINTENDENT REGISTRAR'S DISTRICT or POOR LAW UNION—*continued.*

Number or Numbers of Union in preceding Abstracts.	SUPERINTENDENT REGISTRARS' DISTRICTS or POOR LAW UNIONS.	AREA in Statute Acres.	Population in 1891.	MALES AND FEMALES. Total	Registered in the Quarter ending the last day of Mar.	June.	Sept.	Dec.	MALES. Registered in the Quarter ending the last day of Mar.	June.	Sept.	Dec.	Total	FEMALES. Total	Registered in the Quarter ending the last day of Mar.	June.	Sept.	Dec.
77	Bantry, . .	[illegible]	[illegible]	[illegible]	[illegible]	[illegible]	[illegible]	[illegible]	[illegible]	[illegible]	[illegible]	[illegible]	[illegible]	[illegible]	[illegible]	[illegible]	[illegible]	[illegible]
[illegible]	Bawnboy, . .	[illegible]	[illegible]	[illegible]	[illegible]	[illegible]	[illegible]	[illegible]	[illegible]	[illegible]	[illegible]	[illegible]	[illegible]	[illegible]	[illegible]	[illegible]	[illegible]	[illegible]
[illegible]	Belfast, . .	[illegible]	[illegible]	[illegible]	[illegible]	[illegible]	[illegible]	[illegible]	[illegible]	[illegible]	[illegible]	[illegible]	[illegible]	[illegible]	[illegible]	[illegible]	[illegible]	[illegible]
[illegible]	Belmullet, . .	[illegible]	[illegible]	[illegible]	[illegible]	[illegible]	[illegible]	[illegible]	[illegible]	[illegible]	[illegible]	[illegible]	[illegible]	[illegible]	[illegible]	[illegible]	[illegible]	[illegible]
[illegible]	Borrisokane, .	[illegible]	[illegible]	[illegible]	[illegible]	[illegible]	[illegible]	[illegible]	[illegible]	[illegible]	[illegible]	[illegible]	[illegible]	[illegible]	[illegible]	[illegible]	[illegible]	[illegible]
[illegible]	Boyle, . .	[illegible]	[illegible]	[illegible]	[illegible]	[illegible]	[illegible]	[illegible]	[illegible]	[illegible]	[illegible]	[illegible]	[illegible]	[illegible]	[illegible]	[illegible]	[illegible]	[illegible]
[illegible]	Caherciveen, .	[illegible]	[illegible]	[illegible]	[illegible]	[illegible]	[illegible]	[illegible]	[illegible]	[illegible]	[illegible]	[illegible]	[illegible]	[illegible]	[illegible]	[illegible]	[illegible]	[illegible]
[illegible]	Callan, . .	[illegible]	[illegible]	[illegible]	[illegible]	[illegible]	[illegible]	[illegible]	[illegible]	[illegible]	[illegible]	[illegible]	[illegible]	[illegible]	[illegible]	[illegible]	[illegible]	[illegible]
[illegible]	Carlow, . .	[illegible]	[illegible]	[illegible]	[illegible]	[illegible]	[illegible]	[illegible]	[illegible]	[illegible]	[illegible]	[illegible]	[illegible]	[illegible]	[illegible]	[illegible]	[illegible]	[illegible]
[illegible]	Carrickmacross, .	[illegible]	[illegible]	[illegible]	[illegible]	[illegible]	[illegible]	[illegible]	[illegible]	[illegible]	[illegible]	[illegible]	[illegible]	[illegible]	[illegible]	[illegible]	[illegible]	[illegible]
[illegible]	Carrick-on-Shannon,	[illegible]	[illegible]	[illegible]	[illegible]	[illegible]	[illegible]	[illegible]	[illegible]	[illegible]	[illegible]	[illegible]	[illegible]	[illegible]	[illegible]	[illegible]	[illegible]	[illegible]
[illegible]	Carrick-on-Suir, .	[illegible]	[illegible]	[illegible]	[illegible]	[illegible]	[illegible]	[illegible]	[illegible]	[illegible]	[illegible]	[illegible]	[illegible]	[illegible]	[illegible]	[illegible]	[illegible]	[illegible]
[illegible]	Cashel, . .	[illegible]	[illegible]	[illegible]	[illegible]	[illegible]	[illegible]	[illegible]	[illegible]	[illegible]	[illegible]	[illegible]	[illegible]	[illegible]	[illegible]	[illegible]	[illegible]	[illegible]
[illegible]	Castlebar, . .	[illegible]	[illegible]	[illegible]	[illegible]	[illegible]	[illegible]	[illegible]	[illegible]	[illegible]	[illegible]	[illegible]	[illegible]	[illegible]	[illegible]	[illegible]	[illegible]	[illegible]
[illegible]	Castleblayney, .	[illegible]	[illegible]	[illegible]	[illegible]	[illegible]	[illegible]	[illegible]	[illegible]	[illegible]	[illegible]	[illegible]	[illegible]	[illegible]	[illegible]	[illegible]	[illegible]	[illegible]
[illegible]	Castlecomer, .	[illegible]	[illegible]	[illegible]	[illegible]	[illegible]	[illegible]	[illegible]	[illegible]	[illegible]	[illegible]	[illegible]	[illegible]	[illegible]	[illegible]	[illegible]	[illegible]	[illegible]
[illegible]	Castlederg, . .	[illegible]	[illegible]	[illegible]	[illegible]	[illegible]	[illegible]	[illegible]	[illegible]	[illegible]	[illegible]	[illegible]	[illegible]	[illegible]	[illegible]	[illegible]	[illegible]	[illegible]
[illegible]	Castlereagh, . .	[illegible]	[illegible]	[illegible]	[illegible]	[illegible]	[illegible]	[illegible]	[illegible]	[illegible]	[illegible]	[illegible]	[illegible]	[illegible]	[illegible]	[illegible]	[illegible]	[illegible]
[illegible]	Castletown, . .	[illegible]	[illegible]	[illegible]	[illegible]	[illegible]	[illegible]	[illegible]	[illegible]	[illegible]	[illegible]	[illegible]	[illegible]	[illegible]	[illegible]	[illegible]	[illegible]	[illegible]
[illegible]	Cavan, . .	[illegible]	[illegible]	[illegible]	[illegible]	[illegible]	[illegible]	[illegible]	[illegible]	[illegible]	[illegible]	[illegible]	[illegible]	[illegible]	[illegible]	[illegible]	[illegible]	[illegible]

DEATHS Registered in Ireland in the Four Quarters ending March 31st, June 30th, September 30th, and December 31st, 1866, in each Superintendent Registrar's District or Poor Law Union—*continued*.

Numbers of Dispensary Districts	Superintendent Registrars' Districts or Poor Law Unions	Area in Statute Acres	Population in 1861	Males and Females: Total	Registered in the Quarters ending the last day of: Mar.	June	Sept.	Dec.	Males: Registered in the Quarters ending the last day of: Mar.	June	Sept.	Dec.	Total	Females: Total	Registered in the Quarters ending the last day of: Mar.	June	Sept.	Dec.
[illegible]	[illegible]	[illegible]	[illegible]	[illegible]	[illegible]	[illegible]	[illegible]	[illegible]	[illegible]	[illegible]	[illegible]	[illegible]	[illegible]	[illegible]	[illegible]	[illegible]	[illegible]	[illegible]
[illegible]	[illegible]	[illegible]	[illegible]	[illegible]	[illegible]	[illegible]	[illegible]	[illegible]	[illegible]	[illegible]	[illegible]	[illegible]	[illegible]	[illegible]	[illegible]	[illegible]	[illegible]	[illegible]
[illegible]	[illegible]	[illegible]	[illegible]	[illegible]	[illegible]	[illegible]	[illegible]	[illegible]	[illegible]	[illegible]	[illegible]	[illegible]	[illegible]	[illegible]	[illegible]	[illegible]	[illegible]	[illegible]
[illegible]	[illegible]	[illegible]	[illegible]	[illegible]	[illegible]	[illegible]	[illegible]	[illegible]	[illegible]	[illegible]	[illegible]	[illegible]	[illegible]	[illegible]	[illegible]	[illegible]	[illegible]	[illegible]
[illegible]	[illegible]	[illegible]	[illegible]	[illegible]	[illegible]	[illegible]	[illegible]	[illegible]	[illegible]	[illegible]	[illegible]	[illegible]	[illegible]	[illegible]	[illegible]	[illegible]	[illegible]	[illegible]
[illegible]	[illegible]	[illegible]	[illegible]	[illegible]	[illegible]	[illegible]	[illegible]	[illegible]	[illegible]	[illegible]	[illegible]	[illegible]	[illegible]	[illegible]	[illegible]	[illegible]	[illegible]	[illegible]
[illegible]	[illegible]	[illegible]	[illegible]	[illegible]	[illegible]	[illegible]	[illegible]	[illegible]	[illegible]	[illegible]	[illegible]	[illegible]	[illegible]	[illegible]	[illegible]	[illegible]	[illegible]	[illegible]
[illegible]	[illegible]	[illegible]	[illegible]	[illegible]	[illegible]	[illegible]	[illegible]	[illegible]	[illegible]	[illegible]	[illegible]	[illegible]	[illegible]	[illegible]	[illegible]	[illegible]	[illegible]	[illegible]
[illegible]	[illegible]	[illegible]	[illegible]	[illegible]	[illegible]	[illegible]	[illegible]	[illegible]	[illegible]	[illegible]	[illegible]	[illegible]	[illegible]	[illegible]	[illegible]	[illegible]	[illegible]	[illegible]
[illegible]	[illegible]	[illegible]	[illegible]	[illegible]	[illegible]	[illegible]	[illegible]	[illegible]	[illegible]	[illegible]	[illegible]	[illegible]	[illegible]	[illegible]	[illegible]	[illegible]	[illegible]	[illegible]

DEATHS Registered in Ireland in the Four Quarters ending March 31st, June 30th, September 30th, and December 31st, 1896, in each SUPERINTENDENT REGISTRAR'S DISTRICT or POOR LAW UNION—*continued.*

Number or Numbers of Unions in preceding Accounts.	Superintendent Registrars' Districts or Poor Law Unions.	Area in Statute Acres.	Population in 1891.	Males and Females: Total.	Males and Females: Registered in the Quarter ending the last day of Mar.	June.	Sept.	Dec.	Males: Registered in the Quarter ending the last day of Mar.	June.	Sept.	Dec.	Males: Total.	Females: Total.	Females: Registered in the Quarter ending the last day of Mar.	June.	Sept.	Dec.
[illegible]	Limerick,	[illegible]	[illegible]	[illegible]	[illegible]	[illegible]	[illegible]	[illegible]	[illegible]	[illegible]	[illegible]	[illegible]	[illegible]	[illegible]	[illegible]	[illegible]	[illegible]	[illegible]
[illegible]	Lisburn,	[illegible]	[illegible]	[illegible]	[illegible]	[illegible]	[illegible]	[illegible]	[illegible]	[illegible]	[illegible]	[illegible]	[illegible]	[illegible]	[illegible]	[illegible]	[illegible]	[illegible]
[illegible]	Lismore,	[illegible]	[illegible]	[illegible]	[illegible]	[illegible]	[illegible]	[illegible]	[illegible]	[illegible]	[illegible]	[illegible]	[illegible]	[illegible]	[illegible]	[illegible]	[illegible]	[illegible]
[illegible]	Lisnaskea,	[illegible]	[illegible]	[illegible]	[illegible]	[illegible]	[illegible]	[illegible]	[illegible]	[illegible]	[illegible]	[illegible]	[illegible]	[illegible]	[illegible]	[illegible]	[illegible]	[illegible]
[illegible]	Listowel,	[illegible]	[illegible]	[illegible]	[illegible]	[illegible]	[illegible]	[illegible]	[illegible]	[illegible]	[illegible]	[illegible]	[illegible]	[illegible]	[illegible]	[illegible]	[illegible]	[illegible]
[illegible]	Londonderry,	[illegible]	[illegible]	[illegible]	[illegible]	[illegible]	[illegible]	[illegible]	[illegible]	[illegible]	[illegible]	[illegible]	[illegible]	[illegible]	[illegible]	[illegible]	[illegible]	[illegible]
[illegible]	Longford,	[illegible]	[illegible]	[illegible]	[illegible]	[illegible]	[illegible]	[illegible]	[illegible]	[illegible]	[illegible]	[illegible]	[illegible]	[illegible]	[illegible]	[illegible]	[illegible]	[illegible]
[illegible]	Loughrea,	[illegible]	[illegible]	[illegible]	[illegible]	[illegible]	[illegible]	[illegible]	[illegible]	[illegible]	[illegible]	[illegible]	[illegible]	[illegible]	[illegible]	[illegible]	[illegible]	[illegible]
[illegible]	Lurgan,	[illegible]	[illegible]	[illegible]	[illegible]	[illegible]	[illegible]	[illegible]	[illegible]	[illegible]	[illegible]	[illegible]	[illegible]	[illegible]	[illegible]	[illegible]	[illegible]	[illegible]
[illegible]	Macroom,	[illegible]	[illegible]	[illegible]	[illegible]	[illegible]	[illegible]	[illegible]	[illegible]	[illegible]	[illegible]	[illegible]	[illegible]	[illegible]	[illegible]	[illegible]	[illegible]	[illegible]
[illegible]	Magherafelt,	[illegible]	[illegible]	[illegible]	[illegible]	[illegible]	[illegible]	[illegible]	[illegible]	[illegible]	[illegible]	[illegible]	[illegible]	[illegible]	[illegible]	[illegible]	[illegible]	[illegible]
[illegible]	Mallow,	[illegible]	[illegible]	[illegible]	[illegible]	[illegible]	[illegible]	[illegible]	[illegible]	[illegible]	[illegible]	[illegible]	[illegible]	[illegible]	[illegible]	[illegible]	[illegible]	[illegible]
[illegible]	Manorhamilton,	[illegible]	[illegible]	[illegible]	[illegible]	[illegible]	[illegible]	[illegible]	[illegible]	[illegible]	[illegible]	[illegible]	[illegible]	[illegible]	[illegible]	[illegible]	[illegible]	[illegible]
[illegible]	Midleton,	[illegible]	[illegible]	[illegible]	[illegible]	[illegible]	[illegible]	[illegible]	[illegible]	[illegible]	[illegible]	[illegible]	[illegible]	[illegible]	[illegible]	[illegible]	[illegible]	[illegible]
[illegible]	Milford,	[illegible]	[illegible]	[illegible]	[illegible]	[illegible]	[illegible]	[illegible]	[illegible]	[illegible]	[illegible]	[illegible]	[illegible]	[illegible]	[illegible]	[illegible]	[illegible]	[illegible]
[illegible]	Millstreet,	[illegible]	[illegible]	[illegible]	[illegible]	[illegible]	[illegible]	[illegible]	[illegible]	[illegible]	[illegible]	[illegible]	[illegible]	[illegible]	[illegible]	[illegible]	[illegible]	[illegible]
[illegible]	Mitchelstown,	[illegible]	[illegible]	[illegible]	[illegible]	[illegible]	[illegible]	[illegible]	[illegible]	[illegible]	[illegible]	[illegible]	[illegible]	[illegible]	[illegible]	[illegible]	[illegible]	[illegible]
[illegible]	Mohill,	[illegible]	[illegible]	[illegible]	[illegible]	[illegible]	[illegible]	[illegible]	[illegible]	[illegible]	[illegible]	[illegible]	[illegible]	[illegible]	[illegible]	[illegible]	[illegible]	[illegible]
[illegible]	Monaghan,	[illegible]	[illegible]	[illegible]	[illegible]	[illegible]	[illegible]	[illegible]	[illegible]	[illegible]	[illegible]	[illegible]	[illegible]	[illegible]	[illegible]	[illegible]	[illegible]	[illegible]
[illegible]	Mountbellew,	[illegible]	[illegible]	[illegible]	[illegible]	[illegible]	[illegible]	[illegible]	[illegible]	[illegible]	[illegible]	[illegible]	[illegible]	[illegible]	[illegible]	[illegible]	[illegible]	[illegible]
[illegible]	Mountmellick,	[illegible]	[illegible]	[illegible]	[illegible]	[illegible]	[illegible]	[illegible]	[illegible]	[illegible]	[illegible]	[illegible]	[illegible]	[illegible]	[illegible]	[illegible]	[illegible]	[illegible]
[illegible]	Mullingar,	[illegible]	[illegible]	[illegible]	[illegible]	[illegible]	[illegible]	[illegible]	[illegible]	[illegible]	[illegible]	[illegible]	[illegible]	[illegible]	[illegible]	[illegible]	[illegible]	[illegible]
[illegible]	Naas,	[illegible]	[illegible]	[illegible]	[illegible]	[illegible]	[illegible]	[illegible]	[illegible]	[illegible]	[illegible]	[illegible]	[illegible]	[illegible]	[illegible]	[illegible]	[illegible]	[illegible]
[illegible]	Navan,	[illegible]	[illegible]	[illegible]	[illegible]	[illegible]	[illegible]	[illegible]	[illegible]	[illegible]	[illegible]	[illegible]	[illegible]	[illegible]	[illegible]	[illegible]	[illegible]	[illegible]
[illegible]	Nenagh,	[illegible]	[illegible]	[illegible]	[illegible]	[illegible]	[illegible]	[illegible]	[illegible]	[illegible]	[illegible]	[illegible]	[illegible]	[illegible]	[illegible]	[illegible]	[illegible]	[illegible]
[illegible]	Newcastle,	[illegible]	[illegible]	[illegible]	[illegible]	[illegible]	[illegible]	[illegible]	[illegible]	[illegible]	[illegible]	[illegible]	[illegible]	[illegible]	[illegible]	[illegible]	[illegible]	[illegible]
[illegible]	New Ross,	[illegible]	[illegible]	[illegible]	[illegible]	[illegible]	[illegible]	[illegible]	[illegible]	[illegible]	[illegible]	[illegible]	[illegible]	[illegible]	[illegible]	[illegible]	[illegible]	[illegible]
[illegible]	Newry,	[illegible]	[illegible]	[illegible]	[illegible]	[illegible]	[illegible]	[illegible]	[illegible]	[illegible]	[illegible]	[illegible]	[illegible]	[illegible]	[illegible]	[illegible]	[illegible]	[illegible]
[illegible]	Newtownards,	[illegible]	[illegible]	[illegible]	[illegible]	[illegible]	[illegible]	[illegible]	[illegible]	[illegible]	[illegible]	[illegible]	[illegible]	[illegible]	[illegible]	[illegible]	[illegible]	[illegible]
[illegible]	Oldcastle,	[illegible]	[illegible]	[illegible]	[illegible]	[illegible]	[illegible]	[illegible]	[illegible]	[illegible]	[illegible]	[illegible]	[illegible]	[illegible]	[illegible]	[illegible]	[illegible]	[illegible]
[illegible]	Omagh,	[illegible]	[illegible]	[illegible]	[illegible]	[illegible]	[illegible]	[illegible]	[illegible]	[illegible]	[illegible]	[illegible]	[illegible]	[illegible]	[illegible]	[illegible]	[illegible]	[illegible]
[illegible]	Oughterard,	[illegible]	[illegible]	[illegible]	[illegible]	[illegible]	[illegible]	[illegible]	[illegible]	[illegible]	[illegible]	[illegible]	[illegible]	[illegible]	[illegible]	[illegible]	[illegible]	[illegible]
[illegible]	Parsonstown,	[illegible]	[illegible]	[illegible]	[illegible]	[illegible]	[illegible]	[illegible]	[illegible]	[illegible]	[illegible]	[illegible]	[illegible]	[illegible]	[illegible]	[illegible]	[illegible]	[illegible]
[illegible]	Portumna,	[illegible]	[illegible]	[illegible]	[illegible]	[illegible]	[illegible]	[illegible]	[illegible]	[illegible]	[illegible]	[illegible]	[illegible]	[illegible]	[illegible]	[illegible]	[illegible]	[illegible]
[illegible]	Rathdown,	[illegible]	[illegible]	[illegible]	[illegible]	[illegible]	[illegible]	[illegible]	[illegible]	[illegible]	[illegible]	[illegible]	[illegible]	[illegible]	[illegible]	[illegible]	[illegible]	[illegible]
[illegible]	Rathdrum,	[illegible]	[illegible]	[illegible]	[illegible]	[illegible]	[illegible]	[illegible]	[illegible]	[illegible]	[illegible]	[illegible]	[illegible]	[illegible]	[illegible]	[illegible]	[illegible]	[illegible]
[illegible]	Rathkeale,	[illegible]	[illegible]	[illegible]	[illegible]	[illegible]	[illegible]	[illegible]	[illegible]	[illegible]	[illegible]	[illegible]	[illegible]	[illegible]	[illegible]	[illegible]	[illegible]	[illegible]
[illegible]	Roscommon,	[illegible]	[illegible]	[illegible]	[illegible]	[illegible]	[illegible]	[illegible]	[illegible]	[illegible]	[illegible]	[illegible]	[illegible]	[illegible]	[illegible]	[illegible]	[illegible]	[illegible]
[illegible]	Roscrea,	[illegible]	[illegible]	[illegible]	[illegible]	[illegible]	[illegible]	[illegible]	[illegible]	[illegible]	[illegible]	[illegible]	[illegible]	[illegible]	[illegible]	[illegible]	[illegible]	[illegible]
[illegible]	Scarriff,	[illegible]	[illegible]	[illegible]	[illegible]	[illegible]	[illegible]	[illegible]	[illegible]	[illegible]	[illegible]	[illegible]	[illegible]	[illegible]	[illegible]	[illegible]	[illegible]	[illegible]
[illegible]	Shillelagh,	[illegible]	[illegible]	[illegible]	[illegible]	[illegible]	[illegible]	[illegible]	[illegible]	[illegible]	[illegible]	[illegible]	[illegible]	[illegible]	[illegible]	[illegible]	[illegible]	[illegible]
[illegible]	Skibbereen,	[illegible]	[illegible]	[illegible]	[illegible]	[illegible]	[illegible]	[illegible]	[illegible]	[illegible]	[illegible]	[illegible]	[illegible]	[illegible]	[illegible]	[illegible]	[illegible]	[illegible]
[illegible]	Skull,	[illegible]	[illegible]	[illegible]	[illegible]	[illegible]	[illegible]	[illegible]	[illegible]	[illegible]	[illegible]	[illegible]	[illegible]	[illegible]	[illegible]	[illegible]	[illegible]	[illegible]
[illegible]	Sligo,	[illegible]	[illegible]	[illegible]	[illegible]	[illegible]	[illegible]	[illegible]	[illegible]	[illegible]	[illegible]	[illegible]	[illegible]	[illegible]	[illegible]	[illegible]	[illegible]	[illegible]
[illegible]	Strabane,	[illegible]	[illegible]	[illegible]	[illegible]	[illegible]	[illegible]	[illegible]	[illegible]	[illegible]	[illegible]	[illegible]	[illegible]	[illegible]	[illegible]	[illegible]	[illegible]	[illegible]
[illegible]	Stranorlar,	[illegible]	[illegible]	[illegible]	[illegible]	[illegible]	[illegible]	[illegible]	[illegible]	[illegible]	[illegible]	[illegible]	[illegible]	[illegible]	[illegible]	[illegible]	[illegible]	[illegible]
[illegible]	Strokestown,	[illegible]	[illegible]	[illegible]	[illegible]	[illegible]	[illegible]	[illegible]	[illegible]	[illegible]	[illegible]	[illegible]	[illegible]	[illegible]	[illegible]	[illegible]	[illegible]	[illegible]
[illegible]	Swineford,	[illegible]	[illegible]	[illegible]	[illegible]	[illegible]	[illegible]	[illegible]	[illegible]	[illegible]	[illegible]	[illegible]	[illegible]	[illegible]	[illegible]	[illegible]	[illegible]	[illegible]
[illegible]	Thomastown,	[illegible]	[illegible]	[illegible]	[illegible]	[illegible]	[illegible]	[illegible]	[illegible]	[illegible]	[illegible]	[illegible]	[illegible]	[illegible]	[illegible]	[illegible]	[illegible]	[illegible]
[illegible]	Thurles,	[illegible]	[illegible]	[illegible]	[illegible]	[illegible]	[illegible]	[illegible]	[illegible]	[illegible]	[illegible]	[illegible]	[illegible]	[illegible]	[illegible]	[illegible]	[illegible]	[illegible]
[illegible]	Tipperary,	[illegible]	[illegible]	[illegible]	[illegible]	[illegible]	[illegible]	[illegible]	[illegible]	[illegible]	[illegible]	[illegible]	[illegible]	[illegible]	[illegible]	[illegible]	[illegible]	[illegible]
[illegible]	Tobercurry,	[illegible]	[illegible]	[illegible]	[illegible]	[illegible]	[illegible]	[illegible]	[illegible]	[illegible]	[illegible]	[illegible]	[illegible]	[illegible]	[illegible]	[illegible]	[illegible]	[illegible]
[illegible]	Tralee,	[illegible]	[illegible]	[illegible]	[illegible]	[illegible]	[illegible]	[illegible]	[illegible]	[illegible]	[illegible]	[illegible]	[illegible]	[illegible]	[illegible]	[illegible]	[illegible]	[illegible]
[illegible]	Trim,	[illegible]	[illegible]	[illegible]	[illegible]	[illegible]	[illegible]	[illegible]	[illegible]	[illegible]	[illegible]	[illegible]	[illegible]	[illegible]	[illegible]	[illegible]	[illegible]	[illegible]
[illegible]	Tuam,	[illegible]	[illegible]	[illegible]	[illegible]	[illegible]	[illegible]	[illegible]	[illegible]	[illegible]	[illegible]	[illegible]	[illegible]	[illegible]	[illegible]	[illegible]	[illegible]	[illegible]
[illegible]	Tulla,	[illegible]	[illegible]	[illegible]	[illegible]	[illegible]	[illegible]	[illegible]	[illegible]	[illegible]	[illegible]	[illegible]	[illegible]	[illegible]	[illegible]	[illegible]	[illegible]	[illegible]
[illegible]	Tullamore,	[illegible]	[illegible]	[illegible]	[illegible]	[illegible]	[illegible]	[illegible]	[illegible]	[illegible]	[illegible]	[illegible]	[illegible]	[illegible]	[illegible]	[illegible]	[illegible]	[illegible]
[illegible]	Urlingford,	[illegible]	[illegible]	[illegible]	[illegible]	[illegible]	[illegible]	[illegible]	[illegible]	[illegible]	[illegible]	[illegible]	[illegible]	[illegible]	[illegible]	[illegible]	[illegible]	[illegible]
[illegible]	Waterford,	[illegible]	[illegible]	[illegible]	[illegible]	[illegible]	[illegible]	[illegible]	[illegible]	[illegible]	[illegible]	[illegible]	[illegible]	[illegible]	[illegible]	[illegible]	[illegible]	[illegible]
[illegible]	Westport,	[illegible]	[illegible]	[illegible]	[illegible]	[illegible]	[illegible]	[illegible]	[illegible]	[illegible]	[illegible]	[illegible]	[illegible]	[illegible]	[illegible]	[illegible]	[illegible]	[illegible]
[illegible]	Wexford,	[illegible]	[illegible]	[illegible]	[illegible]	[illegible]	[illegible]	[illegible]	[illegible]	[illegible]	[illegible]	[illegible]	[illegible]	[illegible]	[illegible]	[illegible]	[illegible]	[illegible]
[illegible]	Youghal,	[illegible]	[illegible]	[illegible]	[illegible]	[illegible]	[illegible]	[illegible]	[illegible]	[illegible]	[illegible]	[illegible]	[illegible]	[illegible]	[illegible]	[illegible]	[illegible]	[illegible]

IRELAND.—DEATHS at different AGES registered in

No.	Provinces and Counties.		Total Births.	Total Deaths.	Under 1 year.	1	2	3	4	Total under 5 years.	5-	10-
	IRELAND,	Persons,	[illegible]	[illegible]	[illegible]	[illegible]	[illegible]	[illegible]	[illegible]	[illegible]	[illegible]	[illegible]
		Males,	[illegible]	[illegible]	[illegible]	[illegible]	[illegible]	[illegible]	[illegible]	[illegible]	[illegible]	[illegible]
		Females,	[illegible]	[illegible]	[illegible]	[illegible]	[illegible]	[illegible]	[illegible]	[illegible]	[illegible]	[illegible]
I.	LEINSTER,	Persons,	[illegible]	[illegible]	[illegible]	[illegible]	[illegible]	[illegible]	[illegible]	[illegible]	[illegible]	[illegible]
		Males,	[illegible]	[illegible]	[illegible]	[illegible]	[illegible]	[illegible]	[illegible]	[illegible]	[illegible]	[illegible]
		Females,	[illegible]	[illegible]	[illegible]	[illegible]	[illegible]	[illegible]	[illegible]	[illegible]	[illegible]	[illegible]
II.	MUNSTER,	Persons,	[illegible]	[illegible]	[illegible]	[illegible]	[illegible]	[illegible]	[illegible]	[illegible]	[illegible]	[illegible]
		Males,	[illegible]	[illegible]	[illegible]	[illegible]	[illegible]	[illegible]	[illegible]	[illegible]	[illegible]	[illegible]
		Females,	[illegible]	[illegible]	[illegible]	[illegible]	[illegible]	[illegible]	[illegible]	[illegible]	[illegible]	[illegible]
III.	ULSTER,	Persons,	[illegible]	[illegible]	[illegible]	[illegible]	[illegible]	[illegible]	[illegible]	[illegible]	[illegible]	[illegible]
		Males,	[illegible]	[illegible]	[illegible]	[illegible]	[illegible]	[illegible]	[illegible]	[illegible]	[illegible]	[illegible]
		Females,	[illegible]	[illegible]	[illegible]	[illegible]	[illegible]	[illegible]	[illegible]	[illegible]	[illegible]	[illegible]
IV.	CONNAUGHT,	Persons,	[illegible]	[illegible]	[illegible]	[illegible]	[illegible]	[illegible]	[illegible]	[illegible]	[illegible]	[illegible]
		Males,	[illegible]	[illegible]	[illegible]	[illegible]	[illegible]	[illegible]	[illegible]	[illegible]	[illegible]	[illegible]
		Females,	[illegible]	[illegible]	[illegible]	[illegible]	[illegible]	[illegible]	[illegible]	[illegible]	[illegible]	[illegible]
	I.—LEINSTER.											
1	Carlow,	Persons,	[illegible]	[illegible]	[illegible]	[illegible]	[illegible]	[illegible]	[illegible]	[illegible]	[illegible]	[illegible]
		Males,	[illegible]	[illegible]	[illegible]	[illegible]	[illegible]	[illegible]	[illegible]	[illegible]	[illegible]	[illegible]
		Females,	[illegible]	[illegible]	[illegible]	[illegible]	[illegible]	[illegible]	[illegible]	[illegible]	[illegible]	[illegible]
2	Dublin,	Persons,	[illegible]	[illegible]	[illegible]	[illegible]	[illegible]	[illegible]	[illegible]	[illegible]	[illegible]	[illegible]
		Males,	[illegible]	[illegible]	[illegible]	[illegible]	[illegible]	[illegible]	[illegible]	[illegible]	[illegible]	[illegible]
		Females,	[illegible]	[illegible]	[illegible]	[illegible]	[illegible]	[illegible]	[illegible]	[illegible]	[illegible]	[illegible]
3	Kildare,	Persons,	[illegible]	[illegible]	[illegible]	[illegible]	[illegible]	[illegible]	[illegible]	[illegible]	[illegible]	[illegible]
		Males,	[illegible]	[illegible]	[illegible]	[illegible]	[illegible]	[illegible]	[illegible]	[illegible]	[illegible]	[illegible]
		Females,	[illegible]	[illegible]	[illegible]	[illegible]	[illegible]	[illegible]	[illegible]	[illegible]	[illegible]	[illegible]
4	Kilkenny,	Persons,	[illegible]	[illegible]	[illegible]	[illegible]	[illegible]	[illegible]	[illegible]	[illegible]	[illegible]	[illegible]
		Males,	[illegible]	[illegible]	[illegible]	[illegible]	[illegible]	[illegible]	[illegible]	[illegible]	[illegible]	[illegible]
		Females,	[illegible]	[illegible]	[illegible]	[illegible]	[illegible]	[illegible]	[illegible]	[illegible]	[illegible]	[illegible]
5	King's,	Persons,	[illegible]	[illegible]	[illegible]	[illegible]	[illegible]	[illegible]	[illegible]	[illegible]	[illegible]	[illegible]
		Males,	[illegible]	[illegible]	[illegible]	[illegible]	[illegible]	[illegible]	[illegible]	[illegible]	[illegible]	[illegible]
		Females,	[illegible]	[illegible]	[illegible]	[illegible]	[illegible]	[illegible]	[illegible]	[illegible]	[illegible]	[illegible]
6	Longford,	Persons,	[illegible]	[illegible]	[illegible]	[illegible]	[illegible]	[illegible]	[illegible]	[illegible]	[illegible]	[illegible]
		Males,	[illegible]	[illegible]	[illegible]	[illegible]	[illegible]	[illegible]	[illegible]	[illegible]	[illegible]	[illegible]
		Females,	[illegible]	[illegible]	[illegible]	[illegible]	[illegible]	[illegible]	[illegible]	[illegible]	[illegible]	[illegible]
7	Louth, and Co. of the Town of Drogheda,	Persons,	[illegible]	[illegible]	[illegible]	[illegible]	[illegible]	[illegible]	[illegible]	[illegible]	[illegible]	[illegible]
		Males,	[illegible]	[illegible]	[illegible]	[illegible]	[illegible]	[illegible]	[illegible]	[illegible]	[illegible]	[illegible]
		Females,	[illegible]	[illegible]	[illegible]	[illegible]	[illegible]	[illegible]	[illegible]	[illegible]	[illegible]	[illegible]
8	Meath,	Persons,	[illegible]	[illegible]	[illegible]	[illegible]	[illegible]	[illegible]	[illegible]	[illegible]	[illegible]	[illegible]
		Males,	[illegible]	[illegible]	[illegible]	[illegible]	[illegible]	[illegible]	[illegible]	[illegible]	[illegible]	[illegible]
		Females,	[illegible]	[illegible]	[illegible]	[illegible]	[illegible]	[illegible]	[illegible]	[illegible]	[illegible]	[illegible]
9	Queen's,	Persons,	[illegible]	[illegible]	[illegible]	[illegible]	[illegible]	[illegible]	[illegible]	[illegible]	[illegible]	[illegible]
		Males,	[illegible]	[illegible]	[illegible]	[illegible]	[illegible]	[illegible]	[illegible]	[illegible]	[illegible]	[illegible]
		Females,	[illegible]	[illegible]	[illegible]	[illegible]	[illegible]	[illegible]	[illegible]	[illegible]	[illegible]	[illegible]
10	Westmeath,	Persons,	[illegible]	[illegible]	[illegible]	[illegible]	[illegible]	[illegible]	[illegible]	[illegible]	[illegible]	[illegible]
		Males,	[illegible]	[illegible]	[illegible]	[illegible]	[illegible]	[illegible]	[illegible]	[illegible]	[illegible]	[illegible]
		Females,	[illegible]	[illegible]	[illegible]	[illegible]	[illegible]	[illegible]	[illegible]	[illegible]	[illegible]	[illegible]
11	Wexford,	Persons,	[illegible]	[illegible]	[illegible]	[illegible]	[illegible]	[illegible]	[illegible]	[illegible]	[illegible]	[illegible]
		Males,	[illegible]	[illegible]	[illegible]	[illegible]	[illegible]	[illegible]	[illegible]	[illegible]	[illegible]	[illegible]
		Females,	[illegible]	[illegible]	[illegible]	[illegible]	[illegible]	[illegible]	[illegible]	[illegible]	[illegible]	[illegible]
12	Wicklow,	Persons,	[illegible]	[illegible]	[illegible]	[illegible]	[illegible]	[illegible]	[illegible]	[illegible]	[illegible]	[illegible]
		Males,	[illegible]	[illegible]	[illegible]	[illegible]	[illegible]	[illegible]	[illegible]	[illegible]	[illegible]	[illegible]
		Females,	[illegible]	[illegible]	[illegible]	[illegible]	[illegible]	[illegible]	[illegible]	[illegible]	[illegible]	[illegible]
	II.—MUNSTER.											
13	Clare,	Persons,	[illegible]	[illegible]	[illegible]	[illegible]	[illegible]	[illegible]	[illegible]	[illegible]	[illegible]	[illegible]
		Males,	[illegible]	[illegible]	[illegible]	[illegible]	[illegible]	[illegible]	[illegible]	[illegible]	[illegible]	[illegible]
		Females,	[illegible]	[illegible]	[illegible]	[illegible]	[illegible]	[illegible]	[illegible]	[illegible]	[illegible]	[illegible]

the Year 1896—in the Provinces and Counties.

Deaths.											Provinces and Counties.	No.
[illegible]	[illegible]	[illegible]	[illegible]	[illegible]	[illegible]	[illegible]	[illegible]	[illegible]	[illegible]			
[illegible]	[illegible]	[illegible]	[illegible]	[illegible]	[illegible]	[illegible]	[illegible]	[illegible]	[illegible]	Persons,	Ireland.	
[illegible]	[illegible]	[illegible]	[illegible]	[illegible]	[illegible]	[illegible]	[illegible]	[illegible]	[illegible]	Males,		
[illegible]	[illegible]	[illegible]	[illegible]	[illegible]	[illegible]	[illegible]	[illegible]	[illegible]	[illegible]	Females,		
[illegible]	[illegible]	[illegible]	[illegible]	[illegible]	[illegible]	[illegible]	[illegible]	[illegible]	[illegible]	Persons,	Leinster,	I.
[illegible]	[illegible]	[illegible]	[illegible]	[illegible]	[illegible]	[illegible]	[illegible]	[illegible]	[illegible]	Males,		
[illegible]	[illegible]	[illegible]	[illegible]	[illegible]	[illegible]	[illegible]	[illegible]	[illegible]	[illegible]	Females,		
[illegible]	[illegible]	[illegible]	[illegible]	[illegible]	[illegible]	[illegible]	[illegible]	[illegible]	[illegible]	Persons,	Munster,	II.
[illegible]	[illegible]	[illegible]	[illegible]	[illegible]	[illegible]	[illegible]	[illegible]	[illegible]	[illegible]	Males,		
[illegible]	[illegible]	[illegible]	[illegible]	[illegible]	[illegible]	[illegible]	[illegible]	[illegible]	[illegible]	Females,		
[illegible]	[illegible]	[illegible]	[illegible]	[illegible]	[illegible]	[illegible]	[illegible]	[illegible]	[illegible]	Persons,	Ulster,	III.
[illegible]	[illegible]	[illegible]	[illegible]	[illegible]	[illegible]	[illegible]	[illegible]	[illegible]	[illegible]	Males,		
[illegible]	[illegible]	[illegible]	[illegible]	[illegible]	[illegible]	[illegible]	[illegible]	[illegible]	[illegible]	Females,		
[illegible]	[illegible]	[illegible]	[illegible]	[illegible]	[illegible]	[illegible]	[illegible]	[illegible]	[illegible]	Persons,	Connaught,	IV.
[illegible]	[illegible]	[illegible]	[illegible]	[illegible]	[illegible]	[illegible]	[illegible]	[illegible]	[illegible]	Males,		
[illegible]	[illegible]	[illegible]	[illegible]	[illegible]	[illegible]	[illegible]	[illegible]	[illegible]	[illegible]	Females,		
											I.—Leinster.	
[illegible]	[illegible]	[illegible]	[illegible]	[illegible]	[illegible]	[illegible]	[illegible]	[illegible]	[illegible]	Persons,	Carlow,	1
[illegible]	[illegible]	[illegible]	[illegible]	[illegible]	[illegible]	[illegible]	[illegible]	[illegible]	[illegible]	Males,		
[illegible]	[illegible]	[illegible]	[illegible]	[illegible]	[illegible]	[illegible]	[illegible]	[illegible]	[illegible]	Females,		
[illegible]	[illegible]	[illegible]	[illegible]	[illegible]	[illegible]	[illegible]	[illegible]	[illegible]	[illegible]	Persons,	Dublin,	2
[illegible]	[illegible]	[illegible]	[illegible]	[illegible]	[illegible]	[illegible]	[illegible]	[illegible]	[illegible]	Males,		
[illegible]	[illegible]	[illegible]	[illegible]	[illegible]	[illegible]	[illegible]	[illegible]	[illegible]	[illegible]	Females,		
[illegible]	[illegible]	[illegible]	[illegible]	[illegible]	[illegible]	[illegible]	[illegible]	[illegible]	[illegible]	Persons,	Kildare,	3
[illegible]	[illegible]	[illegible]	[illegible]	[illegible]	[illegible]	[illegible]	[illegible]	[illegible]	[illegible]	Males,		
[illegible]	[illegible]	[illegible]	[illegible]	[illegible]	[illegible]	[illegible]	[illegible]	[illegible]	[illegible]	Females,		
[illegible]	[illegible]	[illegible]	[illegible]	[illegible]	[illegible]	[illegible]	[illegible]	[illegible]	[illegible]	Persons,	Kilkenny,	4
[illegible]	[illegible]	[illegible]	[illegible]	[illegible]	[illegible]	[illegible]	[illegible]	[illegible]	[illegible]	Males,		
[illegible]	[illegible]	[illegible]	[illegible]	[illegible]	[illegible]	[illegible]	[illegible]	[illegible]	[illegible]	Females,		
[illegible]	[illegible]	[illegible]	[illegible]	[illegible]	[illegible]	[illegible]	[illegible]	[illegible]	[illegible]	Persons,	King's,	5
[illegible]	[illegible]	[illegible]	[illegible]	[illegible]	[illegible]	[illegible]	[illegible]	[illegible]	[illegible]	Males,		
[illegible]	[illegible]	[illegible]	[illegible]	[illegible]	[illegible]	[illegible]	[illegible]	[illegible]	[illegible]	Females,		
[illegible]	[illegible]	[illegible]	[illegible]	[illegible]	[illegible]	[illegible]	[illegible]	[illegible]	[illegible]	Persons,	Longford,	6
[illegible]	[illegible]	[illegible]	[illegible]	[illegible]	[illegible]	[illegible]	[illegible]	[illegible]	[illegible]	Males,		
[illegible]	[illegible]	[illegible]	[illegible]	[illegible]	[illegible]	[illegible]	[illegible]	[illegible]	[illegible]	Females,		
[illegible]	[illegible]	[illegible]	[illegible]	[illegible]	[illegible]	[illegible]	[illegible]	[illegible]	[illegible]	Persons,	Louth, and Co. of the Town of Drogheda,	7
[illegible]	[illegible]	[illegible]	[illegible]	[illegible]	[illegible]	[illegible]	[illegible]	[illegible]	[illegible]	Males,		
[illegible]	[illegible]	[illegible]	[illegible]	[illegible]	[illegible]	[illegible]	[illegible]	[illegible]	[illegible]	Females,		
[illegible]	[illegible]	[illegible]	[illegible]	[illegible]	[illegible]	[illegible]	[illegible]	[illegible]	[illegible]	Persons,	Meath,	8
[illegible]	[illegible]	[illegible]	[illegible]	[illegible]	[illegible]	[illegible]	[illegible]	[illegible]	[illegible]	Males,		
[illegible]	[illegible]	[illegible]	[illegible]	[illegible]	[illegible]	[illegible]	[illegible]	[illegible]	[illegible]	Females,		
[illegible]	[illegible]	[illegible]	[illegible]	[illegible]	[illegible]	[illegible]	[illegible]	[illegible]	[illegible]	Persons,	Queen's,	9
[illegible]	[illegible]	[illegible]	[illegible]	[illegible]	[illegible]	[illegible]	[illegible]	[illegible]	[illegible]	Males,		
[illegible]	[illegible]	[illegible]	[illegible]	[illegible]	[illegible]	[illegible]	[illegible]	[illegible]	[illegible]	Females,		
[illegible]	[illegible]	[illegible]	[illegible]	[illegible]	[illegible]	[illegible]	[illegible]	[illegible]	[illegible]	Persons,	Westmeath,	10
[illegible]	[illegible]	[illegible]	[illegible]	[illegible]	[illegible]	[illegible]	[illegible]	[illegible]	[illegible]	Males,		
[illegible]	[illegible]	[illegible]	[illegible]	[illegible]	[illegible]	[illegible]	[illegible]	[illegible]	[illegible]	Females,		
[illegible]	[illegible]	[illegible]	[illegible]	[illegible]	[illegible]	[illegible]	[illegible]	[illegible]	[illegible]	Persons,	Wexford,	11
[illegible]	[illegible]	[illegible]	[illegible]	[illegible]	[illegible]	[illegible]	[illegible]	[illegible]	[illegible]	Males,		
[illegible]	[illegible]	[illegible]	[illegible]	[illegible]	[illegible]	[illegible]	[illegible]	[illegible]	[illegible]	Females,		
[illegible]	[illegible]	[illegible]	[illegible]	[illegible]	[illegible]	[illegible]	[illegible]	[illegible]	[illegible]	Persons,	Wicklow,	12
[illegible]	[illegible]	[illegible]	[illegible]	[illegible]	[illegible]	[illegible]	[illegible]	[illegible]	[illegible]	Males,		
[illegible]	[illegible]	[illegible]	[illegible]	[illegible]	[illegible]	[illegible]	[illegible]	[illegible]	[illegible]	Females,		
											II.—Munster.	
[illegible]	[illegible]	[illegible]	[illegible]	[illegible]	[illegible]	[illegible]	[illegible]	[illegible]	[illegible]	Persons,	Clare,	13
[illegible]	[illegible]	[illegible]	[illegible]	[illegible]	[illegible]	[illegible]	[illegible]	[illegible]	[illegible]	Males,		
[illegible]	[illegible]	[illegible]	[illegible]	[illegible]	[illegible]	[illegible]	[illegible]	[illegible]	[illegible]	Females,		

[illegible]	Cork,	Persons	[illegible]	[illegible]	[illegible]	[illegible]
		Males	[illegible]	[illegible]	[illegible]	[illegible]
		Females	[illegible]	[illegible]	[illegible]	[illegible]
[illegible]	Kerry,	Persons	[illegible]	[illegible]	[illegible]	[illegible]
		Males	[illegible]	[illegible]	[illegible]	[illegible]
		Females	[illegible]	[illegible]	[illegible]	[illegible]
[illegible]	Limerick,	Persons	[illegible]	[illegible]	[illegible]	[illegible]
		Males	[illegible]	[illegible]	[illegible]	[illegible]
		Females	[illegible]	[illegible]	[illegible]	[illegible]
[illegible]	Tipperary,	Persons	[illegible]	[illegible]	[illegible]	[illegible]
		Males	[illegible]	[illegible]	[illegible]	[illegible]
		Females	[illegible]	[illegible]	[illegible]	[illegible]
[illegible]	Waterford,	Persons	[illegible]	[illegible]	[illegible]	[illegible]
		Males	[illegible]	[illegible]	[illegible]	[illegible]
		Females	[illegible]	[illegible]	[illegible]	[illegible]
	III.—Ulster.					
[illegible]	Antrim,	Persons	[illegible]	[illegible]	[illegible]	[illegible]
		Males	[illegible]	[illegible]	[illegible]	[illegible]
		Females	[illegible]	[illegible]	[illegible]	[illegible]
[illegible]	Armagh,	Persons	[illegible]	[illegible]	[illegible]	[illegible]
		Males	[illegible]	[illegible]	[illegible]	[illegible]
		Females	[illegible]	[illegible]	[illegible]	[illegible]
[illegible]	Cavan,	Persons	[illegible]	[illegible]	[illegible]	[illegible]
		Males	[illegible]	[illegible]	[illegible]	[illegible]
		Females	[illegible]	[illegible]	[illegible]	[illegible]
[illegible]	Donegal,	Persons	[illegible]	[illegible]	[illegible]	[illegible]
		Males	[illegible]	[illegible]	[illegible]	[illegible]
		Females	[illegible]	[illegible]	[illegible]	[illegible]
[illegible]	Down,	Persons	[illegible]	[illegible]	[illegible]	[illegible]
		Males	[illegible]	[illegible]	[illegible]	[illegible]
		Females	[illegible]	[illegible]	[illegible]	[illegible]
[illegible]	Fermanagh,	Persons	[illegible]	[illegible]	[illegible]	[illegible]
		Males	[illegible]	[illegible]	[illegible]	[illegible]
		Females	[illegible]	[illegible]	[illegible]	[illegible]
[illegible]	Londonderry,	Persons	[illegible]	[illegible]	[illegible]	[illegible]
		Males	[illegible]	[illegible]	[illegible]	[illegible]
		Females	[illegible]	[illegible]	[illegible]	[illegible]
[illegible]	Monaghan,	Persons	[illegible]	[illegible]	[illegible]	[illegible]
		Males	[illegible]	[illegible]	[illegible]	[illegible]
		Females	[illegible]	[illegible]	[illegible]	[illegible]
[illegible]	Tyrone,	Persons	[illegible]	[illegible]	[illegible]	[illegible]
		Males	[illegible]	[illegible]	[illegible]	[illegible]
		Females	[illegible]	[illegible]	[illegible]	[illegible]
	IV.—Connaught.					
[illegible]	Galway,	Persons	[illegible]	[illegible]	[illegible]	[illegible]
		Males	[illegible]	[illegible]	[illegible]	[illegible]
		Females	[illegible]	[illegible]	[illegible]	[illegible]
[illegible]	Leitrim,	Persons	[illegible]	[illegible]	[illegible]	[illegible]
		Males	[illegible]	[illegible]	[illegible]	[illegible]
		Females	[illegible]	[illegible]	[illegible]	[illegible]
[illegible]	Mayo,	Persons	[illegible]	[illegible]	[illegible]	[illegible]
		Males	[illegible]	[illegible]	[illegible]	[illegible]
		Females	[illegible]	[illegible]	[illegible]	[illegible]
[illegible]	Roscommon,	Persons	[illegible]	[illegible]	[illegible]	[illegible]
		Males	[illegible]	[illegible]	[illegible]	[illegible]
		Females	[illegible]	[illegible]	[illegible]	[illegible]
[illegible]	Sligo,	Persons	[illegible]	[illegible]	[illegible]	[illegible]
		Males	[illegible]	[illegible]	[illegible]	[illegible]
		Females	[illegible]	[illegible]	[illegible]	[illegible]

the Year 1856—in the Provinces and Counties.

Deaths.										Provinces and Counties		No.
[illegible]	[illegible]	[illegible]	[illegible]	[illegible]	[illegible]	[illegible]	[illegible]	[illegible]	[illegible]			
										MUNSTER—*continued.*		
[illegible]	[illegible]	[illegible]	[illegible]	[illegible]	[illegible]	[illegible]	[illegible]	[illegible]	[illegible]	Persons,	Cork	[illegible]
[illegible]	[illegible]	[illegible]	[illegible]	[illegible]	[illegible]	[illegible]	[illegible]	[illegible]	[illegible]	Males,		
[illegible]	[illegible]	[illegible]	[illegible]	[illegible]	[illegible]	[illegible]	[illegible]	[illegible]	[illegible]	Females,		
[illegible]	[illegible]	[illegible]	[illegible]	[illegible]	[illegible]	[illegible]	[illegible]	[illegible]	[illegible]	Persons,	Kerry	[illegible]
[illegible]	[illegible]	[illegible]	[illegible]	[illegible]	[illegible]	[illegible]	[illegible]	[illegible]	[illegible]	Males,		
[illegible]	[illegible]	[illegible]	[illegible]	[illegible]	[illegible]	[illegible]	[illegible]	[illegible]	[illegible]	Females,		
[illegible]	[illegible]	[illegible]	[illegible]	[illegible]	[illegible]	[illegible]	[illegible]	[illegible]	[illegible]	Persons,	Limerick	[illegible]
[illegible]	[illegible]	[illegible]	[illegible]	[illegible]	[illegible]	[illegible]	[illegible]	[illegible]	[illegible]	Males,		
[illegible]	[illegible]	[illegible]	[illegible]	[illegible]	[illegible]	[illegible]	[illegible]	[illegible]	[illegible]	Females,		
[illegible]	[illegible]	[illegible]	[illegible]	[illegible]	[illegible]	[illegible]	[illegible]	[illegible]	[illegible]	Persons,	Tipperary	[illegible]
[illegible]	[illegible]	[illegible]	[illegible]	[illegible]	[illegible]	[illegible]	[illegible]	[illegible]	[illegible]	Males,		
[illegible]	[illegible]	[illegible]	[illegible]	[illegible]	[illegible]	[illegible]	[illegible]	[illegible]	[illegible]	Females,		
[illegible]	[illegible]	[illegible]	[illegible]	[illegible]	[illegible]	[illegible]	[illegible]	[illegible]	[illegible]	Persons,	Waterford	[illegible]
[illegible]	[illegible]	[illegible]	[illegible]	[illegible]	[illegible]	[illegible]	[illegible]	[illegible]	[illegible]	Males,		
[illegible]	[illegible]	[illegible]	[illegible]	[illegible]	[illegible]	[illegible]	[illegible]	[illegible]	[illegible]	Females,		
										III.—ULSTER.		
[illegible]	[illegible]	[illegible]	[illegible]	[illegible]	[illegible]	[illegible]	[illegible]	[illegible]	[illegible]	Persons,	Antrim	[illegible]
[illegible]	[illegible]	[illegible]	[illegible]	[illegible]	[illegible]	[illegible]	[illegible]	[illegible]	[illegible]	Males,		
[illegible]	[illegible]	[illegible]	[illegible]	[illegible]	[illegible]	[illegible]	[illegible]	[illegible]	[illegible]	Females,		
[illegible]	[illegible]	[illegible]	[illegible]	[illegible]	[illegible]	[illegible]	[illegible]	[illegible]	[illegible]	Persons,	Armagh	[illegible]
[illegible]	[illegible]	[illegible]	[illegible]	[illegible]	[illegible]	[illegible]	[illegible]	[illegible]	[illegible]	Males,		
[illegible]	[illegible]	[illegible]	[illegible]	[illegible]	[illegible]	[illegible]	[illegible]	[illegible]	[illegible]	Females,		
[illegible]	[illegible]	[illegible]	[illegible]	[illegible]	[illegible]	[illegible]	[illegible]	[illegible]	[illegible]	Persons,	Cavan	[illegible]
[illegible]	[illegible]	[illegible]	[illegible]	[illegible]	[illegible]	[illegible]	[illegible]	[illegible]	[illegible]	Males,		
[illegible]	[illegible]	[illegible]	[illegible]	[illegible]	[illegible]	[illegible]	[illegible]	[illegible]	[illegible]	Females,		
[illegible]	[illegible]	[illegible]	[illegible]	[illegible]	[illegible]	[illegible]	[illegible]	[illegible]	[illegible]	Persons,	Donegal	[illegible]
[illegible]	[illegible]	[illegible]	[illegible]	[illegible]	[illegible]	[illegible]	[illegible]	[illegible]	[illegible]	Males,		
[illegible]	[illegible]	[illegible]	[illegible]	[illegible]	[illegible]	[illegible]	[illegible]	[illegible]	[illegible]	Females,		
[illegible]	[illegible]	[illegible]	[illegible]	[illegible]	[illegible]	[illegible]	[illegible]	[illegible]	[illegible]	Persons,	Down	[illegible]
[illegible]	[illegible]	[illegible]	[illegible]	[illegible]	[illegible]	[illegible]	[illegible]	[illegible]	[illegible]	Males,		
[illegible]	[illegible]	[illegible]	[illegible]	[illegible]	[illegible]	[illegible]	[illegible]	[illegible]	[illegible]	Females,		
[illegible]	[illegible]	[illegible]	[illegible]	[illegible]	[illegible]	[illegible]	[illegible]	[illegible]	[illegible]	Persons,	Fermanagh	[illegible]
[illegible]	[illegible]	[illegible]	[illegible]	[illegible]	[illegible]	[illegible]	[illegible]	[illegible]	[illegible]	Males,		
[illegible]	[illegible]	[illegible]	[illegible]	[illegible]	[illegible]	[illegible]	[illegible]	[illegible]	[illegible]	Females,		
[illegible]	[illegible]	[illegible]	[illegible]	[illegible]	[illegible]	[illegible]	[illegible]	[illegible]	[illegible]	Persons,	Londonderry	[illegible]
[illegible]	[illegible]	[illegible]	[illegible]	[illegible]	[illegible]	[illegible]	[illegible]	[illegible]	[illegible]	Males,		
[illegible]	[illegible]	[illegible]	[illegible]	[illegible]	[illegible]	[illegible]	[illegible]	[illegible]	[illegible]	Females,		
[illegible]	[illegible]	[illegible]	[illegible]	[illegible]	[illegible]	[illegible]	[illegible]	[illegible]	[illegible]	Persons,	Monaghan	[illegible]
[illegible]	[illegible]	[illegible]	[illegible]	[illegible]	[illegible]	[illegible]	[illegible]	[illegible]	[illegible]	Males,		
[illegible]	[illegible]	[illegible]	[illegible]	[illegible]	[illegible]	[illegible]	[illegible]	[illegible]	[illegible]	Females,		
[illegible]	[illegible]	[illegible]	[illegible]	[illegible]	[illegible]	[illegible]	[illegible]	[illegible]	[illegible]	Persons,	Tyrone	[illegible]
[illegible]	[illegible]	[illegible]	[illegible]	[illegible]	[illegible]	[illegible]	[illegible]	[illegible]	[illegible]	Males,		
[illegible]	[illegible]	[illegible]	[illegible]	[illegible]	[illegible]	[illegible]	[illegible]	[illegible]	[illegible]	Females,		
										IV.—CONNAUGHT.		
[illegible]	[illegible]	[illegible]	[illegible]	[illegible]	[illegible]	[illegible]	[illegible]	[illegible]	[illegible]	Persons,	Galway	[illegible]
[illegible]	[illegible]	[illegible]	[illegible]	[illegible]	[illegible]	[illegible]	[illegible]	[illegible]	[illegible]	Males,		
[illegible]	[illegible]	[illegible]	[illegible]	[illegible]	[illegible]	[illegible]	[illegible]	[illegible]	[illegible]	Females,		
[illegible]	[illegible]	[illegible]	[illegible]	[illegible]	[illegible]	[illegible]	[illegible]	[illegible]	[illegible]	Persons,	Leitrim	[illegible]
[illegible]	[illegible]	[illegible]	[illegible]	[illegible]	[illegible]	[illegible]	[illegible]	[illegible]	[illegible]	Males,		
[illegible]	[illegible]	[illegible]	[illegible]	[illegible]	[illegible]	[illegible]	[illegible]	[illegible]	[illegible]	Females,		
[illegible]	[illegible]	[illegible]	[illegible]	[illegible]	[illegible]	[illegible]	[illegible]	[illegible]	[illegible]	Persons,	Mayo	[illegible]
[illegible]	[illegible]	[illegible]	[illegible]	[illegible]	[illegible]	[illegible]	[illegible]	[illegible]	[illegible]	Males,		
[illegible]	[illegible]	[illegible]	[illegible]	[illegible]	[illegible]	[illegible]	[illegible]	[illegible]	[illegible]	Females,		
[illegible]	[illegible]	[illegible]	[illegible]	[illegible]	[illegible]	[illegible]	[illegible]	[illegible]	[illegible]	Persons,	Roscommon	[illegible]
[illegible]	[illegible]	[illegible]	[illegible]	[illegible]	[illegible]	[illegible]	[illegible]	[illegible]	[illegible]	Males,		
[illegible]	[illegible]	[illegible]	[illegible]	[illegible]	[illegible]	[illegible]	[illegible]	[illegible]	[illegible]	Females,		
[illegible]	[illegible]	[illegible]	[illegible]	[illegible]	[illegible]	[illegible]	[illegible]	[illegible]	[illegible]	Persons,	Sligo	[illegible]
[illegible]	[illegible]	[illegible]	[illegible]	[illegible]	[illegible]	[illegible]	[illegible]	[illegible]	[illegible]	Males,		
[illegible]	[illegible]	[illegible]	[illegible]	[illegible]	[illegible]	[illegible]	[illegible]	[illegible]	[illegible]	Females,		

IRELAND.—Deaths at different Ages registered in the year 185[illegible]—in the Superintendent Registrars' Districts in each County.—Males.

I.—Province of Leinster.

Counties and Superintendent Registrars' Districts		Males																					
		[illegible]	[illegible]	Ages at Death																			
No.	1. Carlow Co.																						
[illegible]	[illegible], part of	[illegible]	[illegible]	[illegible]	[illegible]	[illegible]	[illegible]	[illegible]	[illegible]	[illegible]	[illegible]	[illegible]	[illegible]	[illegible]	[illegible]	[illegible]	[illegible]	[illegible]	[illegible]	[illegible]	[illegible]	[illegible]	[illegible]
[illegible]	[illegible], do.	[illegible]	[illegible]	[illegible]	[illegible]	[illegible]	[illegible]	[illegible]	[illegible]	[illegible]	[illegible]	[illegible]	[illegible]	[illegible]	[illegible]	[illegible]	[illegible]	[illegible]	[illegible]	[illegible]	[illegible]	[illegible]	[illegible]
[illegible]	[illegible], do.	[illegible]	[illegible]	[illegible]	[illegible]	[illegible]	[illegible]	[illegible]	[illegible]	[illegible]	[illegible]	[illegible]	[illegible]	[illegible]	[illegible]	[illegible]	[illegible]	[illegible]	[illegible]	[illegible]	[illegible]	[illegible]	[illegible]
[illegible]	New Ross, do.	[illegible]	[illegible]	[illegible]	[illegible]	[illegible]	[illegible]	[illegible]	[illegible]	[illegible]	[illegible]	[illegible]	[illegible]	[illegible]	[illegible]	[illegible]	[illegible]	[illegible]	[illegible]	[illegible]	[illegible]	[illegible]	[illegible]
[illegible]	[illegible], do.	[illegible]	[illegible]	[illegible]	[illegible]	[illegible]	[illegible]	[illegible]	[illegible]	[illegible]	[illegible]	[illegible]	[illegible]	[illegible]	[illegible]	[illegible]	[illegible]	[illegible]	[illegible]	[illegible]	[illegible]	[illegible]	[illegible]
	2. Dublin Co.																						
[illegible]	[illegible]	[illegible]	[illegible]	[illegible]	[illegible]	[illegible]	[illegible]	[illegible]	[illegible]	[illegible]	[illegible]	[illegible]	[illegible]	[illegible]	[illegible]	[illegible]	[illegible]	[illegible]	[illegible]	[illegible]	[illegible]	[illegible]	[illegible]
[illegible]	[illegible], part of	[illegible]	[illegible]	[illegible]	[illegible]	[illegible]	[illegible]	[illegible]	[illegible]	[illegible]	[illegible]	[illegible]	[illegible]	[illegible]	[illegible]	[illegible]	[illegible]	[illegible]	[illegible]	[illegible]	[illegible]	[illegible]	[illegible]
[illegible]	[illegible]	[illegible]	[illegible]	[illegible]	[illegible]	[illegible]	[illegible]	[illegible]	[illegible]	[illegible]	[illegible]	[illegible]	[illegible]	[illegible]	[illegible]	[illegible]	[illegible]	[illegible]	[illegible]	[illegible]	[illegible]	[illegible]	[illegible]
[illegible]	[illegible]	[illegible]	[illegible]	[illegible]	[illegible]	[illegible]	[illegible]	[illegible]	[illegible]	[illegible]	[illegible]	[illegible]	[illegible]	[illegible]	[illegible]	[illegible]	[illegible]	[illegible]	[illegible]	[illegible]	[illegible]	[illegible]	[illegible]
[illegible]	[illegible], pt. of	[illegible]	[illegible]	[illegible]	[illegible]	[illegible]	[illegible]	[illegible]	[illegible]	[illegible]	[illegible]	[illegible]	[illegible]	[illegible]	[illegible]	[illegible]	[illegible]	[illegible]	[illegible]	[illegible]	[illegible]	[illegible]	[illegible]
11	[illegible], do.	[illegible]	[illegible]	[illegible]	[illegible]	[illegible]	[illegible]	[illegible]	[illegible]	[illegible]	[illegible]	[illegible]	[illegible]	[illegible]	[illegible]	[illegible]	[illegible]	[illegible]	[illegible]	[illegible]	[illegible]	[illegible]	[illegible]
	3. Kildare Co.																						
[illegible]	Athy, part of	[illegible]	[illegible]	[illegible]	[illegible]	[illegible]	[illegible]	[illegible]	[illegible]	[illegible]	[illegible]	[illegible]	[illegible]	[illegible]	[illegible]	[illegible]	[illegible]	[illegible]	[illegible]	[illegible]	[illegible]	[illegible]	[illegible]
[illegible]	[illegible], do.	[illegible]	[illegible]	[illegible]	[illegible]	[illegible]	[illegible]	[illegible]	[illegible]	[illegible]	[illegible]	[illegible]	[illegible]	[illegible]	[illegible]	[illegible]	[illegible]	[illegible]	[illegible]	[illegible]	[illegible]	[illegible]	[illegible]
[illegible]	[illegible], do.	[illegible]	[illegible]	[illegible]	[illegible]	[illegible]	[illegible]	[illegible]	[illegible]	[illegible]	[illegible]	[illegible]	[illegible]	[illegible]	[illegible]	[illegible]	[illegible]	[illegible]	[illegible]	[illegible]	[illegible]	[illegible]	[illegible]
[illegible]	[illegible], do.	[illegible]	[illegible]	[illegible]	[illegible]	[illegible]	[illegible]	[illegible]	[illegible]	[illegible]	[illegible]	[illegible]	[illegible]	[illegible]	[illegible]	[illegible]	[illegible]	[illegible]	[illegible]	[illegible]	[illegible]	[illegible]	[illegible]
[illegible]	Naas, do.	[illegible]	[illegible]	[illegible]	[illegible]	[illegible]	[illegible]	[illegible]	[illegible]	[illegible]	[illegible]	[illegible]	[illegible]	[illegible]	[illegible]	[illegible]	[illegible]	[illegible]	[illegible]	[illegible]	[illegible]	[illegible]	[illegible]
	4. Kilkenny Co.																						
[illegible]	[illegible], part of	[illegible]	[illegible]	[illegible]	[illegible]	[illegible]	[illegible]	[illegible]	[illegible]	[illegible]	[illegible]	[illegible]	[illegible]	[illegible]	[illegible]	[illegible]	[illegible]	[illegible]	[illegible]	[illegible]	[illegible]	[illegible]	[illegible]
[illegible]	[illegible], do.	[illegible]	[illegible]	[illegible]	[illegible]	[illegible]	[illegible]	[illegible]	[illegible]	[illegible]	[illegible]	[illegible]	[illegible]	[illegible]	[illegible]	[illegible]	[illegible]	[illegible]	[illegible]	[illegible]	[illegible]	[illegible]	[illegible]
[illegible]	[illegible]	[illegible]	[illegible]	[illegible]	[illegible]	[illegible]	[illegible]	[illegible]	[illegible]	[illegible]	[illegible]	[illegible]	[illegible]	[illegible]	[illegible]	[illegible]	[illegible]	[illegible]	[illegible]	[illegible]	[illegible]	[illegible]	[illegible]
[illegible]	Kilkenny	[illegible]	[illegible]	[illegible]	[illegible]	[illegible]	[illegible]	[illegible]	[illegible]	[illegible]	[illegible]	[illegible]	[illegible]	[illegible]	[illegible]	[illegible]	[illegible]	[illegible]	[illegible]	[illegible]	[illegible]	[illegible]	[illegible]
[illegible]	New Ross, part of	[illegible]	[illegible]	[illegible]	[illegible]	[illegible]	[illegible]	[illegible]	[illegible]	[illegible]	[illegible]	[illegible]	[illegible]	[illegible]	[illegible]	[illegible]	[illegible]	[illegible]	[illegible]	[illegible]	[illegible]	[illegible]	[illegible]
[illegible]	[illegible]	[illegible]	[illegible]	[illegible]	[illegible]	[illegible]	[illegible]	[illegible]	[illegible]	[illegible]	[illegible]	[illegible]	[illegible]	[illegible]	[illegible]	[illegible]	[illegible]	[illegible]	[illegible]	[illegible]	[illegible]	[illegible]	[illegible]
[illegible]	[illegible], part of	[illegible]	[illegible]	[illegible]	[illegible]	[illegible]	[illegible]	[illegible]	[illegible]	[illegible]	[illegible]	[illegible]	[illegible]	[illegible]	[illegible]	[illegible]	[illegible]	[illegible]	[illegible]	[illegible]	[illegible]	[illegible]	[illegible]
[illegible]	[illegible], do.	[illegible]	[illegible]	[illegible]	[illegible]	[illegible]	[illegible]	[illegible]	[illegible]	[illegible]	[illegible]	[illegible]	[illegible]	[illegible]	[illegible]	[illegible]	[illegible]	[illegible]	[illegible]	[illegible]	[illegible]	[illegible]	[illegible]
	5. King's Co.																						
[illegible]	[illegible], part of	[illegible]	[illegible]	[illegible]	[illegible]	[illegible]	[illegible]	[illegible]	[illegible]	[illegible]	[illegible]	[illegible]	[illegible]	[illegible]	[illegible]	[illegible]	[illegible]	[illegible]	[illegible]	[illegible]	[illegible]	[illegible]	[illegible]
[illegible]	[illegible], do.	[illegible]	[illegible]	[illegible]	[illegible]	[illegible]	[illegible]	[illegible]	[illegible]	[illegible]	[illegible]	[illegible]	[illegible]	[illegible]	[illegible]	[illegible]	[illegible]	[illegible]	[illegible]	[illegible]	[illegible]	[illegible]	[illegible]
[illegible]	[illegible], do.	[illegible]	[illegible]	[illegible]	[illegible]	[illegible]	[illegible]	[illegible]	[illegible]	[illegible]	[illegible]	[illegible]	[illegible]	[illegible]	[illegible]	[illegible]	[illegible]	[illegible]	[illegible]	[illegible]	[illegible]	[illegible]	[illegible]
[illegible]	[illegible], do.	[illegible]	[illegible]	[illegible]	[illegible]	[illegible]	[illegible]	[illegible]	[illegible]	[illegible]	[illegible]	[illegible]	[illegible]	[illegible]	[illegible]	[illegible]	[illegible]	[illegible]	[illegible]	[illegible]	[illegible]	[illegible]	[illegible]
[illegible]	[illegible], do.	[illegible]	[illegible]	[illegible]	[illegible]	[illegible]	[illegible]	[illegible]	[illegible]	[illegible]	[illegible]	[illegible]	[illegible]	[illegible]	[illegible]	[illegible]	[illegible]	[illegible]	[illegible]	[illegible]	[illegible]	[illegible]	[illegible]
	6. Longford Co.																						
[illegible]	[illegible], part of	[illegible]	[illegible]	[illegible]	[illegible]	[illegible]	[illegible]	[illegible]	[illegible]	[illegible]	[illegible]	[illegible]	[illegible]	[illegible]	[illegible]	[illegible]	[illegible]	[illegible]	[illegible]	[illegible]	[illegible]	[illegible]	[illegible]
[illegible]	[illegible], do.	[illegible]	[illegible]	[illegible]	[illegible]	[illegible]	[illegible]	[illegible]	[illegible]	[illegible]	[illegible]	[illegible]	[illegible]	[illegible]	[illegible]	[illegible]	[illegible]	[illegible]	[illegible]	[illegible]	[illegible]	[illegible]	[illegible]
[illegible]	Longford	[illegible]	[illegible]	[illegible]	[illegible]	[illegible]	[illegible]	[illegible]	[illegible]	[illegible]	[illegible]	[illegible]	[illegible]	[illegible]	[illegible]	[illegible]	[illegible]	[illegible]	[illegible]	[illegible]	[illegible]	[illegible]	[illegible]
	7. Louth Co. and Co. of Town of Drogheda.																						
[illegible]	[illegible], part of	[illegible]	[illegible]	[illegible]	[illegible]	[illegible]	[illegible]	[illegible]	[illegible]	[illegible]	[illegible]	[illegible]	[illegible]	[illegible]	[illegible]	[illegible]	[illegible]	[illegible]	[illegible]	[illegible]	[illegible]	[illegible]	[illegible]
[illegible]	[illegible], do.	[illegible]	[illegible]	[illegible]	[illegible]	[illegible]	[illegible]	[illegible]	[illegible]	[illegible]	[illegible]	[illegible]	[illegible]	[illegible]	[illegible]	[illegible]	[illegible]	[illegible]	[illegible]	[illegible]	[illegible]	[illegible]	[illegible]
[illegible]	[illegible], do.	[illegible]	[illegible]	[illegible]	[illegible]	[illegible]	[illegible]	[illegible]	[illegible]	[illegible]	[illegible]	[illegible]	[illegible]	[illegible]	[illegible]	[illegible]	[illegible]	[illegible]	[illegible]	[illegible]	[illegible]	[illegible]	[illegible]
	8. Meath Co.																						
[illegible]	[illegible], part of	[illegible]	[illegible]	[illegible]	[illegible]	[illegible]	[illegible]	[illegible]	[illegible]	[illegible]	[illegible]	[illegible]	[illegible]	[illegible]	[illegible]	[illegible]	[illegible]	[illegible]	[illegible]	[illegible]	[illegible]	[illegible]	[illegible]
[illegible]	[illegible], do.	[illegible]	[illegible]	[illegible]	[illegible]	[illegible]	[illegible]	[illegible]	[illegible]	[illegible]	[illegible]	[illegible]	[illegible]	[illegible]	[illegible]	[illegible]	[illegible]	[illegible]	[illegible]	[illegible]	[illegible]	[illegible]	[illegible]
[illegible]	[illegible], do.	[illegible]	[illegible]	[illegible]	[illegible]	[illegible]	[illegible]	[illegible]	[illegible]	[illegible]	[illegible]	[illegible]	[illegible]	[illegible]	[illegible]	[illegible]	[illegible]	[illegible]	[illegible]	[illegible]	[illegible]	[illegible]	[illegible]
[illegible]	[illegible], do.	[illegible]	[illegible]	[illegible]	[illegible]	[illegible]	[illegible]	[illegible]	[illegible]	[illegible]	[illegible]	[illegible]	[illegible]	[illegible]	[illegible]	[illegible]	[illegible]	[illegible]	[illegible]	[illegible]	[illegible]	[illegible]	[illegible]
[illegible]	[illegible], do.	[illegible]	[illegible]	[illegible]	[illegible]	[illegible]	[illegible]	[illegible]	[illegible]	[illegible]	[illegible]	[illegible]	[illegible]	[illegible]	[illegible]	[illegible]	[illegible]	[illegible]	[illegible]	[illegible]	[illegible]	[illegible]	[illegible]
[illegible]	[illegible], do.	[illegible]	[illegible]	[illegible]	[illegible]	[illegible]	[illegible]	[illegible]	[illegible]	[illegible]	[illegible]	[illegible]	[illegible]	[illegible]	[illegible]	[illegible]	[illegible]	[illegible]	[illegible]	[illegible]	[illegible]	[illegible]	[illegible]
[illegible]	[illegible]	[illegible]	[illegible]	[illegible]	[illegible]	[illegible]	[illegible]	[illegible]	[illegible]	[illegible]	[illegible]	[illegible]	[illegible]	[illegible]	[illegible]	[illegible]	[illegible]	[illegible]	[illegible]	[illegible]	[illegible]	[illegible]	[illegible]
[illegible]	[illegible], part of	[illegible]	[illegible]	[illegible]	[illegible]	[illegible]	[illegible]	[illegible]	[illegible]	[illegible]	[illegible]	[illegible]	[illegible]	[illegible]	[illegible]	[illegible]	[illegible]	[illegible]	[illegible]	[illegible]	[illegible]	[illegible]	[illegible]
[illegible]	Trim	[illegible]	[illegible]	[illegible]	[illegible]	[illegible]	[illegible]	[illegible]	[illegible]	[illegible]	[illegible]	[illegible]	[illegible]	[illegible]	[illegible]	[illegible]	[illegible]	[illegible]	[illegible]	[illegible]	[illegible]	[illegible]	[illegible]

IRELAND.—DEATHS at different AGES registered in the year 1896—in the SUPERINTENDENT REGISTRARS' DISTRICTS in each COUNTY.—FEMALES.

I.—PROVINCE OF LEINSTER.

No.	Counties and Superintendent Registrars' Districts	FEMALES [illegible]	[illegible]	Ages at Death. [illegible]	[illegible]	[illegible]	[illegible]	[illegible]	[illegible]	[illegible]	[illegible]	[illegible]	[illegible]	[illegible]	[illegible]	[illegible]	[illegible]	[illegible]	[illegible]	[illegible]	[illegible]	[illegible]
	1. Carlow Co.																					
1	[illegible], part of,	[illegible]	[illegible]	[illegible]	[illegible]	[illegible]	[illegible]	[illegible]	[illegible]	[illegible]	[illegible]	[illegible]	[illegible]	[illegible]	[illegible]	[illegible]	[illegible]	[illegible]	[illegible]	[illegible]	[illegible]	[illegible]
2	[illegible], do.,	[illegible]	[illegible]	[illegible]	[illegible]	[illegible]	[illegible]	[illegible]	[illegible]	[illegible]	[illegible]	[illegible]	[illegible]	[illegible]	[illegible]	[illegible]	[illegible]	[illegible]	[illegible]	[illegible]	[illegible]	[illegible]
3	[illegible], do.,	[illegible]	[illegible]	[illegible]	[illegible]	[illegible]	[illegible]	[illegible]	[illegible]	[illegible]	[illegible]	[illegible]	[illegible]	[illegible]	[illegible]	[illegible]	[illegible]	[illegible]	[illegible]	[illegible]	[illegible]	[illegible]
4	[illegible], do.,	[illegible]	[illegible]	[illegible]	[illegible]	[illegible]	[illegible]	[illegible]	[illegible]	[illegible]	[illegible]	[illegible]	[illegible]	[illegible]	[illegible]	[illegible]	[illegible]	[illegible]	[illegible]	[illegible]	[illegible]	[illegible]
5	[illegible], do.,	[illegible]	[illegible]	[illegible]	[illegible]	[illegible]	[illegible]	[illegible]	[illegible]	[illegible]	[illegible]	[illegible]	[illegible]	[illegible]	[illegible]	[illegible]	[illegible]	[illegible]	[illegible]	[illegible]	[illegible]	[illegible]
	2. Dublin Co.																					
6	[illegible]	[illegible]	[illegible]	[illegible]	[illegible]	[illegible]	[illegible]	[illegible]	[illegible]	[illegible]	[illegible]	[illegible]	[illegible]	[illegible]	[illegible]	[illegible]	[illegible]	[illegible]	[illegible]	[illegible]	[illegible]	[illegible]
7	[illegible], part of,	[illegible]	[illegible]	[illegible]	[illegible]	[illegible]	[illegible]	[illegible]	[illegible]	[illegible]	[illegible]	[illegible]	[illegible]	[illegible]	[illegible]	[illegible]	[illegible]	[illegible]	[illegible]	[illegible]	[illegible]	[illegible]
8	[illegible]	[illegible]	[illegible]	[illegible]	[illegible]	[illegible]	[illegible]	[illegible]	[illegible]	[illegible]	[illegible]	[illegible]	[illegible]	[illegible]	[illegible]	[illegible]	[illegible]	[illegible]	[illegible]	[illegible]	[illegible]	[illegible]
9	[illegible]	[illegible]	[illegible]	[illegible]	[illegible]	[illegible]	[illegible]	[illegible]	[illegible]	[illegible]	[illegible]	[illegible]	[illegible]	[illegible]	[illegible]	[illegible]	[illegible]	[illegible]	[illegible]	[illegible]	[illegible]	[illegible]
10	[illegible]	[illegible]	[illegible]	[illegible]	[illegible]	[illegible]	[illegible]	[illegible]	[illegible]	[illegible]	[illegible]	[illegible]	[illegible]	[illegible]	[illegible]	[illegible]	[illegible]	[illegible]	[illegible]	[illegible]	[illegible]	[illegible]
11	[illegible], do.	[illegible]	[illegible]	[illegible]	[illegible]	[illegible]	[illegible]	[illegible]	[illegible]	[illegible]	[illegible]	[illegible]	[illegible]	[illegible]	[illegible]	[illegible]	[illegible]	[illegible]	[illegible]	[illegible]	[illegible]	[illegible]
	3. Kildare Co.																					
12	[illegible], part of,	[illegible]	[illegible]	[illegible]	[illegible]	[illegible]	[illegible]	[illegible]	[illegible]	[illegible]	[illegible]	[illegible]	[illegible]	[illegible]	[illegible]	[illegible]	[illegible]	[illegible]	[illegible]	[illegible]	[illegible]	[illegible]
13	[illegible], do.,	[illegible]	[illegible]	[illegible]	[illegible]	[illegible]	[illegible]	[illegible]	[illegible]	[illegible]	[illegible]	[illegible]	[illegible]	[illegible]	[illegible]	[illegible]	[illegible]	[illegible]	[illegible]	[illegible]	[illegible]	[illegible]
14	[illegible], do.,	[illegible]	[illegible]	[illegible]	[illegible]	[illegible]	[illegible]	[illegible]	[illegible]	[illegible]	[illegible]	[illegible]	[illegible]	[illegible]	[illegible]	[illegible]	[illegible]	[illegible]	[illegible]	[illegible]	[illegible]	[illegible]
15	[illegible], do.,	[illegible]	[illegible]	[illegible]	[illegible]	[illegible]	[illegible]	[illegible]	[illegible]	[illegible]	[illegible]	[illegible]	[illegible]	[illegible]	[illegible]	[illegible]	[illegible]	[illegible]	[illegible]	[illegible]	[illegible]	[illegible]
16	[illegible], do.,	[illegible]	[illegible]	[illegible]	[illegible]	[illegible]	[illegible]	[illegible]	[illegible]	[illegible]	[illegible]	[illegible]	[illegible]	[illegible]	[illegible]	[illegible]	[illegible]	[illegible]	[illegible]	[illegible]	[illegible]	[illegible]
	4. Kilkenny Co.																					
17	[illegible], part of,	[illegible]	[illegible]	[illegible]	[illegible]	[illegible]	[illegible]	[illegible]	[illegible]	[illegible]	[illegible]	[illegible]	[illegible]	[illegible]	[illegible]	[illegible]	[illegible]	[illegible]	[illegible]	[illegible]	[illegible]	[illegible]
18	[illegible], do.,	[illegible]	[illegible]	[illegible]	[illegible]	[illegible]	[illegible]	[illegible]	[illegible]	[illegible]	[illegible]	[illegible]	[illegible]	[illegible]	[illegible]	[illegible]	[illegible]	[illegible]	[illegible]	[illegible]	[illegible]	[illegible]
19	[illegible]	[illegible]	[illegible]	[illegible]	[illegible]	[illegible]	[illegible]	[illegible]	[illegible]	[illegible]	[illegible]	[illegible]	[illegible]	[illegible]	[illegible]	[illegible]	[illegible]	[illegible]	[illegible]	[illegible]	[illegible]	[illegible]
20	[illegible]	[illegible]	[illegible]	[illegible]	[illegible]	[illegible]	[illegible]	[illegible]	[illegible]	[illegible]	[illegible]	[illegible]	[illegible]	[illegible]	[illegible]	[illegible]	[illegible]	[illegible]	[illegible]	[illegible]	[illegible]	[illegible]
21	[illegible], part of,	[illegible]	[illegible]	[illegible]	[illegible]	[illegible]	[illegible]	[illegible]	[illegible]	[illegible]	[illegible]	[illegible]	[illegible]	[illegible]	[illegible]	[illegible]	[illegible]	[illegible]	[illegible]	[illegible]	[illegible]	[illegible]
22	[illegible]	[illegible]	[illegible]	[illegible]	[illegible]	[illegible]	[illegible]	[illegible]	[illegible]	[illegible]	[illegible]	[illegible]	[illegible]	[illegible]	[illegible]	[illegible]	[illegible]	[illegible]	[illegible]	[illegible]	[illegible]	[illegible]
23	[illegible], part of,	[illegible]	[illegible]	[illegible]	[illegible]	[illegible]	[illegible]	[illegible]	[illegible]	[illegible]	[illegible]	[illegible]	[illegible]	[illegible]	[illegible]	[illegible]	[illegible]	[illegible]	[illegible]	[illegible]	[illegible]	[illegible]
24	[illegible], do.,	[illegible]	[illegible]	[illegible]	[illegible]	[illegible]	[illegible]	[illegible]	[illegible]	[illegible]	[illegible]	[illegible]	[illegible]	[illegible]	[illegible]	[illegible]	[illegible]	[illegible]	[illegible]	[illegible]	[illegible]	[illegible]
	5. King's Co.																					
25	[illegible], part of,	[illegible]	[illegible]	[illegible]	[illegible]	[illegible]	[illegible]	[illegible]	[illegible]	[illegible]	[illegible]	[illegible]	[illegible]	[illegible]	[illegible]	[illegible]	[illegible]	[illegible]	[illegible]	[illegible]	[illegible]	[illegible]
26	[illegible], do.,	[illegible]	[illegible]	[illegible]	[illegible]	[illegible]	[illegible]	[illegible]	[illegible]	[illegible]	[illegible]	[illegible]	[illegible]	[illegible]	[illegible]	[illegible]	[illegible]	[illegible]	[illegible]	[illegible]	[illegible]	[illegible]
27	[illegible], do.,	[illegible]	[illegible]	[illegible]	[illegible]	[illegible]	[illegible]	[illegible]	[illegible]	[illegible]	[illegible]	[illegible]	[illegible]	[illegible]	[illegible]	[illegible]	[illegible]	[illegible]	[illegible]	[illegible]	[illegible]	[illegible]
28	[illegible], do.,	[illegible]	[illegible]	[illegible]	[illegible]	[illegible]	[illegible]	[illegible]	[illegible]	[illegible]	[illegible]	[illegible]	[illegible]	[illegible]	[illegible]	[illegible]	[illegible]	[illegible]	[illegible]	[illegible]	[illegible]	[illegible]
29	[illegible], do.,	[illegible]	[illegible]	[illegible]	[illegible]	[illegible]	[illegible]	[illegible]	[illegible]	[illegible]	[illegible]	[illegible]	[illegible]	[illegible]	[illegible]	[illegible]	[illegible]	[illegible]	[illegible]	[illegible]	[illegible]	[illegible]
	6. Longford Co.																					
30	[illegible], part of,	[illegible]	[illegible]	[illegible]	[illegible]	[illegible]	[illegible]	[illegible]	[illegible]	[illegible]	[illegible]	[illegible]	[illegible]	[illegible]	[illegible]	[illegible]	[illegible]	[illegible]	[illegible]	[illegible]	[illegible]	[illegible]
31	[illegible], do.	[illegible]	[illegible]	[illegible]	[illegible]	[illegible]	[illegible]	[illegible]	[illegible]	[illegible]	[illegible]	[illegible]	[illegible]	[illegible]	[illegible]	[illegible]	[illegible]	[illegible]	[illegible]	[illegible]	[illegible]	[illegible]
32	[illegible]	[illegible]	[illegible]	[illegible]	[illegible]	[illegible]	[illegible]	[illegible]	[illegible]	[illegible]	[illegible]	[illegible]	[illegible]	[illegible]	[illegible]	[illegible]	[illegible]	[illegible]	[illegible]	[illegible]	[illegible]	[illegible]
	7. Louth Co. & Co. of Town of Drogheda.																					
33	[illegible], part of,	[illegible]	[illegible]	[illegible]	[illegible]	[illegible]	[illegible]	[illegible]	[illegible]	[illegible]	[illegible]	[illegible]	[illegible]	[illegible]	[illegible]	[illegible]	[illegible]	[illegible]	[illegible]	[illegible]	[illegible]	[illegible]
34	[illegible], do.	[illegible]	[illegible]	[illegible]	[illegible]	[illegible]	[illegible]	[illegible]	[illegible]	[illegible]	[illegible]	[illegible]	[illegible]	[illegible]	[illegible]	[illegible]	[illegible]	[illegible]	[illegible]	[illegible]	[illegible]	[illegible]
35	[illegible], do.	[illegible]	[illegible]	[illegible]	[illegible]	[illegible]	[illegible]	[illegible]	[illegible]	[illegible]	[illegible]	[illegible]	[illegible]	[illegible]	[illegible]	[illegible]	[illegible]	[illegible]	[illegible]	[illegible]	[illegible]	[illegible]
	8. Meath Co.																					
36	[illegible], part of,	[illegible]	[illegible]	[illegible]	[illegible]	[illegible]	[illegible]	[illegible]	[illegible]	[illegible]	[illegible]	[illegible]	[illegible]	[illegible]	[illegible]	[illegible]	[illegible]	[illegible]	[illegible]	[illegible]	[illegible]	[illegible]
37	[illegible], do.	[illegible]	[illegible]	[illegible]	[illegible]	[illegible]	[illegible]	[illegible]	[illegible]	[illegible]	[illegible]	[illegible]	[illegible]	[illegible]	[illegible]	[illegible]	[illegible]	[illegible]	[illegible]	[illegible]	[illegible]	[illegible]
38	[illegible], do.	[illegible]	[illegible]	[illegible]	[illegible]	[illegible]	[illegible]	[illegible]	[illegible]	[illegible]	[illegible]	[illegible]	[illegible]	[illegible]	[illegible]	[illegible]	[illegible]	[illegible]	[illegible]	[illegible]	[illegible]	[illegible]
39	[illegible], do.	[illegible]	[illegible]	[illegible]	[illegible]	[illegible]	[illegible]	[illegible]	[illegible]	[illegible]	[illegible]	[illegible]	[illegible]	[illegible]	[illegible]	[illegible]	[illegible]	[illegible]	[illegible]	[illegible]	[illegible]	[illegible]
40	[illegible], do.	[illegible]	[illegible]	[illegible]	[illegible]	[illegible]	[illegible]	[illegible]	[illegible]	[illegible]	[illegible]	[illegible]	[illegible]	[illegible]	[illegible]	[illegible]	[illegible]	[illegible]	[illegible]	[illegible]	[illegible]	[illegible]
41	[illegible], do.	[illegible]	[illegible]	[illegible]	[illegible]	[illegible]	[illegible]	[illegible]	[illegible]	[illegible]	[illegible]	[illegible]	[illegible]	[illegible]	[illegible]	[illegible]	[illegible]	[illegible]	[illegible]	[illegible]	[illegible]	[illegible]
42	[illegible]	[illegible]	[illegible]	[illegible]	[illegible]	[illegible]	[illegible]	[illegible]	[illegible]	[illegible]	[illegible]	[illegible]	[illegible]	[illegible]	[illegible]	[illegible]	[illegible]	[illegible]	[illegible]	[illegible]	[illegible]	[illegible]
43	[illegible], part of,	[illegible]	[illegible]	[illegible]	[illegible]	[illegible]	[illegible]	[illegible]	[illegible]	[illegible]	[illegible]	[illegible]	[illegible]	[illegible]	[illegible]	[illegible]	[illegible]	[illegible]	[illegible]	[illegible]	[illegible]	[illegible]
44	[illegible]	[illegible]	[illegible]	[illegible]	[illegible]	[illegible]	[illegible]	[illegible]	[illegible]	[illegible]	[illegible]	[illegible]	[illegible]	[illegible]	[illegible]	[illegible]	[illegible]	[illegible]	[illegible]	[illegible]	[illegible]	[illegible]

IRELAND.—Deaths at different Ages registered in the year 1896—in the Superintendent Registrars' Districts in each County.—Males—continued.

[illegible]

[illegible]	[illegible]

[illegible]

[illegible]	[illegible]

IRELAND.—Deaths at different Ages registered in the year 1896—in the Superintendent Registrars' Districts in each County.—Females—continued.

I.—Province of Leinster—continued.

No.	Counties and Superintendent Registrars' Districts	Females
	9. Queen's Co.	
[illegible]	[illegible]	[illegible]
[illegible]	[illegible]	[illegible]
[illegible]	[illegible]	[illegible]
[illegible]	[illegible]	[illegible]
[illegible]	[illegible]	[illegible]
[illegible]	[illegible]	[illegible]
	10. Westmeath Co.	
[illegible]	[illegible]	[illegible]
[illegible]	[illegible]	[illegible]
[illegible]	[illegible]	[illegible]
[illegible]	[illegible]	[illegible]
[illegible]	[illegible]	[illegible]
[illegible]	[illegible]	[illegible]
	11. Wexford Co.	
[illegible]	[illegible]	[illegible]
[illegible]	[illegible]	[illegible]
[illegible]	[illegible]	[illegible]
[illegible]	[illegible]	[illegible]
[illegible]	[illegible]	[illegible]
	12. Wicklow Co.	
[illegible]	[illegible]	[illegible]
[illegible]	[illegible]	[illegible]
[illegible]	[illegible]	[illegible]
[illegible]	[illegible]	[illegible]
[illegible]	[illegible]	[illegible]

II.—Province of Munster.

No.	Counties and Superintendent Registrars' Districts	Females
	13. Clare Co.	
[illegible]	[illegible]	[illegible]
[illegible]	[illegible]	[illegible]
[illegible]	[illegible]	[illegible]
[illegible]	[illegible]	[illegible]
[illegible]	[illegible]	[illegible]
[illegible]	[illegible]	[illegible]
[illegible]	[illegible]	[illegible]
[illegible]	[illegible]	[illegible]

IRELAND.—[illegible]

[illegible]

IRELAND.—Deaths at different Ages registered in the year 1896—in the Superintendent Registrars' Districts in each County.—Females—continued.

II.—Province of Munster—continued.

No.	Counties and Superintendent Registrars' Districts	Females: Total Births	Total Deaths	Ages at Death: Under 1 year	1	2	3	4	Under 5 years	5-	10-	15-	20-	25-	35-	45-	55-	65-	75-	85-	95 and upwards
	Cork Co.—(continued)																				
[illegible]	[illegible]	[illegible]	[illegible]	[illegible]	[illegible]	[illegible]	[illegible]	[illegible]	[illegible]	[illegible]	[illegible]	[illegible]	[illegible]	[illegible]	[illegible]	[illegible]	[illegible]	[illegible]	[illegible]	[illegible]	[illegible]
[illegible]	[illegible]	[illegible]	[illegible]	[illegible]	[illegible]	[illegible]	[illegible]	[illegible]	[illegible]	[illegible]	[illegible]	[illegible]	[illegible]	[illegible]	[illegible]	[illegible]	[illegible]	[illegible]	[illegible]	[illegible]	[illegible]
[illegible]	[illegible], part of	61	[illegible]	[illegible]	[illegible]	[illegible]	[illegible]	[illegible]	[illegible]	[illegible]	[illegible]	[illegible]	[illegible]	[illegible]	[illegible]	[illegible]	[illegible]	[illegible]	[illegible]	[illegible]	[illegible]
[illegible]	[illegible]	[illegible]	[illegible]	[illegible]	[illegible]	[illegible]	[illegible]	[illegible]	[illegible]	[illegible]	[illegible]	[illegible]	[illegible]	[illegible]	[illegible]	[illegible]	[illegible]	[illegible]	[illegible]	[illegible]	[illegible]
[illegible]	[illegible]	[illegible]	[illegible]	[illegible]	[illegible]	[illegible]	[illegible]	[illegible]	[illegible]	[illegible]	[illegible]	[illegible]	[illegible]	[illegible]	[illegible]	[illegible]	[illegible]	[illegible]	[illegible]	[illegible]	[illegible]
[illegible]	[illegible]	[illegible]	[illegible]	[illegible]	[illegible]	[illegible]	[illegible]	[illegible]	[illegible]	[illegible]	[illegible]	[illegible]	[illegible]	[illegible]	[illegible]	[illegible]	[illegible]	[illegible]	[illegible]	[illegible]	[illegible]
[illegible]	[illegible]	[illegible]	[illegible]	[illegible]	[illegible]	[illegible]	[illegible]	[illegible]	[illegible]	[illegible]	[illegible]	[illegible]	[illegible]	[illegible]	[illegible]	[illegible]	[illegible]	[illegible]	[illegible]	[illegible]	[illegible]
[illegible]	[illegible]	[illegible]	[illegible]	[illegible]	[illegible]	[illegible]	[illegible]	[illegible]	[illegible]	[illegible]	[illegible]	[illegible]	[illegible]	[illegible]	[illegible]	[illegible]	[illegible]	[illegible]	[illegible]	[illegible]	[illegible]
[illegible]	[illegible]	[illegible]	[illegible]	[illegible]	[illegible]	[illegible]	[illegible]	[illegible]	[illegible]	[illegible]	[illegible]	[illegible]	[illegible]	[illegible]	[illegible]	[illegible]	[illegible]	[illegible]	[illegible]	[illegible]	[illegible]
[illegible]	[illegible], pt. of	[illegible]	[illegible]	[illegible]	[illegible]	[illegible]	[illegible]	[illegible]	[illegible]	[illegible]	[illegible]	[illegible]	[illegible]	[illegible]	[illegible]	[illegible]	[illegible]	[illegible]	[illegible]	[illegible]	[illegible]
[illegible]	[illegible]	[illegible]	[illegible]	[illegible]	[illegible]	[illegible]	[illegible]	[illegible]	[illegible]	[illegible]	[illegible]	[illegible]	[illegible]	[illegible]	[illegible]	[illegible]	[illegible]	[illegible]	[illegible]	[illegible]	[illegible]
[illegible]	[illegible]	[illegible]	[illegible]	[illegible]	[illegible]	[illegible]	[illegible]	[illegible]	[illegible]	[illegible]	[illegible]	[illegible]	[illegible]	[illegible]	[illegible]	[illegible]	[illegible]	[illegible]	[illegible]	[illegible]	[illegible]
[illegible]	[illegible], part of	[illegible]	[illegible]	[illegible]	[illegible]	[illegible]	[illegible]	[illegible]	[illegible]	[illegible]	[illegible]	[illegible]	[illegible]	[illegible]	[illegible]	[illegible]	[illegible]	[illegible]	[illegible]	[illegible]	[illegible]
	Kerry Co.																				
[illegible]	[illegible]	[illegible]	[illegible]	[illegible]	[illegible]	[illegible]	[illegible]	[illegible]	[illegible]	[illegible]	[illegible]	[illegible]	[illegible]	[illegible]	[illegible]	[illegible]	[illegible]	[illegible]	[illegible]	[illegible]	[illegible]
[illegible]	[illegible]	[illegible]	[illegible]	[illegible]	[illegible]	[illegible]	[illegible]	[illegible]	[illegible]	[illegible]	[illegible]	[illegible]	[illegible]	[illegible]	[illegible]	[illegible]	[illegible]	[illegible]	[illegible]	[illegible]	[illegible]
[illegible]	[illegible]	[illegible]	[illegible]	[illegible]	[illegible]	[illegible]	[illegible]	[illegible]	[illegible]	[illegible]	[illegible]	[illegible]	[illegible]	[illegible]	[illegible]	[illegible]	[illegible]	[illegible]	[illegible]	[illegible]	[illegible]
[illegible]	[illegible]	[illegible]	[illegible]	[illegible]	[illegible]	[illegible]	[illegible]	[illegible]	[illegible]	[illegible]	[illegible]	[illegible]	[illegible]	[illegible]	[illegible]	[illegible]	[illegible]	[illegible]	[illegible]	[illegible]	[illegible]
[illegible]	[illegible], part of	[illegible]	[illegible]	[illegible]	[illegible]	[illegible]	[illegible]	[illegible]	[illegible]	[illegible]	[illegible]	[illegible]	[illegible]	[illegible]	[illegible]	[illegible]	[illegible]	[illegible]	[illegible]	[illegible]	[illegible]
[illegible]	[illegible]	[illegible]	[illegible]	[illegible]	[illegible]	[illegible]	[illegible]	[illegible]	[illegible]	[illegible]	[illegible]	[illegible]	[illegible]	[illegible]	[illegible]	[illegible]	[illegible]	[illegible]	[illegible]	[illegible]	[illegible]
	Limerick Co.																				
[illegible]	[illegible]	[illegible]	[illegible]	[illegible]	[illegible]	[illegible]	[illegible]	[illegible]	[illegible]	[illegible]	[illegible]	[illegible]	[illegible]	[illegible]	[illegible]	[illegible]	[illegible]	[illegible]	[illegible]	[illegible]	[illegible]
[illegible]	[illegible], part of	[illegible]	[illegible]	[illegible]	[illegible]	[illegible]	[illegible]	[illegible]	[illegible]	[illegible]	[illegible]	[illegible]	[illegible]	[illegible]	[illegible]	[illegible]	[illegible]	[illegible]	[illegible]	[illegible]	[illegible]
[illegible]	[illegible], do.	[illegible]	[illegible]	[illegible]	[illegible]	[illegible]	[illegible]	[illegible]	[illegible]	[illegible]	[illegible]	[illegible]	[illegible]	[illegible]	[illegible]	[illegible]	[illegible]	[illegible]	[illegible]	[illegible]	[illegible]
[illegible]	[illegible], do.	[illegible]	[illegible]	[illegible]	[illegible]	[illegible]	[illegible]	[illegible]	[illegible]	[illegible]	[illegible]	[illegible]	[illegible]	[illegible]	[illegible]	[illegible]	[illegible]	[illegible]	[illegible]	[illegible]	[illegible]
[illegible]	[illegible], do.	[illegible]	[illegible]	[illegible]	[illegible]	[illegible]	[illegible]	[illegible]	[illegible]	[illegible]	[illegible]	[illegible]	[illegible]	[illegible]	[illegible]	[illegible]	[illegible]	[illegible]	[illegible]	[illegible]	[illegible]
[illegible]	[illegible]	[illegible]	[illegible]	[illegible]	[illegible]	[illegible]	[illegible]	[illegible]	[illegible]	[illegible]	[illegible]	[illegible]	[illegible]	[illegible]	[illegible]	[illegible]	[illegible]	[illegible]	[illegible]	[illegible]	[illegible]
[illegible]	[illegible]	[illegible]	[illegible]	[illegible]	[illegible]	[illegible]	[illegible]	[illegible]	[illegible]	[illegible]	[illegible]	[illegible]	[illegible]	[illegible]	[illegible]	[illegible]	[illegible]	[illegible]	[illegible]	[illegible]	[illegible]
[illegible]	[illegible], part of	[illegible]	[illegible]	[illegible]	[illegible]	[illegible]	[illegible]	[illegible]	[illegible]	[illegible]	[illegible]	[illegible]	[illegible]	[illegible]	[illegible]	[illegible]	[illegible]	[illegible]	[illegible]	[illegible]	[illegible]
	Tipperary Co.																				
[illegible]	[illegible]	[illegible]	[illegible]	[illegible]	[illegible]	[illegible]	[illegible]	[illegible]	[illegible]	[illegible]	[illegible]	[illegible]	[illegible]	[illegible]	[illegible]	[illegible]	[illegible]	[illegible]	[illegible]	[illegible]	[illegible]
[illegible]	[illegible], part of	[illegible]	[illegible]	[illegible]	[illegible]	[illegible]	[illegible]	[illegible]	[illegible]	[illegible]	[illegible]	[illegible]	[illegible]	[illegible]	[illegible]	[illegible]	[illegible]	[illegible]	[illegible]	[illegible]	[illegible]
[illegible]	[illegible], do.	[illegible]	[illegible]	[illegible]	[illegible]	[illegible]	[illegible]	[illegible]	[illegible]	[illegible]	[illegible]	[illegible]	[illegible]	[illegible]	[illegible]	[illegible]	[illegible]	[illegible]	[illegible]	[illegible]	[illegible]
[illegible]	[illegible]	[illegible]	[illegible]	[illegible]	[illegible]	[illegible]	[illegible]	[illegible]	[illegible]	[illegible]	[illegible]	[illegible]	[illegible]	[illegible]	[illegible]	[illegible]	[illegible]	[illegible]	[illegible]	[illegible]	[illegible]
[illegible]	[illegible]	[illegible]	[illegible]	[illegible]	[illegible]	[illegible]	[illegible]	[illegible]	[illegible]	[illegible]	[illegible]	[illegible]	[illegible]	[illegible]	[illegible]	[illegible]	[illegible]	[illegible]	[illegible]	[illegible]	[illegible]
[illegible]	[illegible], part of	[illegible]	[illegible]	[illegible]	[illegible]	[illegible]	[illegible]	[illegible]	[illegible]	[illegible]	[illegible]	[illegible]	[illegible]	[illegible]	[illegible]	[illegible]	[illegible]	[illegible]	[illegible]	[illegible]	[illegible]
[illegible]	[illegible]	[illegible]	[illegible]	[illegible]	[illegible]	[illegible]	[illegible]	[illegible]	[illegible]	[illegible]	[illegible]	[illegible]	[illegible]	[illegible]	[illegible]	[illegible]	[illegible]	[illegible]	[illegible]	[illegible]	[illegible]
[illegible]	[illegible], pt. of	[illegible]	[illegible]	[illegible]	[illegible]	[illegible]	[illegible]	[illegible]	[illegible]	[illegible]	[illegible]	[illegible]	[illegible]	[illegible]	[illegible]	[illegible]	[illegible]	[illegible]	[illegible]	[illegible]	[illegible]
[illegible]	[illegible], do.	[illegible]	[illegible]	[illegible]	[illegible]	[illegible]	[illegible]	[illegible]	[illegible]	[illegible]	[illegible]	[illegible]	[illegible]	[illegible]	[illegible]	[illegible]	[illegible]	[illegible]	[illegible]	[illegible]	[illegible]
[illegible]	[illegible]	[illegible]	[illegible]	[illegible]	[illegible]	[illegible]	[illegible]	[illegible]	[illegible]	[illegible]	[illegible]	[illegible]	[illegible]	[illegible]	[illegible]	[illegible]	[illegible]	[illegible]	[illegible]	[illegible]	[illegible]
[illegible]	[illegible], part of	[illegible]	[illegible]	[illegible]	[illegible]	[illegible]	[illegible]	[illegible]	[illegible]	[illegible]	[illegible]	[illegible]	[illegible]	[illegible]	[illegible]	[illegible]	[illegible]	[illegible]	[illegible]	[illegible]	[illegible]
[illegible]	[illegible], do.	[illegible]	[illegible]	[illegible]	[illegible]	[illegible]	[illegible]	[illegible]	[illegible]	[illegible]	[illegible]	[illegible]	[illegible]	[illegible]	[illegible]	[illegible]	[illegible]	[illegible]	[illegible]	[illegible]	[illegible]
	Waterford Co.																				
[illegible]	[illegible], pt. of	[illegible]	[illegible]	[illegible]	[illegible]	[illegible]	[illegible]	[illegible]	[illegible]	[illegible]	[illegible]	[illegible]	[illegible]	[illegible]	[illegible]	[illegible]	[illegible]	[illegible]	[illegible]	[illegible]	[illegible]
[illegible]	[illegible], do.	[illegible]	[illegible]	[illegible]	[illegible]	[illegible]	[illegible]	[illegible]	[illegible]	[illegible]	[illegible]	[illegible]	[illegible]	[illegible]	[illegible]	[illegible]	[illegible]	[illegible]	[illegible]	[illegible]	[illegible]
[illegible]	[illegible]	[illegible]	[illegible]	[illegible]	[illegible]	[illegible]	[illegible]	[illegible]	[illegible]	[illegible]	[illegible]	[illegible]	[illegible]	[illegible]	[illegible]	[illegible]	[illegible]	[illegible]	[illegible]	[illegible]	[illegible]
[illegible]	[illegible]	[illegible]	[illegible]	[illegible]	[illegible]	[illegible]	[illegible]	[illegible]	[illegible]	[illegible]	[illegible]	[illegible]	[illegible]	[illegible]	[illegible]	[illegible]	[illegible]	[illegible]	[illegible]	[illegible]	[illegible]
[illegible]	[illegible]	[illegible]	[illegible]	[illegible]	[illegible]	[illegible]	[illegible]	[illegible]	[illegible]	[illegible]	[illegible]	[illegible]	[illegible]	[illegible]	[illegible]	[illegible]	[illegible]	[illegible]	[illegible]	[illegible]	[illegible]
[illegible]	[illegible], part of	[illegible]	[illegible]	[illegible]	[illegible]	[illegible]	[illegible]	[illegible]	[illegible]	[illegible]	[illegible]	[illegible]	[illegible]	[illegible]	[illegible]	[illegible]	[illegible]	[illegible]	[illegible]	[illegible]	[illegible]
[illegible]	[illegible], do.	[illegible]	[illegible]	[illegible]	[illegible]	[illegible]	[illegible]	[illegible]	[illegible]	[illegible]	[illegible]	[illegible]	[illegible]	[illegible]	[illegible]	[illegible]	[illegible]	[illegible]	[illegible]	[illegible]	[illegible]

IRELAND.—Deaths at different Ages registered in the year 18[illegible]—in the Superintendent Registrars' Districts in each County.—Males—continued.

III.—PROVINCE OF ULSTER.

No.	Counties and Superintendent Registrars' Districts	Males (all columns)
	15. Antrim Co.	
[illegible]	Antrim	[illegible]
[illegible]	Ballycastle	[illegible]
[illegible]	Ballymena	[illegible]
[illegible]	Ballymoney, part of	[illegible]
[illegible]	Belfast, do.	[illegible]
[illegible]	Coleraine, do.	[illegible]
[illegible]	Larne	[illegible]
[illegible]	Lisburn, part of	[illegible]
[illegible]	Lurgan, do.	[illegible]
	16. Armagh Co.	
[illegible]	Armagh, part of	[illegible]
[illegible]	Banbridge, do.	[illegible]
[illegible]	Castleblayney, do.	[illegible]
[illegible]	Dundalk, do.	[illegible]
[illegible]	Lurgan, do.	[illegible]
[illegible]	Newry, do.	[illegible]
	17. Cavan Co.	
[illegible]	[illegible]	[illegible]
[illegible]	[illegible]	[illegible]
[illegible]	[illegible]	[illegible]
[illegible]	[illegible]	[illegible]
[illegible]	[illegible]	[illegible]
[illegible]	[illegible]	[illegible]
[illegible]	[illegible]	[illegible]
[illegible]	[illegible]	[illegible]
	18. Donegal Co.	
[illegible]	[illegible]	[illegible]
[illegible]	[illegible]	[illegible]
[illegible]	[illegible]	[illegible]
[illegible]	[illegible]	[illegible]
[illegible]	[illegible]	[illegible]
[illegible]	[illegible]	[illegible]
[illegible]	[illegible]	[illegible]
[illegible]	[illegible]	[illegible]
[illegible]	[illegible]	[illegible]
[illegible]	[illegible]	[illegible]
	19. Down Co.	
[illegible]	[illegible]	[illegible]
[illegible]	Belfast, do.	[illegible]
[illegible]	[illegible]	[illegible]
[illegible]	[illegible]	[illegible]
[illegible]	[illegible]	[illegible]
[illegible]	[illegible]	[illegible]
[illegible]	[illegible]	[illegible]
[illegible]	[illegible]	[illegible]

IRELAND.—Deaths at different Ages registered in the year 1896—in the Superintendent Registrars' Districts in each County.—Females—*continued*.

III.—PROVINCE OF ULSTER.

No.	Counties and Superintendent Registrars' Districts	Females (all ages and age groups)
	[illegible] Co.	
[illegible]	[illegible]	[illegible]
[illegible]	[illegible]	[illegible]
[illegible]	[illegible]	[illegible]
[illegible]	[illegible]	[illegible]
[illegible]	[illegible]	[illegible]
[illegible]	[illegible]	[illegible]
[illegible]	[illegible]	[illegible]
[illegible]	[illegible]	[illegible]
[illegible]	[illegible]	[illegible]
	[illegible] Co.	
[illegible]	[illegible]	[illegible]
[illegible]	[illegible]	[illegible]
[illegible]	[illegible]	[illegible]
[illegible]	[illegible]	[illegible]
[illegible]	[illegible]	[illegible]
[illegible]	[illegible]	[illegible]
	[illegible] Co.	
[illegible]	[illegible]	[illegible]
[illegible]	[illegible]	[illegible]
[illegible]	[illegible]	[illegible]
[illegible]	[illegible]	[illegible]
[illegible]	[illegible]	[illegible]
[illegible]	[illegible]	[illegible]
[illegible]	[illegible]	[illegible]
[illegible]	[illegible]	[illegible]
	[illegible] Co.	
[illegible]	[illegible]	[illegible]
[illegible]	[illegible]	[illegible]
[illegible]	[illegible]	[illegible]
[illegible]	[illegible]	[illegible]
[illegible]	[illegible]	[illegible]
[illegible]	[illegible]	[illegible]
[illegible]	[illegible]	[illegible]
[illegible]	[illegible]	[illegible]
[illegible]	[illegible]	[illegible]
[illegible]	[illegible]	[illegible]
	[illegible] Co.	
[illegible]	[illegible]	[illegible]
[illegible]	[illegible]	[illegible]
[illegible]	[illegible]	[illegible]
[illegible]	[illegible]	[illegible]
[illegible]	[illegible]	[illegible]
[illegible]	[illegible]	[illegible]
[illegible]	[illegible]	[illegible]
[illegible]	[illegible]	[illegible]

IRELAND.—[illegible] at different Ages registered in the year [illegible]—in the Superintendent Registrars' Districts in each County.—Males—continued.

III.—Province of Ulster—continued.

No.	Counties and Superintendent Registrars' Districts	Males.																			
		[illegible]	[illegible]	Ages at Death.																	
				[illegible]	[illegible]	[illegible]	[illegible]	[illegible]	[illegible]	[illegible]	[illegible]	[illegible]	[illegible]	[illegible]	[illegible]	[illegible]	[illegible]	[illegible]	[illegible]	[illegible]	[illegible]
[illegible]	[illegible] Fermanagh Co.																				
[illegible]	[illegible]	[illegible]	[illegible]	[illegible]	[illegible]	[illegible]	[illegible]	[illegible]	[illegible]	[illegible]	[illegible]	[illegible]	[illegible]	[illegible]	[illegible]	[illegible]	[illegible]	[illegible]	[illegible]	[illegible]	[illegible]
[illegible]	[illegible]	[illegible]	[illegible]	[illegible]	[illegible]	[illegible]	[illegible]	[illegible]	[illegible]	[illegible]	[illegible]	[illegible]	[illegible]	[illegible]	[illegible]	[illegible]	[illegible]	[illegible]	[illegible]	[illegible]	[illegible]
[illegible]	[illegible]	[illegible]	[illegible]	[illegible]	[illegible]	[illegible]	[illegible]	[illegible]	[illegible]	[illegible]	[illegible]	[illegible]	[illegible]	[illegible]	[illegible]	[illegible]	[illegible]	[illegible]	[illegible]	[illegible]	[illegible]
[illegible]	[illegible]	[illegible]	[illegible]	[illegible]	[illegible]	[illegible]	[illegible]	[illegible]	[illegible]	[illegible]	[illegible]	[illegible]	[illegible]	[illegible]	[illegible]	[illegible]	[illegible]	[illegible]	[illegible]	[illegible]	[illegible]
[illegible]	[illegible]	[illegible]	[illegible]	[illegible]	[illegible]	[illegible]	[illegible]	[illegible]	[illegible]	[illegible]	[illegible]	[illegible]	[illegible]	[illegible]	[illegible]	[illegible]	[illegible]	[illegible]	[illegible]	[illegible]	[illegible]
	[illegible] Londonderry Co.																				
[illegible]	[illegible]	[illegible]	[illegible]	[illegible]	[illegible]	[illegible]	[illegible]	[illegible]	[illegible]	[illegible]	[illegible]	[illegible]	[illegible]	[illegible]	[illegible]	[illegible]	[illegible]	[illegible]	[illegible]	[illegible]	[illegible]
[illegible]	[illegible]	[illegible]	[illegible]	[illegible]	[illegible]	[illegible]	[illegible]	[illegible]	[illegible]	[illegible]	[illegible]	[illegible]	[illegible]	[illegible]	[illegible]	[illegible]	[illegible]	[illegible]	[illegible]	[illegible]	[illegible]
[illegible]	[illegible]	[illegible]	[illegible]	[illegible]	[illegible]	[illegible]	[illegible]	[illegible]	[illegible]	[illegible]	[illegible]	[illegible]	[illegible]	[illegible]	[illegible]	[illegible]	[illegible]	[illegible]	[illegible]	[illegible]	[illegible]
[illegible]	[illegible]	[illegible]	[illegible]	[illegible]	[illegible]	[illegible]	[illegible]	[illegible]	[illegible]	[illegible]	[illegible]	[illegible]	[illegible]	[illegible]	[illegible]	[illegible]	[illegible]	[illegible]	[illegible]	[illegible]	[illegible]
[illegible]	[illegible]	[illegible]	[illegible]	[illegible]	[illegible]	[illegible]	[illegible]	[illegible]	[illegible]	[illegible]	[illegible]	[illegible]	[illegible]	[illegible]	[illegible]	[illegible]	[illegible]	[illegible]	[illegible]	[illegible]	[illegible]
	[illegible] Monaghan Co.																				
[illegible]	[illegible]	[illegible]	[illegible]	[illegible]	[illegible]	[illegible]	[illegible]	[illegible]	[illegible]	[illegible]	[illegible]	[illegible]	[illegible]	[illegible]	[illegible]	[illegible]	[illegible]	[illegible]	[illegible]	[illegible]	[illegible]
[illegible]	[illegible]	[illegible]	[illegible]	[illegible]	[illegible]	[illegible]	[illegible]	[illegible]	[illegible]	[illegible]	[illegible]	[illegible]	[illegible]	[illegible]	[illegible]	[illegible]	[illegible]	[illegible]	[illegible]	[illegible]	[illegible]
[illegible]	[illegible]	[illegible]	[illegible]	[illegible]	[illegible]	[illegible]	[illegible]	[illegible]	[illegible]	[illegible]	[illegible]	[illegible]	[illegible]	[illegible]	[illegible]	[illegible]	[illegible]	[illegible]	[illegible]	[illegible]	[illegible]
[illegible]	[illegible]	[illegible]	[illegible]	[illegible]	[illegible]	[illegible]	[illegible]	[illegible]	[illegible]	[illegible]	[illegible]	[illegible]	[illegible]	[illegible]	[illegible]	[illegible]	[illegible]	[illegible]	[illegible]	[illegible]	[illegible]
[illegible]	[illegible]	[illegible]	[illegible]	[illegible]	[illegible]	[illegible]	[illegible]	[illegible]	[illegible]	[illegible]	[illegible]	[illegible]	[illegible]	[illegible]	[illegible]	[illegible]	[illegible]	[illegible]	[illegible]	[illegible]	[illegible]
[illegible]	[illegible]	[illegible]	[illegible]	[illegible]	[illegible]	[illegible]	[illegible]	[illegible]	[illegible]	[illegible]	[illegible]	[illegible]	[illegible]	[illegible]	[illegible]	[illegible]	[illegible]	[illegible]	[illegible]	[illegible]	[illegible]
[illegible]	[illegible]	[illegible]	[illegible]	[illegible]	[illegible]	[illegible]	[illegible]	[illegible]	[illegible]	[illegible]	[illegible]	[illegible]	[illegible]	[illegible]	[illegible]	[illegible]	[illegible]	[illegible]	[illegible]	[illegible]	[illegible]
	[illegible] Tyrone Co.																				
[illegible]	[illegible]	[illegible]	[illegible]	[illegible]	[illegible]	[illegible]	[illegible]	[illegible]	[illegible]	[illegible]	[illegible]	[illegible]	[illegible]	[illegible]	[illegible]	[illegible]	[illegible]	[illegible]	[illegible]	[illegible]	[illegible]
[illegible]	[illegible]	[illegible]	[illegible]	[illegible]	[illegible]	[illegible]	[illegible]	[illegible]	[illegible]	[illegible]	[illegible]	[illegible]	[illegible]	[illegible]	[illegible]	[illegible]	[illegible]	[illegible]	[illegible]	[illegible]	[illegible]
[illegible]	[illegible]	[illegible]	[illegible]	[illegible]	[illegible]	[illegible]	[illegible]	[illegible]	[illegible]	[illegible]	[illegible]	[illegible]	[illegible]	[illegible]	[illegible]	[illegible]	[illegible]	[illegible]	[illegible]	[illegible]	[illegible]
[illegible]	[illegible]	[illegible]	[illegible]	[illegible]	[illegible]	[illegible]	[illegible]	[illegible]	[illegible]	[illegible]	[illegible]	[illegible]	[illegible]	[illegible]	[illegible]	[illegible]	[illegible]	[illegible]	[illegible]	[illegible]	[illegible]
[illegible]	[illegible]	[illegible]	[illegible]	[illegible]	[illegible]	[illegible]	[illegible]	[illegible]	[illegible]	[illegible]	[illegible]	[illegible]	[illegible]	[illegible]	[illegible]	[illegible]	[illegible]	[illegible]	[illegible]	[illegible]	[illegible]
[illegible]	[illegible]	[illegible]	[illegible]	[illegible]	[illegible]	[illegible]	[illegible]	[illegible]	[illegible]	[illegible]	[illegible]	[illegible]	[illegible]	[illegible]	[illegible]	[illegible]	[illegible]	[illegible]	[illegible]	[illegible]	[illegible]
[illegible]	[illegible]	[illegible]	[illegible]	[illegible]	[illegible]	[illegible]	[illegible]	[illegible]	[illegible]	[illegible]	[illegible]	[illegible]	[illegible]	[illegible]	[illegible]	[illegible]	[illegible]	[illegible]	[illegible]	[illegible]	[illegible]
[illegible]	[illegible]	[illegible]	[illegible]	[illegible]	[illegible]	[illegible]	[illegible]	[illegible]	[illegible]	[illegible]	[illegible]	[illegible]	[illegible]	[illegible]	[illegible]	[illegible]	[illegible]	[illegible]	[illegible]	[illegible]	[illegible]
[illegible]	[illegible]	[illegible]	[illegible]	[illegible]	[illegible]	[illegible]	[illegible]	[illegible]	[illegible]	[illegible]	[illegible]	[illegible]	[illegible]	[illegible]	[illegible]	[illegible]	[illegible]	[illegible]	[illegible]	[illegible]	[illegible]
	IV.—PROVINCE OF CONNAUGHT.																				
	[illegible] Galway Co.																				
[illegible]	[illegible]	[illegible]	[illegible]	[illegible]	[illegible]	[illegible]	[illegible]	[illegible]	[illegible]	[illegible]	[illegible]	[illegible]	[illegible]	[illegible]	[illegible]	[illegible]	[illegible]	[illegible]	[illegible]	[illegible]	[illegible]
[illegible]	[illegible]	[illegible]	[illegible]	[illegible]	[illegible]	[illegible]	[illegible]	[illegible]	[illegible]	[illegible]	[illegible]	[illegible]	[illegible]	[illegible]	[illegible]	[illegible]	[illegible]	[illegible]	[illegible]	[illegible]	[illegible]
[illegible]	[illegible]	[illegible]	[illegible]	[illegible]	[illegible]	[illegible]	[illegible]	[illegible]	[illegible]	[illegible]	[illegible]	[illegible]	[illegible]	[illegible]	[illegible]	[illegible]	[illegible]	[illegible]	[illegible]	[illegible]	[illegible]
[illegible]	[illegible]	[illegible]	[illegible]	[illegible]	[illegible]	[illegible]	[illegible]	[illegible]	[illegible]	[illegible]	[illegible]	[illegible]	[illegible]	[illegible]	[illegible]	[illegible]	[illegible]	[illegible]	[illegible]	[illegible]	[illegible]
[illegible]	[illegible]	[illegible]	[illegible]	[illegible]	[illegible]	[illegible]	[illegible]	[illegible]	[illegible]	[illegible]	[illegible]	[illegible]	[illegible]	[illegible]	[illegible]	[illegible]	[illegible]	[illegible]	[illegible]	[illegible]	[illegible]

IRELAND.—DEATHS at different Ages registered in the year 1896—in the Superintendent Registrars' Districts in each County.—Females—continued.

III.—PROVINCE OF ULSTER—continued.

[illegible]	[illegible]	[illegible]	[illegible]	[illegible]	[illegible]	[illegible]	[illegible]	[illegible]	[illegible]	[illegible]	[illegible]	[illegible]	[illegible]	[illegible]	[illegible]	[illegible]	[illegible]	[illegible]	[illegible]	[illegible]	[illegible]
[illegible]	[illegible]	[illegible]	[illegible]	[illegible]	[illegible]	[illegible]	[illegible]	[illegible]	[illegible]	[illegible]	[illegible]	[illegible]	[illegible]	[illegible]	[illegible]	[illegible]	[illegible]	[illegible]	[illegible]	[illegible]	[illegible]

IV.—PROVINCE OF CONNAUGHT.

[illegible]	[illegible]	[illegible]	[illegible]	[illegible]	[illegible]	[illegible]	[illegible]	[illegible]	[illegible]	[illegible]	[illegible]	[illegible]	[illegible]	[illegible]	[illegible]	[illegible]	[illegible]	[illegible]	[illegible]	[illegible]	[illegible]
[illegible]	[illegible]	[illegible]	[illegible]	[illegible]	[illegible]	[illegible]	[illegible]	[illegible]	[illegible]	[illegible]	[illegible]	[illegible]	[illegible]	[illegible]	[illegible]	[illegible]	[illegible]	[illegible]	[illegible]	[illegible]	[illegible]

IRELAND.—DEATHS at different AGES registered in the year 18[illegible]—in the SUPERINTENDENT REGISTRARS' DISTRICTS in each COUNTY.—MALES—*continued.*

IV.—PROVINCE OF CONNAUGHT—*continued.*

No.	Counties and Superintendent Registrars' Districts.	Total Births.	Total Deaths.	Under 1 year	1	2	3	4	Under 5 years	5-	10-	15-	20-	25-	35-	45-	55-	65-	75-	85-	95 and upwards
	27th. Leitrim Co.																				
[illegible]	Ballyshannon (?), pt. of	[illegible]	[illegible]	[illegible]	[illegible]	[illegible]	[illegible]	[illegible]	[illegible]	[illegible]	[illegible]	[illegible]	[illegible]	[illegible]	[illegible]	[illegible]	[illegible]	[illegible]	[illegible]	[illegible]	[illegible]
[illegible]	Bawnboy (?), do.	[illegible]	[illegible]	[illegible]	[illegible]	[illegible]	[illegible]	[illegible]	[illegible]	[illegible]	[illegible]	[illegible]	[illegible]	[illegible]	[illegible]	[illegible]	[illegible]	[illegible]	[illegible]	[illegible]	[illegible]
[illegible]	Carrick-on-Shannon (?), do.	[illegible]	[illegible]	[illegible]	[illegible]	[illegible]	[illegible]	[illegible]	[illegible]	[illegible]	[illegible]	[illegible]	[illegible]	[illegible]	[illegible]	[illegible]	[illegible]	[illegible]	[illegible]	[illegible]	[illegible]
[illegible]	Manorhamilton (?),	[illegible]	[illegible]	[illegible]	[illegible]	[illegible]	[illegible]	[illegible]	[illegible]	[illegible]	[illegible]	[illegible]	[illegible]	[illegible]	[illegible]	[illegible]	[illegible]	[illegible]	[illegible]	[illegible]	[illegible]
[illegible]	Mohill (?),	[illegible]	[illegible]	[illegible]	[illegible]	[illegible]	[illegible]	[illegible]	[illegible]	[illegible]	[illegible]	[illegible]	[illegible]	[illegible]	[illegible]	[illegible]	[illegible]	[illegible]	[illegible]	[illegible]	[illegible]
	28th. Mayo Co.																				
[illegible]	Ballina, part of	[illegible]	[illegible]	[illegible]	[illegible]	[illegible]	[illegible]	[illegible]	[illegible]	[illegible]	[illegible]	[illegible]	[illegible]	[illegible]	[illegible]	[illegible]	[illegible]	[illegible]	[illegible]	[illegible]	[illegible]
[illegible]	Ballinrobe, do.	[illegible]	[illegible]	[illegible]	[illegible]	[illegible]	[illegible]	[illegible]	[illegible]	[illegible]	[illegible]	[illegible]	[illegible]	[illegible]	[illegible]	[illegible]	[illegible]	[illegible]	[illegible]	[illegible]	[illegible]
[illegible]	Belmullet,	[illegible]	[illegible]	[illegible]	[illegible]	[illegible]	[illegible]	[illegible]	[illegible]	[illegible]	[illegible]	[illegible]	[illegible]	[illegible]	[illegible]	[illegible]	[illegible]	[illegible]	[illegible]	[illegible]	[illegible]
[illegible]	Castlebar,	[illegible]	[illegible]	[illegible]	[illegible]	[illegible]	[illegible]	[illegible]	[illegible]	[illegible]	[illegible]	[illegible]	[illegible]	[illegible]	[illegible]	[illegible]	[illegible]	[illegible]	[illegible]	[illegible]	[illegible]
[illegible]	Castlereagh, pt. of	[illegible]	[illegible]	[illegible]	[illegible]	[illegible]	[illegible]	[illegible]	[illegible]	[illegible]	[illegible]	[illegible]	[illegible]	[illegible]	[illegible]	[illegible]	[illegible]	[illegible]	[illegible]	[illegible]	[illegible]
[illegible]	Claremorris,	[illegible]	[illegible]	[illegible]	[illegible]	[illegible]	[illegible]	[illegible]	[illegible]	[illegible]	[illegible]	[illegible]	[illegible]	[illegible]	[illegible]	[illegible]	[illegible]	[illegible]	[illegible]	[illegible]	[illegible]
[illegible]	Killala,	[illegible]	[illegible]	[illegible]	[illegible]	[illegible]	[illegible]	[illegible]	[illegible]	[illegible]	[illegible]	[illegible]	[illegible]	[illegible]	[illegible]	[illegible]	[illegible]	[illegible]	[illegible]	[illegible]	[illegible]
[illegible]	Swineford,	[illegible]	[illegible]	[illegible]	[illegible]	[illegible]	[illegible]	[illegible]	[illegible]	[illegible]	[illegible]	[illegible]	[illegible]	[illegible]	[illegible]	[illegible]	[illegible]	[illegible]	[illegible]	[illegible]	[illegible]
[illegible]	Westport,	[illegible]	[illegible]	[illegible]	[illegible]	[illegible]	[illegible]	[illegible]	[illegible]	[illegible]	[illegible]	[illegible]	[illegible]	[illegible]	[illegible]	[illegible]	[illegible]	[illegible]	[illegible]	[illegible]	[illegible]
	29th. Roscommon Co.																				
[illegible]	Athlone, part of	[illegible]	[illegible]	[illegible]	[illegible]	[illegible]	[illegible]	[illegible]	[illegible]	[illegible]	[illegible]	[illegible]	[illegible]	[illegible]	[illegible]	[illegible]	[illegible]	[illegible]	[illegible]	[illegible]	[illegible]
[illegible]	Ballinasloe, do.	[illegible]	[illegible]	[illegible]	[illegible]	[illegible]	[illegible]	[illegible]	[illegible]	[illegible]	[illegible]	[illegible]	[illegible]	[illegible]	[illegible]	[illegible]	[illegible]	[illegible]	[illegible]	[illegible]	[illegible]
[illegible]	Boyle, do.	[illegible]	[illegible]	[illegible]	[illegible]	[illegible]	[illegible]	[illegible]	[illegible]	[illegible]	[illegible]	[illegible]	[illegible]	[illegible]	[illegible]	[illegible]	[illegible]	[illegible]	[illegible]	[illegible]	[illegible]
[illegible]	Carrick-on-Shannon, do.	[illegible]	[illegible]	[illegible]	[illegible]	[illegible]	[illegible]	[illegible]	[illegible]	[illegible]	[illegible]	[illegible]	[illegible]	[illegible]	[illegible]	[illegible]	[illegible]	[illegible]	[illegible]	[illegible]	[illegible]
[illegible]	Castlereagh, do.	[illegible]	[illegible]	[illegible]	[illegible]	[illegible]	[illegible]	[illegible]	[illegible]	[illegible]	[illegible]	[illegible]	[illegible]	[illegible]	[illegible]	[illegible]	[illegible]	[illegible]	[illegible]	[illegible]	[illegible]
[illegible]	Roscommon, do.	[illegible]	[illegible]	[illegible]	[illegible]	[illegible]	[illegible]	[illegible]	[illegible]	[illegible]	[illegible]	[illegible]	[illegible]	[illegible]	[illegible]	[illegible]	[illegible]	[illegible]	[illegible]	[illegible]	[illegible]
[illegible]	Strokestown,	[illegible]	[illegible]	[illegible]	[illegible]	[illegible]	[illegible]	[illegible]	[illegible]	[illegible]	[illegible]	[illegible]	[illegible]	[illegible]	[illegible]	[illegible]	[illegible]	[illegible]	[illegible]	[illegible]	[illegible]
	30th. Sligo Co.																				
[illegible]	Ballina, part of	[illegible]	[illegible]	[illegible]	[illegible]	[illegible]	[illegible]	[illegible]	[illegible]	[illegible]	[illegible]	[illegible]	[illegible]	[illegible]	[illegible]	[illegible]	[illegible]	[illegible]	[illegible]	[illegible]	[illegible]
[illegible]	Boyle, do.	[illegible]	[illegible]	[illegible]	[illegible]	[illegible]	[illegible]	[illegible]	[illegible]	[illegible]	[illegible]	[illegible]	[illegible]	[illegible]	[illegible]	[illegible]	[illegible]	[illegible]	[illegible]	[illegible]	[illegible]
[illegible]	Dromore West,	[illegible]	[illegible]	[illegible]	[illegible]	[illegible]	[illegible]	[illegible]	[illegible]	[illegible]	[illegible]	[illegible]	[illegible]	[illegible]	[illegible]	[illegible]	[illegible]	[illegible]	[illegible]	[illegible]	[illegible]
[illegible]	Sligo,	[illegible]	[illegible]	[illegible]	[illegible]	[illegible]	[illegible]	[illegible]	[illegible]	[illegible]	[illegible]	[illegible]	[illegible]	[illegible]	[illegible]	[illegible]	[illegible]	[illegible]	[illegible]	[illegible]	[illegible]
[illegible]	Tobercurry,	[illegible]	[illegible]	[illegible]	[illegible]	[illegible]	[illegible]	[illegible]	[illegible]	[illegible]	[illegible]	[illegible]	[illegible]	[illegible]	[illegible]	[illegible]	[illegible]	[illegible]	[illegible]	[illegible]	[illegible]

IRELAND.—Deaths at different Ages registered in the year 1896—in the Superintendent Registrars' Districts in each County.—Females—continued.

IV.—Province of Connaught—continued.

No.	Counties and Superintendent Registrars' Districts	[illegible]	[illegible]	[illegible]	1	2	3	4	[illegible]	5-	10-	15-	20-	25-	35-	45-	55-	65-	75-	85-	[illegible]
	Leitrim Co.																				
[illegible]	[illegible]	[illegible]	[illegible]	[illegible]	[illegible]	[illegible]	[illegible]	[illegible]	[illegible]	[illegible]	[illegible]	[illegible]	[illegible]	[illegible]	[illegible]	[illegible]	[illegible]	[illegible]	[illegible]	[illegible]	[illegible]
[illegible]	[illegible]	[illegible]	[illegible]	[illegible]	[illegible]	[illegible]	[illegible]	[illegible]	[illegible]	[illegible]	[illegible]	[illegible]	[illegible]	[illegible]	[illegible]	[illegible]	[illegible]	[illegible]	[illegible]	[illegible]	[illegible]
[illegible]	[illegible]	[illegible]	[illegible]	[illegible]	[illegible]	[illegible]	[illegible]	[illegible]	[illegible]	[illegible]	[illegible]	[illegible]	[illegible]	[illegible]	[illegible]	[illegible]	[illegible]	[illegible]	[illegible]	[illegible]	[illegible]
[illegible]	[illegible]	[illegible]	[illegible]	[illegible]	[illegible]	[illegible]	[illegible]	[illegible]	[illegible]	[illegible]	[illegible]	[illegible]	[illegible]	[illegible]	[illegible]	[illegible]	[illegible]	[illegible]	[illegible]	[illegible]	[illegible]
[illegible]	[illegible]	[illegible]	[illegible]	[illegible]	[illegible]	[illegible]	[illegible]	[illegible]	[illegible]	[illegible]	[illegible]	[illegible]	[illegible]	[illegible]	[illegible]	[illegible]	[illegible]	[illegible]	[illegible]	[illegible]	[illegible]
	Mayo Co.																				
[illegible]	[illegible]	[illegible]	[illegible]	[illegible]	[illegible]	[illegible]	[illegible]	[illegible]	[illegible]	[illegible]	[illegible]	[illegible]	[illegible]	[illegible]	[illegible]	[illegible]	[illegible]	[illegible]	[illegible]	[illegible]	[illegible]
[illegible]	[illegible]	[illegible]	[illegible]	[illegible]	[illegible]	[illegible]	[illegible]	[illegible]	[illegible]	[illegible]	[illegible]	[illegible]	[illegible]	[illegible]	[illegible]	[illegible]	[illegible]	[illegible]	[illegible]	[illegible]	[illegible]
[illegible]	[illegible]	[illegible]	[illegible]	[illegible]	[illegible]	[illegible]	[illegible]	[illegible]	[illegible]	[illegible]	[illegible]	[illegible]	[illegible]	[illegible]	[illegible]	[illegible]	[illegible]	[illegible]	[illegible]	[illegible]	[illegible]
[illegible]	[illegible]	[illegible]	[illegible]	[illegible]	[illegible]	[illegible]	[illegible]	[illegible]	[illegible]	[illegible]	[illegible]	[illegible]	[illegible]	[illegible]	[illegible]	[illegible]	[illegible]	[illegible]	[illegible]	[illegible]	[illegible]
[illegible]	[illegible]	[illegible]	[illegible]	[illegible]	[illegible]	[illegible]	[illegible]	[illegible]	[illegible]	[illegible]	[illegible]	[illegible]	[illegible]	[illegible]	[illegible]	[illegible]	[illegible]	[illegible]	[illegible]	[illegible]	[illegible]
[illegible]	[illegible]	[illegible]	[illegible]	[illegible]	[illegible]	[illegible]	[illegible]	[illegible]	[illegible]	[illegible]	[illegible]	[illegible]	[illegible]	[illegible]	[illegible]	[illegible]	[illegible]	[illegible]	[illegible]	[illegible]	[illegible]
[illegible]	[illegible]	[illegible]	[illegible]	[illegible]	[illegible]	[illegible]	[illegible]	[illegible]	[illegible]	[illegible]	[illegible]	[illegible]	[illegible]	[illegible]	[illegible]	[illegible]	[illegible]	[illegible]	[illegible]	[illegible]	[illegible]
[illegible]	[illegible]	[illegible]	[illegible]	[illegible]	[illegible]	[illegible]	[illegible]	[illegible]	[illegible]	[illegible]	[illegible]	[illegible]	[illegible]	[illegible]	[illegible]	[illegible]	[illegible]	[illegible]	[illegible]	[illegible]	[illegible]
[illegible]	[illegible]	[illegible]	[illegible]	[illegible]	[illegible]	[illegible]	[illegible]	[illegible]	[illegible]	[illegible]	[illegible]	[illegible]	[illegible]	[illegible]	[illegible]	[illegible]	[illegible]	[illegible]	[illegible]	[illegible]	[illegible]
	Roscommon Co.																				
[illegible]	[illegible]	[illegible]	[illegible]	[illegible]	[illegible]	[illegible]	[illegible]	[illegible]	[illegible]	[illegible]	[illegible]	[illegible]	[illegible]	[illegible]	[illegible]	[illegible]	[illegible]	[illegible]	[illegible]	[illegible]	[illegible]
[illegible]	[illegible]	[illegible]	[illegible]	[illegible]	[illegible]	[illegible]	[illegible]	[illegible]	[illegible]	[illegible]	[illegible]	[illegible]	[illegible]	[illegible]	[illegible]	[illegible]	[illegible]	[illegible]	[illegible]	[illegible]	[illegible]
[illegible]	[illegible]	[illegible]	[illegible]	[illegible]	[illegible]	[illegible]	[illegible]	[illegible]	[illegible]	[illegible]	[illegible]	[illegible]	[illegible]	[illegible]	[illegible]	[illegible]	[illegible]	[illegible]	[illegible]	[illegible]	[illegible]
[illegible]	[illegible]	[illegible]	[illegible]	[illegible]	[illegible]	[illegible]	[illegible]	[illegible]	[illegible]	[illegible]	[illegible]	[illegible]	[illegible]	[illegible]	[illegible]	[illegible]	[illegible]	[illegible]	[illegible]	[illegible]	[illegible]
[illegible]	[illegible]	[illegible]	[illegible]	[illegible]	[illegible]	[illegible]	[illegible]	[illegible]	[illegible]	[illegible]	[illegible]	[illegible]	[illegible]	[illegible]	[illegible]	[illegible]	[illegible]	[illegible]	[illegible]	[illegible]	[illegible]
[illegible]	[illegible]	[illegible]	[illegible]	[illegible]	[illegible]	[illegible]	[illegible]	[illegible]	[illegible]	[illegible]	[illegible]	[illegible]	[illegible]	[illegible]	[illegible]	[illegible]	[illegible]	[illegible]	[illegible]	[illegible]	[illegible]
[illegible]	[illegible]	[illegible]	[illegible]	[illegible]	[illegible]	[illegible]	[illegible]	[illegible]	[illegible]	[illegible]	[illegible]	[illegible]	[illegible]	[illegible]	[illegible]	[illegible]	[illegible]	[illegible]	[illegible]	[illegible]	[illegible]
	Sligo Co.																				
[illegible]	[illegible]	[illegible]	[illegible]	[illegible]	[illegible]	[illegible]	[illegible]	[illegible]	[illegible]	[illegible]	[illegible]	[illegible]	[illegible]	[illegible]	[illegible]	[illegible]	[illegible]	[illegible]	[illegible]	[illegible]	[illegible]
[illegible]	[illegible]	[illegible]	[illegible]	[illegible]	[illegible]	[illegible]	[illegible]	[illegible]	[illegible]	[illegible]	[illegible]	[illegible]	[illegible]	[illegible]	[illegible]	[illegible]	[illegible]	[illegible]	[illegible]	[illegible]	[illegible]
[illegible]	[illegible]	[illegible]	[illegible]	[illegible]	[illegible]	[illegible]	[illegible]	[illegible]	[illegible]	[illegible]	[illegible]	[illegible]	[illegible]	[illegible]	[illegible]	[illegible]	[illegible]	[illegible]	[illegible]	[illegible]	[illegible]
[illegible]	[illegible]	[illegible]	[illegible]	[illegible]	[illegible]	[illegible]	[illegible]	[illegible]	[illegible]	[illegible]	[illegible]	[illegible]	[illegible]	[illegible]	[illegible]	[illegible]	[illegible]	[illegible]	[illegible]	[illegible]	[illegible]
[illegible]	[illegible]	[illegible]	[illegible]	[illegible]	[illegible]	[illegible]	[illegible]	[illegible]	[illegible]	[illegible]	[illegible]	[illegible]	[illegible]	[illegible]	[illegible]	[illegible]	[illegible]	[illegible]	[illegible]	[illegible]	[illegible]

IRELAND.—Deaths at different Ages registered in the year 1898—in the Superintendent Registrars' Districts—Females.

[illegible]	Superintendent Registrars' Districts.	[illegible]	[illegible]	Under 1 year	1	2	3	4	Total under 5 years	5-	10-	15-	20-	25-	35-	45-	55-	65-	75-	85-	[illegible]
[illegible]	[illegible]	[illegible]	[illegible]	[illegible]	[illegible]	[illegible]	[illegible]	[illegible]	[illegible]	[illegible]	[illegible]	[illegible]	[illegible]	[illegible]	[illegible]	[illegible]	[illegible]	[illegible]	[illegible]	[illegible]	[illegible]

IRELAND.—DEATHS at different AGES registered in the year [illegible]—In the SUPERINTENDENT REGISTRARS' DISTRICTS.—MALES—continued.

[illegible]	Superintendent Registrars' Districts.	[illegible]	[illegible]	[illegible]	[illegible]	[illegible]	[illegible]	[illegible]	[illegible]	[illegible]	[illegible]	[illegible]	[illegible]	[illegible]	[illegible]	[illegible]	[illegible]	[illegible]	[illegible]	[illegible]	[illegible]	[illegible]
[illegible]	[illegible]	[illegible]	[illegible]	[illegible]	[illegible]	[illegible]	[illegible]	[illegible]	[illegible]	[illegible]	[illegible]	[illegible]	[illegible]	[illegible]	[illegible]	[illegible]	[illegible]	[illegible]	[illegible]	[illegible]	[illegible]	[illegible]
[illegible]	[illegible]	[illegible]	[illegible]	[illegible]	[illegible]	[illegible]	[illegible]	[illegible]	[illegible]	[illegible]	[illegible]	[illegible]	[illegible]	[illegible]	[illegible]	[illegible]	[illegible]	[illegible]	[illegible]	[illegible]	[illegible]	[illegible]
[illegible]	[illegible]	[illegible]	[illegible]	[illegible]	[illegible]	[illegible]	[illegible]	[illegible]	[illegible]	[illegible]	[illegible]	[illegible]	[illegible]	[illegible]	[illegible]	[illegible]	[illegible]	[illegible]	[illegible]	[illegible]	[illegible]	[illegible]
[illegible]	[illegible]	[illegible]	[illegible]	[illegible]	[illegible]	[illegible]	[illegible]	[illegible]	[illegible]	[illegible]	[illegible]	[illegible]	[illegible]	[illegible]	[illegible]	[illegible]	[illegible]	[illegible]	[illegible]	[illegible]	[illegible]	[illegible]
[illegible]	[illegible]	[illegible]	[illegible]	[illegible]	[illegible]	[illegible]	[illegible]	[illegible]	[illegible]	[illegible]	[illegible]	[illegible]	[illegible]	[illegible]	[illegible]	[illegible]	[illegible]	[illegible]	[illegible]	[illegible]	[illegible]	[illegible]
[illegible]	Dublin, North	[illegible]	[illegible]	[illegible]	[illegible]	[illegible]	[illegible]	[illegible]	[illegible]	[illegible]	[illegible]	[illegible]	[illegible]	[illegible]	[illegible]	[illegible]	[illegible]	[illegible]	[illegible]	[illegible]	[illegible]	[illegible]
[illegible]	Dublin, South	[illegible]	[illegible]	[illegible]	[illegible]	[illegible]	[illegible]	[illegible]	[illegible]	[illegible]	[illegible]	[illegible]	[illegible]	[illegible]	[illegible]	[illegible]	[illegible]	[illegible]	[illegible]	[illegible]	[illegible]	[illegible]
[illegible]	[illegible]	[illegible]	[illegible]	[illegible]	[illegible]	[illegible]	[illegible]	[illegible]	[illegible]	[illegible]	[illegible]	[illegible]	[illegible]	[illegible]	[illegible]	[illegible]	[illegible]	[illegible]	[illegible]	[illegible]	[illegible]	[illegible]
[illegible]	[illegible]	[illegible]	[illegible]	[illegible]	[illegible]	[illegible]	[illegible]	[illegible]	[illegible]	[illegible]	[illegible]	[illegible]	[illegible]	[illegible]	[illegible]	[illegible]	[illegible]	[illegible]	[illegible]	[illegible]	[illegible]	[illegible]
[illegible]	[illegible]	[illegible]	[illegible]	[illegible]	[illegible]	[illegible]	[illegible]	[illegible]	[illegible]	[illegible]	[illegible]	[illegible]	[illegible]	[illegible]	[illegible]	[illegible]	[illegible]	[illegible]	[illegible]	[illegible]	[illegible]	[illegible]
[illegible]	[illegible]	[illegible]	[illegible]	[illegible]	[illegible]	[illegible]	[illegible]	[illegible]	[illegible]	[illegible]	[illegible]	[illegible]	[illegible]	[illegible]	[illegible]	[illegible]	[illegible]	[illegible]	[illegible]	[illegible]	[illegible]	[illegible]

at different Ages registered in the year 1898—in the [illegible] Divisions.—Females—continued.

[illegible]

IRELAND.—[illegible] at different AGES registered in the year [illegible]—in the SUPERINTENDENT REGISTRARS' DISTRICTS.—MALES—continued.

[illegible]	[illegible]	[illegible]	[illegible]	[illegible]	[illegible]	[illegible]	[illegible]	[illegible]	[illegible]	[illegible]	[illegible]	[illegible]	[illegible]	[illegible]	[illegible]	[illegible]	[illegible]	[illegible]	[illegible]	[illegible]	[illegible]	[illegible]
[illegible]	[illegible]	[illegible]	[illegible]	[illegible]	[illegible]	[illegible]	[illegible]	[illegible]	[illegible]	[illegible]	[illegible]	[illegible]	[illegible]	[illegible]	[illegible]	[illegible]	[illegible]	[illegible]	[illegible]	[illegible]	[illegible]	[illegible]
[illegible]	[illegible]	[illegible]	[illegible]	[illegible]	[illegible]	[illegible]	[illegible]	[illegible]	[illegible]	[illegible]	[illegible]	[illegible]	[illegible]	[illegible]	[illegible]	[illegible]	[illegible]	[illegible]	[illegible]	[illegible]	[illegible]	[illegible]
[illegible]	[illegible]	[illegible]	[illegible]	[illegible]	[illegible]	[illegible]	[illegible]	[illegible]	[illegible]	[illegible]	[illegible]	[illegible]	[illegible]	[illegible]	[illegible]	[illegible]	[illegible]	[illegible]	[illegible]	[illegible]	[illegible]	[illegible]

[illegible]

[illegible]

IRELAND.—CAUSES of DEATH at different Periods of Life in the Year [illegible].—MALES.

Class	Causes of Death	All Ages	Ages at Death
	ALL CAUSES,	[illegible]	[illegible]
	(Orders.)		
I.	ZYMOTIC DISEASES,	[illegible]	[illegible]
II.	PARASITIC DISEASES,	[illegible]	[illegible]
III.	DIETETIC	[illegible]	[illegible]
IV.	CONSTITUTIONAL	[illegible]	[illegible]
V.	DEVELOPMENTAL	[illegible]	[illegible]
VI.	LOCAL	[illegible]	[illegible]
VII.	VIOLENCE,	[illegible]	[illegible]
VIII.	ILL-DEFINED AND NOT SPECIFIED CAUSES,	[illegible]	[illegible]
	(Orders.)		
I.	1. [illegible]	[illegible]	[illegible]
	2. [illegible]	[illegible]	[illegible]
	3. [illegible]	[illegible]	[illegible]
	4. [illegible]	[illegible]	[illegible]
	5. [illegible]	[illegible]	[illegible]
	6. [illegible]	[illegible]	[illegible]
II.	Parasitic	[illegible]	[illegible]
III.	Dietetic	[illegible]	[illegible]
IV.	Constitutional	[illegible]	[illegible]
V.	Developmental	[illegible]	[illegible]
VI.	1. Diseases of Nervous System,	[illegible]	[illegible]
	2. [illegible]	[illegible]	[illegible]
	3. [illegible]	[illegible]	[illegible]
	4. [illegible]	[illegible]	[illegible]
	5. [illegible]	[illegible]	[illegible]
	6. [illegible]	[illegible]	[illegible]
	7. [illegible]	[illegible]	[illegible]
	8. [illegible]		
	(a) [illegible]	[illegible]	[illegible]
	(b) [illegible]	[illegible]	[illegible]
	9. [illegible]	[illegible]	[illegible]
	10. [illegible]	[illegible]	[illegible]
VII.	1. Accident or Negligence,	[illegible]	[illegible]
	2. Homicide,	[illegible]	[illegible]
	3. Suicide,	[illegible]	[illegible]
	4. [illegible]	[illegible]	[illegible]
VIII.	Ill-Defined and not Specified Causes,	[illegible]	[illegible]

[continued on page [illegible].]

IRELAND.—CAUSES of DEATH at different Periods of Life in the Year [illegible].—FEMALES.

Class	Causes of Death	Females (All Ages and Ages at Death)
	ALL CAUSES,	[illegible]
	(Classes.)	
I.	SPECIFIC FEBRILE or ZYMOTIC DISEASES,	[illegible]
II.	PARASITIC DISEASES,	[illegible]
III.	DIETETIC	[illegible]
IV.	CONSTITUTIONAL	[illegible]
V.	DEVELOPMENTAL	[illegible]
VI.	LOCAL	[illegible]
VII.	VIOLENCE	[illegible]
VIII.	ILL-DEFINED AND NOT SPECIFIED CAUSES.	[illegible]
	(Orders.)	
I.	1. [illegible]	[illegible]
	2. [illegible]	[illegible]
	3. [illegible]	[illegible]
	4. [illegible]	[illegible]
	5. [illegible]	[illegible]
	6. [illegible]	[illegible]
II.	[illegible]	[illegible]
III.	[illegible]	[illegible]
IV.	[illegible]	[illegible]
V.	[illegible]	[illegible]
VI.	1. [illegible]	[illegible]
	2. [illegible]	[illegible]
	3. [illegible]	[illegible]
	4. [illegible]	[illegible]
	5. [illegible]	[illegible]
	6. [illegible]	[illegible]
	7. [illegible]	[illegible]
	8. [illegible]	[illegible]
	8a. [illegible]	[illegible]
	8b. [illegible]	[illegible]
	9. [illegible]	[illegible]
	10. [illegible]	[illegible]
VII.	1. [illegible]	[illegible]
	2. [illegible]	[illegible]
	3. [illegible]	[illegible]
	4. [illegible]	[illegible]
VIII.	[illegible]	[illegible]

(continued at page [illegible].)

IRELAND.—CAUSES of DEATHS at different Periods of Life in the Year 18[illegible]—MALES

Class	NATURE OF DEATH	MALES: All Ages	Ages at Death: [illegible]	[illegible]	[illegible]	[illegible]	Total under 1 year	1	2	3	4	Total under 5 years	5-	10-	15-	20-	25-	35-	45-	55-	65-	75-	85-	[illegible]
I.	MIASMATIC DISEASES.																							
	Small-pox { Vaccinated,	[illegible]	[illegible]	[illegible]	[illegible]	[illegible]	[illegible]	[illegible]	[illegible]	[illegible]	[illegible]	[illegible]	[illegible]	[illegible]	[illegible]	[illegible]	[illegible]	[illegible]	[illegible]	[illegible]	[illegible]	[illegible]	[illegible]	[illegible]
	Small-pox { Unvaccinated,	[illegible]	[illegible]	[illegible]	[illegible]	[illegible]	[illegible]	[illegible]	[illegible]	[illegible]	[illegible]	[illegible]	[illegible]	[illegible]	[illegible]	[illegible]	[illegible]	[illegible]	[illegible]	[illegible]	[illegible]	[illegible]	[illegible]	[illegible]
	Small-pox { Not stated,	[illegible]	[illegible]	[illegible]	[illegible]	[illegible]	[illegible]	[illegible]	[illegible]	[illegible]	[illegible]	[illegible]	[illegible]	[illegible]	[illegible]	[illegible]	[illegible]	[illegible]	[illegible]	[illegible]	[illegible]	[illegible]	[illegible]	[illegible]
	Chicken-pox,	[illegible]	[illegible]	[illegible]	[illegible]	[illegible]	[illegible]	[illegible]	[illegible]	[illegible]	[illegible]	[illegible]	[illegible]	[illegible]	[illegible]	[illegible]	[illegible]	[illegible]	[illegible]	[illegible]	[illegible]	[illegible]	[illegible]	[illegible]
	Measles,	[illegible]	[illegible]	[illegible]	[illegible]	[illegible]	[illegible]	[illegible]	[illegible]	[illegible]	[illegible]	[illegible]	[illegible]	[illegible]	[illegible]	[illegible]	[illegible]	[illegible]	[illegible]	[illegible]	[illegible]	[illegible]	[illegible]	[illegible]
	Epidemic Rose Rash,	[illegible]	[illegible]	[illegible]	[illegible]	[illegible]	[illegible]	[illegible]	[illegible]	[illegible]	[illegible]	[illegible]	[illegible]	[illegible]	[illegible]	[illegible]	[illegible]	[illegible]	[illegible]	[illegible]	[illegible]	[illegible]	[illegible]	[illegible]
	Scarlet Fever,	[illegible]	[illegible]	[illegible]	[illegible]	[illegible]	[illegible]	[illegible]	[illegible]	[illegible]	[illegible]	[illegible]	[illegible]	[illegible]	[illegible]	[illegible]	[illegible]	[illegible]	[illegible]	[illegible]	[illegible]	[illegible]	[illegible]	[illegible]
	Typhus,	[illegible]	[illegible]	[illegible]	[illegible]	[illegible]	[illegible]	[illegible]	[illegible]	[illegible]	[illegible]	[illegible]	[illegible]	[illegible]	[illegible]	[illegible]	[illegible]	[illegible]	[illegible]	[illegible]	[illegible]	[illegible]	[illegible]	[illegible]
	Relapsing Fever,	[illegible]	[illegible]	[illegible]	[illegible]	[illegible]	[illegible]	[illegible]	[illegible]	[illegible]	[illegible]	[illegible]	[illegible]	[illegible]	[illegible]	[illegible]	[illegible]	[illegible]	[illegible]	[illegible]	[illegible]	[illegible]	[illegible]	[illegible]
	Influenza,	[illegible]	[illegible]	[illegible]	[illegible]	[illegible]	[illegible]	[illegible]	[illegible]	[illegible]	[illegible]	[illegible]	[illegible]	[illegible]	[illegible]	[illegible]	[illegible]	[illegible]	[illegible]	[illegible]	[illegible]	[illegible]	[illegible]	[illegible]
	Whooping-cough,	[illegible]	[illegible]	[illegible]	[illegible]	[illegible]	[illegible]	[illegible]	[illegible]	[illegible]	[illegible]	[illegible]	[illegible]	[illegible]	[illegible]	[illegible]	[illegible]	[illegible]	[illegible]	[illegible]	[illegible]	[illegible]	[illegible]	[illegible]
	Mumps,	[illegible]	[illegible]	[illegible]	[illegible]	[illegible]	[illegible]	[illegible]	[illegible]	[illegible]	[illegible]	[illegible]	[illegible]	[illegible]	[illegible]	[illegible]	[illegible]	[illegible]	[illegible]	[illegible]	[illegible]	[illegible]	[illegible]	[illegible]
	Diphtheria,	[illegible]	[illegible]	[illegible]	[illegible]	[illegible]	[illegible]	[illegible]	[illegible]	[illegible]	[illegible]	[illegible]	[illegible]	[illegible]	[illegible]	[illegible]	[illegible]	[illegible]	[illegible]	[illegible]	[illegible]	[illegible]	[illegible]	[illegible]
	Cerebro-spinal Fever,	[illegible]	[illegible]	[illegible]	[illegible]	[illegible]	[illegible]	[illegible]	[illegible]	[illegible]	[illegible]	[illegible]	[illegible]	[illegible]	[illegible]	[illegible]	[illegible]	[illegible]	[illegible]	[illegible]	[illegible]	[illegible]	[illegible]	[illegible]
	Simple and Ill-defined Fever,	[illegible]	[illegible]	[illegible]	[illegible]	[illegible]	[illegible]	[illegible]	[illegible]	[illegible]	[illegible]	[illegible]	[illegible]	[illegible]	[illegible]	[illegible]	[illegible]	[illegible]	[illegible]	[illegible]	[illegible]	[illegible]	[illegible]	[illegible]
	Enteric Fever,	[illegible]	[illegible]	[illegible]	[illegible]	[illegible]	[illegible]	[illegible]	[illegible]	[illegible]	[illegible]	[illegible]	[illegible]	[illegible]	[illegible]	[illegible]	[illegible]	[illegible]	[illegible]	[illegible]	[illegible]	[illegible]	[illegible]	[illegible]
	Other Miasmatic Diseases,	[illegible]	[illegible]	[illegible]	[illegible]	[illegible]	[illegible]	[illegible]	[illegible]	[illegible]	[illegible]	[illegible]	[illegible]	[illegible]	[illegible]	[illegible]	[illegible]	[illegible]	[illegible]	[illegible]	[illegible]	[illegible]	[illegible]	[illegible]
	DIARRHOEAL DISEASES.																							
	Simple Cholera,	[illegible]	[illegible]	[illegible]	[illegible]	[illegible]	[illegible]	[illegible]	[illegible]	[illegible]	[illegible]	[illegible]	[illegible]	[illegible]	[illegible]	[illegible]	[illegible]	[illegible]	[illegible]	[illegible]	[illegible]	[illegible]	[illegible]	[illegible]
	Diarrhoea, Dysentery,	[illegible]	[illegible]	[illegible]	[illegible]	[illegible]	[illegible]	[illegible]	[illegible]	[illegible]	[illegible]	[illegible]	[illegible]	[illegible]	[illegible]	[illegible]	[illegible]	[illegible]	[illegible]	[illegible]	[illegible]	[illegible]	[illegible]	[illegible]
	MALARIAL DISEASES.																							
	Remittent Fever,	[illegible]	[illegible]	[illegible]	[illegible]	[illegible]	[illegible]	[illegible]	[illegible]	[illegible]	[illegible]	[illegible]	[illegible]	[illegible]	[illegible]	[illegible]	[illegible]	[illegible]	[illegible]	[illegible]	[illegible]	[illegible]	[illegible]	[illegible]
	Ague,	[illegible]	[illegible]	[illegible]	[illegible]	[illegible]	[illegible]	[illegible]	[illegible]	[illegible]	[illegible]	[illegible]	[illegible]	[illegible]	[illegible]	[illegible]	[illegible]	[illegible]	[illegible]	[illegible]	[illegible]	[illegible]	[illegible]	[illegible]
	ZOOGENOUS DISEASES.																							
	Hydrophobia,	[illegible]	[illegible]	[illegible]	[illegible]	[illegible]	[illegible]	[illegible]	[illegible]	[illegible]	[illegible]	[illegible]	[illegible]	[illegible]	[illegible]	[illegible]	[illegible]	[illegible]	[illegible]	[illegible]	[illegible]	[illegible]	[illegible]	[illegible]
	Glanders,	[illegible]	[illegible]	[illegible]	[illegible]	[illegible]	[illegible]	[illegible]	[illegible]	[illegible]	[illegible]	[illegible]	[illegible]	[illegible]	[illegible]	[illegible]	[illegible]	[illegible]	[illegible]	[illegible]	[illegible]	[illegible]	[illegible]	[illegible]
	Splenic Fever,	[illegible]	[illegible]	[illegible]	[illegible]	[illegible]	[illegible]	[illegible]	[illegible]	[illegible]	[illegible]	[illegible]	[illegible]	[illegible]	[illegible]	[illegible]	[illegible]	[illegible]	[illegible]	[illegible]	[illegible]	[illegible]	[illegible]	[illegible]
	Cowpox and other effects of Vaccination,	[illegible]	[illegible]	[illegible]	[illegible]	[illegible]	[illegible]	[illegible]	[illegible]	[illegible]	[illegible]	[illegible]	[illegible]	[illegible]	[illegible]	[illegible]	[illegible]	[illegible]	[illegible]	[illegible]	[illegible]	[illegible]	[illegible]	[illegible]
	VENEREAL DISEASES.																							
	Syphilis,	[illegible]	[illegible]	[illegible]	[illegible]	[illegible]	[illegible]	[illegible]	[illegible]	[illegible]	[illegible]	[illegible]	[illegible]	[illegible]	[illegible]	[illegible]	[illegible]	[illegible]	[illegible]	[illegible]	[illegible]	[illegible]	[illegible]	[illegible]
	Gonorrhoea, Stricture of Urethra,	[illegible]	[illegible]	[illegible]	[illegible]	[illegible]	[illegible]	[illegible]	[illegible]	[illegible]	[illegible]	[illegible]	[illegible]	[illegible]	[illegible]	[illegible]	[illegible]	[illegible]	[illegible]	[illegible]	[illegible]	[illegible]	[illegible]	[illegible]
	SEPTIC DISEASES.																							
	Phagedaena,	[illegible]	[illegible]	[illegible]	[illegible]	[illegible]	[illegible]	[illegible]	[illegible]	[illegible]	[illegible]	[illegible]	[illegible]	[illegible]	[illegible]	[illegible]	[illegible]	[illegible]	[illegible]	[illegible]	[illegible]	[illegible]	[illegible]	[illegible]
	Erysipelas,	[illegible]	[illegible]	[illegible]	[illegible]	[illegible]	[illegible]	[illegible]	[illegible]	[illegible]	[illegible]	[illegible]	[illegible]	[illegible]	[illegible]	[illegible]	[illegible]	[illegible]	[illegible]	[illegible]	[illegible]	[illegible]	[illegible]	[illegible]
	Pyaemia, Septicaemia,	[illegible]	[illegible]	[illegible]	[illegible]	[illegible]	[illegible]	[illegible]	[illegible]	[illegible]	[illegible]	[illegible]	[illegible]	[illegible]	[illegible]	[illegible]	[illegible]	[illegible]	[illegible]	[illegible]	[illegible]	[illegible]	[illegible]	[illegible]
	Puerperal Fever,	[illegible]	[illegible]	[illegible]	[illegible]	[illegible]	[illegible]	[illegible]	[illegible]	[illegible]	[illegible]	[illegible]	[illegible]	[illegible]	[illegible]	[illegible]	[illegible]	[illegible]	[illegible]	[illegible]	[illegible]	[illegible]	[illegible]	[illegible]
II.	PARASITIC DISEASES.																							
	Thrush,	[illegible]	[illegible]	[illegible]	[illegible]	[illegible]	[illegible]	[illegible]	[illegible]	[illegible]	[illegible]	[illegible]	[illegible]	[illegible]	[illegible]	[illegible]	[illegible]	[illegible]	[illegible]	[illegible]	[illegible]	[illegible]	[illegible]	[illegible]
	Other Diseases from Vegetable Parasites,	[illegible]	[illegible]	[illegible]	[illegible]	[illegible]	[illegible]	[illegible]	[illegible]	[illegible]	[illegible]	[illegible]	[illegible]	[illegible]	[illegible]	[illegible]	[illegible]	[illegible]	[illegible]	[illegible]	[illegible]	[illegible]	[illegible]	[illegible]
	Hydatid Disease,	[illegible]	[illegible]	[illegible]	[illegible]	[illegible]	[illegible]	[illegible]	[illegible]	[illegible]	[illegible]	[illegible]	[illegible]	[illegible]	[illegible]	[illegible]	[illegible]	[illegible]	[illegible]	[illegible]	[illegible]	[illegible]	[illegible]	[illegible]
	Other Diseases from Animal Parasites,	[illegible]	[illegible]	[illegible]	[illegible]	[illegible]	[illegible]	[illegible]	[illegible]	[illegible]	[illegible]	[illegible]	[illegible]	[illegible]	[illegible]	[illegible]	[illegible]	[illegible]	[illegible]	[illegible]	[illegible]	[illegible]	[illegible]	[illegible]
III.	DIETETIC DISEASES.																							
	Starvation, Want of Breast Milk,	[illegible]	[illegible]	[illegible]	[illegible]	[illegible]	[illegible]	[illegible]	[illegible]	[illegible]	[illegible]	[illegible]	[illegible]	[illegible]	[illegible]	[illegible]	[illegible]	[illegible]	[illegible]	[illegible]	[illegible]	[illegible]	[illegible]	[illegible]
	Scurvy,	[illegible]	[illegible]	[illegible]	[illegible]	[illegible]	[illegible]	[illegible]	[illegible]	[illegible]	[illegible]	[illegible]	[illegible]	[illegible]	[illegible]	[illegible]	[illegible]	[illegible]	[illegible]	[illegible]	[illegible]	[illegible]	[illegible]	[illegible]
	Intemperance { Chronic Alcoholism,	[illegible]	[illegible]	[illegible]	[illegible]	[illegible]	[illegible]	[illegible]	[illegible]	[illegible]	[illegible]	[illegible]	[illegible]	[illegible]	[illegible]	[illegible]	[illegible]	[illegible]	[illegible]	[illegible]	[illegible]	[illegible]	[illegible]	[illegible]
	Intemperance { Delirium Tremens,	[illegible]	[illegible]	[illegible]	[illegible]	[illegible]	[illegible]	[illegible]	[illegible]	[illegible]	[illegible]	[illegible]	[illegible]	[illegible]	[illegible]	[illegible]	[illegible]	[illegible]	[illegible]	[illegible]	[illegible]	[illegible]	[illegible]	[illegible]
IV.	CONSTITUTIONAL DISEASES.																							
	Rheumatic Fever, Rheumatism of Heart,	[illegible]	[illegible]	[illegible]	[illegible]	[illegible]	[illegible]	[illegible]	[illegible]	[illegible]	[illegible]	[illegible]	[illegible]	[illegible]	[illegible]	[illegible]	[illegible]	[illegible]	[illegible]	[illegible]	[illegible]	[illegible]	[illegible]	[illegible]
	Rheumatism,	[illegible]	[illegible]	[illegible]	[illegible]	[illegible]	[illegible]	[illegible]	[illegible]	[illegible]	[illegible]	[illegible]	[illegible]	[illegible]	[illegible]	[illegible]	[illegible]	[illegible]	[illegible]	[illegible]	[illegible]	[illegible]	[illegible]	[illegible]
	Gout,	[illegible]	[illegible]	[illegible]	[illegible]	[illegible]	[illegible]	[illegible]	[illegible]	[illegible]	[illegible]	[illegible]	[illegible]	[illegible]	[illegible]	[illegible]	[illegible]	[illegible]	[illegible]	[illegible]	[illegible]	[illegible]	[illegible]	[illegible]
	Rickets,	[illegible]	[illegible]	[illegible]	[illegible]	[illegible]	[illegible]	[illegible]	[illegible]	[illegible]	[illegible]	[illegible]	[illegible]	[illegible]	[illegible]	[illegible]	[illegible]	[illegible]	[illegible]	[illegible]	[illegible]	[illegible]	[illegible]	[illegible]
	Cancer,	[illegible]	[illegible]	[illegible]	[illegible]	[illegible]	[illegible]	[illegible]	[illegible]	[illegible]	[illegible]	[illegible]	[illegible]	[illegible]	[illegible]	[illegible]	[illegible]	[illegible]	[illegible]	[illegible]	[illegible]	[illegible]	[illegible]	[illegible]

Continued at page [illegible].

IRELAND.—CAUSES of DEATHS at different Periods of Life in the Year 1896—FEMALES.

Class.	CAUSES OF DEATH.	All Ages.	[illegible]	[illegible]	[illegible]	Total under 1 year.	1	2	3	4	Total under 5 years.	5-	10-	15-	20-	25-	35-	45-	55-	65-	75-	85-	95 and upwards
I.	MIASMATIC DISEASES.																						
	Small-pox: Vaccinated	[illegible]	[illegible]	[illegible]	[illegible]	[illegible]	[illegible]	[illegible]	[illegible]	[illegible]	[illegible]	[illegible]	[illegible]	[illegible]	[illegible]	[illegible]	[illegible]	[illegible]	[illegible]	[illegible]	[illegible]	[illegible]	[illegible]
	Small-pox: Unvaccinated	[illegible]	[illegible]	[illegible]	[illegible]	[illegible]	[illegible]	[illegible]	[illegible]	[illegible]	[illegible]	[illegible]	[illegible]	[illegible]	[illegible]	[illegible]	[illegible]	[illegible]	[illegible]	[illegible]	[illegible]	[illegible]	[illegible]
	Small-pox: No Statement	[illegible]	[illegible]	[illegible]	[illegible]	[illegible]	[illegible]	[illegible]	[illegible]	[illegible]	[illegible]	[illegible]	[illegible]	[illegible]	[illegible]	[illegible]	[illegible]	[illegible]	[illegible]	[illegible]	[illegible]	[illegible]	[illegible]
	Chicken-pox	[illegible]	[illegible]	[illegible]	[illegible]	[illegible]	[illegible]	[illegible]	[illegible]	[illegible]	[illegible]	[illegible]	[illegible]	[illegible]	[illegible]	[illegible]	[illegible]	[illegible]	[illegible]	[illegible]	[illegible]	[illegible]	[illegible]
	Measles	[illegible]	[illegible]	[illegible]	[illegible]	[illegible]	[illegible]	[illegible]	[illegible]	[illegible]	[illegible]	[illegible]	[illegible]	[illegible]	[illegible]	[illegible]	[illegible]	[illegible]	[illegible]	[illegible]	[illegible]	[illegible]	[illegible]
	Epidemic Rose Rash	[illegible]	[illegible]	[illegible]	[illegible]	[illegible]	[illegible]	[illegible]	[illegible]	[illegible]	[illegible]	[illegible]	[illegible]	[illegible]	[illegible]	[illegible]	[illegible]	[illegible]	[illegible]	[illegible]	[illegible]	[illegible]	[illegible]
	Scarlet Fever	[illegible]	[illegible]	[illegible]	[illegible]	[illegible]	[illegible]	[illegible]	[illegible]	[illegible]	[illegible]	[illegible]	[illegible]	[illegible]	[illegible]	[illegible]	[illegible]	[illegible]	[illegible]	[illegible]	[illegible]	[illegible]	[illegible]
	Typhus	[illegible]	[illegible]	[illegible]	[illegible]	[illegible]	[illegible]	[illegible]	[illegible]	[illegible]	[illegible]	[illegible]	[illegible]	[illegible]	[illegible]	[illegible]	[illegible]	[illegible]	[illegible]	[illegible]	[illegible]	[illegible]	[illegible]
	Relapsing Fever	[illegible]	[illegible]	[illegible]	[illegible]	[illegible]	[illegible]	[illegible]	[illegible]	[illegible]	[illegible]	[illegible]	[illegible]	[illegible]	[illegible]	[illegible]	[illegible]	[illegible]	[illegible]	[illegible]	[illegible]	[illegible]	[illegible]
	Influenza	[illegible]	[illegible]	[illegible]	[illegible]	[illegible]	[illegible]	[illegible]	[illegible]	[illegible]	[illegible]	[illegible]	[illegible]	[illegible]	[illegible]	[illegible]	[illegible]	[illegible]	[illegible]	[illegible]	[illegible]	[illegible]	[illegible]
	Whooping Cough	[illegible]	[illegible]	[illegible]	[illegible]	[illegible]	[illegible]	[illegible]	[illegible]	[illegible]	[illegible]	[illegible]	[illegible]	[illegible]	[illegible]	[illegible]	[illegible]	[illegible]	[illegible]	[illegible]	[illegible]	[illegible]	[illegible]
	Mumps	[illegible]	[illegible]	[illegible]	[illegible]	[illegible]	[illegible]	[illegible]	[illegible]	[illegible]	[illegible]	[illegible]	[illegible]	[illegible]	[illegible]	[illegible]	[illegible]	[illegible]	[illegible]	[illegible]	[illegible]	[illegible]	[illegible]
	Diphtheria	[illegible]	[illegible]	[illegible]	[illegible]	[illegible]	[illegible]	[illegible]	[illegible]	[illegible]	[illegible]	[illegible]	[illegible]	[illegible]	[illegible]	[illegible]	[illegible]	[illegible]	[illegible]	[illegible]	[illegible]	[illegible]	[illegible]
	Cerebro-spinal Fever	[illegible]	[illegible]	[illegible]	[illegible]	[illegible]	[illegible]	[illegible]	[illegible]	[illegible]	[illegible]	[illegible]	[illegible]	[illegible]	[illegible]	[illegible]	[illegible]	[illegible]	[illegible]	[illegible]	[illegible]	[illegible]	[illegible]
	Simple and Ill-defined Fever	[illegible]	[illegible]	[illegible]	[illegible]	[illegible]	[illegible]	[illegible]	[illegible]	[illegible]	[illegible]	[illegible]	[illegible]	[illegible]	[illegible]	[illegible]	[illegible]	[illegible]	[illegible]	[illegible]	[illegible]	[illegible]	[illegible]
	Enteric Fever	[illegible]	[illegible]	[illegible]	[illegible]	[illegible]	[illegible]	[illegible]	[illegible]	[illegible]	[illegible]	[illegible]	[illegible]	[illegible]	[illegible]	[illegible]	[illegible]	[illegible]	[illegible]	[illegible]	[illegible]	[illegible]	[illegible]
	Other Miasmatic Diseases	[illegible]	[illegible]	[illegible]	[illegible]	[illegible]	[illegible]	[illegible]	[illegible]	[illegible]	[illegible]	[illegible]	[illegible]	[illegible]	[illegible]	[illegible]	[illegible]	[illegible]	[illegible]	[illegible]	[illegible]	[illegible]	[illegible]
	DIARRHOEAL DISEASES.																						
	Simple Cholera	[illegible]	[illegible]	[illegible]	[illegible]	[illegible]	[illegible]	[illegible]	[illegible]	[illegible]	[illegible]	[illegible]	[illegible]	[illegible]	[illegible]	[illegible]	[illegible]	[illegible]	[illegible]	[illegible]	[illegible]	[illegible]	[illegible]
	Diarrhoea, Dysentery	[illegible]	[illegible]	[illegible]	[illegible]	[illegible]	[illegible]	[illegible]	[illegible]	[illegible]	[illegible]	[illegible]	[illegible]	[illegible]	[illegible]	[illegible]	[illegible]	[illegible]	[illegible]	[illegible]	[illegible]	[illegible]	[illegible]
	MALARIAL DISEASES.																						
	Remittent Fever	[illegible]	[illegible]	[illegible]	[illegible]	[illegible]	[illegible]	[illegible]	[illegible]	[illegible]	[illegible]	[illegible]	[illegible]	[illegible]	[illegible]	[illegible]	[illegible]	[illegible]	[illegible]	[illegible]	[illegible]	[illegible]	[illegible]
	Ague	[illegible]	[illegible]	[illegible]	[illegible]	[illegible]	[illegible]	[illegible]	[illegible]	[illegible]	[illegible]	[illegible]	[illegible]	[illegible]	[illegible]	[illegible]	[illegible]	[illegible]	[illegible]	[illegible]	[illegible]	[illegible]	[illegible]
	ZOOGENOUS DISEASES.																						
	Hydrophobia	[illegible]	[illegible]	[illegible]	[illegible]	[illegible]	[illegible]	[illegible]	[illegible]	[illegible]	[illegible]	[illegible]	[illegible]	[illegible]	[illegible]	[illegible]	[illegible]	[illegible]	[illegible]	[illegible]	[illegible]	[illegible]	[illegible]
	Glanders	[illegible]	[illegible]	[illegible]	[illegible]	[illegible]	[illegible]	[illegible]	[illegible]	[illegible]	[illegible]	[illegible]	[illegible]	[illegible]	[illegible]	[illegible]	[illegible]	[illegible]	[illegible]	[illegible]	[illegible]	[illegible]	[illegible]
	Splenic Fever	[illegible]	[illegible]	[illegible]	[illegible]	[illegible]	[illegible]	[illegible]	[illegible]	[illegible]	[illegible]	[illegible]	[illegible]	[illegible]	[illegible]	[illegible]	[illegible]	[illegible]	[illegible]	[illegible]	[illegible]	[illegible]	[illegible]
	Cow-pox and other effects of Vaccination	[illegible]	[illegible]	[illegible]	[illegible]	[illegible]	[illegible]	[illegible]	[illegible]	[illegible]	[illegible]	[illegible]	[illegible]	[illegible]	[illegible]	[illegible]	[illegible]	[illegible]	[illegible]	[illegible]	[illegible]	[illegible]	[illegible]
	VENEREAL DISEASES.																						
	Syphilis	[illegible]	[illegible]	[illegible]	[illegible]	[illegible]	[illegible]	[illegible]	[illegible]	[illegible]	[illegible]	[illegible]	[illegible]	[illegible]	[illegible]	[illegible]	[illegible]	[illegible]	[illegible]	[illegible]	[illegible]	[illegible]	[illegible]
	Gonorrhoea, Stricture of Urethra	[illegible]	[illegible]	[illegible]	[illegible]	[illegible]	[illegible]	[illegible]	[illegible]	[illegible]	[illegible]	[illegible]	[illegible]	[illegible]	[illegible]	[illegible]	[illegible]	[illegible]	[illegible]	[illegible]	[illegible]	[illegible]	[illegible]
	SEPTIC DISEASES.																						
	Phagedaena	[illegible]	[illegible]	[illegible]	[illegible]	[illegible]	[illegible]	[illegible]	[illegible]	[illegible]	[illegible]	[illegible]	[illegible]	[illegible]	[illegible]	[illegible]	[illegible]	[illegible]	[illegible]	[illegible]	[illegible]	[illegible]	[illegible]
	Erysipelas	[illegible]	[illegible]	[illegible]	[illegible]	[illegible]	[illegible]	[illegible]	[illegible]	[illegible]	[illegible]	[illegible]	[illegible]	[illegible]	[illegible]	[illegible]	[illegible]	[illegible]	[illegible]	[illegible]	[illegible]	[illegible]	[illegible]
	Pyaemia, Septicaemia	[illegible]	[illegible]	[illegible]	[illegible]	[illegible]	[illegible]	[illegible]	[illegible]	[illegible]	[illegible]	[illegible]	[illegible]	[illegible]	[illegible]	[illegible]	[illegible]	[illegible]	[illegible]	[illegible]	[illegible]	[illegible]	[illegible]
	Puerperal Fever	[illegible]	[illegible]	[illegible]	[illegible]	[illegible]	[illegible]	[illegible]	[illegible]	[illegible]	[illegible]	[illegible]	[illegible]	[illegible]	[illegible]	[illegible]	[illegible]	[illegible]	[illegible]	[illegible]	[illegible]	[illegible]	[illegible]
II.	PARASITIC DISEASES.																						
	Thrush	[illegible]	[illegible]	[illegible]	[illegible]	[illegible]	[illegible]	[illegible]	[illegible]	[illegible]	[illegible]	[illegible]	[illegible]	[illegible]	[illegible]	[illegible]	[illegible]	[illegible]	[illegible]	[illegible]	[illegible]	[illegible]	[illegible]
	Other Diseases from Vegetable Parasites	[illegible]	[illegible]	[illegible]	[illegible]	[illegible]	[illegible]	[illegible]	[illegible]	[illegible]	[illegible]	[illegible]	[illegible]	[illegible]	[illegible]	[illegible]	[illegible]	[illegible]	[illegible]	[illegible]	[illegible]	[illegible]	[illegible]
	Hydatid Disease	[illegible]	[illegible]	[illegible]	[illegible]	[illegible]	[illegible]	[illegible]	[illegible]	[illegible]	[illegible]	[illegible]	[illegible]	[illegible]	[illegible]	[illegible]	[illegible]	[illegible]	[illegible]	[illegible]	[illegible]	[illegible]	[illegible]
	Other Diseases from Animal Parasites	[illegible]	[illegible]	[illegible]	[illegible]	[illegible]	[illegible]	[illegible]	[illegible]	[illegible]	[illegible]	[illegible]	[illegible]	[illegible]	[illegible]	[illegible]	[illegible]	[illegible]	[illegible]	[illegible]	[illegible]	[illegible]	[illegible]
III.	DIETETIC DISEASES.																						
	Starvation, Want of Breast Milk	[illegible]	[illegible]	[illegible]	[illegible]	[illegible]	[illegible]	[illegible]	[illegible]	[illegible]	[illegible]	[illegible]	[illegible]	[illegible]	[illegible]	[illegible]	[illegible]	[illegible]	[illegible]	[illegible]	[illegible]	[illegible]	[illegible]
	Scurvy	[illegible]	[illegible]	[illegible]	[illegible]	[illegible]	[illegible]	[illegible]	[illegible]	[illegible]	[illegible]	[illegible]	[illegible]	[illegible]	[illegible]	[illegible]	[illegible]	[illegible]	[illegible]	[illegible]	[illegible]	[illegible]	[illegible]
	Intemperance: Chronic Alcoholism	[illegible]	[illegible]	[illegible]	[illegible]	[illegible]	[illegible]	[illegible]	[illegible]	[illegible]	[illegible]	[illegible]	[illegible]	[illegible]	[illegible]	[illegible]	[illegible]	[illegible]	[illegible]	[illegible]	[illegible]	[illegible]	[illegible]
	Intemperance: Delirium Tremens	[illegible]	[illegible]	[illegible]	[illegible]	[illegible]	[illegible]	[illegible]	[illegible]	[illegible]	[illegible]	[illegible]	[illegible]	[illegible]	[illegible]	[illegible]	[illegible]	[illegible]	[illegible]	[illegible]	[illegible]	[illegible]	[illegible]
IV.	CONSTITUTIONAL DISEASES.																						
	Rheumatic Fever, Rheumatism of Heart	[illegible]	[illegible]	[illegible]	[illegible]	[illegible]	[illegible]	[illegible]	[illegible]	[illegible]	[illegible]	[illegible]	[illegible]	[illegible]	[illegible]	[illegible]	[illegible]	[illegible]	[illegible]	[illegible]	[illegible]	[illegible]	[illegible]
	Rheumatism	[illegible]	[illegible]	[illegible]	[illegible]	[illegible]	[illegible]	[illegible]	[illegible]	[illegible]	[illegible]	[illegible]	[illegible]	[illegible]	[illegible]	[illegible]	[illegible]	[illegible]	[illegible]	[illegible]	[illegible]	[illegible]	[illegible]
	Gout	[illegible]	[illegible]	[illegible]	[illegible]	[illegible]	[illegible]	[illegible]	[illegible]	[illegible]	[illegible]	[illegible]	[illegible]	[illegible]	[illegible]	[illegible]	[illegible]	[illegible]	[illegible]	[illegible]	[illegible]	[illegible]	[illegible]
	Rickets	[illegible]	[illegible]	[illegible]	[illegible]	[illegible]	[illegible]	[illegible]	[illegible]	[illegible]	[illegible]	[illegible]	[illegible]	[illegible]	[illegible]	[illegible]	[illegible]	[illegible]	[illegible]	[illegible]	[illegible]	[illegible]	[illegible]
	Cancer	[illegible]	[illegible]	[illegible]	[illegible]	[illegible]	[illegible]	[illegible]	[illegible]	[illegible]	[illegible]	[illegible]	[illegible]	[illegible]	[illegible]	[illegible]	[illegible]	[illegible]	[illegible]	[illegible]	[illegible]	[illegible]	[illegible]

[continued on page 158.]

IRELAND.—CAUSES of DEATH at different Periods of Life in the Year 18[illegible]—[illegible].

IRELAND.—CAUSES of DEATH at different Periods of Life in the Year 1896—FEMALES—con.

Class.	CAUSES OF DEATH.	All Ages.	[illegible]	[illegible]	[illegible]	[illegible]	Total under 1 year	1	2	3	4	Total under 5 years	5-	10-	15-	20-	25-	35-	45-	55-	65-	75-	85-	95 and upwards
II.—con.	Tabes Mesenterica,	[illegible]	[illegible]	[illegible]	[illegible]	[illegible]	[illegible]	[illegible]	[illegible]	[illegible]	[illegible]	[illegible]	[illegible]	[illegible]	[illegible]	[illegible]	[illegible]	[illegible]	[illegible]	[illegible]	[illegible]	[illegible]	[illegible]	[illegible]
	Tubercular Meningitis (Acute Hydrocephalus),	[illegible]	[illegible]	[illegible]	[illegible]	[illegible]	[illegible]	[illegible]	[illegible]	[illegible]	[illegible]	[illegible]	[illegible]	[illegible]	[illegible]	[illegible]	[illegible]	[illegible]	[illegible]	[illegible]	[illegible]	[illegible]	[illegible]	[illegible]
	Phthisis,	[illegible]	[illegible]	[illegible]	[illegible]	[illegible]	[illegible]	[illegible]	[illegible]	[illegible]	[illegible]	[illegible]	[illegible]	[illegible]	[illegible]	[illegible]	[illegible]	[illegible]	[illegible]	[illegible]	[illegible]	[illegible]	[illegible]	[illegible]
	Other forms of Tuberculosis, Scrofula,	[illegible]	[illegible]	[illegible]	[illegible]	[illegible]	[illegible]	[illegible]	[illegible]	[illegible]	[illegible]	[illegible]	[illegible]	[illegible]	[illegible]	[illegible]	[illegible]	[illegible]	[illegible]	[illegible]	[illegible]	[illegible]	[illegible]	[illegible]
	Purpura, Haemorrhagic Diathesis,	[illegible]	[illegible]	[illegible]	[illegible]	[illegible]	[illegible]	[illegible]	[illegible]	[illegible]	[illegible]	[illegible]	[illegible]	[illegible]	[illegible]	[illegible]	[illegible]	[illegible]	[illegible]	[illegible]	[illegible]	[illegible]	[illegible]	[illegible]
	Anaemia, Chlorosis, Leucocythaemia,	[illegible]	[illegible]	[illegible]	[illegible]	[illegible]	[illegible]	[illegible]	[illegible]	[illegible]	[illegible]	[illegible]	[illegible]	[illegible]	[illegible]	[illegible]	[illegible]	[illegible]	[illegible]	[illegible]	[illegible]	[illegible]	[illegible]	[illegible]
	Diabetes Mellitus,	[illegible]	[illegible]	[illegible]	[illegible]	[illegible]	[illegible]	[illegible]	[illegible]	[illegible]	[illegible]	[illegible]	[illegible]	[illegible]	[illegible]	[illegible]	[illegible]	[illegible]	[illegible]	[illegible]	[illegible]	[illegible]	[illegible]	[illegible]
	Other and undefined Constitutional Diseases,	[illegible]	[illegible]	[illegible]	[illegible]	[illegible]	[illegible]	[illegible]	[illegible]	[illegible]	[illegible]	[illegible]	[illegible]	[illegible]	[illegible]	[illegible]	[illegible]	[illegible]	[illegible]	[illegible]	[illegible]	[illegible]	[illegible]	[illegible]
V.	DEVELOPMENTAL DISEASES.																							
	Premature Birth,	[illegible]	[illegible]	[illegible]	[illegible]	[illegible]	[illegible]	[illegible]	[illegible]	[illegible]	[illegible]	[illegible]	[illegible]	[illegible]	[illegible]	[illegible]	[illegible]	[illegible]	[illegible]	[illegible]	[illegible]	[illegible]	[illegible]	[illegible]
	Atelectasis,	[illegible]	[illegible]	[illegible]	[illegible]	[illegible]	[illegible]	[illegible]	[illegible]	[illegible]	[illegible]	[illegible]	[illegible]	[illegible]	[illegible]	[illegible]	[illegible]	[illegible]	[illegible]	[illegible]	[illegible]	[illegible]	[illegible]	[illegible]
	Cyanosis,	[illegible]	[illegible]	[illegible]	[illegible]	[illegible]	[illegible]	[illegible]	[illegible]	[illegible]	[illegible]	[illegible]	[illegible]	[illegible]	[illegible]	[illegible]	[illegible]	[illegible]	[illegible]	[illegible]	[illegible]	[illegible]	[illegible]	[illegible]
	Spina Bifida,	[illegible]	[illegible]	[illegible]	[illegible]	[illegible]	[illegible]	[illegible]	[illegible]	[illegible]	[illegible]	[illegible]	[illegible]	[illegible]	[illegible]	[illegible]	[illegible]	[illegible]	[illegible]	[illegible]	[illegible]	[illegible]	[illegible]	[illegible]
	Imperforate Anus,	[illegible]	[illegible]	[illegible]	[illegible]	[illegible]	[illegible]	[illegible]	[illegible]	[illegible]	[illegible]	[illegible]	[illegible]	[illegible]	[illegible]	[illegible]	[illegible]	[illegible]	[illegible]	[illegible]	[illegible]	[illegible]	[illegible]	[illegible]
	Cleft Palate, Harelip,	[illegible]	[illegible]	[illegible]	[illegible]	[illegible]	[illegible]	[illegible]	[illegible]	[illegible]	[illegible]	[illegible]	[illegible]	[illegible]	[illegible]	[illegible]	[illegible]	[illegible]	[illegible]	[illegible]	[illegible]	[illegible]	[illegible]	[illegible]
	Other Congenital defects,	[illegible]	[illegible]	[illegible]	[illegible]	[illegible]	[illegible]	[illegible]	[illegible]	[illegible]	[illegible]	[illegible]	[illegible]	[illegible]	[illegible]	[illegible]	[illegible]	[illegible]	[illegible]	[illegible]	[illegible]	[illegible]	[illegible]	[illegible]
	Old Age,	[illegible]	[illegible]	[illegible]	[illegible]	[illegible]	[illegible]	[illegible]	[illegible]	[illegible]	[illegible]	[illegible]	[illegible]	[illegible]	[illegible]	[illegible]	[illegible]	[illegible]	[illegible]	[illegible]	[illegible]	[illegible]	[illegible]	[illegible]
VI.	DISEASES OF NERVOUS SYSTEM.																							
	Inflammation of Brain or its Membranes,	[illegible]	[illegible]	[illegible]	[illegible]	[illegible]	[illegible]	[illegible]	[illegible]	[illegible]	[illegible]	[illegible]	[illegible]	[illegible]	[illegible]	[illegible]	[illegible]	[illegible]	[illegible]	[illegible]	[illegible]	[illegible]	[illegible]	[illegible]
	Apoplexy,	[illegible]	[illegible]	[illegible]	[illegible]	[illegible]	[illegible]	[illegible]	[illegible]	[illegible]	[illegible]	[illegible]	[illegible]	[illegible]	[illegible]	[illegible]	[illegible]	[illegible]	[illegible]	[illegible]	[illegible]	[illegible]	[illegible]	[illegible]
	Softening of Brain,	[illegible]	[illegible]	[illegible]	[illegible]	[illegible]	[illegible]	[illegible]	[illegible]	[illegible]	[illegible]	[illegible]	[illegible]	[illegible]	[illegible]	[illegible]	[illegible]	[illegible]	[illegible]	[illegible]	[illegible]	[illegible]	[illegible]	[illegible]
	Hemiplegia, Brain Paralysis,	[illegible]	[illegible]	[illegible]	[illegible]	[illegible]	[illegible]	[illegible]	[illegible]	[illegible]	[illegible]	[illegible]	[illegible]	[illegible]	[illegible]	[illegible]	[illegible]	[illegible]	[illegible]	[illegible]	[illegible]	[illegible]	[illegible]	[illegible]
	Paralysis Agitans,	[illegible]	[illegible]	[illegible]	[illegible]	[illegible]	[illegible]	[illegible]	[illegible]	[illegible]	[illegible]	[illegible]	[illegible]	[illegible]	[illegible]	[illegible]	[illegible]	[illegible]	[illegible]	[illegible]	[illegible]	[illegible]	[illegible]	[illegible]
	Insanity, General Paralysis of Insane,	[illegible]	[illegible]	[illegible]	[illegible]	[illegible]	[illegible]	[illegible]	[illegible]	[illegible]	[illegible]	[illegible]	[illegible]	[illegible]	[illegible]	[illegible]	[illegible]	[illegible]	[illegible]	[illegible]	[illegible]	[illegible]	[illegible]	[illegible]
	Chorea,	[illegible]	[illegible]	[illegible]	[illegible]	[illegible]	[illegible]	[illegible]	[illegible]	[illegible]	[illegible]	[illegible]	[illegible]	[illegible]	[illegible]	[illegible]	[illegible]	[illegible]	[illegible]	[illegible]	[illegible]	[illegible]	[illegible]	[illegible]
	Epilepsy,	[illegible]	[illegible]	[illegible]	[illegible]	[illegible]	[illegible]	[illegible]	[illegible]	[illegible]	[illegible]	[illegible]	[illegible]	[illegible]	[illegible]	[illegible]	[illegible]	[illegible]	[illegible]	[illegible]	[illegible]	[illegible]	[illegible]	[illegible]
	Convulsions,	[illegible]	[illegible]	[illegible]	[illegible]	[illegible]	[illegible]	[illegible]	[illegible]	[illegible]	[illegible]	[illegible]	[illegible]	[illegible]	[illegible]	[illegible]	[illegible]	[illegible]	[illegible]	[illegible]	[illegible]	[illegible]	[illegible]	[illegible]
	Laryngismus Stridulus,	[illegible]	[illegible]	[illegible]	[illegible]	[illegible]	[illegible]	[illegible]	[illegible]	[illegible]	[illegible]	[illegible]	[illegible]	[illegible]	[illegible]	[illegible]	[illegible]	[illegible]	[illegible]	[illegible]	[illegible]	[illegible]	[illegible]	[illegible]
	Idiopathic Tetanus,	[illegible]	[illegible]	[illegible]	[illegible]	[illegible]	[illegible]	[illegible]	[illegible]	[illegible]	[illegible]	[illegible]	[illegible]	[illegible]	[illegible]	[illegible]	[illegible]	[illegible]	[illegible]	[illegible]	[illegible]	[illegible]	[illegible]	[illegible]
	Paraplegia, Diseases of Spinal Cord,	[illegible]	[illegible]	[illegible]	[illegible]	[illegible]	[illegible]	[illegible]	[illegible]	[illegible]	[illegible]	[illegible]	[illegible]	[illegible]	[illegible]	[illegible]	[illegible]	[illegible]	[illegible]	[illegible]	[illegible]	[illegible]	[illegible]	[illegible]
	Other and undefined Diseases of Brain or Nervous System,	[illegible]	[illegible]	[illegible]	[illegible]	[illegible]	[illegible]	[illegible]	[illegible]	[illegible]	[illegible]	[illegible]	[illegible]	[illegible]	[illegible]	[illegible]	[illegible]	[illegible]	[illegible]	[illegible]	[illegible]	[illegible]	[illegible]	[illegible]
	DISEASES OF ORGANS OF SPECIAL SENSE.																							
	Otitis, Otorrhoea,	[illegible]	[illegible]	[illegible]	[illegible]	[illegible]	[illegible]	[illegible]	[illegible]	[illegible]	[illegible]	[illegible]	[illegible]	[illegible]	[illegible]	[illegible]	[illegible]	[illegible]	[illegible]	[illegible]	[illegible]	[illegible]	[illegible]	[illegible]
	Epistaxis, Diseases of Nose,	[illegible]	[illegible]	[illegible]	[illegible]	[illegible]	[illegible]	[illegible]	[illegible]	[illegible]	[illegible]	[illegible]	[illegible]	[illegible]	[illegible]	[illegible]	[illegible]	[illegible]	[illegible]	[illegible]	[illegible]	[illegible]	[illegible]	[illegible]
	Ophthalmia and Diseases of Eye,	[illegible]	[illegible]	[illegible]	[illegible]	[illegible]	[illegible]	[illegible]	[illegible]	[illegible]	[illegible]	[illegible]	[illegible]	[illegible]	[illegible]	[illegible]	[illegible]	[illegible]	[illegible]	[illegible]	[illegible]	[illegible]	[illegible]	[illegible]
	DISEASES OF CIRCULATORY SYSTEM.																							
	Endocarditis, Valvular Disease,	[illegible]	[illegible]	[illegible]	[illegible]	[illegible]	[illegible]	[illegible]	[illegible]	[illegible]	[illegible]	[illegible]	[illegible]	[illegible]	[illegible]	[illegible]	[illegible]	[illegible]	[illegible]	[illegible]	[illegible]	[illegible]	[illegible]	[illegible]
	Pericarditis,	[illegible]	[illegible]	[illegible]	[illegible]	[illegible]	[illegible]	[illegible]	[illegible]	[illegible]	[illegible]	[illegible]	[illegible]	[illegible]	[illegible]	[illegible]	[illegible]	[illegible]	[illegible]	[illegible]	[illegible]	[illegible]	[illegible]	[illegible]
	Hypertrophy of Heart,	[illegible]	[illegible]	[illegible]	[illegible]	[illegible]	[illegible]	[illegible]	[illegible]	[illegible]	[illegible]	[illegible]	[illegible]	[illegible]	[illegible]	[illegible]	[illegible]	[illegible]	[illegible]	[illegible]	[illegible]	[illegible]	[illegible]	[illegible]
	Angina Pectoris,	[illegible]	[illegible]	[illegible]	[illegible]	[illegible]	[illegible]	[illegible]	[illegible]	[illegible]	[illegible]	[illegible]	[illegible]	[illegible]	[illegible]	[illegible]	[illegible]	[illegible]	[illegible]	[illegible]	[illegible]	[illegible]	[illegible]	[illegible]
	Syncope,	[illegible]	[illegible]	[illegible]	[illegible]	[illegible]	[illegible]	[illegible]	[illegible]	[illegible]	[illegible]	[illegible]	[illegible]	[illegible]	[illegible]	[illegible]	[illegible]	[illegible]	[illegible]	[illegible]	[illegible]	[illegible]	[illegible]	[illegible]
	Aneurism,	[illegible]	[illegible]	[illegible]	[illegible]	[illegible]	[illegible]	[illegible]	[illegible]	[illegible]	[illegible]	[illegible]	[illegible]	[illegible]	[illegible]	[illegible]	[illegible]	[illegible]	[illegible]	[illegible]	[illegible]	[illegible]	[illegible]	[illegible]
	Senile Gangrene,	[illegible]	[illegible]	[illegible]	[illegible]	[illegible]	[illegible]	[illegible]	[illegible]	[illegible]	[illegible]	[illegible]	[illegible]	[illegible]	[illegible]	[illegible]	[illegible]	[illegible]	[illegible]	[illegible]	[illegible]	[illegible]	[illegible]	[illegible]
	Embolism, Thrombosis,	[illegible]	[illegible]	[illegible]	[illegible]	[illegible]	[illegible]	[illegible]	[illegible]	[illegible]	[illegible]	[illegible]	[illegible]	[illegible]	[illegible]	[illegible]	[illegible]	[illegible]	[illegible]	[illegible]	[illegible]	[illegible]	[illegible]	[illegible]
	Phlebitis,	[illegible]	[illegible]	[illegible]	[illegible]	[illegible]	[illegible]	[illegible]	[illegible]	[illegible]	[illegible]	[illegible]	[illegible]	[illegible]	[illegible]	[illegible]	[illegible]	[illegible]	[illegible]	[illegible]	[illegible]	[illegible]	[illegible]	[illegible]
	Varicose Veins,	[illegible]	[illegible]	[illegible]	[illegible]	[illegible]	[illegible]	[illegible]	[illegible]	[illegible]	[illegible]	[illegible]	[illegible]	[illegible]	[illegible]	[illegible]	[illegible]	[illegible]	[illegible]	[illegible]	[illegible]	[illegible]	[illegible]	[illegible]
	Other and undefined Diseases of Heart or Blood-vessels,	[illegible]	[illegible]	[illegible]	[illegible]	[illegible]	[illegible]	[illegible]	[illegible]	[illegible]	[illegible]	[illegible]	[illegible]	[illegible]	[illegible]	[illegible]	[illegible]	[illegible]	[illegible]	[illegible]	[illegible]	[illegible]	[illegible]	[illegible]
	DISEASES OF RESPIRATORY SYSTEM.																							
	Laryngitis,	[illegible]	[illegible]	[illegible]	[illegible]	[illegible]	[illegible]	[illegible]	[illegible]	[illegible]	[illegible]	[illegible]	[illegible]	[illegible]	[illegible]	[illegible]	[illegible]	[illegible]	[illegible]	[illegible]	[illegible]	[illegible]	[illegible]	[illegible]
	Croup,	[illegible]	[illegible]	[illegible]	[illegible]	[illegible]	[illegible]	[illegible]	[illegible]	[illegible]	[illegible]	[illegible]	[illegible]	[illegible]	[illegible]	[illegible]	[illegible]	[illegible]	[illegible]	[illegible]	[illegible]	[illegible]	[illegible]	[illegible]
	Other Diseases of Larynx and Trachea,	[illegible]	[illegible]	[illegible]	[illegible]	[illegible]	[illegible]	[illegible]	[illegible]	[illegible]	[illegible]	[illegible]	[illegible]	[illegible]	[illegible]	[illegible]	[illegible]	[illegible]	[illegible]	[illegible]	[illegible]	[illegible]	[illegible]	[illegible]
	Emphysema, Asthma,	[illegible]	[illegible]	[illegible]	[illegible]	[illegible]	[illegible]	[illegible]	[illegible]	[illegible]	[illegible]	[illegible]	[illegible]	[illegible]	[illegible]	[illegible]	[illegible]	[illegible]	[illegible]	[illegible]	[illegible]	[illegible]	[illegible]	[illegible]

[continued on page 170.]

IRELAND.—CAUSES of DEATH at different Periods of Life in the Year 18[illegible]—MALES—con.

Class	Causes of Death	MALES: All Ages	Ages at Death: Under 1 month	1– months	3– months	Total under 1 year	1	2	3	4	Total under 5 years	5–	10–	15–	20–	25–	35–	45–	55–	65–	75–	85–	95 and upwards
VI.—Local—con.	Diseases of Respiratory System—con.																						
	Bronchitis,	[illegible]	[illegible]	[illegible]	[illegible]	[illegible]	[illegible]	[illegible]	[illegible]	[illegible]	[illegible]	[illegible]	[illegible]	[illegible]	[illegible]	[illegible]	[illegible]	[illegible]	[illegible]	[illegible]	[illegible]	[illegible]	[illegible]
	Pneumonia,	[illegible]	[illegible]	[illegible]	[illegible]	[illegible]	[illegible]	[illegible]	[illegible]	[illegible]	[illegible]	[illegible]	[illegible]	[illegible]	[illegible]	[illegible]	[illegible]	[illegible]	[illegible]	[illegible]	[illegible]	[illegible]	[illegible]
	Pleurisy,	[illegible]	[illegible]	[illegible]	[illegible]	[illegible]	[illegible]	[illegible]	[illegible]	[illegible]	[illegible]	[illegible]	[illegible]	[illegible]	[illegible]	[illegible]	[illegible]	[illegible]	[illegible]	[illegible]	[illegible]	[illegible]	[illegible]
	Other and undefined Diseases of Respiratory System,	[illegible]	[illegible]	[illegible]	[illegible]	[illegible]	[illegible]	[illegible]	[illegible]	[illegible]	[illegible]	[illegible]	[illegible]	[illegible]	[illegible]	[illegible]	[illegible]	[illegible]	[illegible]	[illegible]	[illegible]	[illegible]	[illegible]
	Diseases of Digestive System.																						
	[illegible]	[illegible]	[illegible]	[illegible]	[illegible]	[illegible]	[illegible]	[illegible]	[illegible]	[illegible]	[illegible]	[illegible]	[illegible]	[illegible]	[illegible]	[illegible]	[illegible]	[illegible]	[illegible]	[illegible]	[illegible]	[illegible]	[illegible]
	Dentition,	[illegible]	[illegible]	[illegible]	[illegible]	[illegible]	[illegible]	[illegible]	[illegible]	[illegible]	[illegible]	[illegible]	[illegible]	[illegible]	[illegible]	[illegible]	[illegible]	[illegible]	[illegible]	[illegible]	[illegible]	[illegible]	[illegible]
	Sore-throat, Quinsy,	[illegible]	[illegible]	[illegible]	[illegible]	[illegible]	[illegible]	[illegible]	[illegible]	[illegible]	[illegible]	[illegible]	[illegible]	[illegible]	[illegible]	[illegible]	[illegible]	[illegible]	[illegible]	[illegible]	[illegible]	[illegible]	[illegible]
	Dyspepsia,	[illegible]	[illegible]	[illegible]	[illegible]	[illegible]	[illegible]	[illegible]	[illegible]	[illegible]	[illegible]	[illegible]	[illegible]	[illegible]	[illegible]	[illegible]	[illegible]	[illegible]	[illegible]	[illegible]	[illegible]	[illegible]	[illegible]
	Haematemesis,	[illegible]	[illegible]	[illegible]	[illegible]	[illegible]	[illegible]	[illegible]	[illegible]	[illegible]	[illegible]	[illegible]	[illegible]	[illegible]	[illegible]	[illegible]	[illegible]	[illegible]	[illegible]	[illegible]	[illegible]	[illegible]	[illegible]
	Melaena,	[illegible]	[illegible]	[illegible]	[illegible]	[illegible]	[illegible]	[illegible]	[illegible]	[illegible]	[illegible]	[illegible]	[illegible]	[illegible]	[illegible]	[illegible]	[illegible]	[illegible]	[illegible]	[illegible]	[illegible]	[illegible]	[illegible]
	Diseases of Stomach,	[illegible]	[illegible]	[illegible]	[illegible]	[illegible]	[illegible]	[illegible]	[illegible]	[illegible]	[illegible]	[illegible]	[illegible]	[illegible]	[illegible]	[illegible]	[illegible]	[illegible]	[illegible]	[illegible]	[illegible]	[illegible]	[illegible]
	[illegible]	[illegible]	[illegible]	[illegible]	[illegible]	[illegible]	[illegible]	[illegible]	[illegible]	[illegible]	[illegible]	[illegible]	[illegible]	[illegible]	[illegible]	[illegible]	[illegible]	[illegible]	[illegible]	[illegible]	[illegible]	[illegible]	[illegible]
	Ulceration of Intestine,	[illegible]	[illegible]	[illegible]	[illegible]	[illegible]	[illegible]	[illegible]	[illegible]	[illegible]	[illegible]	[illegible]	[illegible]	[illegible]	[illegible]	[illegible]	[illegible]	[illegible]	[illegible]	[illegible]	[illegible]	[illegible]	[illegible]
	Ileus, Obstruction of Intestine	[illegible]	[illegible]	[illegible]	[illegible]	[illegible]	[illegible]	[illegible]	[illegible]	[illegible]	[illegible]	[illegible]	[illegible]	[illegible]	[illegible]	[illegible]	[illegible]	[illegible]	[illegible]	[illegible]	[illegible]	[illegible]	[illegible]
	Stricture or Strangulation of Intestine	[illegible]	[illegible]	[illegible]	[illegible]	[illegible]	[illegible]	[illegible]	[illegible]	[illegible]	[illegible]	[illegible]	[illegible]	[illegible]	[illegible]	[illegible]	[illegible]	[illegible]	[illegible]	[illegible]	[illegible]	[illegible]	[illegible]
	Intussusception of Intestine	[illegible]	[illegible]	[illegible]	[illegible]	[illegible]	[illegible]	[illegible]	[illegible]	[illegible]	[illegible]	[illegible]	[illegible]	[illegible]	[illegible]	[illegible]	[illegible]	[illegible]	[illegible]	[illegible]	[illegible]	[illegible]	[illegible]
	Hernia,	[illegible]	[illegible]	[illegible]	[illegible]	[illegible]	[illegible]	[illegible]	[illegible]	[illegible]	[illegible]	[illegible]	[illegible]	[illegible]	[illegible]	[illegible]	[illegible]	[illegible]	[illegible]	[illegible]	[illegible]	[illegible]	[illegible]
	Fistula,	[illegible]	[illegible]	[illegible]	[illegible]	[illegible]	[illegible]	[illegible]	[illegible]	[illegible]	[illegible]	[illegible]	[illegible]	[illegible]	[illegible]	[illegible]	[illegible]	[illegible]	[illegible]	[illegible]	[illegible]	[illegible]	[illegible]
	Peritonitis,	[illegible]	[illegible]	[illegible]	[illegible]	[illegible]	[illegible]	[illegible]	[illegible]	[illegible]	[illegible]	[illegible]	[illegible]	[illegible]	[illegible]	[illegible]	[illegible]	[illegible]	[illegible]	[illegible]	[illegible]	[illegible]	[illegible]
	Ascites,	[illegible]	[illegible]	[illegible]	[illegible]	[illegible]	[illegible]	[illegible]	[illegible]	[illegible]	[illegible]	[illegible]	[illegible]	[illegible]	[illegible]	[illegible]	[illegible]	[illegible]	[illegible]	[illegible]	[illegible]	[illegible]	[illegible]
	Gall-stones,	[illegible]	[illegible]	[illegible]	[illegible]	[illegible]	[illegible]	[illegible]	[illegible]	[illegible]	[illegible]	[illegible]	[illegible]	[illegible]	[illegible]	[illegible]	[illegible]	[illegible]	[illegible]	[illegible]	[illegible]	[illegible]	[illegible]
	Cirrhosis of Liver,	[illegible]	[illegible]	[illegible]	[illegible]	[illegible]	[illegible]	[illegible]	[illegible]	[illegible]	[illegible]	[illegible]	[illegible]	[illegible]	[illegible]	[illegible]	[illegible]	[illegible]	[illegible]	[illegible]	[illegible]	[illegible]	[illegible]
	Other Diseases of Liver,	[illegible]	[illegible]	[illegible]	[illegible]	[illegible]	[illegible]	[illegible]	[illegible]	[illegible]	[illegible]	[illegible]	[illegible]	[illegible]	[illegible]	[illegible]	[illegible]	[illegible]	[illegible]	[illegible]	[illegible]	[illegible]	[illegible]
	Other and undefined Diseases of Digestive System,	[illegible]	[illegible]	[illegible]	[illegible]	[illegible]	[illegible]	[illegible]	[illegible]	[illegible]	[illegible]	[illegible]	[illegible]	[illegible]	[illegible]	[illegible]	[illegible]	[illegible]	[illegible]	[illegible]	[illegible]	[illegible]	[illegible]
	Diseases of Lymphatic System and Ductless Glands.																						
	[illegible]	[illegible]	[illegible]	[illegible]	[illegible]	[illegible]	[illegible]	[illegible]	[illegible]	[illegible]	[illegible]	[illegible]	[illegible]	[illegible]	[illegible]	[illegible]	[illegible]	[illegible]	[illegible]	[illegible]	[illegible]	[illegible]	[illegible]
	[illegible]	[illegible]	[illegible]	[illegible]	[illegible]	[illegible]	[illegible]	[illegible]	[illegible]	[illegible]	[illegible]	[illegible]	[illegible]	[illegible]	[illegible]	[illegible]	[illegible]	[illegible]	[illegible]	[illegible]	[illegible]	[illegible]	[illegible]
	Diseases of Thyroid Body,	[illegible]	[illegible]	[illegible]	[illegible]	[illegible]	[illegible]	[illegible]	[illegible]	[illegible]	[illegible]	[illegible]	[illegible]	[illegible]	[illegible]	[illegible]	[illegible]	[illegible]	[illegible]	[illegible]	[illegible]	[illegible]	[illegible]
	Diseases of Supra-renal Capsules	[illegible]	[illegible]	[illegible]	[illegible]	[illegible]	[illegible]	[illegible]	[illegible]	[illegible]	[illegible]	[illegible]	[illegible]	[illegible]	[illegible]	[illegible]	[illegible]	[illegible]	[illegible]	[illegible]	[illegible]	[illegible]	[illegible]
	Diseases of Urinary System.																						
	Acute Nephritis,	[illegible]	[illegible]	[illegible]	[illegible]	[illegible]	[illegible]	[illegible]	[illegible]	[illegible]	[illegible]	[illegible]	[illegible]	[illegible]	[illegible]	[illegible]	[illegible]	[illegible]	[illegible]	[illegible]	[illegible]	[illegible]	[illegible]
	Bright's Disease, Albuminuria,	[illegible]	[illegible]	[illegible]	[illegible]	[illegible]	[illegible]	[illegible]	[illegible]	[illegible]	[illegible]	[illegible]	[illegible]	[illegible]	[illegible]	[illegible]	[illegible]	[illegible]	[illegible]	[illegible]	[illegible]	[illegible]	[illegible]
	[illegible]	[illegible]	[illegible]	[illegible]	[illegible]	[illegible]	[illegible]	[illegible]	[illegible]	[illegible]	[illegible]	[illegible]	[illegible]	[illegible]	[illegible]	[illegible]	[illegible]	[illegible]	[illegible]	[illegible]	[illegible]	[illegible]	[illegible]
	Suppression of Urine,	[illegible]	[illegible]	[illegible]	[illegible]	[illegible]	[illegible]	[illegible]	[illegible]	[illegible]	[illegible]	[illegible]	[illegible]	[illegible]	[illegible]	[illegible]	[illegible]	[illegible]	[illegible]	[illegible]	[illegible]	[illegible]	[illegible]
	Calculus,	[illegible]	[illegible]	[illegible]	[illegible]	[illegible]	[illegible]	[illegible]	[illegible]	[illegible]	[illegible]	[illegible]	[illegible]	[illegible]	[illegible]	[illegible]	[illegible]	[illegible]	[illegible]	[illegible]	[illegible]	[illegible]	[illegible]
	Haematuria,	[illegible]	[illegible]	[illegible]	[illegible]	[illegible]	[illegible]	[illegible]	[illegible]	[illegible]	[illegible]	[illegible]	[illegible]	[illegible]	[illegible]	[illegible]	[illegible]	[illegible]	[illegible]	[illegible]	[illegible]	[illegible]	[illegible]
	Diseases of Bladder and of Prostate,	[illegible]	[illegible]	[illegible]	[illegible]	[illegible]	[illegible]	[illegible]	[illegible]	[illegible]	[illegible]	[illegible]	[illegible]	[illegible]	[illegible]	[illegible]	[illegible]	[illegible]	[illegible]	[illegible]	[illegible]	[illegible]	[illegible]
	Other and undefined Diseases of Urinary System,	[illegible]	[illegible]	[illegible]	[illegible]	[illegible]	[illegible]	[illegible]	[illegible]	[illegible]	[illegible]	[illegible]	[illegible]	[illegible]	[illegible]	[illegible]	[illegible]	[illegible]	[illegible]	[illegible]	[illegible]	[illegible]	[illegible]
	Diseases of Organs of Generation.																						
	Ovarian Disease,	[illegible]	[illegible]	[illegible]	[illegible]	[illegible]	[illegible]	[illegible]	[illegible]	[illegible]	[illegible]	[illegible]	[illegible]	[illegible]	[illegible]	[illegible]	[illegible]	[illegible]	[illegible]	[illegible]	[illegible]	[illegible]	[illegible]
	Diseases of Uterus and Vagina,	[illegible]	[illegible]	[illegible]	[illegible]	[illegible]	[illegible]	[illegible]	[illegible]	[illegible]	[illegible]	[illegible]	[illegible]	[illegible]	[illegible]	[illegible]	[illegible]	[illegible]	[illegible]	[illegible]	[illegible]	[illegible]	[illegible]
	Disorders of Menstruation,	[illegible]	[illegible]	[illegible]	[illegible]	[illegible]	[illegible]	[illegible]	[illegible]	[illegible]	[illegible]	[illegible]	[illegible]	[illegible]	[illegible]	[illegible]	[illegible]	[illegible]	[illegible]	[illegible]	[illegible]	[illegible]	[illegible]
	Pelvic Abscess,	[illegible]	[illegible]	[illegible]	[illegible]	[illegible]	[illegible]	[illegible]	[illegible]	[illegible]	[illegible]	[illegible]	[illegible]	[illegible]	[illegible]	[illegible]	[illegible]	[illegible]	[illegible]	[illegible]	[illegible]	[illegible]	[illegible]
	Perineal Abscess,	[illegible]	[illegible]	[illegible]	[illegible]	[illegible]	[illegible]	[illegible]	[illegible]	[illegible]	[illegible]	[illegible]	[illegible]	[illegible]	[illegible]	[illegible]	[illegible]	[illegible]	[illegible]	[illegible]	[illegible]	[illegible]	[illegible]
	Diseases of Testes, Penis, Scrotum, &c.	[illegible]	[illegible]	[illegible]	[illegible]	[illegible]	[illegible]	[illegible]	[illegible]	[illegible]	[illegible]	[illegible]	[illegible]	[illegible]	[illegible]	[illegible]	[illegible]	[illegible]	[illegible]	[illegible]	[illegible]	[illegible]	[illegible]

[continued at page [illegible].]

IRELAND.—CAUSES of DEATHS at different Periods of Life in the Year 1896—FEMALES—con.

Class.	CAUSES OF DEATH.	FEMALES. All Ages.	Ages at Death. 0–3 months	3–6 months	6–12 months	Total under 1 Year.	1	2	3	4	Total under 5 Years.	5–	10–	15–	20–	25–	35–	45–	55–	65–	75–	85–	95 and upwards
VI.—contd.	DISEASES OF RESPIRATORY SYSTEM—contd.																						
	Bronchitis,	[illegible]	[illegible]	[illegible]	[illegible]	[illegible]	[illegible]	[illegible]	[illegible]	[illegible]	[illegible]	[illegible]	[illegible]	[illegible]	[illegible]	[illegible]	[illegible]	[illegible]	[illegible]	[illegible]	[illegible]	[illegible]	[illegible]
	Pneumonia,	[illegible]	[illegible]	[illegible]	[illegible]	[illegible]	[illegible]	[illegible]	[illegible]	[illegible]	[illegible]	[illegible]	[illegible]	[illegible]	[illegible]	[illegible]	[illegible]	[illegible]	[illegible]	[illegible]	[illegible]	[illegible]	[illegible]
	Pleurisy,	[illegible]	[illegible]	[illegible]	[illegible]	[illegible]	[illegible]	[illegible]	[illegible]	[illegible]	[illegible]	[illegible]	[illegible]	[illegible]	[illegible]	[illegible]	[illegible]	[illegible]	[illegible]	[illegible]	[illegible]	[illegible]	[illegible]
	Other and undefined Diseases of Respiratory System.	[illegible]	[illegible]	[illegible]	[illegible]	[illegible]	[illegible]	[illegible]	[illegible]	[illegible]	[illegible]	[illegible]	[illegible]	[illegible]	[illegible]	[illegible]	[illegible]	[illegible]	[illegible]	[illegible]	[illegible]	[illegible]	[illegible]
	DISEASES OF DIGESTIVE SYSTEM.																						
	Stomatitis,	[illegible]	[illegible]	[illegible]	[illegible]	[illegible]	[illegible]	[illegible]	[illegible]	[illegible]	[illegible]	[illegible]	[illegible]	[illegible]	[illegible]	[illegible]	[illegible]	[illegible]	[illegible]	[illegible]	[illegible]	[illegible]	[illegible]
	Dentition,	[illegible]	[illegible]	[illegible]	[illegible]	[illegible]	[illegible]	[illegible]	[illegible]	[illegible]	[illegible]	[illegible]	[illegible]	[illegible]	[illegible]	[illegible]	[illegible]	[illegible]	[illegible]	[illegible]	[illegible]	[illegible]	[illegible]
	Sore-throat, Quinsy,	[illegible]	[illegible]	[illegible]	[illegible]	[illegible]	[illegible]	[illegible]	[illegible]	[illegible]	[illegible]	[illegible]	[illegible]	[illegible]	[illegible]	[illegible]	[illegible]	[illegible]	[illegible]	[illegible]	[illegible]	[illegible]	[illegible]
	Dyspepsia,	[illegible]	[illegible]	[illegible]	[illegible]	[illegible]	[illegible]	[illegible]	[illegible]	[illegible]	[illegible]	[illegible]	[illegible]	[illegible]	[illegible]	[illegible]	[illegible]	[illegible]	[illegible]	[illegible]	[illegible]	[illegible]	[illegible]
	Hæmatemesis,	[illegible]	[illegible]	[illegible]	[illegible]	[illegible]	[illegible]	[illegible]	[illegible]	[illegible]	[illegible]	[illegible]	[illegible]	[illegible]	[illegible]	[illegible]	[illegible]	[illegible]	[illegible]	[illegible]	[illegible]	[illegible]	[illegible]
	Melæna,	[illegible]	[illegible]	[illegible]	[illegible]	[illegible]	[illegible]	[illegible]	[illegible]	[illegible]	[illegible]	[illegible]	[illegible]	[illegible]	[illegible]	[illegible]	[illegible]	[illegible]	[illegible]	[illegible]	[illegible]	[illegible]	[illegible]
	Diseases of Stomach,	[illegible]	[illegible]	[illegible]	[illegible]	[illegible]	[illegible]	[illegible]	[illegible]	[illegible]	[illegible]	[illegible]	[illegible]	[illegible]	[illegible]	[illegible]	[illegible]	[illegible]	[illegible]	[illegible]	[illegible]	[illegible]	[illegible]
	Enteritis,	[illegible]	[illegible]	[illegible]	[illegible]	[illegible]	[illegible]	[illegible]	[illegible]	[illegible]	[illegible]	[illegible]	[illegible]	[illegible]	[illegible]	[illegible]	[illegible]	[illegible]	[illegible]	[illegible]	[illegible]	[illegible]	[illegible]
	Ulceration of Intestine,	[illegible]	[illegible]	[illegible]	[illegible]	[illegible]	[illegible]	[illegible]	[illegible]	[illegible]	[illegible]	[illegible]	[illegible]	[illegible]	[illegible]	[illegible]	[illegible]	[illegible]	[illegible]	[illegible]	[illegible]	[illegible]	[illegible]
	Ileus, Obstruction of Intestine,	[illegible]	[illegible]	[illegible]	[illegible]	[illegible]	[illegible]	[illegible]	[illegible]	[illegible]	[illegible]	[illegible]	[illegible]	[illegible]	[illegible]	[illegible]	[illegible]	[illegible]	[illegible]	[illegible]	[illegible]	[illegible]	[illegible]
	Stricture or Strangulation of Intestine,	[illegible]	[illegible]	[illegible]	[illegible]	[illegible]	[illegible]	[illegible]	[illegible]	[illegible]	[illegible]	[illegible]	[illegible]	[illegible]	[illegible]	[illegible]	[illegible]	[illegible]	[illegible]	[illegible]	[illegible]	[illegible]	[illegible]
	Intussusception of Intestine,	[illegible]	[illegible]	[illegible]	[illegible]	[illegible]	[illegible]	[illegible]	[illegible]	[illegible]	[illegible]	[illegible]	[illegible]	[illegible]	[illegible]	[illegible]	[illegible]	[illegible]	[illegible]	[illegible]	[illegible]	[illegible]	[illegible]
	Hernia,	[illegible]	[illegible]	[illegible]	[illegible]	[illegible]	[illegible]	[illegible]	[illegible]	[illegible]	[illegible]	[illegible]	[illegible]	[illegible]	[illegible]	[illegible]	[illegible]	[illegible]	[illegible]	[illegible]	[illegible]	[illegible]	[illegible]
	Fistula,	[illegible]	[illegible]	[illegible]	[illegible]	[illegible]	[illegible]	[illegible]	[illegible]	[illegible]	[illegible]	[illegible]	[illegible]	[illegible]	[illegible]	[illegible]	[illegible]	[illegible]	[illegible]	[illegible]	[illegible]	[illegible]	[illegible]
	Peritonitis,	[illegible]	[illegible]	[illegible]	[illegible]	[illegible]	[illegible]	[illegible]	[illegible]	[illegible]	[illegible]	[illegible]	[illegible]	[illegible]	[illegible]	[illegible]	[illegible]	[illegible]	[illegible]	[illegible]	[illegible]	[illegible]	[illegible]
	Ascites,	[illegible]	[illegible]	[illegible]	[illegible]	[illegible]	[illegible]	[illegible]	[illegible]	[illegible]	[illegible]	[illegible]	[illegible]	[illegible]	[illegible]	[illegible]	[illegible]	[illegible]	[illegible]	[illegible]	[illegible]	[illegible]	[illegible]
	Gallstones,	[illegible]	[illegible]	[illegible]	[illegible]	[illegible]	[illegible]	[illegible]	[illegible]	[illegible]	[illegible]	[illegible]	[illegible]	[illegible]	[illegible]	[illegible]	[illegible]	[illegible]	[illegible]	[illegible]	[illegible]	[illegible]	[illegible]
	Cirrhosis of Liver,	[illegible]	[illegible]	[illegible]	[illegible]	[illegible]	[illegible]	[illegible]	[illegible]	[illegible]	[illegible]	[illegible]	[illegible]	[illegible]	[illegible]	[illegible]	[illegible]	[illegible]	[illegible]	[illegible]	[illegible]	[illegible]	[illegible]
	Other Diseases of Liver,	[illegible]	[illegible]	[illegible]	[illegible]	[illegible]	[illegible]	[illegible]	[illegible]	[illegible]	[illegible]	[illegible]	[illegible]	[illegible]	[illegible]	[illegible]	[illegible]	[illegible]	[illegible]	[illegible]	[illegible]	[illegible]	[illegible]
	Other and undefined Diseases of Digestive System.	[illegible]	[illegible]	[illegible]	[illegible]	[illegible]	[illegible]	[illegible]	[illegible]	[illegible]	[illegible]	[illegible]	[illegible]	[illegible]	[illegible]	[illegible]	[illegible]	[illegible]	[illegible]	[illegible]	[illegible]	[illegible]	[illegible]
	DISEASES OF LYMPHATIC SYSTEM AND DUCTLESS GLANDS.																						
	Diseases of Spleen,	[illegible]	[illegible]	[illegible]	[illegible]	[illegible]	[illegible]	[illegible]	[illegible]	[illegible]	[illegible]	[illegible]	[illegible]	[illegible]	[illegible]	[illegible]	[illegible]	[illegible]	[illegible]	[illegible]	[illegible]	[illegible]	[illegible]
	Diseases of Lymphatic System,	[illegible]	[illegible]	[illegible]	[illegible]	[illegible]	[illegible]	[illegible]	[illegible]	[illegible]	[illegible]	[illegible]	[illegible]	[illegible]	[illegible]	[illegible]	[illegible]	[illegible]	[illegible]	[illegible]	[illegible]	[illegible]	[illegible]
	Diseases of Thyroid Body,	[illegible]	[illegible]	[illegible]	[illegible]	[illegible]	[illegible]	[illegible]	[illegible]	[illegible]	[illegible]	[illegible]	[illegible]	[illegible]	[illegible]	[illegible]	[illegible]	[illegible]	[illegible]	[illegible]	[illegible]	[illegible]	[illegible]
	Diseases of Suprarenal Capsules,	[illegible]	[illegible]	[illegible]	[illegible]	[illegible]	[illegible]	[illegible]	[illegible]	[illegible]	[illegible]	[illegible]	[illegible]	[illegible]	[illegible]	[illegible]	[illegible]	[illegible]	[illegible]	[illegible]	[illegible]	[illegible]	[illegible]
	DISEASES OF URINARY SYSTEM.																						
	Acute Nephritis,	[illegible]	[illegible]	[illegible]	[illegible]	[illegible]	[illegible]	[illegible]	[illegible]	[illegible]	[illegible]	[illegible]	[illegible]	[illegible]	[illegible]	[illegible]	[illegible]	[illegible]	[illegible]	[illegible]	[illegible]	[illegible]	[illegible]
	Bright's Disease, Albuminuria,	[illegible]	[illegible]	[illegible]	[illegible]	[illegible]	[illegible]	[illegible]	[illegible]	[illegible]	[illegible]	[illegible]	[illegible]	[illegible]	[illegible]	[illegible]	[illegible]	[illegible]	[illegible]	[illegible]	[illegible]	[illegible]	[illegible]
	Uræmia,	[illegible]	[illegible]	[illegible]	[illegible]	[illegible]	[illegible]	[illegible]	[illegible]	[illegible]	[illegible]	[illegible]	[illegible]	[illegible]	[illegible]	[illegible]	[illegible]	[illegible]	[illegible]	[illegible]	[illegible]	[illegible]	[illegible]
	Suppression of Urine,	[illegible]	[illegible]	[illegible]	[illegible]	[illegible]	[illegible]	[illegible]	[illegible]	[illegible]	[illegible]	[illegible]	[illegible]	[illegible]	[illegible]	[illegible]	[illegible]	[illegible]	[illegible]	[illegible]	[illegible]	[illegible]	[illegible]
	Calculus,	[illegible]	[illegible]	[illegible]	[illegible]	[illegible]	[illegible]	[illegible]	[illegible]	[illegible]	[illegible]	[illegible]	[illegible]	[illegible]	[illegible]	[illegible]	[illegible]	[illegible]	[illegible]	[illegible]	[illegible]	[illegible]	[illegible]
	Hæmaturia,	[illegible]	[illegible]	[illegible]	[illegible]	[illegible]	[illegible]	[illegible]	[illegible]	[illegible]	[illegible]	[illegible]	[illegible]	[illegible]	[illegible]	[illegible]	[illegible]	[illegible]	[illegible]	[illegible]	[illegible]	[illegible]	[illegible]
	Diseases of Bladder and of Prostate,	[illegible]	[illegible]	[illegible]	[illegible]	[illegible]	[illegible]	[illegible]	[illegible]	[illegible]	[illegible]	[illegible]	[illegible]	[illegible]	[illegible]	[illegible]	[illegible]	[illegible]	[illegible]	[illegible]	[illegible]	[illegible]	[illegible]
	Other and undefined Diseases of Urinary System.	[illegible]	[illegible]	[illegible]	[illegible]	[illegible]	[illegible]	[illegible]	[illegible]	[illegible]	[illegible]	[illegible]	[illegible]	[illegible]	[illegible]	[illegible]	[illegible]	[illegible]	[illegible]	[illegible]	[illegible]	[illegible]	[illegible]
	DISEASES OF ORGANS OF GENERATION.																						
	Ovarian Disease,	[illegible]	[illegible]	[illegible]	[illegible]	[illegible]	[illegible]	[illegible]	[illegible]	[illegible]	[illegible]	[illegible]	[illegible]	[illegible]	[illegible]	[illegible]	[illegible]	[illegible]	[illegible]	[illegible]	[illegible]	[illegible]	[illegible]
	Diseases of Uterus and Vagina,	[illegible]	[illegible]	[illegible]	[illegible]	[illegible]	[illegible]	[illegible]	[illegible]	[illegible]	[illegible]	[illegible]	[illegible]	[illegible]	[illegible]	[illegible]	[illegible]	[illegible]	[illegible]	[illegible]	[illegible]	[illegible]	[illegible]
	Disorders of Menstruation,	[illegible]	[illegible]	[illegible]	[illegible]	[illegible]	[illegible]	[illegible]	[illegible]	[illegible]	[illegible]	[illegible]	[illegible]	[illegible]	[illegible]	[illegible]	[illegible]	[illegible]	[illegible]	[illegible]	[illegible]	[illegible]	[illegible]
	Pelvic Abscess,	[illegible]	[illegible]	[illegible]	[illegible]	[illegible]	[illegible]	[illegible]	[illegible]	[illegible]	[illegible]	[illegible]	[illegible]	[illegible]	[illegible]	[illegible]	[illegible]	[illegible]	[illegible]	[illegible]	[illegible]	[illegible]	[illegible]
	Perineal Abscess,	[illegible]	[illegible]	[illegible]	[illegible]	[illegible]	[illegible]	[illegible]	[illegible]	[illegible]	[illegible]	[illegible]	[illegible]	[illegible]	[illegible]	[illegible]	[illegible]	[illegible]	[illegible]	[illegible]	[illegible]	[illegible]	[illegible]
	Diseases of Vulva, Penis, Scrotum, &c.	[illegible]	[illegible]	[illegible]	[illegible]	[illegible]	[illegible]	[illegible]	[illegible]	[illegible]	[illegible]	[illegible]	[illegible]	[illegible]	[illegible]	[illegible]	[illegible]	[illegible]	[illegible]	[illegible]	[illegible]	[illegible]	[illegible]

[continued at page [illegible].]

IRELAND.—CAUSES of DEATH at different Periods of Life in the Year 1864—MALES—con.

Class.	CAUSES OF DEATH.	All Ages.	Ages at Death.
VI.—con.	Childbirth, see Metria.		
	Paramenia,	[illegible]	[illegible]
	Puerperal Mania,	[illegible]	[illegible]
	Puerperal Convulsions,	[illegible]	[illegible]
	Placenta praevia, Flooding,	[illegible]	[illegible]
	Phlegmasia Dolens,	[illegible]	[illegible]
	Other and undefined accidents of Childbirth.	[illegible]	[illegible]
	Diseases of Organs of Locomotion.		
	Caries, Necrosis,	[illegible]	[illegible]
	Arthritis, Ostitis, Synovitis,	[illegible]	[illegible]
	Other and undefined Diseases of Organs of Locomotion.	[illegible]	[illegible]
	Diseases of Integumentary System.		
	Carbuncle,	[illegible]	[illegible]
	Phlegmon, Cellulitis,	[illegible]	[illegible]
	Lupus,	[illegible]	[illegible]
	Ulcer, Ecthyma,	[illegible]	[illegible]
	Eczema,	[illegible]	[illegible]
	Pemphigus,	[illegible]	[illegible]
	Other and undefined Diseases of Integumentary System.	[illegible]	[illegible]
VII.	Accident or Negligence.		
	In Mines and Quarries,	[illegible]	[illegible]
	Vehicles and Horses,	[illegible]	[illegible]
	Ships, Boats, and Docks (not Drowning).	[illegible]	[illegible]
	Building Operations,	[illegible]	[illegible]
	Machinery,	[illegible]	[illegible]
	Weapons & Implements,	[illegible]	[illegible]
	Fire and Scalds,	[illegible]	[illegible]
	Poison, Poisonous Vapours,	[illegible]	[illegible]
	Drowning,	[illegible]	[illegible]
	Suffocation,	[illegible]	[illegible]
	Falls,	[illegible]	[illegible]
	Weather Agencies,	[illegible]	[illegible]
	Otherwise, or not stated,	[illegible]	[illegible]
	Homicide,	[illegible]	[illegible]
	Suicide,	[illegible]	[illegible]
	Execution,	[illegible]	[illegible]
VIII.	Ill-defined and Not Specified Causes.		
	Dropsy,	[illegible]	[illegible]
	Debility, Atrophy, Inanition,	[illegible]	[illegible]
	Mortification,	[illegible]	[illegible]
	Tumour,	[illegible]	[illegible]
	Abscess,	[illegible]	[illegible]
	Haemorrhage,	[illegible]	[illegible]
	Sudden Deaths (cause unascertained).	[illegible]	[illegible]
	Other ill-defined and not specified causes.	[illegible]	[illegible]

IRELAND.—CAUSES of DEATHS at different Periods of Life in the Year 1896—FEMALES—con.

Class.	CAUSES OF DEATH.	FEMALES. All Ages	Ages at Death. [illegible]	[illegible]	[illegible]	Total under 1 year	1	2	3	4	Total under 5 years	5-	10-	15-	20-	25-	35-	45-	55-	65-	75-	85-	95 and upwards
VI.—con.	DISEASES OF PARTURITION.																						
	Abortion, Miscarriage,	[illegible]	.	.	.	.	.	.	.	.	.	.	.	.	[illegible]	[illegible]	17	[illegible]	.	.	.	.	.
	Puerperal Mania,	[illegible]	.	.	.	.	.	.	.	.	.	.	.	[illegible]	[illegible]	[illegible]	[illegible]	.	.	.	.	.	.
	Puerperal Convulsions,	[illegible]	.	.	.	.	.	.	.	.	.	.	.	[illegible]	[illegible]	[illegible]	[illegible]	.	.	.	.	.	.
	Placenta praevia, Flooding,	[illegible]	.	.	.	.	.	.	.	.	.	.	.	[illegible]	[illegible]	[illegible]	[illegible]	[illegible]	.	.	.	.	.
	Phlegmasia Dolens,	[illegible]	.	.	.	.	.	.	.	.	.	.	.	.	[illegible]	[illegible]	[illegible]	[illegible]	.	.	.	.	.
	Other and undefined Accidents of Childbirth,	[illegible]	.	.	.	.	.	.	.	.	.	.	.	[illegible]	[illegible]	117	[illegible]	[illegible]	.	.	.	.	.
	DISEASES OF ORGANS OF LOCOMOTION.																						
	Caries, Necrosis,	[illegible]	.	.	.	.	.	.	.	[illegible]	[illegible]	[illegible]	[illegible]	[illegible]	[illegible]	[illegible]	[illegible]	[illegible]	[illegible]	[illegible]	[illegible]	.	.
	Arthritis, Ostitis, Periostitis,	[illegible]	.	.	.	.	.	.	[illegible]	.	[illegible]	.	[illegible]	.	[illegible]	[illegible]	[illegible]	[illegible]	[illegible]	[illegible]	[illegible]	[illegible]	.
	Other and undefined Diseases of Organs of Locomotion,	[illegible]	[illegible]	.	.	[illegible]	.	[illegible]	[illegible]	.	[illegible]	.	[illegible]	[illegible]	.	[illegible]	[illegible]	[illegible]	[illegible]	[illegible]	[illegible]	.	.
	DISEASES OF INTEGUMENTARY SYSTEM.																						
	Carbuncle,	[illegible]	.	.	.	.	.	.	.	.	.	.	.	.	.	.	.	.	[illegible]	[illegible]	.	.	.
	Phlegmon, Cellulitis,	[illegible]	[illegible]	[illegible]	.	[illegible]	[illegible]	.	.	.	[illegible]	.	.	[illegible]	[illegible]	[illegible]	[illegible]	[illegible]	[illegible]	[illegible]	.	[illegible]	.
	Lupus,	[illegible]	.	.	.	.	.	.	.	.	.	.	.	.	.	[illegible]	[illegible]	[illegible]	.	[illegible]	.	.	.
	Ulcer, Bedsore,	[illegible]	.	.	.	.	[illegible]	.	.	.	[illegible]	.	.	[illegible]	.	.	[illegible]	[illegible]	[illegible]	[illegible]	[illegible]	[illegible]	.
	Eczema,	[illegible]	.	[illegible]	[illegible]	[illegible]	[illegible]	[illegible]	.	.	[illegible]	.	.	.	.	.	.	[illegible]	.	[illegible]	.	.	.
	Pemphigus,	[illegible]	[illegible]	.	.	[illegible]	.	.	.	.	[illegible]	.	.	.	.	.	.	[illegible]	.	.	.	.	.
	Other and undefined Diseases of Integumentary System,	[illegible]	[illegible]	[illegible]	[illegible]	[illegible]	.	[illegible]	.	.	[illegible]	.	.	.	.	.	.	.	[illegible]	.	.	[illegible]	.
VII.	ACCIDENT OR NEGLIGENCE.																						
	In Mines and Quarries,	.	.	.	.	.	.	.	.	.	.	.	.	.	.	.	.	.	.	.	.	.	.
	Vehicles and Horses,	[illegible]	.	.	[illegible]	[illegible]	[illegible]	[illegible]	[illegible]	.	[illegible]	[illegible]	.	[illegible]	[illegible]	[illegible]	.	[illegible]	[illegible]	[illegible]	.	.	[illegible]
	Ships, Boats, and Docks (not Drowning),	.	.	.	.	.	.	.	.	.	.	.	.	.	.	.	.	.	.	.	.	.	.
	Building Operations,	.	.	.	.	.	.	.	.	.	.	.	.	.	.	.	.	.	.	.	.	.	.
	Machinery,	[illegible]	.	.	.	.	.	[illegible]	.	.	[illegible]	.	.	[illegible]	.	.	.	.	.	.	.	.	.
	Weapons & Implements,	[illegible]	.	.	.	.	.	.	.	.	.	[illegible]	.	.	.	[illegible]	.	.	.	.	.	.	.
	Burns and Scalds,	[illegible]	[illegible]	.	[illegible]	[illegible]	[illegible]	[illegible]	[illegible]	[illegible]	[illegible]	[illegible]	[illegible]	[illegible]	[illegible]	[illegible]	[illegible]	[illegible]	[illegible]	[illegible]	[illegible]	[illegible]	.
	Poison, Poisonous Vapours,	[illegible]	.	.	.	.	[illegible]	[illegible]	[illegible]	[illegible]	[illegible]	[illegible]	[illegible]	.	.	[illegible]	[illegible]	.	.	.	.	.	.
	Drowning,	[illegible]	[illegible]	.	.	[illegible]	[illegible]	[illegible]	[illegible]	.	[illegible]	[illegible]	[illegible]	[illegible]	[illegible]	[illegible]	[illegible]	[illegible]	[illegible]	[illegible]	.	.	.
	Suffocation,	[illegible]	[illegible]	[illegible]	[illegible]	[illegible]	[illegible]	[illegible]	.	[illegible]	[illegible]	.	.	[illegible]	.	.	.	[illegible]	[illegible]	[illegible]	.	.	.
	Falls,	[illegible]	[illegible]	.	.	[illegible]	.	.	[illegible]	.	[illegible]	[illegible]	[illegible]	.	.	[illegible]	[illegible]	[illegible]	[illegible]	[illegible]	[illegible]	[illegible]	.
	Weather Agencies,	[illegible]	.	.	.	.	.	.	.	.	.	.	[illegible]	.	.	[illegible]	[illegible]	[illegible]	[illegible]	[illegible]	.	.	.
	Otherwise, or not Stated,	[illegible]	[illegible]	.	[illegible]	[illegible]	[illegible]	[illegible]	[illegible]	.	[illegible]	[illegible]	[illegible]	[illegible]	[illegible]	[illegible]	[illegible]	[illegible]	11	14	[illegible]	[illegible]	.
	Homicide,	17	[illegible]	.	.	[illegible]	.	.	.	.	[illegible]	.	.	.	.	[illegible]	[illegible]	.	[illegible]	.	[illegible]	.	.
	Suicide,	[illegible]	.	.	.	.	.	.	.	.	.	.	.	[illegible]	[illegible]	[illegible]	[illegible]	[illegible]	[illegible]	[illegible]	.	.	.
	Execution,	.	.	.	.	.	.	.	.	.	.	.	.	.	.	.	.	.	.	.	.	.	.
VIII.	ILL-DEFINED AND NOT SPECIFIED CAUSES.																						
	Dropsy,	[illegible]	[illegible]	[illegible]	[illegible]	[illegible]	[illegible]	.	[illegible]	.	[illegible]	[illegible]	[illegible]	[illegible]	[illegible]	[illegible]	[illegible]	[illegible]	[illegible]	[illegible]	[illegible]	[illegible]	.
	Debility, Atrophy, Inanition,	[illegible]	[illegible]	[illegible]	[illegible]	[illegible]	[illegible]	[illegible]	[illegible]	[illegible]	[illegible]	[illegible]	[illegible]	[illegible]	[illegible]	[illegible]	[illegible]	[illegible]	[illegible]	[illegible]	[illegible]	[illegible]	.
	Mortification,	[illegible]	.	.	.	.	.	.	.	.	.	.	.	.	.	.	[illegible]	[illegible]	.	.	.	.	.
	Tumour,	[illegible]	.	.	.	.	.	.	.	.	.	.	.	.	[illegible]	[illegible]	.	[illegible]	[illegible]	[illegible]	[illegible]	.	[illegible]
	Abscess,	[illegible]	[illegible]	.	[illegible]	[illegible]	.	[illegible]	.	.	[illegible]	.	.	[illegible]	.	[illegible]	[illegible]	[illegible]	[illegible]	[illegible]	[illegible]	.	.
	Haemorrhage,	[illegible]	[illegible]	.	.	[illegible]	[illegible]	.	.	.	[illegible]	[illegible]	.	.	.	[illegible]	[illegible]	[illegible]	[illegible]	.	.	.	.
	Sudden (cause unascertained),	17	.	.	.	.	.	.	.	.	.	.	.	.	[illegible]	[illegible]	[illegible]	[illegible]	[illegible]	[illegible]	.	.	.
	Other ill-defined and not specified causes,	[illegible]	7	[illegible]	[illegible]	[illegible]	[illegible]	[illegible]	[illegible]	[illegible]	[illegible]	[illegible]	[illegible]	[illegible]	[illegible]	[illegible]	[illegible]	[illegible]	[illegible]	[illegible]	[illegible]	.	.

IRELAND.—CAUSES of DEATHS at different Periods of Life, in the Year 1906.—
MALES and FEMALES.

Class.	CAUSES OF DEATH.	MALES AND FEMALES.																					
		All Ages.	Ages at Death.																				
			[illegible]	[illegible]	[illegible]	Total under 1 year.	1	2	3	4	Total under 5 years.	5-	10-	15-	20-	25-	35-	45-	55-	65-	75-	85-	[illegible]
	ALL CAUSES,	[illegible]	[illegible]	[illegible]	[illegible]	[illegible]	[illegible]	[illegible]	[illegible]	[illegible]	[illegible]	[illegible]	[illegible]	[illegible]	[illegible]	[illegible]	[illegible]	[illegible]	[illegible]	[illegible]	[illegible]	[illegible]	[illegible]
	(Classes.)																						
I.	SPECIFIC FEBRILE or ZYMOTIC DISEASES,	[illegible]	[illegible]	[illegible]	[illegible]	[illegible]	[illegible]	[illegible]	[illegible]	[illegible]	[illegible]	[illegible]	[illegible]	[illegible]	[illegible]	[illegible]	[illegible]	[illegible]	[illegible]	[illegible]	[illegible]	[illegible]	[illegible]
II.	PARASITIC DISEASES,	[illegible]	[illegible]	[illegible]	[illegible]	[illegible]	[illegible]	[illegible]	[illegible]	[illegible]	[illegible]	[illegible]	[illegible]	[illegible]	[illegible]	[illegible]	[illegible]	[illegible]	[illegible]	[illegible]	[illegible]	[illegible]	[illegible]
III.	DIETETIC,	[illegible]	[illegible]	[illegible]	[illegible]	[illegible]	[illegible]	[illegible]	[illegible]	[illegible]	[illegible]	[illegible]	[illegible]	[illegible]	[illegible]	[illegible]	[illegible]	[illegible]	[illegible]	[illegible]	[illegible]	[illegible]	[illegible]
IV.	CONSTITUTIONAL,	[illegible]	[illegible]	[illegible]	[illegible]	[illegible]	[illegible]	[illegible]	[illegible]	[illegible]	[illegible]	[illegible]	[illegible]	[illegible]	[illegible]	[illegible]	[illegible]	[illegible]	[illegible]	[illegible]	[illegible]	[illegible]	[illegible]
V.	DEVELOPMENTAL,	[illegible]	[illegible]	[illegible]	[illegible]	[illegible]	[illegible]	[illegible]	[illegible]	[illegible]	[illegible]	[illegible]	[illegible]	[illegible]	[illegible]	[illegible]	[illegible]	[illegible]	[illegible]	[illegible]	[illegible]	[illegible]	[illegible]
VI.	LOCAL,	[illegible]	[illegible]	[illegible]	[illegible]	[illegible]	[illegible]	[illegible]	[illegible]	[illegible]	[illegible]	[illegible]	[illegible]	[illegible]	[illegible]	[illegible]	[illegible]	[illegible]	[illegible]	[illegible]	[illegible]	[illegible]	[illegible]
VII.	VIOLENCE,	[illegible]	[illegible]	[illegible]	[illegible]	[illegible]	[illegible]	[illegible]	[illegible]	[illegible]	[illegible]	[illegible]	[illegible]	[illegible]	[illegible]	[illegible]	[illegible]	[illegible]	[illegible]	[illegible]	[illegible]	[illegible]	[illegible]
VIII.	ILL-DEFINED AND NOT SPECIFIED CAUSES,	[illegible]	[illegible]	[illegible]	[illegible]	[illegible]	[illegible]	[illegible]	[illegible]	[illegible]	[illegible]	[illegible]	[illegible]	[illegible]	[illegible]	[illegible]	[illegible]	[illegible]	[illegible]	[illegible]	[illegible]	[illegible]	[illegible]
	(Orders.)																						
I.	1. Miasmatic Diseases,	[illegible]	[illegible]	[illegible]	[illegible]	[illegible]	[illegible]	[illegible]	[illegible]	[illegible]	[illegible]	[illegible]	[illegible]	[illegible]	[illegible]	[illegible]	[illegible]	[illegible]	[illegible]	[illegible]	[illegible]	[illegible]	[illegible]
	2. Diarrhoeal,	[illegible]	[illegible]	[illegible]	[illegible]	[illegible]	[illegible]	[illegible]	[illegible]	[illegible]	[illegible]	[illegible]	[illegible]	[illegible]	[illegible]	[illegible]	[illegible]	[illegible]	[illegible]	[illegible]	[illegible]	[illegible]	[illegible]
	3. Malarial,	[illegible]	[illegible]	[illegible]	[illegible]	[illegible]	[illegible]	[illegible]	[illegible]	[illegible]	[illegible]	[illegible]	[illegible]	[illegible]	[illegible]	[illegible]	[illegible]	[illegible]	[illegible]	[illegible]	[illegible]	[illegible]	[illegible]
	4. Zoogenous,	[illegible]	[illegible]	[illegible]	[illegible]	[illegible]	[illegible]	[illegible]	[illegible]	[illegible]	[illegible]	[illegible]	[illegible]	[illegible]	[illegible]	[illegible]	[illegible]	[illegible]	[illegible]	[illegible]	[illegible]	[illegible]	[illegible]
	5. Venereal,	[illegible]	[illegible]	[illegible]	[illegible]	[illegible]	[illegible]	[illegible]	[illegible]	[illegible]	[illegible]	[illegible]	[illegible]	[illegible]	[illegible]	[illegible]	[illegible]	[illegible]	[illegible]	[illegible]	[illegible]	[illegible]	[illegible]
	6. Septic,	[illegible]	[illegible]	[illegible]	[illegible]	[illegible]	[illegible]	[illegible]	[illegible]	[illegible]	[illegible]	[illegible]	[illegible]	[illegible]	[illegible]	[illegible]	[illegible]	[illegible]	[illegible]	[illegible]	[illegible]	[illegible]	[illegible]
II.	Parasitic,	[illegible]	[illegible]	[illegible]	[illegible]	[illegible]	[illegible]	[illegible]	[illegible]	[illegible]	[illegible]	[illegible]	[illegible]	[illegible]	[illegible]	[illegible]	[illegible]	[illegible]	[illegible]	[illegible]	[illegible]	[illegible]	[illegible]
III.	Dietetic,	[illegible]	[illegible]	[illegible]	[illegible]	[illegible]	[illegible]	[illegible]	[illegible]	[illegible]	[illegible]	[illegible]	[illegible]	[illegible]	[illegible]	[illegible]	[illegible]	[illegible]	[illegible]	[illegible]	[illegible]	[illegible]	[illegible]
IV.	Constitutional,	[illegible]	[illegible]	[illegible]	[illegible]	[illegible]	[illegible]	[illegible]	[illegible]	[illegible]	[illegible]	[illegible]	[illegible]	[illegible]	[illegible]	[illegible]	[illegible]	[illegible]	[illegible]	[illegible]	[illegible]	[illegible]	[illegible]
V.	Developmental,	[illegible]	[illegible]	[illegible]	[illegible]	[illegible]	[illegible]	[illegible]	[illegible]	[illegible]	[illegible]	[illegible]	[illegible]	[illegible]	[illegible]	[illegible]	[illegible]	[illegible]	[illegible]	[illegible]	[illegible]	[illegible]	[illegible]
VI.	1. Diseases of Nervous System,	[illegible]	[illegible]	[illegible]	[illegible]	[illegible]	[illegible]	[illegible]	[illegible]	[illegible]	[illegible]	[illegible]	[illegible]	[illegible]	[illegible]	[illegible]	[illegible]	[illegible]	[illegible]	[illegible]	[illegible]	[illegible]	[illegible]
	2. " Organs of Special Sense,	[illegible]	[illegible]	[illegible]	[illegible]	[illegible]	[illegible]	[illegible]	[illegible]	[illegible]	[illegible]	[illegible]	[illegible]	[illegible]	[illegible]	[illegible]	[illegible]	[illegible]	[illegible]	[illegible]	[illegible]	[illegible]	[illegible]
	3. " Circulatory System,	[illegible]	[illegible]	[illegible]	[illegible]	[illegible]	[illegible]	[illegible]	[illegible]	[illegible]	[illegible]	[illegible]	[illegible]	[illegible]	[illegible]	[illegible]	[illegible]	[illegible]	[illegible]	[illegible]	[illegible]	[illegible]	[illegible]
	4. " Respiratory System,	[illegible]	[illegible]	[illegible]	[illegible]	[illegible]	[illegible]	[illegible]	[illegible]	[illegible]	[illegible]	[illegible]	[illegible]	[illegible]	[illegible]	[illegible]	[illegible]	[illegible]	[illegible]	[illegible]	[illegible]	[illegible]	[illegible]
	5. " Digestive System,	[illegible]	[illegible]	[illegible]	[illegible]	[illegible]	[illegible]	[illegible]	[illegible]	[illegible]	[illegible]	[illegible]	[illegible]	[illegible]	[illegible]	[illegible]	[illegible]	[illegible]	[illegible]	[illegible]	[illegible]	[illegible]	[illegible]
	6. " Lymphatic System and Ductless Glands,	[illegible]	[illegible]	[illegible]	[illegible]	[illegible]	[illegible]	[illegible]	[illegible]	[illegible]	[illegible]	[illegible]	[illegible]	[illegible]	[illegible]	[illegible]	[illegible]	[illegible]	[illegible]	[illegible]	[illegible]	[illegible]	[illegible]
	7. " Urinary System,	[illegible]	[illegible]	[illegible]	[illegible]	[illegible]	[illegible]	[illegible]	[illegible]	[illegible]	[illegible]	[illegible]	[illegible]	[illegible]	[illegible]	[illegible]	[illegible]	[illegible]	[illegible]	[illegible]	[illegible]	[illegible]	[illegible]
	8. " Reproductive System —																						
	(a) " Organs of Generation,	[illegible]	[illegible]	[illegible]	[illegible]	[illegible]	[illegible]	[illegible]	[illegible]	[illegible]	[illegible]	[illegible]	[illegible]	[illegible]	[illegible]	[illegible]	[illegible]	[illegible]	[illegible]	[illegible]	[illegible]	[illegible]	[illegible]
	(b) " Parturition,	[illegible]	[illegible]	[illegible]	[illegible]	[illegible]	[illegible]	[illegible]	[illegible]	[illegible]	[illegible]	[illegible]	[illegible]	[illegible]	[illegible]	[illegible]	[illegible]	[illegible]	[illegible]	[illegible]	[illegible]	[illegible]	[illegible]
	9. " Locomotive System,	[illegible]	[illegible]	[illegible]	[illegible]	[illegible]	[illegible]	[illegible]	[illegible]	[illegible]	[illegible]	[illegible]	[illegible]	[illegible]	[illegible]	[illegible]	[illegible]	[illegible]	[illegible]	[illegible]	[illegible]	[illegible]	[illegible]
	10. " Integumentary System,	[illegible]	[illegible]	[illegible]	[illegible]	[illegible]	[illegible]	[illegible]	[illegible]	[illegible]	[illegible]	[illegible]	[illegible]	[illegible]	[illegible]	[illegible]	[illegible]	[illegible]	[illegible]	[illegible]	[illegible]	[illegible]	[illegible]
VII.	1. Accident or Negligence,	[illegible]	[illegible]	[illegible]	[illegible]	[illegible]	[illegible]	[illegible]	[illegible]	[illegible]	[illegible]	[illegible]	[illegible]	[illegible]	[illegible]	[illegible]	[illegible]	[illegible]	[illegible]	[illegible]	[illegible]	[illegible]	[illegible]
	2. Homicide,	[illegible]	[illegible]	[illegible]	[illegible]	[illegible]	[illegible]	[illegible]	[illegible]	[illegible]	[illegible]	[illegible]	[illegible]	[illegible]	[illegible]	[illegible]	[illegible]	[illegible]	[illegible]	[illegible]	[illegible]	[illegible]	[illegible]
	3. Suicide,	[illegible]	[illegible]	[illegible]	[illegible]	[illegible]	[illegible]	[illegible]	[illegible]	[illegible]	[illegible]	[illegible]	[illegible]	[illegible]	[illegible]	[illegible]	[illegible]	[illegible]	[illegible]	[illegible]	[illegible]	[illegible]	[illegible]
	4. Execution,	[illegible]	[illegible]	[illegible]	[illegible]	[illegible]	[illegible]	[illegible]	[illegible]	[illegible]	[illegible]	[illegible]	[illegible]	[illegible]	[illegible]	[illegible]	[illegible]	[illegible]	[illegible]	[illegible]	[illegible]	[illegible]	[illegible]
VIII.	Ill-defined and not specified Causes,	[illegible]	[illegible]	[illegible]	[illegible]	[illegible]	[illegible]	[illegible]	[illegible]	[illegible]	[illegible]	[illegible]	[illegible]	[illegible]	[illegible]	[illegible]	[illegible]	[illegible]	[illegible]	[illegible]	[illegible]	[illegible]	[illegible]

IRELAND.—CAUSES of DEATHS at different Periods of Life in the Year 1896—MALES and FEMALES—continued.

Class	Causes of Death	All Ages	[illegible]	[illegible]	[illegible]	Total under 1 year	1	2	3	4	Total under 5 years	5-	10-	15-	20-	25-	35-	45-	55-	65-	75-	85-	95 and upwards
I.	Miasmatic Diseases																						
	Small-pox, Vaccinated	[illegible]	[illegible]	[illegible]	[illegible]	[illegible]	[illegible]	[illegible]	[illegible]	[illegible]	[illegible]	[illegible]	[illegible]	[illegible]	[illegible]	[illegible]	[illegible]	[illegible]	[illegible]	[illegible]	[illegible]	[illegible]	[illegible]
	Small-pox, Unvaccinated	[illegible]	[illegible]	[illegible]	[illegible]	[illegible]	[illegible]	[illegible]	[illegible]	[illegible]	[illegible]	[illegible]	[illegible]	[illegible]	[illegible]	[illegible]	[illegible]	[illegible]	[illegible]	[illegible]	[illegible]	[illegible]	[illegible]
	Small-pox, No statement	[illegible]	[illegible]	[illegible]	[illegible]	[illegible]	[illegible]	[illegible]	[illegible]	[illegible]	[illegible]	[illegible]	[illegible]	[illegible]	[illegible]	[illegible]	[illegible]	[illegible]	[illegible]	[illegible]	[illegible]	[illegible]	[illegible]
	Chicken-pox	[illegible]	[illegible]	[illegible]	[illegible]	[illegible]	[illegible]	[illegible]	[illegible]	[illegible]	[illegible]	[illegible]	[illegible]	[illegible]	[illegible]	[illegible]	[illegible]	[illegible]	[illegible]	[illegible]	[illegible]	[illegible]	[illegible]
	Measles	[illegible]	[illegible]	[illegible]	[illegible]	[illegible]	[illegible]	[illegible]	[illegible]	[illegible]	[illegible]	[illegible]	[illegible]	[illegible]	[illegible]	[illegible]	[illegible]	[illegible]	[illegible]	[illegible]	[illegible]	[illegible]	[illegible]
	Epidemic Rose Rash	[illegible]	[illegible]	[illegible]	[illegible]	[illegible]	[illegible]	[illegible]	[illegible]	[illegible]	[illegible]	[illegible]	[illegible]	[illegible]	[illegible]	[illegible]	[illegible]	[illegible]	[illegible]	[illegible]	[illegible]	[illegible]	[illegible]
	Scarlet Fever	[illegible]	[illegible]	[illegible]	[illegible]	[illegible]	[illegible]	[illegible]	[illegible]	[illegible]	[illegible]	[illegible]	[illegible]	[illegible]	[illegible]	[illegible]	[illegible]	[illegible]	[illegible]	[illegible]	[illegible]	[illegible]	[illegible]
	Typhus	[illegible]	[illegible]	[illegible]	[illegible]	[illegible]	[illegible]	[illegible]	[illegible]	[illegible]	[illegible]	[illegible]	[illegible]	[illegible]	[illegible]	[illegible]	[illegible]	[illegible]	[illegible]	[illegible]	[illegible]	[illegible]	[illegible]
	Relapsing Fever	[illegible]	[illegible]	[illegible]	[illegible]	[illegible]	[illegible]	[illegible]	[illegible]	[illegible]	[illegible]	[illegible]	[illegible]	[illegible]	[illegible]	[illegible]	[illegible]	[illegible]	[illegible]	[illegible]	[illegible]	[illegible]	[illegible]
	Influenza	[illegible]	[illegible]	[illegible]	[illegible]	[illegible]	[illegible]	[illegible]	[illegible]	[illegible]	[illegible]	[illegible]	[illegible]	[illegible]	[illegible]	[illegible]	[illegible]	[illegible]	[illegible]	[illegible]	[illegible]	[illegible]	[illegible]
	Whooping-cough	[illegible]	[illegible]	[illegible]	[illegible]	[illegible]	[illegible]	[illegible]	[illegible]	[illegible]	[illegible]	[illegible]	[illegible]	[illegible]	[illegible]	[illegible]	[illegible]	[illegible]	[illegible]	[illegible]	[illegible]	[illegible]	[illegible]
	Mumps	[illegible]	[illegible]	[illegible]	[illegible]	[illegible]	[illegible]	[illegible]	[illegible]	[illegible]	[illegible]	[illegible]	[illegible]	[illegible]	[illegible]	[illegible]	[illegible]	[illegible]	[illegible]	[illegible]	[illegible]	[illegible]	[illegible]
	Diphtheria	[illegible]	[illegible]	[illegible]	[illegible]	[illegible]	[illegible]	[illegible]	[illegible]	[illegible]	[illegible]	[illegible]	[illegible]	[illegible]	[illegible]	[illegible]	[illegible]	[illegible]	[illegible]	[illegible]	[illegible]	[illegible]	[illegible]
	[illegible] Fever	[illegible]	[illegible]	[illegible]	[illegible]	[illegible]	[illegible]	[illegible]	[illegible]	[illegible]	[illegible]	[illegible]	[illegible]	[illegible]	[illegible]	[illegible]	[illegible]	[illegible]	[illegible]	[illegible]	[illegible]	[illegible]	[illegible]
	Simple and ill-defined Fever	[illegible]	[illegible]	[illegible]	[illegible]	[illegible]	[illegible]	[illegible]	[illegible]	[illegible]	[illegible]	[illegible]	[illegible]	[illegible]	[illegible]	[illegible]	[illegible]	[illegible]	[illegible]	[illegible]	[illegible]	[illegible]	[illegible]
	Enteric Fever	[illegible]	[illegible]	[illegible]	[illegible]	[illegible]	[illegible]	[illegible]	[illegible]	[illegible]	[illegible]	[illegible]	[illegible]	[illegible]	[illegible]	[illegible]	[illegible]	[illegible]	[illegible]	[illegible]	[illegible]	[illegible]	[illegible]
	Other Miasmatic Diseases	[illegible]	[illegible]	[illegible]	[illegible]	[illegible]	[illegible]	[illegible]	[illegible]	[illegible]	[illegible]	[illegible]	[illegible]	[illegible]	[illegible]	[illegible]	[illegible]	[illegible]	[illegible]	[illegible]	[illegible]	[illegible]	[illegible]
	Diarrhoeal Diseases																						
	Simple Cholera	[illegible]	[illegible]	[illegible]	[illegible]	[illegible]	[illegible]	[illegible]	[illegible]	[illegible]	[illegible]	[illegible]	[illegible]	[illegible]	[illegible]	[illegible]	[illegible]	[illegible]	[illegible]	[illegible]	[illegible]	[illegible]	[illegible]
	Diarrhoea, Dysentery	[illegible]	[illegible]	[illegible]	[illegible]	[illegible]	[illegible]	[illegible]	[illegible]	[illegible]	[illegible]	[illegible]	[illegible]	[illegible]	[illegible]	[illegible]	[illegible]	[illegible]	[illegible]	[illegible]	[illegible]	[illegible]	[illegible]
	Malarial Diseases																						
	Remittent Fever	[illegible]	[illegible]	[illegible]	[illegible]	[illegible]	[illegible]	[illegible]	[illegible]	[illegible]	[illegible]	[illegible]	[illegible]	[illegible]	[illegible]	[illegible]	[illegible]	[illegible]	[illegible]	[illegible]	[illegible]	[illegible]	[illegible]
	Ague	[illegible]	[illegible]	[illegible]	[illegible]	[illegible]	[illegible]	[illegible]	[illegible]	[illegible]	[illegible]	[illegible]	[illegible]	[illegible]	[illegible]	[illegible]	[illegible]	[illegible]	[illegible]	[illegible]	[illegible]	[illegible]	[illegible]
	Zoogenous Diseases																						
	Hydrophobia	[illegible]	[illegible]	[illegible]	[illegible]	[illegible]	[illegible]	[illegible]	[illegible]	[illegible]	[illegible]	[illegible]	[illegible]	[illegible]	[illegible]	[illegible]	[illegible]	[illegible]	[illegible]	[illegible]	[illegible]	[illegible]	[illegible]
	Glanders	[illegible]	[illegible]	[illegible]	[illegible]	[illegible]	[illegible]	[illegible]	[illegible]	[illegible]	[illegible]	[illegible]	[illegible]	[illegible]	[illegible]	[illegible]	[illegible]	[illegible]	[illegible]	[illegible]	[illegible]	[illegible]	[illegible]
	Splenic Fever	[illegible]	[illegible]	[illegible]	[illegible]	[illegible]	[illegible]	[illegible]	[illegible]	[illegible]	[illegible]	[illegible]	[illegible]	[illegible]	[illegible]	[illegible]	[illegible]	[illegible]	[illegible]	[illegible]	[illegible]	[illegible]	[illegible]
	Cowpox and other effects of Vaccination	[illegible]	[illegible]	[illegible]	[illegible]	[illegible]	[illegible]	[illegible]	[illegible]	[illegible]	[illegible]	[illegible]	[illegible]	[illegible]	[illegible]	[illegible]	[illegible]	[illegible]	[illegible]	[illegible]	[illegible]	[illegible]	[illegible]
	Venereal Diseases																						
	Syphilis	[illegible]	[illegible]	[illegible]	[illegible]	[illegible]	[illegible]	[illegible]	[illegible]	[illegible]	[illegible]	[illegible]	[illegible]	[illegible]	[illegible]	[illegible]	[illegible]	[illegible]	[illegible]	[illegible]	[illegible]	[illegible]	[illegible]
	Gonorrhoea, Stricture of Urethra	[illegible]	[illegible]	[illegible]	[illegible]	[illegible]	[illegible]	[illegible]	[illegible]	[illegible]	[illegible]	[illegible]	[illegible]	[illegible]	[illegible]	[illegible]	[illegible]	[illegible]	[illegible]	[illegible]	[illegible]	[illegible]	[illegible]
	Septic Diseases																						
	Phagedaena	[illegible]	[illegible]	[illegible]	[illegible]	[illegible]	[illegible]	[illegible]	[illegible]	[illegible]	[illegible]	[illegible]	[illegible]	[illegible]	[illegible]	[illegible]	[illegible]	[illegible]	[illegible]	[illegible]	[illegible]	[illegible]	[illegible]
	Erysipelas	[illegible]	[illegible]	[illegible]	[illegible]	[illegible]	[illegible]	[illegible]	[illegible]	[illegible]	[illegible]	[illegible]	[illegible]	[illegible]	[illegible]	[illegible]	[illegible]	[illegible]	[illegible]	[illegible]	[illegible]	[illegible]	[illegible]
	Pyaemia, Septicaemia	[illegible]	[illegible]	[illegible]	[illegible]	[illegible]	[illegible]	[illegible]	[illegible]	[illegible]	[illegible]	[illegible]	[illegible]	[illegible]	[illegible]	[illegible]	[illegible]	[illegible]	[illegible]	[illegible]	[illegible]	[illegible]	[illegible]
	Puerperal Fever	[illegible]	[illegible]	[illegible]	[illegible]	[illegible]	[illegible]	[illegible]	[illegible]	[illegible]	[illegible]	[illegible]	[illegible]	[illegible]	[illegible]	[illegible]	[illegible]	[illegible]	[illegible]	[illegible]	[illegible]	[illegible]	[illegible]
II.	Parasitic Diseases. Thrush	[illegible]	[illegible]	[illegible]	[illegible]	[illegible]	[illegible]	[illegible]	[illegible]	[illegible]	[illegible]	[illegible]	[illegible]	[illegible]	[illegible]	[illegible]	[illegible]	[illegible]	[illegible]	[illegible]	[illegible]	[illegible]	[illegible]
	Other Diseases from Vegetable Parasites	[illegible]	[illegible]	[illegible]	[illegible]	[illegible]	[illegible]	[illegible]	[illegible]	[illegible]	[illegible]	[illegible]	[illegible]	[illegible]	[illegible]	[illegible]	[illegible]	[illegible]	[illegible]	[illegible]	[illegible]	[illegible]	[illegible]
	Hydatid Disease	[illegible]	[illegible]	[illegible]	[illegible]	[illegible]	[illegible]	[illegible]	[illegible]	[illegible]	[illegible]	[illegible]	[illegible]	[illegible]	[illegible]	[illegible]	[illegible]	[illegible]	[illegible]	[illegible]	[illegible]	[illegible]	[illegible]
	Other Diseases from Animal Parasites	[illegible]	[illegible]	[illegible]	[illegible]	[illegible]	[illegible]	[illegible]	[illegible]	[illegible]	[illegible]	[illegible]	[illegible]	[illegible]	[illegible]	[illegible]	[illegible]	[illegible]	[illegible]	[illegible]	[illegible]	[illegible]	[illegible]
III.	Dietetic Diseases. Starvation, Want of Breast Milk	[illegible]	[illegible]	[illegible]	[illegible]	[illegible]	[illegible]	[illegible]	[illegible]	[illegible]	[illegible]	[illegible]	[illegible]	[illegible]	[illegible]	[illegible]	[illegible]	[illegible]	[illegible]	[illegible]	[illegible]	[illegible]	[illegible]
	Scurvy	[illegible]	[illegible]	[illegible]	[illegible]	[illegible]	[illegible]	[illegible]	[illegible]	[illegible]	[illegible]	[illegible]	[illegible]	[illegible]	[illegible]	[illegible]	[illegible]	[illegible]	[illegible]	[illegible]	[illegible]	[illegible]	[illegible]
	Alcoholism, Chronic Alcoholism	[illegible]	[illegible]	[illegible]	[illegible]	[illegible]	[illegible]	[illegible]	[illegible]	[illegible]	[illegible]	[illegible]	[illegible]	[illegible]	[illegible]	[illegible]	[illegible]	[illegible]	[illegible]	[illegible]	[illegible]	[illegible]	[illegible]
	Alcoholism, Delirium Tremens	[illegible]	[illegible]	[illegible]	[illegible]	[illegible]	[illegible]	[illegible]	[illegible]	[illegible]	[illegible]	[illegible]	[illegible]	[illegible]	[illegible]	[illegible]	[illegible]	[illegible]	[illegible]	[illegible]	[illegible]	[illegible]	[illegible]
IV.	Constitutional Diseases. [illegible]	[illegible]	[illegible]	[illegible]	[illegible]	[illegible]	[illegible]	[illegible]	[illegible]	[illegible]	[illegible]	[illegible]	[illegible]	[illegible]	[illegible]	[illegible]	[illegible]	[illegible]	[illegible]	[illegible]	[illegible]	[illegible]	[illegible]
	Rheumatic Fever, Rheumatism of Heart	[illegible]	[illegible]	[illegible]	[illegible]	[illegible]	[illegible]	[illegible]	[illegible]	[illegible]	[illegible]	[illegible]	[illegible]	[illegible]	[illegible]	[illegible]	[illegible]	[illegible]	[illegible]	[illegible]	[illegible]	[illegible]	[illegible]
	Rheumatism	[illegible]	[illegible]	[illegible]	[illegible]	[illegible]	[illegible]	[illegible]	[illegible]	[illegible]	[illegible]	[illegible]	[illegible]	[illegible]	[illegible]	[illegible]	[illegible]	[illegible]	[illegible]	[illegible]	[illegible]	[illegible]	[illegible]
	Gout	[illegible]	[illegible]	[illegible]	[illegible]	[illegible]	[illegible]	[illegible]	[illegible]	[illegible]	[illegible]	[illegible]	[illegible]	[illegible]	[illegible]	[illegible]	[illegible]	[illegible]	[illegible]	[illegible]	[illegible]	[illegible]	[illegible]
	Rickets	[illegible]	[illegible]	[illegible]	[illegible]	[illegible]	[illegible]	[illegible]	[illegible]	[illegible]	[illegible]	[illegible]	[illegible]	[illegible]	[illegible]	[illegible]	[illegible]	[illegible]	[illegible]	[illegible]	[illegible]	[illegible]	[illegible]
	Cancer	[illegible]	[illegible]	[illegible]	[illegible]	[illegible]	[illegible]	[illegible]	[illegible]	[illegible]	[illegible]	[illegible]	[illegible]	[illegible]	[illegible]	[illegible]	[illegible]	[illegible]	[illegible]	[illegible]	[illegible]	[illegible]	[illegible]

IRELAND.—CAUSES of DEATHS at different Periods of Life in the Year 18[illegible].—MALES and FEMALES—*contd.*

Class.	Causes of Death.	All Ages.	[illegible]	[illegible]	[illegible]	Total under 1 year.	1	2	3	4	Total under 5 years.	[illegible]	[illegible]	[illegible]	[illegible]	[illegible]	[illegible]	[illegible]	[illegible]	[illegible]	[illegible]	[illegible]	[illegible]	[illegible]
		MALES AND FEMALES.																						
IV.—*contd.*	[illegible]	[illegible]	[illegible]	[illegible]	[illegible]	[illegible]	[illegible]	[illegible]	[illegible]	[illegible]	[illegible]	[illegible]	[illegible]	[illegible]	[illegible]	[illegible]	[illegible]	[illegible]	[illegible]	[illegible]	[illegible]	[illegible]	[illegible]	[illegible]
	[illegible]	[illegible]	[illegible]	[illegible]	[illegible]	[illegible]	[illegible]	[illegible]	[illegible]	[illegible]	[illegible]	[illegible]	[illegible]	[illegible]	[illegible]	[illegible]	[illegible]	[illegible]	[illegible]	[illegible]	[illegible]	[illegible]	[illegible]	[illegible]
	[illegible]	[illegible]	[illegible]	[illegible]	[illegible]	[illegible]	[illegible]	[illegible]	[illegible]	[illegible]	[illegible]	[illegible]	[illegible]	[illegible]	[illegible]	[illegible]	[illegible]	[illegible]	[illegible]	[illegible]	[illegible]	[illegible]	[illegible]	[illegible]
	[illegible]	[illegible]	[illegible]	[illegible]	[illegible]	[illegible]	[illegible]	[illegible]	[illegible]	[illegible]	[illegible]	[illegible]	[illegible]	[illegible]	[illegible]	[illegible]	[illegible]	[illegible]	[illegible]	[illegible]	[illegible]	[illegible]	[illegible]	[illegible]
	[illegible]	[illegible]	[illegible]	[illegible]	[illegible]	[illegible]	[illegible]	[illegible]	[illegible]	[illegible]	[illegible]	[illegible]	[illegible]	[illegible]	[illegible]	[illegible]	[illegible]	[illegible]	[illegible]	[illegible]	[illegible]	[illegible]	[illegible]	[illegible]
	[illegible]	[illegible]	[illegible]	[illegible]	[illegible]	[illegible]	[illegible]	[illegible]	[illegible]	[illegible]	[illegible]	[illegible]	[illegible]	[illegible]	[illegible]	[illegible]	[illegible]	[illegible]	[illegible]	[illegible]	[illegible]	[illegible]	[illegible]	[illegible]
	[illegible]	[illegible]	[illegible]	[illegible]	[illegible]	[illegible]	[illegible]	[illegible]	[illegible]	[illegible]	[illegible]	[illegible]	[illegible]	[illegible]	[illegible]	[illegible]	[illegible]	[illegible]	[illegible]	[illegible]	[illegible]	[illegible]	[illegible]	[illegible]
	[illegible]	[illegible]	[illegible]	[illegible]	[illegible]	[illegible]	[illegible]	[illegible]	[illegible]	[illegible]	[illegible]	[illegible]	[illegible]	[illegible]	[illegible]	[illegible]	[illegible]	[illegible]	[illegible]	[illegible]	[illegible]	[illegible]	[illegible]	[illegible]
V.	DEVELOPMENTAL DISEASES.																							
	Premature Birth	[illegible]	[illegible]	[illegible]	[illegible]	[illegible]	[illegible]	[illegible]	[illegible]	[illegible]	[illegible]	[illegible]	[illegible]	[illegible]	[illegible]	[illegible]	[illegible]	[illegible]	[illegible]	[illegible]	[illegible]	[illegible]	[illegible]	[illegible]
	Atelectasis	[illegible]	[illegible]	[illegible]	[illegible]	[illegible]	[illegible]	[illegible]	[illegible]	[illegible]	[illegible]	[illegible]	[illegible]	[illegible]	[illegible]	[illegible]	[illegible]	[illegible]	[illegible]	[illegible]	[illegible]	[illegible]	[illegible]	[illegible]
	Cyanosis	[illegible]	[illegible]	[illegible]	[illegible]	[illegible]	[illegible]	[illegible]	[illegible]	[illegible]	[illegible]	[illegible]	[illegible]	[illegible]	[illegible]	[illegible]	[illegible]	[illegible]	[illegible]	[illegible]	[illegible]	[illegible]	[illegible]	[illegible]
	Spina Bifida	[illegible]	[illegible]	[illegible]	[illegible]	[illegible]	[illegible]	[illegible]	[illegible]	[illegible]	[illegible]	[illegible]	[illegible]	[illegible]	[illegible]	[illegible]	[illegible]	[illegible]	[illegible]	[illegible]	[illegible]	[illegible]	[illegible]	[illegible]
	Imperforate Anus	[illegible]	[illegible]	[illegible]	[illegible]	[illegible]	[illegible]	[illegible]	[illegible]	[illegible]	[illegible]	[illegible]	[illegible]	[illegible]	[illegible]	[illegible]	[illegible]	[illegible]	[illegible]	[illegible]	[illegible]	[illegible]	[illegible]	[illegible]
	Cleft Palate, Harelip	[illegible]	[illegible]	[illegible]	[illegible]	[illegible]	[illegible]	[illegible]	[illegible]	[illegible]	[illegible]	[illegible]	[illegible]	[illegible]	[illegible]	[illegible]	[illegible]	[illegible]	[illegible]	[illegible]	[illegible]	[illegible]	[illegible]	[illegible]
	Other Malformations	[illegible]	[illegible]	[illegible]	[illegible]	[illegible]	[illegible]	[illegible]	[illegible]	[illegible]	[illegible]	[illegible]	[illegible]	[illegible]	[illegible]	[illegible]	[illegible]	[illegible]	[illegible]	[illegible]	[illegible]	[illegible]	[illegible]	[illegible]
	Old Age	[illegible]	[illegible]	[illegible]	[illegible]	[illegible]	[illegible]	[illegible]	[illegible]	[illegible]	[illegible]	[illegible]	[illegible]	[illegible]	[illegible]	[illegible]	[illegible]	[illegible]	[illegible]	[illegible]	[illegible]	[illegible]	[illegible]	[illegible]
VI.	DISEASES OF NERVOUS SYSTEM.																							
	[illegible]	[illegible]	[illegible]	[illegible]	[illegible]	[illegible]	[illegible]	[illegible]	[illegible]	[illegible]	[illegible]	[illegible]	[illegible]	[illegible]	[illegible]	[illegible]	[illegible]	[illegible]	[illegible]	[illegible]	[illegible]	[illegible]	[illegible]	[illegible]
	Apoplexy	[illegible]	[illegible]	[illegible]	[illegible]	[illegible]	[illegible]	[illegible]	[illegible]	[illegible]	[illegible]	[illegible]	[illegible]	[illegible]	[illegible]	[illegible]	[illegible]	[illegible]	[illegible]	[illegible]	[illegible]	[illegible]	[illegible]	[illegible]
	[illegible]	[illegible]	[illegible]	[illegible]	[illegible]	[illegible]	[illegible]	[illegible]	[illegible]	[illegible]	[illegible]	[illegible]	[illegible]	[illegible]	[illegible]	[illegible]	[illegible]	[illegible]	[illegible]	[illegible]	[illegible]	[illegible]	[illegible]	[illegible]
	[illegible]	[illegible]	[illegible]	[illegible]	[illegible]	[illegible]	[illegible]	[illegible]	[illegible]	[illegible]	[illegible]	[illegible]	[illegible]	[illegible]	[illegible]	[illegible]	[illegible]	[illegible]	[illegible]	[illegible]	[illegible]	[illegible]	[illegible]	[illegible]
	[illegible]	[illegible]	[illegible]	[illegible]	[illegible]	[illegible]	[illegible]	[illegible]	[illegible]	[illegible]	[illegible]	[illegible]	[illegible]	[illegible]	[illegible]	[illegible]	[illegible]	[illegible]	[illegible]	[illegible]	[illegible]	[illegible]	[illegible]	[illegible]
	[illegible]	[illegible]	[illegible]	[illegible]	[illegible]	[illegible]	[illegible]	[illegible]	[illegible]	[illegible]	[illegible]	[illegible]	[illegible]	[illegible]	[illegible]	[illegible]	[illegible]	[illegible]	[illegible]	[illegible]	[illegible]	[illegible]	[illegible]	[illegible]
	Chorea	[illegible]	[illegible]	[illegible]	[illegible]	[illegible]	[illegible]	[illegible]	[illegible]	[illegible]	[illegible]	[illegible]	[illegible]	[illegible]	[illegible]	[illegible]	[illegible]	[illegible]	[illegible]	[illegible]	[illegible]	[illegible]	[illegible]	[illegible]
	Epilepsy	[illegible]	[illegible]	[illegible]	[illegible]	[illegible]	[illegible]	[illegible]	[illegible]	[illegible]	[illegible]	[illegible]	[illegible]	[illegible]	[illegible]	[illegible]	[illegible]	[illegible]	[illegible]	[illegible]	[illegible]	[illegible]	[illegible]	[illegible]
	Convulsions	[illegible]	[illegible]	[illegible]	[illegible]	[illegible]	[illegible]	[illegible]	[illegible]	[illegible]	[illegible]	[illegible]	[illegible]	[illegible]	[illegible]	[illegible]	[illegible]	[illegible]	[illegible]	[illegible]	[illegible]	[illegible]	[illegible]	[illegible]
	[illegible]	[illegible]	[illegible]	[illegible]	[illegible]	[illegible]	[illegible]	[illegible]	[illegible]	[illegible]	[illegible]	[illegible]	[illegible]	[illegible]	[illegible]	[illegible]	[illegible]	[illegible]	[illegible]	[illegible]	[illegible]	[illegible]	[illegible]	[illegible]
	[illegible]	[illegible]	[illegible]	[illegible]	[illegible]	[illegible]	[illegible]	[illegible]	[illegible]	[illegible]	[illegible]	[illegible]	[illegible]	[illegible]	[illegible]	[illegible]	[illegible]	[illegible]	[illegible]	[illegible]	[illegible]	[illegible]	[illegible]	[illegible]
	[illegible]	[illegible]	[illegible]	[illegible]	[illegible]	[illegible]	[illegible]	[illegible]	[illegible]	[illegible]	[illegible]	[illegible]	[illegible]	[illegible]	[illegible]	[illegible]	[illegible]	[illegible]	[illegible]	[illegible]	[illegible]	[illegible]	[illegible]	[illegible]
	[illegible]	[illegible]	[illegible]	[illegible]	[illegible]	[illegible]	[illegible]	[illegible]	[illegible]	[illegible]	[illegible]	[illegible]	[illegible]	[illegible]	[illegible]	[illegible]	[illegible]	[illegible]	[illegible]	[illegible]	[illegible]	[illegible]	[illegible]	[illegible]
	DISEASES OF ORGANS OF SPECIAL SENSE.																							
	[illegible]	[illegible]	[illegible]	[illegible]	[illegible]	[illegible]	[illegible]	[illegible]	[illegible]	[illegible]	[illegible]	[illegible]	[illegible]	[illegible]	[illegible]	[illegible]	[illegible]	[illegible]	[illegible]	[illegible]	[illegible]	[illegible]	[illegible]	[illegible]
	[illegible]	[illegible]	[illegible]	[illegible]	[illegible]	[illegible]	[illegible]	[illegible]	[illegible]	[illegible]	[illegible]	[illegible]	[illegible]	[illegible]	[illegible]	[illegible]	[illegible]	[illegible]	[illegible]	[illegible]	[illegible]	[illegible]	[illegible]	[illegible]
	[illegible]	[illegible]	[illegible]	[illegible]	[illegible]	[illegible]	[illegible]	[illegible]	[illegible]	[illegible]	[illegible]	[illegible]	[illegible]	[illegible]	[illegible]	[illegible]	[illegible]	[illegible]	[illegible]	[illegible]	[illegible]	[illegible]	[illegible]	[illegible]
	DISEASES OF CIRCULATORY SYSTEM.																							
	[illegible]	[illegible]	[illegible]	[illegible]	[illegible]	[illegible]	[illegible]	[illegible]	[illegible]	[illegible]	[illegible]	[illegible]	[illegible]	[illegible]	[illegible]	[illegible]	[illegible]	[illegible]	[illegible]	[illegible]	[illegible]	[illegible]	[illegible]	[illegible]
	[illegible]	[illegible]	[illegible]	[illegible]	[illegible]	[illegible]	[illegible]	[illegible]	[illegible]	[illegible]	[illegible]	[illegible]	[illegible]	[illegible]	[illegible]	[illegible]	[illegible]	[illegible]	[illegible]	[illegible]	[illegible]	[illegible]	[illegible]	[illegible]
	[illegible]	[illegible]	[illegible]	[illegible]	[illegible]	[illegible]	[illegible]	[illegible]	[illegible]	[illegible]	[illegible]	[illegible]	[illegible]	[illegible]	[illegible]	[illegible]	[illegible]	[illegible]	[illegible]	[illegible]	[illegible]	[illegible]	[illegible]	[illegible]
	Angina Pectoris	[illegible]	[illegible]	[illegible]	[illegible]	[illegible]	[illegible]	[illegible]	[illegible]	[illegible]	[illegible]	[illegible]	[illegible]	[illegible]	[illegible]	[illegible]	[illegible]	[illegible]	[illegible]	[illegible]	[illegible]	[illegible]	[illegible]	[illegible]
	Syncope	[illegible]	[illegible]	[illegible]	[illegible]	[illegible]	[illegible]	[illegible]	[illegible]	[illegible]	[illegible]	[illegible]	[illegible]	[illegible]	[illegible]	[illegible]	[illegible]	[illegible]	[illegible]	[illegible]	[illegible]	[illegible]	[illegible]	[illegible]
	Aneurism	[illegible]	[illegible]	[illegible]	[illegible]	[illegible]	[illegible]	[illegible]	[illegible]	[illegible]	[illegible]	[illegible]	[illegible]	[illegible]	[illegible]	[illegible]	[illegible]	[illegible]	[illegible]	[illegible]	[illegible]	[illegible]	[illegible]	[illegible]
	[illegible]	[illegible]	[illegible]	[illegible]	[illegible]	[illegible]	[illegible]	[illegible]	[illegible]	[illegible]	[illegible]	[illegible]	[illegible]	[illegible]	[illegible]	[illegible]	[illegible]	[illegible]	[illegible]	[illegible]	[illegible]	[illegible]	[illegible]	[illegible]
	[illegible]	[illegible]	[illegible]	[illegible]	[illegible]	[illegible]	[illegible]	[illegible]	[illegible]	[illegible]	[illegible]	[illegible]	[illegible]	[illegible]	[illegible]	[illegible]	[illegible]	[illegible]	[illegible]	[illegible]	[illegible]	[illegible]	[illegible]	[illegible]
	[illegible]	[illegible]	[illegible]	[illegible]	[illegible]	[illegible]	[illegible]	[illegible]	[illegible]	[illegible]	[illegible]	[illegible]	[illegible]	[illegible]	[illegible]	[illegible]	[illegible]	[illegible]	[illegible]	[illegible]	[illegible]	[illegible]	[illegible]	[illegible]
	[illegible]	[illegible]	[illegible]	[illegible]	[illegible]	[illegible]	[illegible]	[illegible]	[illegible]	[illegible]	[illegible]	[illegible]	[illegible]	[illegible]	[illegible]	[illegible]	[illegible]	[illegible]	[illegible]	[illegible]	[illegible]	[illegible]	[illegible]	[illegible]
	[illegible]	[illegible]	[illegible]	[illegible]	[illegible]	[illegible]	[illegible]	[illegible]	[illegible]	[illegible]	[illegible]	[illegible]	[illegible]	[illegible]	[illegible]	[illegible]	[illegible]	[illegible]	[illegible]	[illegible]	[illegible]	[illegible]	[illegible]	[illegible]
	DISEASES OF RESPIRATORY SYSTEM.																							
	Laryngitis	[illegible]	[illegible]	[illegible]	[illegible]	[illegible]	[illegible]	[illegible]	[illegible]	[illegible]	[illegible]	[illegible]	[illegible]	[illegible]	[illegible]	[illegible]	[illegible]	[illegible]	[illegible]	[illegible]	[illegible]	[illegible]	[illegible]	[illegible]
	Croup	[illegible]	[illegible]	[illegible]	[illegible]	[illegible]	[illegible]	[illegible]	[illegible]	[illegible]	[illegible]	[illegible]	[illegible]	[illegible]	[illegible]	[illegible]	[illegible]	[illegible]	[illegible]	[illegible]	[illegible]	[illegible]	[illegible]	[illegible]
	[illegible]	[illegible]	[illegible]	[illegible]	[illegible]	[illegible]	[illegible]	[illegible]	[illegible]	[illegible]	[illegible]	[illegible]	[illegible]	[illegible]	[illegible]	[illegible]	[illegible]	[illegible]	[illegible]	[illegible]	[illegible]	[illegible]	[illegible]	[illegible]

IRELAND.—CAUSES of DEATH at different Periods of Life in the Year [illegible]—MALES and FEMALES—continued.

Class	Causes of Death	All Ages	Males and Females: Ages at Death																					
			[illegible]	[illegible]	[illegible]	Total under 1 year	1	2	3	4	Total under 5 years	5-	10-	15-	20-	25-	35-	45-	55-	65-	75-	85-	95-	[illegible]
VI.—contd.	Diseases of Respiratory System—contd.																							
	[illegible]	[illegible]	[illegible]	[illegible]	[illegible]	[illegible]	[illegible]	[illegible]	[illegible]	[illegible]	[illegible]	[illegible]	[illegible]	[illegible]	[illegible]	[illegible]	[illegible]	[illegible]	[illegible]	[illegible]	[illegible]	[illegible]	[illegible]	[illegible]
	Bronchitis	[illegible]	[illegible]	[illegible]	[illegible]	[illegible]	[illegible]	[illegible]	[illegible]	[illegible]	[illegible]	[illegible]	[illegible]	[illegible]	[illegible]	[illegible]	[illegible]	[illegible]	[illegible]	[illegible]	[illegible]	[illegible]	[illegible]	[illegible]
	Pneumonia	[illegible]	[illegible]	[illegible]	[illegible]	[illegible]	[illegible]	[illegible]	[illegible]	[illegible]	[illegible]	[illegible]	[illegible]	[illegible]	[illegible]	[illegible]	[illegible]	[illegible]	[illegible]	[illegible]	[illegible]	[illegible]	[illegible]	[illegible]
	Pleurisy	[illegible]	[illegible]	[illegible]	[illegible]	[illegible]	[illegible]	[illegible]	[illegible]	[illegible]	[illegible]	[illegible]	[illegible]	[illegible]	[illegible]	[illegible]	[illegible]	[illegible]	[illegible]	[illegible]	[illegible]	[illegible]	[illegible]	[illegible]
	Other and unclassified Diseases of Respiratory System	[illegible]	[illegible]	[illegible]	[illegible]	[illegible]	[illegible]	[illegible]	[illegible]	[illegible]	[illegible]	[illegible]	[illegible]	[illegible]	[illegible]	[illegible]	[illegible]	[illegible]	[illegible]	[illegible]	[illegible]	[illegible]	[illegible]	[illegible]
	Diseases of Digestive System.																							
	[illegible]	[illegible]	[illegible]	[illegible]	[illegible]	[illegible]	[illegible]	[illegible]	[illegible]	[illegible]	[illegible]	[illegible]	[illegible]	[illegible]	[illegible]	[illegible]	[illegible]	[illegible]	[illegible]	[illegible]	[illegible]	[illegible]	[illegible]	[illegible]
	[illegible]	[illegible]	[illegible]	[illegible]	[illegible]	[illegible]	[illegible]	[illegible]	[illegible]	[illegible]	[illegible]	[illegible]	[illegible]	[illegible]	[illegible]	[illegible]	[illegible]	[illegible]	[illegible]	[illegible]	[illegible]	[illegible]	[illegible]	[illegible]
	Sore Throat, Quinsy	[illegible]	[illegible]	[illegible]	[illegible]	[illegible]	[illegible]	[illegible]	[illegible]	[illegible]	[illegible]	[illegible]	[illegible]	[illegible]	[illegible]	[illegible]	[illegible]	[illegible]	[illegible]	[illegible]	[illegible]	[illegible]	[illegible]	[illegible]
	Dyspepsia	[illegible]	[illegible]	[illegible]	[illegible]	[illegible]	[illegible]	[illegible]	[illegible]	[illegible]	[illegible]	[illegible]	[illegible]	[illegible]	[illegible]	[illegible]	[illegible]	[illegible]	[illegible]	[illegible]	[illegible]	[illegible]	[illegible]	[illegible]
	Haematemesis	[illegible]	[illegible]	[illegible]	[illegible]	[illegible]	[illegible]	[illegible]	[illegible]	[illegible]	[illegible]	[illegible]	[illegible]	[illegible]	[illegible]	[illegible]	[illegible]	[illegible]	[illegible]	[illegible]	[illegible]	[illegible]	[illegible]	[illegible]
	Melaena	[illegible]	[illegible]	[illegible]	[illegible]	[illegible]	[illegible]	[illegible]	[illegible]	[illegible]	[illegible]	[illegible]	[illegible]	[illegible]	[illegible]	[illegible]	[illegible]	[illegible]	[illegible]	[illegible]	[illegible]	[illegible]	[illegible]	[illegible]
	Diseases of Stomach	[illegible]	[illegible]	[illegible]	[illegible]	[illegible]	[illegible]	[illegible]	[illegible]	[illegible]	[illegible]	[illegible]	[illegible]	[illegible]	[illegible]	[illegible]	[illegible]	[illegible]	[illegible]	[illegible]	[illegible]	[illegible]	[illegible]	[illegible]
	Enteritis	[illegible]	[illegible]	[illegible]	[illegible]	[illegible]	[illegible]	[illegible]	[illegible]	[illegible]	[illegible]	[illegible]	[illegible]	[illegible]	[illegible]	[illegible]	[illegible]	[illegible]	[illegible]	[illegible]	[illegible]	[illegible]	[illegible]	[illegible]
	Obstruction of Intestine	[illegible]	[illegible]	[illegible]	[illegible]	[illegible]	[illegible]	[illegible]	[illegible]	[illegible]	[illegible]	[illegible]	[illegible]	[illegible]	[illegible]	[illegible]	[illegible]	[illegible]	[illegible]	[illegible]	[illegible]	[illegible]	[illegible]	[illegible]
	[illegible]	[illegible]	[illegible]	[illegible]	[illegible]	[illegible]	[illegible]	[illegible]	[illegible]	[illegible]	[illegible]	[illegible]	[illegible]	[illegible]	[illegible]	[illegible]	[illegible]	[illegible]	[illegible]	[illegible]	[illegible]	[illegible]	[illegible]	[illegible]
	[illegible]	[illegible]	[illegible]	[illegible]	[illegible]	[illegible]	[illegible]	[illegible]	[illegible]	[illegible]	[illegible]	[illegible]	[illegible]	[illegible]	[illegible]	[illegible]	[illegible]	[illegible]	[illegible]	[illegible]	[illegible]	[illegible]	[illegible]	[illegible]
	[illegible]	[illegible]	[illegible]	[illegible]	[illegible]	[illegible]	[illegible]	[illegible]	[illegible]	[illegible]	[illegible]	[illegible]	[illegible]	[illegible]	[illegible]	[illegible]	[illegible]	[illegible]	[illegible]	[illegible]	[illegible]	[illegible]	[illegible]	[illegible]
	Fistula	[illegible]	[illegible]	[illegible]	[illegible]	[illegible]	[illegible]	[illegible]	[illegible]	[illegible]	[illegible]	[illegible]	[illegible]	[illegible]	[illegible]	[illegible]	[illegible]	[illegible]	[illegible]	[illegible]	[illegible]	[illegible]	[illegible]	[illegible]
	Peritonitis	[illegible]	[illegible]	[illegible]	[illegible]	[illegible]	[illegible]	[illegible]	[illegible]	[illegible]	[illegible]	[illegible]	[illegible]	[illegible]	[illegible]	[illegible]	[illegible]	[illegible]	[illegible]	[illegible]	[illegible]	[illegible]	[illegible]	[illegible]
	Ascites	[illegible]	[illegible]	[illegible]	[illegible]	[illegible]	[illegible]	[illegible]	[illegible]	[illegible]	[illegible]	[illegible]	[illegible]	[illegible]	[illegible]	[illegible]	[illegible]	[illegible]	[illegible]	[illegible]	[illegible]	[illegible]	[illegible]	[illegible]
	Gallstones	[illegible]	[illegible]	[illegible]	[illegible]	[illegible]	[illegible]	[illegible]	[illegible]	[illegible]	[illegible]	[illegible]	[illegible]	[illegible]	[illegible]	[illegible]	[illegible]	[illegible]	[illegible]	[illegible]	[illegible]	[illegible]	[illegible]	[illegible]
	[illegible]	[illegible]	[illegible]	[illegible]	[illegible]	[illegible]	[illegible]	[illegible]	[illegible]	[illegible]	[illegible]	[illegible]	[illegible]	[illegible]	[illegible]	[illegible]	[illegible]	[illegible]	[illegible]	[illegible]	[illegible]	[illegible]	[illegible]	[illegible]
	Other Diseases of Liver	[illegible]	[illegible]	[illegible]	[illegible]	[illegible]	[illegible]	[illegible]	[illegible]	[illegible]	[illegible]	[illegible]	[illegible]	[illegible]	[illegible]	[illegible]	[illegible]	[illegible]	[illegible]	[illegible]	[illegible]	[illegible]	[illegible]	[illegible]
	Other and undefined Diseases of Digestive System	[illegible]	[illegible]	[illegible]	[illegible]	[illegible]	[illegible]	[illegible]	[illegible]	[illegible]	[illegible]	[illegible]	[illegible]	[illegible]	[illegible]	[illegible]	[illegible]	[illegible]	[illegible]	[illegible]	[illegible]	[illegible]	[illegible]	[illegible]
	Diseases of Lymphatic System and Ductless Glands.																							
	Diseases of Spleen	[illegible]	[illegible]	[illegible]	[illegible]	[illegible]	[illegible]	[illegible]	[illegible]	[illegible]	[illegible]	[illegible]	[illegible]	[illegible]	[illegible]	[illegible]	[illegible]	[illegible]	[illegible]	[illegible]	[illegible]	[illegible]	[illegible]	[illegible]
	Dis. of Lymphatic System	[illegible]	[illegible]	[illegible]	[illegible]	[illegible]	[illegible]	[illegible]	[illegible]	[illegible]	[illegible]	[illegible]	[illegible]	[illegible]	[illegible]	[illegible]	[illegible]	[illegible]	[illegible]	[illegible]	[illegible]	[illegible]	[illegible]	[illegible]
	Dis. of Thyroid Body	[illegible]	[illegible]	[illegible]	[illegible]	[illegible]	[illegible]	[illegible]	[illegible]	[illegible]	[illegible]	[illegible]	[illegible]	[illegible]	[illegible]	[illegible]	[illegible]	[illegible]	[illegible]	[illegible]	[illegible]	[illegible]	[illegible]	[illegible]
	Dis. of Suprarenal Capsules	[illegible]	[illegible]	[illegible]	[illegible]	[illegible]	[illegible]	[illegible]	[illegible]	[illegible]	[illegible]	[illegible]	[illegible]	[illegible]	[illegible]	[illegible]	[illegible]	[illegible]	[illegible]	[illegible]	[illegible]	[illegible]	[illegible]	[illegible]
	Diseases of Urinary System.																							
	Acute Nephritis	[illegible]	[illegible]	[illegible]	[illegible]	[illegible]	[illegible]	[illegible]	[illegible]	[illegible]	[illegible]	[illegible]	[illegible]	[illegible]	[illegible]	[illegible]	[illegible]	[illegible]	[illegible]	[illegible]	[illegible]	[illegible]	[illegible]	[illegible]
	Bright's Disease, Albuminuria	[illegible]	[illegible]	[illegible]	[illegible]	[illegible]	[illegible]	[illegible]	[illegible]	[illegible]	[illegible]	[illegible]	[illegible]	[illegible]	[illegible]	[illegible]	[illegible]	[illegible]	[illegible]	[illegible]	[illegible]	[illegible]	[illegible]	[illegible]
	Uraemia	[illegible]	[illegible]	[illegible]	[illegible]	[illegible]	[illegible]	[illegible]	[illegible]	[illegible]	[illegible]	[illegible]	[illegible]	[illegible]	[illegible]	[illegible]	[illegible]	[illegible]	[illegible]	[illegible]	[illegible]	[illegible]	[illegible]	[illegible]
	Suppression of Urine	[illegible]	[illegible]	[illegible]	[illegible]	[illegible]	[illegible]	[illegible]	[illegible]	[illegible]	[illegible]	[illegible]	[illegible]	[illegible]	[illegible]	[illegible]	[illegible]	[illegible]	[illegible]	[illegible]	[illegible]	[illegible]	[illegible]	[illegible]
	Calculus	[illegible]	[illegible]	[illegible]	[illegible]	[illegible]	[illegible]	[illegible]	[illegible]	[illegible]	[illegible]	[illegible]	[illegible]	[illegible]	[illegible]	[illegible]	[illegible]	[illegible]	[illegible]	[illegible]	[illegible]	[illegible]	[illegible]	[illegible]
	Haematuria	[illegible]	[illegible]	[illegible]	[illegible]	[illegible]	[illegible]	[illegible]	[illegible]	[illegible]	[illegible]	[illegible]	[illegible]	[illegible]	[illegible]	[illegible]	[illegible]	[illegible]	[illegible]	[illegible]	[illegible]	[illegible]	[illegible]	[illegible]
	Diseases of Bladder and of Prostate	[illegible]	[illegible]	[illegible]	[illegible]	[illegible]	[illegible]	[illegible]	[illegible]	[illegible]	[illegible]	[illegible]	[illegible]	[illegible]	[illegible]	[illegible]	[illegible]	[illegible]	[illegible]	[illegible]	[illegible]	[illegible]	[illegible]	[illegible]
	Other and undefined Diseases of Urinary System	[illegible]	[illegible]	[illegible]	[illegible]	[illegible]	[illegible]	[illegible]	[illegible]	[illegible]	[illegible]	[illegible]	[illegible]	[illegible]	[illegible]	[illegible]	[illegible]	[illegible]	[illegible]	[illegible]	[illegible]	[illegible]	[illegible]	[illegible]
	Diseases of Organs of Generation.																							
	[illegible]	[illegible]	[illegible]	[illegible]	[illegible]	[illegible]	[illegible]	[illegible]	[illegible]	[illegible]	[illegible]	[illegible]	[illegible]	[illegible]	[illegible]	[illegible]	[illegible]	[illegible]	[illegible]	[illegible]	[illegible]	[illegible]	[illegible]	[illegible]
	Diseases of Uterus and Vagina	[illegible]	[illegible]	[illegible]	[illegible]	[illegible]	[illegible]	[illegible]	[illegible]	[illegible]	[illegible]	[illegible]	[illegible]	[illegible]	[illegible]	[illegible]	[illegible]	[illegible]	[illegible]	[illegible]	[illegible]	[illegible]	[illegible]	[illegible]
	[illegible]	[illegible]	[illegible]	[illegible]	[illegible]	[illegible]	[illegible]	[illegible]	[illegible]	[illegible]	[illegible]	[illegible]	[illegible]	[illegible]	[illegible]	[illegible]	[illegible]	[illegible]	[illegible]	[illegible]	[illegible]	[illegible]	[illegible]	[illegible]
	Pelvic Abscess	[illegible]	[illegible]	[illegible]	[illegible]	[illegible]	[illegible]	[illegible]	[illegible]	[illegible]	[illegible]	[illegible]	[illegible]	[illegible]	[illegible]	[illegible]	[illegible]	[illegible]	[illegible]	[illegible]	[illegible]	[illegible]	[illegible]	[illegible]
	Perineal Abscess	[illegible]	[illegible]	[illegible]	[illegible]	[illegible]	[illegible]	[illegible]	[illegible]	[illegible]	[illegible]	[illegible]	[illegible]	[illegible]	[illegible]	[illegible]	[illegible]	[illegible]	[illegible]	[illegible]	[illegible]	[illegible]	[illegible]	[illegible]
	[illegible]	[illegible]	[illegible]	[illegible]	[illegible]	[illegible]	[illegible]	[illegible]	[illegible]	[illegible]	[illegible]	[illegible]	[illegible]	[illegible]	[illegible]	[illegible]	[illegible]	[illegible]	[illegible]	[illegible]	[illegible]	[illegible]	[illegible]	[illegible]

IRELAND.—CAUSES of DEATHS at different Periods of Life in the Year 1864—MALES and FEMALES—continued.

DEATHS of Males and Females from different Causes registered in IRELAND, and in each of the FOUR PROVINCES, in the Year 18[illegible].

Class	CAUSES OF DEATH.	IRELAND.			LEINSTER.			MUNSTER.			ULSTER.			CONNAUGHT.		
		Males	Fem.	Total	Males	Fem.	Total	Males	Fem.	Total	Males	Fem.	Total	Males	Fem.	Total
	ALL CAUSES, ...	[illegible]	[illegible]	[illegible]	[illegible]	[illegible]	[illegible]	[illegible]	[illegible]	[illegible]	[illegible]	[illegible]	[illegible]	[illegible]	[illegible]	[illegible]
	(CLASSES.)															
I.	SPECIFIC FEBRILE OR ZYMOTIC DISEASES, ...	[illegible]	[illegible]	[illegible]	[illegible]	[illegible]	[illegible]	[illegible]	[illegible]	[illegible]	[illegible]	[illegible]	[illegible]	[illegible]	[illegible]	[illegible]
II.	PARASITIC DISEASES, . .	[illegible]	[illegible]	[illegible]	[illegible]	[illegible]	[illegible]	[illegible]	[illegible]	[illegible]	[illegible]	[illegible]	[illegible]	[illegible]	[illegible]	[illegible]
III.	DIETETIC . . .	[illegible]	[illegible]	[illegible]	[illegible]	[illegible]	[illegible]	[illegible]	[illegible]	[illegible]	[illegible]	[illegible]	[illegible]	[illegible]	[illegible]	[illegible]
IV.	CONSTITUTIONAL . . .	[illegible]	[illegible]	[illegible]	[illegible]	[illegible]	[illegible]	[illegible]	[illegible]	[illegible]	[illegible]	[illegible]	[illegible]	[illegible]	[illegible]	[illegible]
V.	DEVELOPMENTAL . . .	[illegible]	[illegible]	[illegible]	[illegible]	[illegible]	[illegible]	[illegible]	[illegible]	[illegible]	[illegible]	[illegible]	[illegible]	[illegible]	[illegible]	[illegible]
VI.	LOCAL . . .	[illegible]	[illegible]	[illegible]	[illegible]	[illegible]	[illegible]	[illegible]	[illegible]	[illegible]	[illegible]	[illegible]	[illegible]	[illegible]	[illegible]	[illegible]
VII.	VIOLENT, ...	[illegible]	[illegible]	[illegible]	[illegible]	[illegible]	[illegible]	[illegible]	[illegible]	[illegible]	[illegible]	[illegible]	[illegible]	[illegible]	[illegible]	[illegible]
VIII.	ILL-DEFINED AND NOT SPECIFIED CAUSES, ...	[illegible]	[illegible]	[illegible]	[illegible]	[illegible]	[illegible]	[illegible]	[illegible]	[illegible]	[illegible]	[illegible]	[illegible]	[illegible]	[illegible]	[illegible]
	(ORDERS.)															
I.	1. Miasmatic Diseases, . . .	[illegible]	[illegible]	[illegible]	[illegible]	[illegible]	[illegible]	[illegible]	[illegible]	[illegible]	[illegible]	[illegible]	[illegible]	[illegible]	[illegible]	[illegible]
	2. Diarrhoeal	[illegible]	[illegible]	[illegible]	[illegible]	[illegible]	[illegible]	[illegible]	[illegible]	[illegible]	[illegible]	[illegible]	[illegible]	[illegible]	[illegible]	[illegible]
	3. Malarial	[illegible]	[illegible]	[illegible]	[illegible]	[illegible]	[illegible]	[illegible]	[illegible]	[illegible]	[illegible]	[illegible]	[illegible]	[illegible]	-	[illegible]
	4. Zoogenous	[illegible]	[illegible]	[illegible]	[illegible]	[illegible]	[illegible]	[illegible]	[illegible]	[illegible]	[illegible]	[illegible]	[illegible]	[illegible]	[illegible]	[illegible]
	5. Venereal	[illegible]	[illegible]	[illegible]	[illegible]	[illegible]	[illegible]	[illegible]	[illegible]	[illegible]	[illegible]	[illegible]	[illegible]	[illegible]	[illegible]	[illegible]
	6. Septic	[illegible]	[illegible]	[illegible]	[illegible]	[illegible]	[illegible]	[illegible]	[illegible]	[illegible]	[illegible]	[illegible]	[illegible]	[illegible]	[illegible]	[illegible]
II.	Parasitic Diseases, . . .	[illegible]	[illegible]	[illegible]	[illegible]	[illegible]	[illegible]	[illegible]	[illegible]	[illegible]	[illegible]	[illegible]	[illegible]	[illegible]	[illegible]	[illegible]
III.	Dietetic Diseases, . . .	[illegible]	[illegible]	[illegible]	[illegible]	[illegible]	[illegible]	[illegible]	[illegible]	[illegible]	[illegible]	[illegible]	[illegible]	[illegible]	[illegible]	[illegible]
IV.	Constitutional Diseases, . .	[illegible]	[illegible]	[illegible]	[illegible]	[illegible]	[illegible]	[illegible]	[illegible]	[illegible]	[illegible]	[illegible]	[illegible]	[illegible]	[illegible]	[illegible]
V.	Developmental Diseases, . .	[illegible]	[illegible]	[illegible]	[illegible]	[illegible]	[illegible]	[illegible]	[illegible]	[illegible]	[illegible]	[illegible]	[illegible]	[illegible]	[illegible]	[illegible]
VI.	1. Diseases of Nervous System, .	[illegible]	[illegible]	[illegible]	[illegible]	[illegible]	[illegible]	[illegible]	[illegible]	[illegible]	[illegible]	[illegible]	[illegible]	[illegible]	[illegible]	[illegible]
	2. " Organs of Special Sense, .	[illegible]	[illegible]	[illegible]	[illegible]	[illegible]	[illegible]	[illegible]	[illegible]	[illegible]	[illegible]	[illegible]	[illegible]	[illegible]	[illegible]	[illegible]
	3. " Circulatory System, .	[illegible]	[illegible]	[illegible]	[illegible]	[illegible]	[illegible]	[illegible]	[illegible]	[illegible]	[illegible]	[illegible]	[illegible]	[illegible]	[illegible]	[illegible]
	4. " Respiratory System, .	[illegible]	[illegible]	[illegible]	[illegible]	[illegible]	[illegible]	[illegible]	[illegible]	[illegible]	[illegible]	[illegible]	[illegible]	[illegible]	[illegible]	[illegible]
	5. " Digestive System, . .	[illegible]	[illegible]	[illegible]	[illegible]	[illegible]	[illegible]	[illegible]	[illegible]	[illegible]	[illegible]	[illegible]	[illegible]	[illegible]	[illegible]	[illegible]
	6. " Lymphatic System and Ductless Glands, .	[illegible]	[illegible]	[illegible]	[illegible]	[illegible]	[illegible]	[illegible]	[illegible]	[illegible]	[illegible]	[illegible]	[illegible]	[illegible]	[illegible]	[illegible]
	7. " Urinary System, . .	[illegible]	[illegible]	[illegible]	[illegible]	[illegible]	[illegible]	[illegible]	[illegible]	[illegible]	[illegible]	[illegible]	[illegible]	[illegible]	[illegible]	[illegible]
	8. " Reproductive System,—															
	(a) " Organs of Generation, .	-	[illegible]	[illegible]	[illegible]	[illegible]	[illegible]	[illegible]	[illegible]	[illegible]	[illegible]	[illegible]	[illegible]	[illegible]	[illegible]	[illegible]
	(b) " Parturition, . .	-	[illegible]	[illegible]	-	[illegible]	[illegible]	-	[illegible]	[illegible]	-	[illegible]	[illegible]	-	[illegible]	[illegible]
	9. " Locomotive System, .	[illegible]	[illegible]	[illegible]	[illegible]	[illegible]	[illegible]	[illegible]	[illegible]	[illegible]	[illegible]	[illegible]	[illegible]	[illegible]	[illegible]	[illegible]
	10. " Integumentary System, .	[illegible]	[illegible]	[illegible]	[illegible]	[illegible]	[illegible]	[illegible]	[illegible]	[illegible]	[illegible]	[illegible]	[illegible]	[illegible]	[illegible]	[illegible]
VII.	1. Accident or Negligence, . .	[illegible]	[illegible]	[illegible]	[illegible]	[illegible]	[illegible]	[illegible]	[illegible]	[illegible]	[illegible]	[illegible]	[illegible]	[illegible]	[illegible]	[illegible]
	2. Homicide, . . .	[illegible]	[illegible]	[illegible]	[illegible]	[illegible]	[illegible]	[illegible]	[illegible]	[illegible]	[illegible]	[illegible]	[illegible]	[illegible]	-	[illegible]
	3. Suicide, . . .	[illegible]	[illegible]	[illegible]	[illegible]	[illegible]	[illegible]	[illegible]	[illegible]	[illegible]	[illegible]	[illegible]	[illegible]	[illegible]	[illegible]	[illegible]
	4. Execution, . . .	-	-	-	-	-	-	-	-	-	-	-	-	-	-	-
VIII.	Ill-defined and not Specified Causes, ...	[illegible]	[illegible]	[illegible]	[illegible]	[illegible]	[illegible]	[illegible]	[illegible]	[illegible]	[illegible]	[illegible]	[illegible]	[illegible]	[illegible]	[illegible]

DEATHS from different causes registered in IRELAND, and in each of the FOUR PROVINCES, in the Year [illegible]—*continued.*

Class.	CAUSES OF DEATH.	IRELAND.			LEINSTER.			MUNSTER.			ULSTER.			CONNAUGHT.		
		Males.	Fem.	Total.	Males.	Fem.	Total.	Males.	Fem.	Total.	Males.	Fem.	Total.	Males.	Fem.	Total.
I.	MIASMATIC DISEASES.															
	Small Pox — Vaccinated,	[illegible]	[illegible]	[illegible]	[illegible]	[illegible]	[illegible]	[illegible]	[illegible]	[illegible]	[illegible]	[illegible]	[illegible]	[illegible]	[illegible]	[illegible]
	Small Pox — Unvaccinated,	[illegible]	[illegible]	[illegible]	[illegible]	[illegible]	[illegible]	[illegible]	[illegible]	[illegible]	[illegible]	[illegible]	[illegible]	[illegible]	[illegible]	[illegible]
	Small Pox — Not described,	[illegible]	[illegible]	[illegible]	[illegible]	[illegible]	[illegible]	[illegible]	[illegible]	[illegible]	[illegible]	[illegible]	[illegible]	[illegible]	[illegible]	[illegible]
	Chickenpox,	[illegible]	[illegible]	[illegible]	[illegible]	[illegible]	[illegible]	[illegible]	[illegible]	[illegible]	[illegible]	[illegible]	[illegible]	[illegible]	[illegible]	[illegible]
	Measles,	[illegible]	[illegible]	[illegible]	[illegible]	[illegible]	[illegible]	[illegible]	[illegible]	[illegible]	[illegible]	[illegible]	[illegible]	[illegible]	[illegible]	[illegible]
	Epidemic Rose Rash,	[illegible]	[illegible]	[illegible]	[illegible]	[illegible]	[illegible]	[illegible]	[illegible]	[illegible]	[illegible]	[illegible]	[illegible]	[illegible]	[illegible]	[illegible]
	Scarlet Fever,	[illegible]	[illegible]	[illegible]	[illegible]	[illegible]	[illegible]	[illegible]	[illegible]	[illegible]	[illegible]	[illegible]	[illegible]	[illegible]	[illegible]	[illegible]
	Typhus,	[illegible]	[illegible]	[illegible]	[illegible]	[illegible]	[illegible]	[illegible]	[illegible]	[illegible]	[illegible]	[illegible]	[illegible]	[illegible]	[illegible]	[illegible]
	Relapsing Fever,	[illegible]	[illegible]	[illegible]	[illegible]	[illegible]	[illegible]	[illegible]	[illegible]	[illegible]	[illegible]	[illegible]	[illegible]	[illegible]	[illegible]	[illegible]
	Influenza,	[illegible]	[illegible]	[illegible]	[illegible]	[illegible]	[illegible]	[illegible]	[illegible]	[illegible]	[illegible]	[illegible]	[illegible]	[illegible]	[illegible]	[illegible]
	Whooping Cough,	[illegible]	[illegible]	[illegible]	[illegible]	[illegible]	[illegible]	[illegible]	[illegible]	[illegible]	[illegible]	[illegible]	[illegible]	[illegible]	[illegible]	[illegible]
	Mumps,	[illegible]	[illegible]	[illegible]	[illegible]	[illegible]	[illegible]	[illegible]	[illegible]	[illegible]	[illegible]	[illegible]	[illegible]	[illegible]	[illegible]	[illegible]
	Diphtheria,	[illegible]	[illegible]	[illegible]	[illegible]	[illegible]	[illegible]	[illegible]	[illegible]	[illegible]	[illegible]	[illegible]	[illegible]	[illegible]	[illegible]	[illegible]
	Cerebro-spinal Fever,	[illegible]	[illegible]	[illegible]	[illegible]	[illegible]	[illegible]	[illegible]	[illegible]	[illegible]	[illegible]	[illegible]	[illegible]	[illegible]	[illegible]	[illegible]
	Simple and Ill-defined Fever,	[illegible]	[illegible]	[illegible]	[illegible]	[illegible]	[illegible]	[illegible]	[illegible]	[illegible]	[illegible]	[illegible]	[illegible]	[illegible]	[illegible]	[illegible]
	Enteric Fever,	[illegible]	[illegible]	[illegible]	[illegible]	[illegible]	[illegible]	[illegible]	[illegible]	[illegible]	[illegible]	[illegible]	[illegible]	[illegible]	[illegible]	[illegible]
	Other Miasmatic Diseases,	[illegible]	[illegible]	[illegible]	[illegible]	[illegible]	[illegible]	[illegible]	[illegible]	[illegible]	[illegible]	[illegible]	[illegible]	[illegible]	[illegible]	[illegible]
	DIARRHOEAL DISEASES.															
	Simple Cholera,	[illegible]	[illegible]	[illegible]	[illegible]	[illegible]	[illegible]	[illegible]	[illegible]	[illegible]	[illegible]	[illegible]	[illegible]	[illegible]	[illegible]	[illegible]
	Diarrhoea, Dysentery,	[illegible]	[illegible]	[illegible]	[illegible]	[illegible]	[illegible]	[illegible]	[illegible]	[illegible]	[illegible]	[illegible]	[illegible]	[illegible]	[illegible]	[illegible]
	MALARIAL DISEASES.															
	Remittent Fever,	[illegible]	[illegible]	[illegible]	[illegible]	[illegible]	[illegible]	[illegible]	[illegible]	[illegible]	[illegible]	[illegible]	[illegible]	[illegible]	[illegible]	[illegible]
	Ague,	[illegible]	[illegible]	[illegible]	[illegible]	[illegible]	[illegible]	[illegible]	[illegible]	[illegible]	[illegible]	[illegible]	[illegible]	[illegible]	[illegible]	[illegible]
	ZOOGENOUS DISEASES.															
	Hydrophobia,	[illegible]	[illegible]	[illegible]	[illegible]	[illegible]	[illegible]	[illegible]	[illegible]	[illegible]	[illegible]	[illegible]	[illegible]	[illegible]	[illegible]	[illegible]
	Glanders,	[illegible]	[illegible]	[illegible]	[illegible]	[illegible]	[illegible]	[illegible]	[illegible]	[illegible]	[illegible]	[illegible]	[illegible]	[illegible]	[illegible]	[illegible]
	Anthrax, Splenic Fever,	[illegible]	[illegible]	[illegible]	[illegible]	[illegible]	[illegible]	[illegible]	[illegible]	[illegible]	[illegible]	[illegible]	[illegible]	[illegible]	[illegible]	[illegible]
	[illegible]	[illegible]	[illegible]	[illegible]	[illegible]	[illegible]	[illegible]	[illegible]	[illegible]	[illegible]	[illegible]	[illegible]	[illegible]	[illegible]	[illegible]	[illegible]
	VENEREAL DISEASES.															
	Syphilis,	[illegible]	[illegible]	[illegible]	[illegible]	[illegible]	[illegible]	[illegible]	[illegible]	[illegible]	[illegible]	[illegible]	[illegible]	[illegible]	[illegible]	[illegible]
	Gonorrhoea, Stricture of Urethra,	[illegible]	[illegible]	[illegible]	[illegible]	[illegible]	[illegible]	[illegible]	[illegible]	[illegible]	[illegible]	[illegible]	[illegible]	[illegible]	[illegible]	[illegible]
	SEPTIC DISEASES.															
	Phagedaena,	[illegible]	[illegible]	[illegible]	[illegible]	[illegible]	[illegible]	[illegible]	[illegible]	[illegible]	[illegible]	[illegible]	[illegible]	[illegible]	[illegible]	[illegible]
	Erysipelas,	[illegible]	[illegible]	[illegible]	[illegible]	[illegible]	[illegible]	[illegible]	[illegible]	[illegible]	[illegible]	[illegible]	[illegible]	[illegible]	[illegible]	[illegible]
	Pyaemia, Septicaemia,	[illegible]	[illegible]	[illegible]	[illegible]	[illegible]	[illegible]	[illegible]	[illegible]	[illegible]	[illegible]	[illegible]	[illegible]	[illegible]	[illegible]	[illegible]
	Puerperal Fever,	[illegible]	[illegible]	[illegible]	[illegible]	[illegible]	[illegible]	[illegible]	[illegible]	[illegible]	[illegible]	[illegible]	[illegible]	[illegible]	[illegible]	[illegible]
II.	PARASITIC DISEASES.															
	Thrush,	[illegible]	[illegible]	[illegible]	[illegible]	[illegible]	[illegible]	[illegible]	[illegible]	[illegible]	[illegible]	[illegible]	[illegible]	[illegible]	[illegible]	[illegible]
	Other Diseases from Vegetable Parasites,	[illegible]	[illegible]	[illegible]	[illegible]	[illegible]	[illegible]	[illegible]	[illegible]	[illegible]	[illegible]	[illegible]	[illegible]	[illegible]	[illegible]	[illegible]
	Hydatid Disease,	[illegible]	[illegible]	[illegible]	[illegible]	[illegible]	[illegible]	[illegible]	[illegible]	[illegible]	[illegible]	[illegible]	[illegible]	[illegible]	[illegible]	[illegible]
	Other Diseases from Animal Parasites,	[illegible]	[illegible]	[illegible]	[illegible]	[illegible]	[illegible]	[illegible]	[illegible]	[illegible]	[illegible]	[illegible]	[illegible]	[illegible]	[illegible]	[illegible]
III.	DIETETIC DISEASES.															
	Starvation, Want of Breast Milk,	[illegible]	[illegible]	[illegible]	[illegible]	[illegible]	[illegible]	[illegible]	[illegible]	[illegible]	[illegible]	[illegible]	[illegible]	[illegible]	[illegible]	[illegible]
	Scurvy,	[illegible]	[illegible]	[illegible]	[illegible]	[illegible]	[illegible]	[illegible]	[illegible]	[illegible]	[illegible]	[illegible]	[illegible]	[illegible]	[illegible]	[illegible]
	Intemperance — Chronic Alcoholism,	[illegible]	[illegible]	[illegible]	[illegible]	[illegible]	[illegible]	[illegible]	[illegible]	[illegible]	[illegible]	[illegible]	[illegible]	[illegible]	[illegible]	[illegible]
	Intemperance — Delirium Tremens,	[illegible]	[illegible]	[illegible]	[illegible]	[illegible]	[illegible]	[illegible]	[illegible]	[illegible]	[illegible]	[illegible]	[illegible]	[illegible]	[illegible]	[illegible]
IV.	CONSTITUTIONAL DISEASES.															
	Rheumatic Fever, Rheumatism of Heart,	[illegible]	[illegible]	[illegible]	[illegible]	[illegible]	[illegible]	[illegible]	[illegible]	[illegible]	[illegible]	[illegible]	[illegible]	[illegible]	[illegible]	[illegible]
	Rheumatism,	[illegible]	[illegible]	[illegible]	[illegible]	[illegible]	[illegible]	[illegible]	[illegible]	[illegible]	[illegible]	[illegible]	[illegible]	[illegible]	[illegible]	[illegible]
	Gout,	[illegible]	[illegible]	[illegible]	[illegible]	[illegible]	[illegible]	[illegible]	[illegible]	[illegible]	[illegible]	[illegible]	[illegible]	[illegible]	[illegible]	[illegible]
	Rickets,	[illegible]	[illegible]	[illegible]	[illegible]	[illegible]	[illegible]	[illegible]	[illegible]	[illegible]	[illegible]	[illegible]	[illegible]	[illegible]	[illegible]	[illegible]
	Cancer,	[illegible]	[illegible]	[illegible]	[illegible]	[illegible]	[illegible]	[illegible]	[illegible]	[illegible]	[illegible]	[illegible]	[illegible]	[illegible]	[illegible]	[illegible]
	Tabes Mesenterica,	[illegible]	[illegible]	[illegible]	[illegible]	[illegible]	[illegible]	[illegible]	[illegible]	[illegible]	[illegible]	[illegible]	[illegible]	[illegible]	[illegible]	[illegible]
	Tubercular Meningitis (Acute Hydrocephalus),	[illegible]	[illegible]	[illegible]	[illegible]	[illegible]	[illegible]	[illegible]	[illegible]	[illegible]	[illegible]	[illegible]	[illegible]	[illegible]	[illegible]	[illegible]

Deaths from different Causes registered in Ireland, and in each of the Four Provinces, in the year 1896—continued.

Class	Causes of Death	Ireland Males	Ireland Fem.	Ireland Total	Leinster Males	Leinster Fem.	Leinster Total	Munster Males	Munster Fem.	Munster Total	Ulster Males	Ulster Fem.	Ulster Total	Connaught Males	Connaught Fem.	Connaught Total
IV.—con.	Phthisis	[illegible]	[illegible]	[illegible]	[illegible]	[illegible]	[illegible]	[illegible]	[illegible]	[illegible]	[illegible]	[illegible]	[illegible]	[illegible]	[illegible]	[illegible]
	Other forms of Tuberculous Disease, Scrofula	[illegible]	[illegible]	[illegible]	[illegible]	[illegible]	[illegible]	[illegible]	[illegible]	[illegible]	[illegible]	[illegible]	[illegible]	[illegible]	[illegible]	[illegible]
	[illegible]	[illegible]	[illegible]	[illegible]	[illegible]	[illegible]	[illegible]	[illegible]	[illegible]	[illegible]	[illegible]	[illegible]	[illegible]	[illegible]	[illegible]	[illegible]
	[illegible]	[illegible]	[illegible]	[illegible]	[illegible]	[illegible]	[illegible]	[illegible]	[illegible]	[illegible]	[illegible]	[illegible]	[illegible]	[illegible]	[illegible]	[illegible]
	Diabetes Mellitus	[illegible]	[illegible]	[illegible]	[illegible]	[illegible]	[illegible]	[illegible]	[illegible]	[illegible]	[illegible]	[illegible]	[illegible]	[illegible]	[illegible]	[illegible]
	Other [illegible] Diseases	[illegible]	[illegible]	[illegible]	[illegible]	[illegible]	[illegible]	[illegible]	[illegible]	[illegible]	[illegible]	[illegible]	[illegible]	[illegible]	[illegible]	[illegible]
V.	Developmental Diseases.															
	Premature Birth	[illegible]	[illegible]	[illegible]	[illegible]	[illegible]	[illegible]	[illegible]	[illegible]	[illegible]	[illegible]	[illegible]	[illegible]	[illegible]	[illegible]	[illegible]
	Atelectasis	[illegible]	[illegible]	[illegible]	[illegible]	[illegible]	[illegible]	[illegible]	[illegible]	[illegible]	[illegible]	[illegible]	[illegible]	[illegible]	[illegible]	[illegible]
	Cyanosis	[illegible]	[illegible]	[illegible]	[illegible]	[illegible]	[illegible]	[illegible]	[illegible]	[illegible]	[illegible]	[illegible]	[illegible]	[illegible]	[illegible]	[illegible]
	Spina Bifida	[illegible]	[illegible]	[illegible]	[illegible]	[illegible]	[illegible]	[illegible]	[illegible]	[illegible]	[illegible]	[illegible]	[illegible]	[illegible]	[illegible]	[illegible]
	Imperforate Anus	[illegible]	[illegible]	[illegible]	[illegible]	[illegible]	[illegible]	[illegible]	[illegible]	[illegible]	[illegible]	[illegible]	[illegible]	[illegible]	[illegible]	[illegible]
	Cleft Palate, Hare-lip	[illegible]	[illegible]	[illegible]	[illegible]	[illegible]	[illegible]	[illegible]	[illegible]	[illegible]	[illegible]	[illegible]	[illegible]	[illegible]	[illegible]	[illegible]
	Other Congenital Defects	[illegible]	[illegible]	[illegible]	[illegible]	[illegible]	[illegible]	[illegible]	[illegible]	[illegible]	[illegible]	[illegible]	[illegible]	[illegible]	[illegible]	[illegible]
	Old Age	[illegible]	[illegible]	[illegible]	[illegible]	[illegible]	[illegible]	[illegible]	[illegible]	[illegible]	[illegible]	[illegible]	[illegible]	[illegible]	[illegible]	[illegible]
VI.	Diseases of Nervous System.															
	Inflammation of Brain or its Membranes	[illegible]	[illegible]	[illegible]	[illegible]	[illegible]	[illegible]	[illegible]	[illegible]	[illegible]	[illegible]	[illegible]	[illegible]	[illegible]	[illegible]	[illegible]
	Apoplexy	[illegible]	[illegible]	[illegible]	[illegible]	[illegible]	[illegible]	[illegible]	[illegible]	[illegible]	[illegible]	[illegible]	[illegible]	[illegible]	[illegible]	[illegible]
	Softening of Brain	[illegible]	[illegible]	[illegible]	[illegible]	[illegible]	[illegible]	[illegible]	[illegible]	[illegible]	[illegible]	[illegible]	[illegible]	[illegible]	[illegible]	[illegible]
	Hemiplegia, Brain Paralysis	[illegible]	[illegible]	[illegible]	[illegible]	[illegible]	[illegible]	[illegible]	[illegible]	[illegible]	[illegible]	[illegible]	[illegible]	[illegible]	[illegible]	[illegible]
	[illegible]	[illegible]	[illegible]	[illegible]	[illegible]	[illegible]	[illegible]	[illegible]	[illegible]	[illegible]	[illegible]	[illegible]	[illegible]	[illegible]	[illegible]	[illegible]
	Insanity (General Paralysis of Insane)	[illegible]	[illegible]	[illegible]	[illegible]	[illegible]	[illegible]	[illegible]	[illegible]	[illegible]	[illegible]	[illegible]	[illegible]	[illegible]	[illegible]	[illegible]
	Chorea	[illegible]	[illegible]	[illegible]	[illegible]	[illegible]	[illegible]	[illegible]	[illegible]	[illegible]	[illegible]	[illegible]	[illegible]	[illegible]	[illegible]	[illegible]
	Epilepsy	[illegible]	[illegible]	[illegible]	[illegible]	[illegible]	[illegible]	[illegible]	[illegible]	[illegible]	[illegible]	[illegible]	[illegible]	[illegible]	[illegible]	[illegible]
	Convulsions	[illegible]	[illegible]	[illegible]	[illegible]	[illegible]	[illegible]	[illegible]	[illegible]	[illegible]	[illegible]	[illegible]	[illegible]	[illegible]	[illegible]	[illegible]
	Laryngismus Stridulus	[illegible]	[illegible]	[illegible]	[illegible]	[illegible]	[illegible]	[illegible]	[illegible]	[illegible]	[illegible]	[illegible]	[illegible]	[illegible]	[illegible]	[illegible]
	Idiopathic Tetanus	[illegible]	[illegible]	[illegible]	[illegible]	[illegible]	[illegible]	[illegible]	[illegible]	[illegible]	[illegible]	[illegible]	[illegible]	[illegible]	[illegible]	[illegible]
	Paraplegia, Diseases of Spinal Cord	[illegible]	[illegible]	[illegible]	[illegible]	[illegible]	[illegible]	[illegible]	[illegible]	[illegible]	[illegible]	[illegible]	[illegible]	[illegible]	[illegible]	[illegible]
	Other and undefined Diseases of Brain or Nervous System	[illegible]	[illegible]	[illegible]	[illegible]	[illegible]	[illegible]	[illegible]	[illegible]	[illegible]	[illegible]	[illegible]	[illegible]	[illegible]	[illegible]	[illegible]
	Diseases of Organs of Special Sense.															
	Otitis, Otorrhoea	[illegible]	[illegible]	[illegible]	[illegible]	[illegible]	[illegible]	[illegible]	[illegible]	[illegible]	[illegible]	[illegible]	[illegible]	[illegible]	[illegible]	[illegible]
	Epistaxis and Dis. of Nose	[illegible]	[illegible]	[illegible]	[illegible]	[illegible]	[illegible]	[illegible]	[illegible]	[illegible]	[illegible]	[illegible]	[illegible]	[illegible]	[illegible]	[illegible]
	Ophthalmia and Dis. of Eye	[illegible]	[illegible]	[illegible]	[illegible]	[illegible]	[illegible]	[illegible]	[illegible]	[illegible]	[illegible]	[illegible]	[illegible]	[illegible]	[illegible]	[illegible]
	Diseases of Circulatory System.															
	Endocarditis, Valvular Disease	[illegible]	[illegible]	[illegible]	[illegible]	[illegible]	[illegible]	[illegible]	[illegible]	[illegible]	[illegible]	[illegible]	[illegible]	[illegible]	[illegible]	[illegible]
	Pericarditis	[illegible]	[illegible]	[illegible]	[illegible]	[illegible]	[illegible]	[illegible]	[illegible]	[illegible]	[illegible]	[illegible]	[illegible]	[illegible]	[illegible]	[illegible]
	Hypertrophy of Heart	[illegible]	[illegible]	[illegible]	[illegible]	[illegible]	[illegible]	[illegible]	[illegible]	[illegible]	[illegible]	[illegible]	[illegible]	[illegible]	[illegible]	[illegible]
	Angina Pectoris	[illegible]	[illegible]	[illegible]	[illegible]	[illegible]	[illegible]	[illegible]	[illegible]	[illegible]	[illegible]	[illegible]	[illegible]	[illegible]	[illegible]	[illegible]
	Syncope	[illegible]	[illegible]	[illegible]	[illegible]	[illegible]	[illegible]	[illegible]	[illegible]	[illegible]	[illegible]	[illegible]	[illegible]	[illegible]	[illegible]	[illegible]
	Aneurism	[illegible]	[illegible]	[illegible]	[illegible]	[illegible]	[illegible]	[illegible]	[illegible]	[illegible]	[illegible]	[illegible]	[illegible]	[illegible]	[illegible]	[illegible]
	Senile Gangrene	[illegible]	[illegible]	[illegible]	[illegible]	[illegible]	[illegible]	[illegible]	[illegible]	[illegible]	[illegible]	[illegible]	[illegible]	[illegible]	[illegible]	[illegible]
	Embolism, Thrombosis	[illegible]	[illegible]	[illegible]	[illegible]	[illegible]	[illegible]	[illegible]	[illegible]	[illegible]	[illegible]	[illegible]	[illegible]	[illegible]	[illegible]	[illegible]
	Phlebitis	[illegible]	[illegible]	[illegible]	[illegible]	[illegible]	[illegible]	[illegible]	[illegible]	[illegible]	[illegible]	[illegible]	[illegible]	[illegible]	[illegible]	[illegible]
	Varicose Veins	[illegible]	[illegible]	[illegible]	[illegible]	[illegible]	[illegible]	[illegible]	[illegible]	[illegible]	[illegible]	[illegible]	[illegible]	[illegible]	[illegible]	[illegible]
	Other, and undefined Diseases of Heart or Circulatory System	[illegible]	[illegible]	[illegible]	[illegible]	[illegible]	[illegible]	[illegible]	[illegible]	[illegible]	[illegible]	[illegible]	[illegible]	[illegible]	[illegible]	[illegible]
	Diseases of Respiratory System.															
	Laryngitis	[illegible]	[illegible]	[illegible]	[illegible]	[illegible]	[illegible]	[illegible]	[illegible]	[illegible]	[illegible]	[illegible]	[illegible]	[illegible]	[illegible]	[illegible]
	Croup	[illegible]	[illegible]	[illegible]	[illegible]	[illegible]	[illegible]	[illegible]	[illegible]	[illegible]	[illegible]	[illegible]	[illegible]	[illegible]	[illegible]	[illegible]
	Other Diseases of Larynx and Trachea	[illegible]	[illegible]	[illegible]	[illegible]	[illegible]	[illegible]	[illegible]	[illegible]	[illegible]	[illegible]	[illegible]	[illegible]	[illegible]	[illegible]	[illegible]
	Emphysema, Asthma	[illegible]	[illegible]	[illegible]	[illegible]	[illegible]	[illegible]	[illegible]	[illegible]	[illegible]	[illegible]	[illegible]	[illegible]	[illegible]	[illegible]	[illegible]
	Bronchitis	[illegible]	[illegible]	[illegible]	[illegible]	[illegible]	[illegible]	[illegible]	[illegible]	[illegible]	[illegible]	[illegible]	[illegible]	[illegible]	[illegible]	[illegible]
	Pneumonia	[illegible]	[illegible]	[illegible]	[illegible]	[illegible]	[illegible]	[illegible]	[illegible]	[illegible]	[illegible]	[illegible]	[illegible]	[illegible]	[illegible]	[illegible]
	Pleurisy	[illegible]	[illegible]	[illegible]	[illegible]	[illegible]	[illegible]	[illegible]	[illegible]	[illegible]	[illegible]	[illegible]	[illegible]	[illegible]	[illegible]	[illegible]
	Other, and undefined Diseases of Respiratory System	[illegible]	[illegible]	[illegible]	[illegible]	[illegible]	[illegible]	[illegible]	[illegible]	[illegible]	[illegible]	[illegible]	[illegible]	[illegible]	[illegible]	[illegible]

DEATHS from different Causes registered in IRELAND, and in each of the FOUR PROVINCES, in the Year [illegible]—*continued.*

Order.	CAUSES OF DEATH.	IRELAND.			Leinster.			Munster.			Ulster.			Connaught.		
		Males.	Fem.	Total.	Males.	Fem.	Total.	Males.	Fem.	Total.	Males.	Fem.	Total.	Males.	Fem.	Total.
VI.—[illegible]	DISEASES OF DIGESTIVE SYSTEM.															
	Dentition	[illegible]	[illegible]	[illegible]	[illegible]	[illegible]	[illegible]	[illegible]	[illegible]	[illegible]	[illegible]	[illegible]	[illegible]	[illegible]	[illegible]	[illegible]
	[illegible]	[illegible]	[illegible]	[illegible]	[illegible]	[illegible]	[illegible]	[illegible]	[illegible]	[illegible]	[illegible]	[illegible]	[illegible]	[illegible]	[illegible]	[illegible]
	Sore Throat, Quinsy	[illegible]	[illegible]	[illegible]	[illegible]	[illegible]	[illegible]	[illegible]	[illegible]	[illegible]	[illegible]	[illegible]	[illegible]	[illegible]	[illegible]	[illegible]
	Dyspepsia	[illegible]	[illegible]	[illegible]	[illegible]	[illegible]	[illegible]	[illegible]	[illegible]	[illegible]	[illegible]	[illegible]	[illegible]	[illegible]	[illegible]	[illegible]
	Haematemesis	[illegible]	[illegible]	[illegible]	[illegible]	[illegible]	[illegible]	[illegible]	[illegible]	[illegible]	[illegible]	[illegible]	[illegible]	[illegible]	[illegible]	[illegible]
	Melaena	[illegible]	[illegible]	[illegible]	[illegible]	[illegible]	[illegible]	[illegible]	[illegible]	[illegible]	[illegible]	[illegible]	[illegible]	[illegible]	[illegible]	[illegible]
	Diseases of Stomach	[illegible]	[illegible]	[illegible]	[illegible]	[illegible]	[illegible]	[illegible]	[illegible]	[illegible]	[illegible]	[illegible]	[illegible]	[illegible]	[illegible]	[illegible]
	Enteritis	[illegible]	[illegible]	[illegible]	[illegible]	[illegible]	[illegible]	[illegible]	[illegible]	[illegible]	[illegible]	[illegible]	[illegible]	[illegible]	[illegible]	[illegible]
	Ulceration of Intestines	[illegible]	[illegible]	[illegible]	[illegible]	[illegible]	[illegible]	[illegible]	[illegible]	[illegible]	[illegible]	[illegible]	[illegible]	[illegible]	[illegible]	[illegible]
	Hernia, Obstruction of Intestine	[illegible]	[illegible]	[illegible]	[illegible]	[illegible]	[illegible]	[illegible]	[illegible]	[illegible]	[illegible]	[illegible]	[illegible]	[illegible]	[illegible]	[illegible]
	Stricture or Strangulation of Intestine	[illegible]	[illegible]	[illegible]	[illegible]	[illegible]	[illegible]	[illegible]	[illegible]	[illegible]	[illegible]	[illegible]	[illegible]	[illegible]	[illegible]	[illegible]
	Intussusception of Intestine	[illegible]	[illegible]	[illegible]	[illegible]	[illegible]	[illegible]	[illegible]	[illegible]	[illegible]	[illegible]	[illegible]	[illegible]	[illegible]	[illegible]	[illegible]
	Ileus	[illegible]	[illegible]	[illegible]	[illegible]	[illegible]	[illegible]	[illegible]	[illegible]	[illegible]	[illegible]	[illegible]	[illegible]	[illegible]	[illegible]	[illegible]
	Fistula	[illegible]	[illegible]	[illegible]	[illegible]	[illegible]	[illegible]	[illegible]	[illegible]	[illegible]	[illegible]	[illegible]	[illegible]	[illegible]	[illegible]	[illegible]
	Peritonitis	[illegible]	[illegible]	[illegible]	[illegible]	[illegible]	[illegible]	[illegible]	[illegible]	[illegible]	[illegible]	[illegible]	[illegible]	[illegible]	[illegible]	[illegible]
	Ascites	[illegible]	[illegible]	[illegible]	[illegible]	[illegible]	[illegible]	[illegible]	[illegible]	[illegible]	[illegible]	[illegible]	[illegible]	[illegible]	[illegible]	[illegible]
	Gallstones	[illegible]	[illegible]	[illegible]	[illegible]	[illegible]	[illegible]	[illegible]	[illegible]	[illegible]	[illegible]	[illegible]	[illegible]	[illegible]	[illegible]	[illegible]
	Cirrhosis of Liver	[illegible]	[illegible]	[illegible]	[illegible]	[illegible]	[illegible]	[illegible]	[illegible]	[illegible]	[illegible]	[illegible]	[illegible]	[illegible]	[illegible]	[illegible]
	Other Diseases of Liver	[illegible]	[illegible]	[illegible]	[illegible]	[illegible]	[illegible]	[illegible]	[illegible]	[illegible]	[illegible]	[illegible]	[illegible]	[illegible]	[illegible]	[illegible]
	Other and undefined Diseases of Digestive System	[illegible]	[illegible]	[illegible]	[illegible]	[illegible]	[illegible]	[illegible]	[illegible]	[illegible]	[illegible]	[illegible]	[illegible]	[illegible]	[illegible]	[illegible]
	DISEASES OF LYMPHATIC SYSTEM AND DUCTLESS GLANDS.															
	Diseases of Spleen	[illegible]	[illegible]	[illegible]	[illegible]	[illegible]	[illegible]	[illegible]	[illegible]	[illegible]	[illegible]	[illegible]	[illegible]	[illegible]	[illegible]	[illegible]
	Dis. of Lymphatic System	[illegible]	[illegible]	[illegible]	[illegible]	[illegible]	[illegible]	[illegible]	[illegible]	[illegible]	[illegible]	[illegible]	[illegible]	[illegible]	[illegible]	[illegible]
	Dis. of Thyroid Body	[illegible]	[illegible]	[illegible]	[illegible]	[illegible]	[illegible]	[illegible]	[illegible]	[illegible]	[illegible]	[illegible]	[illegible]	[illegible]	[illegible]	[illegible]
	Dis. of Suprarenal Capsules	[illegible]	[illegible]	[illegible]	[illegible]	[illegible]	[illegible]	[illegible]	[illegible]	[illegible]	[illegible]	[illegible]	[illegible]	[illegible]	[illegible]	[illegible]
	DISEASES OF URINARY SYSTEM.															
	Acute Nephritis	[illegible]	[illegible]	[illegible]	[illegible]	[illegible]	[illegible]	[illegible]	[illegible]	[illegible]	[illegible]	[illegible]	[illegible]	[illegible]	[illegible]	[illegible]
	Bright's Disease, Albuminuria	[illegible]	[illegible]	[illegible]	[illegible]	[illegible]	[illegible]	[illegible]	[illegible]	[illegible]	[illegible]	[illegible]	[illegible]	[illegible]	[illegible]	[illegible]
	Uraemia	[illegible]	[illegible]	[illegible]	[illegible]	[illegible]	[illegible]	[illegible]	[illegible]	[illegible]	[illegible]	[illegible]	[illegible]	[illegible]	[illegible]	[illegible]
	Suppression of Urine	[illegible]	[illegible]	[illegible]	[illegible]	[illegible]	[illegible]	[illegible]	[illegible]	[illegible]	[illegible]	[illegible]	[illegible]	[illegible]	[illegible]	[illegible]
	Calculus	[illegible]	[illegible]	[illegible]	[illegible]	[illegible]	[illegible]	[illegible]	[illegible]	[illegible]	[illegible]	[illegible]	[illegible]	[illegible]	[illegible]	[illegible]
	Haematuria	[illegible]	[illegible]	[illegible]	[illegible]	[illegible]	[illegible]	[illegible]	[illegible]	[illegible]	[illegible]	[illegible]	[illegible]	[illegible]	[illegible]	[illegible]
	Diseases of Bladder and of Prostate	[illegible]	[illegible]	[illegible]	[illegible]	[illegible]	[illegible]	[illegible]	[illegible]	[illegible]	[illegible]	[illegible]	[illegible]	[illegible]	[illegible]	[illegible]
	Other and undefined Diseases of Urinary System	[illegible]	[illegible]	[illegible]	[illegible]	[illegible]	[illegible]	[illegible]	[illegible]	[illegible]	[illegible]	[illegible]	[illegible]	[illegible]	[illegible]	[illegible]
	DISEASES OF ORGANS OF GENERATION.															
	Ovarian Disease	[illegible]	[illegible]	[illegible]	[illegible]	[illegible]	[illegible]	[illegible]	[illegible]	[illegible]	[illegible]	[illegible]	[illegible]	[illegible]	[illegible]	[illegible]
	Disease of Uterus and Vagina	[illegible]	[illegible]	[illegible]	[illegible]	[illegible]	[illegible]	[illegible]	[illegible]	[illegible]	[illegible]	[illegible]	[illegible]	[illegible]	[illegible]	[illegible]
	Disorders of Menstruation	[illegible]	[illegible]	[illegible]	[illegible]	[illegible]	[illegible]	[illegible]	[illegible]	[illegible]	[illegible]	[illegible]	[illegible]	[illegible]	[illegible]	[illegible]
	Pelvic Abscess	[illegible]	[illegible]	[illegible]	[illegible]	[illegible]	[illegible]	[illegible]	[illegible]	[illegible]	[illegible]	[illegible]	[illegible]	[illegible]	[illegible]	[illegible]
	Perineal Abscess	[illegible]	[illegible]	[illegible]	[illegible]	[illegible]	[illegible]	[illegible]	[illegible]	[illegible]	[illegible]	[illegible]	[illegible]	[illegible]	[illegible]	[illegible]
	Diseases of Testes, Penis, Scrotum, &c.	[illegible]	[illegible]	[illegible]	[illegible]	[illegible]	[illegible]	[illegible]	[illegible]	[illegible]	[illegible]	[illegible]	[illegible]	[illegible]	[illegible]	[illegible]
	DISEASES OF PARTURITION.															
	Abortion, Miscarriage	[illegible]	[illegible]	[illegible]	[illegible]	[illegible]	[illegible]	[illegible]	[illegible]	[illegible]	[illegible]	[illegible]	[illegible]	[illegible]	[illegible]	[illegible]
	Puerperal Mania	[illegible]	[illegible]	[illegible]	[illegible]	[illegible]	[illegible]	[illegible]	[illegible]	[illegible]	[illegible]	[illegible]	[illegible]	[illegible]	[illegible]	[illegible]
	Puerperal Convulsions	[illegible]	[illegible]	[illegible]	[illegible]	[illegible]	[illegible]	[illegible]	[illegible]	[illegible]	[illegible]	[illegible]	[illegible]	[illegible]	[illegible]	[illegible]
	Placenta praevia, Flooding	[illegible]	[illegible]	[illegible]	[illegible]	[illegible]	[illegible]	[illegible]	[illegible]	[illegible]	[illegible]	[illegible]	[illegible]	[illegible]	[illegible]	[illegible]
	Phlegmasia Dolens	[illegible]	[illegible]	[illegible]	[illegible]	[illegible]	[illegible]	[illegible]	[illegible]	[illegible]	[illegible]	[illegible]	[illegible]	[illegible]	[illegible]	[illegible]
	Other and undefined Accidents of Childbirth	[illegible]	[illegible]	[illegible]	[illegible]	[illegible]	[illegible]	[illegible]	[illegible]	[illegible]	[illegible]	[illegible]	[illegible]	[illegible]	[illegible]	[illegible]
	DISEASES OF ORGANS OF LOCOMOTION.															
	Caries, Necrosis	[illegible]	[illegible]	[illegible]	[illegible]	[illegible]	[illegible]	[illegible]	[illegible]	[illegible]	[illegible]	[illegible]	[illegible]	[illegible]	[illegible]	[illegible]
	Arthritis, Ostitis, Periostitis	[illegible]	[illegible]	[illegible]	[illegible]	[illegible]	[illegible]	[illegible]	[illegible]	[illegible]	[illegible]	[illegible]	[illegible]	[illegible]	[illegible]	[illegible]
	Other and undefined Diseases of Organs of Locomotion	[illegible]	[illegible]	[illegible]	[illegible]	[illegible]	[illegible]	[illegible]	[illegible]	[illegible]	[illegible]	[illegible]	[illegible]	[illegible]	[illegible]	[illegible]

DEATHS from different CAUSES registered in IRELAND, and in each of the FOUR PROVINCES, in the Year 1896—*continued*.

Class.	CAUSES OF DEATH.	IRELAND.			LEINSTER.			MUNSTER.			ULSTER.			CONNAUGHT.		
		Males.	Fem.	Total.	Males.	Fem.	Total.	Males.	Fem.	Total.	Males.	Fem.	Total.	Males.	Fem.	Total.
[illegible]	DISEASES OF INTEGUMENTARY SYSTEM.															
	Carbuncle,	[illegible]	[illegible]	[illegible]	[illegible]	[illegible]	[illegible]	[illegible]	[illegible]	[illegible]	[illegible]	[illegible]	[illegible]	[illegible]	[illegible]	[illegible]
	Phlegmon, Cellulitis,	[illegible]	[illegible]	[illegible]	[illegible]	[illegible]	[illegible]	[illegible]	[illegible]	[illegible]	[illegible]	[illegible]	[illegible]	[illegible]	[illegible]	[illegible]
	Lupus,	[illegible]	[illegible]	[illegible]	[illegible]	[illegible]	[illegible]	[illegible]	[illegible]	[illegible]	[illegible]	[illegible]	[illegible]	[illegible]	[illegible]	[illegible]
	Ulcer, Bedsore,	[illegible]	[illegible]	[illegible]	[illegible]	[illegible]	[illegible]	[illegible]	[illegible]	[illegible]	[illegible]	[illegible]	[illegible]	[illegible]	[illegible]	[illegible]
	Eczema,	[illegible]	[illegible]	[illegible]	[illegible]	[illegible]	[illegible]	[illegible]	[illegible]	[illegible]	[illegible]	[illegible]	[illegible]	[illegible]	[illegible]	[illegible]
	Pemphigus,	[illegible]	[illegible]	[illegible]	[illegible]	[illegible]	[illegible]	[illegible]	[illegible]	[illegible]	[illegible]	[illegible]	[illegible]	[illegible]	[illegible]	[illegible]
	Other and unspecified Diseases of Integumentary System,	[illegible]	[illegible]	[illegible]	[illegible]	[illegible]	[illegible]	[illegible]	[illegible]	[illegible]	[illegible]	[illegible]	[illegible]	[illegible]	[illegible]	[illegible]
VII.	ACCIDENT OR NEGLIGENCE.															
	In Mines and Quarries,	[illegible]	[illegible]	[illegible]	[illegible]	[illegible]	[illegible]	[illegible]	[illegible]	[illegible]	[illegible]	[illegible]	[illegible]	[illegible]	[illegible]	[illegible]
	Vehicles and Horses,	[illegible]	[illegible]	[illegible]	[illegible]	[illegible]	[illegible]	[illegible]	[illegible]	[illegible]	[illegible]	[illegible]	[illegible]	[illegible]	[illegible]	[illegible]
	Ships, Boats and Docks (not Drowning),	[illegible]	[illegible]	[illegible]	[illegible]	[illegible]	[illegible]	[illegible]	[illegible]	[illegible]	[illegible]	[illegible]	[illegible]	[illegible]	[illegible]	[illegible]
	Building Operations,	[illegible]	[illegible]	[illegible]	[illegible]	[illegible]	[illegible]	[illegible]	[illegible]	[illegible]	[illegible]	[illegible]	[illegible]	[illegible]	[illegible]	[illegible]
	Machinery,	[illegible]	[illegible]	[illegible]	[illegible]	[illegible]	[illegible]	[illegible]	[illegible]	[illegible]	[illegible]	[illegible]	[illegible]	[illegible]	[illegible]	[illegible]
	Weapons and Implements,	[illegible]	[illegible]	[illegible]	[illegible]	[illegible]	[illegible]	[illegible]	[illegible]	[illegible]	[illegible]	[illegible]	[illegible]	[illegible]	[illegible]	[illegible]
	Burns and Scalds,	[illegible]	[illegible]	[illegible]	[illegible]	[illegible]	[illegible]	[illegible]	[illegible]	[illegible]	[illegible]	[illegible]	[illegible]	[illegible]	[illegible]	[illegible]
	Poison, from Poisons,	[illegible]	[illegible]	[illegible]	[illegible]	[illegible]	[illegible]	[illegible]	[illegible]	[illegible]	[illegible]	[illegible]	[illegible]	[illegible]	[illegible]	[illegible]
	Drowning,	[illegible]	[illegible]	[illegible]	[illegible]	[illegible]	[illegible]	[illegible]	[illegible]	[illegible]	[illegible]	[illegible]	[illegible]	[illegible]	[illegible]	[illegible]
	Suffocation,	[illegible]	[illegible]	[illegible]	[illegible]	[illegible]	[illegible]	[illegible]	[illegible]	[illegible]	[illegible]	[illegible]	[illegible]	[illegible]	[illegible]	[illegible]
	Falls,	[illegible]	[illegible]	[illegible]	[illegible]	[illegible]	[illegible]	[illegible]	[illegible]	[illegible]	[illegible]	[illegible]	[illegible]	[illegible]	[illegible]	[illegible]
	Weather Agencies,	[illegible]	[illegible]	[illegible]	[illegible]	[illegible]	[illegible]	[illegible]	[illegible]	[illegible]	[illegible]	[illegible]	[illegible]	[illegible]	[illegible]	[illegible]
	Otherwise or not stated,	[illegible]	[illegible]	[illegible]	[illegible]	[illegible]	[illegible]	[illegible]	[illegible]	[illegible]	[illegible]	[illegible]	[illegible]	[illegible]	[illegible]	[illegible]
	Homicide,	[illegible]	[illegible]	[illegible]	[illegible]	[illegible]	[illegible]	[illegible]	[illegible]	[illegible]	[illegible]	[illegible]	[illegible]	[illegible]	[illegible]	[illegible]
	Suicide,	[illegible]	[illegible]	[illegible]	[illegible]	[illegible]	[illegible]	[illegible]	[illegible]	[illegible]	[illegible]	[illegible]	[illegible]	[illegible]	[illegible]	[illegible]
	Execution,	[illegible]	[illegible]	[illegible]	[illegible]	[illegible]	[illegible]	[illegible]	[illegible]	[illegible]	[illegible]	[illegible]	[illegible]	[illegible]	[illegible]	[illegible]
VIII.	ILL-DEFINED AND NOT SPECIFIED CAUSES.															
	Dropsy,	[illegible]	[illegible]	[illegible]	[illegible]	[illegible]	[illegible]	[illegible]	[illegible]	[illegible]	[illegible]	[illegible]	[illegible]	[illegible]	[illegible]	[illegible]
	Debility, Atrophy, Inanition,	[illegible]	[illegible]	[illegible]	[illegible]	[illegible]	[illegible]	[illegible]	[illegible]	[illegible]	[illegible]	[illegible]	[illegible]	[illegible]	[illegible]	[illegible]
	Mortification,	[illegible]	[illegible]	[illegible]	[illegible]	[illegible]	[illegible]	[illegible]	[illegible]	[illegible]	[illegible]	[illegible]	[illegible]	[illegible]	[illegible]	[illegible]
	Tumour,	[illegible]	[illegible]	[illegible]	[illegible]	[illegible]	[illegible]	[illegible]	[illegible]	[illegible]	[illegible]	[illegible]	[illegible]	[illegible]	[illegible]	[illegible]
	Abscess,	[illegible]	[illegible]	[illegible]	[illegible]	[illegible]	[illegible]	[illegible]	[illegible]	[illegible]	[illegible]	[illegible]	[illegible]	[illegible]	[illegible]	[illegible]
	Haemorrhage,	[illegible]	[illegible]	[illegible]	[illegible]	[illegible]	[illegible]	[illegible]	[illegible]	[illegible]	[illegible]	[illegible]	[illegible]	[illegible]	[illegible]	[illegible]
	Sudden Death (cause unascertained),	[illegible]	[illegible]	[illegible]	[illegible]	[illegible]	[illegible]	[illegible]	[illegible]	[illegible]	[illegible]	[illegible]	[illegible]	[illegible]	[illegible]	[illegible]
	Other ill-defined and not specified causes,	[illegible]	[illegible]	[illegible]	[illegible]	[illegible]	[illegible]	[illegible]	[illegible]	[illegible]	[illegible]	[illegible]	[illegible]	[illegible]	[illegible]	[illegible]

TOTAL NUMBER OF DEATHS.—NUMBER of PERSONS who died (1), in INFIRMARIES [illegible] OWN HOMES, &c.; NUMBER of DEATHS from the [illegible]

	PROVINCES AND COUNTIES.	Total Number of Deaths.	In Infirmaries, Hospitals, and Private Asylums	In Public Lunatic Asylums	In Workhouses	At their own Homes, &c.	[illegible]	[illegible]	[illegible]	[illegible]	[illegible]	[illegible]	[illegible]	[illegible]
	IRELAND,	[illegible]	[illegible]	[illegible]	[illegible]	[illegible]	[illegible]	[illegible]	[illegible]	[illegible]	[illegible]	[illegible]	[illegible]	[illegible]
No.	PROVINCES.													
I.	LEINSTER,	[illegible]	[illegible]	[illegible]	[illegible]	[illegible]	[illegible]	[illegible]	[illegible]	[illegible]	[illegible]	[illegible]	[illegible]	[illegible]
II.	MUNSTER,	[illegible]	[illegible]	[illegible]	[illegible]	[illegible]	[illegible]	[illegible]	[illegible]	[illegible]	[illegible]	[illegible]	[illegible]	[illegible]
III.	ULSTER,	[illegible]	[illegible]	[illegible]	[illegible]	[illegible]	[illegible]	[illegible]	[illegible]	[illegible]	[illegible]	[illegible]	[illegible]	[illegible]
IV.	CONNAUGHT,	[illegible]	[illegible]	[illegible]	[illegible]	[illegible]	[illegible]	[illegible]	[illegible]	[illegible]	[illegible]	[illegible]	[illegible]	[illegible]
1	Carlow,	[illegible]	[illegible]	[illegible]	[illegible]	[illegible]	[illegible]	[illegible]	[illegible]	[illegible]	[illegible]	[illegible]	[illegible]	[illegible]
2	Dublin,	[illegible]	[illegible]	[illegible]	[illegible]	[illegible]	[illegible]	[illegible]	[illegible]	[illegible]	[illegible]	[illegible]	[illegible]	[illegible]
3	Kildare,	[illegible]	[illegible]	[illegible]	[illegible]	[illegible]	[illegible]	[illegible]	[illegible]	[illegible]	[illegible]	[illegible]	[illegible]	[illegible]
4	Kilkenny,	[illegible]	[illegible]	[illegible]	[illegible]	[illegible]	[illegible]	[illegible]	[illegible]	[illegible]	[illegible]	[illegible]	[illegible]	[illegible]
5	King's,	[illegible]	[illegible]	[illegible]	[illegible]	[illegible]	[illegible]	[illegible]	[illegible]	[illegible]	[illegible]	[illegible]	[illegible]	[illegible]
6	Longford,	[illegible]	[illegible]	[illegible]	[illegible]	[illegible]	[illegible]	[illegible]	[illegible]	[illegible]	[illegible]	[illegible]	[illegible]	[illegible]
7	Louth, and Co. of the Town of Drogheda,	[illegible]	[illegible]	[illegible]	[illegible]	[illegible]	[illegible]	[illegible]	[illegible]	[illegible]	[illegible]	[illegible]	[illegible]	[illegible]
8	Meath,	[illegible]	[illegible]	[illegible]	[illegible]	[illegible]	[illegible]	[illegible]	[illegible]	[illegible]	[illegible]	[illegible]	[illegible]	[illegible]
9	Queen's,	[illegible]	[illegible]	[illegible]	[illegible]	[illegible]	[illegible]	[illegible]	[illegible]	[illegible]	[illegible]	[illegible]	[illegible]	[illegible]
10	Westmeath,	[illegible]	[illegible]	[illegible]	[illegible]	[illegible]	[illegible]	[illegible]	[illegible]	[illegible]	[illegible]	[illegible]	[illegible]	[illegible]

and SPECIAL HOSPITALS; (2), in PUBLIC LUNATIC ASYLUMS; (3), in WORKHOUSES; and (4), at their
NUMBER of INQUESTS in the PROVINCES, COUNTIES, and SUPERINTENDENT
in IRELAND in 1896.

DEATHS.

Constitutional Diseases.					Local Diseases. Diseases of							Violence.				All other Causes	Number of Inquests	PROVINCES and COUNTIES.
[illegible]	[illegible]	[illegible]	[illegible]	[illegible]	[illegible]	[illegible]	[illegible]	[illegible]	[illegible]	[illegible]	[illegible]	[illegible]	[illegible]	[illegible]	[illegible]	[illegible]	[illegible]	
[illegible]	[illegible]	[illegible]	[illegible]	[illegible]	[illegible]	[illegible]	[illegible]	[illegible]	[illegible]	[illegible]	[illegible]	[illegible]	[illegible]	[illegible]	.	[illegible]	[illegible]	IRELAND.
																		PROVINCES
[illegible]	[illegible]	[illegible]	[illegible]	[illegible]	[illegible]	[illegible]	[illegible]	[illegible]	[illegible]	[illegible]	[illegible]	[illegible]	[illegible]	[illegible]	.	[illegible]	[illegible]	LEINSTER.
[illegible]	[illegible]	[illegible]	[illegible]	[illegible]	[illegible]	[illegible]	[illegible]	[illegible]	[illegible]	[illegible]	[illegible]	[illegible]	[illegible]	[illegible]	.	[illegible]	[illegible]	MUNSTER.
[illegible]	[illegible]	[illegible]	[illegible]	[illegible]	[illegible]	[illegible]	[illegible]	[illegible]	[illegible]	[illegible]	[illegible]	[illegible]	[illegible]	[illegible]	.	[illegible]	[illegible]	ULSTER.
[illegible]	[illegible]	[illegible]	[illegible]	[illegible]	[illegible]	[illegible]	[illegible]	[illegible]	[illegible]	[illegible]	[illegible]	[illegible]	[illegible]	[illegible]	.	[illegible]	[illegible]	CONNAUGHT.
OF LEINSTER.																		
[illegible]	[illegible]	[illegible]	[illegible]	[illegible]	[illegible]	[illegible]	[illegible]	[illegible]	[illegible]	[illegible]	[illegible]	[illegible]	[illegible]	[illegible]	.	[illegible]	[illegible]	Carlow.
[illegible]	[illegible]	[illegible]	[illegible]	[illegible]	[illegible]	[illegible]	[illegible]	[illegible]	[illegible]	[illegible]	[illegible]	[illegible]	[illegible]	[illegible]	.	[illegible]	[illegible]	Dublin.
[illegible]	[illegible]	[illegible]	[illegible]	[illegible]	[illegible]	[illegible]	[illegible]	[illegible]	[illegible]	[illegible]	[illegible]	[illegible]	[illegible]	[illegible]	.	[illegible]	[illegible]	Kildare.
[illegible]	[illegible]	[illegible]	[illegible]	[illegible]	[illegible]	[illegible]	[illegible]	[illegible]	[illegible]	[illegible]	[illegible]	[illegible]	[illegible]	[illegible]	-	[illegible]	[illegible]	Kilkenny.
[illegible]	[illegible]	[illegible]	[illegible]	[illegible]	[illegible]	[illegible]	[illegible]	[illegible]	[illegible]	[illegible]	[illegible]	[illegible]	[illegible]	[illegible]	-	[illegible]	[illegible]	King's.
[illegible]	[illegible]	[illegible]	[illegible]	[illegible]	[illegible]	[illegible]	[illegible]	[illegible]	[illegible]	[illegible]	[illegible]	[illegible]	[illegible]	[illegible]	.	[illegible]	[illegible]	Longford.
[illegible]	[illegible]	[illegible]	[illegible]	[illegible]	[illegible]	[illegible]	[illegible]	[illegible]	[illegible]	[illegible]	[illegible]	[illegible]	[illegible]	[illegible]	.	[illegible]	[illegible]	Louth, & Co. of the Town of Drogheda.
[illegible]	[illegible]	[illegible]	[illegible]	[illegible]	[illegible]	[illegible]	[illegible]	[illegible]	[illegible]	[illegible]	[illegible]	[illegible]	[illegible]	[illegible]	.	[illegible]	[illegible]	Meath.
[illegible]	[illegible]	[illegible]	[illegible]	[illegible]	[illegible]	[illegible]	[illegible]	[illegible]	[illegible]	[illegible]	[illegible]	[illegible]	[illegible]	[illegible]	.	[illegible]	[illegible]	Queen's.
[illegible]	[illegible]	[illegible]	[illegible]	[illegible]	[illegible]	[illegible]	[illegible]	[illegible]	[illegible]	[illegible]	[illegible]	[illegible]	[illegible]	[illegible]	.	[illegible]	[illegible]	Westmeath.
[illegible]	[illegible]	[illegible]	[illegible]	[illegible]	[illegible]	[illegible]	[illegible]	[illegible]	[illegible]	[illegible]	[illegible]	[illegible]	[illegible]	[illegible]	-	[illegible]	[illegible]	Wexford.
[illegible]	[illegible]	[illegible]	[illegible]	[illegible]	[illegible]	[illegible]	[illegible]	[illegible]	[illegible]	[illegible]	[illegible]	[illegible]	[illegible]	[illegible]	.	[illegible]	[illegible]	Wicklow.
OF MUNSTER.																		
[illegible]	[illegible]	[illegible]	[illegible]	[illegible]	[illegible]	[illegible]	[illegible]	[illegible]	[illegible]	[illegible]	[illegible]	[illegible]	[illegible]	[illegible]	.	[illegible]	[illegible]	Clare.
[illegible]	[illegible]	[illegible]	[illegible]	[illegible]	[illegible]	[illegible]	[illegible]	[illegible]	[illegible]	[illegible]	[illegible]	[illegible]	[illegible]	[illegible]	.	[illegible]	[illegible]	Cork.
[illegible]	[illegible]	[illegible]	[illegible]	[illegible]	[illegible]	[illegible]	[illegible]	[illegible]	[illegible]	[illegible]	[illegible]	[illegible]	[illegible]	[illegible]	.	[illegible]	[illegible]	Kerry.
[illegible]	[illegible]	[illegible]	[illegible]	[illegible]	[illegible]	[illegible]	[illegible]	[illegible]	[illegible]	[illegible]	[illegible]	[illegible]	[illegible]	[illegible]	.	[illegible]	[illegible]	Limerick.
[illegible]	[illegible]	[illegible]	[illegible]	[illegible]	[illegible]	[illegible]	[illegible]	[illegible]	[illegible]	[illegible]	[illegible]	[illegible]	[illegible]	[illegible]	.	[illegible]	[illegible]	Tipperary.
[illegible]	[illegible]	[illegible]	[illegible]	[illegible]	[illegible]	[illegible]	[illegible]	[illegible]	[illegible]	[illegible]	[illegible]	[illegible]	[illegible]	[illegible]	.	[illegible]	[illegible]	Waterford.
OF ULSTER.																		
[illegible]	[illegible]	[illegible]	[illegible]	[illegible]	[illegible]	[illegible]	[illegible]	[illegible]	[illegible]	[illegible]	[illegible]	[illegible]	[illegible]	[illegible]	.	[illegible]	[illegible]	Antrim.
[illegible]	[illegible]	[illegible]	[illegible]	[illegible]	[illegible]	[illegible]	[illegible]	[illegible]	[illegible]	[illegible]	[illegible]	[illegible]	[illegible]	[illegible]	.	[illegible]	[illegible]	Armagh.
[illegible]	[illegible]	[illegible]	[illegible]	[illegible]	[illegible]	[illegible]	[illegible]	[illegible]	[illegible]	[illegible]	[illegible]	[illegible]	[illegible]	[illegible]	.	[illegible]	[illegible]	Cavan.
[illegible]	[illegible]	[illegible]	[illegible]	[illegible]	[illegible]	[illegible]	[illegible]	[illegible]	[illegible]	[illegible]	[illegible]	[illegible]	[illegible]	[illegible]	.	[illegible]	[illegible]	Donegal.
[illegible]	[illegible]	[illegible]	[illegible]	[illegible]	[illegible]	[illegible]	[illegible]	[illegible]	[illegible]	[illegible]	[illegible]	[illegible]	[illegible]	[illegible]	.	[illegible]	[illegible]	Down.
[illegible]	[illegible]	[illegible]	[illegible]	[illegible]	[illegible]	[illegible]	[illegible]	[illegible]	[illegible]	[illegible]	[illegible]	[illegible]	[illegible]	[illegible]	.	[illegible]	[illegible]	Fermanagh.
[illegible]	[illegible]	[illegible]	[illegible]	[illegible]	[illegible]	[illegible]	[illegible]	[illegible]	[illegible]	[illegible]	[illegible]	[illegible]	[illegible]	[illegible]	.	[illegible]	[illegible]	Londonderry.
[illegible]	[illegible]	[illegible]	[illegible]	[illegible]	[illegible]	[illegible]	[illegible]	[illegible]	[illegible]	[illegible]	[illegible]	[illegible]	[illegible]	[illegible]	.	[illegible]	[illegible]	Monaghan.
[illegible]	[illegible]	[illegible]	[illegible]	[illegible]	[illegible]	[illegible]	[illegible]	[illegible]	[illegible]	[illegible]	[illegible]	[illegible]	[illegible]	[illegible]	.	[illegible]	[illegible]	Tyrone.
OF CONNAUGHT.																		
[illegible]	[illegible]	[illegible]	[illegible]	[illegible]	[illegible]	[illegible]	[illegible]	[illegible]	[illegible]	[illegible]	[illegible]	[illegible]	[illegible]	[illegible]	.	[illegible]	[illegible]	Galway.
[illegible]	[illegible]	[illegible]	[illegible]	[illegible]	[illegible]	[illegible]	[illegible]	[illegible]	[illegible]	[illegible]	[illegible]	[illegible]	[illegible]	[illegible]	.	[illegible]	[illegible]	Leitrim.
[illegible]	[illegible]	[illegible]	[illegible]	[illegible]	[illegible]	[illegible]	[illegible]	[illegible]	[illegible]	[illegible]	[illegible]	[illegible]	[illegible]	[illegible]	.	[illegible]	[illegible]	Mayo.
[illegible]	[illegible]	[illegible]	[illegible]	[illegible]	[illegible]	[illegible]	[illegible]	[illegible]	[illegible]	[illegible]	[illegible]	[illegible]	[illegible]	[illegible]	.	[illegible]	[illegible]	Roscommon.
[illegible]	[illegible]	[illegible]	[illegible]	[illegible]	[illegible]	[illegible]	[illegible]	[illegible]	[illegible]	[illegible]	[illegible]	[illegible]	[illegible]	[illegible]	.	[illegible]	[illegible]	Sligo.

TOTAL NUMBER OF [illegible]

and Special Hospitals; (3), in Public Lunatic Asylums; (2), in Workhouses, and (4), at their Number of Inquests in the Provinces, Counties, and Superintendent in Ireland in 1896—*continued.*

Poor Law Unions arranged Alphabetically.

Deaths																		
Constitutional Diseases					Local Diseases							Violence				All other Causes	Inquests	Superintendent Registrar's Districts or Poor Law Unions
[illegible]	[illegible]	[illegible]	[illegible]	[illegible]	[illegible]	[illegible]	[illegible]	[illegible]	[illegible]	[illegible]	[illegible]	[illegible]	[illegible]	[illegible]	[illegible]	[illegible]	[illegible]	[illegible]
[illegible]	[illegible]	[illegible]	[illegible]	[illegible]	[illegible]	[illegible]	[illegible]	[illegible]	[illegible]	[illegible]	[illegible]	[illegible]	[illegible]	[illegible]	[illegible]	[illegible]	[illegible]	[illegible]
[illegible]	[illegible]	[illegible]	[illegible]	[illegible]	[illegible]	[illegible]	[illegible]	[illegible]	[illegible]	[illegible]	[illegible]	[illegible]	[illegible]	[illegible]	[illegible]	[illegible]	[illegible]	[illegible]
[illegible]	[illegible]	[illegible]	[illegible]	[illegible]	[illegible]	[illegible]	[illegible]	[illegible]	[illegible]	[illegible]	[illegible]	[illegible]	[illegible]	[illegible]	[illegible]	[illegible]	[illegible]	[illegible]
[illegible]	[illegible]	[illegible]	[illegible]	[illegible]	[illegible]	[illegible]	[illegible]	[illegible]	[illegible]	[illegible]	[illegible]	[illegible]	[illegible]	[illegible]	[illegible]	[illegible]	[illegible]	[illegible]

TOTAL NUMBER OF DEATHS.—NUMBER OF PERSONS who died (1), in INFIRMARIES and GENERAL [illegible] OWN HOMES, &c.; NUMBER OF DEATHS from the PRINCIPAL CAUSES; and [illegible] REGISTRARS' DISTRICTS

[illegible] REGISTRARS' DISTRICTS, &c.

SUPERINTENDENT REGISTRARS' DISTRICTS OR POOR LAW UNIONS.	Total Number of Deaths.	[illegible]	[illegible]	[illegible]	[illegible]	[illegible]	[illegible]	[illegible]	[illegible]	[illegible]	[illegible]	[illegible]	[illegible]	[illegible]	[illegible]	[illegible]	[illegible]	[illegible]
[illegible]	[illegible]	[illegible]	[illegible]	[illegible]	[illegible]	[illegible]	[illegible]	[illegible]	[illegible]	[illegible]	[illegible]	[illegible]	[illegible]	[illegible]	[illegible]	[illegible]	[illegible]	[illegible]

and Special Hospitals; (2), in Public Lunatic Asylums; (3), in Workhouses; and (4), as their Number of Inquests in the Provinces, Counties, and Superintendents in Ireland in 1896—*continued*.

Poor Law Unions arranged Alphabetically.

Deaths.

Constitutional Diseases					Local Diseases							Violence				All other Causes	Number of Inquests	Superintendent Registrars' Districts or Poor Law Unions
[illegible]	[illegible]	[illegible]	[illegible]	[illegible]	[illegible]	[illegible]	[illegible]	[illegible]	[illegible]	[illegible]	[illegible]	[illegible]	[illegible]	[illegible]	[illegible]			
[illegible]	[illegible]	[illegible]	[illegible]	[illegible]	[illegible]	[illegible]	[illegible]	[illegible]	[illegible]	[illegible]	[illegible]	[illegible]	[illegible]	[illegible]	[illegible]	[illegible]	[illegible]	[illegible]
[illegible]	[illegible]	[illegible]	[illegible]	[illegible]	[illegible]	[illegible]	[illegible]	[illegible]	[illegible]	[illegible]	[illegible]	[illegible]	[illegible]	[illegible]	[illegible]	[illegible]	[illegible]	[illegible]
[illegible]	[illegible]	[illegible]	[illegible]	[illegible]	[illegible]	[illegible]	[illegible]	[illegible]	[illegible]	[illegible]	[illegible]	[illegible]	[illegible]	[illegible]	[illegible]	[illegible]	[illegible]	[illegible]
[illegible]	[illegible]	[illegible]	[illegible]	[illegible]	[illegible]	[illegible]	[illegible]	[illegible]	[illegible]	[illegible]	[illegible]	[illegible]	[illegible]	[illegible]	[illegible]	[illegible]	[illegible]	[illegible]
[illegible]	[illegible]	[illegible]	[illegible]	[illegible]	[illegible]	[illegible]	[illegible]	[illegible]	[illegible]	[illegible]	[illegible]	[illegible]	[illegible]	[illegible]	[illegible]	[illegible]	[illegible]	[illegible]
[illegible]	[illegible]	[illegible]	[illegible]	[illegible]	[illegible]	[illegible]	[illegible]	[illegible]	[illegible]	[illegible]	[illegible]	[illegible]	[illegible]	[illegible]	[illegible]	[illegible]	[illegible]	[illegible]
[illegible]	[illegible]	[illegible]	[illegible]	[illegible]	[illegible]	[illegible]	[illegible]	[illegible]	[illegible]	[illegible]	[illegible]	[illegible]	[illegible]	[illegible]	[illegible]	[illegible]	[illegible]	[illegible]
[illegible]	[illegible]	[illegible]	[illegible]	[illegible]	[illegible]	[illegible]	[illegible]	[illegible]	[illegible]	[illegible]	[illegible]	[illegible]	[illegible]	[illegible]	[illegible]	[illegible]	[illegible]	[illegible]
[illegible]	[illegible]	[illegible]	[illegible]	[illegible]	[illegible]	[illegible]	[illegible]	[illegible]	[illegible]	[illegible]	[illegible]	[illegible]	[illegible]	[illegible]	[illegible]	[illegible]	[illegible]	[illegible]
[illegible]	[illegible]	[illegible]	[illegible]	[illegible]	[illegible]	[illegible]	[illegible]	[illegible]	[illegible]	[illegible]	[illegible]	[illegible]	[illegible]	[illegible]	[illegible]	[illegible]	[illegible]	[illegible]
[illegible]	[illegible]	[illegible]	[illegible]	[illegible]	[illegible]	[illegible]	[illegible]	[illegible]	[illegible]	[illegible]	[illegible]	[illegible]	[illegible]	[illegible]	[illegible]	[illegible]	[illegible]	[illegible]
[illegible]	[illegible]	[illegible]	[illegible]	[illegible]	[illegible]	[illegible]	[illegible]	[illegible]	[illegible]	[illegible]	[illegible]	[illegible]	[illegible]	[illegible]	[illegible]	[illegible]	[illegible]	[illegible]
[illegible]	[illegible]	[illegible]	[illegible]	[illegible]	[illegible]	[illegible]	[illegible]	[illegible]	[illegible]	[illegible]	[illegible]	[illegible]	[illegible]	[illegible]	[illegible]	[illegible]	[illegible]	[illegible]
[illegible]	[illegible]	[illegible]	[illegible]	[illegible]	[illegible]	[illegible]	[illegible]	[illegible]	[illegible]	[illegible]	[illegible]	[illegible]	[illegible]	[illegible]	[illegible]	[illegible]	[illegible]	[illegible]
[illegible]	[illegible]	[illegible]	[illegible]	[illegible]	[illegible]	[illegible]	[illegible]	[illegible]	[illegible]	[illegible]	[illegible]	[illegible]	[illegible]	[illegible]	[illegible]	[illegible]	[illegible]	[illegible]
[illegible]	[illegible]	[illegible]	[illegible]	[illegible]	[illegible]	[illegible]	[illegible]	[illegible]	[illegible]	[illegible]	[illegible]	[illegible]	[illegible]	[illegible]	[illegible]	[illegible]	[illegible]	[illegible]
[illegible]	[illegible]	[illegible]	[illegible]	[illegible]	[illegible]	[illegible]	[illegible]	[illegible]	[illegible]	[illegible]	[illegible]	[illegible]	[illegible]	[illegible]	[illegible]	[illegible]	[illegible]	[illegible]
[illegible]	[illegible]	[illegible]	[illegible]	[illegible]	[illegible]	[illegible]	[illegible]	[illegible]	[illegible]	[illegible]	[illegible]	[illegible]	[illegible]	[illegible]	[illegible]	[illegible]	[illegible]	[illegible]
[illegible]	[illegible]	[illegible]	[illegible]	[illegible]	[illegible]	[illegible]	[illegible]	[illegible]	[illegible]	[illegible]	[illegible]	[illegible]	[illegible]	[illegible]	[illegible]	[illegible]	[illegible]	[illegible]
[illegible]	[illegible]	[illegible]	[illegible]	[illegible]	[illegible]	[illegible]	[illegible]	[illegible]	[illegible]	[illegible]	[illegible]	[illegible]	[illegible]	[illegible]	[illegible]	[illegible]	[illegible]	[illegible]
[illegible]	[illegible]	[illegible]	[illegible]	[illegible]	[illegible]	[illegible]	[illegible]	[illegible]	[illegible]	[illegible]	[illegible]	[illegible]	[illegible]	[illegible]	[illegible]	[illegible]	[illegible]	[illegible]
[illegible]	[illegible]	[illegible]	[illegible]	[illegible]	[illegible]	[illegible]	[illegible]	[illegible]	[illegible]	[illegible]	[illegible]	[illegible]	[illegible]	[illegible]	[illegible]	[illegible]	[illegible]	[illegible]
[illegible]	[illegible]	[illegible]	[illegible]	[illegible]	[illegible]	[illegible]	[illegible]	[illegible]	[illegible]	[illegible]	[illegible]	[illegible]	[illegible]	[illegible]	[illegible]	[illegible]	[illegible]	[illegible]
[illegible]	[illegible]	[illegible]	[illegible]	[illegible]	[illegible]	[illegible]	[illegible]	[illegible]	[illegible]	[illegible]	[illegible]	[illegible]	[illegible]	[illegible]	[illegible]	[illegible]	[illegible]	[illegible]
[illegible]	[illegible]	[illegible]	[illegible]	[illegible]	[illegible]	[illegible]	[illegible]	[illegible]	[illegible]	[illegible]	[illegible]	[illegible]	[illegible]	[illegible]	[illegible]	[illegible]	[illegible]	[illegible]
[illegible]	[illegible]	[illegible]	[illegible]	[illegible]	[illegible]	[illegible]	[illegible]	[illegible]	[illegible]	[illegible]	[illegible]	[illegible]	[illegible]	[illegible]	[illegible]	[illegible]	[illegible]	[illegible]
[illegible]	[illegible]	[illegible]	[illegible]	[illegible]	[illegible]	[illegible]	[illegible]	[illegible]	[illegible]	[illegible]	[illegible]	[illegible]	[illegible]	[illegible]	[illegible]	[illegible]	[illegible]	[illegible]
[illegible]	[illegible]	[illegible]	[illegible]	[illegible]	[illegible]	[illegible]	[illegible]	[illegible]	[illegible]	[illegible]	[illegible]	[illegible]	[illegible]	[illegible]	[illegible]	[illegible]	[illegible]	[illegible]
[illegible]	[illegible]	[illegible]	[illegible]	[illegible]	[illegible]	[illegible]	[illegible]	[illegible]	[illegible]	[illegible]	[illegible]	[illegible]	[illegible]	[illegible]	[illegible]	[illegible]	[illegible]	[illegible]
[illegible]	[illegible]	[illegible]	[illegible]	[illegible]	[illegible]	[illegible]	[illegible]	[illegible]	[illegible]	[illegible]	[illegible]	[illegible]	[illegible]	[illegible]	[illegible]	[illegible]	[illegible]	[illegible]
[illegible]	[illegible]	[illegible]	[illegible]	[illegible]	[illegible]	[illegible]	[illegible]	[illegible]	[illegible]	[illegible]	[illegible]	[illegible]	[illegible]	[illegible]	[illegible]	[illegible]	[illegible]	[illegible]
[illegible]	[illegible]	[illegible]	[illegible]	[illegible]	[illegible]	[illegible]	[illegible]	[illegible]	[illegible]	[illegible]	[illegible]	[illegible]	[illegible]	[illegible]	[illegible]	[illegible]	[illegible]	[illegible]
[illegible]	[illegible]	[illegible]	[illegible]	[illegible]	[illegible]	[illegible]	[illegible]	[illegible]	[illegible]	[illegible]	[illegible]	[illegible]	[illegible]	[illegible]	[illegible]	[illegible]	[illegible]	[illegible]
[illegible]	[illegible]	[illegible]	[illegible]	[illegible]	[illegible]	[illegible]	[illegible]	[illegible]	[illegible]	[illegible]	[illegible]	[illegible]	[illegible]	[illegible]	[illegible]	[illegible]	[illegible]	[illegible]
[illegible]	[illegible]	[illegible]	[illegible]	[illegible]	[illegible]	[illegible]	[illegible]	[illegible]	[illegible]	[illegible]	[illegible]	[illegible]	[illegible]	[illegible]	[illegible]	[illegible]	[illegible]	[illegible]
[illegible]	[illegible]	[illegible]	[illegible]	[illegible]	[illegible]	[illegible]	[illegible]	[illegible]	[illegible]	[illegible]	[illegible]	[illegible]	[illegible]	[illegible]	[illegible]	[illegible]	[illegible]	[illegible]
[illegible]	[illegible]	[illegible]	[illegible]	[illegible]	[illegible]	[illegible]	[illegible]	[illegible]	[illegible]	[illegible]	[illegible]	[illegible]	[illegible]	[illegible]	[illegible]	[illegible]	[illegible]	[illegible]
[illegible]	[illegible]	[illegible]	[illegible]	[illegible]	[illegible]	[illegible]	[illegible]	[illegible]	[illegible]	[illegible]	[illegible]	[illegible]	[illegible]	[illegible]	[illegible]	[illegible]	[illegible]	[illegible]
[illegible]	[illegible]	[illegible]	[illegible]	[illegible]	[illegible]	[illegible]	[illegible]	[illegible]	[illegible]	[illegible]	[illegible]	[illegible]	[illegible]	[illegible]	[illegible]	[illegible]	[illegible]	[illegible]
[illegible]	[illegible]	[illegible]	[illegible]	[illegible]	[illegible]	[illegible]	[illegible]	[illegible]	[illegible]	[illegible]	[illegible]	[illegible]	[illegible]	[illegible]	[illegible]	[illegible]	[illegible]	[illegible]
[illegible]	[illegible]	[illegible]	[illegible]	[illegible]	[illegible]	[illegible]	[illegible]	[illegible]	[illegible]	[illegible]	[illegible]	[illegible]	[illegible]	[illegible]	[illegible]	[illegible]	[illegible]	[illegible]
[illegible]	[illegible]	[illegible]	[illegible]	[illegible]	[illegible]	[illegible]	[illegible]	[illegible]	[illegible]	[illegible]	[illegible]	[illegible]	[illegible]	[illegible]	[illegible]	[illegible]	[illegible]	[illegible]
[illegible]	[illegible]	[illegible]	[illegible]	[illegible]	[illegible]	[illegible]	[illegible]	[illegible]	[illegible]	[illegible]	[illegible]	[illegible]	[illegible]	[illegible]	[illegible]	[illegible]	[illegible]	[illegible]
[illegible]	[illegible]	[illegible]	[illegible]	[illegible]	[illegible]	[illegible]	[illegible]	[illegible]	[illegible]	[illegible]	[illegible]	[illegible]	[illegible]	[illegible]	[illegible]	[illegible]	[illegible]	[illegible]

DEATHS.—NUMBER of PERSONS who died (1), in INSTITUTIONS and [illegible] ; NUMBER of DEATHS from the PRINCIPAL CAUSES ; and [illegible] REGISTRARS' DISTRICTS

SUPERINTENDENT REGISTRARS' DISTRICTS, OR

Total Number of Deaths	Number of Persons who died: In Infirmaries and Hospitals [illegible]	In Prisons, Constabulary Barracks	In Workhouses and Workhouse Hospitals	In Other Public Institutions, &c.	Deaths from the Principal Diseases: Small Pox	Measles	Scarlatina	Typhus	[illegible]	[illegible]	[illegible]	[illegible]	[illegible]	[illegible]	[illegible]	[illegible]	[illegible]
[illegible]	[illegible]	[illegible]	[illegible]	[illegible]	[illegible]	[illegible]	[illegible]	[illegible]	[illegible]	[illegible]	[illegible]	[illegible]	[illegible]	[illegible]	[illegible]	[illegible]	[illegible]
[illegible]	[illegible]	[illegible]	[illegible]	[illegible]	[illegible]	[illegible]	[illegible]	[illegible]	[illegible]	[illegible]	[illegible]	[illegible]	[illegible]	[illegible]	[illegible]	[illegible]	[illegible]
[illegible]	[illegible]	[illegible]	[illegible]	[illegible]	[illegible]	[illegible]	[illegible]	[illegible]	[illegible]	[illegible]	[illegible]	[illegible]	[illegible]	[illegible]	[illegible]	[illegible]	[illegible]
[illegible]	[illegible]	[illegible]	[illegible]	[illegible]	[illegible]	[illegible]	[illegible]	[illegible]	[illegible]	[illegible]	[illegible]	[illegible]	[illegible]	[illegible]	[illegible]	[illegible]	[illegible]
[illegible]	[illegible]	[illegible]	[illegible]	[illegible]	[illegible]	[illegible]	[illegible]	[illegible]	[illegible]	[illegible]	[illegible]	[illegible]	[illegible]	[illegible]	[illegible]	[illegible]	[illegible]
[illegible]	[illegible]	[illegible]	[illegible]	[illegible]	[illegible]	[illegible]	[illegible]	[illegible]	[illegible]	[illegible]	[illegible]	[illegible]	[illegible]	[illegible]	[illegible]	[illegible]	[illegible]
[illegible]	[illegible]	[illegible]	[illegible]	[illegible]	[illegible]	[illegible]	[illegible]	[illegible]	[illegible]	[illegible]	[illegible]	[illegible]	[illegible]	[illegible]	[illegible]	[illegible]	[illegible]
[illegible]	[illegible]	[illegible]	[illegible]	[illegible]	[illegible]	[illegible]	[illegible]	[illegible]	[illegible]	[illegible]	[illegible]	[illegible]	[illegible]	[illegible]	[illegible]	[illegible]	[illegible]
[illegible]	[illegible]	[illegible]	[illegible]	[illegible]	[illegible]	[illegible]	[illegible]	[illegible]	[illegible]	[illegible]	[illegible]	[illegible]	[illegible]	[illegible]	[illegible]	[illegible]	[illegible]
[illegible]	[illegible]	[illegible]	[illegible]	[illegible]	[illegible]	[illegible]	[illegible]	[illegible]	[illegible]	[illegible]	[illegible]	[illegible]	[illegible]	[illegible]	[illegible]	[illegible]	[illegible]

and Special Hospitals; (2), in Public Lunatic Asylums; (3), in Workhouses; and (4), at their
Number of Lunatics in the Provinces, Counties, and Superintendent
in Ireland in 1896—continued.

Poor Law Unions arranged Alphabetically.

[illegible]	[illegible]	[illegible]	[illegible]	[illegible]	[illegible]	[illegible]	[illegible]	[illegible]	[illegible]	[illegible]	[illegible]	[illegible]	[illegible]	[illegible]	[illegible]	[illegible]	[illegible]	[illegible]
[illegible]	[illegible]	[illegible]	[illegible]	[illegible]	[illegible]	[illegible]	[illegible]	[illegible]	[illegible]	[illegible]	[illegible]	[illegible]	[illegible]	[illegible]	[illegible]	[illegible]	[illegible]	[illegible]
[illegible]	[illegible]	[illegible]	[illegible]	[illegible]	[illegible]	[illegible]	[illegible]	[illegible]	[illegible]	[illegible]	[illegible]	[illegible]	[illegible]	[illegible]	[illegible]	[illegible]	[illegible]	[illegible]
[illegible]	[illegible]	[illegible]	[illegible]	[illegible]	[illegible]	[illegible]	[illegible]	[illegible]	[illegible]	[illegible]	[illegible]	[illegible]	[illegible]	[illegible]	[illegible]	[illegible]	[illegible]	[illegible]
[illegible]	[illegible]	[illegible]	[illegible]	[illegible]	[illegible]	[illegible]	[illegible]	[illegible]	[illegible]	[illegible]	[illegible]	[illegible]	[illegible]	[illegible]	[illegible]	[illegible]	[illegible]	[illegible]

TOTAL NUMBER OF DEATHS.—NUMBER of PERSONS who died (1), in INFIRMARIES and GENERAL ... OWN HOMES, &c.; NUMBER of DEATHS from the PRINCIPAL CAUSES; and ... REGISTRARS' DISTRICTS

SUPERINTENDENT REGISTRARS' DISTRICTS, OR

[illegible]	[illegible]	[illegible]	[illegible]	[illegible]	[illegible]	[illegible]	[illegible]	[illegible]	[illegible]	[illegible]	[illegible]	[illegible]	[illegible]	[illegible]	[illegible]	[illegible]	[illegible]
[illegible]	[illegible]	[illegible]	[illegible]	[illegible]	[illegible]	[illegible]	[illegible]	[illegible]	[illegible]	[illegible]	[illegible]	[illegible]	[illegible]	[illegible]	[illegible]	[illegible]	[illegible]
[illegible]	[illegible]	[illegible]	[illegible]	[illegible]	[illegible]	[illegible]	[illegible]	[illegible]	[illegible]	[illegible]	[illegible]	[illegible]	[illegible]	[illegible]	[illegible]	[illegible]	[illegible]
[illegible]	[illegible]	[illegible]	[illegible]	[illegible]	[illegible]	[illegible]	[illegible]	[illegible]	[illegible]	[illegible]	[illegible]	[illegible]	[illegible]	[illegible]	[illegible]	[illegible]	[illegible]
[illegible]	[illegible]	[illegible]	[illegible]	[illegible]	[illegible]	[illegible]	[illegible]	[illegible]	[illegible]	[illegible]	[illegible]	[illegible]	[illegible]	[illegible]	[illegible]	[illegible]	[illegible]
[illegible]	[illegible]	[illegible]	[illegible]	[illegible]	[illegible]	[illegible]	[illegible]	[illegible]	[illegible]	[illegible]	[illegible]	[illegible]	[illegible]	[illegible]	[illegible]	[illegible]	[illegible]
[illegible]	[illegible]	[illegible]	[illegible]	[illegible]	[illegible]	[illegible]	[illegible]	[illegible]	[illegible]	[illegible]	[illegible]	[illegible]	[illegible]	[illegible]	[illegible]	[illegible]	[illegible]
[illegible]	[illegible]	[illegible]	[illegible]	[illegible]	[illegible]	[illegible]	[illegible]	[illegible]	[illegible]	[illegible]	[illegible]	[illegible]	[illegible]	[illegible]	[illegible]	[illegible]	[illegible]
[illegible]	[illegible]	[illegible]	[illegible]	[illegible]	[illegible]	[illegible]	[illegible]	[illegible]	[illegible]	[illegible]	[illegible]	[illegible]	[illegible]	[illegible]	[illegible]	[illegible]	[illegible]
[illegible]	[illegible]	[illegible]	[illegible]	[illegible]	[illegible]	[illegible]	[illegible]	[illegible]	[illegible]	[illegible]	[illegible]	[illegible]	[illegible]	[illegible]	[illegible]	[illegible]	[illegible]
[illegible]	[illegible]	[illegible]	[illegible]	[illegible]	[illegible]	[illegible]	[illegible]	[illegible]	[illegible]	[illegible]	[illegible]	[illegible]	[illegible]	[illegible]	[illegible]	[illegible]	[illegible]
[illegible]	[illegible]	[illegible]	[illegible]	[illegible]	[illegible]	[illegible]	[illegible]	[illegible]	[illegible]	[illegible]	[illegible]	[illegible]	[illegible]	[illegible]	[illegible]	[illegible]	[illegible]
[illegible]	[illegible]	[illegible]	[illegible]	[illegible]	[illegible]	[illegible]	[illegible]	[illegible]	[illegible]	[illegible]	[illegible]	[illegible]	[illegible]	[illegible]	[illegible]	[illegible]	[illegible]
[illegible]	[illegible]	[illegible]	[illegible]	[illegible]	[illegible]	[illegible]	[illegible]	[illegible]	[illegible]	[illegible]	[illegible]	[illegible]	[illegible]	[illegible]	[illegible]	[illegible]	[illegible]
[illegible]	[illegible]	[illegible]	[illegible]	[illegible]	[illegible]	[illegible]	[illegible]	[illegible]	[illegible]	[illegible]	[illegible]	[illegible]	[illegible]	[illegible]	[illegible]	[illegible]	[illegible]
[illegible]	[illegible]	[illegible]	[illegible]	[illegible]	[illegible]	[illegible]	[illegible]	[illegible]	[illegible]	[illegible]	[illegible]	[illegible]	[illegible]	[illegible]	[illegible]	[illegible]	[illegible]
[illegible]	[illegible]	[illegible]	[illegible]	[illegible]	[illegible]	[illegible]	[illegible]	[illegible]	[illegible]	[illegible]	[illegible]	[illegible]	[illegible]	[illegible]	[illegible]	[illegible]	[illegible]
[illegible]	[illegible]	[illegible]	[illegible]	[illegible]	[illegible]	[illegible]	[illegible]	[illegible]	[illegible]	[illegible]	[illegible]	[illegible]	[illegible]	[illegible]	[illegible]	[illegible]	[illegible]
[illegible]	[illegible]	[illegible]	[illegible]	[illegible]	[illegible]	[illegible]	[illegible]	[illegible]	[illegible]	[illegible]	[illegible]	[illegible]	[illegible]	[illegible]	[illegible]	[illegible]	[illegible]
[illegible]	[illegible]	[illegible]	[illegible]	[illegible]	[illegible]	[illegible]	[illegible]	[illegible]	[illegible]	[illegible]	[illegible]	[illegible]	[illegible]	[illegible]	[illegible]	[illegible]	[illegible]
[illegible]	[illegible]	[illegible]	[illegible]	[illegible]	[illegible]	[illegible]	[illegible]	[illegible]	[illegible]	[illegible]	[illegible]	[illegible]	[illegible]	[illegible]	[illegible]	[illegible]	[illegible]
[illegible]	[illegible]	[illegible]	[illegible]	[illegible]	[illegible]	[illegible]	[illegible]	[illegible]	[illegible]	[illegible]	[illegible]	[illegible]	[illegible]	[illegible]	[illegible]	[illegible]	[illegible]
[illegible]	[illegible]	[illegible]	[illegible]	[illegible]	[illegible]	[illegible]	[illegible]	[illegible]	[illegible]	[illegible]	[illegible]	[illegible]	[illegible]	[illegible]	[illegible]	[illegible]	[illegible]

and Special Hospitals; (2), in Public Lunatic Asylums; (3), in Workhouses; and (4), at their Number of Inquests in the Provinces, Counties, and Superintendent In Ireland in 1896—*continued.*

Poor Law Unions arranged Alphabetically.

[illegible]	[illegible]	[illegible]	[illegible]	[illegible]	[illegible]	[illegible]	[illegible]	[illegible]	[illegible]	[illegible]	[illegible]	[illegible]	[illegible]	[illegible]	[illegible]	[illegible]	[illegible]	[illegible]	Superintendent Registrars' Districts or Poor Law Unions.
[illegible]	[illegible]	[illegible]	[illegible]	[illegible]	[illegible]	[illegible]	[illegible]	[illegible]	[illegible]	[illegible]	[illegible]	[illegible]	[illegible]	[illegible]	[illegible]	[illegible]	[illegible]	[illegible]	[illegible]
[illegible]	[illegible]	[illegible]	[illegible]	[illegible]	[illegible]	[illegible]	[illegible]	[illegible]	[illegible]	[illegible]	[illegible]	[illegible]	[illegible]	[illegible]	[illegible]	[illegible]	[illegible]	[illegible]	[illegible]
[illegible]	[illegible]	[illegible]	[illegible]	[illegible]	[illegible]	[illegible]	[illegible]	[illegible]	[illegible]	[illegible]	[illegible]	[illegible]	[illegible]	[illegible]	[illegible]	[illegible]	[illegible]	[illegible]	[illegible]
[illegible]	[illegible]	[illegible]	[illegible]	[illegible]	[illegible]	[illegible]	[illegible]	[illegible]	[illegible]	[illegible]	[illegible]	[illegible]	[illegible]	[illegible]	[illegible]	[illegible]	[illegible]	[illegible]	[illegible]
[illegible]	[illegible]	[illegible]	[illegible]	[illegible]	[illegible]	[illegible]	[illegible]	[illegible]	[illegible]	[illegible]	[illegible]	[illegible]	[illegible]	[illegible]	[illegible]	[illegible]	[illegible]	[illegible]	[illegible]
[illegible]	[illegible]	[illegible]	[illegible]	[illegible]	[illegible]	[illegible]	[illegible]	[illegible]	[illegible]	[illegible]	[illegible]	[illegible]	[illegible]	[illegible]	[illegible]	[illegible]	[illegible]	[illegible]	[illegible]
[illegible]	[illegible]	[illegible]	[illegible]	[illegible]	[illegible]	[illegible]	[illegible]	[illegible]	[illegible]	[illegible]	[illegible]	[illegible]	[illegible]	[illegible]	[illegible]	[illegible]	[illegible]	[illegible]	[illegible]
[illegible]	[illegible]	[illegible]	[illegible]	[illegible]	[illegible]	[illegible]	[illegible]	[illegible]	[illegible]	[illegible]	[illegible]	[illegible]	[illegible]	[illegible]	[illegible]	[illegible]	[illegible]	[illegible]	[illegible]
[illegible]	[illegible]	[illegible]	[illegible]	[illegible]	[illegible]	[illegible]	[illegible]	[illegible]	[illegible]	[illegible]	[illegible]	[illegible]	[illegible]	[illegible]	[illegible]	[illegible]	[illegible]	[illegible]	[illegible]
[illegible]	[illegible]	[illegible]	[illegible]	[illegible]	[illegible]	[illegible]	[illegible]	[illegible]	[illegible]	[illegible]	[illegible]	[illegible]	[illegible]	[illegible]	[illegible]	[illegible]	[illegible]	[illegible]	[illegible]
[illegible]	[illegible]	[illegible]	[illegible]	[illegible]	[illegible]	[illegible]	[illegible]	[illegible]	[illegible]	[illegible]	[illegible]	[illegible]	[illegible]	[illegible]	[illegible]	[illegible]	[illegible]	[illegible]	[illegible]
[illegible]	[illegible]	[illegible]	[illegible]	[illegible]	[illegible]	[illegible]	[illegible]	[illegible]	[illegible]	[illegible]	[illegible]	[illegible]	[illegible]	[illegible]	[illegible]	[illegible]	[illegible]	[illegible]	[illegible]
[illegible]	[illegible]	[illegible]	[illegible]	[illegible]	[illegible]	[illegible]	[illegible]	[illegible]	[illegible]	[illegible]	[illegible]	[illegible]	[illegible]	[illegible]	[illegible]	[illegible]	[illegible]	[illegible]	[illegible]
[illegible]	[illegible]	[illegible]	[illegible]	[illegible]	[illegible]	[illegible]	[illegible]	[illegible]	[illegible]	[illegible]	[illegible]	[illegible]	[illegible]	[illegible]	[illegible]	[illegible]	[illegible]	[illegible]	[illegible]
[illegible]	[illegible]	[illegible]	[illegible]	[illegible]	[illegible]	[illegible]	[illegible]	[illegible]	[illegible]	[illegible]	[illegible]	[illegible]	[illegible]	[illegible]	[illegible]	[illegible]	[illegible]	[illegible]	[illegible]
[illegible]	[illegible]	[illegible]	[illegible]	[illegible]	[illegible]	[illegible]	[illegible]	[illegible]	[illegible]	[illegible]	[illegible]	[illegible]	[illegible]	[illegible]	[illegible]	[illegible]	[illegible]	[illegible]	[illegible]
[illegible]	[illegible]	[illegible]	[illegible]	[illegible]	[illegible]	[illegible]	[illegible]	[illegible]	[illegible]	[illegible]	[illegible]	[illegible]	[illegible]	[illegible]	[illegible]	[illegible]	[illegible]	[illegible]	[illegible]
[illegible]	[illegible]	[illegible]	[illegible]	[illegible]	[illegible]	[illegible]	[illegible]	[illegible]	[illegible]	[illegible]	[illegible]	[illegible]	[illegible]	[illegible]	[illegible]	[illegible]	[illegible]	[illegible]	[illegible]
[illegible]	[illegible]	[illegible]	[illegible]	[illegible]	[illegible]	[illegible]	[illegible]	[illegible]	[illegible]	[illegible]	[illegible]	[illegible]	[illegible]	[illegible]	[illegible]	[illegible]	[illegible]	[illegible]	[illegible]
[illegible]	[illegible]	[illegible]	[illegible]	[illegible]	[illegible]	[illegible]	[illegible]	[illegible]	[illegible]	[illegible]	[illegible]	[illegible]	[illegible]	[illegible]	[illegible]	[illegible]	[illegible]	[illegible]	[illegible]
[illegible]	[illegible]	[illegible]	[illegible]	[illegible]	[illegible]	[illegible]	[illegible]	[illegible]	[illegible]	[illegible]	[illegible]	[illegible]	[illegible]	[illegible]	[illegible]	[illegible]	[illegible]	[illegible]	[illegible]
[illegible]	[illegible]	[illegible]	[illegible]	[illegible]	[illegible]	[illegible]	[illegible]	[illegible]	[illegible]	[illegible]	[illegible]	[illegible]	[illegible]	[illegible]	[illegible]	[illegible]	[illegible]	[illegible]	[illegible]

POPULATION in 1891; TOTAL NUMBER of DEATHS in the YEAR 1898—NUMBER of PERSONS who died (B), in WORKHOUSES; and (4), at their OWN HOMES, &c.; NUMBER of DEATHS from the and the respective REGISTRATION DISTRICTS in which the PRINCIPAL [illegible] 1891 [illegible] are situated; with CORRESPONDING DETAILS for

No.	Registration Districts, &c.	Towns [illegible]	Population [illegible] in 1891	Total Number of Deaths in 1898	Deaths of Persons who died: In Hospitals [illegible]	In Public Lunatic Asylums	In Workhouses [illegible]	At their own Homes, &c.	[illegible]	[illegible]	[illegible]	[illegible]	[illegible]	[illegible]	[illegible]	[illegible]	[illegible]	[illegible]
	Province of LEINSTER.																	
1	[illegible]	[illegible]	[illegible]	[illegible]	[illegible]	[illegible]	[illegible]	[illegible]	[illegible]	[illegible]	[illegible]	[illegible]	[illegible]	[illegible]	[illegible]	[illegible]	[illegible]	[illegible]
2	Dublin Registration District	[illegible]	[illegible]	[illegible]	[illegible]	[illegible]	[illegible]	[illegible]	[illegible]	[illegible]	[illegible]	[illegible]	[illegible]	[illegible]	[illegible]	[illegible]	[illegible]	[illegible]
3	Drogheda	[illegible]	[illegible]	[illegible]	[illegible]	[illegible]	[illegible]	[illegible]	[illegible]	[illegible]	[illegible]	[illegible]	[illegible]	[illegible]	[illegible]	[illegible]	[illegible]	[illegible]
4	Kilkenny	Kilkenny	[illegible]	[illegible]	[illegible]	[illegible]	[illegible]	[illegible]	[illegible]	[illegible]	[illegible]	[illegible]	[illegible]	[illegible]	[illegible]	[illegible]	[illegible]	[illegible]
5	Wexford	Wexford	[illegible]	[illegible]	[illegible]	[illegible]	[illegible]	[illegible]	[illegible]	[illegible]	[illegible]	[illegible]	[illegible]	[illegible]	[illegible]	[illegible]	[illegible]	[illegible]
6	Total of [illegible] Registration Districts		[illegible]	[illegible]	[illegible]	[illegible]	[illegible]	[illegible]	[illegible]	[illegible]	[illegible]	[illegible]	[illegible]	[illegible]	[illegible]	[illegible]	[illegible]	[illegible]
7	Remaining portion of Province		[illegible]	[illegible]	[illegible]	[illegible]	[illegible]	[illegible]	[illegible]	[illegible]	[illegible]	[illegible]	[illegible]	[illegible]	[illegible]	[illegible]	[illegible]	[illegible]
8	Total, Leinster		[illegible]	[illegible]	[illegible]	[illegible]	[illegible]	[illegible]	[illegible]	[illegible]	[illegible]	[illegible]	[illegible]	[illegible]	[illegible]	[illegible]	[illegible]	[illegible]
	Province of MUNSTER.																	
9	Cork [illegible]	Cork	[illegible]	[illegible]	[illegible]	[illegible]	[illegible]	[illegible]	[illegible]	[illegible]	[illegible]	[illegible]	[illegible]	[illegible]	[illegible]	[illegible]	[illegible]	[illegible]
10	Limerick [illegible]	Limerick	[illegible]	[illegible]	[illegible]	[illegible]	[illegible]	[illegible]	[illegible]	[illegible]	[illegible]	[illegible]	[illegible]	[illegible]	[illegible]	[illegible]	[illegible]	[illegible]
11	Waterford [illegible]	Waterford	[illegible]	[illegible]	[illegible]	[illegible]	[illegible]	[illegible]	[illegible]	[illegible]	[illegible]	[illegible]	[illegible]	[illegible]	[illegible]	[illegible]	[illegible]	[illegible]
12	Total of [illegible] Registration Districts		[illegible]	[illegible]	[illegible]	[illegible]	[illegible]	[illegible]	[illegible]	[illegible]	[illegible]	[illegible]	[illegible]	[illegible]	[illegible]	[illegible]	[illegible]	[illegible]
13	Remaining portion of Province		[illegible]	[illegible]	[illegible]	[illegible]	[illegible]	[illegible]	[illegible]	[illegible]	[illegible]	[illegible]	[illegible]	[illegible]	[illegible]	[illegible]	[illegible]	[illegible]
14	Total, Munster		[illegible]	[illegible]	[illegible]	[illegible]	[illegible]	[illegible]	[illegible]	[illegible]	[illegible]	[illegible]	[illegible]	[illegible]	[illegible]	[illegible]	[illegible]	[illegible]
	Province of ULSTER.																	
15	Armagh	Armagh	[illegible]	[illegible]	[illegible]	[illegible]	[illegible]	[illegible]	[illegible]	[illegible]	[illegible]	[illegible]	[illegible]	[illegible]	[illegible]	[illegible]	[illegible]	[illegible]
16	Belfast [illegible]	Belfast	[illegible]	[illegible]	[illegible]	[illegible]	[illegible]	[illegible]	[illegible]	[illegible]	[illegible]	[illegible]	[illegible]	[illegible]	[illegible]	[illegible]	[illegible]	[illegible]
17	[illegible]	[illegible]	[illegible]	[illegible]	[illegible]	[illegible]	[illegible]	[illegible]	[illegible]	[illegible]	[illegible]	[illegible]	[illegible]	[illegible]	[illegible]	[illegible]	[illegible]	[illegible]
18	Londonderry [illegible]	Londonderry	[illegible]	[illegible]	[illegible]	[illegible]	[illegible]	[illegible]	[illegible]	[illegible]	[illegible]	[illegible]	[illegible]	[illegible]	[illegible]	[illegible]	[illegible]	[illegible]
19	Lurgan [illegible]	Lurgan	[illegible]	[illegible]	[illegible]	[illegible]	[illegible]	[illegible]	[illegible]	[illegible]	[illegible]	[illegible]	[illegible]	[illegible]	[illegible]	[illegible]	[illegible]	[illegible]
20	Newry [illegible]	Newry	[illegible]	[illegible]	[illegible]	[illegible]	[illegible]	[illegible]	[illegible]	[illegible]	[illegible]	[illegible]	[illegible]	[illegible]	[illegible]	[illegible]	[illegible]	[illegible]
21	Total of [illegible] Registration Districts		[illegible]	[illegible]	[illegible]	[illegible]	[illegible]	[illegible]	[illegible]	[illegible]	[illegible]	[illegible]	[illegible]	[illegible]	[illegible]	[illegible]	[illegible]	[illegible]
22	Remaining portion of Province		[illegible]	[illegible]	[illegible]	[illegible]	[illegible]	[illegible]	[illegible]	[illegible]	[illegible]	[illegible]	[illegible]	[illegible]	[illegible]	[illegible]	[illegible]	[illegible]
23	Total, Ulster		[illegible]	[illegible]	[illegible]	[illegible]	[illegible]	[illegible]	[illegible]	[illegible]	[illegible]	[illegible]	[illegible]	[illegible]	[illegible]	[illegible]	[illegible]	[illegible]
	Province of CONNAUGHT.																	
24	Galway [illegible]	Galway	[illegible]	[illegible]	[illegible]	[illegible]	[illegible]	[illegible]	[illegible]	[illegible]	[illegible]	[illegible]	[illegible]	[illegible]	[illegible]	[illegible]	[illegible]	[illegible]
25	Sligo [illegible]	Sligo	[illegible]	[illegible]	[illegible]	[illegible]	[illegible]	[illegible]	[illegible]	[illegible]	[illegible]	[illegible]	[illegible]	[illegible]	[illegible]	[illegible]	[illegible]	[illegible]
26	Total of [illegible] Registration Districts		[illegible]	[illegible]	[illegible]	[illegible]	[illegible]	[illegible]	[illegible]	[illegible]	[illegible]	[illegible]	[illegible]	[illegible]	[illegible]	[illegible]	[illegible]	[illegible]
27	Remaining portion of Province		[illegible]	[illegible]	[illegible]	[illegible]	[illegible]	[illegible]	[illegible]	[illegible]	[illegible]	[illegible]	[illegible]	[illegible]	[illegible]	[illegible]	[illegible]	[illegible]
28	Total, Connaught		[illegible]	[illegible]	[illegible]	[illegible]	[illegible]	[illegible]	[illegible]	[illegible]	[illegible]	[illegible]	[illegible]	[illegible]	[illegible]	[illegible]	[illegible]	[illegible]
29	Ireland	[illegible] Registration Districts	[illegible]	[illegible]	[illegible]	[illegible]	[illegible]	[illegible]	[illegible]	[illegible]	[illegible]	[illegible]	[illegible]	[illegible]	[illegible]	[illegible]	[illegible]	[illegible]
30		Remaining portion of the Country	[illegible]	[illegible]	[illegible]	[illegible]	[illegible]	[illegible]	[illegible]	[illegible]	[illegible]	[illegible]	[illegible]	[illegible]	[illegible]	[illegible]	[illegible]	[illegible]
31		Total	[illegible]	[illegible]	[illegible]	[illegible]	[illegible]	[illegible]	[illegible]	[illegible]	[illegible]	[illegible]	[illegible]	[illegible]	[illegible]	[illegible]	[illegible]	[illegible]

(1), in Infirmaries and General and Special Hospitals; (2), in Public Lunatic Asylums; Principal Causes; and Number of Inquests; in the Dublin Registration District Urban Sanitary Districts (those with a Population of 10,000 or upwards, in the remaining portion of each Province.

DEATHS. Diseases.			Constitutional Diseases.						Local Diseases.								Violence.				Inquests	No.
[illegible]	[illegible]	[illegible]	[illegible]	[illegible]	[illegible]	[illegible]	[illegible]	[illegible]	[illegible]	[illegible]	[illegible]	[illegible]	[illegible]	[illegible]	[illegible]	[illegible]	[illegible]	[illegible]	[illegible]	[illegible]	[illegible]	[illegible]
[illegible]	[illegible]	[illegible]	[illegible]	[illegible]	[illegible]	[illegible]	[illegible]	[illegible]	[illegible]	[illegible]	[illegible]	[illegible]	[illegible]	[illegible]	[illegible]	[illegible]	[illegible]	[illegible]	[illegible]	[illegible]	[illegible]	[illegible]
[illegible]	[illegible]	[illegible]	[illegible]	[illegible]	[illegible]	[illegible]	[illegible]	[illegible]	[illegible]	[illegible]	[illegible]	[illegible]	[illegible]	[illegible]	[illegible]	[illegible]	[illegible]	[illegible]	[illegible]	[illegible]	[illegible]	[illegible]
[illegible]	[illegible]	[illegible]	[illegible]	[illegible]	[illegible]	[illegible]	[illegible]	[illegible]	[illegible]	[illegible]	[illegible]	[illegible]	[illegible]	[illegible]	[illegible]	[illegible]	[illegible]	[illegible]	[illegible]	[illegible]	[illegible]	[illegible]
[illegible]	[illegible]	[illegible]	[illegible]	[illegible]	[illegible]	[illegible]	[illegible]	[illegible]	[illegible]	[illegible]	[illegible]	[illegible]	[illegible]	[illegible]	[illegible]	[illegible]	[illegible]	[illegible]	[illegible]	[illegible]	[illegible]	[illegible]
[illegible]	[illegible]	[illegible]	[illegible]	[illegible]	[illegible]	[illegible]	[illegible]	[illegible]	[illegible]	[illegible]	[illegible]	[illegible]	[illegible]	[illegible]	[illegible]	[illegible]	[illegible]	[illegible]	[illegible]	[illegible]	[illegible]	[illegible]
[illegible]	[illegible]	[illegible]	[illegible]	[illegible]	[illegible]	[illegible]	[illegible]	[illegible]	[illegible]	[illegible]	[illegible]	[illegible]	[illegible]	[illegible]	[illegible]	[illegible]	[illegible]	[illegible]	[illegible]	[illegible]	[illegible]	[illegible]
[illegible]	[illegible]	[illegible]	[illegible]	[illegible]	[illegible]	[illegible]	[illegible]	[illegible]	[illegible]	[illegible]	[illegible]	[illegible]	[illegible]	[illegible]	[illegible]	[illegible]	[illegible]	[illegible]	[illegible]	[illegible]	[illegible]	[illegible]

TABLE showing the Monthly and Yearly Rainfall at Dublin during the Twenty-one Years 1876 to 1896, inclusive; with the Means for the Twenty Years 1876 to 1895.

Year.	January.	February.	March.	April.	May.	June.	July.	August.	September.	October.	November.	December.	Total for Year.
	Inches.	Inches.	Inches.	Inches.	Inches.	Inches.	Inches.	Inches.	Inches.	Inches.	Inches.	Inches.	Inches.
1876,	[illegible]	[illegible]	[illegible]	[illegible]	[illegible]	[illegible]	[illegible]	[illegible]	[illegible]	[illegible]	[illegible]	[illegible]	[illegible]
1877,	[illegible]	[illegible]	[illegible]	[illegible]	[illegible]	[illegible]	[illegible]	[illegible]	[illegible]	[illegible]	[illegible]	[illegible]	[illegible]
[illegible]	[illegible]	[illegible]	[illegible]	[illegible]	[illegible]	[illegible]	[illegible]	[illegible]	[illegible]	[illegible]	[illegible]	[illegible]	[illegible]
[illegible]	[illegible]	[illegible]	[illegible]	[illegible]	[illegible]	[illegible]	[illegible]	[illegible]	[illegible]	[illegible]	[illegible]	[illegible]	[illegible]
[illegible]	[illegible]	[illegible]	[illegible]	[illegible]	[illegible]	[illegible]	[illegible]	[illegible]	[illegible]	[illegible]	[illegible]	[illegible]	[illegible]
[illegible]	[illegible]	[illegible]	[illegible]	[illegible]	[illegible]	[illegible]	[illegible]	[illegible]	[illegible]	[illegible]	[illegible]	[illegible]	[illegible]
[illegible]	[illegible]	[illegible]	[illegible]	[illegible]	[illegible]	[illegible]	[illegible]	[illegible]	[illegible]	[illegible]	[illegible]	[illegible]	[illegible]
[illegible]	[illegible]	[illegible]	[illegible]	[illegible]	[illegible]	[illegible]	[illegible]	[illegible]	[illegible]	[illegible]	[illegible]	[illegible]	[illegible]
[illegible]	[illegible]	[illegible]	[illegible]	[illegible]	[illegible]	[illegible]	[illegible]	[illegible]	[illegible]	[illegible]	[illegible]	[illegible]	[illegible]
[illegible]	[illegible]	[illegible]	[illegible]	[illegible]	[illegible]	[illegible]	[illegible]	[illegible]	[illegible]	[illegible]	[illegible]	[illegible]	[illegible]
[illegible]	[illegible]	[illegible]	[illegible]	[illegible]	[illegible]	[illegible]	[illegible]	[illegible]	[illegible]	[illegible]	[illegible]	[illegible]	[illegible]
[illegible]	[illegible]	[illegible]	[illegible]	[illegible]	[illegible]	[illegible]	[illegible]	[illegible]	[illegible]	[illegible]	[illegible]	[illegible]	[illegible]
[illegible]	[illegible]	[illegible]	[illegible]	[illegible]	[illegible]	[illegible]	[illegible]	[illegible]	[illegible]	[illegible]	[illegible]	[illegible]	[illegible]
[illegible]	[illegible]	[illegible]	[illegible]	[illegible]	[illegible]	[illegible]	[illegible]	[illegible]	[illegible]	[illegible]	[illegible]	[illegible]	[illegible]
[illegible]	[illegible]	[illegible]	[illegible]	[illegible]	[illegible]	[illegible]	[illegible]	[illegible]	[illegible]	[illegible]	[illegible]	[illegible]	[illegible]
[illegible]	[illegible]	[illegible]	[illegible]	[illegible]	[illegible]	[illegible]	[illegible]	[illegible]	[illegible]	[illegible]	[illegible]	[illegible]	[illegible]
[illegible]	[illegible]	[illegible]	[illegible]	[illegible]	[illegible]	[illegible]	[illegible]	[illegible]	[illegible]	[illegible]	[illegible]	[illegible]	[illegible]
[illegible]	[illegible]	[illegible]	[illegible]	[illegible]	[illegible]	[illegible]	[illegible]	[illegible]	[illegible]	[illegible]	[illegible]	[illegible]	[illegible]
[illegible]	[illegible]	[illegible]	[illegible]	[illegible]	[illegible]	[illegible]	[illegible]	[illegible]	[illegible]	[illegible]	[illegible]	[illegible]	[illegible]
[illegible]	[illegible]	[illegible]	[illegible]	[illegible]	[illegible]	[illegible]	[illegible]	[illegible]	[illegible]	[illegible]	[illegible]	[illegible]	[illegible]
Means,	[illegible]	[illegible]	[illegible]	[illegible]	[illegible]	[illegible]	[illegible]	[illegible]	[illegible]	[illegible]	[illegible]	[illegible]	[illegible]
1896,	[illegible]	[illegible]	[illegible]	[illegible]	[illegible]	[illegible]	[illegible]	[illegible]	[illegible]	[illegible]	[illegible]	[illegible]	[illegible]

* February, 18[illegible], was the driest month of the twenty-one years. † December, 18[illegible], was the month of [illegible] rainfall.
‡ November, 18[illegible], was the wettest month of the twenty-one years. § Heaviest rainfall in 24 hours [illegible] inches, on October [illegible], 18[illegible].

TABLE showing the Monthly and Yearly Number of Rainy Days* at Dublin during the Twenty-one Years 1876 to 1896, inclusive; with the Means for the Twenty Years 1876 to 1895.

Year.	January.	February.	March.	April.	May.	June.	July.	August.	September.	October.	November.	December.	Total Rainy Days
1876,	[illegible]	[illegible]	[illegible]	[illegible]	[illegible]	[illegible]	[illegible]	[illegible]	[illegible]	[illegible]	[illegible]	[illegible]	[illegible]
1877,	[illegible]	[illegible]	[illegible]	[illegible]	[illegible]	[illegible]	[illegible]	[illegible]	[illegible]	[illegible]	[illegible]	[illegible]	[illegible]
[illegible]	[illegible]	[illegible]	[illegible]	[illegible]	[illegible]	[illegible]	[illegible]	[illegible]	[illegible]	[illegible]	[illegible]	[illegible]	[illegible]
[illegible]	[illegible]	[illegible]	[illegible]	[illegible]	[illegible]	[illegible]	[illegible]	[illegible]	[illegible]	[illegible]	[illegible]	[illegible]	[illegible]
[illegible]	[illegible]	[illegible]	[illegible]	[illegible]	[illegible]	[illegible]	[illegible]	[illegible]	[illegible]	[illegible]	[illegible]	[illegible]	[illegible]
[illegible]	[illegible]	[illegible]	[illegible]	[illegible]	[illegible]	[illegible]	[illegible]	[illegible]	[illegible]	[illegible]	[illegible]	[illegible]	[illegible]
[illegible]	[illegible]	[illegible]	[illegible]	[illegible]	[illegible]	[illegible]	[illegible]	[illegible]	[illegible]	[illegible]	[illegible]	[illegible]	[illegible]
[illegible]	[illegible]	[illegible]	[illegible]	[illegible]	[illegible]	[illegible]	[illegible]	[illegible]	[illegible]	[illegible]	[illegible]	[illegible]	[illegible]
[illegible]	[illegible]	[illegible]	[illegible]	[illegible]	[illegible]	[illegible]	[illegible]	[illegible]	[illegible]	[illegible]	[illegible]	[illegible]	[illegible]
[illegible]	[illegible]	[illegible]	[illegible]	[illegible]	[illegible]	[illegible]	[illegible]	[illegible]	[illegible]	[illegible]	[illegible]	[illegible]	[illegible]
[illegible]	[illegible]	[illegible]	[illegible]	[illegible]	[illegible]	[illegible]	[illegible]	[illegible]	[illegible]	[illegible]	[illegible]	[illegible]	[illegible]
[illegible]	[illegible]	[illegible]	[illegible]	[illegible]	[illegible]	[illegible]	[illegible]	[illegible]	[illegible]	[illegible]	[illegible]	[illegible]	[illegible]
[illegible]	[illegible]	[illegible]	[illegible]	[illegible]	[illegible]	[illegible]	[illegible]	[illegible]	[illegible]	[illegible]	[illegible]	[illegible]	[illegible]
[illegible]	[illegible]	[illegible]	[illegible]	[illegible]	[illegible]	[illegible]	[illegible]	[illegible]	[illegible]	[illegible]	[illegible]	[illegible]	[illegible]
[illegible]	[illegible]	[illegible]	[illegible]	[illegible]	[illegible]	[illegible]	[illegible]	[illegible]	[illegible]	[illegible]	[illegible]	[illegible]	[illegible]
[illegible]	[illegible]	[illegible]	[illegible]	[illegible]	[illegible]	[illegible]	[illegible]	[illegible]	[illegible]	[illegible]	[illegible]	[illegible]	[illegible]
[illegible]	[illegible]	[illegible]	[illegible]	[illegible]	[illegible]	[illegible]	[illegible]	[illegible]	[illegible]	[illegible]	[illegible]	[illegible]	[illegible]
[illegible]	[illegible]	[illegible]	[illegible]	[illegible]	[illegible]	[illegible]	[illegible]	[illegible]	[illegible]	[illegible]	[illegible]	[illegible]	[illegible]
1894,	[illegible]	[illegible]	[illegible]	[illegible]	[illegible]	[illegible]	[illegible]	[illegible]	[illegible]	[illegible]	[illegible]	[illegible]	[illegible]
[illegible]	[illegible]	[illegible]	[illegible]	[illegible]	[illegible]	[illegible]	[illegible]	[illegible]	[illegible]	[illegible]	[illegible]	[illegible]	[illegible]
Means,	[illegible]	[illegible]	[illegible]	[illegible]	[illegible]	[illegible]	[illegible]	[illegible]	[illegible]	[illegible]	[illegible]	[illegible]	[illegible]
1896,	[illegible]	[illegible]	[illegible]	[illegible]	[illegible]	[illegible]	[illegible]	[illegible]	[illegible]	[illegible]	[illegible]	[illegible]	[illegible]

* [illegible]
‡ [illegible] month of the twenty-one years. [illegible]
† [illegible] month of the twenty-one years. Rainfall [illegible] inches.
§ [illegible]

TABLE showing the Temperature of the Air in Dublin in the Twenty-one Years 1876–1896, and the Average Temperature for the Twenty Years 1876 to 1895, inclusive, as recorded by Dr. J. W. Moore.

Years.	January.	February.	March.	April.	May.	June.	July.	August.	September.	October.	November.	December.	Year.
[illegible]	[illegible]	[illegible]	[illegible]	[illegible]	[illegible]	[illegible]	[illegible]	[illegible]	[illegible]	[illegible]	[illegible]	[illegible]	[illegible]
1877,	[illegible]	[illegible]	[illegible]	[illegible]	[illegible]	[illegible]	[illegible]	[illegible]	[illegible]	[illegible]	[illegible]	[illegible]	[illegible]
[illegible]	[illegible]	[illegible]	[illegible]	[illegible]	[illegible]	[illegible]	[illegible]	[illegible]	[illegible]	[illegible]	[illegible]	[illegible]	[illegible]
[illegible]	[illegible]	[illegible]	[illegible]	[illegible]	[illegible]	[illegible]	[illegible]	[illegible]	[illegible]	[illegible]	[illegible]	[illegible]	[illegible]
[illegible]	[illegible]	[illegible]	[illegible]	[illegible]	[illegible]	[illegible]	[illegible]	[illegible]	[illegible]	[illegible]	[illegible]	[illegible]	[illegible]
[illegible]	[illegible]	[illegible]	[illegible]	[illegible]	[illegible]	[illegible]	[illegible]	[illegible]	[illegible]	[illegible]	[illegible]	[illegible]	[illegible]
[illegible]	[illegible]	[illegible]	[illegible]	[illegible]	[illegible]	[illegible]	[illegible]	[illegible]	[illegible]	[illegible]	[illegible]	[illegible]	[illegible]
[illegible]	[illegible]	[illegible]	[illegible]	[illegible]	[illegible]	[illegible]	[illegible]	[illegible]	[illegible]	[illegible]	[illegible]	[illegible]	[illegible]
[illegible]	[illegible]	[illegible]	[illegible]	[illegible]	[illegible]	[illegible]	[illegible]	[illegible]	[illegible]	[illegible]	[illegible]	[illegible]	[illegible]
[illegible]	[illegible]	[illegible]	[illegible]	[illegible]	[illegible]	[illegible]	[illegible]	[illegible]	[illegible]	[illegible]	[illegible]	[illegible]	[illegible]
[illegible]	[illegible]	[illegible]	[illegible]	[illegible]	[illegible]	[illegible]	[illegible]	[illegible]	[illegible]	[illegible]	[illegible]	[illegible]	[illegible]
[illegible]	[illegible]	[illegible]	[illegible]	[illegible]	[illegible]	[illegible]	[illegible]	[illegible]	[illegible]	[illegible]	[illegible]	[illegible]	[illegible]
[illegible]	[illegible]	[illegible]	[illegible]	[illegible]	[illegible]	[illegible]	[illegible]	[illegible]	[illegible]	[illegible]	[illegible]	[illegible]	[illegible]
[illegible]	[illegible]	[illegible]	[illegible]	[illegible]	[illegible]	[illegible]	[illegible]	[illegible]	[illegible]	[illegible]	[illegible]	[illegible]	[illegible]
[illegible]	[illegible]	[illegible]	[illegible]	[illegible]	[illegible]	[illegible]	[illegible]	[illegible]	[illegible]	[illegible]	[illegible]	[illegible]	[illegible]
[illegible]	[illegible]	[illegible]	[illegible]	[illegible]	[illegible]	[illegible]	[illegible]	[illegible]	[illegible]	[illegible]	[illegible]	[illegible]	[illegible]
[illegible]	[illegible]	[illegible]	[illegible]	[illegible]	[illegible]	[illegible]	[illegible]	[illegible]	[illegible]	[illegible]	[illegible]	[illegible]	[illegible]
[illegible]	[illegible]	[illegible]	[illegible]	[illegible]	[illegible]	[illegible]	[illegible]	[illegible]	[illegible]	[illegible]	[illegible]	[illegible]	[illegible]
[illegible]	[illegible]	[illegible]	[illegible]	[illegible]	[illegible]	[illegible]	[illegible]	[illegible]	[illegible]	[illegible]	[illegible]	[illegible]	[illegible]
[illegible]	[illegible]	[illegible]	[illegible]	[illegible]	[illegible]	[illegible]	[illegible]	[illegible]	[illegible]	[illegible]	[illegible]	[illegible]	[illegible]
Average,	[illegible]	[illegible]	[illegible]	[illegible]	[illegible]	[illegible]	[illegible]	[illegible]	[illegible]	[illegible]	[illegible]	[illegible]	[illegible]
[illegible]	[illegible]	[illegible]	[illegible]	[illegible]	[illegible]	[illegible]	[illegible]	[illegible]	[illegible]	[illegible]	[illegible]	[illegible]	[illegible]

POPULATION OF IRELAND (including Army, Navy, and Merchant Seamen on shore or in port) estimated to the middle of each of the Seventy-five Years 1822 to 1896, inclusive:—

[illegible]	Estimated Population.			[illegible]	Estimated Population.			[illegible]	Estimated Population.		
	Persons.	Males.	Females.		Persons.	Males.	Females.		Persons.	Males.	Females.
[illegible]	[illegible]	[illegible]	[illegible]	[illegible]	[illegible]	[illegible]	[illegible]	[illegible]	[illegible]	[illegible]	[illegible]
[illegible]	[illegible]	[illegible]	[illegible]	[illegible]	[illegible]	[illegible]	[illegible]	[illegible]	[illegible]	[illegible]	[illegible]
[illegible]	[illegible]	[illegible]	[illegible]	[illegible]	[illegible]	[illegible]	[illegible]	[illegible]	[illegible]	[illegible]	[illegible]
[illegible]	[illegible]	[illegible]	[illegible]	[illegible]	[illegible]	[illegible]	[illegible]	[illegible]	[illegible]	[illegible]	[illegible]
[illegible]	[illegible]	[illegible]	[illegible]	[illegible]	[illegible]	[illegible]	[illegible]	[illegible]	[illegible]	[illegible]	[illegible]
[illegible]	[illegible]	[illegible]	[illegible]	[illegible]	[illegible]	[illegible]	[illegible]	[illegible]	[illegible]	[illegible]	[illegible]
[illegible]	[illegible]	[illegible]	[illegible]	[illegible]	[illegible]	[illegible]	[illegible]	[illegible]	[illegible]	[illegible]	[illegible]
[illegible]	[illegible]	[illegible]	[illegible]	[illegible]	[illegible]	[illegible]	[illegible]	[illegible]	[illegible]	[illegible]	[illegible]
[illegible]	[illegible]	[illegible]	[illegible]	[illegible]	[illegible]	[illegible]	[illegible]	[illegible]	[illegible]	[illegible]	[illegible]
[illegible]	[illegible]	[illegible]	[illegible]	[illegible]	[illegible]	[illegible]	[illegible]	[illegible]	[illegible]	[illegible]	[illegible]
[illegible]	[illegible]	[illegible]	[illegible]	[illegible]	[illegible]	[illegible]	[illegible]	[illegible]	[illegible]	[illegible]	[illegible]
[illegible]	[illegible]	[illegible]	[illegible]	[illegible]	[illegible]	[illegible]	[illegible]	[illegible]	[illegible]	[illegible]	[illegible]
[illegible]	[illegible]	[illegible]	[illegible]	[illegible]	[illegible]	[illegible]	[illegible]	[illegible]	[illegible]	[illegible]	[illegible]
[illegible]	[illegible]	[illegible]	[illegible]	[illegible]	[illegible]	[illegible]	[illegible]	[illegible]	[illegible]	[illegible]	[illegible]
[illegible]	[illegible]	[illegible]	[illegible]	[illegible]	[illegible]	[illegible]	[illegible]	[illegible]	[illegible]	[illegible]	[illegible]
[illegible]	[illegible]	[illegible]	[illegible]	[illegible]	[illegible]	[illegible]	[illegible]	[illegible]	[illegible]	[illegible]	[illegible]
[illegible]	[illegible]	[illegible]	[illegible]	[illegible]	[illegible]	[illegible]	[illegible]	[illegible]	[illegible]	[illegible]	[illegible]
[illegible]	[illegible]	[illegible]	[illegible]	[illegible]	[illegible]	[illegible]	[illegible]	[illegible]	[illegible]	[illegible]	[illegible]
[illegible]	[illegible]	[illegible]	[illegible]	[illegible]	[illegible]	[illegible]	[illegible]	[illegible]	[illegible]	[illegible]	[illegible]
[illegible]	[illegible]	[illegible]	[illegible]	[illegible]	[illegible]	[illegible]	[illegible]	[illegible]	[illegible]	[illegible]	[illegible]
[illegible]	[illegible]	[illegible]	[illegible]	[illegible]	[illegible]	[illegible]	[illegible]	[illegible]	[illegible]	[illegible]	[illegible]
[illegible]	[illegible]	[illegible]	[illegible]	[illegible]	[illegible]	[illegible]	[illegible]	[illegible]	[illegible]	[illegible]	[illegible]
[illegible]	[illegible]	[illegible]	[illegible]	[illegible]	[illegible]	[illegible]	[illegible]	[illegible]	[illegible]	[illegible]	[illegible]
[illegible]	[illegible]	[illegible]	[illegible]	[illegible]	[illegible]	[illegible]	[illegible]	[illegible]	[illegible]	[illegible]	[illegible]
[illegible]	[illegible]	[illegible]	[illegible]	[illegible]	[illegible]	[illegible]	[illegible]	[illegible]	[illegible]	[illegible]	[illegible]

NOTE.—This Table has been constructed for the years [illegible]

[illegible]

[illegible]

[illegible]

[illegible]

[illegible]

AGES of the POPULATION in IRELAND according to the Census Returns of 1861, 1871, 1881, and 1891.

Periods.	Sexes.	Ages—Years.														Total.
		[illegible]	[illegible]	[illegible]	[illegible]	[illegible]	[illegible]	[illegible]	[illegible]	[illegible]	[illegible]	[illegible]	[illegible]	[illegible]	[illegible]	
1861.	Males	[illegible]	[illegible]	[illegible]	[illegible]	[illegible]	[illegible]	[illegible]	[illegible]	[illegible]	[illegible]	[illegible]	[illegible]	[illegible]	[illegible]	[illegible]
	Females	[illegible]	[illegible]	[illegible]	[illegible]	[illegible]	[illegible]	[illegible]	[illegible]	[illegible]	[illegible]	[illegible]	[illegible]	[illegible]	[illegible]	[illegible]
	Total	[illegible]	[illegible]	[illegible]	[illegible]	[illegible]	[illegible]	[illegible]	[illegible]	[illegible]	[illegible]	[illegible]	[illegible]	[illegible]	[illegible]	[illegible]
1871.	Males	[illegible]	[illegible]	[illegible]	[illegible]	[illegible]	[illegible]	[illegible]	[illegible]	[illegible]	[illegible]	[illegible]	[illegible]	[illegible]	[illegible]	[illegible]
	Females	[illegible]	[illegible]	[illegible]	[illegible]	[illegible]	[illegible]	[illegible]	[illegible]	[illegible]	[illegible]	[illegible]	[illegible]	[illegible]	[illegible]	[illegible]
	Total	[illegible]	[illegible]	[illegible]	[illegible]	[illegible]	[illegible]	[illegible]	[illegible]	[illegible]	[illegible]	[illegible]	[illegible]	[illegible]	[illegible]	[illegible]
1881.	Males	[illegible]	[illegible]	[illegible]	[illegible]	[illegible]	[illegible]	[illegible]	[illegible]	[illegible]	[illegible]	[illegible]	[illegible]	[illegible]	[illegible]	[illegible]
	Females	[illegible]	[illegible]	[illegible]	[illegible]	[illegible]	[illegible]	[illegible]	[illegible]	[illegible]	[illegible]	[illegible]	[illegible]	[illegible]	[illegible]	[illegible]
	Total	[illegible]	[illegible]	[illegible]	[illegible]	[illegible]	[illegible]	[illegible]	[illegible]	[illegible]	[illegible]	[illegible]	[illegible]	[illegible]	[illegible]	[illegible]
1891.	Males	[illegible]	[illegible]	[illegible]	[illegible]	[illegible]	[illegible]	[illegible]	[illegible]	[illegible]	[illegible]	[illegible]	[illegible]	[illegible]	[illegible]	[illegible]
	Females	[illegible]	[illegible]	[illegible]	[illegible]	[illegible]	[illegible]	[illegible]	[illegible]	[illegible]	[illegible]	[illegible]	[illegible]	[illegible]	[illegible]	[illegible]
	Total	[illegible]	[illegible]	[illegible]	[illegible]	[illegible]	[illegible]	[illegible]	[illegible]	[illegible]	[illegible]	[illegible]	[illegible]	[illegible]	[illegible]	[illegible]

* [illegible]

INDEX TO SUPERINTENDENT REGISTRARS' DISTRICTS.

[The following Index furnishes a reference to the Number or Numbers of each Superintendent Registrar's District in the Tables of Abstracts contained in this Report, in which the numbers run consecutively from 1 to 131.]*

* [illegible]

INDEX TO REGISTRARS' DISTRICTS.

[The Number or Numbers against each Registrar's District in the Third Column refers to the page or pages in which the Total Births, Illegitimate Births, Deaths, &c., in the District during the year are given.]

Registrars' Districts.	Superintendent Registrars' Districts.	Page.	Registrars' Districts.	Superintendent Registrars' Districts.	Page.	Registrars' Districts.	Superintendent Registrars' Districts.	Page.
[illegible]	[illegible]	[illegible]	[illegible]	[illegible]	[illegible]	[illegible]	[illegible]	[illegible]

Registrars' Districts.	Superintendent Registrars' Districts.	Page.	Registrars' Districts.	Superintendent Registrars' Districts.	Page.	Registrars' Districts.	Superintendent Registrars' Districts.	Page.
[illegible]	[illegible]	[illegible]	[illegible]	[illegible]	[illegible]	[illegible]	[illegible]	[illegible]

PROSECUTIONS for OFFENCES against the REGISTRATION ACTS during the Financial Year 1876–77.

The total number of offences against the Registration Acts which were reported by local Officers, and came under investigation in the General Register Office, during the year ended 31st March, 1877, amounted to 761. As regards many of these, the defaulters came forward and complied with the requirements of the law, on becoming aware that proceedings against them were in contemplation, and in a large number of cases it was found that no proceedings could be taken against the responsible parties, as the legal time for doing so had elapsed.

However, after careful inquiry into the circumstances of each case, and on consideration of the evidence available, prosecutions were directed against the offenders in 117 cases. In [illegible] of these the parties were convicted and punished; in [illegible] cases the proceedings were abandoned, the parties (in most cases) paying the costs of court and complying with the law; in 8 cases the summonses were dismissed, and in 7 cases the result has not as yet been reported to the Registrar-General.

Among the offences dealt with were the following:—Neglect to register births; neglect to register deaths; neglect to furnish certificates of marriages; failure of Coroner to furnish certificate of inquest; giving false information as to age at death, as to the cause of death, and as to duration of illness; giving false information as to births, viz., registering illegitimate children as legitimate, and misrepresenting date of birth; falsifying Medical certificate of cause of death; falsifying extracts from Registers.

The following are a few examples of these cases:—

J. G. was prosecuted at Ballinamuck Petty Sessions for refusing to register his child's birth. He was convicted and fined 20s. and costs.

H. C. was prosecuted at the Metropolitan Police Courts for neglecting to register her child's birth. She was fined 10s. and costs.

M. H. was prosecuted at Killimore Petty Sessions for neglecting to register a death. She was fined 5s. and costs.

R. J. M. was prosecuted at the Belfast Police Court for giving false information when registering the death of his wife. He was fined 10s., and 12s. 6d. costs.

R. B. was prosecuted at the Metropolitan Police Courts for giving false information when registering a death. He was fined £3, and £3 costs.

A Coroner was prosecuted for neglecting to furnish to the Registrar a Certificate of the finding of the Jury in an Inquest held by him. He was fined £1, with 8s. 6d. costs, or 14 days' imprisonment.

It is to be regretted that, despite the measures adopted by the Department for the punishment of offenders, several Registrars report that they believe false information is frequently given to them, especially in cases of deaths.

The modus operandi in one class of offence appears to be as follows:—where a member of a family is entered in a Friendly Society or Industrial Assurance Company, the age is frequently given as much below the real age in order to reduce the amount of the premium payable. After a time the person dies, and then the registry is falsified so as to suit the statements previously made to the Society or Company.

However, it sometimes happens that the informant overlooks the fact that the age in the register should correspond with the age in the policy, and, in order to obtain the money, another criminal act is then necessary, namely, making a declaration before a magistrate, altering the age correctly given in the register to an incorrect age, to agree with the age in the policy.

Although the greatest pains have been taken to obtain evidence in these cases to convict the offenders, it is to be regretted that on many occasions the proceedings had to be abandoned for want of documentary proof of age, though no reasonable doubt existed that the offence had been committed.

In several cases the age of a deceased person has been successfully proved from a marriage register, giving the age at time of marriage, and in other cases the age inserted or proposed to be inserted in the register, has been proved to be impossible from the records of the births or baptisms of the children of the deceased; but of course, as a rule, the absence of reliable records of birth or baptism of old persons, makes it exceedingly difficult to deal with cases affecting them.

In addition to the above mentioned, there were a number of cases during the year in which proceedings were taken under the 26 & 27 Vic., cap. 90, before the magistrates at Petty Sessions for corrections in marriage registers, the summonses in these cases being issued at the instance of local Registration Officers.

A sum of £150 was provided in the estimate to meet legal charges. The total cost of the legal service of the Department during the year was £120 11s. 6d., of which sum £90 5s. 5d. was paid for local professional assistance, and £17 [illegible]s. for mileage to the Registrars.

www.ingramcontent.com/pod-product-compliance
Lightning Source LLC
Chambersburg PA
CBHW030549040726
47497CB00008B/2640